BOOKS BY TAYLOR CALDWELL

THE BALANCE WHEEL
LET LOVE COME LAST
MELISSA
THERE WAS A TIME
THIS SIDE OF INNOCENCE
THE WIDE HOUSE
THE FINAL HOUR
THE TURNBULLS
THE ARM AND THE DARKNESS
THE STRONG CITY
THE EARTH IS THE LORD'S
THE EAGLES GATHER
DYNASTY OF DEATH

CHARLES SCRIBNER'S SONS

THE BALANCE WHEEL

THE
BALANCE
WHEEL

BY

TAYLOR CALDWELL

Leyden, Mass. 01337

Reprinted 1975 by Special Arrangement
With Taylor Caldwell and Charles Scribner & Sons

Library of Congress Catalog Card Number 75-634
ISBN Number 0-88411-153-9

FOREWORD

THE CHARACTERS in this novel do not exist in actuality, nor have they existed. Nor is there a city called Andersburg anywhere in America, to my knowledge.

Nevertheless, my characters are a composite of many people, inasmuch as human passions, hopes, dreams, aspirations, evils and virtues differ only in degree in all men. A man's love for his son, and his fears for him during wars or rumors of wars, are common to all fathers, and a man's struggle to preserve his business can be duplicated a thousand times in every city in America. An American's determination that the Republic he loves so well shall be defended by him to the death is, I hope and pray, the basic determination of most Americans. This book, then, is a true story even if the actual characters have never existed.

As for the national and international events recorded in this book, they are absolutely true. The plot against America, both internally and externally, actually did begin as far back as 1910. It goes on, still. Perhaps it will always go on, for we are the last stronghold of freedom in the world. Perhaps the struggle to destroy the Republic will become even more desperate and violent in the years ahead, both in Washington and in Europe, in the little cities like "Andersburg" and in the great capitals of the world, in the councils of men who meet in secret and in the bold public utterances of the domestic and foreign enemies of America.

The reader will not encounter the full pattern of this plot in the history books of our schools. But if he is willing to take a little time and go to his local library, he will discover the whole terrible story in several factual books, carefully indexed and annotated. He will find that the mighty blow struck at man's liberty and dignity resounded in the first World War. The blow succeeded, and we witnessed the rise of Hitler and Stalin. The second World War was an even mightier blow, and it succeeded to an enormous extent. We are witnessing the advance of Communism both in Europe and in America.

If we are to survive as a free Republic it will be necessary for all Americans to know the real causes of these two disastrous wars, and not the false ones offered to the people.

TAYLOR CALDWELL

January, 1951

PART ONE

Common sense is instinct, and enough of it is genius.

—H. W. SHAW

CHAPTER I

THERE WAS only one thing about Phyllis which annoyed Charles: she invariably served him sherry when he called on Sunday afternoons. She was a very perceptive woman; he sometimes wondered why she had never guessed, during all these years, that he disliked sherry.

It was not that sherry was repulsive to him. He thought the color very intriguing; the bouquet was pleasant. The taste was even more pleasant. But the wine disagreed with him. However, he sometimes thought, in more indulgent moments, that it was not the sherry which frequently produced his biliousness but his contact, on these Sunday afternoons, with his brother, Wilhelm, whom he persisted in calling Willie. Wilhelm's cold fury, on these occasions, never failed to give Charles considerable satisfaction.

On this afternoon, Charles was very pleased, indeed. Phyllis, Wilhelm's wife, had apologized for her husband's absence and had explained that Wilhelm was at the moment engaged in the very careful and excruciating task of supervising the hanging of the latest addition to his private gallery, a Van Gogh. "It arrived this morning, and Wilhelm had left distinct instructions that no matter when it came, midnight or Sunday or dawn, he was to be notified," she told Charles. "So it came just two hours ago, and he went down to the station for it, himself, and carried it back in the carriage, in his arms." She smiled affectionately, and she narrowed her eyes in a certain way which always made something stir achingly in her brother-in-law. "Nothing would do but to drag Gordon out of his lair over the stables to help hang the painting."

She added, her eyes still dancing between the narrowed lids: "He'll be down very soon, however. He's stopped scolding, so I imagine he's studying the effect now."

"Or maybe he's hanged Gordon for his clumsiness, and is preparing a defense," Charles said. "Of course, he'd be absolutely convinced that any jury would sympathize with him."

Phyllis laughed. They were having a very light conversation, as usual. They were rarely serious, when they were together. Many years ago, when they had been very young, they never had been anything else. It seemed to Charles that in those days they were always discussing some weighty matter or other. However, apparently the matters had not been

3

weighty enough for Phyllis, and he had, involuntarily, betrayed a secret boredom. In the end, Phyllis had broken her engagement to him and had married his brother, who could be always depended upon never to laugh at anything at all. He still possessed, in considerable measure, this very dubious virtue, though he was now thirty-eight.

Charles hoped that Wilhelm's preoccupation with the Van Gogh would keep him absent for a long time. He might not have to see his brother until the moment of his leaving. That would be very agreeable. In the meantime, as he sipped his very fine sherry, he looked about him, as he always looked about him in this house, and particularly in this room. He had to admit that Wilhelm had taste.

The hot summer sun filtered softly through lengths of fine Venetian lace which covered the long arched windows of the room. Wilhelm had bought this lace, personally, in Italy; he had had it made especially to fit these windows. The delicate webs mellowed the sunlight, diffused it. The room was large and long, and cool, though heat blazed outside. It was panelled in ivory wood, traced over with a faint silver design consisting of a vase with rising leaves. Between the panels, the walls had been hung with a dim, silvery-gold brocade, in a leaf design also. The same motif had been followed diligently in the narrow molding which separated the walls from the ceiling, and this was overlaid with subdued gold. A similar molding had been set in the ivory ceiling some three feet from the margins. It gleamed unobtrusively in the soft light.

Wilhelm had agonized over every object in this room before purchasing it, just as he had agonized over every other room in his house. In fact, it had taken him well over twelve years to complete the furnishings, and even now he was not quite satisfied and brooded in dissatisfaction over trifles which were not "exactly right." To Charles, everything in the house was admirable and excellent, and especially here, in the music room. He never called it the "music room" though it undoubtedly had a piano in ivory and gold. He called it, to himself, "Phyllis' room." It fitted Phyllis perfectly, though she had chosen nothing in it. Wilhelm, it was, who had bought this faded dove-gray rug in France, with its central circle traced in a thin line of dark blue, and enclosing a design of large, pale blue acanthus leaves, the same design repeated on the four corners of the rug. It had taken Wilhelm two months of anguish to find the proper rug, and doubtless, thought Charles, he had given dealers a hellish time of it. He had most probably, in some French minds, dissipated the myth that Americans were gaudy and careless spenders, for Wilhelm was not only a perfectionist but parsimonious, also.

On each side of an immense white marble fireplace stood slender stands of gold-colored marble, supporting large cloisonné vases of the utmost beauty. Over the fireplace hung a very idealized portrait of Charles' and Wilhelm's father, painted by a fine Italian artist from a photograph. Charles often thought that Emil Wittmann would have laughed aloud at this portrait, which presented him as a grave and stately gentleman of fifty-five, holding a book in white and slender hands. Charles, remembering his father's hands, brown and square and sturdy, would be moved to some silent inner profanity.

Once, Charles, remembering how those hands could thump with telling force on a young backside, and how expert they were with tools and machinery, wondered if Wilhelm had not deliberately changed the hands in order to forget Emil's "grossness" and healthy reality. Perhaps he wanted to forget that Emil had had little patience with any literature except the Bible and Shakespeare and Goethe and Erasmus. Just as he had had the hands changed, so had he had the face changed. It was recognizable as Emil Wittmann, Charles had to admit, but old Emil had never had those aesthetically pale cheeks, that artistic, brooding expression, those very sensitive shadows about his mouth.

Perhaps there had been a craving, a longing, in the young Wilhelm, for an ideal father, according to his own needs. Emil had revolted his son, but his son would not be denied a father, and he had created this one in his secret hunger. I can be fanciful, myself, thought Charles, sipping his sherry and looking at the portrait, and though I may be wrong about the whole thing I can find it pathetic.

It was notable that Wilhelm had never had an idealized portrait of his mother painted from a photograph. Nothing could ever have been done about Gretchen Wittmann, short, round, hopelessly of sound peasant stock, and hopelessly cheerful.

All at once, in that sunlit room today, Charles could smell his mother's kitchen again and see the glimmer of the copper pots on the brick walls. He could see the slaughtered suckling pig on the white kitchen table, and his mother's hands, firmly stuffing the little animal. Sage and onion, spicy and mouth-watering.

He became aware that Phyllis had been speaking, and he started slightly. "I'm sorry," he said, "I was thinking of something."

"You were looking at Papa Wittmann's portrait," said Phyllis. She was laughing gently. "I know; it annoys you, doesn't it?"

Charles considered for a moment or two. "No," he replied finally. "Perhaps he looked that way to Wilhelm. To tell the truth, Phyllis, I was thinking of my mother. She was a wonderful cook, though not an overly dainty one. But you never knew her."

He looked at Phyllis. He was suddenly surprised, for all at once it seemed to him that Phyllis reminded him acutely of his mother. He had never thought so before, and there was no reason to think so now. No two women, in appearance at least, could be so dissimilar. Phyllis was all tall, fine and slender grace, too thin, perhaps, for modern taste, which demanded a figure of noble proportions. To some people, she might seem brittle; to Charles, she was discriminating and subtle, of a nervous acuteness which was also gentle and beautifully poised. She was rarely impatient with anyone, however trying, for she possessed great sympathy, a trait which expressed itself in her large blue eyes and full white lids. At thirty-four, her slender face was still unlined; there was humor in it, and repose. Charles thought he had never seen so lovely a forehead, with the bronze-colored hair rising in a high wave above it. Pearls glimmered in her beautiful ears and about her long neck. She now never bought a frock or a gown or a hat without Wilhelm's supervision, and Charles had to admit that Wilhelm's taste in women's clothing was also impeccable.

No, there was nothing about Phyllis which would set a sane mind to believing that she resembled Gretchen Wittmann. Phyllis' wide and palely colored mouth, vibrant yet restrained, had nothing in common with Gretchen's round red lips, pursed and judicious, or merry. Gretchen had had a thick and bulbous nose; Phyllis' nose was arched, the nostrils delicately flaring. Those eyes, so brilliantly intelligent, so shining, so quick to flicker and narrow and change, were not in the least, not even in expression, like Gretchen's strenuous brown eyes, a little small, and given to direct staring.

"I first knew you about six months after your mother had died, just after I had finished my senior year at Vassar," said Phyllis. She was regarding him thoughtfully. "I've never even seen a photograph of your mother, Charles. Yet I have an idea you resemble her a good deal. Don't you?"

"My father used to say there was some resemblance," he admitted.

She continued to study him. In the last five years or so she had thought of Charles as "the balance wheel," the strong wheel which kept a most complex and delicate machine in motion and in order, which regulated all the other parts, equalized them. Certainly, such a wheel was the very axis of a family composed of such unstable elements as Wilhelm, Friederich and Jochen Wittmann, not to speak of a business which demanded constant energy, initiative, ingenuity and common sense. Emil Wittmann had left to his sons a firmly established tool-making factory, but it was Charles (or Karl, as Friederich insisted upon calling his oldest brother) who had so expanded and enlarged it and made it so prosperous in Andersburg. Even during the panic of 1907, it had made money, had paid dividends and had stood securely. Now, in 1913, the possibilities of its continued growth were enormous, in spite of Wilhelm, Friederich and Jochen. It had kept its reputation for integrity and reliability, again in spite of the other three men, and most especially in spite of Jochen, who was so avaricious and so expedient.

Phyllis had known Emil Wittmann. All at once, as she studied Charles, she wished she had known Gretchen, too. Though Charles was somewhat above average height, he had a square and solid sturdiness of body, full of health and quiet vitality. Once, she had come to dislike this sturdiness; she had been very young, and she had finally been convinced that Charles had very little "soul."

She looked away from him now, and poured another cup of tea for herself. She slipped a sliver of lemon into her tea, and then a lump of sugar. She did all this, automatically, and a little tensely. Why had she ever thought Charles had no "soul"? Because he had had only two years of college, and then had refused to continue with an education which he had believed "nonsense" for himself? Because he had swallowed yawns when she had read poetry to him? Because he was always so realistic? I was such a—Phyllis began to think, then stopped herself sternly. The small muscles of her fingers tightened about her spoon.

"What's the matter, Phyllis?" asked Charles, seeing the change on her face.

She looked up at him with an effort, and smiled. "Why, nothing at all," she replied. She glanced at the gilt clock on the mantelpiece. "Really, it's almost five, and Wilhelm still hasn't come down. I think I'll send for him."

"Oh, let him alone with his Van Gogh! If he is interrupted now, he'll be murderous." Charles laughed. He put down his glass. The sherry was already burning in his stomach. He'd be bilious tomorrow. Salts, he thought, gloomily.

But Phyllis would not let him go, though he was standing now. She said, hastily: "I haven't asked about Jimmy. How is he? I haven't seen him for weeks, and you know how fond I am of him, Charles."

"Yes." He smiled down at her. "And Jimmy likes you, too, Phyllis. Jim's interested in the factory, though he's only seventeen."

"He's such a nice boy," murmured Phyllis. (She could not let him go, just yet. He must continue to stand near her, so strongly, so solidly, his hands in his pockets, and standing like this, far back on his heels, as she always remembered him standing.) "You've done so well for him, Charles. You're everything to him."

"He wouldn't like you to call him 'a boy,'" said Charles. "He thinks he's quite a man, you know."

Phyllis thought of Charles' wife, Mary, who had died three years ago. Mary had been her own friend, at Vassar, a dark and lively young girl, with a face which could change from extreme mirth to seriousness in a single moment. A dear, pretty girl—Mary. Phyllis had loved her.

Charles unobtrusively glanced at his watch. If he went now, he would escape seeing his brother. He still had to call upon his other brothers. It was a duty visit he paid to their homes once a month. He straightened his dark tie with a quick movement of his short broad fingers. The little clock chimed five.

Phyllis saw she could not keep him. Why had she ever thought him "undistinguished, ordinary"? He was not a handsome man. Wilhelm often called him "coarse." He had a broad full face, somewhat highly colored, a broad nose, a big full mouth, and smooth brown hair. There was no elegance in him. Yet Phyllis repeated to herself: 'Why did I ever think him ordinary?'

It was just then that a maid came in to say that Mr. Wittmann had sent her to ask Mr. Charles Wittmann please not to leave, that he wished to see him and that he would join him, almost immediately.

Phyllis sat down. She ordered fresh tea. Her voice was somewhat absent. Charles sat down, also. There was something tense in the room. It disturbed him. He reached for his sherry glass, without thinking. "Well," he said, and looked, frowning, at the clock.

CHAPTER II

As HE WAITED for his brother, Charles wondered vaguely if something was "wrong" with Phyllis. Then his speculations became less vague. Phyllis had changed considerably, he recalled, during the past few months or so, but he had not become so conscious of it until today.

Once he had loved her, but had not enjoyed her company, for, when young, she had been too enthusiastic, too determined in her efforts to be stimulating, too erratic for his conservative taste.

It was strange, but marriage to Wilhelm, whom everyone had considered ideal for young Phyllis Chatham, then the belle of Andersburg, Pennsylvania, and even of Philadelphia, had changed Phyllis astonishingly. Before she was thirty, she had lost her eager solemnity and formidable interest in "art," and had become less interested in all the theories which had surged and ebbed and flowed during the very early years of the new century. Her humor became more dominant; she acquired a restfulness of character, and the basic animation of her nature had become enchanting. Charles had come to enjoy her company; she entertained him with her light comments, which he found most feminine. He no longer loved her, though he felt a deep affection for her. Suddenly, it came to Charles that Phyllis was unhappy.

He looked at her sharply, as they waited for Wilhelm. Was she really thinner and paler? Of course, she was thirty-four, and mature, and women changed with the years more than men did, and more noticeably. She had no anxieties that he, Charles, knew of; she was still extremely in love with Wilhelm. It was all nonsense, though there was a possibility that she was disappointed because she was childless.

That was it. Charles remembered that Phyllis always looked fondly at James, his son, that she never forgot his birthday, and was always delighted when the boy accompanied his father on a visit. She wanted, and needed, children. Charles was very sorry for her. It was not her fault that she had no family; from the very beginning, Wilhelm had expressed his open dislike for children, and had said that he never intended to have any. No child would ever ruffle the perfect order of his home or disturb his meditations and his long hours alone with himself in his library or gallery. He and Phyllis, he frequently said, had the "ideal" life, a completely "adult" life. They were truly companions, harmonious and considerate.

What would life be like for him, Charles, without Jimmy? The very thought was intolerable. He could not conceive of life without his son. He put down the glass of sherry after a distasteful glance at it. Why could not Mary have lived? Why had she and their little newborn daughter died together? It had been senseless. If the doctor had remained but five minutes longer, he would have been able to stop that hemorrhage which had killed Mary; he would have been able to restore breathing in the baby. The nurse had been inadequate in this double crisis. The child had suddenly died while the distracted nurse had tried to staunch that horrible, bursting hemorrhage in the mother.

"Charles," said Phyllis.

"Eh?" Charles lifted his head. She saw the heavy gravity on his face.

"You are thinking of Mary, aren't you, Charles?" Her voice was very gentle.

"How did you know?" He tried to smile at her. Then he looked at the windows, through which the August sun was shining so urgently. "It was on a day like this when she died. I remember. It was a very hot day. And the birth had been difficult for her. She was never very strong."

Phyllis stood up quickly, and walked down the length of the room to a distant window. She stood there, and fingered the lace edge of the Venetian curtain. "Poor Charles," she murmured.

"Well," he said. He added, after a moment: "I could have had less. I might not have had Mary even as long as I did."

"You loved her very much, didn't you?"

"No one could have helped loving Mary," he answered. He was uncomfortable. He never liked to talk about Mary, even now. What was wrong with Phyllis?

She stood in profile to him, far down the room. She was definitely thinner; her whole body had acquired a fine and delicate contour. He had always known that Phyllis was pretty; now with the light beating on her face, lying in a pool of gold in the hollow of her throat, she was beautiful. The blue-and-white teagown gave her a frail quality, and though she stood so still, he sensed her restlessness.

She turned to him. It was a swift movement, and impetuous. Something was trembling on her face, like reflected light. It was then that Wilhelm came in, and Charles was unaccountably relieved.

"Good," said Wilhelm, in his quick and slightly irritable voice. "I thought you wouldn't wait, Charles. It was that damned Gordon. Calls himself a 'handyman,' and can't even strike a nail straight. How are you, Charles? How is the tool factory?"

"I'm all right," said Charles, smiling. "The factory? You hardly ever go there, except when the directors meet. You're always there then, however," he added, with a friendly malice. "By the way, the next meeting is on Thursday. You'll be there."

"Yes. I understand something important is going to be discussed." He looked at his wife. "I hope you have some tea for me, Phyllis?" What was Phyllis doing, standing there so silent by the window? The natural irritability of his voice lessened.

Phyllis moved towards her husband. Now everything about her was tranquil. She gave him a look of affection. "Are we to see the Van Gogh?"

"Well, I certainly don't intend to let Charles leave without seeing it," he replied.

Charles said: "Yes, there's something important coming up on Thursday. I hope to have a talk with you about it before we all meet." He frowned for a moment. He looked at Wilhelm acutely. Wilhelm was concentrating on the sugar his wife was dropping into his tea. "That's enough, Phyllis," he said. "You know I never take but one lump, and here you are, trying to give me two."

Wilhelm glanced at his brother over his thin shoulder. " 'Talk with me about it?' " he repeated. "Why? We'll discuss it at the meeting."

Charles was silent. He had the ability to look more solid than ordinary on certain occasions. Now he sat like a rock in his chair. Wilhelm helped himself to a tea wafer, sat down with precise neatness on a small gilt settee not too near his brother. He said: "This is one of Van Gogh's best. Even you will have to admit that, Charles, when you see it."

Charles said: "What do I know of painting?"

"Oh, I know you like Victorian photographic 'art'! Obvious. And meaningless, except when it is sickeningly pretty."

"So was Renaissance art. You've said so, yourself—Willie."

Wilhelm's mouth became disagreeable. But he ignored the "Willie," as he always did. "Yes, I've said so. I admit it had its place—in its time. But not now. Victorian art is only an imitation of Renaissance art, with an overlay of Puritanism. Or Presbyterianism. Why modern artists cling to it I really don't know. Vapid imitators. There's that Matthew Prescott. Another imitator. Do you know something? I could have bought one of his pictures for less than what I paid for this Van Gogh! This shows that the public taste is definitely growing more intelligent, and discerning."

He looked about the lovely room with satisfaction. "It isn't as though I have no reverence for tradition. This room is all Louis Fifteenth. But it has a timelessness. Victorianism was only an era, sharply defined— and confined. Nothing about it will endure."

"Oh, I don't know," said Charles. He was not interested. Why did Wilhelm evade the question?

"More sherry?" asked Phyllis.

"No, thanks," said Charles. It was getting late, but something must be settled. It was very serious. He had not known how serious it would be. Had Wilhelm not evaded him, he would have taken his leave almost immediately. Wilhelm was usually with him, Charles, in any question which involved Jochen's ideas. It was easy to see that Wilhelm knew of Jochen's new idea and that he did not wish to discuss it with Charles. That was ominous.

Was it possible that Wilhelm needed money? Absurd. He had his large salary as an officer of the company. Phyllis had inherited one hundred and fifty thousand dollars from her grandmother, who had brought her up after her parents' death. Of course, he was always buying his infernal paintings, and this house must cost a fortune to maintain. Moment by moment, Charles became aware of the seriousness of the present situation.

Wilhelm was unobtrusively ignoring him. He was answering Phyllis' interested questions about the Van Gogh. Charles caught words such as "mood," "emotion," "feeling," "intensity of line and color."

Wilhelm sipped his tea with his usual nervous haste. If he could get out of showing Charles the Van Gogh he would now be very satisfied. He felt Charles, sitting there. Charles could feel Wilhelm urging him to leave. He settled himself even deeper in his chair. But he must move cautiously. He was always having to move cautiously with his brothers, and sometimes it was a cursed nuisance. A man got tired.

"I'd like to see the painting," he said. "If it is what you say it is, then it's probably more than worth seeing."

Wilhelm turned to him. He tried to resist, but he was flattered. He wanted Charles to go, but he also wanted Charles to see his new treasure. His uncertainty showed in his lean and narrow face, so dark and volatile. Some ancestor, and not either Emil or Gretchen Wittmann, had given him his slender height, his elegance, the fastidiousness of his appearance. There must have been one high-strung and patrician ancestor in that old German stock, an ancestor who had been a scholar, or a dilettante, like Wilhelm, himself.

Wilhelm was no poseur. He was genuinely patrician. His taste was exquisite. He did not pretend to love "art" in any form. He really appreciated it. Ugliness was dreadful to him, whether in human beings or in landscapes. He wrote significant and brilliant articles for the various magazines devoted to music or painting or literature, and several of these articles had been gathered together in anthologies. He was known to every art society in Europe or America, and dealers knew him well, to their occasional sorrow.

There was one thing he and his brothers had in common: a profound and instinctive respect for money. Charles respected it as evidence of industry and intelligence; Jochen respected it as an absolute thing in itself, and as power; Wilhelm respected it because it enabled him to buy the beautiful things for which he had such a craving. Using these various respects adroitly and cleverly, Charles had been enabled to preserve what his father had left to his sons, and to increase it. He had also used other traits in his brothers' characters to this end.

It must not be an appeal to money now which he must use to hold Wilhelm with him against Jochen. It must be Wilhelm's hatred for ugliness.

Phyllis said: "Do you want me to play something for you while you finish tea, Wilhelm?" She looked at Charles, a clouded look. "Charles?"

Charles was about to say: "Beethoven's 'Moonlight Sonata.'" And then he remembered that this favorite piece of music had once made Wilhelm sneer: "Obvious!" So he said: "Debussy."

Wilhelm put down his cup. He regarded Charles, pleased. Then his face changed and he glanced at the clock on the mantelpiece. Again, he was irresolute. "It's getting late, Phyllis. You know that Charles always visits the others on his calls."

Charles got up and went to one of the windows. He moved his strong and somewhat stolid body with careful leisureliness. "I suppose I should go," he said. "But I always like to spend more time here than anywhere else."

Wilhelm was gratified. But still he resisted. He said: "Thank you. You've told me that before, and I believe you mean it, Charles. That's why it's so hard to understand why you don't sell that hideous house of yours—our father's house—and buy something that has a little attractiveness about it."

Charles wanted to say, as he had often said: "I'm a Philistine. I'm hidebound. You're always telling me that, and it's true. Besides, I like the house." But now he said: "Perhaps you're right. It's dark and cumbersome. And cluttered."

Phyllis' expression became serious. She knew so much about Charles. Something was disturbing him deeply.

Charles was thinking: Jochen's been at him. They've talked together; Joe's determined to have his way, and he's gone behind my back to Willie, even though they detest each other.

He looked through the window consideringly, turning slowly from side to side in order to convey the impression that he was admiring the view.

He said: "My mind's been restricted. But then, I never had your artistic instincts. It's a kind of color-blindness in me, perhaps."

"We can't all be artists," said Wilhelm, and his irritable voice had in it a note of sympathy. "You've done very well with the business, Charles. I don't know what would have happened to it if it hadn't been for you."

Charles' shoulders relaxed a little. He turned back to the room. "Thanks," he said with feeling. "I've done my best. The family's important here, in Andersburg. We have a reputation for reliability and trustworthiness. Our tools can't be excelled anywhere in America, and that is why the biggest concerns come to us. And this city trusts us. That's why I've been thinking of doing something for the city—with a slight profit for all of us." He smiled at Wilhelm.

His brother was immediately intrigued. "What?" he asked.

"That twenty acres we all own jointly, in the name of the company, along the river front."

Wilhelm glanced away. One of his slender hands moved on the arm of the settee, restlessly stroking it. He did not reply. It was not like him to be silent about anything, and Charles' alarm increased.

He said: "The city wants to buy that land from the company. The price offered is not too exciting, I admit. And there's that Connington Steel Company wanting to buy the land for a new mill. You know what that means. They've offered us a big price, and I intended to discuss it with all of you at the meeting. Three times what the city has offered. They'll ruin the waterfront, pollute the water, destroy what is now a beautiful area. They could build somewhere on the outskirts of the city, but they'd find it more convenient to destroy the local water scenery."

Wilhelm's restless hand moved more rapidly. He looked down at his polished boots.

Charles continued: "Andersburg can still boast of an undespoiled waterfront; even the Prescott Lumber Company hasn't ruined it, for it is far down the river. I'm against selling the land to them. We aren't that greedy. We don't want to foul our own nest. Let the Connington buy the Burnsley land five miles back from the city, and keep its dirt and smells and shacks and smoke away from the people of Andersburg."

Wilhelm lifted his cup and extended it to Phyllis. She refilled it. Wilhelm's small thin ears were turning a trifle red. "One lump of sugar, dear," he murmured.

"I have a much better idea," said Charles. "We'll sell the land to the city at its offered low price—if we all agree. On one condition: that it be called the Wittman Civic Park. And on another condition, if you, Wilhelm, would care to undertake the job: that you supervise the planning, lay out the design for the flowers and the trees and the walks, select any statuary, approve any buildings. Only you could do this properly. The park would be a monument to the family; it would be a monument to your taste."

Wilhelm turned to his brother with such abruptness that his cup rattled on its saucer. He was enormously moved and excited. His full dark eyes flashed. "What an idea!" he exclaimed. His egotistical nature quickened. "'The Wittmann Civic Park!' What I could do, if everything were left in my hands! It would be the beauty spot of Pennsylvania!"

Then he stopped. His eyes shifted. He stirred his tea. "But ought we to refuse such an offer from the Connington?" he muttered.

Charles did not answer. He stood there, and let the turmoil rage in Wilhelm.

Wilhelm was sick with the struggle within him. He put down his tea, untasted. He sat on the edge of the settee, his fingers wound together, his shoulders bent.

"Jochen thinks we ought to accept the Connington's offer," said Charles. "But then, Joe lives on Beechwood Road, far from the river. Not like you, who would have the chimneys fuming almost under your nose, down there below. Joe isn't thinking of the terrible drop in property values if the Connington gets our land along the water. What is it to him? It's more money, I admit, and I'm not in the least averse to making money. Incidentally, the Burnsley land is for sale. The Connington hasn't considered it. If we hurry, we can buy it cheaply, then sell it to the Connington. They'll buy it from us, for they want a mill in this area, and though the price will be less than our land along the river, necessarily, it will be a good price. In fact, I'm going to take an option on the Burnsley property tomorrow, in the name of the company, if you agree right now."

Wilhelm stood up, involuntarily. "Buy the land!" he cried. "Don't wait; do it as soon as possible, tomorrow."

He stared at Charles, and the excited light was vivid in his eyes.

Charles' tight muscles relaxed completely. "Good," he said, with respect. "I knew you'd agree, Wilhelm. It's unfortunate for Joe that he's even more color-blind than I am. You remember how he rejected all of your ideas about his house? What did he call them? Well—" and Charles glanced at Phyllis, humorously. "There's a lady present."

Phyllis laughed, and there was a little hysteria in her laughter. "Oh, I know what Isabel said, even if I don't know what Jochen said!"

But Wilhelm, remembering his brother Jochen's remarks about his suggestions, frowned with cold fury. "I've given up Joe," he said. At the sound of that nickname, uttered with disgust, Charles knew that he had completely won. "As for Isabel," continued Wilhelm, who had a touch of femaleness in his character, "we all know that she thinks of nothing but what she calls 'social position.' But then, her father was a butcher, and she wants to live it down."

Charles laughed. "But a very good and very successful butcher. There's nothing wrong with butchering, or with any other kind of business or trade, provided a man is proud of his work, and does his best. It is only Isabel who has made butchering sound contemptible."

Wilhelm regarded Charles almost affectionately. Of all his brothers, Charles was the only one whom Wilhelm respected, despite his deplorable ignorance of the arts and his dreadful house. Wilhelm's excitement was growing. He was visualizing the projected park. He went to a window, held back a curtain and looked down at the river. The park became an actual thing before his eyes. He forgot all about the money, for money to him had always been only a means with which to buy perfect treasures.

The Wittmann Civic Park! It would be, in the end, his own park. He would be remembered as the artist who had designed and created it. A modest bust, but pure and simple and excellent, of himself, in a garden spot, a sort of arbor. He knew just the sculptor in New York—

They all went out of the room and into the small marble-floored hall. A long flight of steep marble stairs rose upwards from it, its balustrade covered with dimmed green velvet. Charles walked up the stairs gingerly, for his soles slipped on the polished white stone. He had often remarked that some day Wilhelm would "break his neck" on these stairs, but he did not make this remark today. He was quietly exuberant. He clung tenaciously to the balustrade, and thought that he had made his city safe from the belching scar of a steel mill on the river front. He did not dislike steel mills, for they were necessary to his own business. But he believed they should not be allowed to ruin the natural beauty of any city. He was proud of Andersburg; it was his home, and he loved it. He wanted it to expand, to become even more prosperous, with new industries and new factories, but he was convinced that it was not necessary to mutilate the residential sections of any town in the name of commerce.

Wilhelm's gallery, though small, could not have been more perfect. Some of the paintings bore famous old names, but Wilhelm had decided, a few years ago, that modern art had become "important." In a carefully selected spot, he had had the Van Gogh hung. The sunset light infused it with brilliance. Charles stood before it, and affected to study it with profound thoughtfulness. But, regrettably, he was only bored. It lacked "finish" for him. The flowers and the fruits, to him, had a crudeness, and he wondered why it was necessary not to paint things as they were. Then he remembered some of the phrases Wilhelm had used to Phyllis about the painting.

"It has a kind of 'emotion' about it," he murmured, rubbing his chin. "I'm not an artist, as I've admitted before. But I'm beginning to see what the man means— A 'mood' perhaps."

Wilhelm was surprised. He stood off from his new treasure, and studied it from every angle. "Definitely a mood," he said. "Van Gogh is all moods. A fleeting aspect—" He looked at Charles challengingly. "There are some who have even been stupid enough to say that Van Gogh, the supreme realist, is a 'surrealist.' Nonsense. You don't believe that, do you?"

Charles had not the slightest idea. But he shook his head solemnly. "Stupid," he repeated.

He knew he had to leave before he made a fool of himself in Wilhelm's sharp eyes. Hurriedly, he again shook hands with his brother, and then with Phyllis. They went down the stairs with him and saw him off in an atmosphere of the utmost cordiality.

Wilhelm and Phyllis went back into the music room. "A little Brahms, darling," said Wilhelm, seating himself. He looked up at Phyllis, and took her hand, and smiled, his nervous face becoming gentle. "Do you know, I have hopes of Charles," he remarked. "Sometimes he is almost perceptive." The Wittmann Civic Park!

"Only you ever caught real glimpses of Charles," answered Phyllis. Suddenly she bent, and kissed her husband's forehead. The thin wrinkles in it smoothed themselves out under her mouth. I do love him, she thought. He is really so sweet. Her eyes became wet, and there was a deep pain in her heart. Wilhelm lifted her hand to his lips, and kissed it.

Then he frowned anxiously. "Phyllis, wait a moment," he said, as she was about to move away towards the piano. "I've been worrying about you. I thought at first it was only my imagination, but you are so pale lately, and sometimes too languid for real health. Do you think," he added, sitting up with new apprehension, "that you could possibly be—"

"No, no, of course not," she answered hastily. "And it is your imagination, dear. But if you wish, I'll see the doctor tomorrow."

Wilhelm sighed. "Well, I'm glad it's not—that."

Phyllis went to the piano. Yes, yes, she thought, I'm glad, too. The keyboard swam before her and for a moment she thought she would burst into tears.

CHAPTER III

CHARLES' NEAT carriage was waiting for him, with its two neat middle-aged horses. He smiled as he sat down on the crimson leather seat. Wilhelm, for all his insistence upon "the modern," was fussily resentful of automobiles, which he called many opprobrious names, such as "filthy" and "stinking." Charles was glad that he had not used his new Oldsmobile—red and bright with brass and utterly dear to Jimmy's heart—in calling upon his brother. It might have destroyed that important moment of understanding between them.

The horses trotted down the narrow but well-kept roads. Sunday visiting had been completed by most people, as it was now slightly after six o'clock. Charles had the road to himself. He leaned back and enjoyed the sight of the small or large mansions lying among their gardens far back from the roads. Here lived the rich "outsiders," the oil and coal "barons," as Friederich called them with hatred. Here also lived the well-to-do residents of Andersburg. It was understood that there was considerable difference between the "outsiders" and the "residents." The outsiders had not been born in Andersburg, and though many of them used their homes as permanent residences now, and only visited their "illicit holdings" at the mines or the oil fields occasionally on business, the fact that they had not been born in this city or its environs forever set them apart from the others.

Andersburg is hidebound, and conservative, like me, thought Charles, without derision. He had many friends among the "outsiders." He found most of them to be very sensible men, and not "brutes," as Wilhelm called them. (Brutes, in Wilhelm's opinion, were men not passionately devoted to one art or another.) Some of their homes might regrettably be without taste, and somewhat flamboyant, but they were comfortable, and the kitchens could always boast a good cook. This alone would have endeared them to Charles

No one was about. He could catch a flash of light here and there on a conservatory roof or wall, or a flutter of a pretty skirt entering a distant door. But it was definitely evening, and the western sky was turning a brilliant red over the mountains across the river. The river reflected the wild color. Barges and boats stood on the scarlet mirror, motionless. The city, brown and white and yellow, curved with the curve of the water, illuminated in its narrow valley. Charles could see it all below him, and to him it was the most beautiful sight in all the world. He had travelled considerably, but still, Andersburg was his home and he never dreamed of living anywhere else. There was no sound about him but the gentle rumbling of the carriage wheels and the twittering of birds and the murmur of the light hot wind in the pines which separated one estate from another. Sometimes he passed large woods of first-growth timber, huge and matted and green and full of rustlings. He lit a cigar with relish. Wilhelm did not like cigars, though he smoked cigarettes with short, nervous puffings. Charles liked his coachman, who was also his man-of-all-work, and he liked that broad back on the perch above him.

He was gathering fortitude for his visit to his brother Friederich. He was often fond of Wilhelm, and Jochen he healthily hated and endlessly watched, but understood. Sometimes they were very friendly with each other. But Charles despised Friederich. There was much about Friederich which he could never understand, and he distrusted what he did not know.

Now Charles frowned. All at once his cigar did not appeal to him, though being thrifty, he continued to smoke it. He forgot the shouldering mountains about him; he no longer heard the birds and the sweet high wind. He was going to see Friederich, and the thought was enough to destroy his sense of well-being. Preoccupied with thoughts of Friederich, he hardly saw that the carriage was quite near the river. He did not see the other carriage, approaching him, until the occupant hailed him.

His own carriage stopped. The two vehicles stood side by side. Charles smiled. "Hello, Oliver," he said to the dark young man in the other carriage. He liked Oliver Prescott, Andersburg's most prominent young lawyer, and one of the directors of the Prescott Lumber Company. He liked the young man's quiet alertness, his direct look and his air of intelligence and integrity. Oliver was in black, for his wife's mother had recently died. Charles also observed that Oliver was not driving his automobile, to which he was much attached. Probably because of mourning, thought Charles, vaguely.

He said: "Liked the way you handled that Tom Murphy business, Oliver."

"Glad you did," said the young lawyer. He smiled, and his face became full of amusement. "But perhaps I ought to thank you, too. I heard you persuaded your brother to accept payment for the damage to his windows. When he was so hell-bent in the beginning for 'justice' and throwing Tom Murphy into jail. For a lifetime, preferably."

Charles stopped smiling, remembering Friederich. He said, reservedly: "Oh, I didn't have much to do with it. I just talked to Fred, that's all. I pointed out to him that Tom Murphy was well liked among the workingmen. Besides, Tom's my best foreman, and I didn't want to lose him." He paused. Friederich was his brother, even if he was a confounded fool. He said: "Well. Tom's a Roman Catholic, and didn't like Fred saying that religion is the opium of the people, or something, and that the Church is the 'enemy' of the 'inevitable Socialistic state,' as Fred calls it. After all, he forgot that Tom might have his convictions, too. He still forgets these things," Charles added. "Well, anyway, I just reminded him that he'd lose much sympathy among the working people in the town if Tom caught it hard, and that quite a number of the men are Catholics, too."

Oliver listened thoughtfully, nodding his head once or twice. He saw Charles was uneasy at discussing his brother. "It's settled, anyway, and that's the main thing," he remarked. "And I don't suppose Tom will break any more windows. Window-breaking, as I told him, was not the way to settle differences or win arguments, even though it's an ancient practice. Tom agreed; besides, it cost him thirty dollars, not to mention my fee for keeping him out of jail."

They laughed together. Charles asked Oliver about his wife and young son, and forgot his discomfort. They parted a few moments later. Now why, thought Charles, couldn't I have had just one brother like that? Why did I have to be cursed with the ones I have?

The carriage was now rolling down a dim, old street of big old houses. The late sun could not penetrate through the enormous elms and chestnuts, so that a cool shadow lay under them. It was a quiet street, a sound middle-class street, this Chestnut Road. The verandahs were deserted, though windows stood wide open. The gardens and stables behind the houses were deep in shadow.

The people took pride in their street. They did not take pride in having Friederich Wittmann as a neighbor. He had bought the "old" Benchley house, but it was "running to seed" since Friederich had moved in after leaving his former home. This was most probably because Friederich was parsimonious, and did not employ a good man for the care of his grounds. He could not get a good man, for, in spite of high Socialistic ideals, he paid miserable wages to anyone whom he could inveigle into working for him. If there is any "grinding of the faces of the poor" Fred's a fine example of it, thought Charles, as his carriage stopped before his brother's house.

He paused a moment before getting out. He looked at his brother's home with distaste, and with quite as much annoyance as the neighbors frequently displayed. There was no sense in having practically no grass at all on the muddy, uneven lawn. But then, grass seed cost money, and if grass were almost totally absent then one did not need to employ anyone regularly to care for it. The big house had once had a portly and prosperous appearance, but now the brown paint was blistered and peeling. The yellow verandah posts had faded to a bilious color, and had cracked. The yellow shutters, too, were neglected. The shingled roof was dark, and Charles suspected that it might leak here and there in a bad rain. If it did, it would be repaired hastily, and as cheaply as possible. The windows were grimy, the lank curtains behind them noticeably dirty. Here the shadow was heaviest and dullest. Possibly just as well, said Charles to himself.

Friederich was not married, and Charles' ring was answered by Friederich's German housekeeper, a fat and untidy old woman with a squat, grim face and hostile eyes blinking behind spectacles with steel rims. She did not like Charles, and Charles quite rightly suspected that she had acquired this point of view from his brother. He was a "baron," an "enemy of the people," though the "poor old devil" hadn't the sense to know that Friederich, as one of the directors of the Wittmann Machine Tool Company, received almost as large a salary as Charles, its president. He saved practically all of it, except what went for the printing and distribution of his infernal pamphlets, and the hiring of the public halls where Friederich addressed the workingmen of Andersburg and other cities in the State. No doubt she thought Friederich gave away his money, if he had any at all, to the "poor" and the "oppressed." And no doubt, Charles further reflected, as he entered the dark and grimy hall, he's implied that to her just as he implies that to his followers.

Again, Charles was exasperated. He tried to quell this emotion. It was no use at all in being exasperated with Friederich. Charles tried to calm himself, but this was almost impossible in the face of the smells which greeted him upon entering what once had been a fine big parlor. The whole house smelled of dirt and dust and slovenliness.

With the memory of Wilhelm's beautiful white Georgian house still bright in his mind, Charles always found Friederich's house newly intolerable on these visits. With disgust, he saw again the ugly cheap brown carpet in the parlor, the mildewed brown walls, the battered old furniture which at its best had never been expensive or good. The black hearth was heaped with ancient ashes, which had not been removed after the last fires. The darkened light which forced its way through the windows added to the gloom and the sense of deterioration. Every stained oaken table was heaped with papers, books and pamphlets; Friederich had not had gas installed in this house, and he used naked oil lamps such as one found in the very poorest of farmhouses far out in the country. The chimneys of the lamps were rarely, if ever, washed; they were smeared with soot. Here and there, mingled with the books and the papers and the lamps, were some of Friederich's pipes. The pipes, at least, were costly and well cared for.

The bookcases near the fireplace were crowded with books on history, philosophy and socialism. They overflowed in piles against the walls.

Though the early summer evening was still very hot outside, it was cold in this room, and musty, as if sun or fire never warmed it. Charles, in the very face of Mrs. Schuele, openly dusted the cracked leather seat of a chair before sitting on it. She informed him, sourly, in "low Dutch," that Mr. Wittmann would be down at once, though he had expected Mr. Karl earlier. She stolidly accepted Charles' frown, then, as he said nothing, she lumbered away, rattling the frayed, bead portieres at the doorway in her passing. For some moments after she had gone the rattling continued, like the clinking of dice, and the sound rasped Charles' nerves.

While he waited, Charles picked up a book on the cluttered table beside him. *The Growth of Socialism,* by Eugene Debs. He had read all Mr. Debs' books, and had been impressed by the man's burning sincerity, if by his complete ignorance of reality. Quite often, Charles had been moved to agree with Debs' denunciations of injustices, and had been touched by his compassion for suffering. This book was a new one to Charles. Charles scanned a few pages. Then he was disturbed. The man was losing any contact with reality he might ever have had. There was a faint glittering madness in his writing, now.

Here and there, passages were heavily marked and underscored by Friederich's pencil. Charles put aside the book. He looked at the dead cigar in his hand, then threw it angrily into the pile of ashes on the hearth. He thought of Debs, who had once been arrested on a charge of conspiracy to kill. He had been acquitted. But there it was. Kill. Fanaticism inevitably led to hatred and to murder, no matter how high its original ideals, and its faith. It led to madness. Charles, in that cold and dirty room, became cold, himself.

Well, thank God, there was no danger of Socialism in America, and probably no danger of it anywhere else in any free country. Freedom lay in the people, and in their desire for it, and a strong, centralized State was its enemy. Charles thought this, waiting for his brother.

But still, he felt cold. The Constitution of the United States asserted that man's rights came from God. Socialism and its like declared that they should come from the State. That was an evil thing, for governments which dominated peoples were naturally their foes. Well. He was getting himself in a stew for nothing. Socialism was as far away from America as the star Arcturus, and could approach no closer.

There was a fast sound of footsteps approaching, and a fresh smell of aroused dust. Charles involuntarily frowned, recognizing the approach of his brother. He settled himself in his chair obdurately. Friederich burst into the room, and Charles understood, gloomily, that his brother was involved in one of his fits of fanaticism.

Charles' worst apprehensions were confirmed when his brother spoke in a loud but curiously stifled voice; and in German: "Karl! You are late. I suppose you have dawdled the afternoon away with Wilhelm, forgetting, in your interest in his society, that I have a meeting less than two hours from now."

Charles held back his temper. He replied in English: "I'm sorry. I had a matter to discuss with—Willie. I was late getting to his house, too." He spoke mildly. "Well, Fred, I'm here, anyway. I won't keep you, if you're busy."

Friederich stood before him, teetering on his heels. He said, sullenly: "Of course, I can't expect you to remember anything important about me. You're very irritating, you know," he added, in English. "I speak to you in our native language, and you deliberately refuse to answer me in it. Are you ashamed of it, and our inheritance?"

His belligerent attitude aroused Charles' usually latent irascibility. He always tried to be patient with his brothers, for the sake of the company, and his own peace of mind. But very often this was difficult to do. He said: " 'Our native language,' Fred? Our native language is English. We are Americans, not Germans. 'Our inheritance'? It is the inheritance of all Americans—freedom, tolerance and decency."

But Friederich obstinately returned to German: "You are as full of platitudes, my Karl, as a pudding is full of raisins. That is the capitalistic mind. Freedom! Tolerance! Decency!" He flung himself into a chair opposite Charles. "What does a capitalistic society know of these?

An unjust society, where wealth is wrongfully and unevenly distributed?"

O my God! thought Charles. Friederich was even more excited than usual. Ordinarily, he had enough good judgment to enquire about his brother's health, and make some casual remarks. To plunge like this into his favorite subject, and with so much excitement, indicated that he would soon become unbearable, and that something was obsessing him. Charles stirred a little.

But Friederich was ranting again, still in German: "You have no pride in our inheritance. Our father, and our grandparents, left Germany because they could not endure Bismarck and slavery. I ask little of you, except that you remember this with humility, and inspiration."

Charles tried unsuccessfully to control himself. Speaking in English, and in a hard voice, he said: "Fred, you don't know what you're talking about." He paused. You damned little Bismarck, yourself! he thought. "Maybe Pa and his parents came here to get away from Bismarckian Germany. Yes, they did. And why? Because Pa and his Pa were naturally the sort of people who could not live in any atmosphere but one of free enterprise and individually ambitious men, where a man could be left alone to live his own life, and to rise or fall by his own efforts. Pa wanted nothing of anyone or any Government but the chance to develop himself, without interference or paternalism, or busybodyness from a pack of bureaucrats."

Friederich was silent. His glance at Charles steadied, and narrowed. Something was flickering far back in his eyes, those small brown eyes so like Charles', and yet so dissimilar in expression. They had the look of the zealot, the dangerous look of a man madly preoccupied with his own ideas and madly hating those who did not share them. He cleared his throat. Now his eyes had a curiously sly and furtive gleam.

It always annoyed Charles that Friederich resembled him rather closely. They were of a height, though Friederich did not have Charles' somewhat stolid and heavy appearance. He was Charles himself, pared down and attenuated, agitated and fleshless, with the same straight brown hair, the same wide face and heavy mouth. But Charles' usual expression of good-tempered mildness and determination were lacking in Friederich, and, instead, the latter exuded a bellicose tenseness and passion. All the incoherence and vehemence of his narrow nature seemed to leap from him in visible, zigzag waves, even when he sat still like this, and these were enhanced by the untidiness of his clothing, his loosened dark-blue tie, his dusty shoes.

Charles thought, with contempt: I'd look just like him, if I lost my

mind or started to hate something, or someone, or everyone. Joe thinks
Fred is "visionary" and "impractical." Hell. He's as visionary as a
stone, as impractical as a banker! I've never taken Fred too seriously
before. Why am I doing it now? I have an instinct, a feeling—

Charles became alarmed. It was the same alarm he had felt when
he had been with Wilhelm. He said, banally: "Well. How are you,
Fred? After all, it's Sunday afternoon, and a time for friendly
visits."

Friederich said disdainfully, but now he spoke in English: "You do
have a gift for saying the most mediocre things. Safe. You like safety,
don't you?"

"It has its points," agreed Charles. He smiled. "You haven't told me
how you are."

Friederich waved his hand abruptly. "Who cares? Do you? Don't
be a hypocrite." Now his face changed, became charged with malev-
olence. "And how is our precious Wilhelm? Still babbling about 'art'?
Still engrossed with that china figurine of a wife of his? Still living in
his Dresden tower?"

Charles tried to answer indulgently: " 'Dresden tower?' I always
thought they called it an ivory tower. But then, I'm not literary, or
something. Willie's all right. Why do you ask? Haven't you seen him,
yourself, lately?" (China figurine! Phyllis. Why, the confounded
idiot!)

Friederich shifted himself in his chair in such a way that the motion
appeared obscene to Charles' suddenly bilious eyes. "Yes, I had the
pleasure of having dinner in his pretty house two weeks ago," said
Friederich. His words were loaded with ridicule. "What food! Veal
kidneys in wine sauce! Consomme! Something he said was a salad.
The imbecile mixed it himself. Green weeds, with wine vinegar and
olive oil, with a 'soupçon' of garlic. Pretentious ass. Raw fruit and
some disgusting French cheese and black coffee for dessert. Is that a
meal for an honest man?"

Charles' cold resentment vanished as he could not keep himself from
laughing. He, too, was familiar with Wilhelm's table.

"Give me Mrs. Schuele's apfel-kuchen and a pot of her coffee and
you can have a dozen of Wilhelm's meals," Friederich said.

He had a habit of clenching and unclenching his right hand almost
continually, as it lay on the arm of his chair, which always irritated
Charles. He was doing this now. Charles looked away. "At least," said
Friederich, with an air of unwilling tolerance, "you have a good German cook. I grant you that."

"Come to dinner tomorrow night," said Charles, immediately regretting his impulsiveness.

"I'm speaking in Philadelphia tomorrow," said Friederich. "I won't be back until Thursday morning." However, his surliness lessened.

"Willie's got a new Van Gogh," said Charles, unobtrusively glancing at his watch.

Immediately, Friederich became excited again, sitting up tensely in his chair. His eyes glinted. "He would! I asked him for a contribution to the Workman's Unemployed League, and he laughed at me. Told me to tell the poor devils to go to work! Forgot that we've been having a lot of unemployment the last two years, of course. So, he preferred a Van Gogh to feeding a few families, did he? I wonder how he'll feel when—"

" 'Comes the Revolution,' " Charles contributed, with boredom.

Friederich's nostrils flared and his eyes became vicious. "All right, sneer, Karl," he said. "But it'll come, no fear. Bloodless, if possible, bloody, if need be. We've got Wilson now, and the tide against oppressive capitalism is turning."

Charles folded his hands together with a comfortable gesture. "Ah, yes," he murmured. "Incidentally, now that we'll be having a Federal income tax, you'll be taxed, yourself, pretty hard, won't you, Fred?"

The unquiet hand became a hard fist. Friederich sat stiffly, watching his brother.

"Now I," said Charles, conversationally, "don't mind paying an income tax, if that means buying a more efficient Government. But there are some, of course, who are not taking the new income taxes agreeably. Greedy people, and so on."

Friederich cleared his throat. It was a rough sound, and one of his annoying mannerisms. "What?" he said. "I pay income tax? I don't get that much—"

"Oh, yes, you do," said Charles, in the most affectionate manner. "I've been looking over our incomes. You'll pay quite a bit, Fred. But then, you like Mr. Wilson. You know that he is so very anxious to help the workers, don't you? You know, something like the Kaiser has set up in Germany. You've always admired the Kaiser, haven't you?"

The fist became harder, like a rock. Again, Friederich cleared his throat. "I don't think it's fair for me to pay any income taxes, Karl. The company could take care of our taxes."

"The company?" said Charles softly. "Who is the company? You, I, Wilhelm, Jochen. We're the company. We're the stockholders. Are

you suggesting that Wilhelm and I and Jochen pay your taxes, Fred?
You, a bachelor?"

Friederich's large and bony face became ugly. "We could pass along
the taxes to—"

"To whom?" asked Charles, as his brother did not continue. "Should
we lower wages? Do you think we should increase the prices to our
customers, who will inevitably order less from us, and so cut down our
gross income? Or make an inferior product, so we lose customers? Or
throw some of our workers out? I'm open to suggestions, Fred."

Friederich did not answer. The gloomy light in the room deepened.

"Of course," said Charles, "we could make the men work twelve
hours a day, and so get rid of about fifteen men. What do you think?"

The fist opened, and the fingers worked again, furiously. "Some of
the men don't put in a decent day's work," Friederich muttered, uneasily.

Charles smiled grimly. He said: "But you've always maintained that
labor is being 'sweated.' You wouldn't want us to sweat our labor,
would you, Fred? Our men are on a nine-hour day, working many
hours less a week than other men in other factories in Andersburg.
You wouldn't want a twelve-hour day, would you, Fred?"

He waited. But Friederich, caught in his own trap, did not speak.
Charles fingered his watch, and his smile was open. "You've mentioned
income tax before, but you thought it meant the Rockefellers, didn't
you, Fred, or the du Ponts, or the Vanderbilts, or the Morgans. You
didn't think it meant you, too, did you, Fred? But all the time it did
mean you."

Friederich lost control of himself. "Don't call me 'Fred'!" he shouted.
"My name is Friederich! You're goading me, aren't you! Trying to in-
furiate me. Yes, I did think it meant the rich, and I still think it ought
to mean the rich—not us!"

"But we're not exactly poor," said Charles, soothingly. "And, after
all, there are so few multimillionaires in America. Even if we took all
their money from them, it wouldn't mean a dollar extra a week for
every workingman in the country. Someone's got to pay taxes. Everyone ought to, even if he gets only ten dollars a week, or if he gets ten
thousand. That is the democratic way. And you're always saying that
the real democratic way is the true Socialistic way—Fred. So, we'll all
be happy Socialists together, paying taxes for the common good. It
seems that some of your dreams are coming true, doesn't it?"

He had always known that Friederich was greedy. In espousing Socialism, Friederich not only expressed his hatred for better men and

wealthier men, and his envy of them, but he had enlarged his egotism, had acquired an audience. I wonder, thought Charles, watching his brother's face, how much of this he knows, himself. Does he really think he is an idealist?

He enjoyed himself in the silence, but it was a grim enjoyment. Then Mrs. Schuele came in with an untidy tray of strong coffee and apple-cake. Charles transferred his attention to the tray, betrayed by a natural kindness. To stare at Friederich too long, and to see what there was to be seen, would have been too brutal. So Charles studied the stained cups and the coarse cake. Mrs. Schuele pushed aside a pile of books on the nearest oak table with a reverent hand, and put down the tray. "Coffee and two lumps of sugar for me, please," said Charles.

The old woman thrust out her lips, then, as if she had not heard, she stomped out of the room. " 'Comes the Revolution,' " Charles repeated to himself, amused. "Shall I pour the coffee, Friederich?" he asked.

"Thanks," said Friederich, sullenly. Charles lifted the coffeepot. The handle was sticky. The hot liquid came out, smelling of chickory. The cheapest damn coffee! Charles, a coffee lover, lost his appetite. He poured a very small cup for himself. There was pale blue milk, no cream. The sugar was spotted. The cake was dry and fell into stale crumbs at a touch.

Usually, during these visits, Friederich would talk almost constantly of Debs and Socialism. For some reason or other, he did not bring up the subject today. He chewed his cake moodily, staring at nothing, the crumbs falling over his vest and his knees. He was thinking. Sometimes his eyebrows quirked. Charles, his sure instinct once more aroused, again scrutinized him. When Friederich looked like this, he was thinking of only one thing—money.

Charles said, idly: "There's a meeting on Thursday, as you know. The Connington Steel Company wants our land along the river."

Friederich swallowed his cake. He lifted his cup to his lips. "I am going to vote 'no,' " said Charles.

"Why?" The word was explosive. "What's your objection? They'll employ a lot of men, Karl. What's wrong with furnishing employment to hundreds of men, bringing in new workers, if necessary?" Friederich glared at him. "They're offering a good price, too."

Charles shook his head slightly. "Oh, you've forgotten about the Connington, Fred. They've mills, as you know, in Pittsburgh, and in Parkersburg. They sweat their labor."

"I'll help organize them," said Friederich, his eyes sparkling with fervor. "We'll agitate for a closed shop. We—"

"They're a powerful company, Fred. You know that. Pinkertons. They know how to break strikes. They pay the lowest wages. You wouldn't want all that, would you, Fred? The workers who practically worship you here wouldn't like to hear you voted to bring in the Connington, would they?"

Friederich put down his cup on the table with a violent thump. "Don't think you can keep on jeering at me this way, Karl!"

Charles raised his eyebrows. "Jeering? I'm not jeering. I was just going along with you, I thought. Well, then, if you think you can do something about them, let them come in. But not on our land. I'm taking out an option on the Burnsley land, five miles away from the river, and offering it to the Connington. They'll take it, because they want a mill in this area."

"But they won't pay so much for the Burnsley land," blurted Friederich. At his own betrayal, he caught his breath. But Charles did not seem to have noticed.

"Maybe not. But then, if we don't offer them the Burnsley land, which we can buy cheaply, and sell to them for as high a price as possible, and if we don't sell them our river land, they'll buy land from someone else. Or do you object to making an honest dollar, Fred?"

Again, Friederich was silent, and this time with rage.

Charles leaned back in his chair, with an expression of judiciousness. "Now, then, if it were generally known, among the people here, that Friederich Wittmann voted against the Connington getting our river land, and so preserving our water front, it would react in your favor, Fred. Then you could tell the newspapers that you intend to see to it that the houses of any new workers built near the mills, on the Burnsley land, would comply with what you call decent housing. And then we could announce that we're going to sell the river land to the city; they want it, you know. It could be called the Wittmann Civic Park. It could be announced that it would be a park for the people, for their enjoyment. That would make you very popular, Fred. Everyone would think it was your idea. It would be just like you, wouldn't it?"

Friederich stared at him, with as great and as sudden an excitement as Wilhelm had shown. But avarice struggled a little longer in Friederich than it had struggled in Wilhelm, Charles noticed. In the end, as it had done in Wilhelm, egotism won.

"The Wittmann Civic Park!" exclaimed Friederich. He saw the headlines in the newspapers. "Mr. Friederich Wittmann, always a fighter for the common people, has just announced—"

Friederich's knotted fist went to his mouth. He looked at Charles.

Then his eyes narrowed suspiciously. "It doesn't sound like you," he mumbled. "You've got something up your sleeve, Karl."

"No, I haven't." Charles smiled. "I honestly like the idea of the park."

Friederich thought again of his talk with his brother Jochen, only a few days ago. Again, the struggle began in him. Charles watched that struggle.

The Connington Steel Company would employ many workers, now unemployed. They would bring in more. Friederich's field of activity would be widened. He would become even more important. What an opportunity! This, with the park, would make his position invincible, would gain more fame for him.

He removed his fist from his mouth. "I'll vote with you, Karl," he said, with an air of high resolution and self-sacrifice.

Charles nodded. "I knew you would, of course," he said. He stood up. He offered his hand to his brother, who remained seated. Friederich reluctantly took that hand. He was still suspicious. Karl was a "capitalist" and a conservative of the worst kind. But there was one thing certain—he would never do anything that would entail a loss for the company.

Charles put his hands in his pockets. He smiled down at Friederich. "Joe will try to influence you," he said, with an innocent air. "Don't let him. He wants to sell that land to the Connington. But you understand things, now Joe'll do anything for money. You know that. Remember how he contributed to the strike-breaking fund of the Andersburg Forge Company? You didn't speak to him for six months after that, and good for you, too! You remember how disgusted I was with him, myself. And then there was that business about our own company having a closed shop. I went along with you on that."

Friederich muttered something.

"Joe calls you a rabble-rouser," said Charles, indulgently. "But that's just his way. And I didn't like him calling you a crackpot, either. Brothers should stand together, shouldn't they, Fred?"

Friederich's face darkened with anger and hatred. "Jochen was always a swine," he said. Friederich was one who never forgave.

He accompanied his brother to the door. The twilight was clear and fresh even on that tree-sheltered street. Two men, neighbors, well-dressed and stout, were examining the house deliberately and murmuring through puffs of cigar smoke. When they saw Charles, they nodded with friendly smiles, but ignored Friederich. With immense leisure, they looked at the grassless lawns, glanced at the stables behind the house, lifted their hats and went on. Their pompous walk was an insult in itself. Charles held back a smile. But Friederich flushed.

"Interfering rascals," he said. "What business is it of theirs?"

"None at all," agreed Charles. "If grass won't grow, it won't grow, that's all. Good night, Fred."

CHAPTER IV

As CHARLES' carriage rolled on, he could indulge himself in a normally malicious complacency. Well, that settles Joe, he thought. Then he scowled. It seemed to him that he was always "settling" something or other about his brothers, and always rescuing the Company from them, and even the city, itself, in some measure.

Thinking of those brothers, it came to him more clearly than ever that in spite of Friederich's hatred for Jochen, and Jochen's ridicule of Friederich, these two were "closer" than a casual inspection of their relationship would disclose. Just as Willie and I are curiously "close," thought Charles, surprised. The thought intrigued him. Willie and his art! But Wilhelm had been his ally in many contests, and Wilhelm had frequently shown respect for his older brother. For Friederich, Wilhelm had only a cold contempt, and for Jochen he had an even colder detestation.

The long twilight before the dark had set in, and Charles wondered whether or not he could reasonably order his carriage to be turned about and go home. But no, Jochen and Isabel were expecting him, though it was so late. There was nothing to do but to run in for three or four minutes, and then excuse himself. Jimmy was waiting for him. The boy would not eat his own supper until his father returned.

At least, Jochen's house was not too far. Within five minutes, the carriage was rolling briskly down wide Beechwood Road, with its array of pretentious mansions set far back from the street. Though Andersburg had less than one hundred thousand population, it was an unusually wealthy city, and Beechwood Road had taken over the title of "Millionaires' Row" from Schiller Road only a few short years ago. The houses here had a rich aura about them, surrounded as they were by long broad lawns and trees and gardens. Jochen's house was one of the most ostentatious, built of rosy brick with white pillars in a style reminiscent of Southern architecture. It had a mellowed air, though it was only six years old. Isabel might be the daughter of a wealthy butcher (who had finally possessed a large slaughterhouse of his own), but she had taste. Wilhelm might have genuine antiques, and Isabel might have only their excellent reproductions, but at least one could sit on a love-seat or a chair without fear of its collapsing and without uneasily hearing ominous creaks under one. The oriental rugs might not be more than thirty years old, but they had a genuine lustre about them, and no frayed edges, and no delicate repairs. All in all, Charles preferred Jochen's house to Wilhelm's. One could tire very easily of beautiful fragility, but one never tired of beautiful, sturdy warmth, even if books were never in evidence, or one painting of real worth.

The last sunlight touched the top of the high and ancient elms and chestnuts along the street, and rippled faintly on the slate roofs of the great houses. Here and there a lamp or two began to shine through shrubbery. Yes, it was late. He'd stay three minutes only. Charles felt some regret. His brother Jochen had a fine cook, and Isabel never served tea or sherry. Excellent coffee would always be produced, and a plate of marvelous pastries, or, if Charles so signified, a Scotch and soda. Jochen lived largely and rapaciously. Wilhelm's fine and exquisite home became ghostly in Charles' thoughts, and Friederich's repulsive house was happily forgotten.

The carriage rolled up the drive. A light shone through the wide and glittering north window. It was almost time for supper. Charles ran lightly up the shallow white steps of the house and rang the bell.

A crisp young maid admitted him, all black and white muslin. Yes, Mr. and Mrs. Wittmann were in the drawing-room. Isabel and Jochen were waiting for him. Isabel was working on some embroidery, and Jochen was reading one of his endless financial journals, and smoking one of his splendid cigars. The high crystal chandelier had been lighted, and it shone down on all the rich color below it and the well-placed furniture and the expensive Sarouk rugs.

"We'd given you up, Charlie," said Jochen, dropping his papers, and flicking the ash from his cigar. He stood up, and stretched, crudely, and yawned. Isabel smiled at Charles. "You're staying for supper, I hope," she said. She extended her hand to him with a great-lady gesture, and he took it.

"Sorry, Isabel," said Charles. "I was delayed. From the very beginning. I'm just staying a moment or two."

"Scotch?" said Jochen.

"Thanks." Charles sat down in a good, comfortable chair, a chair which Wilhelm would disdainfully have called "bastard Chippendale." "But make it a small one," he added, hypocritically.

Jochen chuckled. He went to a tray on a distant table, where the seltzer stood, and the whiskey. Isabel watched her husband. "We had some very nice cakes," she said. "But we sent them back. Would you like some, Charles?"

"Scotch and cakes?" shouted Jochen. He glanced over his big shoulder affectionately at his wife. "I'll bet Charlie's had all the weak tea and sour coffee and stale cake—or any cake, for that matter—that he wants in one day. Right, Charlie?"

"You're right," smiled Charles. He looked about him. He liked this large room, and its comfort, and its massive beauty, even if he did not like either Jochen or Isabel. He suspected, with good reason, that they did not like him, either, and that he formed a solid part of their conversation with each other. He distrusted Jochen and his wife. He distrusted all hearty men, and he disliked women who gave themselves airs, and whose smiles were always gracious and sly.

He ought to have been ill at ease with these two, but he never was. He was never one for probing into his own emotions, so he did not probe now.

Jochen brought back two glasses which tinkled pleasantly. He gave one to Charles, and sat down with one in his own hand. "Cigar?" he asked. Charles accepted a cigar. There was no doubt of it: these two could make one feel at home, if one overlooked a number of things, such as knowing glances between husband and wife, and false smiles, and affected cordiality.

"Well, how's our Willie, and our Fred?" asked Jochen. "I suppose you've made your rounds?"

"Willie's all right, and Fred—well, Fred was not too bad today," replied Charles, temperately.

Jochen and Isabel gave each other a quick look, and seemed amused. Charles concentrated on his drink.

"And how is dear Phyllis?" asked Isabel, with insincere interest.

Charles was accustomed to these questions. He usually answered them automatically. But all at once, something in Isabel's voice irritated him. He looked at her. "Prettier than ever," he said. "But then, Phyllis was always a beautiful woman. Remember, Joe," he went on, turning to his brother, "when Phyllis was considered the most beautiful girl in Andersburg?"

He knew, without looking again at Isabel, that he had annoyed her, and it pleased him. Jochen laughed. "You always thought so, didn't you?" he said. "Well, I didn't. I like body in women, and Phyllis hasn't any. Not obviously, anyway."

Charles put down his glass deliberately. He knew they were watching him. This was ridiculous, but he felt his heavy anger rising. He stared at the glass he had put down. It was that sherry, and the work he had had to do today, that was making something beat strongly in his chest. Damn them, he wasn't going to let them stir up his liver. He looked at his brother, who was watching him with a wide smile.

Jochen, vice-president of the Wittmann Machine Tool Company, was thirty-six, three years younger than Charles. But he was a bigger man, and was "going to fat," and his brown hair was thinning noticeably. He had the Wittmann broad face, but it was broader than Charles', and his small brown eyes were even smaller, so that at times they appeared hardly more than beads between his thick lids. He had a very high color, which could become apoplectic, and his full Witt-mann mouth had a certain brutishness about it. His large and prominent nose had a reddish tinge, for Jochen loved liquor and good food in unrestricted quantities. He had thick ears, unlike those of any of his brothers, and they flared from his big round head, and were almost as red as his nose. He dressed well, though his clothing just escaped being loud, in Charles' opinion, and he had a clean look in spite of his bulk.

For a few moments, Charles disliked Jochen almost as much as he disliked Friederich. It was queer; he could not put a finger on it. But there it was: Jochen reminded him of Friederich in some obscure way, though Friederich was all fanaticism and Jochen was all expediency. Charles paused, and considered. Could it be that fanaticism and expediency were identical traits?

Charles became aware of the fact that Isabel had been speaking to him. He wanted to say, rudely: "What?" But he was never rude with women, even when he disliked them immensely. So he just listened closely, and tried to discover what she had been saying.

"But, of course, Phyllis was never very robust," Isabel concluded. Charles gathered that she had been remarking on Phyllis' recent appearance.

"She couldn't be presenting Willie with an heir at this late date, could she?" asked Jochen, following his words up with a loud laugh.

Charles remembered that Isabel was nearly two years older than Phyllis, so he said: "Hardly. Too old for that. Wouldn't you say, Isabel?"

"Not too old, certainly," replied Isabel, and in so stiff a voice that Charles was pleased again. "After all, she's only a year younger than myself. Thirty-four, isn't she?"

Her vexation was evident, and this amused Jochen so that he laughed again. She directed a hard glance at him, and his laughter stopped. Charles was even more pleased. He picked up his glass again.

"Two years younger," said Jochen, punishing his wife. "You're thirty-six, Isabel. Never mind. You're the prettiest woman in Andersburg, in my opinion, Sweet; so don't glare."

Isabel was indeed a comely woman. Even Charles admitted that. She was tall and had a full but graceful figure, which was the admiration of herself and her friends and Jochen, and she had very neat ankles which she frequently displayed, and very small feet exquisitely shod. She had a more slender face than one would expect in a woman of her proportions, and her complexion was all white and illusive pink. It was her boast that people frequently suspected her of "painting," but art could not have reproduced those fine tints. Her features were good; she had full hazel eyes with sweeping lashes, a beautiful if somewhat narrow mouth, and a nose without fault. Her high-swept hair was thick and dark, coiled at the back and gleaming. It was strange that all these assets, good in themselves, could express a latent commonness, for not a single feature, taken singly, was coarse.

Charles did not like people who spoke of "good breeding." He thought it precious. Yet all at once he was thinking that Isabel had no "breeding." She was not a lady, and she would never be one, in spite of her dainty airs and her careful mannerisms and her assumed aristocracy. Her father, becoming well to do when she had been sixteen, had sent her to a finishing school in Philadelphia for two years. It had done no good at all, reflected Charles. There were even moments when Isabel forgot her grammar, and became entangled in syntax. But she had brought considerable money to Jochen, and Jochen loved her and admired her, and she had given him children, and it was apparent that she loved Jochen in return and admired him extravagantly. Charles had had it repeated to him, by friends, that Isabel felt it unfair that he, and not Jochen, was president of the Company.

Charles bore her no malice for this. It seemed right and proper to him that a wife should have a good opinion of her husband. So, it was not this that made him dislike her. In the past, his dislike had always been a passive thing; he wondered why it was suddenly active, tonight.

Isabel, forgetting her annoyance, and pleased at her husband's compliment, gave him a gracious smile. She turned to Charles: "How is

Jimmy?" she asked. "I haven't seen him for a month, not since Geraldine's birthday party."

"Jimmy's all right," said Charles, his voice unconsciously warming, as it always did when his son was mentioned.

Jochen looked at his cigar. "The Bachs' kid was telling Geraldine that he thought Jimmy had something on his mind lately. Isn't as interested in football and track meets as he used to be. Well, kids grow up."

Charles was provoked. He was about to reply, but was suddenly silent. Yes, there was "something" about Jimmy these last few months. He, Charles, had dismissed the thought with the easy explanation that Jimmy was becoming a man, and was changing into maturity. Then he recalled that he had often caught Jimmy's quick look, which turned away at once. Charles was uneasy. It was not like Jimmy, who was so devoted to him, and who trusted him so implicitly, not to speak of everything to his father.

Then Charles said: "Boys grow up, as you say, Joe. Maybe he's having his first attack of puppy love. I'll hear about it, eventually, from him."

He thought of Jochen's three girls, Geraldine, May and Ethel. He did not like May and Ethel, who were pretentious and full of baseless snobbery like their mother, and who, even at fourteen and thirteen, were always careful to do the correct and socially acceptable thing. They also had Jochen's malice and greed. Charles disliked their childish voices, affected and stilted. They, with their sister Geraldine, went to the best school for girls in Andersburg, and they made a special study of candidates for their friendship. Social climbers, like their mother, thought Charles. But in their climbing, like Isabel's, they showed no taste. Fine girls of fine and distinguished families, if those families were not particularly wealthy, were quite ignored by May and Ethel.

However, this was not so with Geraldine, who was Charles' favorite, and for whom he had a strong paternal affection. Geraldine might not be so pretty as May and Ethel, but she had a genuine "air." It came to Charles that Geraldine was considerably like her uncle Wilhelm, who, in an unguarded moment, had confessed that if he had ever had children he might have liked a girl like Geraldine. She was not, at sixteen, particularly interested in dress and fashion, for she was studious and grave. Yet Charles had often heard her laugh with Jimmy, and the laugh had been sweet and humorous.

Geraldine was a disappointment to her parents, for she was not socially ambitious. Yet, they were concerned about her. Charles knew, without ever having been conscious of a hint from Isabel or Jochen, that they hoped that Jimmy and Geraldine might marry some day. Certainly, they had reason for such hope, for Jimmy and Geraldine had been playmates all their lives, and Jimmy had recently said that Geraldine was the only girl he knew who had "sense."

Thinking this, he said aloud: "Yes, probably just puppy love. He's at the age for it." He looked at his brother and Isabel. "I hope it's Geraldine."

They smiled at him at once, genuine smiles of pleasure, and so he knew he had been right. "Well, Gerry's just a baby, but we'll see in time, after she's been at Wellesley."

Isabel gave her husband a cold glance. "I wish you wouldn't call her 'Gerry,' Jochen. Geraldine's such a pretty name. I detest nicknames."

Charles knew that the thrust was meant for him, also, so he deliberately said: "Well, I must go, Joe. You remember, Joe, that we've a meeting for Thursday, to discuss the sale of the river land. Think over my idea, Joe, of selling the land to the city. You wouldn't want the Connington to get the land and ruin the water front, would you, Joe?"

Joe did not answer immediately, but his eyes glinted foxily. He's thinking he's got Willie and Fred, thought Charles. He waited innocently for Jochen's reply.

Jochen coughed. "It isn't so very important, Charlie. We'll discuss it Thursday." His manner was careless.

Then Jochen's manner changed, became mean and domineering: "I wanted you to come earlier, Charlie, for a private chat. I'll have to be as quick as possible now, I suppose, Why are you keeping on Tom Murphy, who's a troublemaker? Look here, I don't care about his breaking Fred's window. Fred's a damn fool, but he's our brother. Anyway, I'm not going to discuss Fred and his wild ideas. Fred's basically sound. He likes money, in spite of all his jabbering about Socialism. Socialism is just a kind of disease with him, because he feels inferior to the rest of us." He paused.

Charles was surprised. He knew that Jochen was shrewd, but he had never guessed that he had a kind of rough subtlety, too. Shrewd men who were also subtle could be dangerous.

"It's Tom Murphy I'm interested in," said Jochen, and he gave Charles one of his brutal and unfriendly stares. "Tom Murphy organized the union in our shops."

"A company union," Charles reminded him.

"I don't care what the hell you call it," said Jochen, his voice rising. "It's a union, and I'm against unions. You and Fred cooked it up together. I thought you always laughed at Fred. That's why I don't understand why you supported him in that union thing."

Charles puffed at his cigar. His eyes wandered to Isabel, attractive in her light gray muslin gown. He saw the sparkle of the diamonds on her fingers. She was listening, with her ladylike air of patrician uninterest.

Charles said, slowly: "I believe in unions. You've always known that. We treat our men fairly and decently. We pay good wages. But other companies don't—"

" 'Fairly and decently,' hell!" exclaimed Jochen. "I'd show 'em, if I had the power. But you're the president," he added insultingly. "It's in your hands, most of the time. Unions!"

Charles said: "There is a lesson we've all got to learn, and that is if capitalism is going to survive in America the industrialists will have to get rid of any anachronistic attitudes of employer-and-servant relationships, and will have to think of the welfare of their men. It's a matter of survival, for all of us."

Jochen interrupted him rudely: "I've always said, and maintained, that you're fundamentally a radical, Charlie."

Charles wanted to laugh, wryly. He was a "capitalist" and an "exploiter" to Friederich, and a "radical" to Jochen—Friederich and Jochen, who were so queerly alike! Jochen said: "Well, why don't you laugh? You want to, don't you?"

"I'm not particularly amused," replied Charles.

Jochen went on: "You and your 'benefits'! It's costing us a pretty penny, right out of our pockets. Paying the men full wages for the first week they're sick, or something, or maybe just recovering from a drunk. Bonuses at Christmas. Payments if they're hurt at work, when all the time it is their own damn, stupid, careless fault! And then this rotten union, and Tom Murphy, who's always stirring up trouble—"

"That isn't true," Charles said, quietly. "He's the best foreman we have. Have you forgotten that invention on the lathe he thought up?"

"Well, he invented it on our time. It belongs to us."

"In a way. And we pay him royalties. That's the law. But we're getting off the subject. Tom's all right. He doesn't stir up our men. He just stirs up men in other concerns, who are really exploited and sweated."

"I always said you were a 'radical,' " said Jochen. "Why don't you join Fred and sing the happy song of Socialism together?"

The idea of being mentioned in the same breath with Friederich was so repulsive to Charles that he stood up. He was shorter than

Jochen, and considerably smaller. But when he stood like this, braced on his sturdy legs, with his hands in his pockets, he exuded a curious force and formidableness. Even Jochen could feel it.

Charles said, and he let every word fall strongly and slowly into the room: "Our father's will made me president of this company. You can dislodge me, Joe, only if you can get Willie and Fred to help you, and only if you can get fifty-two percent of the company stock away from me. You can't do it, Joe. And so, while I'm overlooking your insults, I'm not overlooking what is in your mind. You're helpless, Joe. You aren't going to badger me into getting rid of Tom Murphy. You aren't going to get me to destroy the company union. You're not going to prevent me from giving the men the little benefits we give them. And when the time comes—and it might come soon, considering the rise in the cost of living—we'll raise the men's wages. Let's have that clear between us."

Jochen might have stood up. If he had done so, he would have towered some six inches above his brother. But he did not stand up. He contented himself with letting all his hatred glare from his face at his brother. He also tried to impress Charles with his contempt, a contempt he did not actually feel.

"All right, all right!" he shouted. "We're stuck with you, and you roll in that fact like a dog rolls in grass! I'm just your vice-president. I'm nothing. You rub that in all the time. No matter what comes up, I find later that you go behind my back and get Willie and Fred with you. They become mush in your hands." His eyes narrowed cunningly. "There's something sly about you, Charlie. But you'll be sly once too often, one of these days."

Now Charles let himself laugh, and it was genuine laughter. "Don't be an ass, Joe. Look at our company. Times haven't been too good these last two years. But we not only hold our own, but we are making profits, too. I only want the company to prosper. I want it to maintain its reputation for the best precision machine tools in the country. What's wrong with all that?"

But Jochen did not answer. He was biting his lower lip. He's thinking about the river property, and how he's got Willie and Fred with him, thought Charles, with enjoyment.

He knew he was right when Jochen suddenly grinned, and became all expansiveness. "Hell, Charlie, what are we fighting about? We've been over this hundreds of times. But I've been edgy today. No offense meant, even though I still think you're wrong." His grin became wider.

Charles smiled in return. "Well, we all have our own opinions, don't we?"

Isabel had been listening smugly, but when Charles had stood up she had become alarmed. She knew Charles' power; she knew he never forgot insults, and that he could become ruthless. She wanted a marriage between Geraldine and Jimmy. Jimmy was his father's heir. She, knowing all about the coming controversy over the river property, wished Jochen had not antagonized his brother. She felt Charles' hard antagonism, for all his mild words. So she gave Jochen a reproving glance, and said: "I'm really surprised at you, Jochen. Charles drops in for a moment and you begin to fight with him over company matters. It's Sunday, my dear, and this is just a social call. Why don't you reserve your arguments for your offices?"

"I don't mind, Isabel," said Charles, giving her a tolerant smile.

"Isabel's right," said Jochen, heartily. Now he could stand up. He stood beside his personable wife, and put his hand on her shoulder. Then he bent his big stout body and kissed her on the forehead. She looked up at him, fondly. "Not mad at me, are you, Isabel?"

"I think you are a naughty, bad-mannered boy, Jochen," she answered, with a murmuring sound of affection in her voice. "I do hope Charles forgives you."

"Nothing to forgive," answered Charles briskly. "Our arguments mean nothing, do they, Joe?"

"Of course not," said Jochen, with even more heartiness. Now he was full of confidence and hidden triumph. He'd have his own little fun, on Thursday.

Charles asked of Isabel: "Where are the girls? Where's Geraldine?"

Isabel's beautiful breast swelled with pride. "They're having supper with the Weaver girls. Such nice girls, you know, Charles. They are really the leaders of the younger set." She was very pleased that Charles had asked about Geraldine. She knew his fondness for the girl.

"Well, I must be going," said Charles. "It's getting dark, and Jimmy's waiting."

They went to the great white front doors with him, all friendliness and cordiality. Jochen even accompanied him to his carriage. "Where's your automobile?" he asked. "Why run around in this old-fashioned thing, Charlie?"

"I like leisure—sometimes," said Charles.

They parted with the utmost amiability. Jochen returned to his house, looking up for a moment or two at its proud façade complacently. Isabel was waiting for him in the hall, and she was frowning.

"Really, Jochen," she said, as he closed the door. "Why did you quarrel like that with Charles? You know it's a very serious thing, about that river property. You may have Wilhelm and Friederich with you, but Charles can be obstinate, and get into one of his moods. You might have kept things pleasant today."

Jochen kissed her again. "Listen, my darling. You can be pleasant as all hell with old Charlie, all of the time, but when it comes to policy, or anything about the company, he doesn't get into one of his 'moods.' He just steps down, hard. Moods never move Charlie."

He chuckled. "But this time he won't step on anybody. I've got the whole thing, right here in the palm of my hand. I can't wait for Thursday!"

CHAPTER V

ALL IN ALL, it had been a very arduous day, but a day that had been extremely profitable, also. Nevertheless, Charles was exhausted as his carriage rolled down unpretentious if well-kept Bowbridge Avenue where he still lived in his father's old house.

Here the middle-class Quakers and Mennonites and German business men lived, industrious, sober, unimaginative. They had not built on Victorian lines, but their houses had a certain compact uniformity of brick and fieldstone or of wood painted brown or dark green, shuttered and quiet, with broad verandahs and large gardens. The lawns were tidy, the shrubbery excessively neat from diligent pruning. Hedges, like green walls, separated property with great preciseness. One or two more daring families had installed electricity, but in the main the houses were lighted with gas. A few even used oil lamps, and while this was criticized as old-fashioned, the practice was not unduly condemned. Here, as Wilhelm often said, could be found more bead portieres than anywhere else in Andersburg, the most ugly of tremendous mahogany furniture, the heaviest lace curtains, the most ponderous crimson velvet draperies, the darkest rooms and the dullest rugs. And, again quoting Wilhelm, the worst cooks, the most parsimonious of householders.

But, as Charles would reply to Wilhelm, no one on this street had ever become bankrupt, had ever (noticeably) dallied outside his conjugal bed or had overdrawn his bank balance. Bankers highly respected the residents on Bowbridge Avenue, and, at the last, Charles said, this was the most important thing.

Charles had the only automobile on the street. He knew he had excited disapproval with this. The disapproval did not displease him. If it had not been for Jimmy, he would not have bought the automobile. But Jimmy, like so many of the younger people here, to quote their parents, was "restless."

Charles' house was almost exactly like the neighboring houses. It was built of dark-red brick; it had dull-green shutters; it had a big verandah, a garden of rich flowers, a stable. Jochen sometimes told Charles that the furniture in any Bowbridge Avenue house could be exchanged for that of any other, complete with curtains and draperies and silver and glass and china, and the inhabitants would not be aware of the change. Charles agreed, tolerantly. It was his parents' house; he liked it. He knew it was ugly, but it was warm and comfortable. He even liked the whatnots in the corners of the living room, filled with paper weights, Dresden china figurines, little glass gimcracks, and sea shells. These had been his mother's pride. He did not mind the small windows, the overpowering trees, the shutters, the long narrow halls, the steep staircases, the stained-glass window in the front door. To him, it was home, ugly or not. The oppressive mahogany everywhere, banisters, walls, overpowering furniture, did not make him melancholy as they did Wilhelm. The old bathroom, with its marble tiles, marble wash basin and enameled tub enclosed in a mahogany frame, suited him. He had been born here, as all his brothers had been born here. He now slept in his parents' bed, in which he had been born.

The more Wilhelm and Jochen ridiculed the house, the more obstinate did Charles become about it. The more they derided its discomforts, its lack of beauty, the more desirable it became to him. He was fond of the dark green and red plush in his living room, and of the black marble mantelpieces, and the crowded dining room.

His housekeeper would be at her church now, but Charles knew that a cold and nourishing supper had been left for him and Jimmy on the dining-room table. His beer would be waiting in the icebox for him, good refreshing German beer. He let himself into the house, whistling thoughtfully, still thinking of what he had accomplished today.

Young James Wittmann was reading in the parlor as his father came in. Jimmy was not overly given to reading, until lately, Charles thought. Now he read almost all the time. If Jochen had not spoken of the boy that evening, Charles would not have remembered this. He did not know whether to be pleased or displeased at this new studiousness.

The big gas chandelier flared down on the curved mahogany and velvet and Brussels carpeting of the room. Jimmy was huddled on a sofa, with a big book on his knees. As his father entered, he put the book hastily aside. Charles observed that the boy closed the book, almost guiltily. Charles ignored the book, and smiled at his son, who stood up. "Hello, Dad," said the boy. "I thought someone had kept you for supper. But I waited." His smile was boyish and affectionate.

"You know I always come back for supper, Jimmy," said Charles. He sat down, wearily. "I'll rest a minute, and then we'll go into the dining room." Jimmy sat down, slowly, and studied his father.

"How's Uncle Will, and Uncle Fred, and Uncle Joe?" he asked, politely.

"You know how they are," answered Charles, laughing a little.

Jimmy nodded, seriously. "I know. But Uncle Will's not too bad. I'm beginning to like him. I even like some of his pictures." He paused, then he asked: "And how is Aunt Phyllis?" He was much attached to Phyllis, and he looked at his father.

"I thought she seemed a little tired," replied Charles. He shifted uneasily in his chair. "I didn't see Geraldine," he added.

Jimmy smiled. "Gerry," he said. "Gerry's a wonderful girl, even if she's only sixteen."

"Well, you're only seventeen," Charles remarked. "Why, you won't be eighteen until February. Don't try to grow up too fast, Jim." He smiled as he said this, but he looked at Jimmy. There was no holding back growth. His son would soon be a young man. Though still so young, he appeared older than he was. He sometimes forced Charles to admit that he could "pass" for nineteen or twenty. Certainly, he was tall and broad, with excellent shoulders, long arms and legs. He had never been a good student at school, until this last year. Now he excelled. Charles supposed, vaguely, that all boys were like this. Then he recalled that Jimmy had been pressing him lately to write to Harvard. Next year, he would be ready for a university. But Charles had not as yet written. To write would be to admit that his son was preparing to leave him.

He often told himself that possibly all fathers thought their sons the finest creatures in the world, but he was certain that no other boy could approach Jimmy for good temper, intelligence, kindness and maturity of personality. He was like his dead mother, in all this. He also had Mary's curly black hair and her clear, dark complexion, and her sudden bright smile. Everything about Jimmy was alive and vital, without clumsiness or coarseness. A few years later Charles was to say over and over to himself: No one was ever more alive than Jimmy. Jimmy was life, itself.

"What've you been doing while I've been making my rounds, son?"

"Nothing very much, Dad. Just reading." The boy put his big, well-formed hand over his book, as if to protect it. Protect it from whom? From me? thought Charles, dismayed.

"You look tired, Dad," said the boy, suddenly. For some reason or other, he colored. He got up, quickly, and moved to a chair closer to his father. He had a very handsome and masculine young face, and now it was grave. "You've got no one to take care of you, but me," the boy went on, awkwardly. "You ought to have had more kids, Dad."

"You're enough for me," said Charles, smiling with deep affection.

But Jimmy was looking aside. "You ought to have gotten married again, Dad, and had other children, too. Why didn't you marry? Mother's been dead for years."

Charles stopped smiling. "I didn't want to, Jimmy," he said, and his voice was a trifle stern. He waited. "What's wrong, Jimmy? You never talked like this before."

Jimmy tried to laugh, but the attempt was a failure. "I've just been thinking about you, Dad. I—I'm all you have. I'm the only boy in the Wittmann family. Aunt Phyllis won't have any children. Uncle Fred's a bachelor. Uncle Joe has three girls. So I just thought it would be— good—for you to have other sons." He looked down at his hands. "The business needs other sons—your sons, Dad."

Charles was silent. His dismay was growing. He waited for Jimmy to speak again, but the boy sat there, utterly quiet.

Then Charles said: "Well. I still have you, for the company. And Joe's girls will marry, and Joe will doubtless get their husbands into the company."

"But their husbands won't be Wittmanns," muttered Jimmy. "I suppose, some day, I'll marry Gerry."

"Then there'll be Wittmanns, possibly half a dozen of them, in the company," said Charles, heavily trying for lightness.

Jimmy stood up. He looked about him. Then, restlessly, he began to walk up and down the room, his hands in his pockets. Charles watched him, perturbed. The boy's steps quickened. He was frowning, and it was not a boyish frown. His head was bent. An unruly black curl fell over his forehead. He shook it away. Then he stopped directly before his father. His face was greatly distressed.

"Dad, I've got to tell you," he burst out.

Charles said: "Yes, Jimmy. I've known you had something to say. But I thought I'd better wait until you were ready to tell me, yourself."

Jimmy regarded him somberly. "You see, Dad, it's Mother. I was only twelve when she died. And I've been thinking."

Charles sat up in his chair. Mary. This was the second time today that his dead wife had been mentioned. He did not know why he felt so wretched, and so sad. He had believed he had overcome his grief, that he had begun to forget. But the wound had not healed, after all. He said again, very gently: "Yes, Jimmy?"

"It was so senseless, Mother's dying," Jimmy said, rapidly. Anger was fierce in his eyes. "I've been thinking about it for a long time. And the baby died, too. It was carelessness. I know it was. And lots of women, like Mother, die like that. It—it ought to be stopped." He looked at his father, and his anger was more intense. "Dad, have you written to Harvard yet? I didn't tell you, but I must tell you now. I want to be a doctor. I want to specialize in gynecology. I want it more than—more than anything. I don't want to go into the company, Dad. I know this is terrible for you, but I just can't go into the company, not feeling as I feel now. You see, I haven't talked to you very much about Mother. I wanted to help you forget. But I never forgot. I want to save women like Mother."

Charles put his hand slowly to his forehead, and rubbed it. He felt dazed. Dully, he watched his son run to the couch, and snatch up a book. Jimmy presented it to him, thrusting it towards his father with a kind of desperation. "This is what I've been reading all summer, Dad. Osler."

Charles took the book, but he did not open it or look at it. Instead, he looked at Jimmy's hands, clean and strong and slender.

"I know you are thinking: 'He's young. He's restless. He just has a sudden idea, like all kids. He'll get over it.' Dad—"

"I wasn't thinking that, Jimmy."

Jimmy sat down again, suddenly, on the edge of his chair. He leaned towards his father. He wound his fingers together. "I ought to have told you before, Dad. I ought to have told you, two years ago. You see, I've been wanting this almost since Mother died. I know it's right for me to want to be a doctor. It's the only thing I do want."

Charles did not know what to do or say, so he opened the book. But he could not see a single word. The book lay on his knees.

"You're terribly disappointed, aren't you, Dad?" asked Jimmy, wretchedly. "And you think I'm just being sentimental, because of Mother."

"No," said Charles. "No, I'm not thinking that." He went on after a moment: "I'm not going to pretend I'm not disappointed. I am. I thought you liked the shops."

"I tried to, for your sake, Dad."

Charles was deeply touched. He leaned towards his son, and laid his hand on the boy's knee. "Jimmy," he said. Then he could not continue for a few minutes. He coughed. He could finally speak again: "Jimmy, I'm glad you told me. I wouldn't want you to go into the company if you don't want to. That would hurt me more than anything else." He tried to smile. "You would be unhappy, and I couldn't stand that. Jimmy, when a man really wants something, he owes it to himself, and others, to get what he wants. And what you want is—good."

He rubbed his hands over the book. "Good," he repeated. "I'm proud of you, Jimmy. I'm more proud of you than ever. But I wish—"

"You wish I didn't think so much about Mother."

"Well, yes. Yes, that's it. You were so young when she died, son. I had hoped it didn't—hurt—you so much. But I can see now that it did. I haven't been very bright, Jimmy."

Jimmy stood up. He came quickly to his father and put his arm over Charles' shoulders. "Dad," he began, then stopped.

Charles sat very still, so that Jimmy would not remove his arm. "In the end, anyway, when you've become what you want to become, you'll marry Gerry, and then there'll be Wittmanns, for me, for the company, too," he said.

Children. One day they were with you, dependent upon you, loving you. And then the next day they were men and women, and they were gone, and there was nothing left. The house was silent around you, and there were no voices, and you were alone. Next year Jimmy would be in Harvard, and there would be no one here again, not ever. Jimmy would come home for the holidays, but the air of departure would be upon him, as it was on him now. Each year he would go a little farther, and finally, he would not come back. It would be a man who would visit his father, and the boy would only be a memory. Like Mary. Loneliness filled Charles. All his grief came back to him, undiminished. If Mary had lived, there would be a little girl in this house, and Mary, too, and perhaps even a third child. Jimmy's arm was still on his father's shoulder, but now it had no power to lift the sadness from Charles, or drive away the loneliness.

Jimmy removed his arm. Like Charles, he was very intuitive. He felt what Charles was thinking. "I'm so sorry, Dad," he said, brokenly.

Charles aroused himself. "Don't be, son. I'm not. I'm glad. I'm glad," he repeated, with emphasis, seeing the indecision and the sorrow in the boy's face. "Besides, I wasn't thinking of the company."

"I know," said Jimmy, in a low voice. "I know what you are thinking, Dad."

Charles stood up. "I know you do. Well. We'll make all arrangements soon, won't we? In the meantime, Jimmy, I'm hungry. And I hope the beer's good and cold."

He put his hand on his son's shoulder. Jimmy was much taller than he. He kept his hand on Jimmy's shoulder as they went together out of the room. He had never felt so tired as this in all his life.

CHAPTER VI

CHARLES HARDLY slept that night, and so the tiredness was still with him in the morning. His impulse, when getting up, was to eat his breakfast as soon as possible and leave the house before Jimmy came downstairs. But then he knew that Jimmy would be disturbed over this departure from the usual, and would remember the conversation of the night before with wretchedness. So Charles waited for his son, and for Jimmy's tutor, and no mention was made of the subject except when Charles was leaving. He stood up, under Jimmy's anxious scrutiny, and said with as much cheer as possible: "I must be going now. And, Jimmy, I'll write that letter to Harvard today."

Some of the weariness left him when he saw Jimmy's bright smile. Jimmy accompanied him to the door. "You don't mind, Dad, do you?" he asked. "I couldn't stand it if you did. I'd forget the whole thing."

"Nonsense," replied Charles. He tucked his morning paper briskly under his arm. He put his hand briefly on Jimmy's arm. "I thought it was all understood. Now, go back and finish your breakfast. But just remember, I'm proud of you. I always was, you know."

He had the new automobile brought for him, for he had some distance to go to see the farmer who owned the Burnsley land. He had work to do, and so he put aside his personal matters for the time. He thought about the option he would obtain on the Burnsley property, and the meeting on Thursday. Again, remembering Jochen, he smiled a little. He opened his paper and glanced through it. Then he frowned. So, Wilson was confident that the Underwood Tariff Bill would become law this fall, was he? Wilson was probably right. No wonder the country was showing all the signs of an approaching major depression. The new tariff law would reduce percentage of tariff rates from 37% to 27%. Business men expressed their gloom. It was all very well to stimulate European industry, but a man had to think of America, too. The cotton mills, for instance, anticipating a reduction in tariff rates of at least one-third, were already laying off men. Raw wool imports would be on the "free" list, and there would be a reduction of almost two-thirds in the tariff on woolen clothing. More Americans unemployed. Idealism was good, provided the country did not suffer. But once let the idealists run wild and America was in danger.

Charles was not a "party" man, though he was a registered Republican. He voted as he pleased, provided the candidate had "sound" principles. He had no doubt of the integrity of Mr. Wilson. But Mr. Wilson was an idealist, and Charles did not particularly care for idealists, who knew little or nothing about business and reality and human nature. And there was that William Jennings Bryan, now Secretary of State. Another one whose contact with the world was almost non-existent. He was a "peaceful" man, and he had a deep belief in all the Articles of the Hague Convention. Of course, there would never be any major wars again; that was understood. It was only common sense. But still, Mr. Bryan's vociferous reiteration of this made Charles dimly uneasy. Mr. Bryan had announced his plan for a joint commission from every nation to decide upon any quarrel between governments which ordinary diplomatic methods had failed to settle. All very well. But why was Mr. Bryan urging his plan upon the President, as if any such a quarrel had any possible chance of arising?

The heat of the last few days had abated. A sweet fresh wind blew across the fields as Charles' automobile was driven carefully along the newly paved road. Everything shimmered in vivid brightness. The trees moved in a thousand shades of green against the brilliant sky. Cattle stood in their shadows. Distant wheat glittered in tall gold. The automobile rolled past farmhouses deep in flowers and shrubbery. Here and there a man worked in the fields; a dog or two barked wildly after the automobile, which raised yellow dust in the sunlight, and considerable noise.

War. War, with whom? Why these ominous whispers behind the words of public men? Perhaps he, Charles, was too depressed this morning. Hadn't the Anglo-American Treaty of 1908 been dropped by the Senate only last May? Was that good, or bad? Why had Mr. Bryan renewed it, in collaboration with Sir Cecil Spring-Rice? Did they know something no one else seemed to know? There was this trouble with Mexico. But a minor trouble. No one took it very seriously. What had the Anglo-American Treaty to do with this?

It seemed to Charles, suddenly, that when public men talked loudly of peace and neutrality it was time for a people to become very suspicious and careful. Then he shrugged. His mind was muddled this morning. Anglo-American Treaties—and Mexico. They were entirely unrelated. He, Charles, was no politician, but even he could see this. He settled down on the leather seat, though all at once he was not comfortable. Suddenly the passing countryside no longer seemed luminous and beautiful to Charles.

Charles had no objection to the English. The German Empire: Well, the Kaiser was a man of common sense, even though he was ambitious. I'm ambitious myself, thought Charles. But still, there was a point where ambition became madness, an obsession.

And now all this emphasis upon peace. No one had talked of "peace" since the short Spanish-American War. Peace was taken for granted. No one talked very much about sunshine, or air. It was part of living, just as peace was now part of living. Charles looked through the paper again. Here and there, under his sharpened eye, he saw firm beliefs in peace expressed by the British Government, the American Government, the German Government, and even the Balkan Governments. Was it only his imagination, but did all this talk really sound sinister? Was there a hidden disease stirring in the world, this shining August day in 1913?

Charles threw aside his paper, calling himself several uncomplimentary names. And then, without warning, he thought of Jimmy again. But it was not of Jimmy's desire to be a physician of which he thought. "Nonsense," said Charles, aloud. Fortunately, his coachman, now acting as driver of the automobile, did not hear this exclamation. Charles felt foolish. He threw the paper over to the side of the seat, and began to smoke. He concentrated upon the Burnsley matter, and Thursday.

He had no difficulty in obtaining an option for three months. That business concluded, he was driven back to the city, his own city of Andersburg, brawny and busy and full of sturdiness. Of course, unemployment was rising here, as it was rising all over America. But probably it was just a passing flurry, occasioned by the proposed new tariff. The country would adjust itself. America had an immense capacity for adjustment. And though there were many fools who said that all that could be invented had already been invented, these past thirty years, and that everything else would only be "improvements" on existing inventions, Charles was convinced that America was only entering upon an age of invention and that the industrial revolution had only begun to make itself felt. That is why he had privately bought, with his own money and not in the name of the company, a patent for a certain aeroplane steering-control assembly. He had paid only two thousand dollars for the patent. The man who had invented this assembly was now dead.

Charles looked at the innocent blue above him. Only a bird wheeled here and there. Occasionally, but very occasionally, the people were excited by a sudden roaring and a glimpse of some aeroplane from Pittsburgh, a fragile thing out on a "test." Last Fourth of July five aeroplanes had been persuaded to add to the city's festivities by diving and dipping and rising over a somewhat squalid "park" in the suburbs. Charles remembered the inventor whose patent he had bought. The man had assured him it was better than any assembly the Curtiss people made and owned. It had been designed for greater and heavier aeroplanes than the Curtiss factories were making, or contemplating making. So the Curtiss people had not been interested. But Charles had been interested. The inventor had shown him rather wild designs for the "aeroplane of the future." Charles had not laughed. He had only bought the patent, two years ago.

There were times when he smiled at himself a little because of that purchase. But still, so many things could happen. Charles believed in the future, especially the future of America. It was his private opinion that in spite of the might and size of the British Empire, and the growing power of the German Empire, true Empire was moving inexorably to the Americas. The inventor might have been a little mad, but he had said to Charles, his eyes glowing: "The sun is rising west."

He lit a cigar Jochen had pressed on him the night before. No one ever smoked cigars like Jochen's. Rich Havanas, with light sweet aroma. He, Charles, would never buy such expensive cigars, but he enjoyed his brother's, and once or twice, when not invited, he had filched some from Jochen's humidor. Old Joe. Charles forgot all about the newspapers and the aeroplane, and contemplated Jochen's coming consternation with deep pleasure.

The automobile was approaching the Wittmann Machine Tool Company. Charles, over Jochen's protests and ridicule, had landscaped and improved the ground which surrounded the factory. It might be in a neighborhood long abandoned to poor homes and even to slums, but Charles would have his way, and with the company money, too, Jochen had said bitterly. The factory had grown from a small red-brick building, built by Charles' grandfather, and two larger buildings had been added to it by Emil Wittmann. Twelve years ago they had been joined by another building, twice as large as any of the others. Charles had actually called in an architect from Pittsburgh for this work, who had worked with the enthusiastic Wilhelm. The three smaller factories had been thrown together; behind them rose the four-story new building, in perfect proportions. This had not been enough for Charles; he had enlarged the small windows on the older buildings to match the large windows in the new building. All gim-cracks had been removed. There was a clean starkness in the beginning, but now evergreen ivy rippled over the entire factory, which had become one unit. Lawns had been planted, and shade trees, now large and thick and green. Charles had added flower beds, the final disgusting note, according to Jochen.

Then Charles had gone to work on the immediate houses about the factory, which housed most of his workers. He had prevailed upon the men to plant lawns, small trees and shrubs and flowers, to paint their homes and to improve them. When monetary assistance was needed, he gave it. He could do nothing about the houses and the slums beyond this area, but at least, when he looked through his office windows, he had a pleasant immediate view. His men, startled at first, and sus-picious, had finally become excited when one by one Charles had bought the small houses from grudging landlords, and had suggested to the men that they buy them from him in return. He gave them long mortgages, at a low interest rate, and quite often without down pay-ments. He had been younger then, and he had thought that Friederich would approve. But Friederich had said, with Jochen's own avaricious bitterness: "Paternalism!" Friederich, Charles had said, was a trifle in-consistent considering he had no objection to State paternalism.

"How about giving the men the houses then, instead of selling them?" Charles had asked his brother, jokingly. He had not been too startled when Friederich had stared at him with surprised sullenness, and had then walked away in silence. Friederich never spoke about the matter again.

The offices were in the largest, last building. There was a general wait-ing room, a big office filled with clerks and bookkeepers and stenog-raphers, and then the four offices of the brothers, and a directors' room beyond them. Wilhelm came to the offices once a week, where, as treasurer, he signed the pay-roll. Friederich made his appearances less often; he had a head clerk who did almost all his work as secretary. Only Charles and Jochen worked every day. They had the largest offices. Charles' office was the first, beyond the waiting room, a pleasant place with two big windows, a dark-red carpet, a fireplace, a big oak desk, a red-leather sofa, and some good strong chairs.

He stopped at the small office near his where his chief clerk worked industriously. "Hello, Parker," he said. "Anything new this morning?"

Jack Parker rose quickly. He was a thin man, worn but amiable, about fifty years old. "Some telephone calls, sir," he replied. Then he hesitated. "Mrs. Wilhelm Wittmann is in your office, Mr. Wittmann."

Charles took the cigar out of his mouth. Phyllis. "Good," he answered, vaguely. He walked away. Wilhelm was here, of course, to sign the pay-roll checks. Phyllis often called for him in their carriage, either to take him home or to luncheon at the home of a friend. It was nothing new. But she always waited in Wilhelm's office.

Charles found her sitting in one of his comfortable chairs. She smiled at him gayly when he appeared. "Good morning, Charles," she said, in her pretty voice. Her blue eyes sparkled at him, as if with amusement.

"Why, good morning, Phyllis," he answered. He sat down behind his desk. There was a little pile of notes on its wide neatness. He looked at Phyllis, hiding his wonder. But he smiled. "Wilhelm chase you out of his office?"

"No," she answered. Her sparkle was suddenly gone, though her smile remained. She was dressed in a blue linen suit, which matched her eyes. The jacket fell open to reveal a soft white blouse, which was not boned to the jawline, but which revealed her white throat and the glistening pearls around it. She wore a wide straw hat, heaped with blue and pink roses, and there were white kid gloves on her hands, and white slippers on her feet just below the hem of her skirt. A big book lay upon her knees, and she had crossed her hands over it.

Yes, thought Charles, Phyllis was much thinner, and her beautiful face had a tired look in spite of the smile. But the thing that interested him was her air of quiet alertness. It might have been his imagination, but he thought there was a tense expression about her mouth.

"How are you, Charles?" she asked. Her voice was lower than usual.

"Me?" he asked, a little startled. "Well, I suppose. As well as yesterday."

Phyllis studied him with gentle candor. Her bronze brows, the color of her hair, momentarily drew together. She did not look away from him. Her voice dropped even lower. "Wilhelm and I are having luncheon with the Bachs today. I just called for him. He should be finished, soon." She paused. "When I came in, Mr. Parker told me that Jochen was with Wilhelm. The door was shut."

She waited. Charles lifted the notes in his hands, but he did not look at them. Instead, he looked at Phyllis. He did not speak.

"I could have gone in, of course," she continued. "But I thought it might be a business conference of some kind. Mr. Parker said Jochen had been with Wilhelm for nearly an hour. Naturally," she said, and now her face was grave, "I could have waited for Wilhelm in the waiting room. Instead, I told Mr. Parker I would wait in here, and that he was to inform Wilhelm where I was. So," she said, very softly, "Wilhelm would have to come in here for me, when he had done his work."

Charles put down the notes. He pushed them aside. "Thanks, Phyllis," he said. He leaned back in his chair, frowning.

But she was smiling again, her eyes narrowed and tilted. "You don't mind, do you, Charles?"

He picked up a pencil and turned it over and over in his fingers. "Thanks, Phyllis," he said again.

It was nothing, of course. But his instinct was stirring.

"How are you, Phyllis?" he asked, when he became aware that she was watching him too intensely.

"I'm splendid, thank you," she answered.

They could hear the muffled pounding of machinery. The open windows let in a warm puff of wind. A big wagon rolled under the windows, grinding on the gravel. There was a hushed tapping of typewriters in the office across the hall. A train whistled in the distance, at the foot of the mountains which overlooked Andersburg.

"I thought you seemed tired yesterday," murmured Charles.

"You seem tired yourself," she replied.

Charles hesitated. He said: "Jimmy told me last night that he wanted to be a doctor. He's going to Harvard."

Phyllis' face changed. Then she said: "I'm glad, for Jimmy. I always thought Jimmy might want to do something—different. It never appeared natural, to me, for him to come here, Charles."

"No? Why not?"

"It just didn't, Charles. Jimmy is something very special, you know."

"And what's not special about this company?" But Charles smiled.

"Oh, Charles, it's not that! You see, you might often remark that Jimmy is growing up, but I don't think you ever really believed it. Or wanted it. But he is almost a man. And Jimmy has a wonderful mind. You've said that, yourself," she added, quickly. "I've talked to him a great deal."

"Did he ever tell you about—this?" asked Charles, jealously.

"Of course not. But I've known he was thinking of something lately. He's grown quiet and sober. You know how he always was so interested in sports. And then he wasn't."

Charles did not answer. He looked at the pencil in his fingers. All at once, a door opened down the hall, and there was a mingling together of Wilhelm's voice, light and impatient, and Joachen's voice, chuckling and hearty. Phyllis still did not move, but the alertness sharpened in her. She glanced down at the book in her hand. Before Charles could say anything, she had risen, had put the book down before him. Taken aback, he looked at the title: *Gustave Courbet.*

Phyllis was standing beside him. She opened the book to the title page: *Gustave Courbet—His Effect on Manet, Degas and Monet.* It was a beautiful, large, wide book. Charles gaped as Phyllis hastily turned the pages; Charles saw flashes of color. Then the shaking fingers stopped at the portrait of Louise Colet. Charles stared at the reproduction, at the background of dull green, ruddy browns, at the black-gowned woman in the foreground, with her black bonnet and ribbons. But he hardly saw them. He was aware of Phyllis beside him, Phyllis who was breathing quickly, and whose sweet perfume floated all about her. He looked up at her face; it was strained and pale, the lips tremulous, the eyes too bright, the smile too fixed.

"You see how Courbet had abandoned the stilted and Victorian tradition," she said. Her voice was loud and clear. Out of the corner of his eye Charles saw Wilhelm and Jochen on the threshold. Phyllis pretended not to see them. She went on, bending over the book, turning over the pages: "As you said, Charles, there is a magnificent honesty about Courbet's work, a forceful splendor."

Wilhelm was coming into the office, followed by the smiling Jochen. Charles bent over the book. "Yes," he said. "A—a splendor." He caught a line of text: "Courbet's vigor and realism outraged European art circles." Charles said aloud: "Courbet, I can see, outraged Europe with his vigorous realism."

"And who the hell is Courbet?" asked Jochen, genially. Phyllis affected a start of embarrassment. She turned her head and smiled at her husband and brother-in-law. "How are you, Jochen? Wilhelm, I just don't know what we are to do, about Charles, here! Oh, Wilhelm, I thought I'd wait in here with Charles until you had finished your work. What are we going to do about Charles, and this book we bought for the Bachs in New York?"

Wilhelm had come quickly to the desk. But he was looking at Charles with incredulous surprise. "What did you say about Courbet?" he asked, in his irritable voice.

"Why, Phyllis and I were just discussing some of the pictures," said Charles, calmly. He paused, while he searched for a word. "I think, yes, I really think, that Courbet's—"

"You said 'revolutionary,' " interrupted Phyllis on a gay note.

"He was considered so," said Wilhelm. He regarded Charles with even stronger surprise. "What impressed you most, in these reproductions, Charles?"

Fortunately, Charles was blessed with an excellent memory, and an eye for detail. He leaned back in his chair. "That portrait of Louise Colet. Er—natural. Not prettified. Powerful," he added, soberly. "The lights and shadows on the face—realistic."

Jochen was leaning against the desk, across from Charles. He looked at the book inquisitively, cocked his big head in order to try to see the text, or a picture. He said: "Well, who's Courbet? Taken an interest in art lately, Charlie?"

"Could be," responded Charles, in a mild voice. "When I build my new house, I might go in for a few good things."

"Eh?" exclaimed Jochen. "What's that? You're going to give up that mausoleum? I'd like to see the day."

"Well, Wilhelm's almost persuaded me," said Charles, smiling sheepishly. "He'll be sorry, too. I'll leave it in his hands. You've got to admit that Wilhelm has all the taste in the Wittmann family."

Wilhelm was still incredulous. He looked at Jochen, as if for enlightenment, and to Charles' happy relief Jochen was scowling. "I don't know about that," said Jochen. "Many people have said that Isabel's in a class by herself, as far as taste is concerned. We're supposed to have one of the finest houses in Andersburg."

Wilhelm's fine dark brows contracted. A cold expression settled on his face.

Phyllis was standing slight and straight beside her husband. Her hand was upon his arm. "I think Isabel has wonderful taste, myself," she said, smiling at Jochen. "And I sometimes think that reproductions of antiques, which she prefers, are often just as handsome as the originals."

"And don't fall apart, either," said Jochen, appeased.

The contraction of Wilhelm's brows deepened. He turned a thin shoulder away from Jochen. "What's all this about Charles and the book?" he asked of his wife. As usual, the chill aloofness of his face softened when he looked at Phyllis.

Again, Phyllis was gay. "I just showed him the book, and he's practically demanded that I let him keep it."

"Not quite as bad as that," said Charles, apologetically. But he put his hand on the book. "Well, I was just thinking. You could get another for the Bachs. However, if it is a promised present, I'll just have to send to New York or Philadelphia for a copy."

"Oh, you can keep it," Wilhelm said. Again, he scrutinized Charles, and he smiled. "It wasn't promised. I thought they might like it. But I believe I'd prefer you to have it, if that is what you want, Charles."

Jochen, who was no fool, suddenly became conscious of something in the atmosphere. He looked slowly from Wilhelm to Charles, then back to Wilhelm again. He thrust out his bulbous lips.

Charles' hand pressed heavier on the book. "Thanks, Wilhelm," he said, with awkward feeling. "I'll take it home with me, tonight. Jimmy will be interested, too."

"Yes, I know Jimmy will," Phyllis put in, with genuine tenderness. She turned to Wilhelm again. "Do you remember Mrs. Bach saying only recently that Jimmy looked so much like you, darling?"

Wilhelm said scoffingly: "That's ridiculous. It's just that he's dark." But he smiled again, remembering that Jimmy was a very handsome boy.

"I think," began Jochen. But just then Mr. Parker entered the room and announced that he had been told that Mr. Jochen was "wanted" on his telephone. Jochen looked at his brothers swiftly. "I'll take—" he said, and reached for the telephone on Charles' desk. But Charles, pretending not to see or hear, reached for the telephone, himself. "I'd almost forgotten," he said. "Parker, get me Mr. Brighton right away, will you?" He handed the telephone to his clerk.

Jochen stood up, slowly, lifting his bulk away from the desk on which he had been leaning. He said to Wilhelm: "Don't forget Thursday." Without a word to Charles or Phyllis, he walked heavily out of the room.

Imperceptibly, Charles made a gesture towards Mr. Parker. Mr. Parker, a man of long astuteness, put the telephone receiver to his ear, called Mr. Brighton's number. He waited a moment, then said regretfully: "The line is busy, Mr. Wittmann."

"All right. I'll try, myself, in a few moments," said Charles, waving him away. Mr. Parker left the room noiselessly, closed the door behind him.

Wilhelm sat on the corner of the desk, and lit a cigarette with quick, restless movements. "Look here, Charles," he said, "I've just thought of something. Phyllis and I are giving a dinner for a few friends on Friday. One of them is from New York, and is an authority on Monet. Will you come to dinner, and listen to the lecture afterwards?"

Something in Charles relaxed. Inwardly, he could think of nothing more terrible than what his brother had suggested. He smiled with an air of pleasure. "Well, you know how little I know about these things, Wilhelm. But I'd like to learn."

Wilhelm puffed rapidly, then tossed aside the cigarette. He said: "I was just saying to Phyllis, only last night, that I was beginning to have hopes of you, Charles." He stood up.

Charles rose. "Thank you," he said, sincerely. His small brown eyes rested penetratingly upon his brother. "I've taken an option on the Burnsley property, Wilhelm."

There was only the slightest hesitation before Wilhelm said: "Good." He touched Phyllis' hand gently. "Good," he repeated.

"But not a word about the Wittmann Civic Park until Thursday," said Charles. "That'll be for you to announce. And then we'll give it to the newspapers."

Wilhelm tried to hide his gratification. "It was a little embarrassing for me. Jochen came in, just as I was finishing, to talk to me about the selling of the river land to the Connington. He had a few more arguments—"

Charles laughed richly. "But none of them included the beautiful smoke chimneys you'd have almost under your nose, did they?"

Wilhelm's mercurial, black eyes sharpened. "No," he said, with unusual slowness. "They didn't. But they will—on Thursday."

Charles, who did not believe in taking any unnecessary chances, walked out of his office with his brother and Phyllis. He went into the warm August day with them, and stood with them while their carriage was being brought to the door. He never remembered what he said, or what they said to him. But he gave Phyllis a deep glance of gratitude, and she smiled at him swiftly.

The carriage rolled away, and Charles waved. When he returned to his office, Jochen was there again, in one of the chairs. Charles sat down behind his desk. The big book was still there. "Nice of Phyllis and Willie, wasn't it?" he said, indicating the book with a nod of his head.

"Yes, very," replied Jochen, significantly. He stared at Charles. "Who the hell is Courbet? Or perhaps you wouldn't know, eh?"

Charles lifted an eyebrow. "Courbet," he replied, "was born in France, in 1819. He was considered to be a—"

"Revolutionary something-or-other," supplied Jochen with heavy sarcasm.

"In a way, yes." Charles leaned back in his chair. "Anything to discuss, Joe?"

They eyed each other for a long moment in silence. Jochen got to his feet. He pursed his mouth, his head bent, thinking. Then he grinned. He touched his forehead lightly with his hand, in a mock salute. "Not a thing, Charlie, not a thing," he said, and went out of the office.

Charles' face drew itself in lines of formidable tightness after his brother had gone. So. Joe had lost again. Joe knew something had happened in this office, but he did not know what it was. "Damn them all, the confounded idiots," said Charles, aloud, taking up his notes. There was only one consolation: Friederich was out of town and could not be reached by Jochen.

Then Charles put down the notes again, very slowly. The wind blew through the windows. But it could not blow away the lingering scent of Phyllis' perfume. It was in the room, like a sweet and subtle presence. Like Phyllis, herself, with her blue eyes and charming, sensitive mouth. Charles could see her as if she stood there beside him, as she had stood only a short time ago. The lace at her throat had parted a little more, and he had seen the hollow of her throat, filled with soft shadow.

CHAPTER VII

CHARLES WITTMANN was not a man who ever suffered from prolonged fits of despondency. He had his "moods," as Jochen's wife had remarked, but these moods were usually ones of strong quiet anger, and not obstinacy. Nor were they attacks of depression or melancholy, baseless and obscure. He knew he had a liverish condition, and that he often over-ate, and had a fondness for beer. Whenever he was depressed, he could usually find the cause in a too-lavish indulgence in sauerbraten or spareribs, or beer, or cheese-cake.

But on Wednesday the condition he had thought "tiredness" or "disappointment" had become a sort of heavy apprehension and weariness.

He would soon be forty. But forty was the prime of life—or so they said, he thought to himself. Forty. Perhaps he needed a vacation. He had promised himself a vacation all summer, but there had been too much to do. Moreover, there had been Jimmy. He had never taken a vacation without Jimmy, and Jimmy, all summer, had been under tutorship. Still, thought Charles, I ought to have gone to Cape Cod, or perhaps to Atlantic City. A change. We were busy this summer, and I ought to thank God for that, considering conditions. But I could have left the business with Joe for two or three weeks.

He always attacked his work with steady enthusiasm and interest. But today, he just sat behind his desk, letters open before him, and notes of calls. It was half-past nine, and he had just come in. He had been too "tired" this morning to arrive at his usual time, which was half-past eight. Perhaps it was the weather, which had turned very hot again. He got up and went to his windows. By straining his neck and turning his head, he could see the mountains in the distance. They were brilliant green against a glaring sky. It would be even hotter, later. He could hear the thunder of his shops, the crunching of wagons on gravel. He liked that thunder, remembering that many factories, all over the country, were becoming muted. But the thunder could not please him this morning. He stood at the window, yawning, feeling a heaviness all through his body, an aversion for work.

He tried to find the cause of his weariness. There was nothing to worry about—nothing. In the past two days he had recovered from his disappointment about Jimmy. He was not only reconciled now to his son's decision; he was almost elated, and very proud. He was not worried about the meeting on Thursday. Wilhelm and Friederich were with him. He had not over-eaten, lately. He was not "liverish." Definitely, it was the heat. Forty. He went back to his desk and looked at the notes about his calls, written down in Mr. Parker's neat handwriting. A Mr. Walter Lord had called three times, once at eight-thirty, again at nine, and again at nine-twenty. Very important, Mr. Parker had written.

Now, who the hell was Mr. Lord? He pressed the bell on his desk, and Mr. Parker, moving quickly and noiselessly as always, came in promptly. "Who," asked Charles, "is Mr. Lord? I see he's called three times."

"He didn't say, Mr. Wittmann," replied the other man. "I asked him for information. He isn't a salesman. He just said it was extremely important to see you."

"Probably another inventor."

Mr. Parker looked at him seriously. "I was just coming in, sir, when you rang. Mr. Lord is outside, in the waiting room."

"The devil he is! Well, you saw him, Parker. What does he want?"

Mr. Parker was thoughtful. "I've looked him over, sir. He has a briefcase. I wouldn't say he is a lawyer. He's not from Andersburg. I know that. And I wouldn't say he is an inventor. When I talked to him on the telephone, before he came, he sounded very sharp and impatient."

"Is that so?" said Charles, with unusual exasperation. "Well, you know very well, Parker, that I don't see every Tom, Dick, and Harry who chooses to rush in here any time it pleases him. Find out what he wants, who he is, and handle him yourself. Good God, I have no time for strangers."

But Mr. Parker did not go. "I've been with you a long time, Mr. Wittmann. I was with Mr. Emil, too. I've learned something in thirty-five years. I can pick out salesmen, and inventors, and business men at a glance. Mr. Lord isn't any of them. I think," Mr. Parker added, "that you ought to see him, sir. I've never seen anyone like Mr. Lord before. He has a kind of—I should think you'd call it authority, and he's very angry because I wouldn't bring him in here at once."

Charles began: "Well, just tell him he must state his business to you—" Then he stopped. If someone impressed Parker, that someone was of importance. Charles said: "You think I ought to waste my time on him, eh?"

"Yes, sir, I do think so."

Charles shifted in his chair, with annoyance. "Sounds damn mysterious to me. Did he give you his card?"

"No."

"No card?"

"No."

They looked at each other. Charles drew in his lips, thoughtfully. He said, after a few brief moments of consideration: "Send him in. But I warn you, if he's a salesman or something like that—"

Mr. Parker went out. I know, thought Charles, with rising irritability. An insurance man. Parker's getting old. But he watched the door with sudden interest. It opened again. Mr. Parker was admitting a small but upright man, carrying a briefcase. Mr. Parker lingered on the threshold. The stranger turned to him. "You may close the door," he said. Amazingly, Mr. Parker closed the door.

At one glance, Charles understood what Mr. Parker had meant. This man had not only a "kind of authority," but he had the appearance of one who demanded, and secured, instant obedience. There was a swiftness and compactness about him, a hard dignity in spite of his somewhat short stature. He was thin, lean, and well dressed. He wore his clothing as though he were a soldier, an officer. One expected brown eyes in such a brown face, but his eyes were extraordinarily light blue under thick gray brows. His hair was almost white. He had a straight, thin-lipped mouth and a great beak of a nose, and an air of command.

He came at once to Charles' desk, and Charles, to his own surprise, found himself rising and extending his hand. "Mr. Lord?" he said.

Mr. Lord took his hand, shook it briefly. "Mr. Charles Wittmann?" His accent was decidedly not that of Pennsylvania. Rather, it had a Yankee twang.

"I'm Charles Wittmann. Please sit down, Mr. Lord."

Mr. Lord seated himself. He sat in his chair, upright and vigorous. He surveyed Charles with an uncompromising penetration. He said: "Yes. You're what I have heard, Mr. Wittmann. I've been in Andersburg for a week, and I've been investigating you. Quietly, of course."

"You've been investigating me?" Charles could not keep the acerbity from his voice.

Mr. Lord put his briefcase on the desk. He kept his hand on it. Again, he studied Charles. "Not only in this town, but in New York, and Philadelphia. We've gone over your reputation, thoroughly. For weeks. You see, it was very important for us to know all about you, before I came here."

"Who are 'we'?" asked Charles, with angry disturbance. "Look here, Mr. Lord, this all sounds very mysterious to me. Let us get down to business."

The other man said quietly: "My name is not Lord."

He opened the briefcase. He removed a thick sheaf of papers from it. And then again, he scrutinized Charles. "It must be understood at once that my visit here is extremely confidential, Mr. Wittmann, and that it must not be discussed with anyone, not even with your three brothers."

Charles was silent. He waited. Mr. Lord took out a card-case from his pocket, laid it before Charles. Charles looked at it. "Colonel John Grayson." And under it was printed: "Army of the United States. Ordnance Department, Washington, D. C."

Charles uttered an exclamation of surprise. Then it seemed to him that all the apprehensiveness, the uneasy foreboding, of the past few days had become concentrated in this moment, in this vital if elderly man, in this very room. "You are Colonel Grayson?"

"Yes." Colonel Grayson reached over, took the card, returned it to his pocket. Then, while Charles watched, he spread out the papers he had taken from his briefcase. Charles saw red tape and gold seals and letter-heads. "My credentials, Mr. Wittmann," said the Colonel.

Dazed, Charles went through the papers, slowly, one by one. It took considerable time. He could not understand.

He looked at the Colonel. It was odd that he began to remember Mr. William Jennings Bryan, and the confident assertions of peace he had read in the papers on Monday. A sort of confusion pervaded Charles' mind. But again, he only waited. The Colonel, too, was silent, sitting there on the edge of his chair.

"You will notice, from my credentials, that the matter is extremely confidential, and delicate," said the Colonel at last.

"Of course," murmured Charles. He rubbed his cheek. "Of course, Colonel Grayson."

The Colonel said: "My name is Mr. Lord."

"What can I do for you, Mr. Lord?" asked Charles, abruptly.

Mr. Lord let himself lean back, very stiffly, in his chair. "You can do nothing for me, Mr. Wittmann. But you can do a great deal for your country." He paused. "Your father was a German, was he not, sir?"

"Yes. But what of it?"

Mr. Lord said: "You are a German-American."

"I am an American," replied Charles. There was a slight palpitation in his chest. "I was born in America. This is my country."

"Good," said Mr. Lord. "But you have a brother. A Mr. Friederich Wittmann. I understand he considers himself a German, and is a little —shall we say—arrogant about it."

"You said—Mr. Lord, that I can do something for my country," said Charles. The beating against the stiffness of his collar was very strong.

"Your father was a very young man when he came to America, with your grandfather, Walther," said Mr. Lord, as if Charles had not spoken. "They came here because they preferred freedom to regimentation. Am I correct?"

"You are correct." A feeling of suffocation came to Charles.

Mr. Lord took his papers and returned them to his briefcase. He locked the latter carefully. He put it on his knees. He stared at Charles strongly, and his very pale eyes narrowed.

"Mr. Wittmann," he said, "I can tell you very little. You must not ask me for more than I can tell you, for I am not permitted to answer. I can give you only a little information. Within a week or so, perhaps a few days one way or another, you will be approached by an official of one of America's largest manufacturers of armaments. That officer will try to buy from you a certain invention, which you own in your own name. An aeroplane steering-control assembly."

Charles was more dazed than ever.

"You paid two thousand dollars for that invention, Mr. Wittmann. This official will offer you much more. He is prepared to pay you any price you ask."

"Go on," said Charles.

"Mr. Wittmann, you are a free agent. I cannot say to you: 'You are forbidden to sell your patent to this company.' Under the law, Mr. Wittmann, you can tell us to go to hell."

Charles said: "We are not the biggest concern in the country, Mr. Lord. I'm afraid I'm not following you very well. You are not telling me very much, you must admit. Why would this—officer—want my patent?"

"Because it is the best aeroplane steering-control assembly patent so far registered. Because, Mr. Wittmann, this company will want it, and they don't want it for America. They want it for a—for a foreign power, shall we say?"

The beating in Charles' neck had become sickening. But he could speak calmly: "It's done all the time, isn't it? Companies here manufacture for companies abroad. Patents are bought, exchanged, used. We're at peace, Mr. Lord."

"Yes," said the Colonel, very quietly, "we are at peace. Yes, Mr. Wittmann, I grant you that." He waited, his hands gripping his brief-case. "I've told you all I can, Mr. Wittmann. I have asked you not to sell that patent to this unnamed company. That's all."

Charles' mind groped. He felt ponderously stupid. He said: "You have some reason. Yes, you have some reason. All of you."

"I did not say that, Mr. Wittmann. I have told you all I can tell you."

The sense of stupidity increased in Charles. And now, all at once, terror struck him, a quite unreasoning terror, like a blow. He was not well acquainted with fear; it was a stranger to him. He did not know why he should feel so beset and so afraid. He stood up, and looked down at the Colonel, and he put his hands on his desk and leaned on his shaking arms.

"You know something," he said. "And if you know something, you can stop it. Why don't you stop it? Now? Now?"

A change came over the Colonel's face. "I am only a soldier, Mr. Wittmann. I have only my orders to see you, and to talk to you."

Charles repeated: "You know something. Why don't you stop it?"

Then the Colonel turned in his chair and looked at the windows. "Mr. Wittmann, I am not a politician. I follow orders. I read only the newspapers you read. I am told very little more than I have told you. I can only guess. Soldiers, Mr. Wittmann, are supposed to be mechanical creatures. We go where we are sent. We kill when we are told to kill. We are given slogans, bands, flags, uniforms. It is supposed to be enough for us."

Charles heard himself saying: "You wouldn't have come to me if it were only a small matter. Say, the Balkans, or the Chinese. We—we've made a good thing out of China. America isn't just having an attack of conscience. We just laugh at the comic opera of the Balkans. And it isn't Mexico. If—if something happens—Mr. Lord, America will be in it. You know that, don't you?"

The Colonel did not reply.

"Who?" said Charles.

Still, the Colonel did not answer.

"Not England," said Charles, hoarsely. "Not Russia. There's only one other country—"

The Colonel lifted his hand. "Mr. Wittmann, I told you I know nothing."

But Charles said: "We are at peace. The whole world is at peace, except for a few minor little scuffles here and there. If—if something is brewing, we can stop it now. Even if we have to pass laws. We can stop it before it starts."

The Colonel slowly turned to him. "I think I said I wasn't a politician, sir." His eyes were a blue flash in his face. "I know nothing about international politics. I'm only a soldier. There are times, Mr. Wittmann, when it is expedient to make—war. When it is profitable. When the people want it. The people, Mr. Wittmann, can always stop war simply by insisting that they want no war. But they never do, sir. They never do. They like it."

"No."

The Colonel nodded. "Mr. Wittmann, I may be only a soldier, but I am not a man without education. I'm not ignorant of my fellow-man. Neither are you. History, as someone has said, is a dull account of wars. Why, Mr. Wittmann? Were the people led into them by lies, or did they want to believe the lies so that they'd have an excuse for war? Did they, to be very simple about it, just want to kill? Kill anyone, anywhere? The desire to kill is one of man's most explosive and strongest instincts." He regarded Charles with somber curiosity. "You know that, don't you? Civilization is an attempt to guide that instinct into safer channels, such as making machines, goods, and so on. We have tried to substitute business and other competition for war. But there comes a time when the whole thing is blown to hell. Instinct is stronger than civilization, or morals, or religion. And there are men who know that only too well: politicians, armaments makers, Presidents, kings, leaders of the people. Men who will profit by the people's love for war, and who will gain power by it, or financial rewards."

He stood up. They faced each other across the desk. A broad band of sunlight struck through the windows, lay between them, shining.

"The world's in a bad way, Mr. Wittmann," said the Colonel. "The people are restless. Change is brewing. There are a lot of men who don't like the idea of change. They'd prefer to set one nation to killing another nation than to—to let their own people be free. The people aren't as 'contented' as they used to be, either."

He smiled a little. "We're adventurous animals, Mr. Wittmann. Can you suggest any adventure which is more appealing than war? Any other adventure which frees man so thoroughly from a civilization he instinctively hates, because it restrains him and inhibits him? War offers irresponsibility, excitement, murder, hatred, plunder. What would you suggest in its place?"

But Charles could only lean on his shaking arms and say nothing.

The Colonel held his briefcase. Now his smile was gone. "You must give our country some credit, Mr. Wittmann. We are busy visiting men like you, who hold dangerous patents, or who can manufacture dangerous things. We are trying, Mr. Wittmann, trying very hard."

Charles said: "I will say 'no' to anybody. You knew I would. But what of the others?"

The Colonel shrugged eloquently. He said: "The hope of peace is only in the people of the nation. If they don't want it, we can't enforce it. At the end, it rests with them. When there is war between two nations there is never just one guilty party. There are always two. There are ways to stop wars, but I've never yet heard of any nation using them, not once, in all recorded history."

"I have a son," said Charles. He felt weak and undone.

"I have three sons, and six grandsons," said the Colonel. Again he smiled. "My grandsons wouldn't mind a war."

Something about Charles must have moved him. "I can only tell you again, Mr. Wittmann, that there are quite a number of people who are trying to avert any war, or the possibility of any war. That is why I came to you today. Try to remember that. We are doing what you said ought to be done. We are trying to stop things before they have a chance to start."

He waited. Charles' head had sunk between his broad shoulders. The Colonel said: "Again, Mr. Wittmann, I can't insist too strongly that all this is very confidential."

Charles said: "That—patent. It belongs to America." His voice dropped away.

The Colonel nodded. "Good. Of course."

He went towards the door. He began to open it, then stopped. He looked back at Charles. "But, after all, we are at peace."

CHAPTER VIII

THURSDAY WAS an important day. It was also the day when Jochen would again be defeated, as Charles had so often defeated him before. In the past, contemplation of Jochen's coming discomfiture had always given Charles several juicy moments of pleasure and contentment, had added an extra richness to his breakfast and a heightened approval of life as he lived it.

But the importance of this Thursday had become diminished for Charles. Something had gone out of him the past few days. His thoughts wheeled back inexorably to Jimmy. He tried to shrug away his deep inner fear and foreboding. One never knew what those fellers in Washington were up to, especially since Wilson had been elected. One could expect anything. Even a melodramatic visit, such as the Colonel's. All part of the kind of hysterical tension which Wilson and his Cabinet had communicated to the country at large. It was nonsense, of course. It would remain nonsense, until he, Charles, had received that unknown "official" from an "unknown company" which manufactured armaments. Charles could think of no such company except Bouchard and Sons, of Windsor. Windsor was only forty miles away. If anyone—ridiculous!—had any idea of visiting Charles Wittmann of Andersburg, the idea was certainly very faint.

Charles had had dealings with the great Bouchard and Sons in the past. He had manufactured certain precision tools for them, but only in small quantities. They had machine tool shops of their own, enormous ones, in which the Wittmann buildings could be absorbed without noticeable expansion. Then they had placed a large order with Charles about two years ago, and he had received a very gracious and flattering letter from Mr. Jules Bouchard, himself, president of the company, congratulating him on the quality of the merchandise. Charles was inclined to think kindly of Bouchard and Sons, and had hoped for more orders. They had not come, but Charles was certain they would come. After all, he and his own company owned many valuable machine-tool patents. Of course, Charles knew in a very vague and amorphous way that many people, and newspapers, accused Bouchard and Sons of helping to "foment" wars, but Charles had thought the accusations a trifle more than extravagant, and crudely sensational. Armaments makers could never really "foment" wars, in a direct sense. They merely supplied arms for nations who demanded wars. It was all "business," and not in the least sinister.

While dressing, and scowling to himself, Charles was reminded that he had felt depressed even before Colonel Grayson's visit. Why was it? He could not quite remember. It had something to do with the tariff, and that pompous, serious old ass, William Jennings Bryan. While putting the tie-pin into his neat brown tie, Charles suddenly paused, his hands still.

There was no use in trying to "pooh-pooh" the recollection of Colonel Grayson's call. Now little snatches of articles in newspapers and magazines came back to him, small winds of calamity. "Der Tag." That was it. There had been a report, sometime, in some paper, that the German Government had entertained a large group of high-ranking British military and naval men, and a toast had been given—by whom?— to "Der Tag." The Day. What day? Charles sat down on the edge of his bed. His big room with the overpowering dark mahogany furniture was very hot. Sweat broke out on his forehead, and under his collar.

Ominous fragments began to drift through his mind. The New York *Times* European correspondent had recently reported that French newspapers were beginning to publish obscure but inflammatory articles against Germany. It was curious, the *Times* reporter had remarked, but the same articles, "almost word for word," had appeared in German newspapers against France. Very subtle—but there they were. Little prickling suspicions, little dancing points of flame, in a great quiet forest. Then there had been another report, also guarded, to the effect that even the Russian newspapers were asking rhetorical questions about "any future wars," and so were the British, the Austrian, the Greek, the Bulgarian, and the Serbian. Sazaroff. The "merchant of death." Charles put his fist against his wet forehead, and tried to remember. It had all seemed so unimportant and absurd to him. Anyway, all that was in Europe. "Smoking chimneys, peculiar activity," had been reported by the American press, in and about the German armaments firm, Kronk. The munition works at Schultz-Poiret at Le Creusot in Burgundy had shown this "activity" also, and only very recently, and Bedors in Sweden, and Robsons-Strong, in England. "Widespread," said Charles, to himself, sweating. "Too widespread." His knuckles, pressed to his forehead, began to ache. "Something" was going on, as Colonel Grayson had hinted. However, if "something" was going on, it was happening in the capitals of Europe. Sibilant whispers from American newspapers began to return to Charles' memory. He remembered the newspapers he had just recently read. All that talk of peace—. It was that talk which had so depressed him. It was strange, but he knew that he had not consciously linked up the memory of this everlasting peace talk with the memories of what he had been reading—so very casually—for many months. Now everything fell into order, like a baleful pattern. Above that pattern stood the face of his son, Jimmy.

"I don't know. I don't know!" said Charles aloud, with muddled anger. He felt the hot August heat all about him. He heard a knock on his door, and called furiously: "Yes? What is it?"

Apparently the knocker was taken aback at his tone, for the answer was timid: "It's me; Mrs. Meyers, Mr. Wittmann. I wondered if you was sick. It's almost half-past eight."

Charles said, trying to make his voice normal: "All right. You just startled me. I got up late. I'll be down in a few minutes."

He found a fresh handkerchief for himself, then held it stupidly in his hand. He moved his short neck restively. Europe was always seething under the surface. The Kaiser had helped to stabilize the passions of Europe. He was a man of sense, though Charles had little admiration for men who were martinets, and who expressed huge contempt for the people. The Kaiser was not a man to start a great war. Hadn't Teddy Roosevelt mentioned the Kaiser with respect not too long ago? Hadn't the Kaiser entertained him, and hadn't Teddy, himself, spoken of the wonderful sense of security and industry one encountered everywhere in Germany? Yet, once Teddy had said something rather odd. He, Charles, could not quite remember it, but it was something to the effect that "something was brewing" in Europe.

Charles thrust his handkerchief in his pocket. His hand was damp. "Europe, hell!" he exclaimed. But the sound of his own voice could not reassure him. One could not forget Colonel Grayson. One could not forget the implication behind the Colonel's visit. If there was any war, America would be in it. America had recently become friendly— oh, so very friendly!—with England. America, who only very recently had ceased to bait, and jeer, at England on every national holiday, such as the Fourth of July!

Charles shook his head violently. Let's be sensible, he said to himself. I'm getting worked up, probably about nothing.

He went downstairs, where Jimmy was waiting for him among the dark behemoth-like furniture of the dining room. He, Charles, had only to wait. If that mysterious official from an even more mysterious "company" never called upon him, he would forget all this nonsense. "Hello, Jimmy," he said to his son. Jimmy rose at his father's entrance. Ever since Sunday night the boy's eyes had searched his face anxiously whenever he had seen him. Charles did not know why he should feel so irritated at Jimmy, when he again caught that glance of concern and worry. But he smiled determinedly, sat down, shook out his big white napkin. "Hot again today, isn't it?"

Jimmy sat down. "Mrs. Meyers and I were wondering about you, Dad," he said.

"Stop worrying!" Charles exploded. Then seeing Jimmy's bewilderment, he controlled himself. "Look here, Jimmy, you've got to stop it. I'm all right. I'm not 'disappointed.' I'm damned glad about your decision. Now, let it alone, will you? I can't have you following me around like a lost dog any more, son."

Jimmy had turned bright red. He was not accustomed to hearing Charles scold him, nor to seeing his father's eyes so angry when they looked at him.

"I'm sorry," he muttered, hurt. What was wrong with Dad? Why was he so unnerved these last few days? "It was just that you're late, and today's the day you talk about the river property. You remember you told me about it?"

"I always tell you about everything," said Charles, remorseful. There was his morning paper at his plate; he pushed it away. "It's the heat, Jimmy. And everything." He smiled at the boy again. "I'm not worrying about the river property."

Jimmy returned his smile. But furtively, he glanced at his father. Dad was pale; he looked tired and strained. Jimmy had few memories of his father which were not strong, controlled, even serene. Until recently.

Elsie Meyers, a round little ball of a woman, came in with Charles' bacon and eggs and coffee. She was a widow of fifty, and had been Charles' housekeeper for many years. She kept her eyes down, and her lips pursed, as she placed the plate before Charles. She, too, was hurt. Charles sighed. "Mrs. Meyers," he said, "I shouldn't have shouted at you, I know. But I didn't sleep well. It was the heat."

"Yes, Mr. Wittmann," she replied, with dignity. But she was mollified. It wasn't like Mr. Wittmann to lose his temper. She, too, gave Charles a furtive glance. "You ought've taken a vacation this summer, Mr. Wittmann," she remarked. "You look tired."

"I'm not tired, Elsie." Then Charles looked at Jimmy. "I've an idea. How about you and me going fishing over the week-end, eh?"

Jimmy was overjoyed. Jimmy was young; he was only seventeen. Nothing could happen to Jimmy. Let Europe seethe, let the whisperers whisper. It had nothing to do with Jimmy. Then Charles, about to drink his coffee, let the cup go back to its saucer, untouched.

What had Grayson said? Murder. Kill. Men's love for war.

Charles lifted the cup to his mouth and drank slowly. He said: "How's the tutoring coming along, Jimmy? By the way, what are you studying just now? History?"

"Sometimes," replied Jimmy. "It's part of what I have to make up from last year, when I had no sense."

Charles attacked his breakfast. He made his tone casual: "I never particularly liked history. Sort of stupid, in a way, all those wars. Why can't people live in peace?"

"Well, we haven't really had a war since the Civil War, Dad. You can hardly call the Spanish-American fracas a war, can you?"

"The Balkans are always simmering." said Charles

"It seems to me they always did." Jimmy laughed.

The food was dry in Charles' mouth. "Well, America will never be in a war again, thank God. But what if she did, Jim? What would you think of it?"

Jimmy frowned, thoughtfully. "Well, it's impossible, of course. Who would we fight? Who would want to fight us? Nobody. None of the major countries would ever want any more wars. They'd have too much to lose, because any modern war would become too big for any nation to handle. That's what Mr. Trevor says, anyway."

"But what would you think of it?" Charles persisted.

"I?" Jimmy was surprised. "Well, Dad, to tell the truth, I can't imagine us in a war with anybody." He considered his father's suggestion more closely. "Still, if we were attacked, I'd like to help defend America. Of course," he added.

"But how would you feel about killing other men, Jimmy?"

"Killing?" repeated Jimmy. "Why, Dad, I don't think I could kill anybody. Unless, of course, we were attacked. Even then, I'd hate it. Yes," he went on, with young vehemence, "I'd hate it. I don't think I'd ever get over it."

Powerful relief filled Charles. Grayson was wrong. People did not instinctively desire to kill, to murder. Here was a young feller, and he'd "hate" it.

"But then," Jimmy was saying, "I'll be a doctor, and I suppose I have a doctor's mind. Doctors want to save, not murder." Jimmy leaned his elbow on the table, and rested his chin in his hand, thoughtfully. The morning light, muted through the trees, struck through the window and lay on the wide angle of his young jaw.

Charles could not finish his breakfast. He pushed a piece of toast around his plate, then dropped it. How could he have forgotten the joy and excitement in the country during the Spanish-American War? How could he have forgotten how he and his own young friends had fought imaginary "Indian" wars, and had revelled in combat and fighting? The fury, the happy race, the impersonal hate, the stimulation, the freeing of some dark and primitive instinct! He, himself, would never feel all that again, for he had become a man, and he was a father. But what of the millions, the hundreds of millions, of young men everywhere, all over the world, who would delight in war, who would go lusting after it with a lust far beyond the desire for a woman? How could he, Charles, have forgotten that so soon?

"What's the matter, Dad?" asked Jimmy, with alarm.

"I was just thinking," Charles answered, and he heard his own voice stifled and unnatural even to his own ears. "I was just thinking that man is the only species on earth which bands together to kill his own kind. I suppose," he added, heavily, "that's what's behind crusades, 'holy' wars, 'defense of country,' everything—just wanting to kill. We're bad; man should never have been created."

Jimmy's alarm increased. There was silence in the room. It was there a long time before Charles became aware of it. When he saw his son's face, he wanted to smile, he wanted to say something light and sensible. But he could not. He could only stand up and sigh.

"Well, I've got to go, Jimmy," he said.

A man tried to live a placid, well-ordered, and useful life, meeting each problem with prudence and detachment. He liked calmness and sense, despising hysteria and emotionalism. He had proved to himself that this was the only intelligent way to live, and he had discovered that by living like this he remained master of all circumstance, and nothing disturbed him overmuch.

Then a day, or days, arrived, and everything was in disorder. He could control nothing, not even his own thoughts. Some center in his life, or the life about him, disintegrated, and flew apart. He suddenly realized that he was not only not master of himself, but was not master of circumstance.

So Charles thought, on the way to his office. A week ago everything had been tranquil in his life. His brothers were sources of annoyance to him at times, true; but they were also sources of amused interest. Jochen had even furnished a kind of excitement for him. Strategy was one of Charles' most potent characteristics, and he liked to exercise it. It gave him a feeling of well-being, of power, of control. Wilhelm's eccentricities were the spice of his life; Friederich might bore him, but there was an unpredictability about Friederich's absurdities which nullified the ennui he aroused in Charles.

The shops were doing well. So, everything, until very lately, had been proceeding according to a sensible man's desire. Life had been mastered; it went through its paces with the easy obedience of a loping circus horse, alert for the crack of the whip of the master.

Then all at once the circus horse, plump, dappled, clean and well-mannered, had changed into a wild and savage beast. A few words here and there, disconnected; a melodramatic visit from an unknown Army officer; a whisper, a movement in the dark. But in consequence, life had become dangerous and sinister.

Charles struggled with himself. His mind, always so disciplined, was in a wordless panic. I'm just tired. A little rest, perhaps. A change of scene. Everything will straighten itself out. But he knew he was not tired; he knew everything had moved, shifted. There was a terror loose in the world, somewhere. He could feel it. All about him were sunshine and amiable people going about their business in the streets. He tried to concentrate upon this. But it was like looking on the bright-colored and happy façade of a nightmare, knowing that something horrible was mounting and shaping behind it, which would soon topple over the painted front and reveal churning chaos.

"Nonsense," was Charles' favorite word. He repeated it to himself like a litany as he walked into the offices. But it had no power to exorcise the shapeless fear in him. However, when he entered the directors' room, and found his brothers impatiently waiting for him, he had so far controlled himself that he seemed almost as usual.

"You're late, Charlie," Jochen said, looking at his watch. "Bad night, eh?"

Friederich gave him a surly but reassuringly furtive glance. "I never knew you to be late before, Karl."

"And I am meeting some friends from New York at twelve," said Wilhelm, pointedly. "Of all mornings, you ought to have been here on time, Charles."

"Sorry," said Charles, curtly. He sat down on his chair, at the head of the neat polished table. He studied his brothers. Then he was sick of them. He wanted nothing but to be rid of them, to hide himself somewhere, to try to get his thoughts into some kind of order.

Jochen said, yawning: "Did you see the paper? Leon Bouchard's in town. At the Imperial Hotel. Just passing through, the paper said, on the way to Windsor. Wouldn't surprise me if he's behind the Connington deal for getting our river property. Say, what's the matter, Charlie?"

For Charles was gripping the edge of the table so tightly that his whitened knuckles showed in the brilliant August light. "Leon Bouchard?"

"Why, you remember Mr. Bouchard," said Jochen, his alert senses making him sit up. "You remember they invited us to visit their big plants in Windsor, when they gave us that juicy order two years ago. You went, and I went with you. Leon's the quiet one, the square short one. The vice-president. Mr. Jules was out of town—you remember. Leon showed us around the plant. You know."

"How long has he been here? How long is he staying?"

Jochen chuckled. "Thinking of wangling an order out of him? That's dandy. Go to it, Charlie. How long's he been here? The paper said since yesterday evening. Came in late. Seeing that he was so nice to us, I've been thinking we ought to invite him out to see our own shops. A mouse showing an elephant, in a way. But we're all right, if I do say so, myself. And he could do worse than having dinner at my house."

"Your house," said Wilhelm, with elegant consideration. "Why not mine? I'm having a dinner for some friends tomorrow. What do you think of my inviting him, Charlie?"

"No," said Charles. His hands gripped the table harder. "No," he repeated.

All of his brothers looked at him, surprised. He saw their faces so clearly, Jochen's big and flushed and gross, Wilhelm's fine-drawn and dark and patrician, Friederich's surly and suspicious. Their faces seemed to advance upon him like nightmares; he wanted to put up his hand to protect himself. "No," he said again. Now his voice sounded more normal. "There's no use running after Mr. Bouchard. If he wants anything, he'll find us. Ridiculous—toadying to him. Undignified."

"I agree with Charles," said Wilhelm. He looked meaningly at his thin gold watch, beautifully inlaid with enamel. A French watch.

"I hate the Bouchards," said Friederich. "The most reactionary bastards in the country. Why doesn't the Government get its anti-trust laws out against them? They have subsidiaries all over the damn country. They control too much."

Jochen gave him an irate look, then remembering the business of the morning, he subsided. "I don't know," he said. "We're in the business of selling our machine tools. It wouldn't do any harm to remind Mr. Bouchard we're alive—and willing."

"No," said Charles. The panic was rioting in him. "Let him make the advances, in this instance." He turned to Friederich. "I don't like the Bouchards much, either—Friederich." He spoke carefully. "We can get along without their business."

"And their money, too, of course," said Jochen angrily. "What's the matter with you, Charlie? You skipped off fast enough, two years ago, when they invited us. Beamed all over. Almost curtsied to Bouchard. Almost rubbed your hands."

Wilhelm and Friederich were now observing Charles with uncertainty.

Friederich cleared his throat with that rasping sound which Charles always found so intolerable. "It does seem—" he said. Wilhelm tapped aristocratic fingers on the table. "It wouldn't do much harm, I think, to remind him of our existence."

"He knows," said Charles. "Yes," he said, "he knows."

Jochen's tiny brown eyes narrowed upon his brother. "What's the matter, Charlie?" he asked, in a very soft tone.

Now Charles was afraid. Once arouse the tenacious Jochen, and everything was lost. Deliberately, he changed the expression on his face to one of good humor. "Let me think about it," he said. "Frankly, I'm more concerned just now about our immediate business. Later, I'll think about Mr. Bouchard. Men like him hate to be coerced. I remember Mr. Leon Bouchard. Independent and reserved. He would hate crude methods."

Wilhelm nodded. Friederich seemed restive. Jochen said nothing.

"Now," said Charles, looking at the single sheet of paper before him, "let's discuss that river property matter. Joe, you still think we should sell to the Connington?"

"Why not? They offer a big price. And big prices aren't something to be sneered at these days."

"But—on the river front. You know I've always wanted to preserve the river front for the people. We haven't any right to help destroy it, and make it ugly."

"To hell with the people," said Jochen, easily, winking at Wilhelm. "Who cares about them? Besides, it will bring more business into town. Andersburg could use a few more industries. And the Connington are a big concern."

Friederich turned to him. "What do you mean: 'To hell with the people'?" His bony face, so wide and pale, had darkened.

Charles could forget Bouchard and Sons now, for a few minutes. Joe had put his foot into it. Jochen saw this at once. He became flustered. He drew out his silver cigar case, chose a cigar, lit it carefully. "Oh, now," he said, carelessly. "Don't get on your high horse, Fred. I was really thinking of the work the Connington would create, for everybody. They'd even bring in more men, and more men mean more trade for Andersburg, and house-building—everything."

Wilhelm broke in, in his precise and disdainful voice: "Everything. Yes. Especially chimneys practically under my nose."

Jochen stared at him formidably. "They'd be far down, Willie. Too far down, almost, for you to see them. Besides, it's a big tract of land. They could build their plant out of sight of your house, around the bend." Again, he concentrated upon Wilhelm. "What's the matter with you? You were strong for it only a week ago. Think of the price, Willie. That's the main thing."

"Think," broke in Charles, "of the Wittmann Civic Park."

Jochen swung in his chair to him. "Eh? What are you talking about, Charlie?"

Charles could lean back now. "I've been thinking of accepting the offer of the city for that property, to be made into a park. I've thought of insisting that it be called the Wittmann Civic Park, in honor of our family. A park for the people."

Jochen stared at him. Then he said, very slowly, spacing his words: "What the hell are you talking about?"

"I can visualize it," said Charles. "The river, the park, the trees, the grass. The Wittmann Civic Park. Stone pillars, at the entrance. 'The Wittmann Civic Park' on it on a bronze plaque, perhaps, or just chiselled into the stone. 'In memory of Walther and Emil Wittmann.' Very nice. And what a view from your window, Wilhelm."

"Well, good," said Jochen, sneeringly. "And a loss of two-thirds in hard cash. Keep the Connington out. Let us remain a backward town. Keep it tight."

"I," said Charles, "have taken an option on the Burnsley property. It's just right for the Connington. Best piece of land around here, and the only land for sale. The Connington will take it, and they'll keep their dirty chimneys and their shacks away from the city. Moreover, they'd be right near the railroad. That would be an inducement, too."

Jochen was breathless with rage. He tried to gather the eyes of his other brothers to him. But they would not look at him. So. Old Charlie with his idiot schemes, again.

"The Connington won't pay as big a price for that damn Burnsley land!" shouted Jochen.

"But, with the sale of the river property to the city, and the amount the Connington will pay us for the Burnsley land, we'll have almost the same profit," said Charles. "And we won't have a ruined waterfront, either." He looked at Jochen. "Why do you want to ruin the view? Why do you want the city covered with smoke? Haven't you any pride in your home town, Joe?"

Wilhelm sat in his chair, thin, dark, and exquisite. "Charles is right. He's usually right. So, I vote with him, when and if this thing ever gets to a vote."

Jochen was breathing heavily. His color was almost apoplectic. So, old Charlie had been sneaking behind his back, had he? There was no help for him, Jochen, in Wilhelm. But there was that half-witted Fred— Jochen turned to Friederich. "Look here," he said roughly. "You have some intelligence, Fred. Look at it sensibly. We can't be sure the Connington would want that Burnsley property. They might get mad at us for even suggesting it. Old Charlie saves all his cash; he's a miser. He has enough if he doesn't do another day's work in his life. A miser. But some of us aren't so unconcerned about money. Some of us think of our city, and what it will mean for the Connington to be here. More employment. More business. More money for everybody."

"The Wittmann Civic Park," said Charles gently.

Jochen glanced at him, and it was a murderous glance. "You! I don't know what you've got up your sleeve, but I bet it wouldn't bear inspection." He turned again to Friederich, over whom he had such enormous and obscure influence. "Let's have some sense here, Fred. You could do a lot of work among the men the Connington would bring here."

"And you might talk to the Connington about the Pinkertons, too," interjected Charles. "You remember the strike-breakers you got here in 1910, Joe, when I took Jimmy to Europe? A nasty business, wasn't it? I couldn't do anything about it, you thought. But Friederich cabled me. You remember cabling me, don't you, Friederich, asking me for help, and telling me about it?"

"I remember," said Friederich, bitterly. He gave Jochen a hating look. "And you cabled back, Karl, that the strike-breakers were to be called off, and that I was to do all the negotiating with and for the men, about the union."

"I do detest disorders," said Wilhelm. "I was against the strike-breakers from the beginning, as you know, Jochen. However, I think we weren't talking about that just now. It is not like you, Charles, to be irrelevant."

"I'm not in the least irrelevant," said Charles blandly. Jochen sat there, furious and already defeated. "Let us get to a vote, and get it over with. I vote 'no' to letting the Connington have our land. Well, Joe, what about you?"

"I vote 'yes'!" bellowed Jochen. He appeared about to burst with rage. "And if any one of you has any intelligence, you'll vote 'yes' too!"

"Then, I haven't any 'intelligence,'" said Wilhelm, aloofly. "I vote 'no.'"

Friederich was silent. This disconcerted Charles. Friederich was unclenching and clenching his hands in that distraught way of his.

"Friederich," said Charles. "You don't want the Pinkertons here, do you? You know the reputation of the Pinkertons."

"You don't give a damn about the Pinkertons!" exclaimed Jochen. "Don't dance around Fred, in your sly way. You're quite ready to sell the Burnsley property to them, aren't you, Pinkertons or not? You're a stinking hypocrite, Charlie!"

Charles saw that the situation was becoming difficult. How had he been so stupid as to overlook this contingency? Mr. Parker, who had been taking notes unobtrusively down at the foot of the table, paused in his writing and regarded Charles with disturbed sympathy.

Then Charles spoke carefully: "You're wrong. I do care about the Pinkertons. And I'm hoping that Friederich might do something about organizing a union among the Connington men."

That settled it. Friederich blurted out: "I vote with Karl. No."

Jochen was aghast. He flung himself against the back of his chair. He glared at each of his brothers in turn. "I can't believe it," he said, finally, as if stunned. "All that money. You can't push a thing like that aside, without decent consideration. And none of the considerations you've advanced, any of you, have any sense. It—it's ridiculous. Grown men don't act this way."

He narrowed his attention upon Wilhelm, in his intense agitation. "Willie, when I talked to you last week you saw the whole thing my way. You agreed that the offer was not to be refused. You wanted a special meeting called—"

Charles' face stiffened. "A little irregular, isn't it, discussing such a matter privately?"

But Jochen ignored him. "Well, Willie? What made you change your mind?"

Wilhelm's cold urbanity was only slightly disturbed. He lit another of his endless cigarettes, every movement delicate. He puffed rapidly. "Shall we say I changed my mind?"

"So, Charlie smelled a rat—"

"I did," agreed Charles.

"—and he talked you out of it," ended Jochen, grimly. "He can always twist you around his little finger. You never see it, but he can do it."

"Very quaint," said Wilhelm lightly. But he had colored. "I am not going to change my mind, again, Jochen. I voted 'no' and I mean it." Almost without interest, he concluded: "And please don't call me 'Willie.' "

Charles saw that the excitable Friederich was deeply uneasy. He was regarding Jochen with his intense fixity of expression. When Jochen turned to him he almost flinched.

"You, Fred. I want you to consider it again. All that money. And you've let this fox of a Charlie talk you out of part of what should be yours."

"You're wrong," said Charles. "Friederich has only understood his duty towards the people of our city. He knows how the people will feel when our plans for the Wittmann Civic Park are announced."

"Shut up about that infernal park!" cried Jochen. "That's just a scheme of yours! You've got something else in mind, and I want to know what it is!"

Charles turned his head to Friederich. "Have I ever lied to you? Do you believe, too, that I am lying now?"

"No," said Friederich, unwillingly. But he gnawed his under lip. "No, Karl, I don't think you are lying. I think you want the park. And," he struggled with himself, "I want it, too. But there's the company to consider. Do we lose much money by refusing the Connington offer?"

"Very little, if anything. I can strike a good bargain, Friederich. But even more than the bargain is the family's integrity and reputation." Charles spread his hands. "You don't want to change your vote again, do you, Friederich?"

Friederich again struggled. However, he said: "I gave my vote."

Charles looked at Mr. Parker. "You have recorded the votes?"

Mr. Parker answered: "I have, Mr. Wittmann."

"I can't believe it," said Jochen, honestly incredulous and shocked.

Friederich was unhappy. Wilhelm saw this, and was amused. He decided to come to Charles' rescue, though the issue was already settled. He said: "The city will believe it was all Friederich's idea—Friederich, the lover of the common man, the worker for the comman man's welfare." He blew a fine stream of smoke upwards. "Well, the newspaper men are waiting outside. Shall we tell them that Friederich Wittmann, who bleeds for the people, has decided that our property be made into a park for them, or shall we tell them that he has denied them the park?"

Friederich gave him a savage look. "I believe my vote is recorded," he said.

Jochen contemplated his defeat somberly. He contemplated Charles. Then all at once he lost his temper completely. He said to Friederich: "You, too. He winds you around his finger. You're dingy, smudgy wax in his hands, do you know that?"

Now Charles could smile, with some return of normal pleasure. It was really too bad of old Joe to speak like that, even though his adjectives had been very telling. Friederich turned a dull crimson.

"Wax!" he said. "Yet you let Karl bring in that labor-saving machinery, so that we could discharge fifteen men! Or was that your idea, Jochen?"

Jochen was dumfounded. Curse the fool! One never knew when one had him. He had raised no objection to the money-saving involved, though he had protested weakly at the discharging of the tool-makers. What a liar, a hypocrite, a dreamer!

"I think," said Charles, amiably, "that it also ought to be thoroughly understood, since we are now wading deep into policy, that Friederich was responsible, in part, for our benefits to the men, in the way of incomes while ill, assistance with medical expenses, and paid vacations. You remember the conferences we had about all that, Friederich?"

Wilhelm's amusement was growing. With the utmost solemnity, he remarked: "I think the men are very grateful to Friederich."

"So!" shouted Jochen. "It all comes out now! I thought it was all Charlie's doing. So you had a part in it, did you, Freddie?"

Confused, badgered, and smarting, Friederich could not speak. Charles said, seriously: "A man can't do his best work if he is worrying about his family, and the doctors' bills, or if he will have a job next week. Friederich understood that."

Jochen pointed a big blunt finger at Charles, and bawled: "He won't work at all, unless he's worried about tomorrow! Yes, let's get into 'policy,' before we're ruined by your scheme, Charlie. Damn it, don't you know that insecurity is the mother of ambition?"

Now that the issue of the river property had been disposed of, Charles could speak his mind. "You have a point there," he smiled.

Friederich found his voice, and he looked revengefully at Charles. "Insecurity, on the contrary, is the breeder of disorder and revolution."

Said Wilhelm, lightly: "You Socialists, then, should be breeders of insecurity. You want disorder and revolution, don't you, so that you'll come into your own?"

Friederich stared at this most hated brother. "What do you mean by my 'own'?"

"Personal power, that's what he means," exclaimed Jochen. "Willie's right. Power you can't get, Fred, by working in the orderly and established frame-work of a free society, because you haven't the brains or resourcefulness."

Charles began to feel happier by the moment. Friederich would remember this day. He nodded his head, very slightly. Joe was right, naturally, and Friederich would never forgive him.

With almost incoherent rage, Friederich replied to Jochen: "What do you mean by a 'free' society? A society where a few are oppressively rich, and maintain their riches by exploitation? Where a man can make a fortune while other men remain poor?"

Jochen could not forget his defeat. Friederich was the weakest of his brothers. He attacked him viciously: "How can a man make a fortune? By having a better idea than his stupider brothers, or more ambition, or more inventiveness, or doing harder work. You Socialists would like to take away incentive. You think that would punish superior men for daring to be brighter than inferior men, such as yourself. But you're careful about the company, aren't you, most of the time? You'll always be careful about that, because you know that your bank accounts would suffer if we were ever fool enough to put your ideas into actual functioning, here!"

Charles said to himself: Maybe I've underestimated Joe's intelligence. He said, aloud: "Well, Americans have a lot of common sense, Joe, and they're realistic. We haven't anything to fear, in spite of some—flighty —ideas."

Wilhelm stood up, all languid elegance, and again looked at his watch. "We never have a meeting without its finally degenerating into one of these fruitless arguments. You bore me, I'm afraid. I'm not interested in Friederich's darling 'average man.' In so far as I am concerned, the average man isn't of importance, nor his squalid average intelligence, or talents."

Charles said: "Wait a moment, Wilhelm. There's no average man, either physically or mentally. That's muddled thinking, and I'm surprised at you. Each man is an individual, and his problems, to a certain extent, are all unique. That is why a capitalistic-democratic society like ours is the best of all societies."

Jochen sneered: "Really, now."

But Charles went on, doggedly, for the fear was with him again: "Our society is the best because it makes room for variety, and increases variety." He looked quickly at Friederich: "I've a few ideas, though, and I think they are practical. I think the workers should be encouraged to form some sort of private society within their unions, in which they can create a kind of insurance company protecting themselves against their peculiar hazards. They should pay for all their benefits, themselves, so they'll have a feeling of personal independence and responsibility. Besides, a free country can't exist without its people having pride and courage, and working for their own good without the help of Government."

Friederich did not know what to say. He was trapped by his fanaticism and torn by his own avarice.

Jochen said scornfully: "All right, Charlie. To use your own silly expression: You have a point there. Look at Fred. He's speechless. He can't say a word, and be consistent with what he's always raving about. But what of the things you're already doing for our men, without their lifting a finger for themselves? You've made us a laughing stock."

Charles replied mildly: "I'm hoping our men will finally get my idea, themselves—protective brotherhoods, among the unions. But until all workers are unionized, no one single small union can do much for itself without the help of employers."

Jochen smiled unpleasantly. "So, we lose money."

"Better than having Washington step in with wild theories," said Charles. "I've been reading some of the outbursts of Wilson's hangers-on. Once we let Government into any scheme of 'protecting' the workingman, by penalizing employers, we're on the way to despotism and personal irresponsibility on the part of hundreds of millions of workers. There's a middle course, and we'd better take it."

Friederich found his voice. He turned malevolently on Charles: "Spoken like a true capitalist. Don't you think that employers have a duty towards those who help them make their money?" There was no use in ever attacking Jochen. But one could attack Karl without a slashing attack in return.

Charles answered, slowly: "Let us be sensible about this. I think everyone has a duty towards everyone else. I think I should be respected for employing a man just as much as he should be respected for working for me. It is an honest exchange, an honest relationship. I am a working man, too."

Friederich gave him one of his knowing and cunning smiles: "Everything will be resolved satisfactorily when the Government controls the means of production." His voice took on a note of threat.

Charles studied Friederich consideringly. "Do you want the Government controlling our shops? If it ever does, you know, our incomes will be controlled, too. And I can assure you that they'll be much less than what they are now."

Friederich's face changed. "No. They'll be more."

Charles shook his head. "You're wrong, Fred. Governments, if not sternly controlled by the people, breed whole swarms of incompetent bureaucrats, and bureaucrats are wasteful. Look at the heavy bureaucracy of Germany. It's Germany's curse. And its benefits to German workers keep German workers sweating."

Jochen had been listening intently. He sneered: "Good old Charlie. Agrees with everyone. After a conference with him, we find we've never gotten anywhere, or done anything he didn't want us to do. So, we're right back where we started."

Wilhelm sighed loudly. "I think the newspaper men are getting restless."

But Friederich had fully recovered. Again, in spite of everything, Charles felt Friederich subtly aligning himself with Jochen against him: "Jochen's methods are not always good. But at least he has definite ideas, even if they are sometimes wrong. Karl never has. He just drifts. The policy of laissez-faire."

Jochen stood up. He put his hand on Friederich's shoulder. "There, you have it, Fred! If you didn't have such extreme ideas sometimes, you'd be invaluable to this company. At least, you don't go around smugly, like Charlie, with his temperate, wishy-washy ways. Always careful. Conciliating." He looked at Charles, malignantly. "You think you are very smart, don't you? But one of these days you might, just possibly, of course, be a little too smart."

He turned to Friederich: "All right, Fred. Let's go out and give the newspaper men a happy treat. You can make the announcement."

Wilhelm and Charles watched them go. Wilhelm's frown made fine wrinkles appear in his forehead. He said: "Charles, we had better be careful about those two. Their ideas are as far apart as ideas can ever be, but, fundamentally, they are the same. You think that is a paradox?"

"No," said Charles.

"At the bottom of it all, Charles, they are both 'oppressors,' to use Friederich's vulgar term. And getting down to fundamentals, again: I believe that intrinsically they want to oppress the same people, rule them with the same kind of tyranny, though Friederich calls it Socialism, and Jochen calls it 'business.'"

Wilhelm began to laugh. "So, you are letting Friederich take the credit for the Wittmann Civic Park, are you?"

Charles raised his eyebrows, then laughed, also.

"I don't mind," continued Wilhelm, amused. "I can let him have the credit, if it is of any assistance to you. Except that I design the park, of course."

"You can be sure of that." Charles considered. "Wilhelm, you could be of help to me. And something tells me I'm going to need help." For a moment he contemplated telling Wilhelm of his shapeless fears. But Wilhelm would only be bored, or politely incredulous.

Wilhelm said: "Do I not always do what I can for you, Charles, even against my own convictions, sometimes? I believe in you."

They moved together towards the door, while Mr. Parker shut his notebook.

Wilhelm paused on the threshold with unusually heavy seriousness. "Help you, Charles? Always. You know that." He smiled his mercurial smile. "And now, let us join the Greek chorus of approval for Friederich, and our dear Jochen. I should imagine they are now basking in the reverence of the newspaper men. And, Charles, do not forget Friday night. I am delighted you are coming."

CHAPTER IX

IT SEEMED to Charles, in retrospect, that he had never asked anything exorbitant of life. He had never yearned after the lightning-lit, the sensational, the magnificent, the trumpet-heralded. Fairly good health, tranquillity, something to love, a respectable bank balance, an unimpeachable reputation, a casual peace of mind built on a sound character —these ought to satisfy any man, he had believed.

But now he knew that no one is invulnerable. His world, so good-tempered, so plainly urbane, so quiet, had been shattered. Something in him, never before consciously known, had thrown everything into disorder. He had become vulnerable because he had become suddenly perceptive.

Even his God had been built on his own image, a sensible God, just slightly materialistic, not metaphysical, possibly even a solid business man in His way. Charles was President of the Board of the First Lutheran Church, but he had never been disturbed by religion over-much. Now, as he thought about it, he realized that he had never fully considered God at all.

But something had stirred, and suddenly nothing was "sound," nothing was "sensible." As he sat alone in his office, after his lunch, he began to think about God, confusedly, and all the other matters which had invaded his life with such ominous insistence, and even terror. His brothers were no longer merely nuisances, to be outwitted and manipulated.

He thought about his brother Friederich. Now he began to see Friederich as a man, as a soul, as something hidden and incomprehensible, as something to be pitied. Pitied! He needed help, Charles decided, suddenly. He needed to be helped to gain self-esteem. Friederich might be arrogant, but he had no normal conceit or vanity. A good opinion of one's self made a man courageous, well-balanced, reasonable, and harmless. It also made him constructive. Friederich, Charles decided by some obscure intuition, had a very low opinion of himself, and this made him vengeful, and vengeful men were full of menace. They were also sad and lost men. Charles was not one to feel too much compassion for anyone, for he had not known that most men needed compassion. Now he was full of compassion for Friederich, and he did not known why.

He was also very afraid, and of so many things, each one amorphous and without outline. He remembered that Leon Bouchard was in the city. He remembered that Leon Bouchard had been a quiet man, "deep." He had respected Leon, for Leon had had a matter-of-fact air about him; he had been broad of face and shoulders, somewhat stocky, but potent, with a good color and reserved manners. There had been a thick power about him; Charles had thought that if any murdering was to be done it would be done openly by Leon, with a thrust of a short wide knife.

"Oh, damn," said Charles. Leon Bouchard was in town. But Leon Bouchard had not called him. Colonel Grayson was running after shadows. His telephone rang, which meant that Mr. Parker had considered the call important. Charles looked at the black instrument. He reached for it, then stopped. Then he said again, aloud: "Oh, damn." He lifted the receiver to his ear.

"Mr. Wittmann?" The voice was assured and quick. "This is Mr. Elson Waite, of the Connington Steel Company. Perhaps you remember me? You will remember, too, perhaps, that you promised to inform me of the decision of your company about that river property?"

A weak sense of relief flooded over Charles. Almost eagerly, he said: "Yes, yes, Mr. Waite. Of course. Of course. I didn't know you were in the city. I—I was about to write you, Mr. Waite. We've made our decision. This morning." He heard his voice, uneven, almost stammering.

"Yes, Mr. Wittmann?" The voice was courteous, but a little sharp and patronizing. Good stern annoyance came to Charles. He, Charles Wittmann, might be president of only a middle-sized machine tool company, and Mr. Waite might be an officer of the Connington Steel Company, so monstrously large that they were being investigated by Congress for a possible violation of the anti-trust laws, but Charles Wittmann had his importance also, and his own personal dignity. He was very important, too, to this exigent Mr. Waite, for he had frustrated Mr. Waite.

So, quite coldly, Charles said: "I'm sorry, Mr. Waite, but I have bad news for you. We've voted not to sell you the river property."

He was filled with elation and pleasure. The issue had been of sufficient value so that Mr. Waite, himself, had come to Andersburg. It gave Charles satisfaction to checkmate him, and thus increase his own self-esteem.

There was an incredulous and affronted silence on the part of Mr. Waite. So, thought Charles, you thought it was all settled, and that the little Wittmanns would be only too happy to give you what you wanted. He went on: "No, Mr. Waite. The answer is no."

"I think," said Mr. Waite, "that we offered you a very good price. A very good price, indeed."

Charles kept his voice cool. "I agree with you, Mr. Waite. But still, we have rejected your offer." Then, not knowing why he said it, he added: "Why are you so insistent upon that property, Mr. Waite?"

There was a pause. Was that the murmur of another man in the background? Mr. Waite said: "This is confidential, Mr. Wittmann, and I'll answer your question." He hesitated portentously. "You see, Bouchard and Sons are interested in that property also. For us. They have steel mills of their own, of course, but they will soon need a great deal of steel, and even we—we, the Connington, are not, at the present time, able to give them all they wish. So, you see that it is very important that we have that property."

The Bouchards. The "butchers." They, the Bouchards, needed a "great deal of steel."

"Hello?" said Mr. Waite, vexed at Charles' long silence.

"Yes," said Charles. "Yes, I am here." He waited a second or two. "I think I read that Mr. Leon Bouchard is in town."

"Yes, he is," said Mr. Waite, in a light and friendly voice. "In fact, Mr. Bouchard is here at the Imperial Hotel with me. Mr. Wittmann, could you have dinner with Mr. Bouchard and me, at this hotel? Perhaps we can come to some agreement. When we met here—quite by accident, of course—he mentioned that he intended to see you, if you had time."

"Mr. Bouchard wishes to see me?" Charles spoke thickly.

Again, there was that murmur in the background.

Mr. Waite was all suave indifference. "I'm just surmising, Mr. Wittmann. Perhaps I am wrong. Mr. Bouchard is just passing through. However, we'd like to talk with you, at dinner. Will you give us the pleasure—"

"That is very kind of you," Charles heard himself saying.

"You will come, then?"

A broad ray of sunlight lay across Charles' desk. He looked at it. He was filled with a bitter anger and fear.

"Yes," he said, "I'll come. But you understand, Mr. Waite, that nothing can change our decision? On the other hand, I have another proposition. I have an option on some land five miles beyond the center of the city; on the outskirts. If you want that, you may have it. At a lesser price, of course. But it is desirable property."

"Shall we discuss that at dinner?" asked Mr. Waite, amiably.

Charles hung up the receiver. He sat in his chair and looked at the telephone. He could refuse the Burnsley land to the Connington. But they would buy somewhere else. The Bouchards needed a "great deal of steel." He, Charles, could do nothing. If he refused, he would be quixotic, and nothing more. He was a business man. He was a small business man. The Connington Steel Company and the Bouchards were giants. He could do nothing. To repudiate a profit would benefit no one. Nothing could save—Save what? Charles shook his head over and over. When powerful men decided an issue, little men were powerless. They could only take what profit they could get. Colonel Grayson. Charles could do nothing about the Connington Steel Company. But he could do something about the Bouchards.

He lit one of his own inexpensive cigars. It tasted acrid in his mouth, and he put it down. Then he got up. He felt tired and old. He went in to see Jochen. Jochen was busily signing mail. When he saw Charles, he scowled. "Oh, it's you," he said. He put down his pen. "Remember what I told you, Charlie? You think you are very smart, but one of these days you might be too smart."

"Perhaps." Charles saw that Jochen had his cigar case on his desk. He opened it, took a cigar out, without asking, lit it. Somehow, it did not have quite the same taste as usual. Jochen squinted at him, inquisitively. Something was bothering old Charlie. Jochen waited.

"Mr. Waite, of the Connington, just called me," said Charles.

Jochen was immediately interested. "He did? From Pittsburgh?" He added, with suppressed rage: "And I suppose you gave him the good news, eh?"

"He's right here, in Andersburg." Charles paused. He felt confident again. "He was just 'passing through,' I believe he implied." He looked at Jochen. "And Leon Bouchard is 'just passing through,' also. They invited me to dinner tonight." It was silly, and it was childish, but he could not help feeling a little malice.

"No!" exclaimed Jochen, forgetting his rage. "My God! Maybe the Bouchards will give us some business. Maybe, after all, the Connington will buy that damn Burnsley property! I'll go with you—"

"No," said Charles. The cigar tasted better. "They only invited me. After all, you know, I'm president of this company."

"But, God damn it, I'm vice-president. Why do you always have to hog the limelight, Charlie?"

"They only invited me," said Charles, pleased. He turned away. "Thanks for the cigar, Joe. I'll call you tonight, and tell you the news."

The Imperial Hotel was still the most imposing hotel in Andersburg, though, in 1911, the Pennsylvania House had been built in that city. The Imperial Hotel had a majestic history, even if its crimson plush and scarlet velvet and gilt had suffered some deterioration through the years. Important visitors, remembering its grandeur and comfort, still preferred it to the Pennsylvania House.

It did not surprise Charles to discover that Mr. Elson Waite and Mr. Leon Bouchard occupied a suite together at the Imperial. It was a fine suite, the best, Charles remembered, even if "Victorian" and violent with red velvet and plush. Did they think him such a fool as to believe that they had met here by "accident," and were only "passing through"? All his fears took on sharper form and ominousness.

Mr. Waite, answering his knock, greeted him with great cordiality. He was a tall gray man, inconspicuous in appearance, but with a pair of pale eyes like bits of stone. He had a look of authority and hardness, in spite of his affable manner, and he reminded Charles of Colonel Grayson.

"You don't need an introduction to Mr. Bouchard, Mr. Wittmann," said Mr. Waite, indicating the powerful, stocky man in the background. "You have met, I believe?"

Charles shook hands with Mr. Bouchard. Leon had not changed much in the past two years, except for a slight soft paunch and even more reserve. He had a lethargic air about him, which only increased his impression of potency. Mr. Bouchard looked at him, and smiled: his smile was unexpectedly attractive. He was of French ancestry, but there was nothing quick and Latin about him.

Leon said: "I've been in Chicago, Mr. Wittmann. Then when I found I could get no train until tomorrow, to Windsor, and when I had to remain in Andersburg, I suddenly remembered you."

Mr. Bouchard went on, with heavy graciousness: "Your precision tools are the best in America. I'm not sorry I had to stay over. I think we ought to discuss a certain order I have in mind—"

A bribe, thought Charles. But he was immediately disgusted with himself. Shadows: he was becoming a victim of shadows. He was seeing danger where none existed.

"Any business you can give us, Mr. Bouchard, will be more than appreciated," said Charles, seating himself at Mr. Waite's invitation, and holding his briefcase on his knees.

Mr. Bouchard sat and studied him. "I understand that you haven't suffered much from the present lag in business," he said.

"No. We aren't as busy as I'd like us to be, but we are still in the black." Charles smiled.

"No labor troubles?"

"No. We have a union, a company union, sir."

Mr. Bouchard exchanged a glance with Mr. Waite. Was there a flicker of amusement at him, between these men? Charles remembered that the Bouchards, too, were always having labor troubles. He ought to have felt proud, he knew; it angered him that he could only feel foolish, a small-town manufacturer of no real importance.

Mr. Bouchard said, politely: "You should be congratulated, Mr. Wittmann, that you are able to control your workers so well."

"I don't control them." It was rare for Charles to feel so explosive. "I only treat them decently. The laborer is worthy of his hire, I think the Bible says."

A curious expression passed over Mr. Bouchard's strongly muscled face. "I have a nephew, Peter, who always says that," he remarked. "But Peter isn't interested in our business. He is an idealist."

I am certainly nervous these days, thought Charles. "Idealists don't do any harm, if they are really idealists," he said, lamely.

"But, every man is a hypocrite, according to Frederick the Great," observed Mr. Bouchard. However, he was smiling. "I don't think my nephew, Peter, would harm anyone, and I don't think he is a hypocrite."

Mr. Waite had been listening to this apparently idle conversation with the utmost politeness. He said: "Very interesting. But it is six-fifteen, and I have engaged a table for three in the dining room at six-thirty. Mr. Wittmann, shall we conclude our business immediately, so that we can have a pleasant hour or two downstairs?"

Charles said: "I'm ready. But there is no business to 'conclude,' Mr. Waite. I told you our decision." He opened his briefcase, drew out a diagram which he had prepared only an hour ago. "Please look at this. It is the Burnsley property, on which I have an option."

But Mr. Waite was looking at him intently, though he took the paper. "May I ask when you took this option, Mr. Wittmann?"

Charles said, without hesitation: "Very recently. When I decided we ought not to sell the river property to you."

"And why don't you want to sell us that property?"

"I want to sell it to the city, for a park. The Wittmann Civic Park." It was intolerable that he should feel so sheepish, so stupid, among these men, and why everything he said should sound so silly.

"Oh." Mr. Waite glanced enigmatically at Mr. Bouchard, who did not move, and who did not speak. "The welfare of the city, I see, Mr. Wittmann. Very wonderful. A sort of monument to your family." Simple, ordinary words, but they could make Charles uncomfortable, and make him color.

"Yes," he said, in an unnecessarily defensive voice. "That's it. The city thinks quite well of us. We have a reputation. And we owe something to the city."

Everything he had said would have been approved by anyone, he knew. They were honorable words. Why, then, should he believe that he was amusing these two men, and that they were secretly laughing at him, and making a fool of him? Again, he was angered, and this anger was turned against himself. Stop it, said Charles to himself, sternly. What is happening to me? No wonder they think I am a fool.

He tried for quiet deliberation, in spite of a profound antagonism against the two: "If you buy the Burnsley land, Mr. Waite, and we sell the river property to the city, we'll lose very little."

"But we really do want the river property," said Mr. Waite, with a too meticulous courtesy. "Very convenient for us, for we'll employ barges and flat-boats."

Charles' ears were burning. "If you buy the Burnsley land, you'll be near the railroad. A spur can be easily attached." Mr. Waite had laid down the paper on a table near him. Charles repressed a desire to snatch it and replace it in his briefcase. He could not stop himself saying: "Mr. Waite, a steel mill, such as you plan, would ruin our river front. I happen to live here, and so do my brothers. We don't want our river front to be destroyed, and you would destroy it. No one has the right to disfigure a city, for his own gain."

Mr. Waite said urbanely: "But you don't live near the river, Mr. Wittmann. And I don't believe your brothers do, either. Business is business, you know—"

Now Charles did take the paper. He felt pent and furious. "I gather you aren't interested in the Burnsley land, Mr. Waite. Shall we just say it is all finished, then?"

Mr. Waite smiled. Again, he glanced at Mr. Bouchard. "Really, Mr. Wittmann, you are jumping at conclusions. I didn't say we won't consider the Burnsley land. I am just trying to persuade you about the river property. I haven't met you before but I gathered, from Mr. Bouchard, that you were a reasonable man."

"I'm very reasonable," said Charles, holding down his voice. "I am so reasonable that I like my city, where I was born, and I like the people here. They depend upon me not to do anything which would injure them, even if I am offered a profit. My brothers agree with me—"

"Except one."

These men knew too much about him, Charles. But he made every muscle in his face smooth. "Yes. You are right. But there are three against 'one.' And we have given out our decision to the newspapers."

Mr. Waite held out his hand patiently, a finely manicured hand. "May I see the outline of the Burnsley land, Mr. Wittmann?"

Mr. Waite, who was a gentleman of acumen, had guessed a great deal about Charles. He knew that Charles was uncomfortable, and that he, himself, by his every slight gesture, the very intonations of his voice, was making Charles feel uncouth and awkward. One of these loutish Pennsylvania Dutch, Mr. Waite had said to himself. However, he had also underestimated Charles. So, he did not notice the slight frown on Mr. Bouchard's face. Mr. Bouchard was not a man to underestimate others, and he was annoyed at Mr. Waite, who thought that he could intimidate Charles by cosmopolitan manners and could disturb him by an air of adult tolerance.

Charles gave Mr. Waite the paper. He sat there, hunched slightly forward, looking more solid and obdurate by the moment. Mr. Waite examined the paper casually. "Yes. I can see that it is very close to the railroad. A spur; yes." He smiled at Charles. "Mr. Wittmann, we are prepared to offer you a larger amount for the river property. I will consult with my president, and perhaps we can even raise it to twice the amount."

"No," said Charles. "You haven't enough money to buy that property, Mr. Waite."

Mr. Bouchard, who had been sitting so still and so watchful, said: "I think you are wasting your time, Elson. Mr. Wittmann does not intend to sell the property to you." He passed his hand over his thick rough shock of gray hair. "Am I correct, Mr. Wittmann?"

"You are correct."

Mr. Waite remarked: "Mr. Wittmann, I'm afraid I don't understand. You seem to be taking a very objective business discussion personally."

"That's right. I do take it personally. That property is to be the Wittmann Civic Park."

Mr. Waite was provoked that he had underestimated Charles. He also thought Charles a fool, who, having made a mistake, was mulishly standing by it. Mr. Bouchard said: "You see, Elson. You've been wrong from the very beginning. I suggest you look into this—this Burnsley matter."

Mr. Waite turned to Mr. Bouchard. Charles expected some exasperated remark. But the two men only looked at each other in silence. Then Mr. Waite said, remotely: "Very well, Mr. Wittmann. I accept your decision. What do you want for that Burnsley property?"

Charles had been prepared to name a price which would give him a small but substantial profit. But he had seen the speechless exchange between the other two. So he named a large price, twice as much as he had intended to name, and even more than the Connington Steel Company had offered for the river property. To his surprise, Mr. Bouchard smiled. Mr. Waite was astonished.

"I'm afraid I don't understand, Mr. Wittmann."

"I'm not anxious to sell the Burnsley land, either," said Charles. "In fact, for a long time I've considered building another shop there, myself. I was ready to do you a favor, but, as you said, you have arranged dinner for six-thirty, and it is that now. Take it or leave it, Mr. Waite."

Mr. Bouchard laughed.

Mr. Waite studied Charles. He decided he detested him. "It almost seems as if you wish to keep the Connington out of this territory, Mr. Wittmann."

Charles considered this. He said: "Perhaps you are right, Mr. Waite. We aren't a very large city. We have small industries, here. We are a peaceful people, Quakers, Mennonites, Pennsylvania Germans. We don't consider money of paramount importance. We don't especially want a huge mill like yours, here. You will bring in what we call 'outsiders.' Of an unpredictable kind. Call us conservative, if you wish. Call us suspicious of strangers. You are entitled to your opinion." He cleared his throat. "Mr. Waite, I might call your attention to the fact that if you refuse the Burnsley property you won't buy anything like it near Andersburg. The Mayor of this city is a personal friend of mine. I have many other influential friends here."

Again, Mr. Bouchard laughed. He appeared to be enjoying himself at Mr. Waite's expense. "Come, come," he said. "This is degenerating into something disagreeable. That is not the way to do business. Elson, why don't you agree to Mr. Wittmann's price, and let us go down to dinner?"

So, thought Charles, they want that mill here. They need a "great deal of steel."

Mr. Waite let his face clear. Charles could see him doing it, determinedly. Mr. Waite smiled pleasantly. "Mr. Wittmann, you have us in a very tight place, and I am afraid you are taking advantage of it. However, I'll agree to that property. I'll agree to your price. Shall we shake hands on it?"

"Of course." But Charles did not put out his hand. "But before we do that, suppose you write out an agreement?"

With an air of amused boredom, Mr. Waite went to a distant desk, wrote out an agreement with quick strokes of a pen on the bottom of the paper which Charles had given him. "The company will confirm this within a few days, formally," he said. He had recovered his politeness. Again, he extended his hand, and Charles took it. The hand felt cold and metallic in his own.

They went downstairs together, in the steel-lace elevator, murmuring casually for the benefit of the elevator man. The huge dining room was almost full, a blaze of white tablecloths, red velvet draperies, red plush chairs, crystal chandeliers, and gilt everywhere. Charles knew he ought to feel elated, for he had concluded a "smart" piece of business, a really tremendous piece of business. But instead, he was depressed and very weary. He wanted to be rid of these men. He wanted not to see them, or to be in their company.

Mr. Waite had arranged for a quiet table in a corner, to which they were conducted by an obsequious head-waiter. Charles sat down, in silence, and bitterly contemplated his silver. Mr. Waite and Mr. Bouchard were quite at ease. Mr. Waite, it appeared, had previously arranged for a very fine dinner. Charles, usually vitally interested in food, regarded the excellent roast beef with repulsion. He was not stirred by a mention of the best champagne. If his host and Mr. Bouchard were aware of his taciturn withdrawal, they did not show it. He heard his voice saying a few words. They sounded dull and uninspired, even to himself. I was never a gay conversationalist, he thought, but now I'm really surpassing myself. I sound like a morose bull.

He knew that Mr. Bouchard was not, himself, a man for dinner repartee. But Mr. Bouchard was doing all he could to make the occasion agreeable. He asked astute questions about Charles' business, and listened with more than polite interest. There was an honest kindness in his words, a sincerity. Charles found himself responding, in spite of his suspicions. This man might be a powerful and ruthless personality. It was evident, in the movement of his short thick hands, his quiet strength, his lack of elegance. But he was also a man who could reflect, and have his moments of thoughtfulness. Unwillingly, Charles began to like him. The shadow of Colonel Grayson retreated, became a fantastic memory. But Charles could not like Mr. Waite. Charles decided that not only was Mr. Waite a much lesser man than Mr. Bouchard, but a much shallower one, for all his conversational ability, his smoothness, his authoritative air. He lacked Mr. Bouchard's simple power.

By the time dessert appeared, and the champagne, Charles' tightness had somewhat relaxed. Mr. Bouchard had not spoken of the aeroplane steering-control assembly. He had asked only about Charles' business, had talked only of Andersburg and his good opinion of the city. When Charles asked a question about Bouchard and Sons, Mr. Bouchard answered without hesitation, and with simplicity, as a king might answer about his country, of which he was proud.

Mr. Bouchard offered Charles a cigar. He took it. He sipped his coffee. Mr. Bouchard settled himself easily in his chair, while Mr. Waite concentrated upon his dessert.

"Mr. Wittmann," said Mr. Bouchard, without obliqueness, "I wanted to talk to you about something. Really minor, and of no real importance, perhaps. But we've learned, accidentally, that you have some sort of patent for an aeroplane. You haven't used it, have you? You probably don't intend to use it. And so I'm wondering if you'd be interested in selling that patent to Bouchard and Sons."

CHAPTER X

THERE IT WAS. Charles put down his coffee. Colonel Grayson was no longer a shadow. He was a living if invisible presence. All the vague anxieties which had plagued Charles came back. He said in a low voice: "No."

Mr. Bouchard was puzzled. "Why not, Mr. Wittmann? You manufacture machine tools. You have that aeroplane patent. You aren't thinking of going into that business, are you?" He smiled.

Charles said: "No."

No one spoke. Mr. Waite carefully clipped at his cigar. Mr. Bouchard smoked slowly and contemplatively. Then he said: " 'No,' what, Mr. Wittmann?"

"I mean, I can't sell you that patent."

"You have a previous offer?"

The champagne which Charles had drunk suddenly made him ill. He struggled with his nausea. He heard himself saying: "You might say that I've had a 'previous offer.' "

"H'm." Mr. Bouchard was thoughtful. He puffed at his cigar, looked at it with dislike. "I don't know why I smoke," he commented. "I never cared about it." He put the cigar down in the ash tray. "Mr. Wittmann, I know this sounds inquisitive, but would you mind telling me who made the offer to you?"

Charles raised his eyes. "It was a tentative offer, only."

"A bigger concern than Bouchard?" Mr. Bouchard was politely incredulous.

"No."

"Then—" said Mr. Bouchard, cautiously.

It was a time to keep one's head. Mr. Bouchard had mentioned an "order." It was not Charles' intention to jeopardize that order. But still, he felt very sick. "I just said—Mr. Bouchard, I can't sell you that patent. You seem to know all about it. It's in my name, and not in the name of the company."

"I'm not in the least interested in aeroplanes, and I don't know what all this is about," remarked Mr. Waite, pleasantly. "But Mr. Bouchard is a friend of mine. Put it down as curiosity, Mr. Wittmann, and say that we just are interested in who has made you a 'previous offer.'"

The cigar Charles had been smoking was of even better quality than Jochen's, but Charles could not smoke it now. "I don't talk about my —customers," he said. "All I can say at present is that I can't sell Mr. Bouchard that aeroplane steering-control assembly. You know exactly what it is, don't you Mr. Bouchard?"

Mr. Bouchard considered this for a moment or two. He was frowning at his cigar. He thought: Damn Jules. He ought to have taken care of this, himself. I don't have the subtlety— He said: "Yes, I know exactly what it is, Mr. Wittmann. We've looked over all the patents in Washington. Yours is the best. That is why we are interested. If you refuse, you might regret it. Some other inventor will think up an even better assembly than yours, sometime. Perhaps very soon."

"Then, all you have to do is to wait."

"I'm afraid we can't 'wait.' We hoped to go into production on that patent very soon. We have our own aeroplane factory—a small one, by the way. You see, Mr. Wittmann, we, like you, believe in America, in experimentation. We believe that the aeroplane has a great commercial future. We want to sell our idea to the American people. We think we can persuade the people to use aeroplanes as regularly as they use the railroads. We may be wrong; but we can try. And Bouchard and Sons make very few mistakes."

Charles said, and knew he should not have said it as soon as the words were uttered: "You mean you want the patent for the American people?"

He was sure he was right when he saw the swift and secret glance between Mr. Waite and Mr. Bouchard. Then Mr. Bouchard was saying reasonably: "Why, of course, Mr. Wittmann. Who else?"

(Charles heard Colonel Grayson saying: "We can trust you?")

He said: "Suppose I sold you the patent with the stipulation it was not to be sold abroad, or lent, or exchanged?"

Again, that oblique glance ran between the other two men. Charles cursed himself. But Mr. Bouchard was smiling again: "Well, now, Mr. Wittmann, why should you say that? You know very well that that stipulation would be absurd. You, yourself, have lent patents abroad. For instance, you have a special tool for rifle bores. You lent it to Germany. Or was it England?"

Charles was silent. He felt thick and stupid and dazed. Finally, he muttered: "That was three years ago." He knew that what he was saying was all wrong. He was betraying himself.

Mr. Bouchard appeared to be puzzled. "What does it matter when it was, Mr. Wittmann? You are a business man. You know that there can be no restrictions. Frankly, buying the patent from you was only my idea. A very vague but interesting idea. If we bought it, I don't know if we'd ever use it. Possibly a better one will soon be invented. In the meantime—"

"No," said Charles.

"But you haven't given me a valid reason." Mr. Bouchard waited for Charles to speak, but Charles did not. "Mr. Wittmann, you paid $2,000 for that patent. We are prepared to pay you ten thousand."

Mr. Waite laughed easily, as if he considered the offer absurd. "Leon!" he exclaimed.

"I don't believe you have 'a previous offer,'" said Mr. Bouchard, bluntly.

It was an insult, and Charles knew it. On any other occasion he would have replied in kind. But he knew what he knew, and he knew that the others were suspicious and were trying to goad him. So he kept his voice quiet: "Maybe yes, maybe no. I'm not saying, Mr. Bouchard."

The waiter poured more champagne. Mr. Bouchard and Mr. Waite watched him with interest. "The best champagne I've ever tasted," observed Bouchard.

Charles had gone too far; it did not seem to him that it would hurt to go even further, so great was his panic. "Very good champagne, Mr. Bouchard. But I notice that you haven't drunk any. The waiter had to pour out the first glass he gave you."

Mr. Bouchard laughed, all good-humor. "I always get caught when I try to be polite. No, I don't like wines, or spirits, or any alcohol. It's my failing. I should, though. I'm of French descent."

"French descent," repeated Charles. "Do you like the French people, Mr. Bouchard?"

"I flatter myself I am a very tolerant man, Mr. Wittmann," said Leon, seriously. "I have no racial preferences. When it comes to business, one man's money is as good as another's."

They hope to smoke me out, thought Charles. He gripped the arm of his chair. It was a naïve remark, and a dangerous one, he knew, but he said: "I am an American. I happen to have a preference for Americans."

They had caught him, in spite of himself, or because of his folly, and he knew it. For they were staring at him impassively. Mr. Bouchard said, after an interval: "Mr. Wittmann, I understood you were a German."

"I am of German extraction. My father and my grandfather left Germany because they preferred a free country. I do, too. I am an American, Mr. Bouchard."

Leon had betrayed no Latin characteristics before, but he did so, now. He shrugged, very eloquently. That shrug mysteriously changed his own appearance. His lethargy vanished. His broad and inexpressive face became alive. Yet, he made no gesture, and his voice was still calm: "I'm thinking of America, too, Mr. Wittmann. I'm thinking of American industry, of American expansion and experimentation. That's why I want to buy your patent. And, frankly, I don't understand your inexplicable objection to selling it to me."

Charles paused. "Maybe the patent is very valuable. I want to think about it. I want to do the best for my company. Perhaps we may go into the aeroplane business, ourselves, if it's suddenly so important."

Once again, the peculiar flash passed between Mr. Bouchard and Mr. Waite. They were puzzled, Charles thought, with relief. He had put them off the track.

Mr. Bouchard said: "Well, no one in America is as big as Bouchard and Sons. And I can assure you that no one else would ever make you the offer we are making you now. See here, Mr. Wittmann, I have another idea. Keep your patent. But make the assembly for us. We'll supply you with the necessary materials, if you wish. You can make the assembly for us. It'll be a very large order, I assure you. Rather inconvenient for us, but we are reasonable people."

Charles asked: "Is that the order you mentioned before, Mr. Bouchard?"

Leon shook his head. "No. The sawing machines you made for us a couple of years ago—the patent of which you hold—were excellent. I intend to give you an order for more of them, many more of them. But we'll discuss that later. However, let's be reasonable. You haven't offered a single valid reason why you won't sell us that patent. And I take it you won't make the assembly for us?"

Charles nodded. "You're right, Mr. Bouchard. The patent is mine. I'm not going to sell it. And I'm not going to make the assembly for you. I'm sorry, but I have my reasons."

"You could tell me what they are?"

But Charles shook his head. He had handled this all wrong. They were making him feel so witless and crass and ignorant. And then he knew that this was their intention.

"Mr. Bouchard, you're asking very leading questions. You surely don't expect me, as a business man, to answer them, do you? I've told you all I could: Others have expressed an interest in that patent. I'm a cautious man. I've come to the conclusion that perhaps I could do better, myself, with that patent. I've thought of manufacturing it, myself—"

"For whom?" asked Mr. Bouchard, quickly.

Charles was silenced. He knew he had to speak, however, and to speak naturally. He hated himself for his slow thinking, his measured thinking.

"I don't know. Mr. Bouchard, I have inherited some German characteristics. I'm not volatile. I take time to consider. I do nothing hastily. You might even say I'm cautious, or cunning. That's what the French say about the Germans, don't they?"

"I didn't say that, Mr. Wittmann," replied Mr. Bouchard, gravely. His eyes were very intent, now, upon Charles. They had lost their dull, uninterested expression. "I've never underestimated you. You are a very intelligent man. So, I'm afraid that your evasions aren't impressing me that you are 'cautious' or 'cunning.'"

Charles was terribly afraid. Everything he had done and said had been wrong, all wrong. Bouchard was on the track of something. He was full of suspicion. He was deeply engrossed.

Charles tried to laugh. "You first insult me, then try to flatter me, Mr. Bouchard. I do these things myself, when I'm trying to convince some obdurate customer, or somebody. Usually, it works very well."

But Mr. Bouchard's gravity increased. He leaned his short thick elbows on the table, and bent towards Charles. Mr. Waite was listening with acute intentness.

"Mr. Wittmann," Leon began. He fixed his eyes upon Charles fully. "You have a reason. You won't tell me that reason. That is your own concern. But we have made you a remarkably good offer. You refuse it. I can only come to the conclusion that you have a reason which you can't, or dare not, tell us. Is that so?"

Charles' fear and anger came to his rescue. He forced himself to sound petulant and annoyed when he spoke: "I don't know what you're talking about, Mr. Bouchard. I've told you I wanted to think about that assembly. When some people, including the Bouchards, are interested in my obscure little patent, it makes me wonder what's in the wind. What is in the wind, Mr. Bouchard?"

Mr. Bouchard took his elbows off the table. He looked at Mr. Waite. Now he, himself, was cautious, and apparently indifferent. "To use your own words, Mr. Wittmann, 'I don't know what you're talking about.' Nothing's 'in the wind.' We've had a business discussion. That's all. In the meantime, I can only ask you to 'think' about our offer, and then to write me, or wire me. Will you promise me that?"

A wave of triumphant relief rolled over Charles. He made his voice deliberately dull and prim: "Why, surely, Mr. Bouchard. Anything you say." He saw Mr. Waite smile. He, Charles, was not a violent man, but now he wanted to strike that assured rascal for thinking what he wished him to think. "I'm slow to make decisions, Mr. Bouchard. I'm only a small business man, and I want to do the best for my company."

Mr. Bouchard nodded. "Of course," he agreed.

They all rose. Mr. Bouchard yawned, unaffectedly. "I'm very tired," he remarked. He put his hand on Charles' shoulder in a comradely gesture. "And, Mr. Wittmann: That other order. I'll write you about it immediately after I return to Windsor."

Yes, thought Charles, triumphantly. You'll give me an order.

"No one makes better machine tools than the Wittmanns," said Mr. Bouchard.

Charles tried to look simple. "Thank you, Mr. Bouchard," he said. "We do our best."

They all shook hands with the utmost cordiality. Charles went away.

He had remembered to take his cigar. Mr. Waite and Mr. Bouchard lingered near the table, watching him go.

"An ignoramus," said Mr. Waite. "He's looking for a big profit. I know these stupid Germans."

Mr. Bouchard was frowning, however. "Elson, why do you insist on underestimating that man? He isn't a fool. I know all about Charles Wittmann. Do you know what I think: Someone's been seeing him before—just before we saw him."

"Well, he admitted that. But he'll come to his senses when he discovers no one is going to pay him more than you will for that assembly."

Mr. Bouchard shook his head slowly and thoughtfully. "It isn't that. We've run into the same mysterious thing, here and there, among small business men who hold potentially valuable patents. 'Someone's' interested in balking us. And I think I know who it is, or who they are. However," added Leon, "it won't help. No, it won't help."

CHAPTER XI

IT WAS ONLY ten o'clock when he returned home, but Charles was exhausted. He was so exhausted that he could be glad that Jimmy had already gone to bed. Usually Jimmy waited up for him, to ask him eagerly about everything. But now the house was quiet, with only a single lamp burning in the "parlor." Charles almost fell into his chair. He had won. But his fears were stronger than ever, and more violent. After a while he dragged himself out of his chair, went upstairs to his bedroom, and sat down at his desk.

He wrote to Colonel Grayson, taking a long time in order that anything he said would be obscure and meaningless to anyone interested except the Colonel: "Our mutual friend paid me a very interesting visit. But I am afraid that I disappointed him in some ways. I am not an inspiring conversationalist. I do hope he won't complain to you about my hospitality. He gave me a large order, which I had to refuse, for our business is not equipped to handle it. However, he promised me another order, for the same tools which I supplied him a few years ago.

"It was very good to see you, when you were passing through Andersburg. I only regret that you could not stay longer. Please give my regards to all our friends."

He wrote it on plain stationery. He marked the envelope "personal only." Then he stamped the letter, went out to a mail-box, and deposited it. It was then that he wondered if he had made a mistake in writing the Colonel, no matter how innocuous. But by this time he was so completely exhausted and confused that he could not think. He returned to his dark house, and again fell into a chair. He desperately wanted his bed; he could not get up, however, for some time. It was the champagne, he thought.

Then he said to himself: It's too big a burden for me to carry alone. I wish I had someone to talk to about it, someone I could trust; Mary.

But it was not Mary who rose up before him, comfortingly. It was Phyllis, Phyllis with her bright bronze hair, her twinkling blue eyes. Charles was startled, taken aback. Why should he think of Phyllis, now? I have always thought of Mary, and my need of her. Phyllis! His tired heart was pounding uncomfortably. He was a man of reason. He tried to reason with himself. Of course, it was because Phyllis had helped him so subtly yesterday. But Phyllis' face did not fade. It became thoughtful, clearer, more urgent. Suddenly, Charles wanted her near him; he wanted to tell her what so frightened him these days. He wanted to tell her about Colonel Grayson, and Leon Bouchard, and Elson Waite.

He had always taken Phyllis for granted, as he took Isabel for granted, and his brothers, and his son, and Geraldine. She was part of his life, his family. But it was strange that of all of them he could only think of Phyllis. He remembered her as he had seen her yesterday, with her white throat and her pearls, her blue suit, her flower-heavy straw hat, her thin gentle hands. There was firmness and surety in Phyllis, for all her delicate and feminine appearance. He wanted Phyllis.

His heart was pounding even faster. His need for Phyllis became almost passionate. He wanted Phyllis in this house, sitting opposite him, telling him that he had acted very wisely and astutely, that she was proud of him. He could see the seriousness in her eyes, the graceful movement of her hands. Now there was a hunger in him, divorced from any animal desire. Phyllis would understand. He could trust her.

He put his hand to his head. It was throbbing. I don't know what's the matter with me, he said to himself. Why should I think of Phyllis? I never think of her, except casually, after I have seen her. It—it was a long time ago.

I need a wife. An intelligent and understanding wife. I am lonely.

Even with Jimmy, I am lonely. I ought to have married again. A woman like Phyllis.

He stood up, in his distress. I was never nervous before, he thought. Then he remembered Wilhelm, in his wretchedness. He did not know why the thought of Wilhelm should so shake him. Again, he rubbed his forehead. It's too much for me. I need a rest. Didn't I suggest to Jimmy that we go fishing this week-end? I must talk about it tomorrow.

All his thoughts blurred, became a chaos in his mind. He dragged himself heavily upstairs, undressed with fumbling hands. He fell into bed. He had believed he would immediately fall asleep. But he could not sleep. His bed was very big. It had never seemed too big before. Now it was empty. He put out his hand in an instinctive gesture, as if seeking comfort.

It was then that he heard the telephone ringing stridently downstairs, and, mingling with it the booming tone of the big grandfather clock, striking eleven. Charles sat up in bed. His first impulse was not to answer the call. But the telephone rang insistently. Mrs. Meyers might hear it, upstairs, or Jimmy. Charles stumbled out of bed, found his slippers, went downstairs. He did not wait to light a match, and turn on the gaslight. He found the telephone in the hall. It was Jochen who was calling him.

"What the devil!" exclaimed Jochen. "You promised to call me tonight, about the Connington's decision. But perhaps you didn't think it important enough, I suppose."

Charles said: "Joe, I'm sorry. I forgot. And then, I just came in. Yes, I saw Mr. Waite. He's agreed to the Burnsley land. I have his informal agreement, which his company will confirm within a few days." Charles leaned against the wall, dizzy. That infernal champagne. He had to make a real physical effort to speak again: "And I gave him a price, and it was twice what they had offered for the river property."

"What!" shouted Jochen, disbelieving. "Hello? Hello? You there, Charlie?" For Charles had not answered.

"I told you," said Charles.

"I can't believe it! Repeat it, Charlie?"

Oh, God, thought Charles. Again he struggled with his dizziness and exhaustion. "You heard me, Joe. Twice as much—as for the river property. It—it was a real piece of business. It seems—they want to locate here."

"Well, I'll be damned," said Jochen, in an awed voice. "Charlie, if that's true, then you're a real business man. Twice as much!"

He was elated. "Good old Charlie, the sharper! I wouldn't have believed it."

The street lamplight filtered into the hall through a pattern of dark leaves. "I had to work," said Charles. "I'm tired, Joe. I'll give you all the details tomorrow."

"I'll bet you had to work!" said Jochen, fervently. "Good old Charlie. I wouldn't have believed it. Charlie, what about Bouchard? Anything there?"

"Yes." A suffocating sensation tightened Charles' throat. "He'll send us an order, soon. For that sawing machine of ours."

"Charlie, you're a genius!"

Charles closed his eyes. But he saw chaos behind his lids. He opened them again. "Do you mind if I go to bed, Joe?" he asked.

"But, damn it! All that business, and you want to go to bed! I know, I know. You're 'tired.' But I should think you'd be excited, not 'tired.' What's the matter with you?"

Charles said: "I haven't been feeling well lately."

Jochen tried to sound concerned. "I've suspected that. Your liver, again?"

"Yes."

"You need a vacation."

Charles was silent.

"Well, if you're 'tired,' I'm not," Jochen went on. "Isabel's been waiting to hear, too. I'll tell her. Congratulations, Charlie."

"Thanks." Charles hung up the receiver, abruptly. He still leaned against the wall. He fumbled for the chair he knew was nearby. He sat down, rested his elbows on his knees, covered his face with his hands. Light flared between his fingers, and he looked up. Jimmy was standing near him; he had lit the wall light.

"Dad," he said, his face blotched and rosy from sleep. "I heard the telephone ringing. Dad," he added, quickly, "what's the matter? You look sick."

Charles tried to smile. "Well, candidly, I am. I had some champagne. You know what wines do to me."

Jimmy stood there, tall and coltish in his nightshirt. He frowned, disturbed. "Dad, it wasn't the champagne, was it? I know you, Dad. What's wrong? Why won't you tell me?"

He came nearer to his father, and Charles saw him so clearly, so young, so vivid, so alive. And so threatened. Threatened! I'm losing my mind, thought Charles. But his sickness increased, and he caught the edge of the table on which the telephone stood. "Jimmy," he said, "there's nothing wrong. Why don't you go back to bed? I was in bed, myself, asleep."

But Jimmy was not deceived. He took his father's wrist in his strong fingers. "What's this? What's this?" asked Charles, again trying to smile indulgently. "Trying to practice your medicine on me, when you don't know a thing about it?"

But Jimmy was looking at the minute hand on the clock. His face was intent, sternly worried. He dropped his father's wrist, slowly. He looked long at Charles. "Dad, you've got a terrible pulse-rate. Go to see Dr. Metzger tomorrow. Please."

"I told you, it's only the champagne."

Jimmy said: "You haven't been yourself for days, Dad. It's not the champagne. Why don't you tell me? You usually tell me everything."

Charles bent his head. What could he say? Could he cry out to Jimmy: There's something going on! I don't know what it is! How can I know? But I have a feeling there's something brewing. And, Jimmy, it might cost you your life, and you're all I have. My son, my son.

He could only say: "I've been having some business worries, Jimmy. And I'm not as young as I used to be."

Jimmy stood there, and Charles could feel him, youthful and living. He could feel the strength of him, the innocence. What was happening to him, Charles? Where was the safe world he had known, the world so realistic, so steadfast? Was the terror only in him? Was he, as Jimmy said, "sick"?

"I'll go to old Metzger tomorrow, if that'll be any satisfaction to you, Jim."

"It will. Dad, your color's bad, too. And it isn't your liver. You're not yellow. You're—you're white."

"I'll get a sunburn over the week-end, with you, son. We're to go fishing together, remember?"

Jimmy flushed, moved uneasily. "Dad, I forgot. I promised to play tennis with Gerry, Saturday. And go boating with her, Sunday. I talked to her, today. But, I can tell her—"

"No." Charles stood up. "I'm not sorry, Jimmy. I'll rest, this week-end. I'll just sit and read, out in the garden." They stood there, face to face. Jimmy was much taller than his father. Charles laid his hand on the boy's shoulder. He could feel the firm warmth of his son's flesh through the nightshirt. Somehow, it comforted him, made the terror retreat. "Go to bed, Jimmy," he said, more calmly.

"You work too hard, Dad. There isn't anyone to help you, down there. My uncles are a pack of fools, all of them."

Charles said, hastily: "Now, stop that, Jimmy. In a minute, you're going to say you ought to go into the shops, after all. And I won't have it. Look, it's way after eleven, so let's go to bed, shall we?"

"Let me heat you some milk, Dad. You always know that helps to put you to sleep, when you're tired this way."

Before Charles could protest, Jimmy had walked off, in his bare feet, towards the kitchen. Charles followed. The big old kitchen smelled of freshly scrubbed wood and soap. A tap dripped in the iron sink. The floor felt cool to Charles' feet, even through his slippers. He sat down at the table, which was covered with white oilcloth. The window was open; the sweet night wind blew in, and Charles heard the rustle of the garden trees. A shaft of moonlight lay on the window-sill. Jimmy had turned the gas on in the stove, and had competently filled a small saucepan with milk. Charles could smell it, and it was a comforting odor, and the washed linoleum had a comforting smell, too. Charles sat there and looked at the pattern of it: big yellow and red squares. All at once, he could not stand that pattern. He leaned his head on his hand, shutting away everything but the oilcloth on the table.

Jimmy said: "If there was just someone to help you. Oh, Uncle Joe's all right, I suppose. But he's a—a murderer, isn't he? He doesn't care about the reputation of the shops. He'd do anything for money, manufacture inferior tools—anything. And Uncle Willie thinks the shops are 'vulgar,' even though he collects regularly, of course." Jimmy's voice was bitter. "There, I shouldn't say that, I suppose. I kind of like Uncle Willie. But what about Uncle Fred, and his crazy ideas? He's daffy, most of the time. He's no help."

Charles dropped his hand. "You think Fred has 'crazy' ideas? I didn't think you knew very much about them, Jimmy."

"Well, I do. They aren't intelligent. Or perhaps it's just that Uncle Fred isn't very bright. Remember what he said to me last Fourth of July? 'Nationalism! Dangerous nationalism! And nationalism always leads to war, because it's stimulated by the war-makers.'"

Something began to hum sickeningly in Charles' head. "Fred said that, did he? What did he mean, 'war-makers'?"

Jimmy shrugged. He poured the hot milk into Charles' special cup, a large German cup all gilt and flowers, which had belonged to Emil Wittmann. "How should I know? But you know how Uncle Fred always goes on."

The hot white fluid in the cup nauseated Charles. But he put in his two teaspoons of sugar.

"Uncle Fred is just against everything, Dad. You know. He hates everything. He hates his own country. I don't know why. He likes to make sour remarks, just so people will feel uncomfortable."

Charles said: "But perhaps he sometimes speaks the truth, too, Jimmy. Remember, we talked about wars this morning. Jimmy, if there were a war—"

"I told you, Dad, I couldn't stand killing anyone." Jimmy was smiling. He sat down near his father. "But if there should ever be a war, I'd probably be a doctor by then. And I could help save soldiers. But it's silly. There'd never be a war. What for? With whom?" Jimmy became thoughtful. "Who would dare attack America?"

"But if—if someone did?"

Jimmy's young face turned grim. "Why, then, I suppose I'd fight. I'd even kill. It would hurt, but I'd kill. We're a wonderful country, Dad, and we're worth fighting for."

Charles said: "Perhaps there are—men—who try to foment wars, for profit. Men without conscience, who conspire with men like themselves, even in foreign countries. For profit."

Jimmy was incredulous. "Dad, that's impossible."

Charles was silent. Suddenly, he remembered old Ernest Barbour, who had built up an empire, which was now called Bouchard and Sons by his nephews. He remembered when old Ernest had died. Hadn't some English nobleman, Lord Kilby, said in a newspaper interview: "If Ernest Barbour had contributed a serum or a treatment for the cure of cancer, diabetes, syphilis, or tuberculosis, which would have saved a million lives from premature death or torture, his name would have been known only to a few, and those he had benefited would have remained in ignorance even of his identity— But this man manufactured death and ruin, created an immense fortune on the bones of battlefields, suborned honor and the integrity of government, bought generals and politicians and journalists and kings, with a cynicism that is inhuman, frightful to contemplate.—Every war that is brewing, and will be brewed in the ominous future, was born in his brain, for the sole purpose of increasing his wealth and his power.— If the foolish world has a prayer to be said on the passing of this man, it will be: 'Deliver us from this Evil.'"

But Ernest Barbour was dead. His nephews owned and controlled what he had built. They were a great company, which manufactured many things, which invented many things, besides armaments. War was dead. It would never happen again. Bouchards or no Bouchards. The conspirators had been silenced. An enlightened world would never again go to war, would never again be the victim of a Barbour or a Bouchard, a Robsons-Strong, a Kronk, a Bedor's, a Sazoroff—

The whispers became a shout in Charles' mind. The shout was all in this room, full of madness and plots and greed. It was full of the smoke of newly active armaments companies, all over the world. It was full of the subdued talk of many men together, in quiet rooms, Germans, Americans, Englishmen, Frenchmen, Roumanians, Russians, Serbs—

Charles cried: "Jimmy, it isn't impossible!"

He couldn't drink his milk. He stood up, leaned against the table. His head began to spin. "Jimmy, there ought to be a way to stop it, before it gets started. Governments should stop it, in spite of politicians and liars and thieves—"

Jimmy was staring at him, aghast. "What are you talking about, Dad? I don't understand."

Charles put the back of his hand against his forehead. "They'll make it so plausible, when they're ready. There'll be nothing else for us to do but fight. There'll be no way out." He stammered: "We'd have to fight, after they'd arranged it. Or die. But what would that matter to them? They're all in it, together. They're an empire, all of them, everywhere, and they hate the rest of us."

Oh, God, what am I saying? thought Charles, distracted. He was so tired. He heard Colonel Grayson's voice: "There are times when it is expedient to make war—When the people want it." Charles said, incoherently: "People shouldn't want war. America should never want war. That's what I mean, Jimmy. America should halt wars before they begin. America should understand—"

"What?" asked Jimmy, when Charles stopped speaking.

"—that wars are plotted, deliberately. Behind closed doors. By men who will ostensibly become enemies, when a war occurs. By men who know that the people love war, and cater to that love."

He was actually panting. "Jimmy," he said. "No group of men, anywhere, can make a war, no matter how they try, and no matter how they want a profit out of a war. Only peoples, at the end, make wars."

Jimmy considered his father's words with alarmed seriousness. "Well, Americans would never want any war. They'd just laugh at anyone who would suggest it."

"Unless, Jimmy, they'd be deceived into believing that war was necessary."

Jimmy was puzzled. "But Dad, there've been good wars, too, you know. For freedom."

Charles did not know why he was so desperate. He shook his head. "Look, Jimmy. Good causes don't need wars. They might take a little extra time, they might demand more understanding, but they don't need mass-murder. We can stop the causes of war. We can stop the arming of potentially dangerous nations, who, in their turn, are being deceived and incited. Deliberately. By evil men."

Jimmy drew an invisible pattern on the table oilcloth with his forefinger. "Dad, what about the Civil War? Don't you think that was necessary?"

"No, Jimmy. Slavery was becoming untenable in the South. The South knew that. It was only a matter of time until it would have been abolished everywhere. One by one, the Southern States would have abolished it. But the North kept harassing the South. Someone, some men, were harassing the Southern States. Then it became all confused. The South was indignant; it seemed to them that they must withdraw from the Union, in order to preserve their dignity and self-respect. And that war was eventually not fought to free the slaves but to preserve the Union. Even Lincoln admitted that."

The clock boomed twelve. They could hear its notes, shaking the house ever so slightly, a faint vibration.

Jimmy looked at his father in an intense silence. Finally, he said, with uncertainty: "Dad, you don't think there's going to be a war, do you? With anyone?"

The boy was greatly disturbed.

"No! No!" Charles exclaimed. "Jimmy, I'm sorry. I—I'm all confused, these days. I have the strangest thoughts. I don't know what to think, Jimmy. I suppose I'm just tired." He added: "Wars aren't simple, Jimmy. It—it gets all complicated."

He went out of the kitchen, abruptly, with lame and heavy legs. Jimmy turned off the lights. They stood at the foot of the stairs. Again, Charles put his hand on his son's shoulder. "Forget what I said, won't you, Jimmy? I don't know anything. Not a thing. Not a thing," he repeated, with loud emphasis.

They climbed the stairs together, arm in arm. They parted upstairs. Charles said: "Go to sleep, Jimmy. I'm afraid I'm not myself, these days."

Then he was alone in his bed, his empty bed, and he was ill with a terrible illness. He was only a little man. He could do nothing. He lay there, hour after hour, looking at the darkness. Finally, he saw the gray light of morning at the windows. He said to himself: Only a little man. I can't do much, but what I can do I'll do, so help me God. My son, my son.

CHAPTER XII

CHARLES DID NOT SLEEP. He, usually so calm, so derisive of hysteria and excitement, so "balanced" and good-tempered, could not sleep at all. He remembered so many things he had forgotten, words from school-books, from newspapers. "There can be no successful appeal from the ballot to the bullet," Lincoln had said. And in the end, the bullets had been stronger. Had not Bismarck shouted: "Better pointed bullets than pointed speeches. The great questions of the day are not decided by speeches and majority votes, but by blood and iron." And Martin Luther: "War is the greatest plague that can afflict humanity; it destroys religion, it destroys states, it destroys families. Any scourge is preferable to it." And Jefferson: "War is as much a punishment to the punisher as to the sufferer."

A little man. I am only a little man. What can men like me do? thought Charles, as the first sun began to shine through his windows. Millions of men like me, all over the world, and we can do nothing. The workingman has his unions; the great corporations have their advisers; the criminals have their lawyers; the churches have their priests and their ministers; the nations have their ambassadors. But who can speak for men like me, men who abhor war, men who detest murder? How can we ignore our Governments, and speak to each other, and say to each other, as Benjamin Franklin said: "There never was a good war or a bad peace." Let our politicians curse each other, but let us laugh together, and say: You are my brother. I have no quarrel with you. Do not let your son kill my son, for we have nothing but our children.

To fathers, war was not an "adventure," as Colonel Grayson had said. It was the death of life. The young men, the very young men, should be ignored, as the statesmen should be ignored. Let the young man find his adventure in living, and not in murder; let the statesman find his glory in just legislation, and not among slogans. No man, thought Charles, should be permitted to vote before he is thirty, or until he is the father of sons. Some way, sometime, there might come a day when men like himself, Charles, would outlaw war, when they would band together in every nation to destroy the haters of men who would have men killed for profit or because they wished personal power.

Charles began to detest himself because he had deliberately lived so circumscribed, so well-ordered, so selfish, a life. He wished he knew more. Somewhere, he had read about the Quakers. They would take part in no wars. They calmly refused to be embroiled in wars. So, there was a beginning. One had only to join with the Quakers. There were quakers in Pennsylvania, in Andersburg. He knew no one else who had any honest religious principles, except, perhaps, the pastor of his church, Mr. Joseph Haas.

Charles was President of the Board of his church, and influential among its members. Mr. Haas was his personal friend. Charles had serenely taken it for granted that decent men went to church; he had never asked himself if anyone ever believed, fully and with all his heart, in what Mr. Haas had to say in his pulpit. He had never asked this of himself. Now he understood that he had always approved of churches because he had had a vague idea that they were "necessary," though why they were "necessary" he had not wondered. He had not liked men who belonged to no church. They had lacked "stability," for him. But "stability" was not faith; it was not even security. It could be shaken and destroyed, and it could end in a roaring chaos, and God could be lost in the smoke of guns.

He looked at his alarm clock. In a moment it would ring. He shut it off. The churches. Why didn't the churches stop war? Or were they as helpless as himself, when the peoples wanted war, and gloried and delighted in it, and screamed idiotic slogans, and demanded that men like the Bouchards provide them with the weapons of murder?

So many things to think about, and so many things in ambush.

But it was a lovely morning, as golden and fresh as a new apple, as sweet as honey. Charles stood by his window. He saw the dark green trees, the green lawns, the children already at play in the cool shadows, the brisk housewives already sweeping their verandahs. It was so peaceful. The night with its terrors lay behind him, in this room.

He drew a deep breath of the scented air, pushing aside the curtains in order to do so. Shadows. Whispers. He had been "hysterical" all week. Perhaps it was his liver, after all. That patent. Perhaps Mr. Bouchard had really been sincere in wanting that patent for "experimentation." Perhaps Colonel Grayson was only a fearful old man. Perhaps all this talk of peace was really honest talk of peace.

He was pale but quiet when he went down to breakfast. Jimmy was waiting for him; he looked at his father anxiously. But Charles smiled. "Hello, Jimmy. Sorry the telephone woke you. It was just your uncle Joe, who wanted to know if I had concluded some business I had last night. So, you are playing tennis with Gerry, are you, today? Why not ask her to remain for dinner?" Then he remembered that he had accepted Wilhelm's invitation for tonight, and he was annoyed. He sat down. "I had almost forgotten, but I'm having dinner at your Uncle Willie's house. Ask Gerry to stay, anyway. Or isn't that proper, even though Mrs. Meyers will be here?"

Jimmy did not answer for a moment. He gazed at his father soberly. Then he said: "Oh, it's all right, I suppose. I'll call up Aunt Isabel, and ask her." Why didn't his father speak of that conversation last night? But Charles was looking with approval at a dish of sliced bananas and cream which Mrs. Meyers had placed before him.

"Not cream, Dad," said Jimmy. "You know what Dr. Metzger said about cream, and your liver."

Charles laughed. "I'm going to have cream, anyway. Now, Jimmy, you aren't a doctor yet. Let me enjoy my breakfast. I happen to be hungry."

Jimmy watched his father. He, himself, was unusually silent. But he was relieved when Charles refused eggs. So, it was Dad's liver, after all. Jimmy brightened. "It won't be too hot for tennis today, after I get through my lessons," he said. Charles ate his hot oatmeal with relish. "No, I think it'll be just cool enough," he said. His spoon scraped the plate. He looked down at it, thoughtfully. "Jimmy, why don't you ever go to the church's Wednesday nights' get-togethers?"

Jimmy was surprised. "Why, I don't know, Dad. They just bored me. Hardly anyone goes any more."

Charles looked at him. He had a sudden impulse to say: Jimmy, do you believe in God? But that would startle Jimmy, who was so intelligent and humorous. He had never once spoken of God, to Jimmy. He had never said a prayer with Jimmy. All his son's instructions in religious observances had come from his church. Had Mary ever taught him his bed-time prayers? Charles felt foolish, as if he had been about to say something childish, or undignified.

Why? said a voice in Charles. He put down his spoon. Mrs. Meyers poured his coffee for him. Charles felt Jimmy's eyes upon him.

"I think," he said, in an offhand manner, "that you ought to take some part in the church's activities, son, besides going with me to services on Sunday mornings."

"Why, Dad?"

Charles shrugged. "Well," he murmured. "It might look well," he added, lamely.

"To whom?"

"Well, it would, anyway," said Charles, irritably.

"I'm not interested in doing things that 'might look well,'" said Jimmy. He was coloring. "I'm sorry. Dad. You are insulted. I ought to have remembered that you like doing what you think is the 'right thing.'"

A week ago, Charles would have laughed. But now he did not laugh. "Is that what you think of me, Jimmy, only wanting to do the right thing for the sake of appearances?"

Jimmy's young jaw set. "You once told me, Dad, that it was very necessary to keep up appearances. That it was the respectable thing to do."

Yes, I said that, thought Charles. I said that, imbecile that I am.

Jimmy's dark eyes were very intent. He was resting his chin on his hand and studying Charles. "I'm afraid I didn't make myself very clear," said Charles, with uncertainty. "I think I meant that decent men do certain things because they are correct and expected. Setting a good example."

"To whom?"

"Good God, Jimmy!" exclaimed Charles. "What's the matter with you? What are churches for? For everybody. And men of responsibility want others to go to churches, too. It—it's stabilizing."

"It's respectable," said Jimmy.

Charles stood up, and Jimmy stood up, also. They looked at each other.

"I thought," Charles said, "that we understood each other, Jimmy."

"We do, Dad," answered the boy, earnestly. "But something's happened that is bothering you, and you want to talk to me about it, and you don't know how." He paused. He put his hand on his father's arm, and smiled shyly: "Yes, Dad, I do believe in God. That's what you wanted to know, wasn't it?"

Charles stared at him speechlessly, his pale face turning red.

"You want me to believe in God, don't you, Dad? Mother taught me prayers, before she died, and I learned about God in Sunday school But all that didn't make me really believe in Him. It—it was just knowing." He became even more shy. "You see, there's a difference between 'believing' in God, and 'knowing' about Him."

"I—" began Charles. Then he said, very simply: "I'm glad, Jimmy.

I really am." He turned aside. "You see, son, I don't know. I thought I knew everything it was necessary for a man like me to know, but I've found out I know nothing at all."

He was at his desk at nine o'clock. He sat there and looked at the pile of his mail. But he was hardly aware of it. He was saying again to himself: "I know nothing at all."

A week ago he had been worried over nothing; he had thought very little of anything, except his son and his work. A good, safe, orderly life. And now it was all gone. Something vague and terrible had entered it. The thought of God had entered it too. It was very unsettling.

He attacked his pile of mail. There was a thin brown paper envelope, with no return address upon it, among his letters. It was marked "Personal," so Mr. Parker had not opened it. Charles tore it open. A paper fell out: *The Menace*. There were three slight pamphlets, also: "The Roman Catholic Church's Plan for World Slavery." "Dangerous Errors of the Papacy." "Freedom or Subjugation." Frowning, Charles returned to *The Menace*. It was a newspaper of half a dozen pages. He read the headlines: "The Catholic Church Renews its Attacks on American Institutions in Boston." He ran his eye rapidly over sub-headlines. He read a paragraph here and there. According to the paper, the Roman Catholic Church had secret organizations all over the world, the Jesuits, who were plotting world-wide destruction of "free Protestantism," and the "return of the bloody Inquisition." Then Charles noticed that someone had printed something in pencil on top of the paper: "Please read these and remember Tom Murphy."

Hate. It was here with him, again, in this pleasant sunlit office of his. It was breathing over his shoulder. It was reflected back to him from his shining window. Hate. The thing which had been silently and darkly let loose in the world had not been his nightmare, had not been conjured up by his "liver." It was alive. It was everywhere.

He pushed a bell on his desk, and Mr. Parker entered. Charles kept his face expressionless. "Parker, will you go into the shops and tell Tom Murphy I want to see him at once?"

Who had sent him these slimy things? His brother Friederich? No. Someone else in Andersburg had sent him this paper, these pamphlets. Someone who hated, who lurked in shadows, and grimaced, and hated. And he was not alone.

Tom Murphy came in, pulling off his workman's cap. He was a slender and keen-faced man of thirty-five, with light hair and prominent blue eyes, a blunt nose and a mouth that was always ready for laughter. But he was not smiling now. He was a foreman, and his blue overalls were very clean and starched, for he had a meticulous little wife.

"Good morning, Mr. Wittmann," he said. "You sent for me?"

His eyes were cold and proud. Charles hesitated.

"Yes, I did, Tom."

"I see." Tom spoke quietly. "You want to tell me you're going to fire me, after all, for breaking Mr. Fred's windows, even though you helped keep me out of jail?"

Charles held *The Menace* in his hands. "No," he said. "Don't be a damned fool, Tom. I wasn't even thinking of that."

"I was drunk. But I was mad, too," said Tom. He pushed back a lock of his hair. "I had five beers that night. But I was mad, too."

Charles could not help smiling. "Tom, Mr. Fred doesn't want you to go, either."

Tom was astonished. "He doesn't?" Then he narrowed his eyes. "Mr. Wittmann, if Mr. Fred doesn't want me to be kicked out it was because of you. Well, I thanked you before, I think. I want to thank you again."

Charles never before had asked an employee to sit down in his presence. It "wasn't done," even among employers who had respect for those they employed. But Charles said: "Sit down, Tom. I want to talk with you about something."

Surprised and uncertain, Tom lowered himself into a chair. Charles pushed the paper across the desk, and the pamphlets. "Tom, did you ever see, or hear, of anything like these before?"

Tom took them in his big clever hands. But he only glanced at them, briefly. He laid them down on the desk. "Someone sent them to you, Mr. Wittmann? I see there's something printed on the top, about me."

Charles repeated: "Did you ever see, or hear, of anything like these before?"

Tom's face had darkened with repugnance and loathing. "Yes, sir, I did. Lots of times. They're all over the town. Sometimes they're pushed under my door. Sometimes I find them in my mail-box. So do the other fellers. And some of the fellers bring them here and grin over them, in corners, and then hide them when they see me coming. Me and the other Catholics in the factory."

"You mean," said Charles, incredulously, "that this has been going on and I didn't know anything about it?"

Tom could not help smiling. But he said, gravely: "I guess so, Mr. Wittmann. Everybody knows about them. They come faster and faster. Even our priest, Father Hagerty, knows about 'em. He gets lots in his mail-box. And I heard he got a letter telling him to get out of town, too. That's why we've got a policeman going the rounds, especially on Sunday. At Mass." He studied Charles sternly. "I guess you didn't know about them before because you're a decent gentleman, Mr. Wittmann."

But Charles was thinking of the little white Catholic church in the poorer section of Andersburg. There were not many Catholics in this city, which had a Quaker and Pennsylvania "Dutch" Protestant population. So, this church, of which he had rarely thought before, had to have a policeman to guard it!

"And we have a sexton around, all the time, through the week," Tom was saying. "A big, ugly Irishman. We're afraid someone will—will . . ."

"Befoul it?"

"I guess you'd call it that," answered Tom, after considering the word. "Yes, sir."

Charles was stunned. His kindly, serene little city, his city built on sedate and tolerant Quaker traditions, his friendly little city where he had believed everyone was safe, and which the obscenities of men had never disgraced before!

"But even with the police, and the sexton, someone broke a couple of the stained-glass windows," Tom said. "Nobody knows when it was done. It wasn't even in the papers. Father Hagerty," Tom continued, bitterly, "was proud of them windows. They came from Italy, and they cost a lot of money. It took Father Hagerty two years to get enough money for 'em. And now they're gone."

He added, morosely: "It was right after I broke Mr. Fred's windows. Maybe I gave somebody the idea."

But Charles did not smile. He looked at the paper and the pamphlets on his desk. He said, dully: "I suppose these things go all over the country, too."

"Yes, sir. I got a brother in Boston, and a cousin in Philadelphia, and my wife's got a brother in Detroit and another in Indianapolis. Them things are all over. And more and more of 'em all the time. It's getting bad."

"Someone pays for them," said Charles. "Someone wants them. Someone is trying to—to stir up hatred in America." He leaned back in his chair. All his weariness was heavy on him again, all his sickness. "Why? Who is behind it? But you wouldn't know, would you, Tom?"

Tom shook his head. "No, sir, I wouldn't. It all began about two years ago. At least, that's the first time I ever heard of 'em."

"Some people are paying out a lot of money for this," said Charles. "It costs money. Especially to cover a whole country with papers and pamphlets, like these. I wonder."

He remembered seeing Father Francis Hagerty once or twice, on the streets, a shy man with a timid face, a young man. Certainly not a man who could fight a thing like this, robustly and with anger. Charles remembered his gentle brown eyes and unobtrusive ways. Who had called his attention to this priest, and named him? Charles could not remember.

Charles examined the pamphlets. They had been printed in Boston, and the paper was good, the print excellent. There was money behind all this, a lot of money. A lot of money never came from one man. It always came from many men.

Charles examined the other pamphlets. No trash, these, no "butcher" paper. The authors were men of mind. And they had been hired. By whom? Who was determined to destroy America, in one way or another?

"We got a parochial school, just a little one, with five Sisters,' said Tom. "It's got so bad the mothers have got to go for the kids. My wife goes for my two girls every day. The other kids throw stones at 'em. They dumped manure—somebody—on Father Hagerty's verandah one night. It was them pamphlets, and that paper, Mr. Wittmann, that got people stirred up."

He sighed. "Something's happened to this town, Mr. Wittmann. Funny you never knew about it before. I was born here, and it was always a nice town. Until about two years ago. And I hear from my folks that it's the same in their towns, too."

Charles scratched his temple. He still could hardly believe it. William Penn. The Constitution of the United States. "With liberty and justice for all . . ."

Tom stood up. "Guess I'd better get back, Mr. Wittmann. There was a job I was seeing about." But he waited, seriously.

"All right, Tom," said Charles. "Go back to the shops." He tried to smile. "I do hope you believe, though, that hardly anyone would pay attention to this filthy stuff. Not Americans, anyway."

Tom shook his head, slowly. "I'd like to believe it, sir. But I can't. It's too big. And people always want to hate somethin'. I found that out." He blushed.

After Tom had gone, Charles called Mr. Haas, his minister.

PART TWO

The world is my country, all mankind are my brethren, and to do good is my religion . . .

THOMAS PAINE

CHAPTER XIII

THE REVEREND Joseph Haas was very pleased to see Charles Wittmann, but slightly surprised, this Friday morning. He had been working on his sermon, but he put down his pen willingly. If something had brought Charles out at eleven o'clock of a weekday to see his minister, then that something must be of great importance. Men like Charles never do anything out of the ordinary, reflected the minister.

The rectory was very pleasant, a large white house of wood, with green shutters. The furniture was agreeable; the study was excellent, with its panelled walls of knotted pine and bookshelves and comfortable brown leather furniture. The desk, of gleaming mahogany, had been a personal present from Charles last Christmas.

Mr. Haas greeted Charles with fondness. "Well, well, Charles," he said, shaking hands vigorously. "Delighted to see you."

"Hope I'm not intruding, Mr. Haas," said Charles. "I won't take up much of your time. Perhaps only fifteen minutes." He let his minister lead him to a chair. He liked Mr. Haas, who was a big stout man with a kindly, happy face and a pair of shrewd gray eyes. Mr. Haas was his own age; they had much in common, for they were both realistic. But now Charles looked at Mr. Haas keenly. What did he know about anyone? Did Mr. Haas believe in the God he spoke of with such restrained respect on Sundays? Did he honestly believe in the Fatherhood of God and the brotherhood of man, and decency?

Charles wished he had paid more attention, in the past, to Mr. Haas' sermons. He thought he remembered that the sermons had always been well-delivered, scholarly, and sincere. But he honestly could not remember exactly what they had been about, except that they never seemed to antagonize anyone, or cause anyone to discuss them later. It must be very hard to be a minister, Charles thought, as Mr. Haas seated himself, beaming. It must be a hard life. All the women, with their problems and their malices and their pious jealousies, and all the men with their different ideas of what an ideal minister should be, and the Sunday-school teachers who must dislike some of the other teachers, and the marriages that ought not to take place, and the children who must be controlled. And all the endless, maddening diplomacy, moving warily, talking tactfully, smoothing constantly, showing no one parishioner more attention than another, displaying a bland impartiality all the time, deftly side-stepping awkward issues, and never, never letting anyone suspect that one was tired, disgruntled, weary, disgusted or bored, worried about mercenary matters, or, very likely discouraged.

He probably despises some of us, shudders at some of us—and probably some of us sicken him almost to death, thought Charles. He had never looked at his minister as a man, before, a man with personal miseries and heart-breaks and anxieties. That beaming face, with the shining glasses, that friendly smile—what did it hide? Charles wanted to say: Don't mind me. Don't remember who I am. It must hurt you too much, thinking of all of us.

Mr. Haas noticed the penetrating look in Charles' eyes, the tenseness of Charles' face. "What's the matter, Charles?" he asked quietly. "Is there something wrong? Something I can do?"

Charles considered this. He said, suddenly: "It's just occurred to me that you're always asking that of somebody, Mr. Haas. I wonder how many people have asked you that, or if they meant it, or would do anything for you if you really did ask."

Mr. Haas was taken aback. He removed his glasses, and polished them with a spotless handkerchief. He said, trying to smile again: "Well, now, Charles, it's a minister's duty to take care of his flock. He knows, with surety, that his own troubles are in the hands of God, but not every man in the congregation has that assurance."

Charles thought about this, with his usual slow thoroughness. "Do you know," he said, finally, "I've been a member of this church all my life. And all the time I don't think I thought about—about . . ." He stopped, mortified.

"About God," said Mr. Haas, gently. He sighed. "Yes. But that's not unusual, Charles. And perhaps it's not your fault, entirely. There's something dynamic which has left our churches, Charles," he said, gravely. "Something evangelistic, in the real sense. Something vivid and living. Now almost all churches, especially churches like ours which have a large number of business and professional men in the congregation, are just social gatherings of a sober kind. Nothing must ever be said that would annoy anyone, arouse anyone, or excite anyone. Vitalistic religion is almost—almost indecent, Charles, in our churches these days."

Charles was silent, but he was listening intently, and he was nodding. "Yes," he said.

"But"—Mr. Haas smiled almost sadly—"it would be far easier on a minister if he were not always so afraid of his congregation."

Charles looked down at the papers in his hands. He was greatly depressed. He had come to ask for information, to ask a favor. But ministers were "afraid" of their people.

"What is it, Charles?" asked Mr. Haas, concerned.

Charles said: "I came here today to ask you to do something, and to raise hell, if necessary." He was embarrassed. "Sorry."

Mr. Haas looked at his desk. He said, almost inaudibly: "I'd like to do that, sometimes, Charles. 'To raise hell,' as you say."

"I shouldn't ask it of you, Mr. Haas. It would be too much."

"Tell me, Charles," said Mr. Haas. He clasped his hands together on the desk.

Charles put the paper and the pamphlets before his minister without speaking. Mr. Haas took them up. But he glanced at them only briefly, and then he flung them aside as if they were filthy and intolerable things.

"You've seen this sort of stuff before, Mr. Haas."

"Yes. I've received it, many times. It comes to me every week. I get the pamphlets, too. I throw them away at once."

Charles said: "And you've never spoken of them to anyone, never tried to stop it?"

Mr. Haas said: "Charles, no decent person ever notices this sort of thing—this offal. I know that nearly everyone in Andersburg has received this paper, either by subscription, or without it. And the pamphlets, too. It's been going on for a long time." He waited. But Charles did not speak. "It's dirty, Charles. But one has only to ignore things like this, and they die of themselves. Silence, Charles, that's all."

Charles said, sternly: "I don't agree with you, Mr. Haas. Ignoring a disease doesn't dispose of it. It just grows more malignant if not treated."

Mr. Haas averted his head slightly. "Charles, I've never seen you so disturbed before. It isn't like you. You mustn't let things like these— Charles, we live in the twentieth century, but there are still some residues, here and there, of ancient intolerances and ignorance. Education will soon eradicate them. It won't be very long, I'm sure, before all religious and racial hatreds will disappear."

Charles exclaimed: "Education! I don't believe it. You can't 'educate' the bestiality out of men."

Mr. Haas shook his head. "Once, when I was just a young minister, I came across something like this in a very small town. It was my first church. I denounced the dirty sheet. Do you know what happened?

Many of the people in my church, who had never heard of the paper before, immediately sent for it. It made matters much worse, and the lies spread."

Charles gathered himself stolidly together, forced his minister to look at him. "I am being impertinent, I know, Mr. Haas. But when you 'denounced' similar lies, did you tell your people that they were committing a sin—against God and man—by reading them, and that a man who believes and spreads lies is a liar, himself, and contemptible?"

Mr. Haas faintly colored. "I didn't use such strong language, Charles."

"You didn't say that the purchasers of lies, the spreaders of lies and hate, are not worthy to be Americans, that they are destroyers of America, and detestable in the sight of God?"

"Good heavens, Charles! No minister should threaten, or use a verbal whip!"

"Why not? Why not, when hate threatens America and freedom and religion?"

"Charles, you are saying some fantastic things!"

"So," said Charles, thoughtfully. He waited a moment. "Let me put it this way: You can say to any religion, or to any race: 'There are rascals, liars, thieves, perjurers, brutes, and murderers among you. You have, among you, the lowest and most degenerate of human beasts, who hate all other men.' And you'd be right, Mr. Haas.

"We all know that criminals and scoundrels are everywhere, and are not confined to any race or religion. They are universal. Admitting that does no harm. But the danger comes when we confine our accusations to any one race, to any one religion, and insist that that race or religion is completely evil, and we, the accusers, are all without stain."

He waited for Mr. Haas to speak, but the minister only nodded slowly and gravely. So Charles went on: "When things like this paper, these pamphlets, come out, there is always something, someone, behind it. There is always a calculating and coldly hating organization. There are always plotters, with a purpose."

"Charles! Do you actually believe . . . ?"

Charles said, relentlessly: "Plotters. With a purpose. Disruption. Confusion. Beclouding some important issue, or attempting to turn the people's attention from something which is happening, or about to happen, so that the people will be disorganized by their own mutual antagonisms, divided by their hatreds, and so be unable to act in unison against the thing that threatens all of them."

He waited for the minister to speak, but Mr. Haas was full of dumb consternation and incredulity.

"You've read about bull-fighters, Mr. Haas. If the bull is after one fighter, his fellow fighter waves his cloak in the bull's face, and distracts it."

Mr. Haas could hardly lift his voice above a whisper: "What do you mean, Charles?"

Charles stood up. This sickening tremor along his nerves! "I don't know, Mr. Haas. I just—feel it. I want you to help, Mr. Haas. You can speak of these pamphlets, this paper, this Sunday, from your pulpit. And you can tell the congregation that perhaps it is subterfuge—these lies—to hide that something which may be brewing in hidden places."

"Charles! They'd think I was mad. I might even—"

"Lose your church? No, Mr. Haas. You won't. I have too much influence here, in the church, in Andersburg." He leaned against the desk, bent towards the pale minister. "There's another thing you can tell the congregation on Sunday, and that is that haters have only one thing in mind: Destruction. Slavery of both the haters and the hated."

Mr. Haas' large, stout face quivered. All at once, he was deeply alarmed.

Charles wiped his damp hands on his handkerchief. "You were saying, Mr. Haas, that something vital has gone out of our churches. Help it return."

Mr. Haas sighed. He looked at Charles, and his eyes were terribly weary. "Charles, I sometimes think that if Christ had not been crucified He would eventually have died of a broken heart."

He stood up, gave Charles his hand. "Charles, I'll do what I can. It may not help, but I'll do it. You will hear me, yourself, on Sunday."

Charles took the other man's hand. He said, very quietly: "I've just remembered something. You know, my father was very devoted to this country. And he was always quoting Alexander Hamilton: 'It is of great importance in a republic not only to guard against the oppression of its rulers, but to guard one part of society against the injustice of the other part.'"

The minister laughed sadly. "But at the last, it is always up to the people, themselves."

CHAPTER XIV

Mr. Ralph Grimsley, editor and owner of the Andersburg *Clarion,* greeted Charles with immense cheeriness. He was a slight, spry little man, very bald, very dark, and very shrewd and quizzical. "Well, well, if it isn't old Charlie, himself!" he exclaimed, shaking hands. "Sit down. Hell of a hot day, isn't it? Well, well. Glad you came; suppose it's about the Wittmann Civic Park. Big thing, Charlie. One of the biggest things ever happened in these parts. First time any company ever did anything for the town. Now, just sit and tell me about it."

Charles patiently supplied details as they occurred to him. Ralph Grimsley was one of his best friends, a man for a story in high hot letters, but a man of integrity, also. Charles was very cautious when it came to the matter of the Connington Steel Company. The Connington, he said, understood at once when Charles had told Mr. Elson Waite his decision about the Park. "Mr. Waite," said Charles, "thought it extremely good. That's for publication, Ralph. Extremely good. Approved of it, highly."

Mr. Grimsley grinned. "I bet he did. Looking for orders or goodwill or something, Charlie?"

Charles assumed an expression of great propriety. "Well, you know how to quote me." He laughed. "You can also add that Mr. Waite agreed to the Burnsley land in order that the river property might be preserved for the people—also the people who'll be working for the Connington here."

"I'll send him a copy of this interview," said Mr. Grimsley. "Bet he'll have it reprinted in Pittsburgh and all over, too, to show that the Connington is really just a lover of the toiler and knows its social responsibilities."

After a while Charles showed him *The Menace* and the pamphlets. Mr. Grimsley's face wrinkled with disgust. He pushed the papers aside. He looked at Charles. "Well?" he asked.

"That paper has a big circulation in Andersburg, Ralph?"

"Yes. Bigger than the *Clarion.*" Mr. Grimsley spat into his spittoon. "People would rather read dirty stuff even than stuff about their own town and their neighbors."

Mr. Grimsley stared at Charles with more intentness. "You've got an idea, haven't you, Charlie?"

"I have. I've been to see our minister. He is going to talk about it, Sunday. Have a reporter at the service, Ralph."

"You mean Mr. Haas—our nice, genial, society minister—is actually going to talk about this paper? I don't believe it! He's too genteel. Or maybe he'd be afraid he'd get someone mad at him."

"He's going to speak, nevertheless," said Charles. "I have his promise. You see, I have convinced him that something is behind it, something of terrible importance." Charles talked quietly for several minutes, while Mr. Grimsley listened, perched on his chair like a black-eyed, quick-witted spider. And then, after Charles had spoken, he sat there, his chin on his collar.

"Maybe I'm wrong," said Charles. "But I can't make myself believe that, in spite of all my efforts."

Mr. Grimsley filled his pipe carefully, lit it, took a few deep puffs. His eyes wandered restlessly about the room. Charles waited. He waited a considerable time.

"No," said Mr. Grimsley, meditatively, at last. "I don't think you have been imagining all these things."

"No?" said Charles, somberly. "I wish you'd said I was."

Mr. Grimsley got to his feet and scuttled to a battered cabinet at the far end of his office. He brought out a large book. He opened it. On its broad pages he had pasted a number of long and short reports of international news.

"All of these've appeared in the Andersburg *Clarion,* and in the Philadelphia and New York newspapers. Read 'em, Charlie. You get these papers. And after you've read 'em, you tell me if you ever stopped to think about them—even if you consciously saw 'em."

Charles began to skim over the items:

One of them was dated June 15th, 1913: "Since June 8th, the Emperor William II of Germany has been joyously celebrating the twenty-fifth anniversary of his accession to the throne— The Emperor repeatedly asserted that throughout his reign he has advocated peace in spite of the fact that at any time he had been powerful enough to precipitate a war—"

One was dated in July: "King Victor Emmanuel of Italy has been in close conference with the German Emperor at Kiel, on confidential matters—"

"Chancellor von Bethmann-Hollweg denounced those who have been calling the attention of the German people to the immense profits made on Government contracts by the Kronk works. He declared that it was 'absolutely essential' to the safety of the German Empire that certain large armaments orders be given to Kronk, even though no war is contemplated now or in the near future which would involve Germany. 'However,' said the Chancellor, 'if such an unforeseen event did transpire, the Fatherland would necessarily, though with sorrow, be embroiled. It would concern the honor of the German people.'

"The Chancellor further stated: 'The important point is that into the place of European Turkey, whose state life has become inactive, there have entered certain States which exhibit a disturbing active vitality. There is one thing without doubt: If it should ever come to a European conflagration which sets Slaventum against Germanentum, it would be for us a disadvantage that the position in the balance of forces, which was occupied heretofore by European Turkey, is now filled in part by Slav states.' "

Charles looked up swiftly. The editor nodded. "Go on, Charlie. Read what you should have read, or remembered, quite some time ago."

"The new German army bills increase the military force by 4,000 officers, 15,000 non-commissioned officers, 11,700 men, and 27,000 horses."

"Certain incidents are occurring in Zabern, Alsace. The Emperor has expressed his concern—"

"London, June—: Lord Bedford-Marshall gave it as his considered opinion that a great danger to British trade lies in the last report that German manufacturers have invaded traditional British markets abroad, and are consistently underselling British products in many countries. 'Though,' said Lord Bedford-Marshall, 'these products are quite inferior to British exports. Nevertheless, the invasion continues, and no Briton who is seriously concerned with the future of British export trade can afford to overlook this threat.' "

"Stockholm, August—: The Swedish people are determined that in the event of any conflict between major nations of Europe they will remain strictly neutral."

Mr. Grimsley put his ink-stained index finger on the report from London. "There," he said, softly, "you have it. That's what it always comes to."

Charles closed the book, slowly. Mr. Grimsley leaned back in his creaking swivel-chair, hooked his little thumbs in his suspender-straps. His eyes followed the movements of a fly that buzzed at a window. "Two-thirds of the world half-starving, waiting for goods. But they don't have the cash. Only the 'traditional' markets have it. No one tries to think up a way so two-thirds of the world can have the goods and the food, and pay for 'em in some manner. No, the other third just talks in Parliament, or at Kiel, and 'expresses concern.' Or appropriates money for armaments and larger armies and talks of 'honor' or whispers plots to kill off competitors. And in all corners, everywhere, there are men busy inventing slogans—"

Charles said: "But not in America. Surely not in America!"

Mr. Grimsley pulled at his wrinkled lip. "Don't be too sure, Charlie. There's only one thing you can be sure of in this world, and that is that man is a devil. And remember, there's always a lot of money to be made when there's trouble, and who can resist money?"

He swung towards Charles, and stabbed him in the chest with his finger. "There's something else, Charlie. Has it ever occurred to you that maybe there's some people in some of all these countries who hate freedom, and are afraid of it, and want to see it destroyed? How long has freedom, as we know it in America, really been flourishing? Not very long, Charlie. Behind this century or two of liberty lie two thousand centuries of active slavery of the whole world, a slavery perpetuated by a few powerful men. Do you think, as a lot of fools think, that 'democracy marches on,' and that soon the whole world will be free —free as we know freedom?" Mr. Grimsley shook his head violently. "Know what I think? I think that some few men, in every nation, everywhere, have their private plots to destroy freedom, not only where it exists in Europe, but where it exists in America. And while they're doing the destroying, they think, they'll make a heap of money.

"And how can they start? By making wars. Getting the people to hate each other, feeding them lies, inciting them. Playing up to the people's love for war and murder. Giving them wars, and while they're killing, taking their freedom away from them."

Charles thought of Colonel Grayson. It seemed to him that this untidy editorial office had become very hot.

"If they can't stir up a war, Charlie," said Mr. Grimsley morosely, "they'll be lost. Their dream of destroying the growing threat of liberty everywhere will die. They'll do all they can to prevent that."

He tapped *The Menace* and the pamphlets which lay on his desk. "Charlie, there's the decoy, while the dirty work goes on behind the scenes. I don't know, but I'd bet anything that other religions, or maybe races, are being attacked in other countries, just like this."

Charles shook his head, over and over, as if he could not stop. Mr. Grimsley watched him, and he did not smile.

"There's nothing, I suppose," said Charles, in an empty voice, "that men like myself can do."

"I don't know, Charlie. Honest to God, I don't know. Maybe it's too late for anybody to do anything, especially only a few men. But you can remember something if you want to. Tom Paine said: 'An army of principles will penetrate where an army of soldiers cannot; neither the ocean, the Channel, nor the Rhine can arrest its progress; it will march on the horizon of the world, and it will conquer.'

"But that won't stop murder—now," muttered Charles.

"Maybe not." Mr. Grimsley looked at Charles soberly. "You're thinking of your boy, Jimmy, aren't you?"

CHAPTER XV

CHARLES' BIG RED and brass automobile created considerable excitement in the poor and shabby quarter of the city where the Reverend Francis X. Hagerty lived and had his Church of Our Lady of Sorrows. It had no sooner stopped before the little gray house than a troop of urchins crowded about it, wondering, and excited and respectful.

The church was next door, small, white, wooden, very neat and modest, with a large gilt cross on its steeple. The doors stood wide open to its dim coolness. Charles hesitated, then entered the church. He was immediately impressed by the intense cleanliness of the interior, the brilliant white of the altar cloth, the small but exquisite statues. Curiously, he walked about the church. An old woman or two, and an old man and a young housewife, were kneeling in the pews; Charles heard the faint click of beads. He saw a few candles burning in red glasses; he saw the light on the altar. There was the slightest scent of incense in the air, like a breath. There were eight tall thin windows in the church; six of them were of finely stained glass; two were of plain window glass. He looked at the latter, and frowned.

He thought: Our own churches should be open like this, every day. It is a very nice thing. Why should religious observances be restricted to one day in the week? Why should God be remembered only on the seventh day? Perhaps that is what is wrong with us.

He had never until now questioned the cozy materialism of the twentieth century. Goods, and the production of them, business and trade, honor and respectability: these had been enough. Now he saw they were not enough. The indestructible element which ought to sustain them had been left out; one violent thrust and the whole agreeable structure could be hurled down.

A little tired woman of about sixty answered the bell of the priest's house, wiping her worn hands on her apron. She saw the blazing red of the automobile at the curb; she did not know Charles, but she saw that he was a gentleman, and that his clothing was expensive. This all frightened her. She was even more frightened when he told her his name and said that he'd like very much to see Father Hagerty, if the latter was not busy.

She stammered, "Why, yes, Mr. Wittmann. I'm Mrs. Hagerty. I'm the Father's mother. He'll be glad to see you. No. He isn't busy just now. He's in the garden, out back."

Why should the rich and important Mr. Wittmann come to see her son? She remembered the threats, the broken windows, the offal on her spotless verandah. Charles said, kindly: "I just want to talk with him for a few moments." He paused. He said quickly, then: "It's about those windows in the church. I'm very sorry about that. Hoodlums, of course. I thought perhaps Father Hagerty might be interested in having them restored."

She could only stare at him speechlessly. With humorous gloom Charles wondered how much windows like that would cost. But the poor woman had been so frightened and he had had to say something to reassure her. He lifted his hat; she still could not speak, though there were tears now in her eyes. "Don't bother to call him. I'll join him in the garden."

He let her lead him through the house, which was small and poorly furnished, but clean and bright and redolent of wax. She stumbled once or twice in her confusion. She opened the back door for him, and still unable to speak she pointed to the young priest in his shirt-sleeves, working in his garden.

The garden, in contrast with the house, was rich and opulent with color. Garden tools lay about on the green grass. Fruit trees against a distant brick wall were heavy with ripening fruit. The priest looked up as Charles approached. In a shrill and trembling voice, from the door-steps, Mrs. Hagerty called out: "It's Mr. Wittmann!"

Father Hagerty put down his spade. Yes, he was as Charles remembered, shy and unobtrusive, with a very sensitive face and brown eyes, intelligent and quiet. He rubbed his hands on his handkerchief. "Mr. Wittmann," he said, simply. He offered his hand.

Charles shook his hand, which was calloused. No, he thought, he is definitely not a fighter. Why hadn't his bishop sent a brawny man to Andersburg, a staunch man, instead of this young and retiring feller? And then Charles saw the priest's eyes.

Charles said: "I do hope you'll pardon this unannounced visit, Father Hagerty. I won't stay long. But the matter is important. No, please don't bother. We can talk right here."

Father Hagerty said: "Let us sit down, then, Mr. Wittmann, under that tree." There was a large elm tree directly in the center of the yard, and under it were two wicker chairs. They sat down together. Charles looked about him, just faintly embarrassed.

"You have a fine garden here," he said.

The priest smiled, with gratification. He could not imagine why Charles had come to see him, and he was uncertain and alarmed. But he saw that Charles had no intention of being anything but friendly.

"It's a great pleasure to me," said the priest. "The flowers all go to the charity wards in the hospital, and the church, and those who are ill at home, and the chronic invalids. It keeps me very busy," he added.

Had Charles come to suggest that he leave Andersburg, or something equally impossible? Father Hagerty looked at him with grave candor. Charles knew almost exactly what he was thinking. He said: "I've just been in your church. It's very beautiful." He hesitated. "I can't tell you how much I regret those windows being broken. A drunken fool, probably. I am wondering if you'd mind if I contributed something towards their restoration?"

Amazed, Father Hagerty said: "That is very good of you, Mr. Wittmann. I was very proud of those windows. Moreover, they cost my people a good deal of money—"

"I'll send you my check for three hundred dollars," said Charles.

Father Hagerty was much moved. Charles went on, smiling: "You see, Andersburg is my home, my city. I'm proud of it. I want to stay proud of it. I'll see if a collection can't be taken up at my own church, too, for those windows. There are a lot of decent people here, Father Hagerty. I'd like you to believe that."

The priest smiled. "But I do, sir. I never doubted it."

Then Charles showed him *The Menace* and the pamphlets. The priest's expression changed to one of sorrow. "I see you are familiar with this foul stuff," said Charles.

"Yes." The young priest's distress increased.

Charles said: "I've just talked to my minister, Mr. Haas. He is going to deliver a sermon about all this, on Sunday. And I've talked to the editor of the *Clarion*. He will send a reporter to my church on Sunday, to report the sermon."

Father Hagerty considered this in silence. Then he said: "Mr. Wittmann, I can't tell you how much I appreciate all this. But I don't think it will do any good, though I understand the kindness of your motives. I also am more than delighted that the Reverend Mr. Haas wishes to deliver that sermon. But I still think that it won't do any good. It will bring the whole issue before the people, arouse everybody—"

Charles laughed patiently. "That's exactly what Mr. Haas said. Bring it out into the open. Expose these things for the lies they are. Make the people ashamed that they ever read them."

The priest shook his head. "Mr. Wittmann, I think it is better to ignore the whole thing. Men are innately good. Eventually, they discover that lies are lies. If one just ignores—"

"Father Hagerty," interrupted Charles, "I want you to answer just one question for me. I understand that this paper and pamphlets like these began to appear in small quantities about two years ago. They were 'ignored,' weren't they? No one spoke of them editorially or in the pulpit?"

"No."

"Well, then, they were 'ignored.' And did they die out, Father Hagerty, or did their distribution increase?"

The priest put his hands upon his thin knees. "I see what you mean, sir. You are right. They were ignored, and they came faster and faster."

"Somewhere," said Charles, "I read that lies cannot stand, because they have no legs, but that they can fly, because they have wings. And so they can go a great distance.

"Someone manufactured those lies, Father Hagerty. And there is always a purpose in lies. In most cases, it is only malice. It is my belief that in this case it is organized hatred—for a purpose."

Father Hagerty looked at him with consternation. "I'm afraid I don't understand, Mr. Wittmann. What would be that 'purpose'?"

"I don't know, yet. But there is a purpose. I, myself, am seriously convinced that the purpose behind the lies is to set one American against another."

"But why?"

Charles shook his head wearily. "I'm not quite sure, as I said. Once divide a people, set it to hating its own members, and they are off guard. I don't know who the plotters are, but I can assure you they are waiting for the day, the right day of sufficient confusion and disruption. Then the purpose will be accomplished, the people deceived, and ready for anything."

The priest considered this somberly. Once or twice he glanced at Charles quickly, as if about to speak, then he resumed his thinking. He rubbed his damp cheek with the back of his hand; it left a mud stain upon it. This made him appear very young, and Charles was touched.

"I don't know if these lies, this hatred, can be halted, Father Hagerty. It's probably gone too far. What can any man of good will do, in a world where there is so little good will? But at least we can try." He stood up. The priest looked at his garden sadly, in silence.

"Father Hagerty," said Charles, gently, "your people know of these lies, don't they? There is something you can do: You can urge them not to hate, in return. That is very important. In the end, it might be even more important than you can believe just now."

He, too, looked at the garden blazing in the hot sun.

"You can tell them that the American people are being distracted from something which is very terrible, but which is growing right up before them. The plotters don't want the people to guess the plot."

"You frighten me," murmured the priest. He stood up. Helplessly, he stared at the ground.

"Good. I want men like you, millions of men like you, to be 'frightened.' I want them to know." He held out his hand. "You see, Father Hagerty, America is in some frightful danger. I think the whole world is in danger."

Father Hagerty took his hand. He tried to smile, but it was a mournful attempt.

"I am beginning to see—a little," he said.

CHAPTER XVI

CHARLES CAME home a little earlier than usual the next day because of Wilhelm's dinner. He wished to bathe and freshen himself for what he knew would be an exhausting evening.

He found Jimmy and Geraldine, his niece, in the garden, contentedly eating early golden apples under the shade of a great walnut tree. They were doing nothing, and doing it with joy. Jimmy lay sprawled on the cool green grass; Geraldine sat near him, her thin young arms wrapped about her knees. Charles could hear only the lightest murmur of desultory conversation. Sun filtered down through the branches of the tree and lay in bright streaks on Geraldine's straight black hair, which fell in heavy lengths upon her shoulders. Her thin, clear profile was sharply defined. Charles thought again, with surprise, how much she resembled Wilhelm. A dear girl, he thought, a lovely girl.

He called to the children, and waved his hand. "No," he said, "don't get up. I'm going to rest and dress, Jimmy, then I'm going to dinner at your Uncle Willie's. How are you, Gerry?"

The girl turned her face towards him, and smiled. "I'm wonderful, Uncle Charlie. Jimmy and I are just talking. I'm staying for dinner. Mother said I could." He saw the shine of her great, dark eyes, the glimmer of her pretty teeth.

Charles nodded, and retreated. But he stood in the doorway and watched the children, who had resumed their consumption of apples, and their talk which was as drowsy and murmurous as the sound of bees. Surely nothing, nothing, could threaten them, in their grave innocence, their certainty that all was well in their world, their trust. Their trust in whom? In me? thought Charles, as he went into the house. But what can I do? Nothing. What can any of us do in the face of "traditional markets" and Emperors who celebrate their "peaceful reigns," and Chancellors who talk of Germanentum and Slaventum, and a world of people who instinctively want to kill?

Charles called Phyllis. "Charles?" she said. "Oh, Charles, you aren't calling to say you can't come?" Her voice was humorous, but underneath it he thought be detected dismay.

"Of course I'm coming," he said. He had never before realized how much he liked her voice. He could see her so clearly, and something strengthened in him. "Not that I'm going to add anything inspirational to the conversation, you know."

She laughed. "Poor Charles," she said, softly. She laughed again.

"I suppose there'll be something to drink before dinner?"

"Drink? Why, of course. If you want it." She sounded a little puzzled.

"Yes. I want whiskey. Quietly, and behind a door, if necessary. But whiskey. Perhaps even a lot of it."

He waited for her laughter, but it did not come. Instead, there was only a humming on the line. After a few moments, he said, tentatively: "Phyllis?"

"Yes, Charles." Her voice was a little faint. Then she said more clearly: "Is it as bad as that?"

He said, bitterly: "Yes."

"Perhaps you can tell me, tonight."

"If we have a chance. Phyllis," he said more normally, "who the hell is, or was, Monet? I thought you might give me some information before I arrived."

He could see her smiling again. "He still 'is,' Charles. He's a French

Impressionist painter. He paints things in different 'lights.' For instance, he painted the Cathedral of Rouen in them."

"The same Cathedral?"

"The very same. Also, he exhibited some pictures called 'Le Bassin aux Nympheas,' in 1900. That is what they're going to talk about, tonight. But don't worry about it. Just talk about the different lights on the Cathedral. Casually. Don't let them draw you out. Just toss it into the conversation, then retreat. Poor Charles," she added, and laughed ever so gently. "Come at quarter to seven, instead of seven, and I'll see you get the whiskey before the others arrive."

"It sounds as if I'm going to need the whiskey," said Charles, with gloom.

"Frankly, Charles, I don't think any of them, except Wilhelm and Mr. Bartholemew, know very much about Monet, and even Mr. Bartholemew doesn't know too much. He is to give the talk, after all, and he'll say a lot of things which you needn't try to follow." She dropped her voice, and again it was humorous. "You know, Charles, I've been waiting a long time for you to tell me that you detest sherry. I always knew you did. But you are so polite, or something."

Now he could laugh, and with his involuntary laughter much of his anxiety lessened. "So, you've been teasing right along, have you, with that damned sherry?"

They laughed together. Charles felt almost gay. He could see Phyllis' blue eyes, sparkling.

"I'm sorry about the dinner, though," said Phyllis, very frankly. "It's the kind you don't like. Wilhelm ordered it, especially, the poor darling, and has been fussing at the chef all afternoon. You wouldn't like a ham sandwich with the whiskey, would you?"

"I might, I really might. But not with lettuce."

When he went upstairs his burden did not feel so heavy. He could still hear Phyllis' voice. Then he remembered that he was thinking a great deal of Phyllis these days. Phyllis, whom he had once wanted to marry.

He looked at himself in his mirror as he removed his collar and tie. He said to himself: I ought to have married Phyllis, after all. The thought shook him. He stood there, stupidly, with the tie in his hand, and a sickening desolation made his heart thump. No, no, he cried to himself. I had Mary, and I loved Mary. What is the matter with me these days?

But he could not shake off his devastating distress. He could stop thinking of Phyllis, but he could not stop the nebulous misery which hung in his mind. Once, he had the impulse to call his brother's home and plead sudden illness. Then he was revolted by the cowardly idea, and humiliated that he should think of it. Excuses were craven things, if they were used to avoid facing a necessary issue. This issue must be faced. He had once loved Phyllis; in a way, it was very possible that he had never recovered from this love. He remembered his delight in her presence, the deep sympathy and understanding between them. This was not a recent development; it had always been with him.

So, he had once loved her. And then he had loved Mary, and had married her. Never once, during the years of his marriage, had he ever believed that he had not loved her. He loved her still, as a dear memory. He looked at the photograph of her on his dresser, in its gilt frame, and he saw the lively young face, and he said to it, in his inner silence: I loved you, Mary, my dear. But now I see I never loved you as I loved Phyllis. As I am terribly afraid I love her, still, and have always loved her.

It was out now, and he could face it with his own kind of dogged resolution. He could not control what was "brewing" in an evil world, but he could control, sternly, any outward indication that he loved Phyllis. There was no use in deceiving himself that he could, by any effort of his will, "forget" Phyllis, for there was no way of avoiding her. He would simply have to acknowledge that he loved her.

One accepted such things, and made no one else miserable because of them. So he bathed and dressed as deliberately as always, and his face, in the mirror, might be a trifle set but it was calm.

The children were coming in to dinner as he came downstairs. Jimmy said, sympathetically: "We have pepper-pot, tonight, Dad. And dump cake."

"Well, we don't need to eat all of it," said Gerry, smiling at her uncle affectionately. "We can leave some of it for Uncle Charlie."

Yes, a lovely girl, with something that was much more than beauty in her fine features and large eyes. Plain, her mother called her. Plain! Isabel was a fool. Jochen, however, had not been a fool when he had spoken of his daughter's intelligence, but he had been stupid when he had confessed that she had no charm.

Charles put his arm about the girl, and she put her arm about him.

"Yes, save me some of the pepper-pot, and the cake," he said to his son, but he looked down at Gerry, and smiled. One of these days she might be his daughter. He hoped so, fervently.

His old carriage was waiting. He settled himself down in it. Then, as he often did when things became somewhat unmanageable for him, he consciously emptied his mind. The misery might remain, but he allowed no tangible object to arise in his mind to which the misery might attach itself definitely.

The brass sunset over the green mountains was there for him to see, and he forced himself to see it. As the carriage climbed the mountain roads the air became fresher and purer. Then he had a wide view of the river below, brazen, also, curving around the city. He made himself see it objectively. If something threatened it, it was strong enough to resist. "Yes," he said, aloud, and strongly.

Like his city, he, too, could resist his own released torment. Storms blew up in men as they did in cities; if the foundations were well laid, the storm did little damage. He knew his strength, and even if he could find no comfort in himself, he could find resistance.

He found Phyllis alone, waiting for him. She greeted him with a conspirator's laugh. "I have a ham sandwich for you, and whiskey," she said. "Wilhelm's still dressing. He won't be down for ten minutes. But do hurry, Charles." There was the sandwich and the whiskey on the delicate, round marble table. Charles looked at them, and felt revulsion. He said: "Awfully kind of you, Phyllis," and sat down, and took up the sandwich and the whiskey. She sat near him, smiling, and shaking her head.

"Jellied soup, and lobster à la Newburg," she confessed. "And asparagus vinaigrette, and a wine mousse, and demi-tasse."

Charles took a deep drink of the whiskey. Then he took another, and the tall glass of liquor and soda was empty. Phyllis watched. She said, gently: "Would you like another, Charles?"

"Yes, please."

She prepared another drink for him. Charles was in trouble, in grave trouble. She could not ask him, she knew that. If he wished her to know he would tell her. However, Charles rarely told anyone his troubles. She saw that he had replaced the sandwich, untouched, on the plate. She made no comment.

He held the glass, and tried to make his voice light: "The heat's been too much for me. I can't eat very much of anything these days."

Phyllis nodded. Little ringlets, the color of bronze, curled on her forehead, and on her nape, moist and bright. The heat had brought a flush to her cheeks. But her blue eyes, though smiling and crinkling, seemed tired. Her mauve silk dress clung to her slender and pretty figure and outlined her arms. Her throat was bare, but there was a froth of airy lace over her breast. Wilhelm had evidently chosen this gown, too; it blended so well with the delicate yellows of the room, the

creamy panelled walls, the deeper mauve rug. Even the flowers had
been carefully selected; golden roses in crystal vases stood on the mantelpiece, with every green leaf precisely flaring. The French doors stood
open to the sweet evening air, cooling and freshening after the day's
glare of sun. Charles could see the gardens beyond, the dark vivid
grass, the great silent trees, the beautiful flower beds burning with late
summer flowers. He liked this room he sat in almost as much as he
liked the "music room." He liked the view of the mountain beyond,
almost purple, now, as the sun sank.

Once or twice Phyllis had used the word "étude." He did not know
what it meant, but it had a curious connotation for him. Cool evening
light, soft and dim; silence; lofty graciousness and elusive nobility. He
had always been afraid that "étude" did not mean these, so he had
never investigated. He put down his glass. He could not look at
Phyllis. He said, with deliberation. "What is an étude, Phyllis?"

She answered: "A finished composition, Charles. A study, in a way,
a technical exercise in music."

There. One had only to approach romanticism or fear or pain,
definitely, and they all lost their mystery, and in losing their mystery
they lost much of their power to exalt or destroy. He saw, now, that
he had never wanted before to know what an étude was because he
had sentimentally wanted to keep its mystery, the mystery which surrounded his repressed love for Phyllis.

"A finished composition," he repeated.

"One complete in itself," she added.

He discovered that he was looking at her in the bright dusk of the
room. Complete in itself. The étude had not lost its mystery, after all,
and all his pain returned to him. Why did she sit like that, regarding
him so directly, so sadly? She sat gracefully on the small gilt chair, her
white hands clasped in her mauve lap, and her sadness was like the
evening shadow outside.

She said in a very low voice, as if thinking of something else: "I was
glad to hear you had your way about the river property, Charles."

She was helping him! He said: "Yes." He told himself she was helping him because she recognized that he was tired. He repeated: "Yes."
He stared at his emptied glass. The whiskey was affecting him. Usually,
it gave him a sense of exhilaration; now he could feel nothing but
desolation and loss.

He said: "When I'm tired, this way, all sorts of things come back to
me. I was thinking of Mary, tonight."

Phyllis smiled. "Dear Mary," she murmured.

"I suppose a man never really gets over something like—that," he said, and he knew his voice was louder than it should be, and had a note of desperation in it.

Phyllis nodded. "That's quite understandable. No one ever forgets anyone he has loved. Never. It always comes back, when one least expects it. And very often when one doesn't want it to come back. Sometimes, too, it returns so very—"

But Wilhelm was entering the room now. There was a swish of mauve skirts as Phyllis stood up. The untouched ham sandwich disappeared magically out of sight, as did the glass. Phyllis then almost ran to her husband, and twined her arm in his. "Charles came a little earlier," she said to Wilhelm, and stood on tiptoe to kiss his cheek.

Wilhelm, elegant in his black, brushed his lips against his wife's hair. Then he said to Charles: "Yes, you are the first, Charles. I hope you won't be bored."

Charles stood beside his chair, and looked at Wilhelm and Phyllis, standing so close together. "I don't expect to be," he said. Should he throw in that business now about the cathedral and all its "lights"? "I'm really interested in Monet." He went on, hurriedly: "I believe I saw one of his paintings of the Cathedral of Rouen."

"Which one?" asked Wilhelm, surprised, and very pleased. "And where?"

Phyllis interrupted with light deftness: "Oh, Wilhelm! Sometimes you don't listen. Charles told you about it at least three years ago. He saw it in New York. It was Monet's third study." She glanced at Charles. "Is that right, Charles?"

"Yes. That's it."

Wilhelm frowned. "I'm afraid I don't remember. You see, Charles, I always thought you weren't interested in Impressionist painting, or in any painting, in fact." He bent his head, thinking. "The third study. Was that the one of the evening light, or the early morning, or at an angle?"

Dismayed, Charles saw that he had used his meagre information too soon. But Phyllis said, laughing: "Why, Wilhelm, don't you know? Of course you do!"

Wilhelm bridled. "Certainly. I ought to have remembered. Stupid of me to forget."

They heard the door-bell ringing, and the steps of the maid. "Our guests are coming," said Phyllis, gayly. "I do hope your headache is quite gone, darling."

"Have you a headache today?" asked Charles, quickly, breathing easier. "I've had one, too. It's the heat, I suppose. I've been having them very often, lately, however. I suppose I should go to Dr. Mower. But I'm afraid he'll recommend bifocals."

"At your age?" said Wilhelm, annoyed, remembering that Charles was his senior by only fourteen months.

"It's not a matter of age, always," said Phyllis. "My aunt never wore bifocals, even at seventy."

The guests came in, in a body, five couples. Charles knew them only slightly. They were the elegantes of Andersburg, the dilettantes, like Wilhelm. But they were all reassuringly wealthy, retired coal "barons" or other business men. Their average age was fifty, or even a little more. Then Charles was intrigued. He had never wondered before why most of Wilhelm's friends were so much older than himself. Now, he saw. Wilhelm was afraid of growing old. In contrast with these other men he was young, quick, and vivid. Poor old Willie, thought Charles, almost fondly. In fourteen months he'll be looking forty in the face, too. It's going to be a wrench for him.

In some obscure fashion the sudden perception of this weakness of Wilhelm's increased Charles' affection for his brother, and as his affection became stronger his own pain unaccountably abated in some measure.

The room was aflutter with blue, rose, white, and yellow dresses, rustling like a soft wind among the solid black of the men. If the other male guests were surprised to see Charles there they did not show it. They greeted him with restrained courtesy, commented on the weather. Then they were helpless. They could talk to Charles about nothing. They were retired. They were trying their best to forget their former businesses. They were patrons of the arts. What could they say to this man who so very solidly recalled the days of bitter struggle, strategy, and competition? They thought of the offices they had abandoned, of hours of sudden gross exhilaration or victory. They thought of all this, and they eyed Charles resentfully. They sipped at their small glasses of sherry, and saw he drank none. A whiskey man, they thought. Possibly even beer. Nostalgia gnawed at them. They held their sherry glasses to the newly lit light of the chandelier, and squinted like connoisseurs.

Their ladies, in their late forties or early fifties, did not feel in the least resentful of Charles. They liked him. One or two chided him for sending regrets to some of their dinner parties. A short stout matron, who was not intensely interested in Monet, or in any artist, in fact, said to him, roundly: "Why aren't you ever seen about, Charles? Do you try to avoid us?"

"No, Mrs. Holt. No, indeed. But it seems I'm always so busy these days."

Busy. The men brooded on this. Of course, he would be "busy," they thought with some vindictiveness. Everyone knew that he was really "the whole thing" at the Wittmann Machine Tool Company. Not a thought in his head but profits and competitors and machines and business. Probably took account books home with him at nights. Noisy office; noisy factory behind him. All that coming and going, and letter-writing and reading and activity. The guests were more resentful than ever.

Mr. Bartholemew, a large booming man, was saying, near Charles: "I've a very fine paper here, if I must admit it myself, Wilhelm. Monet, when you think of him—" He was again surprised to find Charles here. "Oh," he said. "Charles, do you know anything about Monet? I mean, do you really know anything about him, or are you going to be intolerably bored?"

Phyllis could not help saying, mischievously: "Oh, Charles is simply fascinated with Monet. All about the different studies of the Cathedral at Rouen." Then seeing Charles' dismay, she added: "But, then, Henry, you are going into all that, yourself, aren't you?"

"Yes, my dear Phyllis, certainly." But Mr. Bartholemew was staring disbelievingly at Charles.

Dinner was fortunately then announced. Charles was so enormously relieved to find himself not seated next to Phyllis that he even attacked the jellied soup. But after a spoonful or two he abandoned it. Then came the lobster à la Newburg. Lobster was one dish of which he held a very low opinion. Wilhelm was telling someone how the lobsters had been shipped to him in ice, and how his chef had insisted upon too much sherry. He had almost discharged the ignoramus. The guests nodded. The two or three who were resentful of Charles became resentful of the lobster, too. A spareribs man. One could tell that, easily. His complexion was too red.

Deserting the lobster, Charles tried the sauce. He deserted this, too, very quickly. There was really nothing he could eat but bread, and there had been only a single roll on his plate, and there was not a damned piece of butter in sight. In the interests of the company he had certainly let himself in for an infernal evening. The exquisite, fragile dining-room was becoming too hot; the cool evening did not penetrate here. Charles drank a glass of water, dejectedly. But he was very polite to the ladies on each side of him. He was glad that Mrs. Holt sat at his right. The lady at his left did not talk about Monet, either.

The rest of the evening promised to be even more appalling. He had no pleasant cushions of thought and reflection on which to drowse while the talk went on about him or before him. He could not think of his son without that swell of unfamiliar panic; he could not think of the shops without thinking of that damnable aeroplane steering-control assembly and the Bouchards and Colonel Grayson and the things which Mr. Grimsley had shown him in the newspapers, which he—infernal fool!—had hardly noticed before. He could not occupy himself with a cigar and look at Phyllis and feel a warm pleasure and contentment. He could not look at Wilhelm and watch his mercurial movements, his grimaces, his quick gestures, and be amused at the watching. He had only two subjects to fall back upon: Friederich and Jochen, and when he thought of these two brothers, it was with a kind of malaise.

The balance wheel. That is what so many had called him, he remembered. Oh, it was easy enough to be a "balance wheel" in one's own orbit. But when one was flung outside that orbit into the terrible confusion of vague but inimical disaster, where one had no control over anything, then one was no longer a balance wheel, not even among his own hopeless thoughts. "A man of resolution," his grandfather had once told him, "is a man whom nothing can hurt." But his grandfather had had somewhere to go, to get away from sinister men. There was no place in the world where one could go now. The circle was closed by the wolves.

What then? Courage? He felt that inwardly he was in a crouch, turning his head from side to side in utter darkness, his fists impotently clenched.

The party moved, laughing and gay, into the music room, with Charles somberly bringing up the rear. The air in this room was cooler. But all at once Charles was seized by claustrophobia. He couldn't breathe. The sleek pale walls appeared to crowd in upon him. A small gilt chair was being pushed towards him; he sat down. Phyllis was beside him, and she was smiling at him, though she only smiled with her lips. He felt her concern. He said: "A very nice dinner." He did not know how pale his face was under the glittering chandelier.

Phyllis said, very gently: "There is an old saying, that when evils cannot be cured they must be endured."

Her voice was almost a whisper. Her hand brushed his arm briefly. And then before he could answer her, she had turned to her neighbor, Mr. Holt, and was saying in a bright tone: "So much cooler, don't you think?"

Endured. But sometimes there was an end to endurance, a place where a man had no fortitude left, because fighting did no good.

He became aware that Mr. Bartholemew had been speaking for some time. Apparently he, Charles, was behaving properly. He was staring at Mr. Bartholemew with something which must pass for concentration. Mr. Bartholemew's attitude was pompous; his mouth moved, but Charles could not hear a single thing he was saying. People were nodding approvingly about Charles; he nodded, too. Then he remembered what Phyllis had said. Yes, he thought, his lips pressed together, I suppose I can endure. I suppose I could go on living, no matter what happened. I suppose they'd call that courage.

He was very tired. His tiredness was a strong ache all over his body.

He had not liked school, and so had not continued at college. But he remembered something Ovid had written: "Neither can the wave which has passed be called back; nor can the hour which has gone by return." He had not thought of Ovid for years, if he had ever consciously thought of him. Why, then, did that majestic and dolorous phrase return to him now?

Had "the hour" gone by? He knew, all at once, that it had gone, and that he could do nothing about it, could never have done anything about it, but that if millions of men like himself had known in time they could have prevented the birth of that hour, could have stood in the path of the wave and built a wall of stones against it. But it was too late, now.

People were clapping softly about him. He clapped, too. He saw their faces, politely enthusiastic. But Wilhelm was scowling. Wilhelm was preparing to give a short rebuttal to Mr. Bartholemew's talk on Monet. Oh, God, thought Charles, watching his brother take Mr. Bartholemew's place.

Wilhelm was talking in his swift, irritable voice, and with elegant gestures. Phyllis leaned towards Charles. He bent towards her. "Eh? I'm sorry," he muttered.

"Oh, Charles," she was whispering. "I don't know what it is, but you are so strong, Charles."

He looked at her slender face and he thought how beautiful it was, and a horrible despondency clutched him. He shook his head slightly. "No," he said. "Not this time, Phyllis."

Why was she so concerned about him? Why did she look so wretched? She was whispering again: "I know it's another aphorism, but Cicero did say that a man of courage is also full of faith."

He pondered on this. Then he said: "I have no faith. I see now that I never did. Except in myself. And it isn't enough, Phyllis."

"It never was," she answered.

But in what could a man have faith? thought Charles, on the way home. God? God had retreated into opaque mists. He was no longer a super-business man, with an orderly mind, and everything under control. He was a Mystery. If He existed. Charles had never before questioned that; respectable people accepted God naturally, or appeared to do so. If God existed, did He care what happened to this little world of men, this dangerous world of men? Charles could not believe He did.

Faith, then, in one's ability to survive? A barren faith. But that was all that was left. "An army of principles?" How many multitudes would have to die before that army became a reality?

CHAPTER XVII

THE WITTMAN MACHINE Tool Company was one of the few companies in Andersburg which permitted its workers the luxury of a Saturday afternoon holiday. This was the source of a great deal of bitterness between Jochen and Charles, and Charles had obtained this concession five years ago only after a prolonged struggle with his youngest brother.

However, Jochen, to express his fury at this "anarchistic" concession, usually remained to work alone in the offices after Charles had gone. Charles knew that Jochen did not enjoy this; the silence behind him in the shops must be intolerable. The silence of the offices was also something not easy to bear. However, Jochen always appeared to be most busy when Charles called in to say goodbye, as he did today.

Charles saw that his brother was signing mail. Joe, he reminded himself, would not only have to sign the mail (which could have waited in most cases until Monday) but he had to seal the envelopes himself, stamp them, and mail them. But Charles had a deep suspicion that the moment everyone was gone he, himself, stayed only an hour or so longer.

He stood in the doorway and watched Jochen. It was one o'clock. Half an hour ago the offices and the factory had emptied themselves with happy joy, for it was a most sultry day and there were pleasant little beaches and picnic plots along the river. Jochen pretended to be unaware of Charles' presence, until Charles said, pleasantly: "Hot, isn't it? Well, until Monday, then, Joe, unless you are going to church tomorrow."

Jochen glanced up, and frowned. "Oh, Charlie. Off so soon?"

It was the usual ritual. Charles looked at his watch. "Three minutes after one," he said. "I thought it was half-past twelve. Everybody's gone. What are you doing, Joe, that couldn't wait until Monday?"

"I," said Jochen, sarcastically, "am praying. I'm also being 'honorable.'"

Charles laughed. Once he had quoted someone to the effect that to labor was to pray, and that there was honor in work.

"Pray tomorrow; it's Sunday. And be honorable every day, besides Saturday afternoon."

Jochen put down his pen. "I suppose that is just a remark, and means nothing?"

"Nothing at all." Charles surveyed his brother thoughtfully, then smiled. "I'm going down to Baker's Bend this afternoon, for a swim. You know how cool it is there. But I'll probably call you here before I go. Say, about three or half-past."

Jochen's expression changed. "Why?"

Charles waved an airy hand. "Just to see if that Bouchard order might come in. They work Saturday afternoons, too, you know."

"You know damn well if the order had been sent it would have arrived this morning," said Jochen, angrily. "There's no mail delivery this afternoon. So don't bother to call me. Bouchard wouldn't send a telegram."

Feeling pleased for a moment or two, Charles went away. He remembered that Geraldine had artlessly mentioned that her parents had been invited to a garden party this afternoon at three o'clock. Charles wondered if Jochen would remain in the office. He doubted it. Still, it was a happy possibility, in view of his own remark, and the heat of the day. Charles could think of nothing more pleasant than Jochen sitting here and waiting for his call, which would, of course, never come.

He went to see Dr. Metzger, for he had promised Jimmy to do so, and he wished to be reassured about his health. Dr. Metzger examined him minutely, then slapped him on the bare shoulder. He sat down, and studied Charles with deep thoughtfulness.

"All right, Charlie, what's wrong?" he asked.

"I thought you'd tell me that. Nerves; liver; heart; lungs. All the things that can go wrong with a man."

"There's nothing wrong—that way. I mean, you have something on your mind, and it's raising hell with you. You know what I mean."

Charles dressed. "You know how business is, Gustave. And getting worse. All over the country. That ought to worry anybody."

"But not you," said Dr. Metzger, shrewdly. "You're doing pretty well. All right, Charlie. I'm not a father-confessor. You don't have to tell me what's bothering you. But something is. Beyond that, you are fine."

"Good. Jimmy wanted to know. You've heard Jimmy is going to study medicine?"

"Yes. Wonderful boy, your Jimmy. Called me up this morning to give me a full list of your symptoms." The doctor smiled, then became serious. "Look here, Charlie, you're still a young man, hardly forty. But something's bearing down on you, and it isn't your business, and it isn't your boy. I don't know what it is. You're rock, Charlie. But even rock can crumble. I'm not saying you are about to do that, but whatever it is that is bothering you, come to grips with it."

Then he stared, surprised at his own words. "I never thought I'd ever have to tell you that, Charlie!"

He walked with Charles to the door. "Just remember this: Things are never quite as bad as we imagine they are, or will be." He was again surprised. He had never thought Charles Wittmann particularly gifted with imagination. But, there was that blood pressure, and men without imagination rarely had high blood pressure. The doctor said: "Find someone you can talk to, Charlie. You've got a very close mouth, I know. But sometimes closed mouths hold back explosions; they can't hold them back forever. Even if you can't do anything about what's bothering you, talk to someone—anybody you can trust—about it. It's a wonderful help."

There's no one I can trust, thought Charles, thinking of his brothers. Wilhelm, who would be bored and incredulous? Friederich, the fanatic, who would scream his incoherences? Jochen, who would laugh at him? A wife, thought Charles. A man ought to have a wife, a good wife, with tenderness and understanding. Phyllis.

There it came again, that name, and the face it conjured up before him, and the outraged and involuntary sense of loss and desolation. It all came on him when he least expected it, like an enemy striking from behind a quiet bush. He began to examine his own thoughts desperately, as he was driven towards home. Phyllis, Colonel Grayson, the Bouchards, the feeling of being cornered and imprisoned: What had happened to him that he could not shake off what must be shaken off if he were to retain his health and courage?

The automobile was driven past a large empty lot where a number of young boys were playing baseball. Charles remembered that Jimmy was away with his cousin. There was no one at home, for Mrs. Meyers had been given the afternoon off. He wanted nothing to eat. He turned his head and watched the boys as long as he could see them. They were Jimmy's age, or a little younger; he could hear their shouts, the click of a ball against a bat. He caught glimpses of their faces, eager, laughing, excited, combative. Good. While they were young, let them sweat off their passion for conflict, like this; when they were older, let them think of ways to supply all men with work and goods and peace. This was an "adventure" for mature minds. And there was science, and the mysterious province of the human spirit to explore, and the nature of man—and the nature of God. Let the people into the cloisters; let them think with the scholars, the biologists, the theologians, the philosophers. Don't wall up the mighty places with stone, thought Charles. Let the people in. They might have something to contribute which "superior" men might never think of.

Christ had taken simple men from the sea and the hills and the land, and with them had evolved an Idea whose grandeur and magnificence and nobility had never been imagined by all the doctors and the lawyers and the philosophers, in all their quiet places and their colonnades. Nor from the men He had chosen had come the idea that it was necessary to kill in order to preserve "traditional markets." He had not taught murder, nor had He spoken of blood and iron, and the "honor" of peoples, and the making of weapons. He had left all this to the pale and evil men of the world. He had let the people in, and He had let in liberty and the dignity of man, and love, and the majesty of the human soul.

I've never thought, myself, of these things before, Charles confessed. But if millions of men like me—"an army of principles." It was not impossible.

He did not want to go home. He did not want to go to Baker's Bend, after all, where his particular club had its bath-house. He heard a gramophone blaring from an open window. The city was hot, sweltering. Even the trees could not lessen the heat of the streets. Panting men and women and children sat on verandah steps and watched his automobile go by. He wanted to be cool, and he wanted to be alone.

He asked his driver to take him to the foot of the mountains, and there dismissed him. He slowly walked up Mountain Road in the general direction of Wilhelm's house. Finally, he could see the red tile roof of the house, high in the distance. Then he abruptly made a turn to his right and walked along a very small winding country road, old and overgrown with bushes, grass, and weeds. But all at once it was cooler, and it was profoundly still. Old elms and maples and chestnuts met together in a green mass over Charles' head; the damp earth exhaled a cool sweetness. Here and there, as the trees opened, he saw the hot blue of the summer sky, and the road became brown and dry. He hurried through these openings to the green shadow beyond. Birds, disturbed by his passage, cried shrilly. He saw squirrels racing through the high grass; now he reached a natural grove of evergreens, and the ground was covered with thick and yielding old needles. Clumps of wild flowers, blue and yellow and scarlet, bloomed here and there.

Charles took off his hat; there was a scented wind high here in the quiet places. But he liked best the silence, the absence of human voices. There were no houses near this abandoned road; no sign of any living thing but the birds and the squirrels. Progressively, the air became cooler as he climbed. He knew this road well; he had walked along it literally hundreds of times, as a boy, and as a man. He knew where a spring was; he saw it now, bubbling among thick grasses. He lay down in the grass and drank of the spring; it had a faint sulphur taste. It recalled his boyhood to him, and the peace of his boyhood. It recalled his father to his memory, big, red-faced, gross and hearty Emil, who believed— What had Emil believed? In freedom, in the inevitable triumph of man over indecency and cruelty. In God.

Charles, in his youth, had thought his father somewhat naïve. Old men talk of God, he had thought, but young men talk of life. The mineral taste of the spring was very refreshing, as he lay in the grass. Now he began to wonder if his father had been as naïve as he had thought. No, Emil knew his Goethe as well as his Bible, and his Lessing, and his Spinoza. Charles thought of the huge old books in his house, old German books full of mighty and sonorous phrases. When had he last looked at them? He could not remember. He could hardly read German, now, without slow difficulty. Why did everyone think that it was naïve, or senile, to think of God, these days? He himself, had vaguely thought so, also, until he had smelled the terror which was beginning to envelop the world so silently, so inexorably.

There were fundamentals. When men went too far from fundamentals they encountered the dragons of fear, disorder, complexity, doubt, and confusion. They thought they had become civilized. But, in fact, they had lost nothing of their bestiality, their animalism.

Emil and his father had left Germany because they hated the "Statism" of Bismarck. Charles sat up, abruptly. Emil had believed that the rights of man came from God, not from the State. Statism. Could it be that everywhere in the world there was a plot developing secretly against that heroic belief that man's rights came from God? How best to destroy that belief, to reduce the world of men to serfdom under a State? By war, by religious and racial disorders, by confusing laws, by conspiracy? Charles listened to the silence of the woods about him. Peace. Who, anywhere, could overwhelm the peace of the world, could deliberately plot against liberty, could conspire to force Statism or Socialism upon men, and hope for success? Once or twice Friederich had spoken of Marxism to Charles, of a weird and incredible thing called Communism. But even the Germans, so disciplined, so exact, and so obedient a people, were beginning to rebel against the regimentation of that egotistic man, the Kaiser. There were those strikes in Hamburg, and other cities. There was a tide of Germans coming to America again, as they had come after Bismarck. No, liberty and democracy were growing, not declining. Let the plotters plot—if indeed there were plotters—and it would all come to nothing. That monster with the two heads, Statism and Communism, lived only in the disordered minds of a few murderous men.

Charles had it all settled, now. He stood up. He waited for his old feeling of surety to return, his old sturdiness and placidity. But they did not come back.

He went on. He knew there was a clearing at a little distance, a circular place of grass, surrounded by trees. He made for it, almost desperately. He had only to lie there, and perhaps sleep a little, and he would be of one piece again. There was an open place, he remembered, in that circle, through which one could see the long wooded slope of the green mountain tumbling down to the city below, and the river. He had sometimes thought that if this had been a Latin country a shrine would have been erected in that small glade, in the midst of cool, green, and watery light, in the center of sweet silence and peace. Shrines. Why, there ought to be shrines everywhere in America! What had the Greeks chiselled on an altar? "To the Unknown God." But there would never be altars like that in America, thought Charles, listlessly. We have become a materialistic country.

He came to the glade, and there was Phyllis sitting there alone, with her back against a great old tree, a book down in the grass beside her. Her white linen dress was very vivid in the green and sunless quiet.

She had not heard Charles coming; she was looking emptily before her, and her face was mournful and still.

"Phyllis!" Charles exclaimed. She looked up. Something flashed into her eyes, deep and brilliant.

"Charles," she said.

He stood there, foolishly, his hat dangling in his hand. He had only to go towards Phyllis, and speak easily, but he could only stand there. All at once the silence in the little circle was portentous, meaningful. It was enchanted. It was a dusky dream, with no other color but Phyllis' white dress and bright hair, and Charles standing on the edge of the circle, quite unable to say anything and Phyllis only looking at him.

It seemed that a long time had passed, to Charles, before he could say: "I didn't know anyone was here." It was a silly thing to say, he thought, incoherently.

"I often come here, Charles." Phyllis was smiling. "It's restful."

He went towards her then. He said: "Where's Willie?"

"He went to Philadelphia this morning." She was still smiling, but there was no pink in her cheeks or lips. "It was to get a birthday present for you, Charles."

He sat down near her. "A birthday present," he repeated, as if he did not understand. "For me."

"Yes. You have one next month. Or have you forgotten?"

He laid his hat carefully down beside him. "One doesn't try to remember his fortieth birthday." He spoke carefully. She was watching him, and her smile made her eyes tilt and crinkle in her pale face.

"It's an etching by Van Gogh," she said.

"Eh?" he muttered. Then he thought over what she had said. He sat there, in his staid clothing, his bent knees stiff. He said: "An etching by Van Gogh." He felt stupid and thick, staring at his knees. He felt them trembling.

"Or a sketch of Monet's," she added, gently. "I do hope you won't mind, Charles, and that you'll like it."

The trees closed them in, except for that one break before them, which overlooked the city. The slightest wind fluttered the leaves above them, turned them white for a moment or two. A bird cried far up in the branches.

"Why should I mind?" asked Charles, still staring at his knees. "There's nothing wrong in knowing something outside of your own— your own narrow orbit. I've been thinking I've never really known very much. It wouldn't hurt me to know something about Monet or Van Gogh or Debussy. It wouldn't decrease my interest in my business. It might even give me something to think about." He turned his head. Phyllis' expression was sad but intent. "You see, Phyllis," he continued, "if a man thinks only of a few things, especially those things that concern him closely, he has nothing to think about when—when trouble comes, for instance." He frowned. "I don't think I've said what I mean."

"You mean, he hasn't any inner resources."

"Yes. That's right. I've never had any inner resources, Phyllis. And now, when I need to think of something else—well, you might say of impersonal concern, I haven't anything very much."

She studied his broad Wittmann face, and saw his quiet desperation. Her first impulse was to say something absurd and consoling. But she could not insult him like that. So she said: "I think you have more than you believe you have, even if your life has been a little restricted by your business interests."

"I thought they were pretty much of everything," he said. He pulled up a few blades of grass, and looked at them soberly.

"And now?" asked Phyllis, softly.

He glanced at her, then looked at the grass again. There was such loneliness in him, such bereavement. "Well, what I thought was secure isn't so secure. Maybe. I'm not very good at talking, Phyllis. I can't put my thoughts into words. I've lost something. Maybe it's my self-confidence. No, that isn't exactly what I mean."

"You mean, certitude."

He nodded his head. "Yes. Certitude. I've lost that."

"But no one ever has it, really, Charles."

"I thought I had." He was surprised. He repeated: "I thought I had. Do you mean to say, Phyllis, that no one has any certitude at all?"

She shook her head. "No one, Charles."

He broke each blade of grass carefully, threw it aside. "I didn't know," he said. Phyllis did not speak. He said, again: "I didn't know." He looked at her. "You had a very nice party last night."

She laughed a little. "I thought Wilhelm's talk was better than Mr. Bartholomew's."

"Yes."

The silence again closed in upon them, isolated them. Out of the corner of his eye Charles could see the edge of Phyllis' white dress, her slender ankles, and pretty feet. He pulled up another handful of the grass.

"I didn't hear a word either of them said," he admitted, suddenly.

He waited for her to laugh again. But when she didn't laugh he turned to her. "That was a rude thing to say, and I'm sorry. I was thinking about something else."

"I know, Charles."

"I thought perhaps it might be my health," he said lamely. "I just came from seeing Metzger. It wasn't my health. He says."

She nodded. Then she said: "You don't have to tell me if you don't want to, Charles. I wish I could help, however. You know that."

"Yes, Phyllis. I do know it."

He crossed his arms on his knees and stared before him. Suddenly, he thought of that elusive word: étude. Finished. Complete. Something was complete, in this circle with him. His misery and fear and insecurity left him. His tired lethargy lifted. He bent his chin on his arms. "I'd like to tell you about it, Phyllis, and I'd like you to tell me, afterwards, that I'm a fool."

"I'd like to hear," she said, simply.

And then he told her as much as he could of the past week, but he did not tell her of Colonel Grayson. But he told her of the things he had read, the thoughts he had had; he told her about Mr. Haas and Jimmy and Father Hagerty, of Friederich, and all his shapeless terrors, and the Bouchards. His voice went on and on in the green silence, pouring out of him in a flood of release. He knew that what he could not express fully she understood completely. He did not know how long he talked, but he suspected that it was at least for half an hour, and she never interrupted him once.

"So, there it is," he said, finally. "It's all been deviling me all week. I've been looking for someone to tell me I'm a fool. I thought Grimsley would. But he didn't. He just showed me those items, which I'd missed, or overlooked."

He dropped his arms from his knees, and turned to Phyllis again. "Now, please tell me I'm a fool, and there's nothing."

Phyllis was very grave and quiet. She smoothed her white dress. "Wilhelm and I were all over Europe eighteen months ago, you remember, Charles."

"Yes?"

"I'm afraid you're right. I knew there was something wrong. Everything felt precarious to me. I didn't know why. I asked Wilhelm about it, and he said I had 'nerves.' I tried to think so. But it wasn't 'nerves.' There is, as you've said, Charles, something brewing. Something central and strong and fixed has flown apart. You felt it, in Europe, in the people. I might even say, in the very sunlight, and the shadows in the streets of London, and Berlin and Paris. But I don't think anyone actually knew, or believed—"

Charles said: "No. They can see it coming. But usually it's too late to do anything about it, because they never watched for the signs, or the signs were hidden from them." He brushed his knees. "Well. There it is. And there's nothing I, personally, can do. That's what's so desperate about it."

Phyllis said: "Charles. You talk as if you were alone. Do you know, Charles, how very much alone you've always been? And you've deliberately kept yourself alone, and now you can't believe that what you feel and instinctively fear is feared and felt by others."

She spoke so kindly, almost tenderly, yet he heard something else under her words. He said: "You sound as if you were—reproaching—me, in a way, Phyllis." He waited a moment, and considered what she had told him. "I never thought of it like that. I thought I was alone. I ought to have remembered that no one ever has a truly unique thought."

"Someone you can talk to—someone you can trust," Dr. Metzger had told him.

Phyllis leaned towards him, her hands in the grass. As the duskiness increased in the circle her hair brightened, and her face brightened, also, so near his.

"Charles, you're a wonderful man. You are the kind of man who has built America. The man of initiative, pride, resourcefulness, and enterprise. You inherited a business, and increased it. You have an unassailable reputation for integrity. You are not the president of a great corporation; you are a business man who owns his own business, who asks only the privilege of working as best he can, without interference, and with dignity. All that you are, and all that you have done, has a kind of greatness. And it's the kind of greatness which America dares not lose."

He had flushed at what she had said, with embarrassment. "Yes? What can I do?"

He could see the dim green light on her face, and her smile. "Charles, Shakespeare said something once:

" 'Be just and fear not:
        Let all the ends thou aim'st at be thy country's,
        Thy God's, and truth's.' "

He was so moved that he could say nothing. He could only look into her eyes.

"Men like you, Charles, have enemies. I don't know who they are. Perhaps they are the men whom your brother Friederich worships so extravagantly: the men who would debase the spirit of men for the good of what they call the State, or 'collectivist society.' Perhaps they are men who would like to enslave all the people."

Charles pondered over this. Her voice, in spite of its quiet, had held vehemence and certainty. Then he shook his head. "Why can't we do something before disaster comes? Why can't we be wise before the fact?"

"Because your very nature prohibits it. Men like you don't band together. Only the wicked men gather together and have a definite program. But, at the end, you do get together, in your desperation."

"In the meantime—"

"You can do nothing, Charles, except your best, and wait. And you, yourself, can begin to fight a certain self-satisfied complacency in your own thoughts—a materialism. Do you know that we have become a very materialistic world? Yes, I can see you've thought of that, too."

She put her fingers over his, and pressed them. He did not stir. The touch of her hand was suddenly almost unbearable in its sweetness and comfort.

"Think about the materialism of this century, Charles," she said, with strong earnestness. "And talk about it with other business men like yourself. It's a disease, you see. Feel—be emotional—Charles, about your place in the world. You have always had a tremendous sense of responsibility, but it has been an unemotional one, a materialistic one. There's no time to be lost."

Charles tried to keep his hand very still, so that she would not become aware that her hand was holding his.

"Grimsley was quoting Tom Paine, to me," he said. "Something about 'an army of principles.'"

She nodded. "Yes. I know what Tom Paine says. And be glad that you are part of that 'army of principles.' You'll win, some day, because your principles are truth."

Nothing had been settled. There was nothing he could do. He could not shout out to the world that it was in danger. But he was no longer alone or desolate or so desperate. "Be just and fear not." Perhaps if many men thought of the good of their country, and God, and truth, it would eventually be all right, even if all the terrors came, and the death and the ruin.

"You have such fortitude, Charles," Phyllis was saying, very softly. "And fortitude is so much nobler than endurance, which is just a dogged natural instinct. You can suffer anything, Charles, and you won't go down, because you are the best which the world has ever produced."

He colored again. "Now, Phyllis. That sounds extravagant."

She pressed his hand again, laughed a little, and removed her hand. "I believe in you, Charles, I always did. And so many others do, even if they don't know it yet."

She glanced at her watch; its enamelled cover caught the fading light. "It's nearly five!"

He stood up, brushing the grass from his clothing. Then he gave Phyllis his hand. She took it simply, and he helped her to her feet. They were standing close together. Phyllis began to smile. Then the smile left her face, and her eyes widened with what he knew, without any doubt at all, was a terrible suffering. "Charles," she said, and then could not speak.

He thought: She knows I love her, and she loves me, too. We never stopped loving each other, all these years, in spite of everything.

He thought all this so clearly, so quietly. There was a sort of inevitability about this final realization between them. But he knew that it was also inevitable that they must never speak of it. So they looked at each other in that silence, and drew upon their individual resistance.

"I'll walk with you to the house, Phyllis," he said. "And don't let Willie know—know that you've told me about the gift he's buying for my birthday."

She nodded. "No, Charles. I won't let Wilhelm know."

CHAPTER XVIII

They came out onto the crooked country road together. They walked in silence. But to Charles the silence had a fullness, a richness, even if it was sad and confused. He was not alone; if he was desolate, it was a desolation which was shared. One could stand pain, if there was someone present who suffered also.

He could see, out of the corner of his eye, the flutter of Phyllis' skirt, the slight motion of her hand. Once or twice her fingers brushed his, accidentally. She, too, did not speak. He heard her light footstep on the earth, her breath. They walked through a blaze of evening sunshine, and then into the green shadow. Then they emerged onto Mountain Road, and saw the red roof of Wilhelm's house in the distance above them.

There was the sound of wheels, and hoofs. They stood at the side of the road to let the approaching carriage pass. Then Charles saw that the carriage held his brother Jochen and Isabel. Isabel's printed parasol, which matched her "garden dress," was tilted over her handsome head, and she was laughing maliciously and Jochen was grinning. Evidently they were returning from the garden party at some home on the mountain, and having great fun over either their hosts or the guests.

"It's Jochen and Isabel," said Phyllis. She lifted her hand and waved gayly. Charles, annoyed that the sweetness of the last hour was being destroyed, frowned. Jochen, calling to his coachman to stop, was surprised. He was also alerted by Charles' expression. As for Isabel, she stopped laughing, and stared.

"Well, well," said Jochen. The carriage drew abreast of Charles and Phyllis. Jochen leaned over the side, and said, in a mincing voice: "Fancy seeing you here!" He grinned again.

"'Fancy seeing you,'" repeated Charles. "I thought you were working this afternoon. Playing hookey, eh?"

"I worked late," said Jochen, defensively. "But there was this damned party. Never saw such a set of bores. Wasted all this time. But the Brownes are important people, you know."

"Are they?" For some reason or other, Charles was increasingly annoyed. Phyllis was talking to Isabel, who mentioned the names of some of the guests, preeningly. Charles listened. Phyllis was smiling gently and tolerantly.

"The Bouchards didn't wire, or call," Jochen was saying.

"We'll hear from them next week," answered Charles, indifferently. Isabel was chatting on and on, bridling, and Phyllis was polite. Why didn't Jochen get out of the carriage? It was only courteous. But he sat there, in his garden-party outfit, and talked of the Bouchards, and looked repeatedly at Phyllis with a curious gleam in his eyes. Charles then noticed that Isabel's own eyes were sliding back and forth between him and Phyllis. It was a way she had, but he had never been so irritated by it before. He thought the sliding look was very quick and knowing, and he said to himself again that he certainly did not like Isabel. He wanted her to be done with her prattling so that he could go on with Phyllis. Why was Phyllis so patient, listening as if Isabel's account of the party was very interesting?

Jochen said: "Been rolling around in the grass, Charlie? You're covered with it."

Isabel's prattle stopped abruptly. Her face, under the shadow of the parasol, was intent. Charles looked down at his prosy suit. It was indeed scattered over with blades of grass. He brushed them off: "We were in the woods," he said. "Sitting and talking."

Phyllis was relieved that the conversation had left the magnificence of the garden party. "Such a hot day," she remarked. "I went into that circle, and Charles came. It was very pleasant."

"I should think it would be," said Isabel, in the softest, slowest voice. She glanced at Jochen. Then, very animatedly, she went on: "Such a romantic place. Jochen and I used to meet there, before we were married. Too." She waited. No one spoke. Phyllis retained her agreeable and charming expression. Charles' boredom increased. It was strange that his instinct, usually so reliable, did not stir, even in the face of his brother's odd expression and Isabel's faint smirk. He saw Isabel's pink tongue secretively moistening her red lips. He only knew that he really actively disliked her.

"Well," he said, glancing at his watch.

Phyllis invited Jochen and Isabel for tea, but Isabel, her eyes endlessly sliding and glinting, laughingly remarked that she and her husband had had all the tea they wished for one day. "But give our love to Wilhelm," she said. "Can we expect you, tomorrow, Phyllis? It's the day you and Wilhelm usually call."

"I'm afraid I'll have to come alone," replied Phyllis. She appeared a little distressed. "I'm so sorry, and I know Wilhelm will be, too. You see, he's in Philadelphia, and I don't expect him back until Monday."

Isabel stared at her. Then she looked at her husband. "I see," she said, thoughtfully.

It came to Charles again that there was something mysteriously gross about Isabel, sitting there so elegantly in her carriage, with her parasol and her Paris frock and her gloves and her dainty air. This grossness was very evident, in Phyllis' presence. Phyllis, who appeared all lightness and gentle serenity. And why was Isabel regarding Phyllis like that, long and slyly, and why was Jochen so alert, staring, too, at Phyllis?

"Well," said Charles, again. "I think we'd better go on, Phyllis. I'll have that tea, or something, with you."

He touched Phyllis' elbow, lightly. It was the touch of a husband, urging, yet protective. Jochen and Isabel saw it.

Graciously, Isabel said goodbye, tilted her parasol in a playful gesture, and Jochen applied two fingers to a hat he had not removed. Charles and Phyllis went on together, not looking back as the carriage rolled away.

Charles' sure instinct had begun, belatedly, to stir, though he could give no name to it. He only knew that he was vaguely uneasy. He said, as he helped Phyllis over some stones in the road: "Joe. And Isabel. They like to be prominent, don't they?" Then he was embarrassed, and covered his embarrassment with a laugh. "No harm in them, though. Just their way of acquiring importance."

Phyllis laughed. "Oh, Charles, don't be so afraid of being malicious! It's only human, and natural. I'm quite often malicious."

He laughed, with her. "I suppose you think I'm an egotist, when I try to be 'tolerant,' don't you?"

She was delighted. "Yes, of course! You are entirely too virtuous, Charles."

He saw her face, merry and sweet. The strain had gone from it, and it was young, and even joyous. He knew that for the first time in many days he, himself, felt a sort of freedom, even a senseless elation. He and Phyllis laughed together uncontrollably, as if they had been having a conversation full of extraordinary humor. Their somber talk in the woods was forgotten. The evening sky was purpling above them; far below, the river was the color of brilliant copper.

But still, the dim uneasiness remained in Charles, behind all the release and the gaiety. They reached the gates of Wilhelm's house, and Charles stopped abruptly. He took off his hat.

"Phyllis, I'm awfully sorry, but I can't stay. You don't mind too much, do you?"

For one moment, she was deeply disappointed. Then she was quiet and still. She put out her hand. "It's perfectly all right, Charles," she said.

He took her hand. He wanted to press it briefly, then let it go. But he could not do it. He wanted to turn, and leave. Instead, he stood there, and as they had looked at each other in the woods so they looked at each other now, gravely and sadly.

"Goodnight, Phyllis," he said.

"Goodnight, Charles." She took her hand from his. He opened the gate for her. He stood and watched her tall slight figure go up the drive. At the bend she glanced back, and paused. She was outlined against the lonely sky. She lifted her hand and waved to him, and he waved in return. Then she continued on her way and there was nothing about him but silence and the evening wind, and the old desolation.

Jochen and Isabel, too, were silent in the carriage as it carefully rolled down the mountain road. Jochen sat on his seat, large and fattish, his lips pursed, his eyes narrowed. Isabel watched him under the parasol. She waited for her husband to speak, but he remained silent. She coughed, delicately. "Well, really, it was rather indiscreet, wasn't it?" she murmured.

"What?" He turned to her. He frowned, but she saw it was pretense. "Charles and Phyllis."

"What about them?"

She lowered her voice so the coachman could not hear. "Of course, it's nothing at all, but people could—misinterpret. They ought to be more careful. It's just as well no one else saw them, but us, isn't it? Others might not understand."

"There's nothing to understand," said Jochen, with immense carelessness. "Old Charlie's an innocent," he added.

Isabel gave her light laugh. "Perhaps not so innocent." She paused. "I sometimes wonder if he ever regretted marrying Mary. After all he was once engaged to Phyllis, wasn't he?"

"Oh, that's all over. In fact, I don't suppose there ever was anything." Jochen's voice was elaborately offhand.

"But still, it was indiscreet."

They looked at each other, and smiled, and their smiles were not pleasant. Somewhere, in the recesses of Jochen's mind the incident was being carefully filed away. He said: "Best not to mention it to anybody. People talk, you know, Isabel. And there's Gerry. Old Charlie would be kind of mad if it came back to him. Must be careful."

Still, he remembered. He thought of Charles and Phyllis, standing there in the road, near the carriage. It was not mere bad manners which had kept his hat on his head in Phyllis' presence. It was his secret hatred for her, and his contempt for her. There had always been a latent hostility between them. Jochen did not believe that she and Charles were involved in even the slightest intrigue. She, Phyllis, did not have the robustness for it, and as for old Charlie, Jochen thought, the ripest woman would be safe with him.

Jochen said: "Now, don't pout, my precious. Just remember we have to watch out for ourselves."

Isabel understood. She gave Jochen a tender smile, and patted his hand. He squeezed her arm, a warm round arm, and he flushed. There was never a woman to compare with Isabel.

CHAPTER XIX

THAT SATURDAY night Mr. Ralph Grimsley had placed a curious but conspicuous insertion on the front page of every issue of the *Clarion*. No one could miss it; it was outlined by a thick wavy border, calculated to catch the most indifferent eye.

"The Reverend Mr. Joseph Haas, prominent and respected minister of the First Lutheran Church of Andersburg, will give a sermon on a most vital subject at 10:00 o'clock tomorrow morning. It is believed that this sermon is so important, not only to the people of Andersburg, but also to all the American people, that the *Clarion* urges everyone, irrespective of religious denomination, to hear this sermon, and attend the services."

Nothing like this had ever been written in the *Clarion* before, and it aroused immense curiosity and speculation. It was known that Mr. Grimsley had only a cavalier courtesy for Mr. Haas, and that he often spoke of him lightly as "our gilded minister." Everyone said, after reading this item, that the Reverend Mr. Haas must indeed have something of significance to say. Otherwise, Mr. Grimsley would not have inserted the notice.

Consequently, though it was a hot August Sunday, so sultry that one could hardly breathe, and with a blazing sky ominously piled, in the east, with thunderheads, the big white church began to fill as early as half-past nine. Family pews, usually less than half-filled even on religious holidays, soon became congested with the stiff white skirts and shirtwaists and white gloves and big straw hats of the women, and the formal, hot black figures of their husbands.

The ushers had never seen anything like it. There were folding seats tucked away in store-rooms, dusty from disuse. The ushers, by quarter to ten, were sweatingly scurrying to these store-rooms, catching up dust-cloths from closets, and hastily wiping off the chairs, which were to be placed at the rear of the church, and even in the side aisles. At five minutes to ten even these chairs were filled, and a crowd was hovering at the great open doors, looking in vain for seats. The sun poured in through the stained-glass windows, poured in through the doors. Palm-leaf fans made a soft rustling in the decorously murmurous quiet, and could be heard even above the first soft chords of the organ. The church was alive with moving hats and heads; the heat was so great that the perfume of the late roses set in vases near the altar could be detected even in the last pews, and added to the general discomfort. But everyone was excited, everyone crowded up against his neighbor. Not only was practically every member present, but it was obvious that members of other churches were also attending, either as guests of members or just seating themselves at random in the plebeian pews without family plates.

The service began; the choir, obviously excited themselves, were unable to control the tremors in their politely trained voices. But this only added to the momentousness of the occasion. The worshippers stood up, rustling, sat down with louder rustlings, at the proper intervals. The church was tumultuous with a thunder of responses; the brittle sound of the leaves of prayer-books was like the sound of a summer wind.

Charles had brought his son, Jimmy. He was surprised to see his brother Jochen enter the family pew, not only with Isabel, but with his three daughters, Geraldine, May, and Ethel. Jochen did not particularly like Mr. Haas. He had been candid in his opinion that Mr. Haas was "a big, affable rabbit, who never said anything." But Jochen had come. It was apparent that he was annoyed, but it was also apparent that he was curious. He shot Charles a rather sharp glance, nodded, seated himself pompously. This was all foolishness, his meaty shoulders and stiff neck declared. Phyllis had come; she sat near Isabel, all in white. She gave Charles a faint smile; her eyes, he saw, were very serious. She understood. But then, Phyllis always understood everything.

The supreme, paralyzing surprise occurred when Friederich Wittmann arrived just after the service had commenced. Charles, Jochen, Isabel, and Phyllis, stared with round-eyed disbelief. Friederich, surlily ignoring all his relatives, crowded roughly beside his niece Ethel, who regarded him blankly, her mouth open. Friederich was as untidy and dusty as always. Only Charles noticed that he was grimly defiant, that his small brown eyes glittered. He did not open a prayer-book; he did not rise when the others rose. He just sat there, thin arms folded across his chest, glaring at the minister.

Jochen leaned across his wife and sister-in-law and whispered to Charles, underneath the music of the choir, and the responses of the people: "Well, I'll be damned!" Charles smiled slightly, spoke the next response louder. Friederich was not seen to blink as he waited for the minister to begin his sermon. This was his first appearance since the funeral of his father, and now neighbors began to notice him and to whisper behind fans and prayer-books. Friederich ignored them, also, with gigantic contempt.

Charles was uneasy. He was ashamed of his brother's untidy clothing, his soiled collar, his dirty cuffs, his wrinkled tie. Then he was more ashamed of his conservative shame. Why had Friederich come? Did he have the slightest idea of what the subject of the service would be? Charles was positive that only he and the minister knew. He hoped that Friederich would not create any disturbance. If necessary Jochen and he could suppress Friederich, even if Jochen might be violently antagonistic to the sermon.

Mr. Haas' appearance had newly excited the people. Usually he wore a bland sweet expression, full of holiness and gravity, with perhaps a genial twinkle of the eye above it all. He always conducted the services in a most urbane fashion, big and handsome and contained in his august black robes. But now he exuded a tenseness and subdued passion never seen before. He was very pale; he looked older, and very tired, but also very determined. His voice did not quaver; it was very quiet, penetrating, and thoughtful. For the first time since Charles could remember, he was the priest, militant, austere, and firm.

But he is afraid, thought Charles, with a profound shame. He will speak out of his fortitude and his anger and his justice. He will do it all, no matter the consequences to himself; he will not temper his speech; he will speak outright. But still, he is afraid. How terrible it is for a priest to be fearful, not for, but of, his flock.

Mr. Haas held several pamphlets in his hands. The last chords of the organ died away. Now there was a great hush in the church. Mr. Haas looked at his people for a long moment or two. Then Charles saw that the minister was praying; his eyes did not leave the crowded faces below him, but his mouth moved soundlessly.

Then, all at once, Charles saw that Mr. Haas was no longer afraid. He began to read, quietly but sonorously. He turned the pages of the pamphlets, betraying no contempt. His voice was dispassionate. He read excerpt after excerpt, neutrally. The people listened, with eyes and ears intent upon the speaker. They leaned forward, not to miss a word. Some, believing they knew in advance what Mr. Haas would say about these pamphlets, nodded meaningly, smiled maliciously. Charles saw the polite hatred on their faces. Wait, he thought, grimly.

The feeling of drama grew in the church, an almost unbearable tension.

Then, one by one, Mr. Haas let the pamphlets drop to the floor. He moved slightly, and stood upon them. The malicious smiles, here and there, faded, were replaced by frowns, or blankness. Friederich, who had sat motionless, stirred.

Now there was silence in the church. Mr. Haas was no longer speaking. His hands were on the edge of the pulpit. He was leaning on them heavily. He surveyed the people, as if studying them, measuring them, commanding them.

"You have heard me read hatred in this church," said Mr. Haas, and now his voice, breaking the silence, began to mount. "You have heard me read lies and all viciousness and cruelty. You have heard me read the manifesto of the enemy.

"I have quoted the words of the secret enemy in ambush. I have had to profane the sanctity of this Church with the ugly cries of the wicked and the debased, those who would set a man against his brother, a nation against other nations, a people against their Lord and their Savior. You have heard me read the program of murder."

He paused. "There are some among you, I know, who will think I speak extravagantly, and that I ought not to have given any attention to these foul things upon which I stand. You are good people, reasonable, tolerant, just. But you are blind, in spite of this.

"There are many here who would never believe falsehood, and would refuse to hate. But in the end, when hatred becomes widespread, the good are caught in the whirlwind, and they, too, are destroyed by the enemy. In truth, the good are the first victims of the enemy, for evil cannot exist in the presence of virtue.

"We are threatened, all of us, good, bad, and indifferent, by the murderers who have written and issued these pamphlets. There is not a church anywhere, a synagogue, which is not in jeopardy. There is not a man of God, a faithful man, a kind man, a man of integrity, who does not stand in dreadful danger today, this last Sunday of August, in the year of Our Lord 1913."

Again, he paused. Very slowly, and carefully, Charles turned his head and scanned the church. He saw all those faces, very clearly, now, in the brilliant light that streamed through the windows and the doors. He saw moved faces, thoughtful and concerned, faces full of sternness and disgust, dismayed faces, frightened and confused faces. He saw ashamed faces, bent aside and embarrassed, and for these he was more thankful than for all the others. And then, here and there, like sores, like spots of blight, he saw ridiculing or malevolent faces, faces full of hate, defiantly sneering.

The palm-leaf fans were held in petrified hands. No one moved. It was so quiet that everyone could hear the minister draw a long and exhausted breath.

He said: "To set a man against his neighbor, his brother, is an unpardonable thing before the face of God. The Roman Catholic Church has its list of the seven deadly sins, but the deadliest of all sins is hatred, for it not only injures the hated but it destroys the soul of the hater. It sets him apart from his God. It puts him outside the pale of humanity. It brands him with the stigmata of beasthood.

"It is not fashionable, any longer, to believe in a personal devil, just as it is becoming unfashionable in some 'advanced' quarters to smile at the idea of a personal God. But there is indeed a personal devil. Each man who hates is that personal devil. Evil has a way, in this world, of often being more powerful than good. It can reach wider, and it can strike deeper. The supreme terror, hatred, has emptied more churches, devastated more cities, murdered more multitudes, killed more innocents, and evoked more tears and mourning, than the black plague and all the plagues put together. Why this is so I do not understand completely, but I feel it is because it is an evil more intolerable to God than any other evil, and one He will never countenance or forgive. There is no mercy for it, for it is without mercy."

Slowly, he let his eyes roam over the frozen rows of the people. Sternly and accusingly, he picked out the faces that jeered at him silently and malignantly.

His voice rose higher, rang back from the walls:

"It has been suggested to me that this present wave of hatred has a design, and I am inclined to believe that all hatred is organized for a sinister and hidden purpose. The design is as yet dark to me. I pray to Almighty God that it will never be revealed to any of us, that it will fall apart impotently before its perpetrators kill us.

"Let me repeat to you the words of William Penn, the great founder of our State: 'Those people who are not governed by God will be ruled by tyrants.'

"Those who hate are not governed by God. They are in danger of tyrants, or they are the potential tyrants. The enemy of God."

Mr. Haas lifted up his hands in a gesture of simple but terrible warning:

"Those of you who are the enemy—search your hearts. And may God have mercy upon your souls before it is too late."

The choir's voice rolled out into the church, hushed and portentous. It swelled to the ceiling. Mr. Haas stood there, alone, shaken and white, but still indomitable. Then his eyes met those of Charles.

Charles did not look at his relatives. Usually, there were hushed greetings in the aisles when the services were finished, and the people left the church. But no one spoke; hardly anyone bowed. Gravely, and silently, all streamed out into the hot sunlight. Charles went down the walk with his son. Then, halfway down, he stood and waited.

Jochen was red-faced with rage. He came up to Charles and exploded loudly: "Well! Of all the outrageous performances! The minister of a church, our church! My God! There's nothing for him to do now but resign, of course—"

"Why?" asked Charles, blandly.

"Why?" cried Jochen, disbelievingly. A number of Charles' friends, knowing him as the President of the Board, were gathering about him, listening.

"I'm shocked, shocked to the heart. It was disgusting," said Isabel, putting her hand to her breast as if faint. "How dared he talk like that in a church?"

"Why?" repeated Charles.

Now he saw Friederich coming towards him, and he watched him come. Jochen was clamoring again, Isabel was incredulous, Phyllis was silent. But Charles saw only Friederich.

"So," said Friederich, significantly. All the muscles in his face were tremulous with fury. "That's your minister, is it? That's the man you helped appoint, is it?"

"Yes, 'it' is," said Charles. He kept his voice down. More and more people were gathering about the family group now. "I am proud to say he is our minister."

Jochen turned to Friederich. "He's 'proud,' he says. You heard him."

Charles looked at Friederich. "I think Mr. Haas hit home. What do you think, Fred? See, there are our friends, listening. They want to hear what you have to say."

No one spoke, not even the blustering Jochen. All looked at Friederich, and all, including the increasing group about the family, looked at him. He saw them, waiting. His eyelids began to twitch; he clenched his fists. His stare was one glaze of hatred as it fixed itself upon Charles.

"You come so seldom to this church, Fred," said Charles, after he had let Friederich's silence become significant. "We'd like your opinion. Well?"

Jochen opened his mouth. Then he closed it again.

Never had the nervous Friederich been so still. Now Charles detected fear in him, and crafty apprehension, as well as hatred. His sallow skin whitened.

Then, without a word he turned, pushed his way violently through the considerable and increasing crowd about the Wittmanns, and rapidly moved down the walk. All saw him go. People stopped everywhere to look after him, and then to look at Charles. Many joined the crowd, frowning and hesitant.

Charles saw several of the officers of the church among the men. One said, seriously: "Your brother Fred, wasn't it?"

"Yes."

Mr. Schweitzer hesitated. "Strong language, wasn't it? Right for a church sermon, Charlie?"

Charles said: "Do you think a minister shouldn't point out evil to his people, and warn them against it? Do you think he shouldn't imitate Christ?"

Mr. Snyder said, doubtfully: "Well, I don't know, Charlie. After all, maybe what was in those pamphlets is true. I don't know. Don't think I'm bigoted, Charlie. Some of my best friends—"

"Are Catholics," Charles said, quickly. He smiled. He glanced at his fellow officers. They had immense respect for him. "I think we should give him a vote of gratitude, don't you?" added Charles.

Jochen, still uneasy, still puzzled, at what had transpired between Charles and Friederich, said angrily: "I think we should ask him to resign. That performance was disgraceful."

"We go to church to hear of spiritual matters," said Isabel.

Phyllis spoke for the first time. "And evil has nothing to do with the destruction of the human spirit?" she asked gently.

Isabel glanced at her, haughtily. "I really don't understand you, Phyllis. But I hardly think this is the time or the place to discuss this very serious matter. Jochen, shall we go?"

She put her hand on Jochen's arm. He looked about him. "I'm not an officer of this church. But if that man remains here I'll go to another church, where there's some respect for—"

"For what?" asked Charles. "Respect for convention? Is our minister to stand in his pulpit and congratulate us for the 'nice' people we certainly are not? Dare he never call his soul his own, and act with his conscience, or speak the truth as he sees it? Dare he never call his people what they need to be called, or warn them? Is a minister a minister, or a panderer to our high opinion of ourselves?"

He stood there, stolid and braced, his legs apart, his face flushed and quietly aroused.

Mr. Schweitzer said: "When you put it that way, Charlie, of course—"

Mr. Snyder said: "I guess you're right, Charlie." He remembered that Charles had signed a large note for him a year ago, when his hardware business was tottering.

Jochen glared at them. They were smiling at his brother. "I leave this church," he said, sullenly.

"Good," said Charles. "Perhaps you'll be able to find a church where the minister is so afraid of his people that his church is half empty. Plenty of room to move around, Joe. No crowding in the pews. And no one, of course, of any importance."

Isabel flung up her head grandly. "You misunderstood Jochen, Charles," she said, blushing with irritation. "He is naturally perturbed."

Jochen walked away with her, muttering. Isabel's head was high.

Charles surveyed his officers. They were all small business or professional men. "If anyone wants to leave this church, that is his privilege. But news gets around in this town. And there are quite a number of Catholics here, too, and more coming all the time. It might hurt some of us if the Catholics learned we left this church, or persecuted our minister, for defending their rights as Americans."

One of the officers laughed half-heartedly. "And it might annoy our Protestant customers to find out we didn't."

Charles said: "I don't think so. You haven't much respect for your fellow Protestants when you say that, Johnnie. We aren't all liars or hypocrites or haters, you know. Some of us are quite decent people. Or don't you think so?"

"Still, I think the sermon was, well, sensational," put in Mr. Schweitzer, confused.

"Truth usually is," said Charles.

He went away with Jimmy. Jimmy said, softly: "You had a hand in that, didn't you, Dad? I saw you look at Mr. Haas."

Charles laughed a little. He began to bow to the ladies, greeted their husbands. They watched him closely. Then they were relieved. If Charles Wittmann, so dependable, so important, so respected, approved of Mr. Haas' sermon, then it followed that all respectable people should approve of it, also. Certainly, one did not wish to be classed with those whom Mr. Haas had called "outside the pale of humanity." Charles began to hear approbatory comments upon the sermon, meant for his ears.

Very simple people, he thought. Most of us mean well. Very few of us rascals. It only needs a man like Haas to show us the way. But how many are there, like him? Men who are not afraid of their Boards, and the women?

He said to Jimmy: "Don't let your imagination run away with you,

son. Perhaps Mr. Haas just decided to have a little courage, that's all."
He added: "Not even the haters will leave the church. It would make
them so conspicuous. And besides, it's Andersburg's 'society' church!"

CHAPTER XX

WHEN CHARLES and Jimmy reached the curb they saw Wilhelm Wittmann's carriage drawing up. Charles had forgotten Phyllis, but now he
turned to look for her. She was approaching with a lady whom Charles
immediately recognized as Mrs. Braydon Holt, who had sat beside
him at Wilhelm's dinner.

She waved her shut parasol at him, and cried out, loudly: "You,
Charlie Wittmann! Don't you dare run away!"

The many people still lingering turned immediately to look at Mrs.
Braydon Holt with surprise and respect. They had not noticed her
before; she was not a member of this church. In fact, this short, fat
lady in her late forties did not belong to any church at all. This had
always seemed rather "irregular" and baffling, for not only was Mr.
Braydon Holt the wealthiest man in Andersburg, but his wife was the
acknowledged social leader. In a woman less prominent, this would
have invited open censure. But Mrs. Holt was only called "independent" or "peculiar in her ways," and always in a tone of servility. Mr.
Holt, who was not active in business, owned many oil fields in Pennsylvania, and collected modern statuary.

Isabel Wittmann might often suavely boast of her "friendship" with
Mrs. Holt, on the slight basis of having met her once at Wilhelm's
home, and having encountered her once more in a shop. But she was
Phyllis' friend, and Wilhelm's. This, Charles knew. Mrs. Holt had
never concealed her liking for him, either, when she had seen him on
a few occasions, but he had never had "much use" for her husband
who, at fifty-five, ought, Charles believed, to be "doing something useful besides filling his house with chunks of silly stone." Consequently,
he had gone but once to the Holt house, and had been bored to actual
slumber in his chair.

However, he liked Mrs. Holt, though she had a loud, hearty voice,
and, perhaps, in a way, because of it. There was something so direct
about her, so without hypocrisy, even if she shouted when she laughed.
Seeing her now, he liked her more than ever. Her big face was scarlet

under the brim of her wide straw hat, which was laden with bunches of green leaves and stuffed birds. She was proud of having no taste, and her buff-colored linen suit was entirely too small for her figure, which made up in width what it lacked in height. Her light-brown hair was untidily and unsteadily arranged by a series of very visible black hairpins, and blew out in whiffs under her hat. She tried to control them, as she rolled rapidly towards Charles, and the glove on her hand was conspicuously soiled. Her black buttoned boots, out of keeping with her skirts, had scuffed toes. But she had clear blue eyes, round and sharp, a fetching retroussé nose, and a big mouth full of remarkably excellent teeth.

Phyllis could hardly keep up with her, and so she was breathless when she said to Charles: "Minnie came to church with me—"

"Heard it was going to be something worthwhile!" exclaimed Mrs. Holt, unconscious of or indifferent to the stares behind and around her. "How are you, Charlie, you rascal?" And she held out her hand, which he shook heartily. "Your boy?"

"Yes. Jimmy. This is Mrs. Holt, son."

Jimmy bowed gravely while Mrs. Holt gave him a critical scrutiny. "Nice, well-set-up boy," she finally announced. "Doesn't look as if he'd cause you much trouble. Young people usually do, these days, you know. I mean, cause their parents trouble." But she gave the boy a kind smile, and turned briskly to Charles.

"I didn't see you in our pew," said Charles.

She laughed, poked his arm with the handle of her parasol. People were drifting unobtrusively nearer, in order to catch the conversation. Charles was embarrassed; he hated to be overheard. Mrs. Holt went on: "Saw there wasn't going to be any room. Besides, was afraid that other sister-in-law of yours would start exercising her graces on me. Bores me to death, that woman."

Charles was more and more embarrassed, especially when he saw distant, furtive smiles. He cleared his throat, glanced at Phyllis, who said, quickly: "Minnie wasn't at all disappointed in Mr. Haas' sermon. She—"

"Wonderful! Wonderful!" cried Mrs. Holt, with noisy enthusiasm. "Never thought the man had it in him. Always tried to avoid him when I could. Sleek and bland, like a fat, friendly cat. I take it all back now, though. I'd like to tell him what I thought about his sermon. Courageous. Things like that. Honest. Yes, I'd like to tell him—"

"Why don't you, Mrs. Holt?" asked Charles, forgetting the eavesdroppers.

"Eh?" she said, blankly.

"Write him. Or call him on the telephone. Or go to see him, and tell him to his face," said Charles. "Ministers get plenty of criticism, but little praise. He did a—a fine thing, and he ought to be told, especially by people like you, Mrs. Holt."

She pushed out her lips, and frowned thoughtfully. "If I do that, first thing you know he'll be after us to join his church." She shook her head.

"And what would be wrong with that?" asked Charles, smiling.

"Well, I was christened a Presbyterian, for one thing." She shook her head again. "I don't go to church. I never go. You know. Dull, and all that."

"You didn't find it dull, today?"

"Certainly not! Didn't I tell you it was wonderful?"

"Well, Mrs. Holt, if Mr. Haas had people like you in our church, and if he knew he had your support, his sermons might always be 'wonderful.' "

She grinned at him, craftily. "Oh, I know you, Charlie Wittmann." Then she became serious. "In a way, I suppose you're right. Ministers are usually scared to death of their congregations. Must just flatter them, or bore them politely, and never, never make them think or it'll get them mad and they'll be out looking for a new church sooner than you could say Jack Robinson."

She spoke contemptuously in her loud, coarse voice, yet Charles knew there was no real coarseness in her, as there was in Isabel.

"Our ministers would be the honest and militant men most of them are at heart, if we'd just support them and encourage them to speak the truth," said Charles. "Mrs. Holt, you'll call Mr. Haas? Or you'll write him? Or better still, you'll send an open letter to the *Clarion*, expressing your approval?"

She laughed at him, cunningly. "I see," she said. Her grin was wider. "Charlie, you never come to our house, do you?"

She laughed again, and again poked him with her parasol.

But Charles saw she was thinking, and that she was genuinely moved and enthusiastic.

"I'll tell you what, Charlie, I'll write to the *Clarion* about this sermon. Grimsley's a friend of ours. And I'll call your Mr. Haas, and I'll send him a check for a fund, or something. Churches always have 'funds,' don't they? Bottomless needs for funds?"

"Yes, they do," said Charles. The crease of excitement was deepening in his forehead. "See here, Mrs. Holt, you don't have to join our church

if you don't want to. But how about coming to services a few times
a year?"

"You mean, show myself here?"

Charles wished she had not been quite so blunt. The eavesdroppers
had dropped all pretense of being uninterested, and were listening with
frank eagerness. Charles coughed. Phyllis said, gently: "Charles and I
would love to have you with us, Minnie, whenever you'd care to come,
as you came today. That's what he means. We are so fond of you, you
know."

Mrs. Holt now became aware of her audience. She frowned at them,
then suddenly said, more loudly than ever: "I'll certainly come, and
often, if your minister's congregation shows its appreciation of him as
a wise and courageous and decent man! A church like that would get
all my support, whether or not I joined it. I don't suppose there's
another church in this whole town that has a minister like yours!"

"We think so, too," said Phyllis.

"Yes, indeed," said Charles, happily.

He helped the two ladies into the carriage. Mrs. Holt leaned out:
"I'm giving a party week from next Wednesday, Charlie. You be there
now, mind."

"With pleasure," said Charles.

Phyllis, smiling, spoke hurriedly: "I almost forgot, Charles. I had a
telegram from Wilhelm this morning. Will you be home this evening,
after eight? Wilhelm has a painting of Picasso's and he is so excited
over it that he wants to bring it to you at once, instead of waiting for
your birthday."

"What? What?" demanded Mrs. Holt, horrified. "Is Charlie going
in for Impressionism? No!"

"Yes," said Charles. He smiled. "In a way, I suppose you could
call it."

She stared at him with affront. Then all at once she began to smile.
She finally chuckled. "Well, well. But Phyllis, you'd better call Charlie
up ahead of time and give him a little information about Picasso, don't
you think?"

"I intend to do so," said Phyllis, demurely. "In about an hour,
Charles?"

He waved his hat to them as the carriage drove away. In high satisfaction, he walked on with Jimmy.

"Women are wonderful people, son," he remarked. "Really wonderful. They're so damned subtle. We'd still be in caves if it weren't for
them."

Charles was hardly home when his telephone began to ring furiously. Jochen's voice roared into his ear: "I still insist that man should resign, Charlie! Why, what the hell—"

"Why don't *you*?" asked Charles, calmly. "Willie and I would keep the pew. Then Mr. and Mrs. Holt could use it, with us, unless they want a pew of their own."

"What's that?" Jochen was staggered. "What's this about the Holts?"

"Why don't you wait and read the *Clarion* in a day or so? Mrs. Holt was at church, this morning."

"You don't mean she was actually there?" Jochen shouted. "This morning? Speak louder, Charlie, I can't hear you when you mumble like that. I don't believe it!"

"You don't have to. You can just read the *Clarion*. But think it over about leaving the church. We'd like to have the Holts share our pew with us. Let me know tomorrow, will you?" And Charles gently replaced the receiver, leaving Jochen stunned at the other end.

"Yes, yes," said Charles, as he went into the dining room with Jimmy. "All in all, this has been a most satisfactory day."

In a happier state of mind than had been usual with him lately, Charles ate a fine dinner. Just as he was drinking his coffee, Mrs. Meyers announced that Mr. Friederich was on the telephone. Becoming tight-lipped again, Charles answered the call.

Friederich spoke quietly enough, but it was in such a tense voice that Charles guessed that his brother was deeply hysterical with rage. He also spoke in German.

"Karl, I am writing a letter to the *Clarion*. I saw one of their reporters there. I am denouncing Haas, and upholding the information in those pamphlets he had the audacity and impudence to stamp upon. I am giving further information."

Charles gripped the telephone stand, but he answered calmly, in English: "I wouldn't, Fred. I really wouldn't. We have Catholic workmen; only a few, but they are among our best. The company union doesn't believe in religious intolerance. There might be a strike. But even more important is that the Pfeifer Manufacturing Company of Pittsburgh is one of our best customers, and Mr. Pfeifer is a Catholic." Charles had no such information as to the religious persuasion of Mr. Pfeifer, but he knew that Friederich would not doubt his word. "Mr. Pfeifer also has influence among others of our customers, too."

Friederich was silent. Charles could feel his rage, however.

"Of course," said Charles, "I never want to interfere with a man's profound convictions." He paused. "Especially not when the trifling matter of money is concerned."

Charles withdrew his ear quickly when he heard the crash of Friederich's receiver being replaced. His ear hummed. But he smiled again.

CHAPTER XXI

PHYLLIS CALLED a short time later, just as Charles was preparing for his Sunday afternoon nap. She said, softly: "Oh, Charles. Good. Good. So many people have called me, very approvingly, and just very slightly interested in the 'rumor' that Mrs. Holt was at our church today, and is going to send Mr. Haas a check, and a letter to the *Clarion!*"

The sound of her voice struck him to the heart with a sensation of warmth and tenderness. They laughed a little together, with a mixture of kindness and tolerant malice.

Then Phyllis said: "I'll give you the information about Picasso, now. Do you know anything at all about Picasso?"

"Nothing, except that I remember seeing one or two small canvases which Wilhelm has. A lot of cubes, and color, I think. Confusing. Well, tell me."

"He's still alive. He was born in 1881, in Malaga, Spain. He is interested in painting images, rather than 'appearances,' in contrast with the Impressionist school."

"My God, Phyllis, what does that mean?" Charles was alarmed.

"You just need to remember 'images' as opposed to 'appearances,' Charles." Phyllis laughed.

"What's the difference?"

"That, my dear Charles, would require quite a lecture. You might mention 'music' with regard to Picasso's work. Wilhelm is always saying that Picasso produces visible music." She went on, almost pleadingly: "Wilhelm's telegram sounded so excited."

"But, Phyllis. All those images and appearances, and music!"

"Just quote back what he's already said to you about Picasso. Tonight, then, after eight?"

What I do for the damned company! thought Charles, getting into bed. Smoothing down idiots like Joe, threatening idealists like Fred with loss of revenue, learning infernal terms like "images" and "appearances" and "music," for the benefit of Willie.

Then he remembered that he ought to call Mr. Haas. He tramped downstairs again in his worn brown bathrobe and slippers. But Mr. Haas' telephone was constantly busy. Charles called and called for at least fifteen minutes before he was able to get a clear line. Mr. Haas sounded exhausted, almost feverish.

"Charles, you have no idea! The calls that I have been getting for two hours. Everyone has been so kind, so approving, so laudatory. I'd never have believed it. And Mrs. Holt called me. She said she was also writing me, and writing the *Clarion,* and that she was sending me a check to express her approval."

Charles, though pleased, was also intensely ashamed. It was a terrible commentary upon mankind that when a man does his duty it always creates a furor, and that if a minister performs his function as a minister, in its widest sense, all sorts of chicanery and cheapness have to be resorted to to save him from the wrath of his own flock.

He congratulated Mr. Haas, and recommended that the minister rest. Tomorrow, he reminded Mr. Haas, the Haas family was to go to Philadelphia for a long-delayed holiday. Mr. Haas sighed. "And I'm glad that Mr. Zimmermann is taking over the services tonight," he said. "I'm afraid I wouldn't have the strength for it. By the way, Charles, Mr. George Hadden is here with me. He came personally, to give me his congratulation, though, of course, he isn't a member of our congregation."

"Hadden, of the sheet metal works?" Charles was interested.

"Yes. He is a Quaker, you know."

Charles remembered George Hadden, who was also one of his minor customers, a young man who had only recently inherited his father's business. He was a tall and slender and dignified man of about thirty, quiet and reserved, seldom seen about at any social events. "I didn't know he was a Quaker," said Charles. Something was stirring vaguely in his mind.

"He is, indeed. And everyone knows what splendid people the Friends are, Charles. I am very happy."

It was strange that Charles, though content, was unable to rest when he was in his bed in his darkened bedroom. The room was hot, for all the heavy pattern of leaves on the drawn blind. From time to time there was a dull rumble of distant thunder in the air, even if the sun was still bright outside. This was the only sound, however, except for the shrill of the cicadas in the trees. Charles tried to keep his eyes shut, and tried to relax, but he found himself staring at the dark and enormous shapes of his mahogany furniture. They seemed to lurk in the room, ominously, no longer friendly as usual.

Now his contentment was gone. The oppressiveness of the atmosphere began to smother him. His disquiet returned, though without form. It's the thunder, just over the mountain, he thought. The cicadas shrilled louder. The leaf-patterns hardly stirred on the blinds. Then Charles heard the voices of his son and Geraldine Wittmann in the breathless air.

Charles began to speculate upon the children. Their voices soothed him. What did they talk about, these eager and earnest young people? Charles got up, in his nightshirt, left his room, tiptoed into the back bedroom, which was Jimmy's. The room blazed with light, and the window was open. Jimmy and Geraldine were below, under the trees. Jimmy was stretched in the hammock, and Geraldine sat in the grass beside him.

"There never was anybody like Dad," Jimmy was saying, with pride. He was eating a peach, and his words were a little muffled.

"My father's really a darling, too," said Geraldine, slowly.

Charles, peering cautiously from behind the curtain, saw Jimmy give her a tolerant glance. "Oh, yes, naturally."

The two were silent for a few moments. Geraldine did not look particularly happy. Her young, dark face was somewhat grave. Her hands were locked together on her thin knees; her white lawn dress was somewhat rumpled, and her black hair streamed down her back. "I don't think people differ very much," she said, thoughtfully. "They just have different opinions. At the bottom, they are the same."

Jimmy was annoyed. "I don't know about that," he said. "How do people get different opinions? By being different, that's why."

"But difference comes from wants. Your father wants something, Jimmy, and mine wants something else. They both want, however."

"You think if people all wanted the same thing, at the same time, they'd be the same people?"

"Of course, Jimmy."

He fished a peach from some recess behind him, and Geraldine accepted it. They munched together. Jimmy rocked slowly in his hammock. Peach juice ran down the girl's chin. She sighed, "It's so hot," she said. "It feels as if something is threatening, doesn't it?"

Jimmy nodded. Now he was frowning. "Something in the air," he said.

Charles withdrew. He went back to his sweltering bedroom, but not to his bed. He sat in a plush chair and lit a cigar, but did not roll up the blind. Threatening. It was not only the August heat. The smoke curled sluggishly in the gloom. Charles sat very still, listening to the thunder which never retreated, never came nearer. Perhaps it'll stay that way, thought Charles.

Mrs. Meyers did not remain for Sunday supper, though she always laid it out on the dining-room table: slices of roast pork, beef, ham, sausage, and potato salad and rolls wrapped in a white cloth, and a covered cake. Jimmy made coffee for himself and Geraldine. Waiting at the table, Charles could hear their young laughter in the kitchen. Jimmy brought in a glass of very cold beer for his father. He gave Charles a quick and unobtrusive look.

"Couldn't sleep very well today, eh, Dad?"

"I slept very well," said Charles. He stretched out his hand to Geraldine, who sat beside him, and he stroked her long hair affectionately. "You are a sweet child," he said.

"She's terrible," said Jimmy, comfortably. He glanced at his cousin with superior fondness. "She never combs her hair."

He and Geraldine cleared the table, while Charles went into the parlor. He could hear the voices of his neighbors, low and decorous, from adjoining verandahs. He was not in the mood for exchanging any comments with them. A little later, his son and Geraldine entered.

"Do you mind if we close the windows and play the gramophone?" asked Jimmy. "So our neighbors won't be horrified by hearing music on Sunday?"

Charles smiled his assent. The presence of the young people comforted him. Jimmy was fond of classical music; Charles thought it would be a small price to pay for being with his son and niece. But Jimmy put on some very lively and noisy records, and the sound seemed to jump wildly all over the room. Jimmy held out his arms to Geraldine, and the two began to skip convulsively up and down over the carpet, giving a small leap from time to time. Charles watched, much amazed. He thought the dancing very irregular; the boy and girl were clutched together, Jimmy's face in Geraldine's floating hair. He also thought it very ugly and very funny and touchingly innocent. They were so grave and so absorbed of face, while their young legs performed the most amazing and rapid feats.

"What on earth," Charles murmured, when they stopped in the midst of one convulsion to change the record.

"It's the bunny hug," Jimmy informed him. "I'm teaching it to Gerry. She's doing very well," he added, patronizingly. "Of course, it looks awful to you, Dad. You're of the old waltz school."

"You make me sound doddering," said Charles. He stood up. "I think I can do as well as you, Jimmy." And he held out his hand to Geraldine. The boy and girl flashed an amused smile at each other. The music, if it could be called that, screamed out shrilly and with a maddening rhythm. "I've heard ragtime before," said Charles. "Come on, Gerry."

Geraldine tried to dance slowly, with deference for her uncle's great age, but Charles, as if possessed, pulled and pushed her madly up and down the room. Jimmy watched, aghast. Once he called out, feebly: "Your blood pressure, Dad—" But Charles leapt about and Geraldine, breathless, could hardly keep up with him.

The music crashed to a violent stop. Charles, laughing, stood and mopped his wet and scarlet face. Geraldine was quite disheveled, her white dress twisted on her slight body, her black silk stockings wrinkled. Her hair had partially fallen over her face, and she put up her hands to tuck it back under her blue ribbon.

Jimmy began to wind up the gramophone. But he was very anxious. "Uncle Charlie's wonderful," said Geraldine, catching her breath. "He did it better than you, Jimmy."

Charles' heart was pounding, but he felt exhilarated. "I ought to get about and do more of this," he said, trying not to gasp. "You aren't the only young man in the family, Jim."

They were now both looking at him with apprehension. But he laughed, and sat down. He gathered that Jimmy was not only anxious about him, but that he had thought his father's dancing a trifle unseemly. Conservative, remarked Charles to himself, amused. Why do older people always think the young are empty-headed and irresponsible?

"Do you want some more nice, cold beer, or lemonade?" asked Jimmy, tentatively. "Cool you off?"

"I want some nice Scotch," said Charles. "Bring me my bottle, Jim, and a glass of water, too."

Together, the two went out, trying to hide their disapproval of this extraordinary conduct. They came back into the room with Charles' bottle of Scotch and a glass of water. They were more disapproving than ever, and suspicious. Charles loved them. He filled his glass once; then, when it was half empty, he poured more whiskey into it. They still stood there, reproachful, and remote, and watched him.

Geraldine was about to leave when Wilhelm's carriage drove up, and Wilhelm and Phyllis came up the stairs of the verandah. Jimmy ran to open the door for them. He liked his uncle, and had much affection for Phyllis.

Wilhelm, elegant in his black, his air of reserve hardly hiding his excitement, came in carrying a small canvas wrapped in paper. Charles was struck again by the resemblance between Geraldine and Wilhelm. In order to relieve the girl of her shyness in Wilhelm's presence, he said: "Wilhelm, have you ever noticed how much Gerry looks like you? Extraordinary."

"No, I never did," Wilhelm tried for impatience. But he looked with interest at Geraldine, who was flushing. Phyllis said, kindly: "But the darling really does, Wilhelm." She put her arm about the girl. "Look at those eyes, the shape of her face, her nose, her mouth. You might be her father."

"I might. But I'm not," said Wilhelm, smiling a little. He was flattered. He thought that Geraldine was quite pretty. Graciously, he said: "Geraldine's the beauty of her family."

Geraldine blushed very brightly. "Oh, thank you, Uncle Willie, but I'm not really. May and Ethel are so pretty, just like Mama."

"I think they are very coarse-looking girls," said Wilhelm, with calm brutality. "And very ordinary. I'd never be able to pick them out of a dozen other girls; they all look alike. Now you, my dear, have an air."

Geraldine, quite overcome, took her departure. Jimmy went with her, to see her home. Wilhelm was relieved. Phyllis sat down near Charles, but Wilhelm stood in the center of the room, the flat package in his arms. Then he was dissatisfied. "A little light, please," he said.

Charles got up and lit the glass chandelier. He opened the windows; the cool evening air came in. Wilhelm was now unwrapping the canvas. Then, after a slightly dramatic pause, he showed the canvas to Charles. "For your birthday, Charles," he said. "I know it isn't until next month, but I wanted you to enjoy it sooner."

Charles was very touched, but he was also dismayed. The canvas appeared to him to be only a mass of browns and grays, with faint flecks and colors here and there, and only a vague geometrical outline or two. He wondered if he were holding the thing rightside up or not. Now where, in the name of God, would he hang it? But worst of all, what should he say? He could feel Wilhelm, smiling slightly and proudly, waiting for his comment. Then he heard himself muttering: "Ah, yes. More image than appearance. Music—"

Wilhelm, gratified and amazed, said: "Exactly! You've caught the spirit, the very essence of the meaning, and at once. Astounding. You see, Phyllis, sometimes the amateur mind is quicker to grasp essential significance and value in art than the trained one." He lit one of his eternal cigarettes, snapping shut his gold case with a sharp sound. "Charles, frankly, I should never have expected it of you."

I should never have expected it of myself, thought Charles, ruefully. He looked up. Wilhelm was sitting near him, smiling. Charles caught Phyllis' eye. Together, then, they regarded Wilhelm with a sudden and very tender affection, in which there was no feeling of disloyalty or betrayal.

Then Charles made a decision. He said: "Wilhelm, I've got to be fair with you. I don't know a thing about any of—this. Honestly."

Phyllis made a slight gesture of consternation, but Charles gave all his attention to his brother, who was taken aback. Wilhelm began to frown, and his eyes glittered at Charles.

"You see," Charles went on, resolutely, "I just—looked—it all up. About this art business. I know nothing more about it than a—well, a baby."

"Then," said Wilhelm, mortified and angered, "where did you pick up all those learned phrases of yours?"

"I told you—I looked it up."

Wilhelm's thin cheeks tightened. "You've been making a fool of me, I see."

"No. No. Believe me, I haven't." Charles hesitated. "Try to understand, please. I've not had your education, your taste. I know nothing very much about anything, except the business. I've had to devote all my time to it, and it's my life."

Wilhelm was silent. He crossed his long legs; he looked at the tip of his cigarette. Charles gripped the canvas, and leaned towards his brother. Phyllis folded and unfolded her handkerchief in her hands, wretchedly.

"Wilhelm, have I ever played the hypocrite with you?" asked Charles, earnestly.

Wilhelm's face changed. "Of course," he said, coldly. "Many a time."

Charles was, himself, taken aback. Then he saw the slightest and thinnest of smiles on his brother's mouth. Charles laughed weakly.

"But only for the sake of all of us, the company."

"Ah, yes, the company, the sacred company." Wilhelm watched a spiral of smoke rise as it left his lips. It was clear that his hurt was not superficial. "And what would any of us have done without the company? I suppose we must remember that, and remember that you deserve our gratitude." He looked at Charles then, and it was an odd look, and whatever it expressed it was not displeasure or outrage. "I'm trying to be very infuriated with you, Charles, but it seems I cannot."

Charles said: "Thank you, Willie." He tried to catch back the nickname before he said it, but it escaped him. Charles went on: "I am not being a hypocrite when I say that I've lately come to realize how little I know, how narrow my life has become, how restricted and circumscribed. Try to believe me when I tell you that I want to know other things, too. A narrow life leads to narrow thinking. I want to know something about the things you know. And I want you to believe that."

"I believe it," said Wilhelm, very quietly.

Charles laid the canvas on his knees, and spread his hands over it. Wilhelm saw that unconscious gesture. Now, he was touched.

"Charles, you've had a narrow life because it has been too busy a one. You've had to shut yourself away from everything else, so you could keep the company together. Not only because it was our father's company, and not only because you are the president. There are three of us, besides you. Jochen, who is an expedient brute, who would destroy everything for a sudden quick gain, and has no honor; Friederich who is a maniac and an idler, and I—"

He paused, and regarded Charles again with that odd look. "And I, who would not have my art gallery, but for you, or my leisure, or my pleasures. We're not worth your sacrifices, you know—Charles."

Charles was embarrassed. "I've not been sacrificing very much. Don't light up the altars for me, Wilhelm. I've been fulfilling myself in a way. But I see it is a narrow way. In many ways, I'm afraid I'm quite stupid. If I had broadened my life a little, I might not now—"

"Not—what?" asked Wilhelm. His voice was even gentle.

Charles sighed. "It's hard for me to explain. And perhaps I couldn't ever have done much, anyway. But at least I could have seen. It is terrible to be blind. It's, well, it's unpardonable to be blind."

Wilhelm considered this with great concentration. He was a very subtle man. He began to frown again. "I see. I suppose what happened today in our church is part of what you mean. Phyllis told me."

"And—?"

But Wilhelm did not reply immediately. His old expression of impatience and dissatisfaction returned. "I can forgive almost anything but bad taste," he said at last. "A church is hardly the proper place to deliver a diatribe on intolerance."

"Bad taste?" Charles was aroused. "I don't understand. Where, but in a church, is the 'proper place' to attack evils?" Again, he leaned towards his brother. "Wilhelm, I've not only been thinking about art, and all the others things I never knew. I've been reading some of our father's books. And last night I read something which Isocrates said: 'The only sound basis for a nation's prosperity is a religious regard for the rights of others.'"

Wilhelm quickly turned his head and studied him. But he was still impatient. "Perhaps, perhaps. I grant you that your premises are right. Nevertheless, I still think it was in bad taste. I might even be wrong, but there it is. And you were always so circumspect, Charles. I find it hard to believe that you have lent yourself to all this."

"'Lent myself to all this?'" said Charles.

Wilhelm smiled. "Yes. Of course you did. You see, Charles, you never really ever deceived me. During your machinations I was usually taken in by you; I saw the whole pattern later. Very deft. But I could always depend on you to be circumspect, and so I can't understand what happened today."

He stood up, restlessly. "Bad taste," he repeated. "One expects different things of modern churches. Certainly not hectic denunications. Noise. Uproar. Dissension. Upsetting people." He added, discontentedly, and as if personally affronted: "A gentleman tries to avoid controversies. They draw uncouth elements too close to one. The gross, the brutish, the barbarous. Who wishes to acknowledge the existence of such people?"

"They exist. And they are dangerous," said Charles, with strong resolution. "I have found that out, Wilhelm. And they're active; they're being conditioned, being led, for a purpose."

Wilhelm shrugged. "This is very wild talk, Charles, and I am surprised at you. I can only hope that Mr. Haas will return to his former discretion."

"And I hope he will never return to it." Charles stood up. He placed the canvas on his chair, and faced his brother. "Wilhelm, I pray you are right. But I know you are wrong."

Wilhelm scrutinized him, his volatile eyes very penetrating. "Yes, I see you have been aroused out of your rut, haven't you, Charles? But be cautious about it, if only for your own sake."

"Have you ever thought much about Fred?" asked Charles, suddenly.

Distaste flattened Wilhelm's lips. "Friederich? Frankly, no. I dislike thinking about him immensely. He is revolting."

"You've never listened to him? You know nothing of his kind?"

"I don't understand you."

"His kind, I think, is behind what is about to happen to the world, unless enough people can be awakened."

"Friederich? With his Socialism and frenetic ideas?" Wilhelm laughed.

"I mean his kind of mind. They've established contact again, his brand of people. They establish contact every so often, in the history of the world, and then there is a catastrophe."

"Good heavens," murmured Wilhelm. He tried for a light tone of amusement. "You really believe that, don't you, Charlie?"

"Yes," said Charles. "I've been reading history, lately."

"Granting, as I do not, that 'something' is going to happen, what do you think it is?"

Charles hesitated. He looked at Phyllis. "War," he said. And added: "I think."

Now Wilhelm was astounded. "War! You must be out of your mind, Charles!" But Charles did not answer. "Good heavens, Charles, why should there be war? With whom?"

Charles knew that anything he said would only sound ridiculous. However, he said: "I can't tell you everything. Most of what I know is a sort of feeling—But I can tell you this: If there is a war it might precipitate another opportunity for the little minds, a terrible opportunity."

Wilhelm bit his lip. His eyes sparkled with exasperation. "I refuse to talk nonsense with you any longer, Charles. Shall we forget all this?" He picked up the canvas. He affected to become suddenly engrossed in it. He was very disturbed. He looked from the canvas to the wall, then back again, then once again at the wall.

"Now where, among all those monstrosities of stags at bay and garden paths and fountains and etchings of horrible old ruins, are you going to hang my Picasso?" he demanded.

Charles, at first inclined to rage at this peremptory dismissal of what was so frightful to him, now felt his rage die away in his pity for his brother who hated all unpleasantnesses as he hated disease and foulnesses of every kind.

"Over the fireplace," Wilhelm decided at last. "Now, if you'll be so kind as to get me a hammer, Charles."

He fussed a great deal in hanging the canvas with Charles' help. Then he stood back to give it his critical consideration. He shook his head. "Appalling, in these surroundings," he murmured.

Charles silently agreed.

"Blasphemous," said Wilhelm, mournfully. "I wonder what Picasso would think if he could see this work of his among so much sheer trash, so many horrors." He turned to Charles briskly. "You'll simply have to take down those alleged pictures, Charles, or I'll shudder every time I come into this room."

Now Charles saw more clearly than before that his brother was enormously troubled. Wilhelm, too, had much instinct. He wanted to be reassured.

Charles tried to smile.

"I promise you that I'll take down these pictures myself, tomorrow," he said.

Wilhelm's relief was all out of proportion.

"Good!" he exclaimed. He was like a child in his pleasure. "And now, if you'll sit down, Charles, I'll tell you something about Picasso." He smiled. "And a little, perhaps, about Monet, whom you claimed to admire so much."

CHAPTER XXII

THE *Clarion* carried a full account of Mr. Haas' sermon. Mr. Grimsley, the editor, had also written an editorial in his own most pungent and bitter style, and he used all the telling adjectives he could think of during the writing. The editorial was headed: "The Secret Brotherhood."

"It was always from this band that have come the murderers of all the saints and the heroes and the martyrs," the editorial said. "They are born and born again, in every century, and too often, for the peace of the world, they get together, find each other, know each other. They are the Devil's legions, and they have their passwords, their banners and their hidden signals. They are men of all nations.

"There is one way the civilized man can know them, and that is by their hatred. The man who hates other men, the man who is malignant, the man who lies—mark him down. He is one of the secret brotherhood."

Jochen Wittmann made no comment upon this to Charles, on Tuesday. He merely looked sullen and haughty, and kept out of Charles' way.

At four o'clock Monday afternoon, Mr. Parker informed Charles that a gentleman wished to speak to him on the telephone. He had refused to give his name, but he sounded very urgent. Charles impatiently agreed to answer the call. "Who is it?" he demanded.

A young man's voice, subdued and hesitant, came to him: "Father Hagerty, Mr. Wittmann. Is it possible to speak to you without—"

"Yes, of course." Charles nodded to Mr. Parker, who went out of the room and shut the door silently behind him. "Yes, Father Hagerty?" said Charles, in a lower tone.

"I want to thank you, Mr. Wittmann. I tried to reach Mr. Haas but was informed he was not in the city."

"No. He left for Philadelphia."

The priest's voice was clearer, now. "Mr. Wittmann, I have not mentioned it to anyone, nor indeed, did you actually tell me, yourself. But it is known, apparently, that you had asked Mr. Haas to deliver that sermon."

His teeth clenched, Charles looked at the heap of anonymous letters on his desk. He said: "No one knew, actually. But these people have a way of finding things out. They are much subtler than we are. I think there is something in the Bible about the children of darkness being wiser in their generation than the children of light. Isn't there?"

"Yes." The priest paused; now his voice took on a note of distress. "I still wonder if it was wise. Minorities, everywhere, have found that it only increases enmity and hatred for them when they are defended so openly—no matter how nobly, either. You see, I've had my windows broken again, the windows of my front room." He tried to laugh.

"That's nothing." Charles tried to sound cheery. "You received my check for the church window, didn't you? No, no, don't thank me. Just have your parlor windows repaired and send me the bill. By the way, the window at the *Clarion* was broken this afternoon, too. Mr. Grimsley called me half an hour ago. He thinks it very amusing. He is going to make quite a story of it. And Mr. Haas' housekeeper has reported to me, as the President of the Board, that two of Mr. Haas' windows were broken this morning. We're smoking them out, Father Hagerty. This will arouse the decent people in the city."

The priest said: "Perhaps. I don't know, Mr. Wittmann. I don't know what my bishop will say when I write him my report, as I shall have to do."

Charles laughed. "Your most reverend bishop, Father Hagerty, does not control me, nor does he control Mr. Haas, or Mr. Grimsley. Give the bishop my most respectful regards and tell him that we three are going to stop this thing, if it is at all possible to stop it."

Now Father Hagerty laughed. His voice became younger, and livelier. "I shall tell him that, you can be sure! But he is certain to wonder what it is all about—this window-breaking, and all this animosity, in Andersburg." He added: "After all, people are not generally so ugly, Mr. Wittmann."

"How old is your bishop, Father Hagerty?"

The priest was surprised. "I think he is about sixty, Mr. Wittmann."

Charles smiled. "Then he won't 'wonder.' A man of sixty knows that quite a large portion of the human race is detestable. Only young men like you are under the delusion that people are intrinsically 'good.' "

"But they are, sir. The others are only misguided."

"I think your bishop might not agree with you."

Then it was evident that the young man was embarrassed. "I ought not to be taking up your time like this, Mr. Wittmann, but as I said, it is being rumored about that you had a great deal to do with the sermon and that editorial, even though your name was never mentioned. Some of my parishioners have called to ask me if you were about to enter the Church. These are simple and harmless people. But a few who are not simple and harmless—and they know you—are telling me strongly that what you have done, and your motives, are open to question. They tell me that you are 'using' the Church for your own gain, whatever that might be. I am informing you of this now so that if you hear malevolent rumors spread by any Catholics you will be not too indignant. After all, human beings are—"

"So damned human," interrupted Charles. "No, I won't be indignant. I know people."

A few minutes later Charles went into Jochen's office. Jochen looked up at him with sultry surprise. "Well?" he said.

But Charles stood and studied him with long penetration. Jochen glared at him. However, there was nothing furtive in that glare. No, thought Charles, it wasn't Joe.

"Joe," said Charles, "when I saw Mrs. Holt on Sunday she asked me if you and Isabel would care to have dinner at her home a week from Wednesday." God help me, he added to himself, if old Minnie refuses!

Jochen's face cleared astonishingly. He looked at Charles with an expression of amazed delight. "She did? Well, why hasn't she asked us, herself?"

Charles put a note of irritation in his voice: "How the hell should I know? Do I keep a record of your social affairs? Maybe she was just sounding me out, or something."

Jochen sat back in his chair, importantly. "Well, of course, our calendar is usually filled, so perhaps it is understandable. Do you think I should call her, or have Isabel call her?"

With alarm, Charles said: "No. You are right, Joe. I told her that I wouldn't relay the message, so she'll probably write, or call Isabel very soon."

He went back to his office, cursing himself. What had made him say all that to Joe? There was no necessity. But he had acted on his instinct. He immediately called Mrs. Holt, and after an interminable parley with servants Mrs. Holt came briskly to the telephone. "Charlie? Now don't tell me you aren't coming to my party, or I'll stop that check I sent to Mr. Haas! And I wrote those letters you told me to write, and I do think—"

"Mrs. Holt, I'm coming. But will you do a favor for me? Will you call my sister-in-law and ask her and my brother for dinner that night, too? I know this is irregular, and an imposition, but—"

There was a long amazed silence. Then Mrs. Holt uttered a very unladylike exclamation. Then she laughed. Finally, she said: "Up to something, Charlie? All right, I'll call Isabel. And, incidentally, while I'm speaking to her I'll tell her how much I admire your minister." She continued: "But Isabel's such a bore, and you know she is. By the way, the party is for Roger Brinkwell, who is returning to Andersburg."

"Brinkwell? Don't know him."

"Oh, Charlie," said Mrs. Holt, impatiently. "He used to live here. Of course, he is about seven years older than you, and he left Andersburg with his parents when you were six, I should think. They went to Pittsburgh. You must have heard of the Brinkwells of Pittsburgh. You haven't? You're a very ignorant man, Charlie. Roger's been with the Connington Steel ever since he left Yale. He's going to be superintendent of their new mills, here. He and his wife, Pauline, are to be our house guests beginning next Saturday, while they decide where they will live in Andersburg."

Something very vague and unpleasant stirred in Charlies' mind, but it refused to come to the surface.

Mrs. Holt went on: "Roger's wife comes of an old Main Line family in Philadelphia, Charlie. The Brighams. And so Roger and

Pauline are very aristocratic, indeed." Her voice became satirical. "Braydon has something in common with Roger. Roger collects Gobelins."

"Gobelins?"

"Charles, I'm really getting annoyed with you. Tapestries, of course. You don't know anything about tapestries?"

Charles suddenly remembered a very wet and dreary afternoon he had spent in Brussels many years ago, inspecting particularly unattractive tapestries in some castle or other.

Mrs. Holt was telling him more about the Brinkwells, of whom Charles had already formed a very low and prejudiced opinion these last few minutes. "Braydon collects modern sculpture," Mrs. Holt said, "and everybody who collects always seems to find someone else who collects, too. And they become Davids and Jonathans. You ought to collect something, Charlie."

"I've already got a Picasso," said Charles. And on this high note of mutual amusement they said their goodbyes.

Charles returned to his office. He took up the pile of foul and anonymous letters, studied them, wondered again at the perspicacity of the "brotherhood," and tore up the sheets.

Friederich would not have suggested these letters. He might be a madman, a fanatic, and a hater, but he was no coward, and he was never, unfortunately, anonymous.

Why, the damn fool's naïve, too! thought Charles, looking at the torn pile in his basket. He wondered, after thinking that, why he should feel so suddenly relieved, as if a kind of dread had subsided in him.

CHAPTER XXIII

YEARS LATER, in retrospect, it seemed to Charles Wittmann that this September of 1913 was the most beautiful month he had ever known. There was so much that troubled him then, he remembered in those later years, but it was so small in comparison with all the Septembers that followed.

The sweet softness of this September was never forgotten by him. In spite of the things that nagged at his mind, and his vague fears, he could still enjoy this month. Its blueness and greenness, its still and meditative nights, its crickets shrilling peacefully at the golden moon, its long sunlit lengths under the chestnut trees, its vivid gardens, the warmth of its noonday on old brick walls and the roofs of housetops—who could deny that September was the loveliest of months? September turned the hills to heliotrope in the evening, and the sunsets had a great and majestic calm. A faint scent of smoke trailed in the air, and a deep red fire burned in salvias before almost every verandah. The meadows dreamed, the skies were entranced, and the elms turned yellow.

Every thrifty housewife made grape jelly, and the scent of this, and the scent of tomato ketchup bubbling on stoves, became part of the scented wind in the streets. There were mornings that were cool and quiet, and misty, filled with shadowy light that had an aster-colored quality. And there were mornings that quivered with chill gold, and chestnuts fell from the trees and burst open, showing their ruddy hearts.

It was more a feeling than anything else which assured Charles that the hatefulness that had begun to flourish in Andersburg was retreating. No more windows were broken anywhere; copies of *The Menace* were almost impossible to find. Pamphlets ceased to arrive in the mails. A sudden kindness began to show itself among people who formerly had looked at each other coldly or suspiciously. When Father Hagerty modestly reported in the *Clarion* that he hoped all Catholics would respond generously to his plea for support of the new, small Sisters of Charity Hospital, he was stunned by the response. The Catholics of Andersburg were, so far, quite a small minority. They could not, of themselves, have raised such an amazing fund.

The Church Board voted Mr. Haas an increase in salary before he returned from his holiday. It also issued a letter to him expressing its gratitude for his "courage and justice."

Charles could not remember where he had once read: "One just man can save a city." He had thought it idealistic romanticism at one time. Now he was not so sure.

In this September, he could even look forward with equanimity to the dinner at the Holts' home. He remembered the last of the two dinners he had had there. Mrs. Holt had "peculiar" tastes in guests. She mingled old and young together, indiscriminately. Mr. Holt was absent-minded, concerned only with his sculpture, and tending to limit his conversation to fellow collectors of the arts. Charles suspected that Mrs. Holt, with a fine disregard for selecting congenial guests, did all the inviting. There were sure to be young ladies present, from the larger cities, who, in their great darkened eyes and tiny vicious-looking red mouths, were imitating the current, and adored, moving-picture "vampire." They had a tendency to slink, their long tight skirts slit almost to the knee; they rattled with tremendous ropes of wooden beads, of every color; their wrists jingled. Their hair was bushed out about their ears, and swarmed around their cheeks in tendrils. They were really nice girls, and so damned innocent.

There would be young men present, ostentatiously untidy, with solemn eyes, brothers, suitors, and fiancés of the girls, and they talked learnedly of Picasso and Van Gogh and Debussy, and many other things. Sometimes they would sit on the floor near the girls, and smoke cigarettes in long holders, and toss their hair artistically over their fore-heads. Charles would be bored by them, but he would look at them in a kindly way.

Charles did not like untidiness. And so, he did not like these parties. They were infernally disorganized and noisy, and everyone exhibited his ego, and it was always too hot in those gigantic rooms crowded with sculpture and modern paintings, and always too smoky, and the food was served on tables at which everyone helped himself while servants fluttered in the background. A dinner, to Charles, meant a nicely appointed and decorous table, at which everyone sat and was served. This business of everyone filling his plate, casually, and then wander-ing about all over eating messily, seemed anarchistic to Charles.

Mrs. Holt enjoyed her parties, and so left everybody alone, only swooping, occasionally, upon a group, to express her loud opinion, and then diving somewhere else. And everybody also enjoyed her parties. Except, of course, Charles.

Charles liked conversation, too, but usually about business or local events, or the iniquity of the Democrats. None of these subjects were at any time mentioned by the Holts' guests. They did not exist for them. So Charles, fortified only by the thought that Phyllis and Wil-helm would be present, expected nothing of this party but a headache from champagne, an upset stomach, and agonizing boredom. He was even more depressed, when he entered the first of the mighty and clamorous rooms, to see Jochen and Isabel at a distance. He had for-gotten they were to be here. He had arrived in a swarm of other guests, entire strangers to him. Perhaps if he just hovered in the background, he might escape meeting anybody.

But he heard a loud greeting voice over the hubbub, and there was Mrs. Holt, attired in a somewhat soiled and very elaborate white satin gown with sequins, plunging down the length of the parquetry floor, and skidding light-heartedly on an occasional and very valuable prayer-rug in her progress.

"Charlie Wittmann!" she shouted, throwing out both hands to him. Her hair was very precariously dressed; a lock of it fell on her neck, which glittered with diamonds. Ignoring the other new arrivals, she grasped Charles' hands and shook them vigorously. "Lots of your friends, here," she beamed. "But you've got to meet everybody else, too—"

"God forbid," said Charles, with fervor.

"Now, you behave. No sitting off in a corner somewhere, and brooding, the way you did last time. Charlie, why don't you buy yourself a new dinner-jacket? You've grown too fat for that one. Besides, it's green. Charlie, I love you." She put her thick arm through his and began to tug him along. "Everybody'll love you. You are such a perfect anachronism. So nineteenth century. Thank God."

This puzzled Charles, in view of Mrs. Holt's taste in parties. He tried to hold back a little. She chided him: "You're not going to be stubborn, are you? Everybody's dying to meet you."

"I doubt it," said Charles, desperately.

"Oh, come on. Don't be so mulish. Such nice people here. Just don't talk politics. We've got one of Wilson's best friends present, and he hates Republicans. There! There's Phyllis, and Wilhelm, talking to Braydon. You like them, don't you? And, oh yes, here's your friend Oliver Prescott. Oliver!" she shouted, at the back of a young man to the right. "Here's Charlie Wittmann."

Oliver Prescott turned at this thunderous summons, and another young man turned with him. With deep relief, Charles smiled at them. The second young man was George Hadden, the Quaker businessman who had been kind enough to call upon Mr. Haas, personally, to congratulate him upon his sermon.

There was something rustic about Mr. Hadden. He had the shy courtesy of the farmer, the simple reticence. Tall, almost gangling, he looked as ill at ease at this party as Charles, himself, did. His fair hair was neat and clipped very close to his head, in contrast with the long theatrical locks of the other young men present. He had a lanky face, a big nose, a very gentle mouth, and strong, quiet eyes full of kindness, and of such an intense blue that they gave the impression, at first, of being almost black.

"How are you, Oliver?" said Charles. "And you, Mr. Hadden?"

They all shook hands. Charles relaxed a little. These men were younger than himself, but he was happy with them. Though Oliver Prescott was dark and had a repressed look of swift alertness about him, there was some resemblance between him and George Hadden. Charles decided that it was the quality of integrity.

"How's the law, and the lumber business?" he asked of Oliver Prescott. "And where's Barbara?"

Oliver said: "The law's flourishing, and the lumber business is terrible, and Barbie's home with a cold."

Mr. Hadden, smiling, said: "My business is terrible, too. My wife? She's at home; just had a baby, a boy."

"I didn't know," said Charles. But he did not see Mr. Hadden often, and he had met the young man's wife only once. "Congratulations," Charles added.

Mrs. Holt was tugging again at Charles' arm. "Now, come on, and meet everybody else." Charles called over his shoulder, as he was borne along: "I'll see you again." They watched him sympathetically, and nodded.

"Everybody," as Charles suspected, did not love him. Neither did they like him or dislike him. They only paused vaguely in their conversations for the introductions, and forgot him as he was trundled off by their hostess. He forgot them, also. They were just faces.

Charles' feet began to hurt. So far, he had not been thrown into the group containing Jochen and Isabel. He did not see Phyllis and Wilhelm. He asked for them. "Oh, they've gone up to Braydon's special room, where he keeps his best pieces," said Mrs. Holt. "They'll be down immediately. Really, Charles, it's not as hot as all that, so why are you perspiring so? It's that dress collar of yours. Why don't you men realize you get fat? And you smell of mothballs. Never mind. I love you."

Her remarks did not put Charles at his ease, but it was impossible to resist her bluff heartiness. And she was enjoying herself tremendously. There were three huge electric chandeliers in this one room alone, each one blazing, and the windows were all shut, and shrouded against the soft September night in layers of tapestry. Why did the sight of tapestry repulse him anew? There was someone—

"Ah!" screamed Mrs. Holt, urgently pulling at Charles' arm. "There he is! Roger! Roger! You come here at once and meet Charlie Wittmann!"

A man of about forty-seven detached himself from a large group, and came smilingly towards his hostess. Roger Brinkwell. Charles looked at him, and hated him. He knew Roger Brinkwell. He had known him all his life; he had known dozens of Roger Brinkwells, and he hated each one separately and violently, and in the same way.

"How do you do, Mr. Wittmann?" asked Roger Brinkwell, with amiable politeness. "You don't remember me, do you? But then, you were about six or seven when I left Andersburg. But I remember you very well, and all your little brothers."

Charles stared at him, and slowly every muscle became like stone in his face. "I don't remember you, Mr. Brinkwell," he said. But I know your kind, he thought.

"I lived right around the corner," said Mr. Brinkwell. Charles continued to stare at him, and now his eyes became small and narrowed. Mr. Brinkwell appeared slightly surprised at this scrutiny.

Yes, thought Charles, I've always known you—and hated you. You might be a lawyer or a janitor or a mechanic or a salesman or shopkeeper. Anything. You can be an Englishman or a German, an American or an Italian, a Frenchman or a Swede. On the surface. But you are always you, no matter when you arrive.

They were all alike. They were always small men, never above five foot five, and sometimes even a trifle shorter. They were over-active men, like beetles, Charles thought, aggressive and aware. Usually they were compact, or even slender, as this manifestation was. In contrast with the rest of their bodies they had big round heads, out of proportion —big hard heads like balls—and almost invariably they had a large quantity of crisp dark hair, crinkled and very much alive. They had nimble, cruel faces, maliciously humorous and vivid, and merciless eyes which never softened in spite of frequent and rapid smiles on very mobile lips. Their noses were almost always big, of the "Roman" type, hard and bony, and they had wide, high and bony foreheads with heavy black brows. Their chins were definite, and pugnacious. When their expressions were not jeering, they were malevolent, no matter what they said, no matter how courteous they were, or to whom they were speaking.

"You seem to be remembering me, Mr. Wittmann. Or, I suppose I should call you Charlie, as I used to do, said Mr. Brinkwell, smiling.

I never forgot you, thought Charles. And you hate me, you hate my kind, as much as I hate you.

He continued to look at Mr. Brinkwell. In spite of their general air of restless activity, these men seldom used their hands to add color to their speech. All their expressiveness was in their terrible natures, which were also pouncing and dangerous, and in their constantly darting eyes.

They moved quickly and unerringly, like trained dancers, and never were they stupid. A race apart, these vigilant and treacherous men, without honor, without any decent human instinct. Their conversation was never dull, but always quick and witty. Never once had Charles encountered them among physicians, or on the boards of charity organizations, or in churches.

Charles never hated a man without just cause. Why did he hate the Roger Brinkwells? In some forgotten corner of his mind, in some forgotten memory as a child, lay the first perception and knowledge of these men. Then he remembered Roger Brinkwell, suddenly and clearly, and his long hatred of the other man's type became comprehensible to him.

Roger Brinkwell had been the only child of his parents. His father had been a surgeon of very high repute, a kindly man. His mother had been something else, entirely. Charles remembered her. He remembered that the Roger Brinkwells customarily married the kind of woman Roger's mother had been, and he knew that Roger's wife must be like that, also.

Now Charles faintly remembered that Mrs. Brinkwell had inherited a very great deal of money from a distant relative, and she had forced her husband to leave Andersburg. The neighbors had called her "uppity," and were glad when she had left. A stupid woman.

Now the memory was becoming clearer. Roger had been very popular with the local boys of his own age. But he had been a galling and cold-blooded tormentor of younger children. He had had particularly sought out little Charlie Wittmann for his persecutions, with a kind of relentless humor.

"You were a humorless, fat little fellow, Charlie," said Mr. Brinkwell, in a very amiable and laughing voice. "You had three brothers, Willie, Joe and Fred."

You set your dog on Fred, thought Charles, and remembered Friederich's dreadful terror, and the blood on the small arm, and Roger's laughter. They always laughed, did these people.

Mrs. Holt looked uneasily at Charles. Now, what was the matter with him? She had never seen such an expression on Charlie's face before; it was really horrible, even if it was so quiet. Fred, Charles was thinking, and now he knew a great deal more.

If Mrs. Holt was surprised by the still ferocity of Charles' eyes, Roger Brinkwell was not. He had forgotten the incident of the dog. He was only remembering that he hated the Charles Wittmanns of the world, and never enjoyed anything so much as injuring them. Almost always, they came to look at him like this, with set jaws and eyes that fixed themselves upon him, as if in recognition.

He smiled. "I hear two of your brothers are here, Joe and Willie," he said.

"Yes," said Charles. He stood there, immovable, and the two men regarded each other in the mutual acknowledgment of hatred.

"Waite's told me all about you," said Roger Brinkwell. He smiled, as if at the memory of a fine joke. "He said you've done very well with your father's business. He thinks very highly of you, and said to give you his regards."

Charles said nothing.

"And now I'm home again," continued the other man, lightly. "We're to begin building on that land we bought from you—Charlie. Very soon."

"So you do remember Roger, Charlie?" asked Mrs. Holt.

Charles turned to her. "Yes, Mrs. Holt. I remember."

It was with a deep sensation of relief that Mrs. Holt said: "Well, here is Pauline, too. Pauline, this is Mr. Wittmann, a very dear friend of mine." She repeated, turning to look directly at Brinkwell, and at the tall woman who was with them now: "A very dear friend of mine."

CHAPTER XXIV

PAULINE BRINKWELL was exactly the kind of woman Roger's mother had been, and she was exactly as Charles had known she would be.

Roger Brinkwell's kind liked only a certain type of woman. They were the lovers of the faceless but pretty women, with meek, downcast eyes, and lips that were constantly being moistened by the tips of furtive tongues. The Roger Brinkwells preferred the fair women, of diluted paleness, and with ashen hair and rather watery blue eyes, taller than themselves, and with pallid personalities. Did they know that these women, pliant and withdrawing, were almost as dangerous as themselves, and as conscienceless?

Mrs. Brinkwell was no frump. She had even a good figure, and she dressed unobtrusively and with a subdued style. Her jewelry was restrained, her blanched hair dressed becomingly in a classic way. Her gown was of the palest blue, the color of her eyes, and she wore turquoises in her ears and in wide gold bracelets on her arms. Her voice had a trailing and uncertain timbre, and the gloved hand she extended to Charles was weak in its pressure.

She gave Charles an absent glance, but he was not deceived. She, like Roger, was ridiculing him, and despising him. She said: "Dear Minnie's told us so much about you, Mr. Wittmann, and Roger remembers you. You must have gone to school together, or church?"

"Oh, Charlie's a lot younger than me," said Mr. Brinkwell, amused. "We did go to the same church, or rather, Sunday-school. Didn't we?"

"Do you go to church?" asked Charles.

Roger laughed. "No, honestly, I'm an agnostic. But Pauline's very strict about such things. You must tell her about our old church. I hear your minister is a—a rather remarkable man. That is what Minnie told us. We'll have to meet him."

He was already restless. His shoulders moved. His eyes glinted at Charles, and Charles felt himself becoming stolid and immovable in his usual fashion. Once I was afraid of you, he thought. All of the kind which is you. But not any more, thank God. I know how to fight you.

Pauline was studying him curiously, beneath her drooping lids, and with a distant air of patronage.

Mrs. Holt, who felt so much and knew so much intuitively, said: "Roger's got a boy, too, Charlie. He's here, tonight. Why there he is, over there."

Charles turned indolently and saw a young man at a little distance, a young man very much like Pauline, pale and without color, and listless. He was talking to a girl who was trying to impress him.

"Your son looks like you, Mrs. Brinkwell," Charles said, and he allowed his tone to say what he could not put into words. The drooping eyelids lifted, and the watery quality beneath them congealed.

Mrs. Holt took Charles' arm again. Then they all saw Wilhelm and Phyllis. Phyllis wore a long tight dress of the lightest pink, and her bright hair was caught up under two blush roses. Mr. Holt was with them. They saw Charles, and Phyllis smiled.

"Phyllis and Wilhelm," said Mrs. Holt.

Roger Brinkwell had dismissed Wilhelm after one glance. But he was looking at Phyllis with keen dislike, instinctive and immediate.

"Who are they?" murmured Pauline.

"My brother Wilhelm, and his wife, Phyllis," said Charles, and his voice was loud and hard. Pauline appeared startled, and murmured something faintly. Two or three people, passing, stopped at the sound of Charles' voice, as if they, too, were startled by its quality, which carried through and over the surrounding hubbub.

Mr. Holt, who was always distracted and vague of mind, said at once: "How do you do, Charles. Wilhelm tells me you have acquired a Picasso. Now, while I— Oh, very sorry, Minnie, very sorry, indeed. Mrs. Wittmann, Mrs. Brinkwell. Wilhelm, you probably remember Roger." Mr. Holt having ended the introductions returned to Charles: "That particular Picasso, now, is in his old mood—"

Wilhelm coolly inspected Roger Brinkwell. He knew at once that here was not a man he could ever like, though Mrs. Holt was telling him that the feller collected Gobelins. Wilhelm had no objection to Gobelins, except that one definitely did not go in for tapestries these days. As for Mrs. Brinkwell, she had ceased to exist for Wilhelm the moment he had shaken her hand, and had released it.

"Have we met before, somewhere?" asked Wilhelm, politely, but without interest.

"Why, yes," said Roger, with amusement. "You perhaps wouldn't remember, of course. You were about five or so. I lived around the corner from you, on Broadhurst Road. My parents took me to Pittsburgh, and I'm now with the Connington Steel, and I've returned here to be their superintendent in Andersburg. We'll all be together, again, Willie, as in the old days."

Charles felt a small happiness at the use of this nickname. Wilhelm became very reserved and fastidious. Nevertheless, it was evident that he was interested.

"Indeed," said Wilhelm. "You're building on that Burnsley land we sold to you, I suppose. An excellent spot. Yes, yes, Mrs. Holt told us, I believe. My dear," and he turned to Phyllis, "Mrs. Holt spoke to us of Mr. and Mrs. Brinkwell?"

You know damn well she did, thought Charles, even more happily.

Very demurely, Phyllis nodded. Wilhelm put on an air of satisfaction. "I seldom forget a name," he assured Roger, whose expression was becoming very alive and unpleasant.

Mrs. Brinkwell, meanwhile, had been inspecting Phyllis thoroughly, in her languorous way. She decided that Phyllis' gown was undoubtedly from Paris, that it was very unbecoming, that the roses in Phyllis' hair were unusual and therefore vulgar, that Phyllis was too thin, and that Roger disliked her. Roger always disliked these nervous women.

"Now, about that Picasso of yours, Charles," said Mr. Holt. "I confess I don't know too much about Picasso, myself, but from Wilhelm's description, I think—"

"Now, don't begin, please, Braydon," said Mrs. Holt. She threw a swift glance at her guests. "Roger, Pauline, there are a number of people who are dying to meet you. They just came in. Braydon, do come and greet your new guests."

She smiled at Charles and Phyllis and Wilhelm. "Now, don't you three run off somewhere and talk Picasso. I'll be back in just a few moments."

When they were alone, Wilhelm said: "That feller, that Brinkwell. Loathsome."

"You think so—too?" asked Charles, quickly.

"Certainly. Collects Gobelins. But it isn't that. It is something else. I'm not exactly a sloth, myself, but he's too quick, if you know what I mean."

"He knew us when we were children," said Charles, nodding. His fondness for Wilhelm became almost passionate. "I just remembered. You wouldn't, Wilhelm. You were too young." He paused. "He set his dog, once, on Fred."

Wilhelm might regard his brother Friederich, without love, but he was a Wittmann. He turned to watch the retreating backs of the Brinkwells. He said, quietly: "So. I don't remember it, but it's very likely. He's the kind. I doubt very much he's even a collector. Probably does it to give himself éclat, or something. Yes, definitely loathsome. What do you think, Phyllis?"

"It's very strange," said Phyllis without hesitation, "but it seems to me I've always hated the kind of man he is. I've met quite a few of them. One sat behind me in school, and he used to pinch me, and he always laughed when he did it."

Wilhelm dismissed the Brinkwells. He frowned at Charles. "Now will you tell me why Jochen and Isabel are here? I know Mrs. Holt doesn't care much for them. Are you behind this, Charles?"

Charles was so soothed by the conversation that he said at once: "Yes. Don't ask me why, Wilhelm. I don't know. It was just—"

"I know: your instinct. You've told me about it before." Wilhelm smiled.

"Its an infernal nuisance," continued Wilhelm. "I hope your instinct is right. It seems a little—shall we say—unbalanced, these days. We've been avoiding them from the moment we saw them at a distance. It isn't that I particularly dislike Jochen, but Isabel is extremely boring."

Charles said: "I promised to go back to Oliver Prescott and George Hadden. They are here, too." And he hurried away, after smiling at Phyllis.

He found George Hadden and Oliver Prescott hidden behind a piece of statuary; in this haven they were discussing something with much seriousness. They welcomed him, and suggested, as the rooms were hot and noisy, that they go out upon the terrace. No one noticed them go.

The September night was calm and dark and moonless, and very cool. The terrace was deserted. The men stood in silence for a few moments, listening to the high mountain wind among the trees, which, though hardly turning as yet, had a tattered look in the flood of light from the house windows. Here and there, as boughs blew aside, one caught the twinkle of the lights in distant houses on the mountainside. Everything was so very quiet; even the uproar in the house behind the men hardly reached them. Carriages littered the circular drive. They walked to the edge of the terrace, which ended at the brink of a long downward slope. Far below lay Andersburg, glittering, and they could see the motionless black water around which it curved. From the opposite mountain came the faint moan and tiny thunder of a passing train; a steamboat whistle, and then a series of hoots, came up from the river. Crickets cried in the dusty grass, but there was no sound of any disturbed bird. It was still hardly past summer, but there was a sadness in the night, a nostalgia. Charles thought: I am forty, and my youth has gone. Perhaps I've a lot of years ahead of me. But still, my youth is gone. I don't look forward to next year, the spring, as I used to do. I cherish every day, now.

Oliver was smoking, and so was George Hadden, and Charles fished a cigar from his pocket. They stood and looked down at the city. The wind came to them, stronger, louder.

"Feels like frost, soon," said George Hadden. "Early, this year."

"Hope we don't have a bad winter," said Oliver Prescott. "My farm clients tell me they're having good crops, and if the winter isn't too long they'll have good crops next summer, too. Poor devils, they need it."

Charles said to himself: Not next summer. Only tomorrow. He looked at the two young men. They were much younger than himself. They could speak of coming summers and springs, of crops.

"How many children do you have, George?" he asked.

George Hadden smiled. "A little girl, and this boy. We hope to have more, of course. We've just begun."

"Good," said Charles. "Good. Good."

George Hadden said: "I heard your brother Friederich speak in Philadelphia a few weeks ago, Mr. Wittmann."

"You did?" asked Charles, incredulously, wondering why George had wasted his time.

"Yes, I was there on business, and I read the announcements in the newspapers. So I went. Very interesting," added the young man, thoughtfully.

"Interesting?" repeated Charles, frowning. "Why? How?"

George hesitated. "For many reasons. I'd heard your brother was a good speaker."

"Fred?" said Charles, more incredulous than ever. "Of course, I've never gone to hear him."

"He's good, very good," said George, even more thoughtfully. "Then there was the audience. It was almost as interesting as the speech." He hesitated again. "I hope you won't be annoyed, Mr. Wittmann, when I tell you that your brother seems to draw a—well a very peculiar audience. In some respects."

"I should imagine so," said Charles, wryly. "Go on; tell me, George."

"Well, there were many workmen there. But there was something clean about them. I've noticed that about men who work hard, and with their hands as well as their brains." George smiled slightly. "Honest, I believe the right word is. But there were others. I could pick them out. I knew them, in a way."

Charles came closer to the younger man. "Yes?" he said. "Tell me."

"Well, I could see that these others were unsuccessful professional men, lawyers, perhaps, or doctors, school teachers, newspaper people. Or, I should say, they felt they were unsuccessful, that they deserved more than the world had given them, or they wanted more. It's a kind of man—I'm not very successful in trying to express what I mean."

"I understand, completely," said Charles. "People who lacked the capacity to succeed in any major way, as their fellow professional men had succeeded."

"Inadequate wretches, who knew exactly what they were, and hated the world, and even themselves, for being what they were," suggested Oliver. "Too bad our Founding Fathers, when they spoke of all men being created equal, didn't go on to explain that men should be equal before the law, but that nature hadn't endowed them equally when it came to brains or capacities or imaginations."

George said, reflectively: "Children ought to be taught that, in the schools. Every man has his dignity as a man, and he has his rights, which God has given him. Once, long ago, a man felt he was valuable even if his work was humble. That went, however, with the industrial revolution."

He had a slow and hesitant way of talking, almost apologetic. "When 'work' became a 'commodity' the individual worker lost his dignity and his importance as a man. But now, 'work' has just become hands to be bartered in the market place, and so—" He thought for a moment, feeling his way. "And so man lost, in so far as society is concerned, his magnitude as a soul. That was a terrible thing."

"The industrial revolution emphasized, too much, the importance of money," said Oliver. He looked at Charles. "I've always admired your emphasis on individual craftsmanship, Mr. Wittmann. Your men have respect for themselves."

"I never wanted our business to grow too big," said Charles. "I wanted, always, to have some sort of—call it comradeship—with my men. I'm proud of them, and I've always hoped they knew it. There's a lot of talk about 'mass production,' for the future. Maybe it'll be a good thing, as they say. Give everybody more, and cheaper. But I think what it'll take away will be much more important. However, I don't think we can do anything about it."

"The churches can," said George, somberly. "They can reemphasize, to every man, his personal dignity and stature, no matter what work he does. And they can emphasize the equal importance of any work, just so long as it's honest work."

They were silent, together. Then Charles said: "But tell me about Fred."

George continued: "Well, the workmen were all right. They came to hear your brother, because they work too hard and too long, and for too little money. They have their grievances, and we must admit it. I wasn't worried about them; they'll find their way, eventually. It's the others I was worried about. The—the—"

" 'Little men,' " said Charles. "The inadequate, mediocre men, who knew it."

"Yes." George laughed shortly. "I think everyone was disappointed that night. Your brother didn't talk about the rights of labor. He talked about war."

"War!" exclaimed Charles, stupefied.

George was very serious. "Yes, that's what he said: War. He said it was coming. That it was being 'plotted' all over the world. And that we must be ready to stop it before it begins."

Charles stood there, blank and amazed, and very shaken.

"No one, of course, believed it," said George. "The workmen were only confused, and looked at each other. Now, that's a very funny thing," he reflected. "I just remembered. The other men—not the workmen—looked at each other, too. And it was in a strange sort of way. Almost as if they were satisfied. And hopeful."

Charles was stunned. Then he said, a trifle hoarsely: "You'd think Fred would be happy—in a way—about a war. I don't understand. I've always thought of him as being one of the inadequate ones—"

"Oh, no," said George, slowly and carefully. "He isn't, really, Mr. Wittmann. It's just that nobody's ever tried to tell him he's important, or made him feel that, either."

Charles said nothing. There was a violent disorder in his thoughts, and some shame, some remorse, and urgent anxiety. Then he said: "Did Fred say how he had found out there might be a war?"

"He never goes into details," said George. "He's not the logical, dry type, full of statistics. I believe he once mentioned that his 'instinct' told him more than he actually knew."

"His instinct," repeated Charles. He rubbed his forehead with the back of his hand. "I did hear him say, once, that nationalism and chauvinism were crimes against all men," he muttered. "But I thought it just abstract raving, at the time. But actual war! Soon!"

"Yes. He was very vehement about it. The workmen became more and more confused, and frightened. And the others just sat, and smiled a little." George sighed. "They hated your brother. They knew he wasn't really one of them, after all."

"Not one of them," muttered Charles.

Then all at once his relief was so enormous that he became weak. He leaned against a broad stone pillar on the terrace.

Fred, he thought. I must talk to Fred. But he remembered that Friederich had just gone away for six weeks, on a speaking engagement in many cities and towns. He said urgently, in himself: Tell them, Fred. Warn them. For God's sake, warn them.

George was laughing in his gentle fashion. "I don't think your brother even knows what Socialism really is," he said. "He's looking for something to tie himself to, to give him self-confidence. It's too bad he hasn't any religious faith."

Charles said, quickly and determinedly: "You don't know him, personally, George, do you? Will you meet him when he comes back?"

He looked at the young Quaker's serious face. "Very important," he said.

"Of course, Mr. Wittmann. I'll be glad to know him," said George Hadden. "And now, perhaps, if we can just find Mrs. Holt for a minute or two, I think we'll be able to get away."

PART THREE

Despair doubles our strength.

CHAPTER XXV

But it was not for some time that Charles could speak to his brother Friederich. Nor could he arrange a meeting between Friederich and George Hadden.

At first, there were objective occurrences which prevented this. George Hadden's young wife and little boy took ill, the latter part of October, when Friederich returned to Andersburg. Then Charles was shocked to learn, one morning, that the child had died of a particularly bad form of what was called "la grippe." The mother barely survived. The doctors spoke worriedly of "approaching epidemic forms" of the disease. Many apprentices in the Wittmann shops were incapacitated, as was Tom Murphy, the first foreman, and some of the best skilled workers. Wilhelm, himself, was struck down at Christmas by it, much to his anger. The day before Christmas Friederich pointedly absented himself from his family and went to spend the holidays in consultation with some mysterious friend in Chicago. Charles had heard of this "friend," but he had listened vaguely. Alerted, now, he tried to discover the identity of the man but Friederich eluded him.

On December 30th, when Jimmy was planning exuberantly for the New Year's festivities, he was suddenly stricken by the illness, and on January 4th, 1914, he developed pneumonia. Charles was terribly frightened. For five days he did not go to his office at all but sat with his son, who was attended by nurses. He never forgot those days by Jimmy's bed, for the new year promised to launch itself by way of a particularly evil winter. Jimmy's gasps for breath, his delirious groans mingled with the roar of the blizzard against the window-panes, and so dark was it outside that for several days the light was never turned off in the house on Bowbridge Avenue.

Phyllis, when she could leave Wilhelm during his irritable convalescence, came often to Charles' home, there to sit in silence with him either in Jimmy's room or in the dull, heavy dimness of the parlor. Charles could speak very little, but to have Phyllis there was comfort and solace. She brought him coffee; she spoke with gentleness and surety. There was nothing "cheerful" about her: she tacitly accepted Jimmy's danger, with wisdom but also with unspoken certainty that he would not die.

She was with Charles one early and bitter evening when the crisis came and Dr. Metzger, tired and with drooping shoulders, suddenly announced: "Well, there. It's mostly over now, Charlie. The boy's almost out of danger, thank God." Charles said dully: "Then he was in danger." The doctor nodded. "There were a few times when I thought nothing could be done. But Jimmy's a strong whelp, and he'll be all right. Just care."

The doctor patted the boy's wet cheek. Jimmy had fallen asleep after the crisis; his breathing was nearly natural; the swollen flush had receded. Dr. Metzger pulled the blankets over him and told the nurse not to disturb him for a change of nightshirts until he woke up.

Then he turned to Charles: "Go on downstairs, Charlie, and mix yourself a good drink." He smiled at Phyllis. "Take him down, Phyllis, and perhaps you'd better take one, too. You both look as if you need it." He followed them downstairs to the parlor, and was easily persuaded by Phyllis to have a whiskey and soda.

"Never saw anything like this thing," he said, standing near the fire, a glass in his hand and his rumpled graying hair falling over his forehead. "It's like a plague or something. More deaths than I like to think about, and every doctor rushed to death. Better watch out for yourselves, Phyllis and Charlie." He spoke to them as a doctor speaks to a man and his wife who have just come through terror together. It seemed perfectly natural to him that Phyllis should seem so exhausted in her relief, and so weary. She and Charles sat side by side, as if in mutual comforting, and in relaxation.

Then all at once it occurred to Dr. Metzger that Charles had been all alone but for Phyllis during this ordeal. He knew that Wilhelm was just recovering from his own illness, though he was not Wilhelm's physician. But he had not seen Jochen or Isabel. Young Geraldine had been here only once, and then but for a few moments, standing crying and anguished in the parlor. The doctor frowned. He looked at Charles, sitting there so gray of face, bent over, both hands about his untouched glass.

"My wife reads the society pages," he said, tentatively. "She read where the Brinkwells have bought a house on Mountain Circle, not far from where you live, Phyllis."

Phyllis nodded with dazed indifference. "Do drink that, Charles," she urged. Charles gave her a smile, and obeyed.

"The Wilcox house," added the doctor. "Must be getting a big salary from the Connington, or his wife must be rich. After all, that's a mighty fine, expensive house, and only five years old, and I heard they imported the walnut for the rooms, and the marble. My wife knows all about those things."

But Phyllis was refilling Charles' glass in spite of his feeble protests. "Yes, his wife must be pretty rich. Seems I heard that somewhere," said the doctor.

"Who?" asked Phyllis, bewildered. She had been watching Charles closely, with deep concern, and had hardly listened to Dr. Metzger. "The Brinkwells. The new superintendent of that new steel mill they're building on the Burnsley land. They think the mills will be rolling by mid-summer, the fast way they're building. Biggest thing in Andersburg; almost as big as the one they have in Pittsburgh."

Now Charles came up out of his black exhaustion, the whiskey warming his coldness and lethargy. Dr. Metzger might ramble, sometimes, but there was usually a sharp meaning or implication in his ramblings. And he was looking at the smoldering fire, over which hung Wilhelm's Picasso weirdly shimmering and absurdly out of place in the wintry dusk of this old room.

"You've met the Brinkwells?" asked Charles, slowly.

"I?" Dr. Metzger laughed heartily. "I'm only an old plug-horse. Not fashionable enough for the Brinkwells. They have Landor, who lives near your brother Joe. Landor's a friend of mine in a way: sends me all the patients he suspects can't pay his big fees. Well, anyway, sometimes Landor and I talk."

"Don't you think you ought to lie down before dinner, Charles?" asked Phyllis, anxiously. And then she was silent, for Charles was looking up at the doctor with intent scrutiny.

"Anybody I know at Brinkwell's parties?" asked Charles.

The two men were regarding each other as if Phyllis were not in the room.

"Yes," said Dr. Metzger. "Quite a few. Joe and Isabel were there New Year's Eve. But you know that. You were invited, too."

"No," said Charles, "I wasn't."

Now Phyllis sat with her hands held tightly together on her knee, and only listened.

"Quite a party, I hear," said the doctor, very carefully. He put down his empty glass on the mantelpiece and studied it. "And now my wife tells me that they are giving another one next week; their son's birthday. She read me the list of guests. Joe and Isabel were on that list. All the young folk have been invited to that birthday party. Your brother's girl, Geraldine, Charlie. About seventeen now, isn't she?"

He dropped his arm from the mantelpiece, and sighed. "Well, I've got to get along. Dozen calls or more before dinner. Hope this thing doesn't get out of hand. You can let everybody know, now, Phyllis, that it's safe to visit Jimmy."

"Yes," said Phyllis. She was a little white in the gloom. She said: "Isabel has called every day, and she and Jochen sent flowers for Jimmy, and Geraldine calls at least twice a day. I didn't bother you, Charles, to tell you. I think I'll tell the poor child, now, that Jimmy has passed the crisis."

She stood up, sick at heart. Involuntarily, and simply, she put her hand on Charles' shoulder. He looked up at her, in silence, and then she tried to smile. They forgot Dr. Metzger. Charles reached up and put his hand over Phyllis' and they remained like that for a long moment or two.

The doctor went into the hall, alone, frowning with concern. He pulled his old damp coat on. His horse and buggy stood in the snowy evening outside, and the lights were beginning to flare on. Then Phyllis came into the hall, and the doctor could see that there were tears in her eyes. She reached for the telephone, but before taking off the receiver she said: "Thank you, thank you, Gustave."

She called Jochen's house, asked for Geraldine, and watched the doctor leave the house. As the door opened and shut a furious swirl of wind and snow rushed into the hall. Phyllis shivered. It was Isabel who answered, in her "refined" voice. "Phyllis? I'm so glad to hear from you. I've been calling you very often, but you are never at home. How is Wilhelm?"

Phyllis said: "Wilhelm is almost better, Isabel. As soon as the weather clears a little he will be allowed out." She went on, very quietly: "You know I've been here a lot, Isabel. Mrs. Meyers has told you, and you have asked for Jimmy, and I spoke to you once, myself."

"Are you at Charles'?" asked Isabel, with gracious surprise. "But, of course. I'm so very sorry; we are so busy these days that I keep forgetting. How is dear Jimmy?"

"Jimmy," said Phyllis, "has passed the crisis. I wanted to tell Geraldine. Is she there?"

"So glad," murmured Isabel. "It must have been quite a trial for poor Charles. Jochen hardly sees him, for he just rushes in for an hour or two, when he can spare the time, and rushes home. Geraldine? She is being fitted for her gown for young Kenneth Brinkwell's party next week. I'll give her your message, Phyllis."

"Isabel. It's perfectly all right for Geraldine to visit Jimmy. He's out of danger, and I don't think it will hurt Geraldine to see him, say in a few days, when his strength comes back. Will you tell her that?"

"Certainly." Nothing could have been kinder than Isabel's voice, or more solicitous. "But don't you think a 'few days' might be too soon, Phyllis? I guard the girls so carefully, you know. And with this horrible disease going about a mother must be doubly cautious. Perhaps after Kenneth's party—" She waited. Phyllis was silent. Isabel said: "Phyllis?"

"Yes," said Phyllis, very quietly.

"Do give Wilhelm our love, too. When you go home tonight," said Isabel.

"Yes," said Phyllis. She hung up, and stood in the dark hall, and her heart was beating with fierce anger. She returned to Charles, sitting there so silent, bent over in his chair, his eyes fixed on the dying fire. He heard her come. "You told Gerry, Phyllis?"

"Yes."

Charles sighed. "You know, Phyllis, it takes something like ᵾis to put everything else out of your mind. Well, thank God, anyway." But Phyllis knew that there were many things returning to Charles' mind, and very few of them gave him consolation and relief.

He went with her into the hall and helped her on with her black sealskin coat, and found her muff. A little light from the parlor drifted in here, and Charles could see Phyllis' face, pale and tense. He took her hand, and said: "Phyllis, I'll never forget how you've helped me. Never. There was no one but you."

She tried for lightness: "But Mr. Haas came at least half a dozen times, even if you didn't see him, and Father Hagerty was here twice, and called every day, and Mr. Grimsley haunted the telephone. And there were your other friends, too."

Charles said: "Yes. Yes, of course. But all the time it was only you, here, Phyllis."

She kept her smile, for she was afraid that she would burst into tears. She heard the crackling of her carriage wheels as they drew up on the dry snow outside. "Oh, Charles," she said.

His fingers tightened about hers. "Phyllis," he said. And then he opened the door for her, and she was gone before he could help her down the icy steps. Slowly and heavily, he went upstairs to his son's room. It was filled with flowers, from Mr. Haas, from Wilhelm and Phyllis, and from Jochen and Isabel. There was a large vase of red roses from Mrs. Holt, also, and a still unopened message from her.

But Charles stood beside his sleeping son and looked down at him, his arms hanging at his sides.

Only once did Charles see Friederich, and that was on a white and raging afternoon when the latter appeared briefly at the office. Charles caught a glimpse of his youngest brother, who appeared to have arisen from nowhere, and in rapid passage, now, almost out of the building. Charles ran after him, and caught him near the door. Friederich turned upon him, rather than to him, and Charles was momentarily taken aback by the look of frozen ferocity in Friederich's eyes.

"I've tried to reach you," said Charles, lamely. "I've left messages, these last two weeks or so, at your house. Perhaps Mrs. Schuele didn't give them to you."

Friederich grasped the big brass doorknob. He stared at Charles with inexplicable hatred. He said, in German: "She gave them to me."

"Well," said Charles, helplessly. He added, fumbling: "Jimmy has been very sick. He came downstairs, yesterday, for the first time."

Friederich began to open the door.

"There was someone I wanted you to meet," said Charles, lifting his hand almost pleadingly.

"Karl, there is no one you know whom I should care to meet."

"It's George Hadden, the Quaker. You know. He has that sheet-metal works."

Friederich actually paused, then. "George Hadden?" he asked, with brutal insult. "What would anyone like you know of George Hadden?"

Charles ignored this. "I know him. I'd like to know him better. He heard you in Philadelphia, quite a time ago. He—he admires you." (What the devil was wrong with the fool, now? He had come from the direction of Jochen's offices.) Charles went on: "It was in September when he said he'd like to meet you. But you were gone for six weeks, and then his baby died, and his wife was ill, and then Jimmy came down with 'la grippe.' " Charles began to speak in German, rustily but carefully: "I have told you: he admires you. It is impossible just at this time to ask him to receive anyone. But may I tell him that you will see him later?"

"Are you trying to corrupt him, too, Karl?"

Charles kept his temper. Joe: had Fred been in to see Joe, and why? Was this expression of rage and hatred for him, Charles, or for Joe?

"Friederich," said Charles, patiently, "I do not try to corrupt anyone. You know this, yourself. I am merely giving you his message. If you do not care to meet George Hadden that is your own affair."

Friederich stood there sullenly by the door, his suspicious glare on Charles' face, his hands clenching and unclenching at his sides. He was all irresolution and wariness.

Charles said: "Come into my office a moment."

"I have no time," replied Friederich. Nevertheless, moving slowly and reluctantly, glancing about him as if in furious fear of enemies, he followed Charles back into his office. But he would not sit down.

"You might write Hadden and tell him of this message, or call him," said Charles. The antennae of his mind were groping, carefully. He saw his brother, the thinner and erratic double of himself, grimy and unkempt. Charles shrugged: "I like Hadden, though I've seen him rarely. He doesn't belong to my church, or any of my organizations. But he is a fine fellow."

Friederich grunted. Then Charles saw that he was not only enraged, but extremely uneasy.

Friederich said, as if forced to speak, and the sound of his voice was shrill: "Jochen tells me he wishes to expand our works, but you will not."

"Not yet," said Charles. "I can see no necessity for it, yet. Jochen spoke of it to me two months ago, and I refused, for very definite financial reasons. We received a large order from the Bouchards, yes. But things are not improving, Friederich. There is a sort of suspension of business in the air. A waiting, one might almost say." He had to hesitate, occasionally, to find the correct German word.

Then he saw that Friederich's expression had changed, become darker yet less furious. Friederich also came closer to him. "'A waiting,'" he repeated.

"Yes," said Charles, and looked at his brother intently.

"For what?"

Charles was silent. Then when Friederich repeated the question in a louder and more excited voice, Charles said: "I don't know. Perhaps George Hadden knows."

A tic showed itself on Friederich's right cheek; it made the muscle move rapidly. Now Charles saw his loneliness, his insecurity, and his lostness.

"I think I know," said Friederich, finally. "Yes, I think I know. But it is something I will never tell you, for it would make you happy. It would make you think of profits."

Charles had to control his temper. He had to hold back the contemptuous words: "And you never think of profits?" Instead, he said: "George Hadden is in business. He has no aversion to profits. He is also a Quaker, and an honest man." He waited. He said: "Friederich, perhaps there are things I know, too, which you think I do not know." He stood up. "I have a son, Friederich."

"A son," began Friederich, sneeringly. Then he stopped. He wet his lips. "I—" he began, then was silent.

"Let us help each other; there are things we all ought to tell each other," said Charles.

Friederich turned away. Confusion and irresolution were in his every slow step which he took towards the door. Charles did not follow him. Friederich stood by the door, his head drooping, his sunken profile to his brother. He had drawn in his upper lip under the lower one.

"I cannot see George Hadden for at least four weeks more," he mumbled. "I am leaving tomorrow for Detroit." He was trying to gather himself together; he straightened up. He was trying, Charles saw, to renew his rage. "Jochen has just told me that you will not put your precision jig grinder into production, for some stupid reason or other, that you will listen to no argument."

"I own the patent, Friederich. It is an important one, but as yet in the experimental stage. Yes, I know that the Bouchards would like us to manufacture it for them. They have been writing to me, and I believe they have written to Jochen. But it is not ready. It might never be ready for the Bouchards. They also wish us to lease or sell our patent for gun bores to them. Why, Friederich?"

Avarice, fear and anger suddenly blazed on Friederich's face. Now he was utterly distracted. He pushed back his untidy hair with one smudged palm.

"You are such a liar, Karl!" he cried. "Always, you deliberately try to confuse me!"

So, thought Charles. He used his old weapon against his brother. He goaded him.

"I confuse you?" asked Charles, laughing slightly. "You are the most confused man I ever knew—Fred. You don't know what you want, do you?" He spoke in English now. "Why don't you try to settle for something—either a lot of money, or your ideals?"

Friederich took one step towards him, almost beside himself. "Why do you talk like this to me, as if you knew anything about 'ideals' or anything besides money and profits? I have hateful brothers. I am sick of all of you."

"Including Joe? You've just been with him, haven't you? Had a nice, cosy chat, I suppose."

Friederich's rage overpowered him. "Yes, I talked with him about your obduracy, your cautious clinging to your patents." He stopped. The tic was more pronounced on his face. "But that is not important. You are all fools, all of you. Jochen is a fool today. He wants to change our name, by court order, to Von Wittmann! Wittmann is not enough for that imbecile and his *Gnädige Frau!*"

"What?" exclaimed Charles, incredulously. " 'Von Wittmann!' Why, the infernal damn fool!"

"Yes!" shouted Friederich. He pointed a lean finger at Charles. "And do not lie to me and tell me you are not willing!"

"I certainly am not." Charles was genuinely outraged, and Friederich saw this. This threw him into worse confusion. He cried: "Well, then, if you are not 'willing,' do something about it!"

He caught the door-knob now, opened the door, closed it with a violent bang behind him.

Charles was so angry that his first thought was to go see Jochen. But he knew this was not the clever way. He touched his bell and asked Mr. Parsons to ask Mr. Wittmann to come in.

Jochen came in, jocular, ruddy-faced and all pleasantness. But Charles saw that he was also wary. He said, abruptly: "Have you been talking to Fred about our gun-bore patent and the precision jig grinder?"

Jochen sat down, with a tolerant smile. "Yes, I did. Any objection? After all, he is an officer of the company. Or do you and I keep all our business under our hats?" He laughed. "Not that it mightn't be best, with the kind of brothers we have."

"You know that Fred doesn't know much about the business. You teased him with the idea of more money, didn't you?"

"Why not?" asked Jochen, easily. "He likes it. I like it. You like it. Willie likes it. And we're all Wittmans together." He smiled again. "Now, will you tell me what all this is about? I'm busy, you know. Though not as busy as I could be, thanks to you."

"Don't be so ingenuous. You know I've refused those patents to the Bouchards, that I've refused to expand just now. So why did you try to use Fred against me?"

Jochen became indignant. "Are we all your tame seals? Can't we discuss these things without you standing over us with a whip? If I disagree with your policy I have a perfect right to consult my brother officers to see if we can't do something to persuade you to change your mind. You're acting like a damn fool, Charlie."

"Have you talked to Willie, too?"

Jochen's eyes slid away. "Yes. What if I did? But lately you've got him in the palm of your hand." Jochen's eyes came back to his brother, and they were vindictive and sly. Finally, he smiled. "But there was one thing with which he agreed. Perhaps we'll tell you about it one of these days. After all, it might sound funny—"

He stood up. So, thought Charles. That's all I wanted to know.

Charles shrugged. "I can always wait, contentedly, to hear about your schemes, Joe. They're sure to be amusing. I do like to laugh, sometimes. And I've needed a laugh, lately. Got a cigar?"

Jochen, not pleased, took out his silver cigar-case, opened it, extracted a cigar, and threw it on Charles' desk. "Why don't you buy your own cigars?" he asked. "But no, you're too much of a miser. Anyway, I suppose I ought to be flattered that you like mine." He watched Charles light it. He could not resist saying: "That's even a better brand than mine. Roger Brinkwell gave it to me."

Charles, squinting through the smoke, saw his brother preen with high satisfaction. He nodded, after a few concentrated puffs. "Very good," he conceded. "A little strong. But excellent. You're wonderful friends with the Brinkwells, you and Isabel, aren't you? I hear about it all the time." Charles allowed himself to show that he was impressed. Jochen leaned against the desk. "We're on first-name basis," he said. "But then, we always were."

Again, Charles nodded, comfortably. "I don't suppose Brinkwell likes me. I haven't been invited."

Jochen chuckled. "You're not the society type, Charlie. The grubby business man. Polly likes a little savoir-faire in her guests. Nothing against you personally, of course."

"As you say, I'm not 'society,' Joe." He puffed steadily. "What's the matter with Gerry? She's been to see Jimmy only twice in the past two weeks. Is she sick?"

Jochen colored. He began to move towards the door. "No," he said, airily. "But there's her school, and her dancing classes. Isabel keeps the girls busy with such things. Geraldine's only seventeen. But young Brinkwell, Kenneth, comes to see her quite often. Saturday nights, sometimes." He opened the door, spoke quickly and loudly: "Jimmy going to be able to go back to school, soon?"

Charles sat and smoked for a long time after his brother had gone.

CHAPTER XXVI

JIMMY HAD SO far recovered by the second February Sunday that Dr. Metzger had agreed that the tutor, who had been helping the boy with his lost school work for the past three weeks, might be discharged, and Jimmy might look forward to resuming school the following Monday.

The illness had seemed to hurry the boy towards maturity. He was now eighteen, yet though his strong young life had begun to surge again he had taken on a deeper seriousness. When his fellow-students who visited him talked to him of basketball, and baseball in the spring, he listened with interest but not with the passionate attention he had shown a year ago.

This February Sunday was dark and bitterly gloomy, skeins of snow driving themselves against the windows as they were blown by a violent wind. The furnace gushed up its streams of warm air, but fires had to be lit to offset the extraordinary cold. After dinner, Jimmy sat with a blanket on his knees before the parlor fire and talked with his father. The boy did not show his concern over Charles' worn appearance, his lost weight, his air of abstracted anxiety. Charles did not speak of them, and Jimmy did not ask him. He knew his father. If Charles wished to speak he would do so.

Jimmy was still very thin; his young face so slender, now, so pale, resembled his mother's. His hair had not been cut since his illness; the thick and wiry curls fell on his forehead as Mary's hair had fallen, and now Charles saw that Jimmy's smile was Mary's smile. The old desolation came back to him acutely, and his loneliness. But after all, he said to himself, when it comes down to rock-bottom we're all alone, all of us. Yes, I've heard all that before; it's an old story. But when it occurs to any of us it isn't something we've heard before.

Jimmy had not spoken today, or yesterday, of his cousin Geraldine. It had been ten days since the girl had last come, and then she had run in from school, breathlessly, for only five minutes. Jimmy had told his father of this, frowning slightly. He had added nothing to his brief account, but Charles had seen that Jimmy was disturbed.

The two had not been speaking for nearly an hour. Jimmy was studying; Charles read his newspapers. The gaslights over them flared as little gusts of wind found their way through double windows. It was only four in the afternoon. It was the day that Charles was to visit his brothers. But Friederich was not in the city; Jochen had called that morning to explain that he and Isabel were having "late supper" with the Brinkwells. There was only Wilhelm to visit. Charles smiled faintly. Wilhelm's illness had been trivial compared with Jimmy's, but he clung to his invalidism with the precise fussiness of an old woman. He had always been a hypochondriac, Charles remembered.

"If the storm keeps up, it wouldn't be a good idea for you to go out, Dad," said Jimmy, putting down his book.

Charles said: "I'd be glad of the storm, frankly, if it weren't that I've got to see your uncle about something. Something ridiculous."

Jimmy glanced at the Picasso over the fire. He squinted at it carefully. "I just hope we don't get something else like that, after you've seen Uncle Willie," he said.

Charles laughed. "Now, don't get hidebound, yourself, Jimmy. If we had some kind of artistic intelligence that painting would mean something to us. Or, rather, as your uncle would say, it would mean something especial and private to us, something we read into it ourselves. Sort of obscure, isn't it?"

"It looks to me like a case of piles," said Jimmy, hoping his father would laugh again. It had been a long time since he had heard Charles laugh.

Charles studied the painting. "I've tried and tried," he said, baffled. "I'm learning a little. I know quite a few phrases, and can rattle them off with the best of the connoisseurs. I even surprise myself. But I always seem to prefer something that isn't 'especial and private.' I like something that is universal. One part of me doesn't seem to exist, and it ought to exist, as your uncle says. And that part is 'individuality,' so that any scene, face, event or sound will take on my own unique 'coloration.' I suppose I just don't have any unique coloration."

"Thank God you haven't found out anything that you could use with Uncle Fred," said Jimmy, grinning.

Charles rubbed his chin with his finger. He said, thoughtfully: "There ought to be something, Jim. You wouldn't know of anything, would you? Fred never spoke of something—well, sane—that I could use to get on common ground with him?"

"Is it that bad?" asked Jimmy, concerned. Then when Charles nodded, the boy began to think. He kept shaking his head impatiently. He said at last: "You know that Uncle Fred doesn't know I'm alive, most of the time. Once or twice, I've passed him on the street and he didn't recognize me. But last summer, one day, I saw him carrying a big book, and I spoke to him. You know how he is: always in a hurry, but he actually stopped when I mentioned the book, and was even pleasant. It was a book about Goethe, and he said he belonged to a world Goethe Society."

"Goethe," repeated Charles. He looked at the bookcases which lined each side of the fireplace. His father's books, in German, thick dark books in crimson or brown leather. Among them, he was certain, were many books about Goethe, and written by Goethe. He stood up and examined one or two. He put the books on a table. Tomorrow, he would start reading them. He took out his handkerchief and wiped a fine film of dust off the top book. "This isn't going to be as bad as Impressionist painting," he said. "My father worshipped Goethe. I don't remember much about the whole thing."

"If you knew as much as my uncles do about everything we'd all starve to death," said Jimmy.

Charles put his hand on his son's head, shoved it with rough affection. "They say it takes brains to make money," he said. "But no one believes that, these days. Or perhaps you aren't supposed to care about rent and food and clothing or bills or obligations—if you are intelligent. Grubs like me will take care of you. Or ought to, a lot of people think."

He sat down. "The Puritans used to say: 'He who does not work shall not eat.' But quite a lot of those who call themselves the intelligentsia deny that."

He took up his newspaper again. He was seeing so many things these days, small things easily passed over.

Alsace was still seething over the "Zabern incident." Work was being hurried on the Kiel Canal, and the Kaiser had triumphantly announced that the Hohenzollern Canal would also be opened in the summer, far ahead of schedule. Dr. Liebknecht had accused the Kronk officials of maintaining secret agencies in Berlin whose function it was to bribe German Army and Navy officials to reveal state documents pertaining to new munitions contracts. Munitions? Why? A gentleman high in official circles in Austria had openly, and derisively, expressed his disbelief that Italy would honor the Triple Alliance she had with Germany and Austria. "I recall to the attention of my colleagues what Napoleon has said about the Italians," said the gentleman, with high-bred disgust. Now, what the hell had Napoleon said about the Italians?

"Jimmy," said Charles, "did Napoleon say anything in particular about the Italians? I mean, as far as military commitments or alliances are concerned."

Jimmy screwed up his face, thoughtfully. "I believe Napoleon implied that Italians weren't very much as soldiers, and that you'd need a lot of divisions to watch them, or something, to force them to toe the mark about fighting or honoring military alliances."

"Is that so?" Charles was pleased. "A very intelligent people, the Italians, apparently. So, they wouldn't be much good in a war, eh? Yes, definitely very intelligent people."

"'A nation great in war is great in nothing,'" said Jimmy. "That's what my history teacher told us."

Charles went on reading closely. One hundred million dollars had been appropriated by the French government for military services for a three-year term. Why?

Little things. But they came every day. It was like watching the licking of flames far off in the distance in a great hazy forest. Small flames; just a faint flash once in a while, a puff of smoke, and the flame sank down. But there it was again, in another part of the forest. Soundless, still. The roar of holocaust was not yet loud in the wind. Would it ever be? Where were the fire-fighters?

There is nothing, nothing, that I can do, thought Charles, as he thought so often. I can only watch. He turned to another portion of the paper. Mr. Wilson was still demanding regulation of trusts and monopolies. Good, thought Charles. We small business men and manufacturers should support Wilson in this. Men aren't to be trusted, whether they are soldiers or business men, or anybody. Power goes to men's heads; they become insane.

Someone rang the doorbell, and Charles heard Mrs. Meyers go to the door. Father and son turned their heads in the direction of the sound. They heard Mrs. Meyers' voice, and a younger voice, subdued and hurried. "Gerry," said Jimmy, and his face lighted up so brilliantly that Charles felt sick. The boy put aside his book, shook back his hair.

Geraldine came in. She saw no one but Jimmy, though Charles stood up. She looked at Jimmy, and said: "Oh. I—I was just passing, Jimmy. I thought I'd come in to see you."

"Hello, dear," said Charles, gently.

She started, and turned to him. "Uncle Charlie," she murmured. She stood there, irresolute. She had not allowed Mrs. Meyers to take her wraps. She wore a long brown beaver coat, new and expensive, and her hands were in a beaver muff. There was a wide beaver hat on her head. She had just been permitted to "put up" her hair; it was coiled in a smooth black knot on her neck.

She was very thin, much thinner than she had been last summer, and taller. Her young face was wan and quietly intense, and there were circles under the beautiful dark eyes, as if she had been ill, or sleepless for a long time. Even her mouth had no color, and the corners, as she looked at Charles, were tremulous as though she were trying not to cry.

Jimmy said: "I'm awfully glad you came in, Gerry. Here, sit down."

She sat down, stiffly, her hands still in her muff. Charles, with deep tenderness, said: "We're always glad to see you, Gerry. We've missed you."

Now her mouth became tight with her effort to control her emotion. When Charles went to her to loosen her coat she did not resist. He threw the coat over the back of her chair. She bent her head so that her face was half hidden by her hat.

"I've missed you, too," she said, almost inaudibly.

"But school, and everything," said Charles, sitting down in his chair.

Geraldine did not answer. Jimmy and Charles exchanged a glance of concern and understanding. Jimmy said: "They push you, when you get so far. In school. Don't worry, Gerry. Summer will soon be here."

Charles was conscious of his slow and rising anger. This poor child. He understood what her parents were doing to her. He had never hated Jochen very often, and then only in passing, and almost tolerantly. But now he hated his brother with real strength.

"Things push, Gerry," he said, and leaned over to touch her arm lightly. Its thinness frightened him. "As Jimmy says, don't worry. You just have to keep your head."

The firelight and gaslight glimmered on her rich, crimson velvet dress, and the white lace collar. Charles could see the tenseness in the cords under the fine dark skin of her neck. She would not speak. Charles understood she could not say what she wanted to say, and he respected the child for it.

Then Geraldine lifted her head and looked at her cousin. "Jimmy," she said.

"Yes, Gerry. I know all about it," replied the boy. "It doesn't matter."

Geraldine drew in a deep breath. "I'm so glad you're better, Jimmy. And you'll be going back to school."

"And there's that place where we have hot chocolate after school," said Jimmy. "Hope you've missed me not being there, Gerry."

"Yes," she whispered. And now she was smiling, the most piteous smile.

"I'll meet you there tomorrow afternoon," said Jimmy. "At three, as usual."

She nodded. She was very close to crying. Charles stood up. He said, heartily: "Well, if I'm going to see your uncle, children, I'll have to go now. Will you be here for supper when I come back, Gerry?"

She turned to him, jerkily. "I can't, Uncle Charlie." Her lips shook. "You see, I'm just on my way home from seeing Doris Sidney. I had dinner at her house. I—I promised to be home before Mama and Papa went to—to the Brinkwells. And it's getting late as it is. If I'm not home right away they'll begin to call the Sidneys, and—"

Charles stood beside her. He put his hand on her shoulder. "Well, stay a few minutes with Jimmy, dear."

He went out and shut the door behind him. He fumbled in the semi-dark for his coat and hat. He tried to think of the short walk to the livery stable where he kept his horse and modest carriage in the winter. But he could only think of Jochen and Isabel. So, they wanted Kenneth Brinkwell for this child, did they?

In the parlor, Geraldine was crying, and Jimmy was sitting close beside her and holding her hand and wiping her tears awkwardly with her scrap of a handkerchief.

CHAPTER XXVII

It was extremely unpleasant to be out this cold wintry afternoon, with the carriage wheels slipping on the rising icy roads, and the last of the sun a brazen lake over the opposite mountains, which were as black as coal. But at least it was not snowing here. However, Charles began to feel resentment that he should be out today. He knew this was irrational; he knew that he had only to call Wilhelm, and to explain that the day was too bad for visiting.

In his resentment, it seemed to him that his brothers were becoming more and more unbearable, that it was asking too much of him to stand them much longer. But his logical mind reproached him by reminding him that he was not so much provoked by his brothers as he was desperate, and knew that he could do nothing about his despair.

He was informed, while being relieved of his hat and coat, that
Mr. and Mrs. Wittmann were in the music room. He walked there,
slowly, scowling. He could hear the faint strains of music being played
superbly. Chopin? Mozart? Debussy? He did not care. He just disliked it. He would be "banal," this evening, and ask Phyllis to play
the hymn to the evening star, from Tannhäuser, and Willie be damned.
He disliked everything, even this house, just now. He looked at the
steep marble staircase rising to the dim upper story and hoped that one
of these days Willie would break his neck—or at least his ankle—on
those stairs. It was a wonder someone hadn't done that before.

He was much annoyed to find Wilhelm in a puce-and-gold dressing-
gown, sitting before a neat fire, with a purple afghan over his knees.
Such damn nonsense. The man had gotten over his attack of la grippe
weeks ago. Yet, there he sat, so elegantly, a folded white handkerchief
in the pocket of his dressing-gown, and coughing fastidiously. Phyllis
was at the piano, in a white woolen frock, while her husband listened
with all the absorbed seriousness of a sensitive critic, his slight fingers
beating time on the carved arm of the chair.

"Well," Charles said, coming into the room. Wilhelm turned his head
with a vexed expression, and Charles sat down until Phyllis had finished. The beautiful notes rose and fell like drops of bright frozen
water in the exquisite room. Charles, as usual, tried to find what he
called a "theme" in the music, but it seemed all erratic sound to him,
and his nervousness increased.

Wilhelm sat there, precise and egotistical, his head tilted, listening.
One had to admire his air of aristocracy. Charles tried to admire it. But
again, his resentment returned to him. He was certainly losing control
of himself, he thought. It ought not to matter to him that Wilhelm
knew nothing, nothing at all, of what was happening in the world.

Charles knew he was sitting in his chair very lumpily, and growing
very "solid" with each moment. He wanted Wilhelm to feel this. Then
he saw that Wilhelm was not looking at him; there was something too
obvious in his absorption, too evasive. Charles grunted under his
breath.

Phyllis came to him, smiling faintly, and gave him a glass of sherry.
She had not given him sherry since last August; she had given him
whiskey and soda, even in the face of Wilhelm's light disapproval.

Wilhelm made the first remark, and it was testy. "How is Jimmy?"

"He goes back to his school tomorrow," said Charles, looking with
gloom at the sherry.

"Good," said Wilhelm. He glanced at Phyllis: "Is the tea hot, my dear? You know how I detest lukewarm tea." He said to Charles: "You've had a very bad time, I know. Fortunately, you did not get that abominable illness, yourself."

Charles was about to say: "I didn't have the time." But he stopped the words before he could speak them. Phyllis was sitting near Wilhelm; she was drawing up the afghan; Wilhelm glanced at her fondly, gave his affected cough. "Isn't there a draft, Phyllis?" he asked. "I'm certain I feel one on the back of my neck. La grippe leaves one in a debilitated condition." He sipped his tea, tasting it with the concentration of a connoisseur. "I had this jasmine tea especially imported," he informed Charles. "A pity you don't like it."

The sweet odor of the hot beverage pervaded the room. Perfumed tea, thought Charles, fuming. "I never liked tea," he could not help saying. The winter wind boomed around the house, and the fire flared.

Wilhelm continued to sip as if Charles had made a faux pas of the worst kind, and it was only charitable to ignore it. He said: "I'm glad that Jimmy is better. Now Phyllis can stay home instead of running about in the snow and cold. I sometimes felt quite neglected." He smiled at Phyllis, and his narrow face became gentle. She put her hand over his, and he took it. This affectionate exchange often happened when Charles was present, and it had always touched him. It did not touch him now. He did not know, or would not allow himself to know, why he was suddenly so outraged, and so desolated. He stood up, abruptly, and looked down into the fire.

"And, thank God," said Wilhelm, lifting Phyllis' hand to his lips, and then releasing it, "that detestable woman, Isabel, won't be calling almost every day, asking for Phyllis. She knew very well that Phyllis was with you and Jimmy, yet she was always surprised. But then, she was never anything else but a fool and a scatterbrain."

Charles stood very still on the hearth. The log fell apart in a blaze of brilliant gold. Phyllis said: "She was probably very busy, and never remembered."

"It was most annoying," said Wilhelm, petulantly. "I always disliked her, and I am sure I never concealed my dislike. I couldn't understand why she was so solicitous about me all at once."

Charles said: "But Isabel, as Phyllis says, is so busy these days. She has so many social engagements."

" 'Social engagements,' " scoffed Wilhelm. "Who are Jochen's and her friends? Nobodies. Vulgar bourgeois, like themselves. Come now, Charles, don't be so grim. You know you agree with me."

Charles continued to look at the fire, while Wilhelm watched him curiously. What was wrong with old Charles? Of course, he disliked Jochen and Isabel, but surely he did not hate them? One did not hate one's relatives. It was plebeian. Again, Wilhelm coughed.

He said: "I don't suppose you had time to look at that book about Gauguin, Charles? Very good reproductions, there. No one appreciates the Impressionist painters these days. But the time will come, and it won't be long, I assure you, when Van Gogh and Picasso and Gauguin will be given their due."

Charles had completely forgotten the book about Gauguin. He could not even remember what he had done with it, after Phyllis had brought it to him. He was too disturbed to think of any lie which would placate his brother. One turbulent thought replaced another in his mind. He was not used to turbulent thinking. "Have you thought out the design for the Wittmann Civic Park, Wilhelm?"

Wilhelm smiled and put down his tea-cup. "While I was in bed, and convalescing, I drew up a complete plan. Within a week or two I'll turn it over to the landscape gardeners I have personally selected. It will be a small park, as parks go, but I assure you it will be in the most excellent taste. My only fear is that the populace might injure it. Too bad it can't be a private park."

He added, peevishly: "There are parks in London, and even in New York, which one can enter only by keys belonging to selected people. A most sensible idea." He became irascible. "I can just see the hordes trampling the grass, the perfect paths, lumbering through the flower-beds, defacing the grottoes. Yes, it is too bad, indeed."

"There will be caretakers," said Phyllis.

But Charles was thinking. It was getting dark. He must soon leave. He said: "We'll have to help keep up the park. Think of the people the Connington Steel Company will be bringing into Andersburg. But then, as everyone says, the mill will also bring prosperity to the city, and God knows we need a little prosperity. We are the only company still in the black, here, even if I have refused to lease or sell some of my patents to the Bouchards."

Wilhelm nodded. "Very wise of you, of course, Charles. We'll make more in the long run by keeping the patents to ourselves. Jochen has been badgering me, lately, on the telephone, about what he calls your 'obduracy.' But he is all for the quick profit."

Charles turned to him, slowly. "I'm sorry, in a way, that the Connington is coming here. I'm sorry the Brinkwells are here. I hate Brinkwell. And I think, when you met him, that you didn't like him, either."

"Detested him," agreed Wilhelm, nodding again. He was being as amiable as possible, but Charles felt that his brother was evading him, that he wanted him to leave. Wilhelm said: "Mrs. Brinkwell called a few times, to inquire about my health. I did not talk to her personally. And Phyllis, I believe, has refused her invitations, pleading my illness." He listened to the roar of the mountain wind. "Dreadful weather. I'm very glad you could visit me today, Charles, but I do think you should be thinking of returning home."

Charles said, quietly: "Gerry came to see Jimmy today. She wasn't permitted to do it, until now. And I have an idea Joe and Isabel don't know, though the girl didn't mention it."

"What?" said Wilhelm. "I can't believe it. I always understood, from Jochen, that he hoped there would be a match, there."

Charles looked at his brother. "Yes," he said. "The girl certainly resembles you amazingly, Wilhelm." Wilhelm smiled. Charles went on: "Joe always did have the idea of a 'match,' as you say. But not since the Brinkwells came. They have a son, you know."

"That flabby, colorless young feller?" asked Wilhelm, incredulously.

Phyllis said, as quietly as Charles: "But the Brinkwells have so much money, and they bought that awful Wilcox house, Wilhelm."

Wilhelm was most indignant. "That Wilcox house! I knew it well. An atrocity. I was there only once, when the Wilcoxes owned it, and it revolted me. Such loathsome taste, such crassness. Yes, I know the Brinkwells bought it, and are living in it, of course. It is just like them."

"I think so, too," Charles smiled. "Well, they have the Wilcox house, and their Gobelins. And they have their son. Joe and Isabel are pushing Gerry at him. The child is very wretched, Wilhelm. I don't know why I discuss the matter with you, but she resembles you so much that it's almost as if you were her father."

"Such a lovely, dignified little thing," said Phyllis, sadly.

"And, as you've said, they're intrinsically vulgar people." Charles began to laugh. "You won't believe it," Charles continued, "but the Brinkwells have been suggesting the most ridiculous thing to Joe and Isabel. They've given them the idea of adding a 'von' to our name!"

Wilhelm colored. He looked at his empty tea-cup. Phyllis refilled it. He watched her do this.

Charles turned to look up at his father's portrait. "I wonder what Dad would have thought of that?" he said. "Dad was proud of his name. Yet the Brinkwells, who are such friends of Joe's and Isabel's, are trying to make them ashamed of an honest and upright name—a good name."

THE BALANCE WHEEL   223

"Impossible!" exclaimed Phyllis. Wilhelm frowned at her. He coughed feebly. His color remained high.

"I think it outrageous that people like the Brinkwells should interfere with our family name, and should imply that it's ordinary, or something," said Charles. "But then, Joe has never had any pride. He doesn't know the meaning of the word."

He laughed again. "I'll have to tell this to Minnie Holt. It'll be all over Andersburg in no time, and I can just hear everybody laughing at us."

He watched Wilhelm closely, out of the corner of his eye. Wilhelm von Wittmann. Yes. Charles felt himself losing his temper. "If it goes any further, I'll tell Minnie. It's too good to keep."

Wilhelm, Charles saw, was extremely perturbed. Braydon would be disgusted; he had indicated to Wilhelm that he did not believe that Roger Brinkwell was truly a collector at heart. The Brinkwells! Wilhelm was thinking. So, they were behind this, were they?

He sipped his tea. It was hard to relinquish something which had appealed to him so immensely. But it would be harder to endure ridicule. Wilhelm turned quite pale.

Wilhelm said: "If Jochen becomes Jochen von Wittmann, then he'll be a 'von' all by himself. I never heard anything so absurd."

Now he was very angry. He forgot that he had looked quite benignly on the idea when Jochen had suggested it to him.

"Stupid. Repugnant," he said. "But, something like that would naturally occur to Jochen. Still, I think perhaps it is Isabel's doing. Jochen has a measure of good sense."

Charles nodded, seriously. "I think you are right, Wilhelm. The Brinkwells, and Isabel." He turned from the fire.

He held out his hand to Phyllis, and she smiled at him. "I'm so glad you found out in time, Charles," she said. "But it's unfortunate that poor Wilhelm should be so annoyed just when he is getting well."

Wilhelm was indeed excessively annoyed. When Charles had gone he said to Phyllis: "Jochen did mention it to me two or three weeks ago, when you were visiting Jimmy, my dear. I didn't take him seriously. Will you call Jochen's home, Phyllis, and see if he is there? I must talk to him before another day has gone by."

Jochen and Isabel were still at home, though preparing to leave. Jochen listened in silence to Wilhelm's dignified if angry remarks. Then he said: "Charlie been there this afternoon? I thought so. Fred told him, I suppose. I saw Fred go into his office a few days ago."

"What has that to do with it?" demanded Wilhelm, coldly.

"Nothing. Except that old Charlie's succeeded in wangling you again."

"Nonsense. He has just made me see how absurd the idea is. If I had not been so ill, Jochen, I would have refused the very moment you spoke of it."

Jochen laughed coarsely. "All right, Willie. Go on and play sheep to Charlie's Little Boy Blue. He never fails with you, does he?"

Wilhelm returned to Phyllis. He coughed very hard. She covered his knees with the afghan. "There are times, Phyllis," he informed her, "when I am forced to believe that Jochen has no intelligence at all."

Phyllis kissed him, very gently. "I don't know what Charles would do without you, darling," she said, for she saw that Wilhelm was secretly very resentful against Charles, also. "He relies on you so."

Wilhelm considered this. Then he said, pettishly: "I don't know. Charles is a very subtle man, Phyllis. At times, he is even crafty. I don't always trust him. I don't know why I should have such brothers, I really don't."

For no reason he knew of, he thought of Isabel again, and her suave voice apologizing to him for not remembering that Phyllis was with Charles and his son. "So stupid of me," she had said, not once, but several times. "But I knew you were ill, too, Wilhelm."

Wilhelm said now, to his wife: "I don't know. I have exasperating relatives. That Isabel." He twitched at the afghan discontentedly. He hoped he was not to have a relapse; there was such an uneasiness and heat in him.

CHAPTER XXVIII

CHARLES ALWAYS thought March a most detestable month. There were some, he supposed, who claimed to hear "the bells of spring" in March. He heard only furious blizzards, the whine of gales in cold black trees, the howling in the chimneys of his house. The look of the black-and-white mountains depressed him; the heavy gray sky lowering over them always lowered over his spirits, too. A man who liked movement in the streets and an air of briskness about shops, he abhorred long cold vistas filled with nothing but wind, the brick corners of buildings jutting bleakly over empty pavements, shop-windows reflecting only opposite shop-windows. Sometimes he went into his snow-heaped garden to look hopefully at beds where crocuses were planted. He was always disappointed; it would be at least a week or two more. He examined the twigs of maples and elms. Stiff, small, hard. If anything was happening in those woody nibs he could not feel or see it. He supposed there was, but he was a man who needed evidence.

Jimmy was well, at least, back at school and studying furiously. Perhaps it was this concentrated haste of his son's which made Charles feel that everything was in the same state, lately. A secret but powerful haste. He tentatively inquired among the few sturdy business men he knew, men of medium-sized businesses like his own. They were puzzled. They scratched jaws. Well, now, they didn't rightly know. Maybe there was something— They looked at Charles in bewilderment. What was the matter with old Charlie? He was always so sure and so firm. But here he was, looking much older than he should; after all, the man was only forty or thereabouts. What did he mean: "Something"? A few answered him, frowning in a baffled way. There was the Connington, going up so fast. Usually a plant like that took at least eighteen months. Yet here it was, almost finished. Come to think of it, they'd heard that the steel mills in Pittsburgh were very busy, and they were getting orders for things, long before the season. And the saw-mills, those Prescott mills, were working overtime. Funny.

Charles called up Oliver Prescott, who was a director of the Prescott Lumber Company, a subsidiary of the Northwest Lumber Company. Oliver said: "Yes, you're right, Mr. Wittmann. All right: 'Charlie.' My brother-in-law, Eugene Arnold, would know more about it, but I can tell you, myself, that we've had a lot of big orders recently. Why? I don't know; I only know about the orders. It could be, you know, that we're coming out of the depression, and things are getting better. After all, even depressions don't last indefinitely."

Charles hesitated about calling George Hadden, of the sheet metal works, because of George's bereavement during the previous fall. But George Hadden seemed glad to hear his voice. "I haven't forgotten about meeting your brother Friederich, Mr. Wittmann," he said. "But things—"

"I know," said Charles, with sincere regret.

"Well, there's another on the way, we hope. I'm wondering if that meeting could be arranged sometime next week. Mr. Friederich should be back by then, shouldn't he? And I'd like him to meet my sister, Helen. She has just returned from The Hague. You've never met her." He paused. "I didn't write, or call, but thank you for the flowers, at this late date."

Charles asked him if his company was "doing well." George

answered immediately, pleased: "Yes, indeed. A lot of new orders, from big companies, too. We're very happy. We are calling back all our old workmen. It's been a bad time for the country, this past year or so."

Charles looked at the heap of new orders on his own desk, urgent orders for his best precision tools. He was still looking at them when Mr. Parker came in to inform him that Mrs. Holt wished to speak to him.

She cried at once: "Now, Charles, I know I ought to have waited until you got home, but I think it's important. What? 'Charlie?' Well, yes, I always did call you that, didn't I? But I've been reading some novels recently, about King Charles of England. First or second—I don't remember. But very romantic. What? Yes, I said romantic. Charles is such a reckless name; reminds me of lace collars and velvet and silver buckles. And swords. Things like that."

In spite of his despondency, Charles began to laugh. But Mrs. Holt was defensive. "You're so prosy, my dear. That's why so many people call you Charlie. 'Charlie' sounds solid and obstinate and money-in-the-bank, and no nonsense. I suppose that describes you. I can imagine that nothing ever goes wrong with your ledgers and accounts. I'm going to call you Charles," she added with determination. "Perhaps it will make you feel romantic, yourself. Perhaps you'll even have a love affair, or something, and get married to a perfectly giddy female with golden hair and a past, and buy a house of white stone with white marble inside. And an automobile."

"I have a big red one. But Jimmy drives it all the time."

"Is that so? I've never seen you in it, yourself. Incidentally, have you bought yourself a new dinner jacket yet?"

Charles was alarmed. "I've not been going to parties," he protested.

"Well, you're going to one very soon. A small but late supper party." She laughed. "Not mine, dear Charles. But one given by the Brinkwells. You'll receive an invitation. Now, wait, please. Pauline's been telling me that you've refused all three of the invitations she's sent you. So I suggested that you might accept an invitation to a small and exclusive little party, say at ten o'clock at night."

"Why did you say that?" asked Charles, irately. "Minnie, that's too bad of you. You know I dislike those people."

There was a little silence. Then Mrs. Holt said slowly and carefully: "Charles, I think you ought to accept."

He was about to refuse, in annoyance, then remembered Mrs. Holt's serious voice. He said: "You think I ought to go, eh?"

"Yes. Decidedly."

Charles waited for a moment or two. Finally he said: "I don't suppose you'd know, Minnie, and I realize that Braydon has retired. But would you have the slightest idea if the oil wells Braydon owns are—well, doing much business? Any particular call for oil, say?"

"What? How funny you are—Charles. Have you oil stocks? No? Well, you should buy some. Yes, Braydon mentioned to me only very lately that his oil companies are literally 'booming.' Orders just pouring in, he says. What did you say, Charles? Who is buying the oil? Really, I don't know. But I think it is some exporting company, or companies. For Europe. Do buy yourself some stocks. You're just the kind who would never invest in common stock, I know. But do it now. Never mind. Just remember to buy a new dinner jacket. That other one is so old-fashioned, and green. I want to be proud of you. And," she added, again reverting to her former slow and careful voice: "you'll want to concentrate on something else besides how anarchistic and shabby you might look in your old jacket."

"All right, Minnie. I'll buy the jacket, and I'll go to the Brinkwells."

She said, with affection: "Good. Oh, I'll call you 'Charlie,' again. I just remember that it was a King Charles who had his head cut off by somebody very disagreeable. A vegetarian, or something. I'd hate to see your head cut off, Charlie."

Her laughter was loud, but Charles thought there was a curious subtlety to it. All his imagination, he told himself, as he hung up. For a man who had a reputation for no imagination I'm doing very well, he reflected.

Concentrated, secret haste. New orders, for everyone. Nonsense. The country was just taking an industrial upturn for the better. What did he expect? That the depression had become a permanent thing?

He went into the shops. He was glad that so many of his best men had been recalled; there were even a number of new apprentices. Young men didn't care, these days, about being good artisans, fine craftsmen. It was good to see apprentices once more, seriously applying themselves to learning to make excellent precision tools. Tom Murphy was contented and busy. "I like to hear the shops humming again, Mr. Wittmann," he said, looking at Charles with deep liking and respect. "I thought it'd never happen again. Even orders for warp-tying machines and looms, from the silk companies. I thought we'd never get 'em again. But the best, of course, are precision gear-cutting machines, and the boring machines, and the micrometers and drills, and milling cutters, and reamers. Just like old times, only better. Damn much better."

The young man was elated. His fair-skinned face was flushed; his sandy hair fell over his forehead. He looked about the noisy shops with pride. "And that big order on that patent of yours, Mr. Wittmann, for the micrometers, and the other for the lathes. From the Bouchards. They know good tools when they see 'em; know they can't get better in the whole country. Even if we charge more."

It was hard to be depressed, in the face of this new prosperity. Charles said, absently: "No trouble in getting the new men to join the union, Tom?"

"No, sir. They don't get hired if they don't join. But there was one fellow I wouldn't take, though he was good." Tom frowned. "He said company unions weren't any good. We ought to join one of the others. Maybe so. I don't know. I told him we was satisfied, and he sneered at me."

Charles patted his shoulder. "Well, don't be too stubborn, Tom. Company unions are fine. But perhaps there might come a time when they won't serve the best purpose. Keep an open mind."

When Charles arrived home Jimmy was deep in his books. Charles said: "Now, look here, son. What about the ice-skating? And the hockey you always liked? Studies are good, especially when you have something definite in mind, as you have. But you've never gotten your color back since your illness."

Jimmy might be pale, and he might still be very thin, but his air was vivid and alive. He said: "I'm going ice-skating with Gerry on Saturday. Honest." He scowled. "She never says anything, but I'm getting the idea she has to sneak off, sometimes."

"How is Gerry?" asked Charles. "I miss her. She used to come in almost every day after school, with you."

Jimmy hesitated. He put aside his book, but left a finger in it. "She doesn't look very happy. We don't talk about it. We—we know what we think about each other." He became reserved. "She's busy studying, too. And she thinks she'll be going away to school next September." Jimmy looked at his father, directly. "Have you told Uncle Joe I'm going to Harvard?"

Charles studied his son. "I could tell him it isn't settled. I could even say, later, that I think you've picked some other university."

Jimmy nodded. "Thanks, Dad. You see, there's a school for girls right near Harvard—Uncle Joe's been thinking of it, Gerry says, but Uncle Joe's 'considering' he said."

Charles did not discuss the subject any further. But he was sickened with his hatred. His liver was bad enough, God knows, these days. Something else, however, had been added to his misery. Now, when he felt like this, there would come a vicious spasm in his stomach which would last for hours. Pyloric spasm, Metzger called it. Whatever it was, it was infernally painful. It interfered with the digestion of his favorite dishes. He had had to give up spareribs and sauerkraut. He held that against Jochen, virulently.

After dinner, Jimmy returned to his books. Charles took down a volume of Goethe's in the parlor, and reread a certain verse. He had read it very often. In the beginning he had begun to read Goethe for a special reason; now he read the great sonorous poetry for himself. This sometimes surprised him. But there was something about Goethe which he understood, deeply and simply. Once his father had said that Goethe had brought a tremendous world-dream to the Germans. But Charles believed that Goethe had brought the mightiest of the old German dreams to the world. It was indeed a mighty dream—if an innocent one. A dream that man could be godlike and noble, childlike and infinitely wise, simple and heroic. Charles reflected that this would probably never be possible. He also reflected that no other man, with the exception, perhaps, of Goethe, ever believed it either.

Perhaps Goethe appeals to me because I'm an innocent, too, thought Charles, replacing the book. He had memorized a certain portion of a certain poem. He repeated it to himself, silently, as he put on his hat and coat and gloves and went out into the cold March night. Almost bemused, himself, he remembered other poems, other phrases, other words so luminous, so grand, that he was stirred and touched with emotion. He looked up at the black and windy sky; the white stars burned there, without a moon. The streets were empty and silent, the trees dark and bare. Yet there was a faint milky light, like a lighter shadow in the darkness. Starlight. Charles had never known before that stars could cast light like this, a dreamlike radiance, a mystic gleam. He was at once moved and lonely.

He began to walk faster. He had to keep these treacherous thoughts of his down. There was no sense in longing, in dreaming, in desiring, for there was no hope. He could not always turn away the pain, but he could endure it calmly, and say to it: There's no use. Once he had read that a man could not live without hope. He knew this was nonsense. He was alive, and had no intention of dying. He never allowed himself to imagine that Phyllis was walking beside him, when he walked like this. It was only too possible that she was playing for Wilhelm, or laughing with him, or holding his hand. That was right.

After a considerable time he came to Chestnut Road, and Friederich's house. It was more dilapidated than ever, with no green trees to hide it from the glare of the arc light a little distance away. A dull light burned near one window. Charles climbed the icy wooden steps carefully, holding on to the rusted hand-rail. He tugged on the bell, but it gave out no sound, so he hammered irritably on the splintered door. Friederich, himself, opened it. There was a book in his hand, and he was wearing his overcoat. Charles knew why, at once. The house was cold, as usual. Friederich was too parsimonious to give his furnace much coal, and there was probably no fire on any hearth.

"Karl," said Friederich, in an affronted voice. But he stood aside and let Charles go into the house. The air, here, was heavy, smelling of kerosene, old pork fat, dust, and acrid coffee.

Charles said, in German: "Why are you surprised to see me? You received my note, did you not?"

"Yes. But I did not think you meant you would come tonight. Your note was indefinite. Why should you wish to see me?"

Charles took off his hat, but not his coat. He looked about the cold and dirty parlor, with its heaps of sliding books, its littered tables, its black hearth. Friederich's pipe was smoking in a filthy ash tray. Friederich was wearing glasses with steel rims. Charles had not known that his brother wore glasses. They gave him a forlorn and deserted look, vaguely sad, in spite of his sullen expression. Apparently, too, he was not well, for his color was bad. Then he coughed.

"You have had a cold?" suggested Charles, with mild sympathy.

"Yes. But who would care about that? You, or my other brothers?" Friederich sat down, and Charles took two or three books from the seat of a very dusty chair and sat down, also.

He looked at his brother. Friederich had become wary, as usual, and suspicious. He stared at Charles with intense unfriendliness.

"Have you had the doctor?" asked Charles. He had never felt much concern for Friederich before. It must be the glasses, he thought.

"Everyone has colds," Friederich replied. He peered at Charles, doubting that he had heard sincerity. But Charles' face was genuinely solicitous. Friederich was disturbed at this. He coughed again. "I have a cough mixture, and a tonic," he said. "It is not so bad, now. I am almost well."

Charles thought: He has been sick, and nobody knew, because nobody cared. He hasn't a soul in the world—though he has three brothers. He hates us, and we hate him. This poor devil has never had anyone. Even when we were at home, together, children, he never had anyone, not even our parents.

Charles remembered that during his childhood and boyhood he had suspected, a few times, that Friederich had loved their father deeply and inarticulately. He had never done anything, or said anything, to betray this love. A very terrible thing. Emil had never had any tolerance for the unattractive little boy, and when Brinkwell's dog had torn his arm Emil had shouted to him not to be a "coward." Even their mother, though frightened, had been impatient with his lonely howling.

"I wish I had known," said Charles, thinking of all those past years. "What could you have done? A cold is just a cold," said Friederich. "I could have done something," Charles muttered.

Friederich shifted uneasily in his chair. He was still deeply suspicious. But something about Charles' face and voice had reached him. He repeated that he had a cough mixture and a tonic. It was nothing at all.

"If you are ever ill again, you must send for me. I must ask you to promise that," said Charles.

Friederich took off his glasses. He twiddled them in his fingers. He pursed his lips. He could not understand. He rubbed his nose with the back of a grimy hand. He said, suddenly: "Your son: he is completely well, now?"

"Yes."

"You have been ill, yourself, Karl? You have lost some flesh."

"I have not been ill. But I have been worried."

"Worried?" Friederich was incredulous.

"Yes, Friederich. I need help. Your help."

Friederich stood up, abruptly. All his black suspicions had come back. He said, in a voice that shook: "It is not often that you come to me. You only come when you can use me. And it is always a lie, what you say to me. I discover that later."

Charles did not turn to him. He said: "There is some truth in what you say. And I say again: it has always been for our company. For you, as well as for myself, and Wilhelm, and Jochen."

"Yes, yes, I know that!" said Friederich, harshly. "It is always the same old story, and it is true in many respects. But I am tired of being used." He waited, but Charles did not speak. Friederich threw out his hands. "What is it that you wish me to say, or do?" he exclaimed, with bitterness. "It is not necessary for you to wheedle me or to lie to me, now. I know your methods, Karl."

Charles looked at him then. Friederich's sunken face was twitching. He had replaced the glasses, which again gave him that vulnerable, sad expression.

"I am being honest with you, Friederich," said Charles. "I need your help. I want you to come into the company. You are treasurer, but you rarely do anything. I want you to learn; I want you to be a part of your own company."

Friederich was stunned. "You are lying," he said feebly.

Charles shook his head. "No, I am not."

Friederich became excited. "Why do you ask me this, at this late day? You never wanted me there before. If our father had not left the company to all of us you would never have permitted me to enter these offices, these shops! All of you would have kept me out."

Charles nodded. "Yes. That is quite true. I am not denying it. It was wrong; it was unjust. However, you were never very interested."

"Because none of you ever allowed me to be interested." Friederich began to walk unsteadily up and down the room, huddled in his old and wrinkled coat. "Our father: he was not anxious for me to come. I was always in the way, he told me. I was stupid, he said. I had not the feeling for the shops."

He stopped in front of Charles. "That is what was said to me. I was never wanted—by anyone."

"I know," said Charles.

Friederich put up a trembling hand and scratched his neck. "You know," he repeated.

Charles sighed. "I want you now, Friederich. I do not want to 'use' you. It is necessary for you to be with me. There are dangerous days coming, and I will need your help."

Friederich sat down. He let his arms and hands fall helplessly between his slack knees. He shook his head, over and over. "I am trying to believe you, Karl. It is very hard to do this. I do not understand."

Charles said: "Friederich, listen to me. Do you still have those scars on your arm?"

"Scars?" repeated Friederich.

"You have forgotten? Where the dog bit you?"

Friederich fell back in his chair, as if exhausted. "I have never forgotten. I was only four years old, but I have never forgotten. The pain; the blood. The doctor with the needle. It is a long time ago. But I have hated dogs ever since. I have always been afraid of them."

He sat up, and almost hysterically pulled off his overcoat, his under-coat. Charles saw the soiled shirt underneath. Friederich was rolling it up, and with it came his underwear. The thin dark arm was revealed. There, just above the elbow, was the long whitish scar, jagged and narrow, and gleaming in the light of the kerosene lamp. "There it is!" cried Friederich.

They both looked at the scar, in silence.

Then Friederich said: "Why are you interested in this, now? What is it to you, Karl?" He had turned crimson, as if with shame. He rolled down his sleeves. "Are you laughing at me again?"

"No," said Charles. He waited until Friederich's clothing had been straightened. "I know you think all this is very peculiar. But I have a reason. Do you remember the boy who set the dog on you?"

"The boy?" Friederich, confused by the conversation, shook his head. "Ah, yes, I remember. It was so long ago. There was a boy, certainly. A big boy—"

Bewildered, Friederich waited. But Charles was waiting, also. Friederich again scratched his neck. "Your manner is most peculiar, Karl. You speak as if you knew this boy—this man he is, for it is long ago. He is here in Andersburg. He is very rich, and he married a rich wife. He will live in this, our city."

Friederich's emaciated face stiffened. He put his hand to his covered arm as if he felt the pain he had felt as a child. "Here, in this city," he repeated.

Charles stood up. He said: "We had all forgotten his name, because we were small children. But when I met him I remembered; he recalled his name to me, and where he had lived."

Friederich gripped the arms of his chair and rose slowly. "Who?" he repeated.

"An ugly man, as he had been an ugly boy. In character. What is born in a man is always with him. It is with him today; he would like to set a thousand dogs on a thousand men." Charles pushed his cold hands into his pockets. "His name is Roger Brinkwell, and he will be the new superintendent of the Connington Steel Company, in Andersburg."

Charles had told himself that it was impossible to predict how Friederich would take this news. He had been right. He was prepared for an outburst of rage, for exclamations of incoherent fury. But he was certainly not prepared to see Friederich become scarlet, and to remain in a fixed silence, even after almost a full minute had passed.

Charles said: "You have met him? You have seen him? Is it possible? He is a friend of Jochen's."

Friederich turned away with a short swift gesture which was full of a mysterious violence. He walked rapidly to the windows. He pulled aside a dirty curtain and stared, still in silence, out into the darkness.

Charles watched this curious behavior with alarm. He started after his brother, then stopped halfway. He said: "What is wrong? You have met this man?"

Friederich did not turn. His thin bent back remained motionless. He only said: "I have not met him."

Then he swung about. He pointed one of his lean fingers at his brother. "What a wily liar and plotter you are, Karl! I understand it all. Is there anything you never know? Did you think to deceive me?"

Thunderstruck, Charles almost stammered: "Are you mad? What is wrong with you?" It was not often that he was frightened; he was frightened now.

Now Friederich became extraordinarily excited. "Jochen has told me of this man. It is true that I do not like the Connington Steel Company, for they refuse to recognize a union. It is also true that I will work with the men they employ to organize them. All can be arranged. This, Jochen has told me, has almost been promised me."

Charles stood very still. His hands clenched in his pockets. Friederich must have thought his expression strange, for he forced himself to greater excitement. The finger still pointed at Charles.

"They will bring prosperity to Andersburg. Jochen has said that this mill will give us orders, such orders as you have refused to the Bouchards—"

"I have not refused orders from the Bouchards," said Charles, quietly. "That is a lie. I have refused them only my aeroplane steering-control assembly, and our special gun-boring machine." He watched Friederich closely. "I will never lease or sell these patents to them. That, I have sworn to myself." He showed no excitement of his own, but his heart was behaving painfully. "Jochen has been lying to you. But it appears you prefer to believe him than to believe me."

"Karl! Karl!" said Friederich.

The hating disgust in Friederich's voice frightened Charles more than ever. There was something wrong, something very wrong.

"Great God," said Charles. "Do not look at me like that. I do not know what you mean. Believe me, before God, I do not know what you mean."

Friederich passed Charles, as if he were not present, flung himself down in his chair. Then he looked at his brother, and saw that he was very white, Charles who always had such a good color. A queer uneasiness came to Friederich.

"Jochen warned me," he muttered. He put his soiled hand over his eyes a moment as if very tired and dizzy. "He warned me that you would come to me, when you eventually discovered—"

"What?"

Friederich sighed. Then he went off into a fit of coughing. He almost strangled. Charles' first impulse was to go to him; but he held himself back. He had to know. He wanted to take Friederich by the shoulders and shake him roughly.

"Karl," said Friederich, when he could get his breath, and could speak only hoarsely. "Jochen has told me that you do not like this Brinkwell, that you would, perhaps, come to me with lies about him. You are jealous of our company, Jochen says. I do not quarrel with you about this. But a company can expand, can grow, by—"

"By what?" asked Charles.

"By coöperation. That is what Jochen says: by coöperation." Friederich's uneasiness had mounted to panic. He, too, had his intuitions. He cried out: "You all lie to me! I am just a fool before you! You use me and laugh at me!"

Charles had to sit down. He sat on the edge of his chair, his hands still clenched in his pockets. He stared at the floor, grimly. He said: "Listen to me, and you may tell Jochen if you wish: There shall be no cooperation, in the way that Jochen might have implied to you, between us and Brinkwell. Never, never. I am president; I will fight to my death to prevent that 'cooperation.' "

"You see?" said Friederich. "You knew, and you came to me tonight, and you lied."

Charles did not speak. He could not question Friederich any more, for he knew that the befuddled man had been told as little as possible by Jochen.

My company, thought Charles. What is it that they want of it?

Friederich gave a weak and bitter laugh. "How are your lessons in modernistic painting proceeding, Karl? Have you discovered the difference between Van Gogh and Picasso?"

Charles said: "Yes, there are many things I see, now."

Friederich scratched his cheek. "Your German, Karl. It has immensely improved. You could not have improved it, possibly, with the intention of using it on me?"

Charles stood up again. He walked slowly up and down the room. Friederich watched him. Charles said, without glancing at his brother: "You will never understand. I have had to fight all of you to save our father's company. For years, I have had to fight—"

"Ach, yes," said Friederich, trying to sound cunning. "How you have bustled, Karl. Always, you have bustled. As a very young man you moved so fast in the offices and in the shops. Always so important. Did you know I observed that importance, and hated you?" He added: "And how I laughed." He laughed now, and it was a most pathetic sound.

Charles, though engrossed with his own dread, heard his brother. He stopped before him, began to speak, then closed his mouth. He had a sudden vivid picture of himself, before and after his father's death. Yes, he had "bustled." He had been "important." He might even have been arrogant, with his new responsibilities. And there had been Friederich, young, too, dumbly hoping for recognition, being given none, and finally coming to hate.

Charles said: "Listen to me, Friederich. You may not believe; if you do not, I cannot help it. I have hurt you, perhaps. I did not mean to do it. I was young, and I was egotistical. But our father's company was always first with me. I am sorry I hurt you. I came to you tonight to ask for your help."

He paused. Friederich was fascinated. He began to suck in his lips. He felt for his pipe, and his hand trembled.

Charles went on: "You see, I have a son."

Friederich said, bitterly: "So you have told me before."

But Charles continued: "I want you to think for a moment. You have been to many cities. This depression—it is passing? Tell me if it is so."

Friederich was again deeply confused. "Yes, it is so," he muttered. Then he sat upright in his chair. "What do you mean, Karl?" He was suddenly excited. "No!" he exclaimed. "It is not possible for you to know anything!"

"It could be war," said Charles. He took his hands out of his pockets, gestured slightly, dropped his hands.

Friederich clenched one of his own hands; he pressed one knuckle against his mouth. Over it he stared at Charles feverishly.

"I have a son," repeated Charles. He was so tired; his legs were shaking. "I have been watching, ever since last summer. And I am much afraid. There is something about to happen. There is something moving in the world, and it is terrible. And again, I must say once more: I have a son. I have nothing else."

"You have no proof," said Friederich, almost whispering.

"Nor have you. But I know a little of something, which has been hinted to me in confidence. I cannot tell you about it. I can only say that you must think of this steel mill, and the great speed with which it is being built. As if in preparation."

It was all so hopeless. Charles had heard of fatalism, and he had despised it. But now he knew what it was. "There is nothing very much I can do," he said, and he did not know that he was shaking his head over and over. "I must work alone, as always."

He picked up his hat from a table, shook it mechanically. "Yes, my German has improved. I thought I might need it; I improved it in order to try to reach a common ground with you, for I have felt this thing in the world. I believe George Hadden has felt it, also. I have told you before that he heard you speak. He wishes to meet you now. His sister has just returned from The Hague."

Friederich stood up, the cold pipe in his hands. He began to clean it; he fumbled and the pipe fell. He bent to reach for it, then let it lie. He had turned a sickly color.

"Great God," he said.

"Yes," said Charles. "Grosser Gott."

"I will meet this George Hadden, and his sister," said Friederich. Charles put on his hat. "In this house, or in mine?"

Friederich looked about him, dazedly. Charles wondered if his brother was seeing the filth and disorder for the first time. "Here," said Friederich. "I will ask Mrs. Schuele—" He looked at Charles. "You will want to come, too?"

"No," said Charles, after considering the intonations in his brother's voice. "Not unless you ask me, freely, and of your own will." He took a step or two towards the door. "I am tired of being insulted. I have said all I wish to say." He spoke in English. "Yes, I have tried to reach you, as I have said. I have studied Goethe, too, for I heard that you belonged to a world Goethe society. That, I have done. But now I read Goethe for myself, alone."

Friederich's hand rose as if to stop his brother from leaving. He coughed loud and long. He tried to jeer: "So, you have been reading Goethe, for yourself. Tell me, Karl, what is it you have read, that, perhaps, has interested you in Goethe?"

Charles quoted:

> "Wer nie sein Brot mit Tränen ass,
> Wer nie die kummervollen Nächte
> Auf seinem Bette weinend sass,
> Der kennt euch nicht, ihr himmlischen Mächte."

(He who never ate his bread in tears, who never sat weeping on his bed through long nights of anguish, he knows you not, you heavenly powers.)

He waited. But Friederich only looked at him in a deep misery.

Then Charles said, nodding: "Yes, yes. I've said that to myself many times, lately. I'm afraid it's too late for any of us. We can do nothing." He went out of the room, leaving his brother, leaving this ugly house with its grime and its cold. He felt the cold in his very bones. He stumbled down the icy steps outside. Then he heard the door, which he had closed behind him, open. Friederich stood on the threshold, framed in feeble light.

"I shall ask you to come, Karl, when George Hadden is here."

Charles turned. He stood on the sidewalk below. He heard his brother's voice. It was defiant, but it was also pleading, as if the poor man was hopelessly wanting to believe, to reach out, and asking not to be deceived.

"Thanks," said Charles. He walked away, and Friederich stood in the doorway until his brother disappeared.

Yes, thought Charles, walking heavily and tiredly. I reached him. He'll help me, the little he can. It won't be much, perhaps, but it will be something.

There was such a fear in him.

CHAPTER XXIX

ON THE night of the Brinkwells' "small, exclusive party," Mrs. Holt called Charles, an hour before he was to leave his house.

"Charlie, we're down in the city, for dinner with friends," she said in her hearty voice. "We'll pick you up in our limousine and take you to the Brinkwells, and our chauffeur will drive you home, afterwards. Now, Charlie, don't be stuffy. Do you know what I think? You 'independent' people aren't fine characters, after all! It just makes you feel inferior to accept a 'favor' from somebody else, and you simply can't bear to feel inferior. Such conceit. You're such a conceited man, Charlie. Yes, you are, too. So you go around, all puffed up, and being all proper and dreary and trying to be just a monotone."

Charles laughed. Mrs. Holt ran on: "So, we'll pick you up. Did you get a jacket? Good. What's that? You'll drive up in your own automobile? Nonsense. I saw that red horror on the street the other day; your boy, Jimmy, was driving it. Not fitting for you, Charlie. Go on, tell me I'm interfering. Well. Charlie? Do a lot of listening. An awful lot of listening. And don't lose your temper. You never do? Well, sometimes you look mad even if you don't say anything. And, Charlie, I want to see your house. Braydon and I will stop in for a few moments before we all go to the Brinkwells. I've heard your house is just a horror, a real nineteenth century horror. It must be charming."

Charles said to Jimmy: "I love Mrs. Holt. She's a very subtle woman. How do you like my new dinner jacket, son?"

Jimmy, studying at a well-lighted table in the parlor, surveyed the jacket critically, while Charles solemnly rotated. "Quite a gentleman," said the boy. "And no paunch. Dad, what happened to your paunch? You don't eat very much, lately. Mrs. Meyers was complaining tonight, in the kitchen, that you didn't even touch your shoo-fly pie, which used to be your especial favorite."

"I was getting fat," said Charles, hastily. "You've got to admit a dinner jacket looks better on me now than it used to. Sleekness is the thing, so I've heard."

But Jimmy was more anxious than ever. "Dad, do you know that you and Uncle Fred look very much alike? I never saw it until you began to lose weight. You don't want to look like him, do you?"

"Jimmy." Charles sat down, carefully pulling up his trousers. He looked at his new, glittering shoes. "Perhaps I've been wrong about your uncle. In many ways I'm sure of it. It doesn't pay to be too positive about anybody. That's conceit, and stupid."

He was thinking of the call he had had from Friederich two hours ago. The other man's voice had been wary and rough, but it had had, again, that odd note of pleading, of asking not to be deceived again. Friederich had said: "George Hadden and his sister, Miss Helen Hadden, are coming for dinner tomorrow night. I—I'd like you to come, too." Friederich had paused, and then had said irritably: "I've made Mrs. Schuele clean up. She 's been neglecting things, and I've been too busy to see."

Charles had thought very carefully about the invitation. He knew Friederich's chronic suspicion about everyone was still very active. So he had thanked Friederich for the invitation, but had suggested that he come after dinner. "I think it would be best if you and the Haddens had a time to yourselves before I came. I'll come around about eight."

Friederich had protested, but not very vehemently, and Charles had known that by his refusal to come for dinner he had relieved his brother of much of his suspicion.

The telephone rang and Charles answered it. It was Mrs. Holt, again. "Charlie, have you any beer? Braydon loves it, secretly, but no one would ever think of giving him any. He doesn't even know I know he sneaks down to the kitchen at night and helps himself to the servants' beer. I've seen him, once or twice. He washes out the glass and puts it back and hides the bottle. Braydon didn't always collect sculpture, you know." She chuckled.

Charles promised the beer. He inspected and found two cold bottles in the ice-box. He brought out two glasses and placed them on a silver tray in the parlor. Jimmy went up to his room to continue his studies in peace.

The Holts' mighty limousine drew up later, black and glittering. Charles went out into the windy March night to greet them. There was a smell of fecund air in the wind, of life and earthy movement, though it was still very cold. Then he stared. Mrs. Holt, whose sealskin coat was blowing up, had suddenly become a plump, short, blowsy, but reasonable facsimile of Irene Castle. Charles still stared as she and Mr. Holt came into his house. She said, happily: "Now, stop making your eyes bulge, Charlie. Braydon still isn't speaking to me because I had my hair cut off. But so comfortable, you have no idea. No pins, no combs. Just lovely." She put up her black-gloved fat hand and fluffed out the chopped-off mass of her light-brown hair about her big red face, which beamed proudly. The "bob" made her look like a harvest moon with a nimbus. "Daring?" she asked. "And Charlie, what do you think of this gown? Just the very latest. Irene Castle wore the original when she and her husband last appeared in New York."

The dress was even more alarming, to Charles, than the short locks. It was of pink satin, a few shades lighter than Mrs. Holt's face, with a ruffled bodice which made her bosom seem even larger than it was. But the skirt petrified Charles. It flared out over Mrs. Holt's huge hips, so that she appeared almost a yard wide at that point, and then was draped very narrowly to the ankles. This was bad enough, but the front of the skirt was open almost to Mrs. Holt's robust knees, and when she walked one saw her big plump legs, in bright pink silk stockings.

A rope of pearls dangled far below her waist, and there were ropes of pearls about her fat wrists, and pearls and diamonds dripping from her ears almost to her shoulders. She was a remarkable sight, and very pleased with herself. "I'm the first to have this bob and this sort of dress in Andersburg," she said.

"And the last, I hope," said Mr. Holt, with dignified gloom. He was more distant and vague than ever, possibly in order to give the impression of complete detachment from his wife.

"Oh, Braydon," she said, slapping him so vigorously on the arm in her affectionate remonstrance that the poor, thin man tottered for an instant. "You and Charlie. So conservative. Hidebound. Why are men like that? They scream every time a woman changes her styles. I suppose you'd like me to wear an apron, or something, all the time."

Mr. Holt, who was distinctly unhappy, looked pointedly at his wife's skirt. "An apron seems called for," he said.

"Oh, posh. If I were eighteen years old, and wore this dress, your eyes would bulge."

She linked her arm into Charles' arm. "Don't stand there trying to think of something complimentary to say, Charlie. I know you're trying to, and you're all confused. Do show us your house. Yes! So ugly, so wonderful, so anachronistic! Precious."

"Minnie," said Mr. Holt, rebukingly.

But Charles said: "I don't mind. Everybody talks about it, particularly my brothers, Willie and Joe. I like it. It was my father's house, and it's comfortable."

Mrs. Holt left the men and was prowling rapidly around the parlor, inspecting everything, nodding her head as if delighted. "Just like you, Charlie," she said, for a reason inexplicable to Charles. She had stopped before the whatnots and was clapping her hands over the very inexpensive bits of china which Charles' mother had so loved. Charles went over to look at the whatnots, which were filled with tiny china cups, violently painted, little figurines of doubtful artistry, paper-weights with "snow-falls" in them, miniature china trays, china lady's slippers, and small china castles. Mrs. Holt laughed gayly. "Just like you, Charlie!" she repeated.

"How so?" asked Charles, somewhat annoyed.

"Never mind," she answered, soothingly. "You wouldn't understand." Then she halted, shocked. She was staring at the Picasso over the fireplace. "My God!" she screamed. Her mouth fell open. Both men looked at the Picasso. Mr. Holt slowly approached it, putting on his pince-nez.

"Excellent," he muttered. "But of course, not in his present mood. Excellent."

Mrs. Holt rushed to examine the painting at a closer range. "Well, whatever," she said, in a prayerful voice. She swung to Charles, and cried accusingly: "Charlie Wittmann! Have you lost your mind? How perfectly dreadful, revolting!"

Charles said: "My brother Willie gave it to me."

Mr. Holt nodded. "Really wonderful."

Mrs. Holt was gazing at Charles with affront. Then, all at once, she began to smile. She patted Charles' arm gently. "What one has to do!" she murmured.

"What do you mean, Minnie?" asked Mr. Holt, puzzled. But Mrs. Holt sat down in a platform rocker covered with red plush and began to rock, shaking her head a little and smiling sympathetically. She laughed. The draped skirt fell widely apart and her legs were fully exposed. Charles modestly looked aside. She waved her hand at him. "Charlie, have you some beer?"

"Beer?" repeated Mr. Holt, scandalized.

Mrs. Holt eyed him fondly. "Well, Charlie doesn't have those glasses out for water, Braydon. And they're definitely not for sherry—too big." She winked at Charles, who, after glancing at the two glasses, went out in the dark cold "shed," rummaged about for another bottle of beer in the ice-box and brought it back with a third glass. He found Mr. Holt sitting in one of the other rockers, and looking very distinguished, indeed. He saw Mr. Holt regarding the three bottles of beer with a pretense of indifference. Mrs. Holt said: "If Braydon doesn't want a bottle, I'll have two, Charlie."

Mr. Holt became more distinguished than ever. He said: "I am a little thirsty. A glass of cold beer—"

"Braydon gave up beer a long time ago," said Mrs. Holt. She laughed again, a jolly sound. "You see, I was quite the Pennsylvania girl, or, I should say, the Philadelphia girl. But I loved Braydon at first sight." Mr. Holt smiled, self-consciously, and crossed his thin legs. "So vigorous, so fresh, so strong," said Mrs. Holt. "Ah, me. He smelled of oil, too. He was prospecting for it, down near Titusville, and he got a few wells even better than Mr. Rockefeller's, and had sense enough to hold onto them, in spite of Mr. Rockefeller."

Charles poured the beer, carefully refraining from looking at Mr. Holt. But when he unavoidably had to do so, while giving the other man his glass, he found Mr. Holt perceptibly less distinguished in appearance, and smiling. "Yes, yes," said Mr. Holt. "They tried everything, perjury, threats, buying me out, hiring away my workmen, and even setting fire to one of my wells. But I—"

"Stuck," supplied Mrs. Holt, with a glance even more loving than before. Mr. Holt cleared his throat. "I resisted." He studied the frosted glass, smiled again. "Stuck," he said. And put the glass to his lips and drank long and gratefully.

"Then, after we were married, he started to collect stones," said Mrs. Holt.

"Really, Minnie." But Mr. Holt settled down more comfortably in his rocker.

"He thought stones more befitting than anything else. He thought he would fascinate me with his culture," said Mrs. Holt. "And all the time I just loved him."

Mr. Holt turned red. His distant air had disappeared. He even grinned, now. "You were a county belle," he said. He became thoughtful. "But I really like sculpture. I really do."

"Of course," said Mrs. Holt, tenderly. "You can get to like anything in time."

Charles said: "I've learned something about Van Gogh, from my brother Willie. I thought it pretty horrible at first. But now I like those—those strenuous yellows and blues and reds. They—well, they're alive. Sort of. They don't exist, I suppose, and the pictures still seem lopsided, but still I guess they have—"

"A kind of charm," Mrs. Holt nodded. "But give me Sargent, anytime. Or anybody, for that."

Mr. Holt was studying the room. "This looks like my father's house, too," he said. "I like it. Drafty, but the fire makes you sleepy and relaxed. I don't think I like our house," he said suddenly, looking at his wife.

"I do." She was very cheerful. "You can lose your guests in it; so many big rooms. And you can invite so many people that you don't have to say more than a few words to any of them. Just give them plenty to drink and eat, and they're happy, and I'm happy. We all have a nice time." She pondered a moment. "That Wilcox house, where the Brinkwells live. Really dreadful. 'A small mansion,' the newspapers called it. You can't get away from the thing, or forget it. It's on you, all the time. Sometimes I suspect Pauline has no taste."

Charles glanced surreptitiously at his watch; Mrs. Holt saw the gesture. "Oh, I know, Charlie, it's time we should be leaving. But we're enjoying ourselves. What if we're late? It doesn't matter. Our family was more important in Philadelphia than Pauline's." She turned to her husband. "Do you suppose Roger will insist upon showing Charlie all those Gobelins? And that particularly horrid one he has over the fireplace in the big drawing-room?"

"That's early Flemish," said Mr. Holt, reproachfully. He drank the last of the beer. "At least," he conceded, "Roger said it was. I don't know. Frankly, I don't know anything much about tapestries."

"Roger's very buoyant," said Mrs. Holt. She stared blankly at

Charles. "He does everything with so much verve. That big mill. Going up so fast. What do they make in those mills, Braydon?"

Mr. Holt said: "I heard they're going to have a machine tool shop." Then he seemed distressed. He stood up. "It was just mentioned to me, Charles. Nothing—ah, I suppose, important. I know Waite. Elson Waite. The superintendent in Pittsburgh." He was more distressed than ever. "Charles, it was mentioned in confidence. I don't know why I was so—so indiscreet. It just slipped out, unintentionally."

Charles looked at his watch. He found it a little difficult to put it back in his small watch pocket. "Of course," he said. He stood up, also.

Mr. Holt, who was visibly disturbed, helped his wife out of the chair. "Minnie, they make many things in steel mills. Hundreds of things. I can't begin to tell you how many."

He helped Mrs. Holt with her coat. She beamed happily. "So interesting. Business. And so exciting. Just think, Charlie, the Connington here are going to manufacture very special things for the Bouchards, too! So much work for everybody. Didn't you mention that, too, Braydon?"

But Mr. Holt was picking up his hat, and then he was trying to find his gloves.

"Like guns," Mrs. Holt rattled on. "Great big guns. The Bouchards make guns and things," she said to Charles, with that same amiable blankness in her eyes. "And they've given out such big contracts to the Connington; they have steel mills of their own, too. Isn't this mill a sort of subsidiary, in a way, of the Bouchards, Braydon?"

"Minnie," said Mr. Holt. "You don't know anything about business. It is really too bad that you speak of things you heard in Elson's house. You haven't the slightest idea of anything."

"Of course not," she agreed, contentedly.

Mr. Holt, walking to the limousine, was very stately, but silent. Now, Charles. What was it that Roger was always saying about Charles, and others were always saying? Dull. No imagination. No enterprise. Not quick. Mr. Holt hoped this was true. Then, for no reason at all—with the beer agreeably in his stomach, and with his memory of the ugly warm parlor so like his father's—he hoped that it was not true. But Minnie should really hold her tongue; nothing was ever safe with her.

The limousine at the curb glittered and sparkled in the arc-light. It was warm, inside, and vast, and there were fur robes and vases for flowers at the rear windows. Charles settled back, at Mrs. Holt's right hand, while Mr. Holt sat at her left. She chattered happily about nothing at all. Then Charles felt her give his arm a quick urgent squeeze. So. This branch of the Connington in Andersburg was to be a separate corporation, with the Bouchards having controlling interest. No one was to know, apparently. Charles became aware of the savage spasm in his stomach. Even old Holt didn't know the import, Charles thought. The machine-tool shop. Competition.

"Charlie," said Mrs. Holt. "Your dinner jacket is sweet. Just sweet. And you look so handsome in it. Almost as handsome as Braydon."

The limousine passed another arc-light, and Mrs. Holt saw Charles' face. She sighed.

Even if the Brinkwells had not been living in the "Wilcox house" Charles would have disliked it. It was a broad but solid house, of white stone, and had an aggressive atmosphere about it, perched there in a big area which was wooded and would be expensively gardened in the summer. "Bastard Regency," Wilhelm had called it. Charles did not know. He only knew it antagonized him, that it appeared unfriendly, with its little stone balconies around the windows, and the bronze door. Light shone out on the bare black earth; patches of snow remained here still on the mountain, leprous patches. The mountain wind was loud and cold in the empty trees. Far up in the sky curved the icy thread of the new moon.

A butler opened the door for the Holts and Charles. Charles saw the black-and-white marble of the hall floor. The house was warm, yet for Charles it was cold. Nothing could soften this place. They went into a drawing-room sparsely yet elegantly furnished. Charles guessed these were "antiques," these small dainty sofas and chairs and tables. In a white marble fireplace a brisk fire was burning. Faintly colored draperies of velvet were drawn over the long windows. The walls were hung with tapestries.

The other guests were waiting. Charles, with some surprise, saw that these were only Wilhelm and Phyllis, Jochen and Isabel. Roger came up to him and the Holts, all welcoming and jeering smiles, while Pauline trailed languidly after, her big watery blue eyes as cold as the air outside. But she kissed Mrs. Holt, and showed every sign of pleasure, so Charles guessed that the coldness was for him, alone. She shook Mr. Holt's hand graciously, then turned as if her attention had been called to a stranger. "So happy you could come, Mr. Wittmann," she murmured. She gave him her hand, and it was boneless in his. Female, but not feminine, thought Charles, in spite of the floating chiffon draperies and the long pale hair about her paler face.

Roger was jovially clapping him on the shoulder. Charles, who was not conspicuous for height, was pleased that Roger had to reach to make this unwelcome gesture. "Well, well," said Roger. "Thought you had all forgotten about us."

Then he saw Mrs. Holt's dress, and visibly held back an exclamation. "Irene Castle," said Mrs. Holt, placidly. "I had it made. Like it, Roger?"

"Marvelous," he said, enthusiastically.

"Wonderfully becoming," said Pauline. "And as I said before, Minnie, I do love your hair cut short that way."

"Such liars," said Mrs. Holt, comfortably. "You think I look awful. Braydon does. I think I look chic. I'll murder any woman who copies this gown." She added: "I'm learning to tango. Braydon is, too, and he hates it."

Wilhelm and Jochen were standing. Charles had not seen Wilhelm for some time. On the Sunday when he was to call upon Wilhelm and Phyllis he was notified by one of their servants that "Mr. and Mrs. Wittmann have been suddenly called to New York." That had not disturbed Charles. Wilhelm often made these unplanned visits out of town. Then he noticed, now, that Wilhelm was unusually silent, that he did not look directly at him even when he inquired about Charles' health, and that he turned immediately to Mr. Holt and began to talk to him rapidly about something.

What the hell's the matter with him? Charles thought, irascibly. He thought of all the burden of his real and enormous troubles and his acerbity against his brother grew stronger. Phyllis was smiling up at him, beautiful, if thinner than ever, in her simply draped black silk gown. "How are you, Charles?" she was saying, and she gave him her hand.

Phyllis. Charles always braced himself for the pain when he saw Phyllis. It came to him furiously like an animal which recognized that he was unusually vulnerable tonight. It was this pain which made him hold Phyllis' hand very tightly, and keep it. "I am all right," he heard himself saying, "And you, Phyllis?"

"I have had a little cold," she said. "My usual Spring cold." She did, indeed, seem frailer. The lines of her chin had sharpened, and the lines of her cheeks. This made her lovely blue eyes very large. Her bright hair was coiled about her face in a new fashion, and its vividness made her lack of color more evident.

She gently withdrew her hand, but not before a faint pink flush ran over her face. Charles turned, in order to greet his other sister-in-law. It was then that he saw Wilhelm watching him, and Wilhelm's expression was cold and intense, and full of enmity.

This confused Charles. Had old Joe been plotting against him, Charles, with Willie, again? Charles' irritation vanished, was replaced by the familiar alarm. What were they up to, now?

Charles could no longer evade acknowledging the presence of Jochen's wife, Isabel. He had been hating Jochen steadily for some months, and this in itself was disturbing to him, for though he had often hated Jochen it had been a brief emotion and almost good-natured. He saw Jochen daily, but for a long time there had been a tension between them and they rarely discussed anything these days but the business of the shops. Charles had been to the house on Beechwood Road only three times since Christmas. He had stayed but half an hour. He had not been invited for dinner at any time.

Isabel smiled up at him in her aristocratic way, and the smile was malicious. "How are you, Charles?" she asked. It was as if she had some secret and infamous knowledge about him, for her hazel eyes were sly. Apparently something was pleasing her these days; her rosebud complexion was prettier than ever; her dark hair had an extra shine. Her hand, in Charles', was warm and heavy. Her gray satin gown was in fine taste, and very becoming.

"Old Charlie's always all right," said Jochen, boisterously. He was standing beside his wife. "Good old Charlie."

"But not 'Good-time-Charlie,'" said Isabel, with much graciousness. "You are getting so thin, Charles. And so pale. But then you are all working so hard these days, aren't you?"

Charles tried to remember that she was nothing at all. He tried to remember that gentlemen did not hate women, even if they were sisters-in-law.

He said: "Yes, we all work hard."

Mrs. Holt had seated herself in a prominent chair, and the least delicate. She overflowed it. The pink dress looked more remarkable than ever, and her face glowed and reddened. She had waved her hand at Jochen and Isabel, but when she had seen signs that Isabel was thinking of approaching her, she had leaned over the gilt arm of her chair and had immediately begun to speak to Phyllis. Now she called to Charles: "Charlie, do come here. I don't think anybody has really appreciated how handsome you look tonight."

Charles was glad of the call, but he was embarrassed. Everyone looked at him acutely, except Wilhelm, who was making a special effort at lighting a cigarette. Charles went over to Mrs. Holt and she took him by the hand. Then Charles knew that she was making a point, and his fingers tightened about hers. She swung his hand to and fro, lovingly. "I'm getting to like this man very much," she said. "I always did, in fact. Braydon, you ought to be jealous. You needn't; Charlie's four years younger than I. But now, if I were single, and young, I'd take this man out of the widower-class, I really would."

Charles laughed. "And you'd have to ask me only once," he said.

Everybody was looking at them. There was a tense feeling in the room. Roger Brinkwell, standing poised in the center of the room, watched Charles and Mrs. Holt. His alert face sharpened. Pauline stood in a languid, draped fashion against the side of a chair, but there was nothing languid in her eyes. Jochen and Isabel appeared startled. Phyllis seemed happy. Only Wilhelm was abstracted, on the surface, though he was smoking even faster than usual and carefully not looking at Charles.

Mr. Holt said his usual: "Now, Minnie." But he regarded Charles with friendliness. Really a nice feller, this Charles Wittmann, if slow and a little obtuse.

"Well, you see," said Mrs. Holt, still swinging Charles' hand. "This man is very special, to me. And he's got a nice house. Charming. I love it. Wonderful man. What would everybody do without him, in Andersburg?"

She gave the room a wide, beaming smile, gayly unconscious that her legs showed to the knees, or not caring. "If anybody so much as lifted a finger against my boy I'd—well, there just wouldn't be a minute's peace for him in this town any longer."

Then she pushed him away and said: "But go and flirt with the pretty ladies here. Not too much, though, mind. I'm your best girl, Charlie."

"Charles has no best girl," said Isabel, sweetly. "Have you, Charles?"

He started to answer her. But her light-hazel eyes were full of malice and dislike. He finally said, slowly: "Yes, I have. Minnie. And Gerry."

The smile left Isabel's face. A swift glance went between her and Pauline, now. "Really," said Isabel, raising her brows.

"Geraldine's Kenneth's best girl," said Roger, lightly. "Besides, you're too old for her, Charlie."

A servant came in with glasses and sherry. "What's that? Sherry?"

asked Mrs. Holt. "None for me, thanks." She informed the room: "Braydon and I had some beer with Charlie, at his home."

"Now, Minnie," said Mr. Holt.

"Good cold beer," said his wife. "Oh, by the way, Wilhelm, I saw your Picasso," said Mrs. Holt.

Wilhelm took the cigarette from his mouth. He started towards Mrs. Holt, then stopped, as Charles was still near her. But he was no longer so cold and neutral. "Did you, Mrs. Holt? And how did you like it?" His voice was interested.

"It was perfectly horrible," said Mrs. Holt, happily. "Just horrible. Of course. But Braydon admired it."

"Perfect example of Picasso's break with tradition," said Mr. Holt, hastily. "It will be very valuable one of these days."

"I don't see why," said Mrs. Holt. "But I think it was lovely of you, Wilhelm, to give it to Charlie. He explained it very well, to me. Erudite. He'll soon catch up to you, though I hope not." She gave Wilhelm a pleased smile. "So kind of you to give it to Charlie, though. I've always had an idea you two had a lot in common."

"Oh, they have," said Isabel.

Jochen was alarmed. He was no longer afraid of Charles. He, himself, had set some whispers moving in Andersburg, in spite of what he had told Isabel last August. One of these days his brother would be utterly ruined. The stubborn mule would never give in, or even if he did, he would be ruined. But the time had not yet come. Charles was still dangerous to him.

He said, quickly: "Well, Charlie and Willie are near the same age. They always ran around together, as kids. Fred and I have more in common—"

Wilhelm looked at Charles, and the cold enmity was there for the other man to see, and the aversion. What's wrong with him? thought Charles, dismayed. Have they gotten to him about something? Is he in "it" with them?

"Yes," said Charles, "Wilhelm and I always trusted each other. I think we still do."

Wilhelm sipped his sherry. His hand shook a little.

"I think it is because they understand each other so," said Phyllis.

The tension was very strong in the room. Roger Brinkwell let it impress itself upon everybody before he said: "How about looking at some of my tapestries, Charlie? You've never seen them, have you?"

Charles studied that nimble face and cruel mouth. Before he could answer Jochen said: "I wouldn't mind seeing them again, myself."

So, Charles thought. "There is one I like," said Wilhelm. The four men, trailed vaguely by Mr. Holt, left the room. "The best," said Roger, "are in the library."

"But that was a good early Flemish over the mantelpiece," said Charles.

Roger stopped for a moment in the black-and-white hall. He was amazed. Jochen stared blankly. Wilhelm frowned, studied his cigarette. "You noticed it?" asked Roger. "I didn't think you knew anything about tapestries."

"He learns things all the time. Especially when he needs them," said Jochen, meanly.

Charles said hurriedly: "Let us see those Gobelins, Roger."

The library, long and cold and perfectly furnished, was hung with tapestries between the book-cases. Charles was pleased to see that they were every bit as dismal as those he had seen once in Brussels, if smaller. He scrutinized each in turn, nodding to himself, standing off a little, then approaching for a closer look. Jochen watched him, nastily. "Learning, Charlie?" he asked.

"Now those at Versailles—" said Charles.

"You've seen them at Versailles?" asked Roger.

"I spent three days, looking at them," replied Charles, mendaciously.

Roger was uncertain, and he was distrustful. His vivid face was as sharp and quick as an animal's in the lamplight. "I always thought of you as the perfect type of the Pennsylvania Dutchman, Charlie. Not interested in—"

Charles was very grateful. He glanced at Wilhelm. "What's wrong with the Pennsylvania Dutch?" he demanded. "What do you know of them? You're not one of us."

Roger laughed. "I lived among you for quite a while, didn't I?"

"You think we have no culture, eh?"

"I always thought of you as solid. Sauerkraut and beer and brass bands."

Wilhelm frowned. "Thank you," he said.

Roger saw the trap into which Charles had led him. He also saw Charles' smile. He had a moment of consternation. Perhaps Jochen might be wrong. This man might possibly not be the slow thick fool he had been told he was, not only by Jochen but by Waite, also. Roger turned to Wilhelm, with that rapid dancer's movement of his. "I have something special for you to see, too," he said. "A genuine Maurer, practically his first revolt against academic art, poor devil."

"No!" exclaimed Wilhelm. He followed Roger down the room to

where a single picture was hanging on a space uncluttered by tapestries. The others followed. Charles saw a painting on the wall. It looked, he thought, like nothing on earth, an appalling nightmare of what was, if one looked close enough, a complete distortion of the human countenance. Angles, a tiny twisted mouth, a sudden eye appearing where no eye ought to appear, streaks of hard sharp color, like painted sticks, across what might be a human cheek indicated by four vertical lines in different hues. A nose like a miniature lamp-post, running halfway through the eye, with two crooked, horizontal lines slashing far out on either side of the mouth, presumably nostrils. A neck like two bones with nothing in between.

Why, that looks like the sort of thing Jimmy used to draw when he was four years old, Charles thought. All children draw such things.

"Of course," Roger was saying, "this is pure modernism. Everyone despises Maurer just now, but he will be our first great American modernist one of these days. His father, I've heard, has about disowned him. But everyone knows that old Maurer is a traditionalist of the most obstinate and insignificant order."

"Utterly without imagination," said Wilhelm, with an edge of envy in his voice as he reverently studied the painting.

Charles was by now sufficiently conversant with the jargon of modern art to offer a comment. "Extreme," he said. "Don't you think he's trying to surpass Picasso? In my opinion, he's either imitative, or insane."

Wilhelm and Roger regarded him coldly. "He's entirely original," said Wilhelm, momentarily forgetting his hostility. "And everybody who is original is usually regarded as mad by his contemporaries."

Jochen was looking at the painting with complete bewilderment. "How old is Maurer?" he asked, disastrously. Wilhelm and Roger exchanged pitying looks, but did not answer.

Charles said, easily: "Oh, Maurer is a man. His father is a famous painter, himself, but, as Roger and Wilhelm have pointed out, in the academic manner. Young Maurer won the Carnegie gold medal and $1500 first prize, in 1901, for a painting. But more in the traditional mood. A study of a woman. Good vigorous coloring."

About six weeks before he had visited New York, for the express purpose of doing some exigent research on modern painting. Wilhelm's coldness had become evident at that time, and Charles had decided that he ought to please his brother by learning enough by himself to take part in a conversation. Modestly, he pretended to be unaware of Wilhelm's and Roger's frank amazement.

"Met Maurer, in person," continued Charles. "He had just run over from Paris. We had quite a talk." This was a slight exaggeration. Charles had seen Maurer wandering disconsolately about the tiny side-street gallery, which was almost devoid of customers, and, taking pity on the sad-looking man, had pretended enthusiasm—but vague enthusiasm—for the few "horrors" which Maurer had created. Maurer had listened, but he was very intelligent, and he had known that Charles was only trying to be kind. However, he was so grateful for this sympathy that tears had come into his eyes. He had not made a single comment, but had turned away, slowly.

"You talked with him?" asked Wilhelm, disbelievingly.

"Indeed," said Charles, with a mysterious expression. "He had his *An Arrangement* there, too. He didn't seem proud of it, however. We agreed it had been a sort of—a sort of prostitution. Apparently, he had needed the money. Though he was still having a hard time, he felt that the time had come for him to express himself honestly." Charles added thoughtfully: "Tragic. A tragic man. Wouldn't surprise me if he goes the way Van Gogh went, though perhaps without the dramatics."

Jochen glared at him. Wilhelm and Roger listened intently. But Charles had now exhausted his repertoire about Maurer and was afraid of further questions. He wandered away to look at the depressing tapestries again, and assumed an interested air.

"I bought this for only fifty dollars," Roger was saying to Wilhelm. He seemed shaken. Wilhelm, still rather startled, was watching Charles. Then he said to Roger: "Fifty dollars. See here, Roger, you don't go in for this. Tapestries are your métier. I'll be glad to—"

Roger said, smiling: "Now, I'm not selling. Frankly, I'm not an expert like you, Wilhelm. Suppose you send over for it one of these days, or, if you'll allow me, I'll send it to you."

CHAPTER XXX

CHARLES HAD read few novels in his life. In one or two he had come upon the expression: "holding his breath." He had thought that phrase very fanciful. But now he found himself literally holding his breath, after Roger Brinkwell had made his gallant offer of the Maurer to Wilhelm.

Charles affected to be studying the picture with deep attention.

Cupidity. That had always been in his brother. But acceptance would mean more than cupidity. If Wilhelm refused, he would refuse much more than a mere scrabble of distorted lines and ripping color. Charles could feel the three men behind him. He began to sweat between his shoulder-blades, though the big dark room was chilly. He understood that Wilhelm and Brinkwell knew what an acceptance would mean.

Wilhelm did not speak. Roger said, lightly: "Well? I want you to have it. Let me send it to you, Wilhelm."

Charles took a step nearer the Maurer. The lines and colors became a jumble before him.

Then Wilhelm said: "Thank you, Roger." He paused. He added: "But no. I'll buy it from you, but I won't take it."

Charles felt himself breathing. He also felt weak.

Roger was protesting and Wilhelm insisting upon purchasing. Charles heard the petulant desire in his brother's voice, and something else, sharp and wary, and disliking.

"Very well," said Roger, with a surrendering laugh. "You can have it for what I paid for it. Take it with you tonight, if you want to."

"I'll send you my check tomorrow," said Wilhelm, and he sounded reserved.

Good old Willie, thought Charles. He looked over his shoulder at Wilhelm, but Wilhelm was drifting away to join Mr. Braydon, who was studying a distant tapestry. Charles said to Brinkwell, mildly: "It was a good try."

Jochen said: "Eh? You mean a good buy, don't you?"

"That's right," said Charles, and he smiled at Brinkwell.

Roger Brinkwell returned the smile. But he was thinking rapidly. This smug solid fool—or was he a fool? He touched Charles on the arm. "I want to show you something, Charlie," he said. He led the way to a desk at the other end of the room. Wilhelm and Mr. Holt remained in the shadows. They were trying to impress each other, very elegantly, with their limited knowledge of tapestries. Jochen followed Charles and Roger. Roger picked up a frame on his desk. The glass covered some writing in an archaic style. "A letter written on May 30, 1785, by Thomas Jefferson to John Day," said Roger. "A reproduction of the original." He handed the frame to Charles. "It might interest you. In a way, it's a prophecy."

Charles held the frame a little distance from him, and read: "An improvement is made here in the construction of muskets, which it may be interesting to Congress to know, should they at any time propose to procure any. It consists in the making of every part of them so exactly alike that what belongs to any one, may be used for every other musket in the magazine. I went to the workman. He presented me the parts of fifty locks, taken to pieces, and arranged in compartments. I put several together myself, taking pieces at hazard as they came to hand, and they fitted in the most perfect manner. The advantages of this when arms are out of repair, are evident. He effects it by tools of his own contrivance, which at the same time, abridge the work, so that he thinks he shall be able to furnish the musket two livres cheaper than the common price."

Charles read the letter slowly, then started to put it down. But Jochen took it from him. "What is it?" he asked, curiously.

"It seems that Jefferson understood mass-production, and its possibilities, long before anyone else did," said Roger. "Accuracy—interchangeability. We've come a long way since then, but not far enough. The battle for production. That will change America's future, for we understand, or are beginning to understand, the advantages of producing in mass. We have Ford to thank for that, to a great extent."

"Yes. Good old Ford," said Jochen.

Roger had long ago understood that though Jochen was shrewd and cunning he could be managed. But Charles had remained the unknown quantity to Brinkwell.

"You're going into mass-production, in the new mill?" asked Charles. He appeared to show little interest.

"Yes, indeed. Mass-production is the keynote of the Connington," said Roger, enthusiastically. "There's no limit to it. In spite of America's resources, she lags far behind England in industry, and, of course, Germany is ahead of England in production. That's why she's invading all England's markets. That's why she's dangerous. We'll have to compete with her one of these days."

"Good," said Charles. He stood there, growing, thought Roger, more solid every moment, more dull and stupid. Waite was right.

"Why good?" asked Roger.

"Competition is the life-force of all industry," said Charles. He had pushed his hands into his trouser pockets; he was the picture of the peasant Teutonic burgher, out of place in his dinner jacket.

"Yes, I've heard that platitude before."

"You don't think much of it?"

Before answering, Roger lit a cigarette. The flare of the match showed his lively face and squinting eyes. He shook the match, waving it back and forth in the air. "Let's put it like this: We can't permit Germany to get too strong, industrially."

"Why?"

"Why? Because we want the top industrial place. And we'll get it."

"We can get it by producing superior goods, and at a lower price, than Germany produces them," said Charles. "We have the resources. We have the man-power. We have the inventions. It's only a matter of time—"

Roger said, idly: "Maybe a lot of us don't want to take that 'time.' "

The cold and clenching knot now so familiar to Charles these months tightened in his stomach. But he made himself shrug. "It won't be long. We're a new country."

Roger tapped him on the arm, and Charles kept himself from flinching. "Look here, with the exception of a very few American concerns like yours, Charlie, most of our best machine tools come from Germany—"

"That's something we ought to do something about," said Jochen, with heavy humor.

But Charles and Roger ignored him. Charles studied the other man, very thoughtfully. "Yes, that's true, we do get our best machine tools from Germany. But we can soon outstrip Germany. I repeat: it won't be long."

Roger said, with a smile: "It won't be long."

"We'll soon be able to compete with Germany in the world markets for all goods," said Charles. Now he faced Roger directly. "There are two ways of competition between nations. One is barter. The other is —murder."

Roger took his cigarette from his mouth. He held it in his small fingers and looked at it. His forehead wrinkled.

There was a silence. Jochen was uneasy. The conversation had taken a turn which he could not follow. He saw Charles, standing there so obdurate, stocky, so "fixed." He saw Roger's inscrutable face.

Charles said: "Your new plant: What will be your largest production? Munitions?"

Roger put the cigarette back in his mouth. He was gravely alarmed. He had underestimated this bastard. How much did he know?

Roger said, smiling again: "What? Munitions? I don't know yet. The Bouchards make munitions—"

"You wouldn't be intending to produce them for the Bouchards, would you? You wouldn't be a separate corporation, in Andersburg, with the Bouchards having controlling interest, would you?" Charles spoke very quietly, and he looked at Roger with his brown eyes.

Roger regarded him intently. He was too good an actor to show his.

sudden consternation. He knew something, this sullen Dutchman, this hard, medium-sized rock in the path of the Connington Steel Company.

"I don't know anything about that," said Roger. "I'm not told policy."

"No?" said Charles.

Roger did not answer this. Charles repeated: "No? And you the superintendent. Or is your company producing superintendents on a mass-scale, too, to fit in anywhere?"

Roger ground out his cigarette on a silver ash-tray which stood on the desk. Charles watched him as if he were doing something very important and interesting. Roger began to laugh. "I'm afraid you've hit the nail on the head," he remarked. "I'll be taking orders. It's too soon to tell what they'll be." He eyed Charles humorously. "There was something in your voice when you spoke of munitions which has been puzzling me. What objections have you to munitions? They're goods, just like any other goods. They're sold on the open market."

"Yes, I know," said Charles.

"Still, you haven't explained that 'something' in your voice—"

"Was it there?" asked Charles. "Or did you just imagine it? Or would there be a reason for it?"

For the first time Roger became aware that Charles was implacable, that he was a force to contend with, and destroy, if possible.

Roger said: "I may have too much imagination. After all, you're a sensible business man, and you know everything is business." He paused. "You're realistic. You know anyone can buy anything, if he has the price. So why not munitions, if he wants them? Or have you been reading some hysterical books lately?"

Charles rocked slowly on his feet. "I don't read books—much. But I've been thinking, lately, about insanity. There was something that Nietzsche said: 'Insanity in individuals is something rare—but in groups, parties, nations, and epochs, it is the rule.' I've been wondering if the world isn't about to do something insane—say, for profit. Perhaps you'll call that 'business,' too. I'd call it the lust for power. I don't trust men when they become too powerful, and I don't care where they live or who they are."

Roger hummed faintly under his breath.

"You just spoke of mass-production," said Charles. "I suppose that's all right, in a way. Give more people more goods. Create bigger markets for goods. Raise the standard of living; make more things accessible to more people. Let everyone ride in an identical automobile, live in an identical house, use the identical goods, wear the identical clothes, shoes, use the identical furniture. Facelessness. Destroy the individual. Turn him into a belly for goods from a monster assembly-line. That's his function in life, isn't it—a consumer of goods?"

"Well, why not?" demanded Jochen, belligerently.

This time Roger turned to him, and put his hand on his shoulder. "As you say, Joe, 'Why not?'"

Still keeping his hand on Jochen's shoulder, in a familiar way, Roger said to Charles: "I'm afraid you're a sentimentalist after all, Charlie."

"For believing in the individual man, and his right to remain an individual? And there's one thing you've overlooked: craftsmanship. You'll not get around that quality of integrity, in your mass-production."

Roger shook his head, smiling. "You're wrong, Charlie. We will."

Charles set himself more solidly on his feet. "Do you intend to produce machine tools, in your new plant?"

There was a tightening all over Roger's face. But he replied, easily: "We might. It could be a good idea."

Then Charles saw Jochen turning red. All the hatred Charles had been feeling for him these last months was nothing to the hatred he felt now. But he said to Roger:

"Produce them if you want to, of course. But you won't produce the tools I can produce, for all my men are craftsmen, not machines." He did not raise his voice, or change his expression, yet Roger felt a threat in him. "I don't talk loosely about my business, Brinkwell, but I can give you this little information: I own 30% of my best patents in my own name. You can't get around my patents. You'll try, but your customers, even if they buy at a lower price, will know the difference. As for the other 70% of the patents: I have three brothers. You'd have to get their consent, if you'd try to go over my head—in any way."

He looked very slowly and carefully at Jochen, and then at Roger. "A nation can outlive its tyrants, but never its fools. However, there is a way of dealing with fools—if necessary."

For the first time, under pressure of what had been so unexpectedly said by Charles, Roger lost his temper. "Spoken like a German," he said. He dropped his hand from Jochen's arm. "Be careful, Charlie. It might not be so—popular—soon, to be a German."

Charles nodded. "Yes, I've been suspecting that." He looked at Jochen. "I hope you caught these last remarks, Joe."

"Charlie's being ambiguous," said Roger. He had recovered his temper.

Again Charles nodded. "Perhaps." He turned abruptly, and began to walk out of the library. Wilhelm and Mr. Holt had disappeared. Charles wondered if Wilhelm had heard anything of this conversation. If so, it was necessary to reach him as soon as possible, to arrange a meeting. Roger and Jochen watched Charles leave the room, in silence.

Then when they were alone, Jochen said, with rage: "You see how he is. Stupid fool!"

Roger said: "I wonder."

"Look here, Roger, you don't for a minute think old Charlie has any brains, do you? He's sly, but he hasn't an ounce of imagination, or he'd have known you were offering him something."

"Oh, he did," said Roger, easily. "And he refused."

In the meantime, Charles hurried to the great drawing-room, looking for Wilhelm. But at first sight he thought the room was empty. From some distance he heard the laughter of women. The fire was dying down on the cold hearth. The mountain wind assaulted the windows. Then Charles saw Phyllis sitting alone on a settee, her back to him. He went to her at once, almost running. "Phyllis," he said, urgently. She started. He sat down beside her, leaned towards her so he could speak in a very low voice:

"I can't find Wilhelm. There isn't much time, so I've got to talk to you, Phyllis. What's wrong with Willie? He acts as if he hates me, or something. Have I done anything wrong?"

Phyllis' pale face became distressed. She put her hand on Charles' arm. "I don't know, Charles. I've tried to find out. He doesn't even talk about you very much, at home. Yes, there is something wrong. I don't think it's anything you've done, except that perhaps Jochen has been trying to turn him against you, for some purpose."

"Yes, yes, I know the purpose." In his fear, Charles spoke impatiently. "Phyllis, do you know anything at all about what Jochen has said to Willie?"

She shook her head. "No, Charles. Wilhelm doesn't—talk—to me, about these things. He used to, but not now. And he's very distant to me, too. Charles, I'm afraid he suspects that I've tried to help you, in the past. He behaves as if he doesn't trust me any longer." Trouble and pain darkened her eyes. "I don't understand anything, Charles."

"Phyllis, will you tell him I must talk to him, almost immediately? Tomorrow, at your house?"

"Oh, Charles, we're having a dinner party, tomorrow, and you know how it is all day, with Wilhelm, the day of a party. He hardly leaves the kichen." She tried to smile, then the smile went away. "Is it very bad, Charles?"

"Very bad. I can't tell you how bad. That's why I must talk with Willie.'

"Oh, Charles. And day after tomorrow we're going to Philadelphia for a week."

Charles was silent. She saw how grim he was. Her hand tightened on his arm. "You think Wilhelm is avoiding you, don't you, Charles?"

"I know he is. He sent for the pay-roll and the books, and didn't come down to the office for the past three weeks, Phyllis."

He said desperately: "You must find some way so I can talk with him alone, Phyllis."

She bent her head. "I don't know what to do. I suggested you have dinner with us soon, and he was very abrupt about it—Charles, I ought not to be talking about Wilhelm this way. It's disloyal. I only know something is wrong, but what it is I don't know. It seems very terrible. He simply won't talk with you. You'd have to catch him, unawares—"

"Then, you must help me. Call me when he is alone, Phyllis, and at home. Call me at the office, or at my house. Any time. I'll come at once."

"He'll know, then, that I've told you."

"I can't help that. Phyllis?" She lifted her head and looked at him, and her eyes were full of tears. "Phyllis, I'm asking you to help me. You've got to help me. You've never refused before."

She hesitated, because she could not speak for a moment. Then she whispered: "I'll do all I can, Charles. I'll call you."

He put his hand over the hand she still kept on his arm. "Thank you, dear," he said.

It was just at that moment that the ladies came back to the drawing-room through one doorway, and Wilhelm, Mr. Holt, Roger, and Jochen through the doorway leading from the hall. They all saw Charles and Phyllis on the settee together, and they saw that Phyllis' hand, on Charles's arm, had been covered by his.

Isabel shot one swift glance at her husband, and then at Wilhelm. Wilhelm stood very still in the doorway.

"Well, dear me!" cried Isabel, gayly. "What a conspiracy! Are you conspiring with Charles, Phyllis, about anything?"

Charles stood up, too quickly. Phyllis, with a rustle, also rose. They stood side by side, and Phyllis flushed violently. The ladies advanced into the room, and the men came forward, also.

"It looks like a conspiracy," laughed Jochen. "Slipping away from us all, eh? Looks bad, Charlie." And he shook his head with an air of affectionate raillery.

"I don't blame Charles," said Mr. Holt. "If I'd thought of it first I should have been here before him." He left Wilhelm and the other men, approached Phyllis, and gave her a kind smile, and an innocent one.

Pauline trailed languidly towards the fireplace. She regarded Phyllis archly. "So that is why you pleaded you had a headache, you naughty girl." She spoke in the friendliest way, and with indifference. "I wanted to show Minnie and Isabel and Phyllis the tapestry in my bedroom, Roger."

Mrs. Holt had been loitering behind, but her eyes had been busy. She came to Phyllis, looked at her directly and accusingly. "Oh, Phyllis, you haven't told Charlie, after all . . . ?"

Phyllis, who had literally been left without speech, found her voice. "No, Minnie, I didn't. Really, I didn't. You—you mustn't accuse me of such things," she faltered.

Mrs. Holt laughed loud and heartily. "Well, just don't, that's all. It's to be a complete surprise for Charlie, and I'd never have forgiven you, Phyllis."

"I don't like mysteries," said Charles. Something was happening in this damn room which he could not understand. He had been engrossed, in these last moments, in a dismayed study of Wilhelm's face.

"Well, even if you don't like mysteries, you'll have to wait to be told this one," said Mrs. Holt, already wondering what the "mystery" was to be. A statue for that Wittmann Park? Braydon had hundreds. There was that horror, Caesar. Braydon was attached to it, but Charlie must have it. It was just the right size.

Wilhelm said abruptly, and his voice was clear and sharp in the room: "Phyllis, we must really go."

"So must we," said Mrs. Holt. "It's just too horribly late. And listen to that wind! Charlie, you don't mind, do you?"

Charles was silent in the Holt limousine, while Mrs. Holt described, in very outspoken words, the tapestry in Mrs. Brinkwell's bedroom. Mr. Holt chuckled from time to time. Then Mrs. Holt turned to Charles and said: "It was pretty bad, wasn't it, Charlie?"

"Yes, Minnie."

"I thought it would be. When Roger got you to go into the library. Charlie. If there is anything we can do."

Charles began to speak, then closed his mouth. Mrs. Holt waited.

Mr. Holt said: "You mustn't mind Roger, Charles. He can be a little malicious, sometimes. But it is mostly in fun."

"Such fun," said Mrs. Holt. "Well, Charlie?"

"Minnie, I've not very often asked anyone to help me. When the time comes, and I'm afraid it will, I'm going to call on you."

"Good." She squeezed his hand under the fur robe. There was something else she wished to say but it was a delicate subject. One didn't talk about such things to an innocent like Charles.

"I've got to talk with Willie," Charles said, half to himself. "There must be a way." He tried to see Mrs. Holt in the rushing darkness. "Joe's been poisoning his mind against me. I don't know what it is. But Phyllis has promised me to let me know when Willie is alone."

The Wilcox house was not far from the home of Phyllis and Wilhelm. Wilhelm did not speak in the carriage, though Phyllis sat beside him. She felt her husband's withdrawal, his coldness. She did not know he was also desolate. Poor Wilhelm, she thought in her misery. He thinks I have been plotting against him with Charles. If only he would confide in me, as he always did before, and I could tell him about Charles.

Aloud, she said: "Dear Wilhelm. What a dull party." She leaned against him, nestled her cheek on his shoulder. He did not respond. It was then that she felt his desolation. "Oh, Wilhelm!" she cried, "I do love you so, darling."

Do you, Phyllis? he thought. Do you?

He could not stand his own pain. He reached up his gloved hand and rested it against her cheek. She pressed her cheek into it. He thought: She would never deceive me. I know Phyllis.

He said: "And I love you, too, my dear. You'll never know how much."

No, Phyllis would never deceive him. He was certain of that. But there was Charles. Charles was a liar and a plotter, and there was no trusting him, ever.

CHAPTER XXXI

THOUGH THE early spring night was suddenly warm and full of the most exciting scents, Charles was too engrossed in his dread to be aware of it. A strong wind, but mild, blew his coat about him; he clung to his hard black hat, and bent his head. In the moonlight, the grass on lawns showed a faint wild green, and he did not see it.

But when he came to Friederich's house he could not fail, even in his preoccupation, to notice that something had taken place here. The steps had been mended; they had been washed and swept, and were without grit. The windows shone in the arc light, and white lace curtains were stiff and clean behind them. A new brass knocker had been fastened on the door, in the shape of a wolf's head. It appeared very savage, fangs bared, ears pricked, eyes fierce. Charles began to smile. The knocker seemed very pathetic to him, on Friederich's door.

Friederich opened the door, and there was no gush of musty air and the smell of old rancid pork fat. The air was clean, and warm, pleasant with wax and furniture polish. Friederich, himself, had undergone a change, also. He had had his suit pressed; his collar was not wilted, but stood stiff in white splendor almost to his ears, and his black string tie was neatly tied and held by his father's pearl pin. He had shaved well, and there was a look of pleasure about him and excitement.

"Karl," he said, and he spoke in English. He hesitated, then offered Charles his hand, for the first time in his life. Charles accepted that hand, shook it strongly, and was deeply touched. He felt Friederich's palm and fingers; they were dry and thin and slightly tremulous.

Friederich took Charles' coat and hat. "We didn't talk of anything, yet," he said. He added, shyly: "We waited for you."

Then Charles knew that he "had" Friederich, without a doubt. He took Friederich by the arm, and they entered the parlor together. Another change had taken place here. All the books had been replaced in their bookcases, all the tables had been dusted and polished, all the furniture had been brushed. The rug had been cleaned; there was a fire on the hearth. It was a shabby, cheap room, still, but soap had been used here, plenty of cloths and mops.

George Hadden and his sister, Helen, were waiting for Charles. George rose and the young woman, who was about twenty-nine years old, smiled up at him. Charles saw that she was rather short, and plump, with her brother's sandy coloring. Her hair was smoothly brushed back from her round, rosy face into a large neat knob on her neck. It was evident that she wasted no time on style and fashion, for she wore a plain white shirtwaist buttoned high on her throat, and a full long skirt of blue serge, and black buttoned shoes. She also wore pince-nez. But even the glasses could not hide the shining clarity of her blue eyes, and their deep intelligence. There was something sweet and tender about her mouth, something touchingly feminine about her rather broad, upturned nose and dimpled chin. She had capable hands, and a look of calmness and purity.

"George has told me so much about you, Mr. Wittmann," she said, and her voice was gentle. He sat down. Friederich hovered for a moment, then awkwardly sat next to Helen Hadden. Charles was suddenly interested. Friederich had changed extraordinarily. He was hesitant, but it was evident that he was excited. He stared for a long moment or two at Helen's profile, and color came into his waxy cheeks. His arm jerked once or twice, as if he wished to put it along the back of Helen's chair. Then he sat very stiffly, and colored even more.

He said, to Charles: "You ought to have come for dinner, Karl. I—I think it was a good dinner—" His tone was almost pleading.

"Very good," remarked Miss Hadden. She gave him a sweet glance. "All my favorite dishes. Good plain Pennsylvania food."

Charles was surprised. Friederich studied his knees. He cleared his throat. "Mrs. Schuele's niece is an excellent cook," he said.

"And you don't see that wonderful old German china any more," went on Miss Hadden.

So, thought Charles. That's where Mother's best set went to, after all. He just walked off with it, and here I've been looking for it everywhere for years. He kept his face straight, aware that Friederich was now blushing furiously.

"It was my grandmother's," he said, and only Charles heard his feeble defiance. "Then it was my mother's." He paused, then went on, louder: "It was all I ever had, that belonged to the family."

"I know," said Charles. "You've always been so busy, Friederich. Why don't you look over the old house and see if there is anything else you want? I know," he continued: "There's our father's old meerschaum pipe, with the gold and amber stem. I was looking at it only last week, and wondering if you wanted it. But it's a nuisance to keep clean, and you've got a lot of pipes."

"I always wanted it," said Friederich.

Yes, thought Charles. You always did. I remember now. "Then I'll send it to you tomorrow. Jimmy can drop it here on the way to school."

George glanced from one brother to the other, and understood. He wondered which of the two men he pitied the most. He said, to Charles: "I often see—or I should say, hear—your boy tearing around town in that big red automobile of yours, Charles. He's growing up, fast. He doesn't run around with many of his old friends, does he? I see that he's taken up with Mr. Haas' Walter, who's a very serious boy."

"I'd never have thought it of Jimmy," laughed Charles. "Only a year ago he despised young Walter, who is going to be a minister like his father. But now they're close friends, even though Walter is a year older. They're going to Harvard together, they tell me."

George turned to his sister: "Jimmy is Charles' son." Helen nodded pleasantly. She liked Charles. She nodded to Friederich also. Charles decided that Friederich resembled a happy dachshund very closely when Helen looked at him.

The conversation continued to be amiable. Friederich showed no symptoms of wanting to discuss anything of importance. He appeared content only to look at Helen. So Charles turned his attention to George.

"The Connington expects to have its furnaces going in the summer, George. They also expect to have a large machine-tool shop."

"No!" said George, concerned. "In competition, I suppose? But then, they don't have your fine patents."

"Brinkwell is under the impression that price will be a deciding factor, when they make the machine tools, and not quality. He even implied to me that there were ways of getting around patents. And he was insolent enough to hint that as 70% of the patents are held in the name of our company he could influence my brothers."

George, who was usually so peaceable, became angry. "He doesn't know the Wittmanns," he said.

Charles considered this. He knew that Friederich had at last come to attention and was listening. "He might know one," he said.

Friederich burst out vehemently: "Yes! Jochen! He winds Jochen around his little finger. I know!"

George and Charles looked at him. Charles tapped a finger-nail against his teeth. Helen leaned forward in her chair. Friederich began to stammer: "At least, I think so. Jochen told me a few months ago— that—that the Connington wanted to lease or buy some of our patents, and that they would have a wonderful proposition for us when they were ready." He became miserable. "I—I don't know. I don't know anything about business—"

Charles said to George, mildly: "Has Friederich told you that he intends to take an active interest in our shops very soon?"

Helen, who had been informed of much by her brother before coming to Friederich's house, said with warm pleasure: "How wonderful. With Mr. Wittmann's knowledge of social needs, and his experiences among the workers, he will be invaluable, won't he?"

"I've always felt so," said Charles, without blushing in the slightest.

Friederich was looking at Helen, as at a vision. She regarded him admiringly. He took out his handkerchief and wiped his forehead. He stammered again: "Karl said he needed me—I don't know why, exactly. But I'll do all I can."

"What is wrong with Monday?" asked Charles.

Friederich was appalled at the imminence of Monday. But Helen was waiting for his answer. "Monday." He nodded. All at once he was important, valuable. His broad and bony face took on dignity. "I don't know anything." He said this, simply. "But I can learn. I've never taken an active part, and the shops are a mystery to me. But I can learn." He looked at Charles, appealingly.

"It won't take long," said Charles. "Yes, you can help me. I'm going to need your help, Friederich. I've told you that before." Now he said to Helen: "Miss Hadden, you've just returned from Europe, and The Hague. Is there something you can tell us?"

Helen smiled, somewhat sadly. "Someone told me in Europe that when the Quakers appear it is because they scent trouble. I was part of a small delegation, studying peace plans at The Hague. I attended two or three unofficial meetings." Then her round face became stern and troubled. "I talked with many delegates. There is definitely something terrible in the air, in Europe."

Charles said to her, but held his brother's eyes: "Yes? I knew there was something. Perhaps you can give us a little information, Miss Hadden."

"Perhaps I should first begin by saying that what threatens to happen to Europe, and probably to the world, is the result of a universal breakdown of moral responsibility," said Miss Hadden. "We've been discussing this for several years, at Quaker meetings here. The battle for production, as they call it, and the competition among nations in the producing of goods and the struggle for world markets, has caused a decline in spiritual values. Many of us came to the conclusion that when agriculture gives way to industrialism on a wide scale, materialism inevitably follows, unless spiritual values are determinedly cultivated and maintained."

She regarded Charles thoughtfully: "I suppose the industrialization of the world is inevitable. But many of us earnestly want governments to remove the emphasis on materialism and teach the peoples that the benefits of industry can be enjoyed only when they accept the moral responsibility of those benefits." She paused, and the clear eyes behind the glasses became sad. "Even religious leaders don't seem aware of the peril of their people, though the Pope, I believe, recently warned of this."

Friederich was leaning towards her, stiffly. "I don't know much about religion, Miss Hadden," he said, and Charles, with astonishment, heard apology in his brother's voice. Friederich became confused, as Helen looked at him. "I—I've heard clergymen say that strikes, for instance, were against the will of—of 'God,' and that strikers were 'godless.' I was in the mining regions not very long ago." Now he turned bitter. "I wonder if any of those clergymen had ever spent a single day in the mines!"

Helen nodded, gravely. "Yes," she said. "I know. But I'm not speaking of clergymen, Mr. Wittmann. I'm speaking of religion. Quite often they are two entirely different things. I'm a Quaker, but sometimes it seems to me that only the Roman Catholic Church takes an active interest in the welfare of workers. This has created a lot of enemies for the Church, and the accusation that it is 'invading fields' which it ought not to invade, and 'interfering' in politics."

"There is a reason for these accusations," said Charles. "I wonder who those men are, who oppose the activity of the Roman Catholic Church in combating materialism and stimulating religion?"

Helen locked her plump hands together on her knees, and studied them. "I don't know," she said. "But I do know they exist. One of my friends suggested they were 'munitions makers.' But that is simplifying things too much."

She sighed. "People never want to accept the responsibility for death and ruin which they have brought on themselves." She opened her big black leather purse, and brought out a sheaf of papers. "I made a few notes," she said. She studied the papers closely.

"It was all so diffused," she said, after a moment, apologetically. "Information could only be deduced from certain events. For instance, Robsons-Strong, the great munitions firm in England, recently stated —and very jubilantly—that the past year has been an excellent one for orders for projectiles, armor, guns, and other implements of war, and that their mills and factories were operating at their highest capacities, and that prospects for the next six years are unbelievably good. This was reported in the British press, less than two months ago. The naval race, alone, from 1909 to 1912 gave another British company profits of two million six hundred thirty-five pounds, and in 1913, last year, their profit was eight hundred seventy-two thousand pounds."

"These are actual facts?" said Charles.

Helen nodded. "Yes, these are the facts. They were mentioned at The Hague. I could give you more facts, concerning every other nation, too, especially Germany."

She held the papers in her hands, and frowned dejectedly. "It is a curious thing about Germany. I went there after The Hague conferences. There was constant talk of war, and of 'aggressors.' Everyone in Germany accused all other nations of being those 'aggressors.' Now, there is a tension in Germany, because Germany has become prosperous and very industrialized, and is invading all the world markets. She is aware that other nations regard her as dangerous, because of this.

"Then, there is the Kaiser, who is a very proud, excitable, and womanish man. He sees enemies everywhere, even where they don't exist."

Charles stood up. He began to walk up and down the room, his head bent. Friederich said: "I knew. I knew all the time. I felt it." But no one heard him.

"War," said Charles, half to himself. "Yes. I knew it."

Friederich swallowed once or twice, then said aloud, in his high-pitched and stammering voice: "It's more than war. War's just the beginning, the means. It—it's slavery. That's what they want—after a war—slavery, for almost everybody, everywhere."

Charles stopped abruptly in front of him.

"You think I'm a fool!" cried Friederich, defensively.

"No," said Charles. "But, who are 'they'?"

George watched them, puzzled. "Isn't that idea just a little far-fetched, Charlie?"

Charles repeated: "No. It isn't far-fetched." He said to Miss Hadden: "Do you know anything about this?"

She, too, was puzzled. "I'm afraid not, Mr. Wittmann. I only know the facts I have. Who wants 'slavery'?"

She was concerned for him, for he appeared ill. She lifted the papers again. "The whole thing seems to me to be only a struggle for markets. And the press of populations. And the ambitions, and stupidities, of individuals.

"There are some in Germany, around the Kaiser, who are giving him grandiose ideas. Germany can become the most powerful of all the nations, and not only industrially."

She selected a sheet of paper. "Everyone knows, in Europe, that there will be a war. And very soon. But who knows in America? That is the terrible thing. If our Government knew, something might be done."

Charles thought of Colonel Grayson. "Perhaps some know. But we're helpless. We have practically no army, and no navy of any consequence. Who will tell President Wilson? He wouldn't believe it."

Miss Hadden said: "Here are some more facts. Winston Churchill,

First Lord of the Admiralty, has recently announced that England will maintain the sixteen to ten ratio of sea power. He also emphasized that as an ally of France, England's 'interests' would force her to come to the aid of that country if she were invaded. No one questioned who would 'invade' France, or what 'interests' England had in France."

Miss Hadden had a strong yet womanly voice, and she spoke without emotionalism though her face had become very flushed and her eyes were brilliant.

"President Poincaré made a state visit to England last June, and it is more than rumored that he discussed the French budget for the army and for armaments, which had been enormously increased over the preceding years. During the President's visit to England the Russian ambassador was present on numerous occasions, and he discussed the Triple Entente, which, as you know, is composed of Russia, France, and England, and the Triple Alliance, composed of Germany, Austria, and Italy.

"The Kaiser will request, in May, the creation of a petroleum monopoly. We were told this would not be passed by the Reichstag."

"Why not?" asked Friederich, bristling automatically.

Miss Hadden smiled at him, sadly. "I don't know, except that England might have a few friends at court, in Berlin, and possibly quite a few friends in America, who would prefer Germany not to create a petroleum monopoly. Such a monopoly might prevent a war."

Charles thought of what Mrs. Holt had told him, and Braydon's oil wells.

"We didn't take the Balkan war very seriously last summer," said Miss Hadden. "Yet, America could have said: 'These aggressions and petty wars must stop. It is insanity, and insanity in nations is communicable.' By ignoring the Balkan war we've led the powers of Europe to believe that America will stand by, indifferently, no matter what happens on a larger scale."

"And no one in England or France is concerned?" asked Charles. "No one cares, or very few know?"

Miss Hadden looked at him directly. "Oh, yes, many know. They call the Kaiser a Wagnerian imbecile. And they laugh. I talked with a number of members of the British delegation, and the French. They seemed—" and Miss Hadden paused, and then continued slowly and distinctly— "rather pleased, if anything."

"It's not possible to—to understand such villainy," said Friederich. Now his waxy color had returned, and he was sick. Charles studied him somberly.

"Villains, yes, everywhere," said Miss Hadden, in a low voice. "Yet here and there there are men who see the villains. For instance Lord Welby only recently said in London: 'We are in the hands of an organization of politicians, generals, manufacturers of armaments, and journalists. All of them are anxious for unlimited armaments expenditure, and go on inventing war scares to terrify the public and to terrify Ministers of the Crown.' The danger," the girl continued gravely, "is that when war scare after war scare is invented there does come a time when the peoples become conditioned to the idea of war, and a war results."

" 'Politicians, generals, journalists,' " repeated Charles. "And their lackeys, their employees and their employers—the armaments makers."

He began to walk up and down the room in a turmoil of inner sickness and despair. "Why can't all this money paid out for armaments be used to develop remote areas of the world industrially and agriculturally? Why—"

"Because death is more profitable," said Friederich. He stood up beside Miss Hadden, and he wrung his hands together defenselessly.

"Never any money to flood desert regions," said Charles, as if to himself. "Never enough money to throw railroads across all the mountains, or to build cargo ships. Only money for murder. Why? But they have a plan. I know it. I don't know how, but I do."

Charles stopped before her. "I'm not 'simplifying,' Miss Hadden. I'm not accusing the armaments companies of 'creating' wars, though they help. They're in 'business,' you know. You see," he said, looking down at the serious young woman, "to develop undeveloped regions of the world would expand man's freedom. And that's what so many men don't want, and will even create wars to prevent."

He turned away, and said: "Everyone dies but the haters. They never die. They're immortal."

"What? What? Who?" exclaimed Friederich, shrilly.

Charles stood and scrutinized him. Yes, Friederich was an "innocent." He had been "used." He'd seen the face of the enemy many times, and he hadn't recognized it. But how to make this innocent man see?

Charles said to his brother: "None of us can see the plot clearly. They're too clever for that. They don't show themselves; they hide, the hating, scrawny, greedy, malicious bastards! They want power, and hate the rest of the world because they don't have it, aren't fit for it, and would only misuse it."

George Hadden nodded. "Yes, we discussed that before, Charlie."

Helen sighed. "I don't know what it's all about, George. I only know what I've heard and seen in Europe."

Then Friederich blurted out: "I never thought of that! Karl, I think I know what you mean. Now, there's that man I know in Chicago—" He stopped abruptly.

Charles said: "Yes." He turned to Miss Hadden: "You only saw and heard what was on the surface. You saw the bubbles; you didn't see the river underneath."

He thought of his son. He said: "And there's nothing we can do, any of us. We can just slide down to hell, that's all."

George got to his feet, and took his sister gently by the hand. She stood up, obediently. As Charles had known, she was a small woman, but she had great dignity and the presence which only integrity could give.

She gave her hand to Friederich. He took it, but he seemed dazed. She said: "Will you and your brother have dinner with my parents and me, soon, Mr. Wittmann?"

Now Friederich came out of his sick stupor. He said: "Yes, yes, at any time, at any time, Miss Hadden!" He clutched her hand as if he were a child awakening from a dreadful nightmare.

Helen gave him a smile of tenderness and compassion before turning to Charles. Now she was grave again. "Yes, I think I'm beginning to understand," she repeated. "If there is a war, those you spoke about will show themselves. Afterwards. They always do."

She and her brother offered Charles a ride home. But he indicated he wanted to stay for a few moments with Friederich, and they left. When he was alone with Friederich he said:

"That was all important, Fred. And it concerns us too. Whatever happens in the company you've got to trust me. There'll be times you'll be lied to, Friederich, but you've got to trust me."

Friederich had just come back from the door after saying good night to his new friends. He stood at a little distance and looked at his brother, and he rubbed his tremulous hands together, blinking.

"If you don't trust me, we'll lose everything," Charles said. "Not only our company, either."

Friederich continued to rub his hands and to blink. Then he began to cough spasmodically, and the sound was sad to Charles. He waited until the spasm had passed, and Friederich could speak.

"I never trusted you, Karl. Never before this. But—but I think I do, now. But tell me, tell me! Don't hide things from me! Don't—manoeuver!"

"There'll be times I can't tell you everything—not immediately. That's why you've got to trust me."

Friederich suddenly thrust out his hand, stiffly, and Charles took it. "All right, Karl," Friederich said. "I'll trust you."

I hope so, thought Charles. But he was not a very trustful man, himself, and he wondered, drearily.

Friederich smiled shyly, and looked away. He went to the door with his brother. Then Charles saw that he was again uneasy. He cleared his throat, and coughed. "Karl, that friend of mine who lives in Chicago: he is visiting me next week. I think you ought to meet him. Yes," said Friederich, "you must meet him."

CHAPTER XXXII

On Monday morning Charles came to his office earlier than usual, then went into the shops, which were already buzzing and humming and grinding in a fine fervency. He heard the pounding of the machines, the whirring of belts, the scream of metal being assaulted by metal. All these were good sounds, muted so long, but now thundering away as if making up for lost time. Charles loved the metallic smell, the hoarse voices of the men, the sense of movement and the pace of conscientious labor. He stopped to speak to some of the older craftsmen, elderly Germans who still shouted their "jas!" and their "neins!" at each other, and who spoke English with difficulty despite their many years in his service and in his country. Lately, he had begun to speak to them in their native tongue, and this had touched them. There was no man like their Herr President, they said to each other, with devotion. He understood what good work was, and he respected good work and the good worker. There was none of this "hurry, hurry, faster, faster!" which they were hearing of in other factories. How could a man do respectable work with a hammer in his ears? Excellent work was done by men who were admired for their excellence. The Herr President understood dignity.

Charles beckoned to Tom Murphy, who was overseeing some work by a few young apprentices. Tom came to him alertly. "I want Herman Mohn," said Charles. "You come along, Tom." Tom followed him to where another foreman, about forty-eight, was gravely inspecting some new tools. After Tom Murphy, Charles considered Mohn to be his best foreman, a man of German parentage who had inherited the German characteristic of extreme meticulousness. He was a square and solid man, humorless and almost too exact.

Charles said, carefully not glancing at Tom Murphy: "Herman, Mr. Friederich is coming to the shops in about half an hour. He wants to learn the business. He'll be in here about three days, and I want you to give him all your time, and teach him. Of course, he can't learn everything, but I think you can give him a good idea of what all this is about."

"Holy St. Francis!" muttered Tom, too audibly. Charles ignored him.

But Herman gave what Charles had said his ponderous consideration. Then he nodded, without the slightest suspicion of a smile. "Yes, Mr. Wittmann. I'll do my best."

Charles turned to Tom. "I thought it best to turn Mr. Friederich over to Herman. For obvious reasons. Now, Tom, I want you to stay as far away from my brother as possible. Just be tactful. Though I never heard that tact was an Irishman's leading virtue." He smiled, motioned with his head for Tom to follow him again. He found a place in a corner where it was not too noisy. "I brought you along when I spoke to Herman, because I didn't want you to think that I was insulting you in any way, by overlooking you."

"But, good God, Mr. Wittmann, I can't be invisible!" said Tom, irately. "I don't know how it's going to be, with Mr. Friederich here. What does he want to come in here for?"

"Suppose you mind your own business?" said Charles, irritably. "Who owns these shops, anyway?"

Tom began to whistle, then checked himself. "All right, Mr. Wittmann, all right." He added, ruefully. "He hates my guts."

"Well, you did break his windows, if you remember." Charles tried not to smile, and only to sound severe. "That wouldn't endear you to him, under any circumstances."

Tom stared at him thoughtfully. He began to scratch his head. He knew all about the animosities between the brothers. This was something new. Who was behind it, Mr. Charlie, or Mr. Joe?

Charles said: "I thought it about time that Mr. Friederich should take an active interest in what is part of his own factory, at least."

He turned and walked away. Tom watched him go, frowning. Something was wrong with Mr. Charlie, these days. Charles stopped to speak to another man, and Tom saw that his profile was tired and haggard, for all the pleasant things he was saying to his employee.

Tom followed Charles, and when the latter had almost reached the door of the long tunnel that led to the offices, Tom called: "Mr. Wittmann!"

Charles halted, and again he was irritable. "Well, what's the matter now, Tom?"

Irritability was a new thing in Charles, and Tom was disturbed by it. "It's nothing, Mr. Wittmann. I was—well, I was just thinking about something that Father Hagerty said last Sunday."

Charles cocked an eyebrow. "Yes?" he said.

Tom turned a bright scarlet. "Mr. Wittmann, maybe you think I'm taking liberties, or something. But, there was Father Hagerty—"

"A very sincere man," said Charles. He waited, while Tom's face became more and more suffused. "I suppose what you're trying to tell me is that Father Hagerty said something which might apply to me. All right, Tom, what was it?"

Tom miserably twisted his cap in his hands and cursed himself silently. He felt for his pack of Bull Durham, then let his hand drop back to his side. "Go on, smoke if you want to," said Charles. So he waited again while Tom pulled out his tobacco, found his papers, and made himself a cigarette with a deftness somewhat impeded by nervous fingers. Charles said: "Make one for me, too, Tom."

Some of the old Germans, working industriously at a distance, watched this scene with some disapproval. Everyone knew that the Herr President was a fine man and a just employer, but was it not too much that he should smoke with a foreman? Charles leaned against the door, and inhaled the cigarette Tom had made for him. "Not bad," he said, approvingly. "My father rolled his own, too. But he could do it faster, Tom."

"I feel like a damn fool," blurted Tom. "And maybe it'll sound like a kid, me telling you this, Mr. Wittmann. But Father Hagerty said that 'it was very sad that a man seldom prayed until he had come to the end of his resources.'"

Charles laughed a little. "So you think I've come to the end of my resources, eh?"

"Well," said Tom, "you've been looking that way for some time, Mr. Wittmann! And what I really wanted to say was that if there was anything I could do—well, God damn it, you've just got to ask me, that's all!"

Charles did not laugh, now. He rolled the cigarette between his fingers, and watched the smoke rising from it. "I know, Tom," he said, after a few moments of silence.

He opened the door and then closed it behind him. When he arrived at his office he found Jimmy there, and his friend, Walter Haas. Walter was very like his mother, the minister's wife. He was short, and quite stout for a boy of eighteen or so, and had fine blond hair, a bright complexion, large, sober gray eyes, and a gentle mouth. Charles was pleased, if surprised, to see the boys, for it was almost school time.

"Dad, I forgot to ask you for ten dollars for some new books, this morning," said Jimmy, cheerfully. He had almost regained his old color and his vibrant air. He stood at least six inches taller than his friend, and his dark skin, black hair, and vivacious eyes made the contrast between the two so very vivid that Charles wondered what they saw in each other. Jimmy was always so exuberant, and young Walter was always so quiet.

Charles liked young people, without any maudlin sentiment. Lately, he had begun to feel compassion for them. He said to Walter: "How are your father and your mother?"

Walter answered politely: "Very well, thank you, Mr. Wittmann." He said to Jimmy: "We'd better hurry, Jim. It's almost nine o'clock."

Charles gave his son ten dollars, and said: "It seems to me that you're needing a lot of books these days, Jimmy. Or do the hot chocolates and sodas come into the picture?"

Jimmy was hurt. "To be exact, Dad, the books cost nine dollars and fifty cents, and if you want the other fifty cents tonight I'll give them to you."

"I certainly do want them," said Charles. "Tonight. Your allowance is quite enough, son."

Walter listened to this with gravity and approval. Did the youngster ever laugh? thought Charles. What the hell did these two boys talk about? he wondered. Jimmy was virtuously pocketing the ten dollars and throwing his books over his shoulder. Charles remembered that Walter was the only son of his father, though there were three little girls also. The only son, and murder loose in the world. Young sons, everywhere, and men plotting behind great bronze doors.

"What's the matter, Dad?" asked Jimmy, forgetting his hurt virtue.

"Nothing, nothing. If you don't run like mad, son, you'll be late."

The two went off together, Jimmy in a rush and Walter following more sedately.

Charles sat down at his desk, and the weakening sensation of shock, which he was experiencing so often lately, came to him again. He leaned his forehead on the back of his hand, his elbow on the desk. His mail lay before him in a neat pile, opened; there were one or two letters, unopened, which had been marked "personal." He looked at them all, and did not see them.

One mustn't get hysterical, he thought. It didn't do any good to magnify things. If there were terrible ghosts wandering over the earth, who would hear a single man cry out?

The door opened and Friederich came in, hesitantly. Charles looked up, and tried to smile. He saw at once that Friederich was glum and uncertain, and suspicious. "I'm here," said Friederich, unnecessarily. Then: "Good morning, Karl."

Charles answered normally: "Good morning, Friederich." He touched the bell on his desk. "You know Herman Mohn, don't you? He is going to take you around the shops."

Friederich nodded solemnly. "A good man, Herman Mohn. Not a trouble-maker," he added.

Then Charles knew that Friederich wished to talk with him before going into the shops, for his brother began to show symptoms of un-easiness. He plucked at his fingers; he shifted in his chair. But his clothing was neat, his collar stiff and white, and his formerly untidy hair had been cut and well-brushed. Charles said: "Have you heard from the Haddens?"

Friederich smiled reluctantly. "Yes. Miss Hadden invited me to dinner with her and her parents, next Friday." He hesitated. "What must I do, Karl? Is something expected of me? After all, I don't know much about young ladies."

"Flowers. Or a book. Or candy," replied Charles, promptly.

"A book," repeated Friederich.

Charles said hastily: "Well, perhaps not a book." He thought of the volumes of Debs and Belz and others he had seen about Friederich's premises. "Flowers. Girls always like them. And candy for her mother, possibly."

Friederich smiled again. "I hope that Miss Hadden and I may be friends some day. You think she has—has—no aversion for me, Karl?" He was anxious.

"On the contrary," said Charles, with warmth. He considered. Then he said, with an utter disregard for truth: "In fact, I met George Hadden when I took a walk, yesterday. He told me that his sister had spoken of you, and that she considered you a very distinguished man, and even handsome." He regarded his brother benevolently.

Friederich colored, embarrassed. "It's possible Miss Hadden is preju-diced," he said. He smoothed an obviously new tie. Charles saw that his fingers were no longer grimy; the nails had been closely cut, and cleaned, and his shoes were polished. Then Charles had another thought.

"Miss Hadden may be an exceptionally intelligent young lady, but young ladies like to be told flattering things about themselves, and not about their brains," he said. "In fact, if you tell a woman you think she is intelligent she feels insulted."

Friederich was bewildered. "I can't believe that!" he exclaimed.

"Well, I know women. So, if I were you, Friederich, I'd talk about anything else but politics, or world matters, when you see her. Even if she is a Quaker, and a serious young woman, she wouldn't mind it in the least if you mentioned something about her eyes, in a tactful way, of course, or what pretty hands she has, or her smile." He could see Friederich trying to be tactful and gallant, and pressed his lips hard together.

Friederich, on whom the implication of being a man of the world had not been lost, assumed an air of judicious importance and understanding. Then all at once he was dismayed. "But I don't know what to talk about!" he exclaimed.

Charles was moved. "Well, as I said, you can tell her you admire her for her intelligence, but even more as a woman. She's very beautiful, in her own way. And then you can talk about her special interests. Women love to talk about themselves, just as we do. But don't get serious! That's important. And don't tell her very much about yourself. Be mysterious, and strong." Friederich nodded, sat very erect in his chair. It then occurred to Charles that Friederich had spoken not a word of German since he had entered this office.

Friederich stood up. He actually buttoned his coat, carefully. "A very nice suit," said Charles. "Where did you buy it? Philadelphia?"

"No, right here in Andersburg." Friederich's gratification was touching. "Good material," Friederich added. Then he looked at Charles intently, and his broad and bony face became somber. "Karl, have you told Jochen I'm coming in?"

"Not yet. But why should you think that important? Haven't you as good a right to be here as he?"

Every last vestige of suspicion left Friederich. "Yes, of course," he said. He hesitated. "Jochen's not going to like it, however."

"I know. What does it matter? You are treasurer, here. Friederich, you're not finished with Joe. He'll get after you, as I told you. And again, I must ask you to trust me."

Friederich clenched and unclenched his hands, almost desperately. "Yes, Karl. I want to trust you. I've got to trust you. Something tells me I should." He was silent. Then he burst out: "I've not forgotten Brinkwell, and that dog!"

He walked with jerky rapidity to the door, then stopped. Charles waited. His brother turned, and he appeared agitated. "I believe you're being honest with me, Karl. You've influenced me, and I don't know! I've been rereading some of Belz's books and pamphlets, and remembering what you and Miss Hadden said the other night, and now they sound—they sound—"

"Yes," said Charles.

"But I've known him for years! I never doubted his sincerity, his interest in labor, in uncorrupted politics. Karl, you mustn't forget that you're to meet him this week." He opened the door and closed it with a loud bang behind him.

Charles sighed. He had accomplished something of immense value, with Friederich. But it was a delicate thing, and there was no trusting the irrational emotionalism of his brother.

Charles forced himself to look at his mail. Orders, orders, orders. He put aside the orders and looked at the two letters marked "personal" on his desk. Then he became more intent. One was postmarked Washington. He opened it and saw a few impersonal lines of typing, signed "John Lord." He read: "I hope to be in Andersburg the latter part of April and have a little talk with you. I remember our last meeting, and the renewal of our acquaintanceship will be pleasant."

Charles put down the letter. Rain had begun to wash against the windows; they rattled in the spring wind. Now the office, to Charles, seemed unbearably invaded by the roar of the shops. The letter on his desk appeared to him as deadly as a loaded gun.

He picked up the other letter. The handwriting on it seemed familiar. He opened the envelope, and saw that the letter was from Phyllis, and had been sent from Philadelphia.

"I'm afraid we're going to stay a little longer than I expected, Charles. However, Wilhelm has confided a little in me, again. And I'm sorry to say that it seems that Jochen has been poisoning Wilhelm's mind against you. I don't know how, or in what way. He wouldn't tell me. I asked him if you had offended him, and he wouldn't answer me. At any rate, it seems to be affecting Wilhelm's health. He is losing weight and is unhappy. I think he distrusts you about something, and he was always so fond of you, you remember.—I'll call you, as you asked, at the first opportune moment. I think it's very necessary that you and Wilhelm have a talk, as soon as possible."

Charles reread the letter, carefully. Then he struck a match and burned it, and watched it smolder away into ash in his tray. The smoke coiled and twisted, then was gone. But he still stared at the ashes, and he knew that the bitter taste in his mouth was the taste of hatred.

He heard someone outside his door whistling a parody of a hymn sung by Billy Sunday's chorus. Billy Sunday had recently held a "revival" in Andersburg, and some of the more irreverent inhabitants had cleverly changed the tempo of the hymns so that they sounded like the music of fox-trots. Charles was familiar with that whistling; he sat very still in his chair, and waited. The door opened and Jochen came in, whistling even louder. He stopped and smiled at Charles genially. Charles did not return the smile. He did not know that he was leaning forward in his chair, formidably, and that his hands were fists on his desk. But Jochen saw this at once, and his wide smile disappeared.

"Hey!" he said. "You look like a villain in one of the Perils of Pauline episodes! What's the matter?"

He came towards Charles' desk, cautiously, his eyes slightly squinting. "Business off, or something?"

"No," said Charles.

Jochen saw the orders on the desk. He picked them up, a thick sheaf. He inclined his head, contentedly. "Well, it's not business, then, that makes you look like a heavy." He put down the sheaf. He stood by the desk, and Charles saw his new confidence, his secret arrogance. He returned Charles' stare without his usual uneasiness. Not glancing away, he took out his silver cigar case and lit a cigar. Then he sat down.

"What's this damn fool business of Fred out there in the shops?" he asked. "Another one of your games, Charlie?"

Charles unclenched his hands. The fingers ached. He said: "He has a right here, hasn't he? He has a right to learn the business. It's about time."

Jochen's eyes narrowed. He looked at the streaming windows. He began to speak, slowly: "Have you forgotten that Fred's my territory, not yours?"

"Territory?"

"Well, you've got your Willie, and I've got my Fred. No fair poaching." Jochen grinned, then turned fully to his brother.

Charles did not answer. He studied the other man. He had never underestimated Jochen's real capacities. Jochen was cunning. And able. He was a rascal. But he knew his business. He was exigent. But he was shrewd. Now he had become dangerous.

Jochen said: "What'll that idiot do, out in the shops? What's up your sleeve, Charlie? Think you can put any sense into that thick head? Think you can use him? Oh, I know all your little tricks. Making him feel important to the business, then using him. It's no use, Charlie. Stick to your Willie, and I'll stick to my Fred."

He grinned again, slyly.

"Well, play with him, Charlie. But all I have to do is to crook my finger and he comes running. He believes everything I say. Just as Willie believes everything you say. Doesn't he?"

"Does he?" asked Charles. There was something humming furiously in his ears. He felt a strong violence in himself.

"You ought to know. You've used him all the time, against me. You're a bright boy, Charlie, but play with your own toys."

Charles looked at the ash in his tray, and Jochen's eyes followed that glance. "Burning something? A billet-doux?" Jochen laughed. "Old Charlie getting love letters?" He was intrigued by the ashes. He stirred them with his cigar, tried to find a fragment that could be read. Charles watched him. "Something important, eh?"

"Very important," said Charles.

His tone made Jochen look up, alertly. "Business?"

"Business."

"Then, why burn it? I'm vice-president, aren't I? Or have you forgotten?"

"I haven't forgotten."

Jochen started to speak, then stopped. He scrutinized Charles' face; he saw its sallowness; he saw the hard mouth, thinned and spread. He saw Charles' eyes, fixed on him with an expression he had never seen before. Now his confidence left him; his uneasiness came back. His sudden fear made him bluster: "You seem to have forgotten—if that's business smoldering away there. Another Bouchard order you don't want me to see?" Then he noticed the unburned envelope on Charles' desk, and the postmark. His nostrils widened. He looked away, quickly, full of excitement. He had recognized Phyllis' handwriting, for he was a man who noticed every detail, automatically.

"It's very important. But it's not a Bouchard order," said Charles. There was nothing he could do; there was nothing he could say.

He said: "Fred's out there, learning what he ought to have learned long ago. Let him alone, Joe, let him alone. I'm warning you."

"You're warning—" Jochen began to exclaim. Then again, he saw Charles' eyes. He spoke more moderately: "Hell, let him look at the pretty machines, if he wants to. I'm not objecting, except that he'll probably slow up the men. No, I'm not objecting to anything, except that I've got a little warning for you, too. You won't be able to play your tricks on old Freddie. He doesn't trust you as far as he can see you."

Charles thought of Friederich's defenseless eyes, his vulnerability. He stood up, with abruptness. "I want you to know this, Joe," he said. "I want you to know that Fred's sincere about learning the business. Yes, I'm encouraging him. I can't protect him from you, but I think you're going to find it a little hard to lie to him about me. Now."

Jochen took another long puff at his cigar. He was afraid of his brother, even at this moment. "Who does the lying around here? You! I've exposed your tricks a few times, to Willie and Fred, that's all. And I'll go on exposing them." He stood up. He loomed over his brother. He pointed the cigar at him. "You're running this business into the ground, Charlie. You're old-time. We should be expanding, with all these orders. You don't want to expand. You want your tidy little business to remain just a tidy little business."

Charles said: "Brinkwell isn't going to get any of my own patents. And they're the ones he wants. And I think he won't get many, if any, of the others, either. That's what you want to know, isn't it?"

Jochen began to breathe heavily, in his fury. Charles went on: "I'm not leasing or lending any patents to Brinkwell. Nor to the Bouchards. And I'm not selling either Brinkwell or the Bouchards the things they want. I know Brinkwell's been after you, all the time. But I'm here, Joe. I'm still president. I still have my patents. And Joe, I'm watching all the orders. They're not putting any tricks to work. They'll never get what I own by ordering through dummy companies, either. I know where every tool goes."

Damn you, damn you to hell! thought Jochen.

Charles put his palm on his desk so that it could support him, for there was a long trembling running over his body. He knew it was this queer and unfamiliar violence in himself, roaring into a flood, which he would soon not be able to contain, and not want to contain.

If Jochen had not felt so frustrated, so enraged, he might have seen what could have been seen, and exercised his own particular caution. But now he began to shout furiously: "I'll 'remember' nothing but that you're a tight old fool, that you're ruining us, and that someway, somehow, you've got to be shaken loose!"

It's come, thought Charles. The break was inevitable. Nothing could stop it. Even in his violence he had a moment's sick regret.

Jochen's voice rose louder: "Who's been working here all the time, with you? Who's been giving every day to this damned place, and thinking only of how it could be kept going during hard times, and sweating and worrying—with you? Either of those cottonheads, Willie or Fred? What've they ever done for you, for us?"

The violence was surging heavier in Charles, but he could still control himself enough to nod, and to say: "Yes, we've worked together, and the others didn't work. We cut our salaries, to save the business, when the others refused a cut. We've stayed here, day and night, month after month, trying to find out ways and means, so we could survive. We did it, together."

Had Jochen been less than an instinctive bully, he might have listened to this with reason, and might still have come to some terms with Charles. But he thought that Charles' admissions were the admissions of weakness, and he rushed at what he believed was a breach.

"Oh, yes!" he bellowed. "You can be mealy-mouthed, can't you, and 'reasonable,' and admit things, but that wouldn't move you from your damned idiotic stand! Good old balance wheel, not denying anything, but not giving anything, just grinding away at nothing! But I tell you now that I'm not going to stand this. I'm going to do something—"

The rage in Charles gushed up to his face and turned it to a dark crimson. His small eyes began to glitter. He took his hand off his desk, and stood there solidly, and in an implacable silence.

" 'Do something?' " he said, finally. "Such as poisoning Willie's mind against me?"

Jochen was petrified, even in the very midst of his rage. Now he saw Charles clearly, and his old dread of his brother came back to him.

"You'll do nothing," said Charles. "You can lie about me to Willie, or to anybody else, you can play at plots behind my back. But it'll come to nothing. I thought we'd never need to have this out, and that we'd never need to show each other how much we hated each other, and always did. But it's come, now. And so I'm giving you a final warning: I'll smash you, Joe. I'll find some way to smash you, and drive you out. Lift one real finger against me, try to harm me in any way, or put any of yours and Brinkwell's plots into actual action, and I'll smash you. You're a fool, and you don't know what's behind Brinkwell, or you wouldn't care if you did know. But I know. And that's why I'll drive you out if you really try anything."

Jochen could not speak. The cigar shook in his big fingers. He stared at Charles incredulously. When he could talk his voice trembled: "You know what that means, don't you, after what you've said? We're enemies. You've made us into enemies."

"No," said Charles. "You did. And we were always enemies."

Jochen dropped his cigar in the ash-tray. He was sobered, but he had also become as implacable as his brother. The fat's in the fire, he thought. He said: "Do you know what you've been saying? That you'll 'drive' me out? I'm the vice-president of this company; this company belongs to me, too. Have you lost your mind?" His large fat face had lost its ruddy coloring.

"I told you, Joe: I'll smash you, and I'll drive you out. I'm desperate, and I'll stop at nothing. Vice-president or no vice-president, I'll find a way to ruin you."

They looked at each other, and they knew that from this day on there would be not even the smallest sign of friendship between them, nor any pretense of it. Again, in spite of his anger and his violence, Charles could feel regret, remembering all the years he and Jochen had worked together. But Jochen felt only hatred and determination. He was in danger. He would have to strike fast, now, he thought. It was Charles, or he.

He walked out of the office, clumsily and heavily. After quarrels with Charles he usually slammed the door after him. But today he closed it quietly. To Charles, that slight sound was more ominous than any slam, or any exclamation of fury, or any threat.

He said to himself: I must move fast. Very fast. I don't know where, but I must.

Jochen, walking rapidly towards the shops, also said to himself: I must move fast. He opened the thick wooden door and the thundering of the machines engulfed him. He looked about for his brother Friederich. There was the imbecile Socialist, in his shirt-sleeves, and wearing a leather apron, and bending over a machine in the company of Herman Mohn! Jochen braced himself, made himself smile. He sauntered over to his brother, studying Friederich as he came. What had happened to the fool? What had that swine, Charlie, done to him? Friederich's hair was neat, and he had a wondering and absorbed expression, like an idiot confronted by a miracle.

"Interesting, Fred?" asked Jochen, genially.

Friederich lifted his head, saw his brother, and scowled for a moment. "Yes," he said, shortly. "It's very interesting. Herman, you were saying—"

"Wait a minute," said Jochen. He nodded at Herman Mohn, and the foreman retreated to a spot out of hearing. Friederich was annoyed.

He scowled again. Jochen said: "How's old Charlie figuring to use you this time, Fred?"

Friederich straightened himself with dignity. "No one's using me," he answered. "Why don't you go away, Jochen?" He paused. "My opinion is that you've been libeling Karl to me for years. I refuse to listen to you. Others have told me how decent and reliable and honest Karl is, and their opinion, to me, is better than yours."

Jochen heard this unbelievingly. His tool had turned in his hand and had struck at him. His rage came back. "Who's been telling you anything about Charlie? Your Socialist friends, your anarchists, perhaps?"

Friederich, the unstable and easily aroused, lifted an oil-stained finger and shook it in his brother's face. The men nearby listened with discreet avidity, and glanced at each other under lowered lids.

"No!" cried Friederich. "It was George Hadden, and George Hadden is no liar!"

"Hadden? That sly, simpering Quaker?" exclaimed Jochen. "You've got into the hands of that hymn-singing—"

Miss Hadden's face flashed before Friederich. He took a step closer to his brother, and shook his finger directly under Jochen's nose. He almost screamed: "Let me alone! Don't speak to me! Go back to your Brinkwells and your murderers!"

Jochen recoiled from the finger. "Are you crazy?" he demanded, stupefied.

Friederich dropped his hand. He studied his brother. Karl was right; Jochen was a fool, in spite of his industry. So much was clear to him, Friederich, at this moment. He was excited by it. The old fanatical light flashed back into his eyes.

"Go away!" he exclaimed. "Whatever you tell me I'll tell Karl. I'm warning you, Jochen."

He beckoned to Herman Mohn, who came back soberly, but all ears. Jochen could only stand there, completely dumfounded. Then he saw how ridiculous he must appear to all his workmen nearby, who had overheard everything. He walked away; his head was beginning to ache. Something was moving up behind the strong wall of his life, and soon there would be a battering against it.

He returned to his office and called Roger Brinkwell.

PART FOUR

. . . the abomination of desolation . . .
MATTHEW 24:15

CHAPTER XXXIII

THE WINDOWS stood open and the cool April wind poured in, strongly yet sweetly. Charles could smell the life of the April earth, fresh and intensely poignant. The street was quiet outside, for everyone had gone to bed or was dozing in a chair after a heavy Sunday dinner. April sun lay on the window sills, spangled the lace curtains of the parlor, a sun not vivid but alive, a new sun. By turning his head on the cushion of the sofa he could see the outlines of the elm tree on his lawn, the pliant bending of the branches faintly shadowed in green. His father had planted that tree forty years ago, a young sapling. Now its limbs brushed the upper windows of the house. It was a friend. But all its outlines seemed, to Charles, the outlines of silent pain, and the green gauze beginning to show on them was timid life on old sorrow.

Charles had been reading Goethe again, this afternoon. He lifted the book, a slight one, but which had a feel of heaviness in his hand. "What is man— Do not his powers fail when he most requires their use? And whether he soar in joy or sink in sorrow, is not his career in both inevitably arrested?" Charles adjusted his glasses, and read another phrase: ". . . does he not feel compelled to return to a consciousness of his cold, monotonous existence?"

Charles closed the book. No matter what happened, Monday morning always arrived. Possibly that was why Sunday evening always had a melancholy of its own, shadowed and sad. It was the inevitability of the Mondays which wounded a man's spirit. He might be able to stand grief and regret and loss, with some kind of dignity. It was the Mondays, the exigent, toneless, colorless Mondays, the days of renewed monotony, which broke his heart.

For how long, now, had Monday seemed unbearable to him? It hadn't always been this way, he thought. I'm not forty-one, yet, but Mondays do something awful to me. Was it because of Jochen, to whom he never spoke these days except on matters of business, and then only coldly and briefly? Nothing could have prevented the break, Jochen being what he was. But one never broke definitely, and with finality, with a brother, without regret almost as strong as grief. There was nothing I could have done to delay it, Charles told himself. And then he looked at the chair near the fireplace which the young Jochen had always obstinately appropriated for himself on winter Sundays and evenings, and he closed his eyes for a moment. We hated each other, all our lives, he told himself, but there is something between brothers. Did Jochen feel this? Charles, realistically, doubted that he did, or, if he did, he did not understand what it was he was feeling.

The house was full of ghosts. I'll sell the damn thing, thought Charles, and knew he would not.

Jimmy, out with some of his friends, had been born here. But Charles was not thinking of his son. He saw the ghosts of his young brothers, and he was tired and listless with his regret. It was all tied up with his aversion to Mondays, in some way, his shrinking from seeing Jochen, his weariness with Friederich.

It was like having an unexploded bomb, but ticking, in the offices, to have Friederich there. Not that Friederich was too difficult. He had applied himself, not for three days, but a whole week, to the shops, and was now in his own office, studying ledgers and accounts and books about machine tools with his old ferocious absorption. He was always coming in on Charles, excitedly, and trustingly, to have something explained to him. He was forever running back into the shops, with a textbook in his hand, or a magazine issued by some machine-tool company, to identify something for himself. Charles never saw him speak to Jochen. Jochen was a persistent man, yet he apparently made no effort to approach Friederich. He'd given him up, thought Charles, uneasily. It's Willie he's after, now. He thinks I have Fred.

Where were Wilhelm and Phyllis? Charles had heard nothing from either as yet. They couldn't remain in Philadelphia for the rest of their lives! Charles sat up, removed his glasses, rubbed his eyes. He listened to the silence of the house. He had always liked it. Now it oppressed him. Mrs. Meyers had gone for the afternoon, as usual. No one knew when Jimmy would return. I haven't any real friends, I suppose, thought Charles. If I haven't, it's my own fault. I haven't encouraged any closeness, any familiarity. I've been so damned self-sufficient, and this is where it's landed me, in an old house, on an old sofa, on an April afternoon, and with thoughts enough to poison anybody.

A door banged, the back door. Jimmy tiptoed to the door of the parlor, and peered in. "I'm not asleep, son," said Charles, with relief. "But why are you back so early? Mr. Haas chase you away?"

Jimmy coiled himself awkwardly in Jochen's old chair, and gave an exaggerated sigh. "You don't think I'd be at the parsonage on a *Sunday?*" he demanded, outraged. "The whole town's bad enough on a Sunday, but at the parsonage—" He ended his remark with a feeling groan.

Charles laughed. The ghosts had gone away. Young life sat in that chair, eager life that had hopes and plans, and knew nothing about middle-aged Sundays. Jimmy stood up, restlessly. "Mind if I play a few records, Dad?" he asked. He began to crank the gramophone, whistling abstractedly to himself. Charles watched him, and his uneasiness came back. Something was wrong with Jimmy these days, something which made him jumpy and tense.

"Something light, eh?" said Charles, reaching up to close the windows.

"Dad," said Jimmy, with patient tolerance, "you know I don't like that trash. Why, I haven't bought a single popular record since I was young!" Charles lay back on his cushion, vaguely content.

Then his content began to go, for the opening strains of the "piece" were full of muted suffering and sorrow. Higher and higher, stricken with wild despair, the music rose, crying aloud hopelessly, full of unbearable desolation. Charles wanted to speak out, in denial, for the music was his own renewed pain, and it was more than he could stand. Just as he was about to protest, a man's subdued yet powerful voice joined the mourning instruments, and they dropped to the background. The voice did not clamor its agony; it accepted it, made it articulate, expressed it with a resigned and tormented bitterness.

Stop it, said Charles, in himself. Stop it. He wanted to put his hands over his ears, to shut his eyes. But he could only listen, achingly. He could only stare before him and see Phyllis' face. His hunger came rushing at him like a beast, tearing at his flesh. He pushed himself to a sitting position. The waning sun had withdrawn from the window sills; the wind was closer, and it was becoming part of that man's voice so that everything cried out with it and the shadows in the room were postures of anguish.

Then there was silence, except for a grinding sound which Jimmy quickly stopped.

"What—what the devil was that?" asked Charles, hoarsely.

"That?" said Jimmy, indignantly. " 'That' was Caruso. And that song was Massenet's *Élégie*. I bought the record yesterday, and it's wonderful."

"My God," said Charles. "It's terrible. Don't play it when I'm around again, son."

Jimmy's indignation increased. "It's wonderful," he repeated. "It cost me three dollars. Out of my own allowance, too."

"I don't care what it cost you," said Charles.

Jimmy, in eloquent silence, walked away from the gramophone. He sat down. "The trouble with you, Dad, is that you don't know anything about music. No one sings better than Caruso. And the Élégie—well, it's one of the most 'moving' songs in the world. That's what our music teacher says. I think it is, too."

Charles' face was in shadow, and so the boy could not see it. He saw his father take out his handkerchief and mop his face. "It's not warm in here, Dad," said Jimmy. "You haven't a fever, or anything, have you?" he asked, with sudden anxiety. "You haven't been looking well for months." He stood up. "Why don't you let me take your temperature?"

"For God's sake, no," said Charles. "Stop playing the doctor with me, Jimmy. Élégie? What's that? Sounds funereal to me, I think."

Jimmy sat down again. "It is, in a way," he said. "It's a man's—well—lamentation for his dead wife." He considered. "It's in French. He says something about 'bright summer days' being lost forever, and birds, and sunshine. It's all about his grief, and how it's always darkness for him now."

Charles sat with his rumpled white handkerchief in his hands; his shoulders were bent. He looked down at the piece of cloth. "Yes," he said. "Of course."

His very bones felt cold. 'Yes, of course," he repeated. This sinking in him—it wasn't new. It would go away. It was worse this time, but it would go away. Eventually.

"Then you knew what it was?" asked Jimmy.

"Yes," said Charles. I've always known it. And now I know it'll never get any better. I've been fooling myself all this time.

Jimmy stood up, and pushed his hands deep into his trousers' pockets. He began to walk up and down the room, restlessly, his head between his shoulders. It was a long time before Charles became aware of that beating of young feet up and down on the carpet. Then Jimmy stopped before his father. "Dad," he said, "I haven't seen Gerry for two weeks. I want to talk to you about it."

Charles put away his handkerchief. "Is something wrong with her, son?"

Jimmy shook his head. For the first time, Charles saw the boy's misery, and then he knew that he had been vaguely seeing it for sometime.

"I thought she might be sick," said Jimmy. "So I called her house. But someone always said she was at her music lessons, or studying and couldn't be disturbed, or was out. And then on Friday, I got a letter from her." The boy swung his head distressedly, and his thick dark curls fell on his forehead. He pushed them away with impatience. "She said she'd see me soon, when she could. She couldn't explain just yet, she said. But she wrote that Uncle Joe's going to send her to school next September. Mrs. Brinkwell's old school, down on the Hudson. Not near Harvard at all. And this summer, she said, she and Aunt Isabel and May and Ethel were going to stay at Mrs. Brinkwell's house near Philadelphia. It's out in the country, somewhere, on a lake."

The pain had retreated, back in some formless limbo. Charles sat up erect on the sofa, and there was that clutching in his stomach again, the old twisting and spasm.

"Dad," said Jimmy, "has something happened between you and Uncle Joe? Gerry didn't actually say so, but she said you'd had a 'misunderstanding' or something, and maybe it would pass. It can't be serious, can it, Dad?"

"Yes," said Charles. "It's worse than 'serious,' son. It's a break. And nothing can ever mend it. I ought to have told you before. Sit down, Jimmy. I keep forgetting that you're practically a man. I think you should know."

He told Jimmy what had happened. He told nearly all, from the time of Roger Brinkwell's coming. But he did not tell Jimmy of his fears. He implied that it was a matter of patents which he did not want to lease or sell.

When he had finished, Jimmy did not speak. However, he finally began to whistle dolorously. He kept nodding his head as he thought. "I see," he said, at last. "You did the right thing, Dad. I'm glad you did. There wasn't any other way. And now you've got Uncle Fred eagerly rushing around, and Uncle Willie's gone into the silences, through Uncle Joe. It must be hell for you."

"The worst of it is that I don't know where it's going to end," said Charles. "But somehow, worse than anything else is having this happen to you, about Gerry. You're the innocent bystanders, you and Gerry. I wish to God it had never happened. I wish to God Brinkwell had dropped dead before he came here."

"If it hadn't been Mr. Brinkwell, it would've been someone else," said Jimmy. He got up and sat down on the sofa beside his father. "Dad, don't feel about it, like that—I mean, about Gerry and me. We'll find our way. We've got our whole lives. It's you I'm worrying about. So that's why you've looked like the devil for months!" He put his hand on Charles' shoulder. "Worrying yourself to death. Uncle Joe's a fool, and he's got a mouth like a carp, and he's always wanting more money. He'd have sold you out to anyone, sometime. But what could he be doing with Uncle Willie? Why haven't you been up to his house lately, and beating him down and making him listen to sense?"

"Because, as I told you, Jimmy, he's always away."

The warmth of the young hand on his shoulder penetrated to Charles' flesh. It was comfort and tenderness and sturdy affection.

Jimmy frowned. "Sometimes, when he used to be up in the air about something he'd do this to you, Dad. And you've always gotten after him. You could do it now. Don't wait."

Jimmy was looking at the Picasso, and laughing feebly. "You've always gotten around Uncle Willie. Do it soon. Find out if he's at home—today."

The telephone began to ring in the hall, and Jimmy jumped up and ran for it. He thinks it might be Gerry, thought Charles. Then Jimmy was back in the room, beckoning excitedly. "It's Aunt Phyllis, Dad! She wants to talk to you."

Charles went to the telephone. The old trembling had come back. He had to sit down to talk. Jimmy stood near him, and Charles did not see his son.

"Phyllis?" said Charles.

"Charles. Oh, Charles." Her voice came to him gently, and quickly. "You received my letter?"

"Yes. I received your letter, Phyllis." He was talking stupidly; he should be asking her about Wilhelm. But he could only clutch the edge of the table and strain to hear her. "Thanks, Phyllis. How—how are you?"

Jimmy was puzzled. He had never heard his father speak like this, as if he was having difficulty in breathing.

"I'm very well, I suppose, Charles." Phyllis spoke in a lower tone. "Wilhelm's here, downstairs, and I'm taking from upstairs. We're alone. If you want to see him, please come now. We returned only this morning."

"Yes," said Charles.

"Charles? Is there something wrong? You sound very faint—"

Grief, and darkness, and then out of it Phyllis' voice. Charles said: "I'll come at once. Right away." It wasn't death, after all. She was speaking, and for some queer reason, for the past hour, he had believed he would never hear her again. He said: "I thought—I thought you'd gone away, Phyllis— It's like hearing from someone you thought had—"

There was no answer. Charles waited. He leaned forward. "Phyllis? Phyllis?"

"Yes, Charles." Then again: "Oh, Charles."

He heard her replace the receiver. He took his from his ear, and stared at it blankly. He turned it in his hand. From the mouthpiece came a peevish female voice: "Number, please? Number, please?"

Charles hung up. He sat there, his hands planted on his knees. Something made Jimmy retreat silently, and then go upstairs, his young face greatly disturbed.

The telephone rang again, shrilly, and Charles answered at once. It was only Friederich, however. "Karl, I'm sorry that Herbert Belz didn't come last week. But I have a letter from him, which I didn't open until now, and he says that he will be here about the tenth. He's still in Chicago."

Charles decided to drive the big red automobile, himself, to go to his brother's house. Jimmy had taught him to drive very well during the past month. He was putting on his coat and hat when Jimmy came downstairs again. "It was only your uncle Fred," said Charles. "And your aunt says your uncle Willie is at home, alone, and I'm taking your advice and going up to see him at once." He tried to smile. "No, you needn't drive me. I can manage well enough for myself, thank you, son."

"But those mountain roads, Dad. You haven't done much driving on them, and then not on any steep grades."

"Nonsense. I know how to use the brake when necessary."

Jimmy saw that his father was still slightly breathless. "Well, all right. But be careful, Dad," he admonished, with solicitude.

Charles concentrated all his mind and effort on the mountain roads. Considerable work had been done here, under pressure from the people who lived on these slopes, but the roads, though good, were narrow, and the ditches along the side were full of soft spring mud. A slight miscalculation, a slight swerve, a wheel in the thick brown slime, and there was trouble until someone came along with a tow rope in another automobile and tugged one out.

So Charles drove carefully, and negotiated very slowly around curves. He was not too fond of driving; he had discovered, with dismay, that the driver never saw the country, but only the road. So he was almost upon an automobile with its right rear wheel caught in the mud before he saw it.

Why, that was old Harry Hoffman's Ford, of which he was so proud, and which he had bought with the money a presumably grateful Government had given him for the injuries he had suffered during the Spanish-American War. The sad thing about it was that "old Harry" was not really old; in fact, he was younger than Charles. But he had been wounded and he had contracted a tropical disease, and he had become an old man. He used his automobile for the purpose of "hacking" at the station, and was doing well at it.

Charles moved ahead of Harry's automobile, and stopped his own machine. Harry was already hopefully approaching him, and tugging at his chauffeur's hat, another proud possession. "Mr. Wittmann!" he said. "Lucky for me. I'm taking a passenger up to Mr. Brinkwell's house, 'way up there, and I've got stuck."

Charles walked back with him. "I've got a tow-rope," he said. Then he saw that Harry, the small and shrunken former Rough Rider, had been desperately attempting to heap little rocks and pieces of wood under the rear wheel. The man's yellowed face literally dripped with sweat; his hands had become one welter of mud. He was panting with exhaustion. "I've been trying to get her out for nearly half an hour," he said, dismally. "But she sinks in deeper all the time. If someone could've given me a shove from the rear I would've been all right, and on my way by now."

A lady passenger, then. "Well, I've got the tow-rope," said Charles. "I'll hitch it onto yours and I'll pull you out. But I wish there was another man here to help us. You can't push by yourself, Harry."

But Harry nodded confidently. "I've still got my strength," he said. He lowered his voice as he accompanied Charles to the big red car on the road. "That feller in there—he wouldn't help. Don't suppose passengers have to, and he's right in a way. But still—"

Charles looked at Harry, then at the Ford. Harry's breath was raucous in the chill mountain quiet, and his eyes were suffused. Charles went back rapidly to the smaller car and pulled open the door. He saw a man in the rear seat, his hat far down on his forehead; he was smoking impatiently. Charles said, angrily: "If you want to climb the mountains for about three miles or so, with your bag, then you can do it. But if you want to ride, you'll get out and help Harry Hoffman shove from the rear, while I pull with my car. Make up your mind."

The man stirred. "I'm not getting out into that mud," he said. "I'm a passenger. It's the driver's job, not mine."

Charles said: "Well, take your bag and walk. Three miles up or five miles back to the station."

The man stepped out of the car. He was somewhat taller than Charles, and very slender, and it was impossible to say if he were thirty or fifty, for everything about him was neutral. He had a pale, smooth face, light gray eyes, light thin hair, a pointed nose and an expressionless mouth. His clothing was dark gray, and expensive, and his boots were polished. He was a man no one would remember, even after a dozen meetings, unless he had a name which one might urgently wish to remember. He would fade into any anonymous crowd, any static group. Brinkwell. Why hadn't Brinkwell sent down his own automobile and chauffeur to the station?

He spoke and his voice was oddly resonant in the quiet: "With your help, he'll be able to get out well enough."

Charles told himself that if this man's appearance was unremarkable his voice certainly was not. It had power and authority. Charles said: "I'm going up the hill, myself, to visit a relative, and I'll call Mr. Brinkwell from there and tell him to send down someone for you. Unless you're not expected."

The Spring twilight had begun to pour over the mountains, and the man almost faded into it. But Charles remembered the expensive clothing.

The man said indifferently: "I'm expected. Not that it matters. And I don't want to put you to any trouble." He looked distastefully at the sunken wheel of the Ford, then at his gloved hands. Charles' eyes narrowed. "I'll take you up to Mr. Brinkwell's," he said, tentatively.

"No," said the man. He moved his heard sharply in Harry's direction. "You'll have to get on the side with the mud, and I'll push on the road side, when this gentleman has attached his rope."

So, Brinkwell didn't want him known, thought Charles. He went back to his automobile, found the rope in the rear under the seat, and with Harry's help he tied the two motor cars together. "Funny kind of feller, ain't he?" muttered Harry. "Obliging as a sore tooth."

"Ever seen him before, Harry?" Charles almost whispered.

Harry shook his head. "I don't know, Mr. Wittmann. Seems I have, and then it seems I haven't. Or I've seen lots of people just like him. Looks just like everybody else, don't he?"

Yes, thought Charles. Anonymous. The rope was tied, Charles got into his automobile, and Harry returned to the rear of his. Charles put the red automobile into gear, shouted: "Shove!" and the rope tightened between the Oldsmobile and the Ford. He could feel it become taut, and shudder. There was a loud sucking noise, the Oldsmobile roared, swayed, gripped, and ground its wheels on the road. Then it was moving; Charles looked back; the Ford was out of the mud, and shaking all over as if with palsy. An instant later the stranger had disappeared into the Ford and Harry, panting louder than ever, but beaming and stamping his mud-coated shoes on the pavement, came up to thank Charles. "Don't know how long I'd've had to stay there but for you, Mr. Wittmann! I'm certainly lucky."

Charles waved his hand, and went on. He heard the chugging of the Ford behind him. The mountain road divided a short distance ahead, and Charles went to the left, the Ford to the right. For some time, even above the noise of his own automobile Charles could hear that sharp and valiant clatter as the smaller machine climbed.

The red roof of Wilhelm's house began to rise above trees faintly nebulous with green. It seemed to Charles that he had not seen this house for years. It stood there, remote and silent, with the dark mountains behind it, and its whiteness glimmered spectrally in the twilight as Charles approached. It had the air of a house remembered in a dream, strange and unreal and unwelcoming. Charles stopped the automobile at the door, which opened at once. The maid was new, and she looked at Charles inquiringly. "Mr. Wittmann," he said. "I'm Mr. Charles Wittmann."

The girl led him into the hall, murmuring something. But Phyllis appeared suddenly, and exclaimed: "Charles!" The maid retreated, and Phyllis held out her hands to her brother-in-law. "It's so good to see you again, Charles," she said, and smiled, and scrutinized him anxiously in spite of the smile.

He took her hands, and held them hard. She was the only reality in this house for him. The half-light blurred everything in the hall; the steep white staircase was made of unsubstantial smoke, and even the fire was only painted.

"I haven't seen you—for years, and years, Phyllis," said Charles, and tried to laugh. Had this cool and aloof house always echoed like this, or had he just never noticed it before?

Phyllis tried to laugh, also. Her hands had always been fine and slender but now they felt almost bony in Charles' hands. It was probably only the deep purple velvet of her dress which made her face so white in the gloom, and so thin. But the fire sparkled on her rich hair.

"Do come in and sit down with me in the music room, Charles," she said, gently, drawing her hands from his. "You see, I tried to reach you, but Jimmy said you had left. Someone called Wilhelm, just after I had talked with you, and he told me that he had to go out for awhile, possibly until evening. Does it matter so much, Charles?"

"Yes, it matters very much, Phyllis." He stood there, sick with his disappointment. "I just have to talk with Wilhelm. Did he drive?"

"No," said Phyllis, wretchedly. "But you know what a walker Wilhelm is, and so he might be gone for hours. I—I didn't ask him whom he was visiting, or who the caller was. It could be someone very near, or someone down in the city. Sometimes, when he's walked somewhere, and it's a considerable distance, he lets them drive him back. Under grateful protest, of course." She laughed again, and the sound was as wretched as her voice. "I wanted to ask him who it was, but he was so short. Charles, something very terrible is happening to Wilhelm."

Charles was silent. Phyllis waited, then said: "But come and talk to me, and perhaps Wilhelm will be home sooner than we expect."

Charles looked about the hall again. Suddenly he felt its hostility, its withdrawal.

"It's very mild outside, Phyllis," Charles said, abruptly. "Suppose we walk around for a little while, and then come back. If Willie's here, then I'll stay, and talk it out with him."

CHAPTER XXXIV

THEY WALKED slowly over the long, gravelled paths of the garden, and then up a slight slope, and then onto a broad promontory which overlooked the river far below, and the city. There they stood, very close together in a dusk so violet that it seemed less air than an element in itself, still but limitless, reaching from the water to the very sky. The town lights, at the base of the mountain, winked in and out like yellow fireflies, and the river was a purple plain beyond it in the cool spring wind, and the sweet scent of the gardens, newly stirring, came to them strongly.

Beyond the river, and over the opposite mountain, the sky had turned an intense deep cobalt, and now the evening star, pure and white, shone in it with increasing brilliance.

Phyllis stood beside Charles in her seal-skin coat, with a white lace shawl over her head. She listened while he talked. It seemed to him that he talked endlessly, while she did nothing but listen, making no comment, not even turning to him. Her head was bent, and he could not see her face.

"So, there it is," he said, in conclusion. "And don't think, Phyllis, that when I spoke of Brinkwell and his 'mass-production,' that I've anything against big business. It's just that monopolies are dangerous, especially now, with everything that's stirring. They won't think, or believe, men like Brinkwell, that concentration of industry will make it that much easier for Socialism or something else like it to eat them up. The safety of the whole country lies in concerns like mine, in diversity."

Phyllis said: "You're quite desperate, aren't you, Charles?"

"Well, yes, I am."

"And everything you've told me about an impending war, Charles—I believe it. You haven't much proof, but still, I believe it. Charles, you know you can't do anything about it, don't you? Not even ten thousand or a hundred thousand men like you, anywhere."

"Yes, I know."

"And, of course, it would do no good writing Congressmen, or anybody. For those who wouldn't believe you would only laugh at you, and those who would know you're telling the truth would only laugh louder."

"Yes."

They did not speak again, but only looked at the sky beyond them.

Phyllis said, eventually: "Charles, you are desperate about your business, and your son. You can't spend your strength worrying about any impending war; it wouldn't do any good. You must just concentrate on your business, and just hope, and perhaps pray, that if war comes it'll confine itself to Europe, as it's always done before."

Now she turned to him and put her hand on his arm. "Don't think of anything, until you have to, but the business. That's the immediate thing. You know, the Bible does say: 'Sufficient unto the day is the evil thereof.' When you have to face other problems, that'll be time enough."

"But it seems horrible, Phyllis, having to stand by and watch things develop."

"But you can't do anything about it. It's too late, for anybody."

He nodded.

"So, you can only attend to your own immediate affairs, retain your patents, refuse to be harassed by Jochen, and stop seething." She laughed, a little sadly. "Poor Charles. I never thought you'd 'seethe' over anything except the shops."

Charles said: "Do you believe that, Phyllis?"

She dropped her hand. "Not now," she said.

Again, they both stood and looked at the sky, shoulder to shoulder. Charles was very tired; the wind had become cold against his back;

the trees talked louder in it, restlessly. The star in the cobalt sky glittered brighter. Charles thought of the *Élégie*; he could rarely remember any musical selection, but now whole phrases of the song of lamentation returned to him. A man's loss, a man's hopelessness, a man's despair, for everything which had been taken from him.

He said to himself: I must tell Phyllis about it. And he knew he couldn't. It was the most pressing thing in him now, but still he knew he couldn't tell her about it. Then he looked at her. She had covered her face with her hands and she was crying, silently. He watched her, aghast. He moved away a little, and said, roughly, "Don't, Phyllis."

He kept himself from touching her, because he knew that she did not want him to touch her, for, once having touched, it would be too terrible. So he said again, even more roughly: "Don't, Phyllis."

He could not allow her to speak, so he said: "Let's go back to the house. Maybe Willie's there by this time."

After mentioning his brother's name he knew that it was safe to touch her. He took her elbow, and pulled her hand away from her face. She averted it from him, but not before he had seen her tears. He sighed. "Let's go back to the house," he repeated.

They went back, not speaking, in the purplish darkness. They went into the lighted hall, where the fire was very low. A maid came and took their coats. "I'll stay and wait for him," said Charles. "This has to be settled."

It was then that they heard a carriage drive up, outside, and Phyllis cried: "It's Wilhelm! But there's someone with him. Never mind. We'll find a way."

Wilhelm had walked all the way down to the city to Jochen's house. Charles had not encountered him because there was a steep pedestrian country road which dipped from the house on Mountain Circle for some time before it joined the main road.

Wilhelm had walked, rather than driven, because under all his volatile mannerisms and mercurial disposition was a stratum of good, hard, Wittmann common sense. He knew that should he drive he would arrive at Jochen's home in an agitated state of mind which would preclude him from using his very sound gifts of detachment and coolness. He needed time; he needed a walk to give him a perspective. He had a deep capacity for passion, and he suspected it. Moreover, his life-long distrust for Jochen, and his natural distaste for his youngest brother, made him wary, in spite of all he had begun to believe of Charles.

He thought of all that Jochen had told him and hinted to him during the past months, as his tall, black figure moved rapidly down the silent country road. He thought of what he had seen, himself. How much was lies? How much was his own imagination? He detested Jochen; he had his own suspicions that Jochen was using him against Charles in a particularly ugly fashion, and he knew why, to some extent. Thinking of this, he began to feel a cold and bitter rage against both his brothers. The time was past for hints and innuendoes. He was determined to brush aside the sticky webs of lies in the darkness and get at the truth. What if it were what he most feared? Now he thought only of Charles, and it was with hatred.

Jochen, himself, admitted him with a hearty if somewhat somber greeting. Isabel was sitting in the great handsome sitting-room, dressed in gray velvet. She gave him her hand very seriously, and her pretty hazel eyes were sympathetic. Wilhelm wanted to say to his brother: "Can't we be alone?" But that would be too impolite, even for a sister-in-law. Besides, he had a somewhat romantic idea that women were less likely to lie than men, and that they were naturally more compassionate.

Wilhelm sat down, as far from the fire as possible. Lean and dark and withdrawn, he looked at Jochen. Jochen saw, with satisfaction, that Willie might put on an aristocratic and disdainful air of coolness but he was nevertheless deeply disturbed, and that he looked as if he had not slept well for a long time.

Wilhelm regarded his brother and Isabel silently. His long thin fingers began to tap on the carved arm of his chair. Then he said: "Jochen, for months you've been hinting to me that there was—" He paused, with a slight grimace of disgust. "There was," he continued, " 'something' between Charles and my—my wife. And I've told you that it was not true, and that it was an insult to Phyllis, and myself."

Isabel said, with soft quickness: "Oh, Wilhelm, I'm afraid that isn't exactly right. Jochen would never say a word against Phyllis; we not only admire and love her so much, but we'd not suspect her for a moment. She's a lady. Please don't be unjust to poor Jochen."

Wilhelm looked at her with a hard steadiness. "Isabel, it would be impossible to be 'unjust' to Jochen. I've known him much longer than you have."

Jochen scowled. He was alarmed. Isabel was puzzled; she did not quite understand. Then she remembered Wilhelm's tone of voice. "Ambiguous," she murmured.

"Perhaps to you, Isabel. But I don't think it is to Jochen. Is it?" Wilhelm glanced at his brother.

"I suppose you're being subtle," said Jochen. "And I'm not sure that you mean to be complimentary, either."

Wilhelm slapped his palm on the arm of the chair. "I mean I want the truth. That's all, just the truth. You called me, and said you had something circumstantial to tell me. Tell it, and let's get it over."

Jochen looked out of the corner of his eyes at his wife, who prepared to corroborate whatever he said. "Willie," began Jochen, "I've told you for months that we've both heard whisperings about—well, about Charlie, mainly. It's all over Andersburg; you, being Phyllis' husband, wouldn't hear it. It's an old aphorism—"

"About the 'deceived' husband," added Wilhelm, sarcastically, as Jochen hesitated.

"That's just it!" cried Isabel, eagerly. "Phyllis *isn't* deceiving you!"

"How could you insult your own wife like that?" demanded Jochen, outraged.

Wilhelm smiled bitterly. "Go on," he said, in a reasonable voice.

"I've just told you what others have been whispering, and what I've overheard, and what's been told me confidentially: that Charlie's been molesting Phyllis, and embarrassing her with—with—"

"What is melodramatically called 'his attentions,'" interrupted Wilhelm, with contempt. "He's been 'pursuing' her. I love those Victorian phrases. Go on." He thought of Charles and Phyllis in the Brinkwells' drawing-room; he thought of the glances exchanged by his brother and his wife, in his own home. He thought of Phyllis' constant and gentle defense of Charles; he remembered all that he had ever known of how she had influenced him in Charles' favor. There was much that Jochen did not know, or even suspect, but which Jochen's hints had made him see for himself.

"All right, all right, if you want to be humorous," said Jochen, impatiently. "But it doesn't sound right to me to be humorous when a man's wife is being made the subject of gossip and scandal in the town, and without her being in the least at fault, herself, and only a victim. Everybody's laughing behind his hand. The Brinkwells don't know any of us very well, except perhaps Isabel and me." Jochen unconsciously bridled, and Isabel preened in stately fashion. "So, they wouldn't have any reason to be disturbed about anything, unless it was brought to their attention very forcibly. You know Pauline, Wilhelm. Do you think she'd lie?"

"Of course she would," replied Wilhelm. "The woman's a ghastly fraud. And a vulgarian."

Isabel was horrified. But Jochen stopped her with a lift of his hand before she could speak in protest. "Nevertheless, no matter what your opinion of Pauline is, Willie, you've got to admit she hasn't any ulterior motive, and I've never heard her gossip just for the sake of gossip and meanness. In fact, she hasn't gossiped about either old Charlie, or Phyllis. It was just that she heard rumors, and so she came to Isabel one day and she was very upset, and said that—"

"That Isabel 'ought to know' what 'people' were saying," added Wilhelm.

"All right, put it that way, if you want to sneer," said Jochen. "But we've gone over this for months. I didn't believe it at first, myself, and Isabel absolutely refused to believe it. We have family pride, you know."

"Have you?" asked Wilhelm. "Please, don't let us digest and redigest the whole thing. Let us examine absolute facts. You and Isabel saw Charles and Phyllis emerging from the woods last summer. You, Jochen, have seen Phyllis alone with Charles in his office, once or twice. I have, too. Phyllis was with Charles for over a week, when his boy was ill. Who else was there, to help him? I can see, though, that a dirty mind could put quite a significance on that perfectly innocent week. Then, there is that old matter of Charles and Phyllis once being engaged. Then, there are these alleged 'scandalous stories' of which you've told me. You told me other things, as slight as all these. You tell me that Charles is causing Phyllis embarrassment because of his 'pursuit' of her. She hasn't mentioned it to me—"

"Of course she wouldn't," said Jochen, sturdily. "Why should she bother you or make you angry? After all, we're all brothers, and there is the company. But," and he paused gravely, "has she told you that she's written to him lately, at his office?"

Wilhelm's hand became still. "No," he said, flatly, "she hasn't. Has she?"

"Yes. I saw the envelope myself. I recognized her handwriting. After all, I'd know it, after all these years of Christmas presents and notes to Isabel and the girls, wouldn't I? But even that wouldn't be so bad if it weren't for the fact that the envelope was empty, and Charlie had just burned her letter."

Wilhelm's smooth dark skin had become congested with color. "It could have been a friendly note. After all, whenever we are away she writes to all the family, as you know."

"Of course," said Jochen, smoothly. "But why did old Charlie burn it so carefully, then? Why was he so disturbed when I asked him what it was? He could just have said: 'It's from Phyllis.' But he didn't. We both looked at the ashes. Then when I sort of accused him, in a careful way, he became enraged. He jumped to his feet and said if I 'tried' anything he'd 'smash me'!" Jochen jumped to his feet, himself, furious and flaming with the memory of that interview with Charles. Wilhelm watched him. He had been ready to discount much of Jochen's story, but now that he saw the genuine rage of his brother, the hatred in his eyes, he accepted it all. This was no "play-acting." It was the truth. Wilhelm closed his own eyes for a moment.

"'Smash me'! 'Drive me out'!" shouted Jochen. "That's what he said when I asked him what the letter was. He knew I knew. And he threatened me. For a moment I thought the swine had lost his mind! I, the vice-president of the company, his brother! After all my work. God damn it, it was an innocent question, and if he hadn't acted up so I'd not have thought a thing! But he was guilty, and he knew I knew he was guilty, and he was ready to murder me!"

"Why should he have been so careful about burning that letter?" asked Wilhelm. "You say you believe that Phyllis is innocent. Yet, if she had written him a letter which he found it necessary to burn, she isn't innocent."

"Oh, she must be!" wailed Isabel.

Jochen standing there with a red face and big clenched fist, narrowed his eyes. He said: "It's you who're insulting your wife now, Willie. Not we. We refuse to believe what you're implying. Personally, I think Charlie's been pestering Phyllis so much, and probably writing to her in Philadelpha begging her to come back, that she had to write him and tell him off. That's what I think. That's what any decent woman would do. Wouldn't she?" he asked his wife.

"Indeed!" cried Isabel. "And I think that's just what happened, and naturally, Charles couldn't have her letter lying around, and so he destroyed it."

"It's the burning of the letter that I don't understand. Why burn it? Why get in such a rage when I asked him about the ashes, innocently? Why fly up and threaten me when I hinted something? He didn't even pretend to misunderstand me," said Jochen.

Wilhelm was silent.

"If you don't do something about it, I will!" Jochen was shouting again and pointing his finger at Wilhelm. "I'm not going to have these stories circulating around like they are now! There's the family name to think of. It's bad enough that he's ruining the company with his old-fuddy ways, and refusing to listen to any of Brinkwell's suggestions, which would make us really rich. He has to do this thing, and compromise Phyllis—"

Wilhelm stood up. If he didn't get out into the cool air he'd faint, he thought. "I shall go home and think over all this. And then I'll probably decide to talk to Charles, myself."

His knees were uncertain. He put his hand on the back of his chair to steady himself. Phyllis. It was impossible to think of anything foul in connection with Phyllis. It was Charles, and Charles, only.

"Yes, talk to him," said Jochen, jeeringly. "He'll deny everything." He saw Wilhelm's face. "I'll call your carriage," he said.

"I walked. And I'll walk back."

"No, you're in no condition." Jochen put his hand on his brother's shoulder. "I'll take you home. It's dark, now, and it's too far."

The carriage was closed, and comfortable, but Wilhelm sat pulled together as if deadly cold, and did not speak. He heard Jochen as at a distance. "He'll drag us all down—Brinkwell—fortune in it—now he's got that idiot, Fred. He's played with all of us—tricked us—you remember how he's set one of us against another all the time, and laughed at us to himself—it's about time we understood a few things—"

Wilhelm thought: No, Phyllis would never betray me, never. But she looks ill, has looked ill for a long time. What if she doesn't care for me any longer? That would be something I couldn't stand. Charles has been hounding her; yes, I can see it now, and she wouldn't tell me of it, not wanting to hurt me. I mustn't let myself believe for one moment that she cares about him. But why did she write him?

His head was aching; the violence and misery of his thoughts were too much for him. Everything he had, including himself, was nothing while he had to think of losing Phyllis. He moved and looked through the carirage windows. They were rolling up the mountain, steadily, and past clumps of pine trees, and spruces. Jochen's voice was going on and on. I ought to have walked, thought Wilhelm. I can't endure Jochen, I never could. I think I hate him now. I think, in a way, I hate him worse than I do Charles.

They finally reached Mountain Circle, and Wilhelm began to push the fur robes from his knees, when Jochen said in a low and excited voice: "Look! Isn't that old Charlie's red automobile out there, near your door?"

Wilhelm looked, and saw, and sat motionless.

"Did you call him and tell him you were home?" asked Jochen, urgently.

Wilhelm could only shake his head.

"He couldn't have known. I wouldn't have known if you hadn't written me from Philadelphia, Willie, that you'd be in Andersburg this morning. Charlie didn't know? Then, how did he find out?"

He waited, but Wilhelm was still motionless though the carriage was drawing up behind the automobile.

"He found out in some way. Maybe he called you, and when he heard you weren't home he came up at once. That's right! Of course, Phyllis would never have called him to come, under the circumstances."

Wilhelm suddenly flung the robe from his knees, and without waiting for the coachman he opened the door, himself. Jochen lumbered rapidly after him. Wilhelm ran up the low white steps, Jochen following; Wilhelm did not wait for a maid to open the house door, but found his keys, inserted one.

He entered the hall, with Jochen, and there were Phyllis and Charles standing there before the fire, and facing them.

"Wilhelm!" cried Phyllis. "I'm so—" And then she saw her husband's face, and saw Jochen behind him.

"Willie," said Charles.

"Oho," muttered Jochen.

Charles looked at Wilhelm and then at Jochen and then at Wilhelm again. So, he commented to himself. He felt himself stiffening, bracing, and he moved one foot apart from the other so that he stood solidly like one expecting an assault. He pushed out his broad Wittmann chin, and he put his hands in his pockets.

Wilhelm quietly closed the door behind him. The four looked at each other, in silence. Then it came to Wilhelm, who had been about to speak, that the scene which was imminent would be beyond endurance, and too vulgar and base to be permitted. A maid, who had heard the door close, came, and Wilhelm and Jochen gave her their coats and hats. Phyllis stood close to Charles but her eyes were fixed pitifully and questioningly on her husband. It was at Jochen that Charles looked, with implacable hatred.

"Charles," said Wilhelm. Phyllis took a step towards her husband. But he gently held up his hand against her. "No, Phyllis. I want to talk to Charles, alone. Alone," he repeated, glancing at Jochen. "And I want you to stay here with Phyllis, until I've finished."

Phyllis turned her eyes upon Jochen. "No," she said. "I won't stay with Jochen. If you won't let me speak, Wilhelm, I'll go to my room."

She moved away from the men and began to mount the white marble staircase, her head high, one hand holding up her purple skirts. They watched her go.

Then Wilhelm said to Charles: "Please come upstairs with me to the gallery. Then we'll rejoin Jochen. You must not leave until we come down," he said to his other brother. "This must be settled, and at once. It is only fair and just—to everyone concerned."

"I'm willing," said Jochen, with a grin. "I can wait. Take your time, Willie." And he strolled away towards the music room.

Wilhelm and Charles went upstairs together without speaking. Once Charles' foot slipped on the smooth marble, and he almost fell. Wilhelm waited courteously until he had caught himself, then they continued up to the gallery.

CHAPTER XXXV

THE LAMPS in the gallery had been lighted. Wilhelm closed the door behind him and Charles before he saw that Phyllis was there, waiting, her hands clasped together. She came towards her husband and Charles.

"Phyllis," said Wilhelm.

"Don't send me away, dear," she begged. "Let me stay. Charles and I have been talking about—things—for a long time tonight. I want to be here to help him—"

Wilhelm stood and looked at her. It was true, then. They wanted to tell him, together. He moved away, near to a group of pictures on the wall. He said: "No."

"You've got to listen," said Charles. "It's desperately important."

"You've been avoiding Charles so long," pleaded Phyllis, her voice breaking. "It's been too long. For all of us."

Wilhelm leaned against the wall. Phyllis cried: "Oh, poor Wilhelm! You look so ill."

"I'll be as brief as I can," said Charles. "I'm so damned tired of talking, and thinking, and waiting. You'll have to hear me out, Willie. Then, do what you want to do. I'll have done my best to make you understand."

Wilhelm's slight black shoulders pressed the wall; he dropped his head. It wasn't possible to stand it; he couldn't give up Phyllis. If everyone would only go away for a while he might be able to think more clearly, to fight down this pain.

Phyllis ran to him, and caught him by the arm. "You wouldn't talk to Charles, before we went away, darling. Before that, he asked me for my help, in getting you alone. But then we went to Philadelphia. I wrote him from there and told him I'd call him immediately when we returned, so he could come up at once. And so, I called him this afternoon."

Wilhelm moved his head slightly, and looked at his wife. "You called him, Phyllis?"

"Yes, yes!" she exclaimed, pressing his arm. "I told you. I kept my promise, which I had written to him from Philadelphia. I'm sorry it had to be so underhand, but when you hear what he has to say you'll understand. I—"

"You wrote from Philadelphia?" repeated Wilhelm.

"Yes! Dear, do try to listen. I know you're very tired, but you must listen. I had to write Charles, just as I had to call him today. And then you went out. Charles arrived shortly after you left. He was so sick with disappointment that he wanted to leave, but I kept him here in hopes you'd return shortly. And then you came back with Jochen!"

Charles came closer to his brother. "Yes, it had to be Joe, didn't it? It had to be that liar and scoundrel. You couldn't have called me, of course. I'm only the president of the company, to be conspired against behind my back, and libelled. I always thought you were with me, Willie. But Joe's gotten to you at last, hasn't he?"

"Oh, no," said Phyllis, turning to Charles. "Wilhelm would never betray you or plot against you with Jochen. You must believe me, Charles. You can't wrong Wilhelm that way."

Charles said: "The time's come when I can't afford to be too 'nice,' Phyllis. Everything I have has got to be laid out on the table for Willie to see. I don't know what Joe's been saying to him, all these weeks, and now I don't care. I'm going to give him facts. If he's juvenile enough not to listen, then we'll all go down to hell, together."

Wilhelm could not speak. They waited for him, Phyllis almost crying. His shoulders slipped on the wall. Then he saw the deep concern of his wife and Charles for him, the affection in their eyes, and the dismayed glance they gave each other. They moved nearer to him, watching him anxiously.

"Oh, darling," said Phyllis, and took her husband's hand and held it tightly.

"Will you give me, say, ten minutes?" Charles asked. "Then I'll go away and you can talk it all out cozily with Joe, and destroy everything I've worked for all my life."

It was all a lie, thought Wilhelm. All a filthy lie. There was nothing to it, ever. Jochen's brought me to this, and lied about my wife and my brother, and I've listened. What can I say to them? How can I even look at them?

His head swam with his passionate relief, and with his self-disgust, and his anger and humiliation. He pushed his shoulders away from the wall. He tried to speak, and then could only put his arm around Phyllis, and stand there.

Charles was puzzled. There was something going on here which he could not understand. A moment ago Willie had looked as if he was about to collapse. Now he was standing upright, holding Phyllis, and there was some color coming back into his cheeks. Charles said to Phyllis: "When you wrote me you didn't say anything about Willie being ill or anything in Philadelphia."

"He hasn't been well since he had that influenza, Charles. I wrote you that, too."

"Well," said Charles, sighing. "Look here, sit down, Willie. Let's all sit down. I'm not leaving here until I've had my say. Why didn't you talk to me about it? Why did you have to hide? Because Joe was lying to you, and you believed it?"

"Yes. I believed him," said Wilhelm. Now he could speak, and it was with enormous bitterness. "Never mind. Yes, let us sit down."

There were some small chairs placed near the walls under the pictures. Phyllis sat beside her husband, and Charles perched on a chair and faced them. The gallery was cold; the lights were cold on the pictures. At the end of the room a bust of Socrates gravely stared down the long aisle.

"Before you begin," said Wilhelm, "I'd like to ask you something, Charles. Jochen told me this afternoon you had threatened to 'smash' him and 'drive' him out of the company. Why?"

Charles laughed shortly. "Yes, I told him that, and I meant it. I still mean it. He's not going to destroy what I've built up. No."

"I see," said Willie, thoughtfully. Phyllis' hand was warm in his. She smiled at him with deep tenderness. "I see," he repeated. Then he looked at Charles. "Go on. Tell me. Tell me as much as possible. You won't tell me everything, I know, but do your discreet best." And then he actually smiled.

They laughed a little, together. Charles said: "I've been talking to Phyllis about all this for months. I tried to talk to you, too, but you wouldn't listen; that was the time you gave me the Picasso."

"The first time you mentioned it was when we were in the woods that afternoon, last summer," said Phyllis. "I was terribly frightened. You remember, Charles?"

"I remember," said Charles. He had planted one hand on each spread knee, and sat there solidly, nodding.

"Go on," said Wilhelm. "He's waiting down there, and I have a few things to say to him. In private."

So Charles began to talk, as he had talked to Phyllis that afternoon, and when he paused for a moment Phyllis quoted him to Wilhelm, and Charles nodded again. Wilhelm listened intently, holding his wife's hand, and watching the lamplight in her earnest eyes.

Then Charles, gray with tiredness, stopped and mopped his face. He and Phyllis waited for Wilhelm to speak. But Wilhelm sat in silence.

"I've got Fred," Charles repeated, when his brother remained silent. "For how long only God knows. You know Fred, Willie. He might bolt any day over to Joe again. In the meantime, he's seeing Helen Hadden, and George and I are both working on her, and I think the poor devil's in love with the girl. She seems to like him. If I can only keep him in hand for a while longer, and if I can be sure you're with me, we'll save our company. Even if Brinkwell does have his own machine-tool shops."

"So, you think Brinkwell wants our patents?" said Wilhelm. "Yes, I see. And you're determined, for perfectly good reasons of your own, not to let him have them. Naturally. You aren't suspecting that if we comply with what he wants we'd soon be a Connington subsidiary, are you?"

Charles looked at him, and then he jumped to his feet with a savage exclamation. "What a damned fool I've been! Of course, that's what would happen! That's what's behind it all! And I never saw it, never once! There it was, right before my eyes, and I never saw it!" He was stupefied.

Phyllis said to Wilhelm: "You see, now, how much Charles has needed you."

Charles said, violently: "So, that's what it is! You're right, Phyllis, I've been spreading myself out, worrying about something I'll never be able to help, and here was the company sliding down to hell behind my back!" He shouted at Wilhelm: "How could you have seen it at once, and I couldn't?"

Wilhelm leaned back negligently in his chair. "My dear Charles, it's obvious. Of course, it would take some little time, even if we leased or lent those patents to Brinkwell, but eventually there we'd be—a neat subsidiary of the Connington, Fred completely immobilized, myself impotent, and Jochen— Let us consider Jochen. The Wittmann Machine Tool Company is too small for our young brother. He has his eyes on something much bigger. What could that be? Assistant superintendent to Brinkwell, perhaps? Or—perhaps—general manager of our own shops. And you, Charles?"

Wilhelm held up his hand, and his ring flashed in the lamplight. "Charles, please. Let's be sensible. Let's think this over quietly."

Charles exclaimed: "It's the humiliation of the thing that I can't stand! 'Be sensible,' you say, and all the time he's been plotting to ruin us!"

"He hasn't been able to do it yet. And he never will," said Wilhelm. "He'll stoop to anything, believe me. I know it only too well. But now that we know, we can stop it. We must concentrate on keeping Friederich with us, though, as you said, it's like holding a time bomb in your hand."

For the first time in his life he felt securely strong, and even superior to Charles, who had not seen what was obvious. Poor Charles. Wilhelm felt his old affection for his brother return to him, deeper and warmer than ever. However, he held back an inclination to incite Charles to further rage with gentle ridicule, for he remembered what he had believed of him, and of Phyllis, only a little more than an hour ago. "I must talk to Jochen alone. Let us go downstairs. Please wait for me, Charles. When I've finished with Jochen I want you to join us."

He stood up. "What do you think we should do to Jochen?"

"I don't know," said Charles, boiling. "I know what I'd like to do to him. Kick him out!"

Wilhelm smiled leniently. "We might be able to get to that, one of these days. Yes, I think we might. I have a small matter of my own I'd like to settle with him. No, I can't tell you, Charles. It's too mortifying—" Phyllis was standing beside him. "Too mortifying. Too shameful," added Wilhelm. "And then, again, he might become so enraged, when he finds out that we know all about him, that he might, very possibly, say something so unpardonable that he couldn't remain with the company."

Wilhelm considered this, no longer smiling. "Come down with us, Phyllis. Stay with Charles, while I talk to Jochen. I think, in your presence, after we've had a talk, that Jochen will hold his tongue. I don't think any of us is quite ready, just now, to 'kick him out,' as Charles says."

"I am," said Charles. They walked to the door, then Charles paused.

"I don't like mysteries, Willie. What has he been telling you? I've got to know."

Wilhelm turned, and looked at his brother. "No," he said. "No. That's something I'll never tell you, Charles. For if I did you could never be friends with me again. You'd despise me, and you'd be right. I don't want that to happen." He looked at Phyllis. "You'd despise me, too, my dear. That would be even worse for me."

He quickly opened the door, and Charles and Phyllis followed him. Charles said: "And to think that all the time I was thinking that Brinkwell was just wanting to set up his shops in competition with us! And all the time—"

They reached the stairway together, then stopped. Jochen, having become uneasy at the long delay, and the silence upstairs, had come back into the hall. He was standing there below, squinting up at them in the subdued light.

"Well," he said, trying to see.

Wilhelm drew back and let Phyllis precede him. She went down a few steps and Charles, near the banister, and Wilhelm, near the wall, followed her, side by side.

It was Wilhelm's intention to be dignified, and not to make a scene before his wife. But as he went down the stairs with Charles his hatred and anger became too much for him, and his shame. He did not want Jochen to be near Phyllis, or even to look at her. It was too much! So, he began to hurry, to catch up with Phyllis. "Don't—" he exclaimed.

It was then that he slipped on the glimmering marble stairs.

Charles instinctively threw out a hand to catch him, but it was too late. Wilhelm's sleeve was torn from his fingers as Wilhelm went hurtling past him. Phyllis, hearing Wilhelm's exclamation and Charles' cry, turned just in time to see her husband flying headlong down the stairs. She drew back with a scream as he neared her, his arms flaying. Then a moment later he had crashed below her, on the last steps, almost at Jochen's feet.

Charles stood paralyzed on the stairway. He heard Phyllis screaming, over and over. He saw his brother lying huddled together, motionless, face down, a broken body in rumpled black. He gripped the balustrade, for his legs were weakening with horror and disbelief. He could not move. Dazed, he watched Phyllis running down the stairs. He saw her kneeling beside Wilhelm, her violet gown spread all about her. She was still screaming. And he could not move.

Jochen looked at the man near his feet. Then, very slowly, he lifted his eyes to Charles.

"So, that's how you settled it," he said.

It was terrible, to hear Phyllis screaming like that. Charles wanted to go to her. But the stairs were wavering before him, and he had to sit down to save himself from falling, also.

CHAPTER XXXVI

COLONEL GRAYSON looked at Charles sympathetically. "I know it's hard for you to think of anything just now," he said. "I wouldn't have bothered you, but time's pressing, and we must be prepared."

Charles nodded. He looked at the papers which Colonel Grayson had placed before him; they were copies of certain patents he held in his own name and in the name of the company. But it was difficult to see; it was difficult to focus, or to care.

"When I read of your brother's death, I delayed for three weeks," said the colonel.

"Yes," said Charles, in a dull voice. He tried to look over the papers; he moved his glasses on his nose. The papers were without meaning. He shifted them about a little, then his hand just lay on them.

"A terrible blow to you," continued the colonel.

Charles said nothing. "A terrible blow." Willie. Willie in the burial plot beside his parents. It wasn't possible. Willie with his "modern art," his elegance, his affectations, his fastidiousness, his mercurial delight in living: it wasn't possible. It had happened six weeks ago, but still Charles could not believe it. Wilhelm had lived for five hours after his fall, though he had never regained consciousness. Charles would never forget those five hours of waiting. Charles took off his glasses and rubbed the red spot on his nose. During those five hours it had begun to rain, and finally there had been a thunderstorm. He would never hear thunder again without seeing Wilhelm's dying face, and without hearing Phyllis' smothered weeping. "A broken neck," the doctor had said. He had tried to console Charles and Phyllis, while Jochen had stood at a distance. "He didn't suffer," the doctor had said. How could he know? The dying have no voice. Charles looked at the copies of his patents.

"No," he said.

Colonel Grayson frowned, though he was still sympathetic.

"Perhaps I haven't made it clear to you, Mr. Wittmann," he began.

"You've made it clear that when the Amalgamated Steel Company in Pittsburgh asks for these patents I should lease them to them," he said. "The answer is 'no.'"

The colonel shifted his slight body in his chair. "Why not, Mr. Wittmann?"

It was difficult to talk, and it was an actual physical effort which involved strain. "I've been thinking of my brother Wilhelm," he said. "You wouldn't understand, Colonel Grayson, when I say that I just thought to myself: 'The dying never have a voice.'"

The colonel considered this seriously. Then he said: "I think I do understand. But—"

"Since you were here last August, I've been doing a lot of reading, and a lot of questioning," Charles interrupted. "I know what's in the wind. No one, but no one, is going to get any of my patents for any such purpose. The Amalgamated makes munitions, doesn't it, just like the Connington? My patents won't ever be used to make munitions, Colonel Grayson."

The colonel was silent, smoking. Charles stood up, and thrust his hands deep in his pockets. "Who are the Amalgamated making munitions for, if they are making munitions now?" he asked.

"They aren't making munitions, not just yet, Mr. Wittmann. But if they do—"

"Germany?" said Charles.

"No. Not Germany."

"For England, perhaps, and France, or possibly Russia?"

"Mr. Wittmann," said the colonel, "I'm not in a position to tell you anything. Frankly, I know very little, anyway. The Amalgamated may never ask for your patents. I hope not. We're doing everything we can in Washington."

"But you didn't do enough, in time."

"I know what you're thinking of, Mr. Wittmann. I remember the conversation we had last August very clearly. You'll remember that I said that some things happen no matter what is done, or what is tried. Maybe what we both don't want to happen never will. I admit our State Department is inadequate, and that they're confused with rumors—"

Charles broke in: "You may not know it, but the Connington Steel Company, which has just opened here in Andersburg, has been trying to get these patents from me for months. Maybe they know more than our 'inadequate' State Department seems to know."

"Very possibly," said the colonel, gravely.

"They knew. Everyone in Europe knew. I've been reading, as I said, Colonel Grayson. I've been asking questions. Everyone knew but our State Department. Or didn't it?"

"Mr. Wittmann, I'm a military man, not a member of the State Department. If our State Department knows, it doesn't want to believe. And then again, it may be right. Nothing may happen."

"Even though the Connington, and the Bouchards, are sure it will?"

The colonel rolled his cigarette in his fingers. "You can't be certain of that."

"Not with actual quotations from them—no. But I had a talk this winter with Brinkwell. I know what he tried to get from my brother Jochen. I stopped that. Brinkwell and I understand each other very well."

The colonel sighed. "All right, Mr. Wittmann, suppose we grant your premise that there'll be a war in Europe." He hesitated. "I returned from a visit to Germany two months ago.

"I'm thinking of the Germans, Mr. Wittmann. Have you been to Germany recently? No? There's been a change in Germany. I've talked to people close to the Kaiser. The man is definitely insane. Do you know anything about insanity, Mr. Wittmann? I do. Insanity is contagious. Ten years ago the Germans were an enthusiastic nation, proud of what they had done, full of ambition, hopeful. They had a right to be. Now they've caught insanity from their Kaiser."

The colonel smiled wryly. "I'm not a scholar, Mr. Wittmann. But I remember something Epicurus said: 'Nothing is enough for the man to whom enough is too little.'"

"He's being pushed, goaded, manoeuvered—"

The colonel gave Charles a sharp glance. "Perhaps. Knowing what I know about European tensions and ambitions and hates and envies, I can say 'perhaps.' But you can't 'goad, push or manoeuver' a sane man into anything, or a sane nation. A nation can be proud, but not proud enough to plan for world conquest, or even to want it."

"You think the Kaiser wants it?"

"Yes. Definitely. He's out of his mind. And he's afraid; that's part of his insanity. Perhaps other nations are deliberately frightening the Kaiser. Yes. Because they want Germany to commit suicide, which is the real name for war."

"And you want me to lease my patents, if they are called for, to help in a general suicide?"

The coloned frowned.

Charles said: "I've been reading. I've found out a lot of things. The munitions makers of Europe are very active, and have been active for the past three years."

"But if they had no potential market, they wouldn't be active, Mr. Wittmann. Let us say they 'smell' a bad situation coming up, an explosive situation."

He waited for Charles to speak, but Charles was silent. He continued: "Do you know what Friedrich von Bernhardi recently said? 'The inevitableness, the idealism, and the blessing of war, as an indispensable and stimulating law of development, must be repeatedly emphasized.' That is the sort of thing he tells the Kaiser, and the Kaiser is listening."

"Now, Colonel Grayson, let me tell you something Bonar Law just said: 'There is no such thing as an inevitable war. If war comes it will be from failure of human wisdom.' "

The colonel smiled sourly. "Yes, I can see that you've been reading, Mr. Wittmann. 'Human wisdom'? Can you mention one instance of human wisdom, anywhere, in the whole history of man?" He gave Charles a long, hard look. "Why did your grandfather, and your father, leave Germany?"

Charles did not answer.

"Do you want the condition which existed, and now exists again, in Germany, to spread all over Europe, Mr. Wittmann?"

"Is it existing?"

"Yes, it is. Now." He looked at the copies of the patents. "France is free; Scandinavia is free; England is free— Don't you prefer that kind of freedom to the kind of thing which now prevails in Germany?"

Charles sat down. His face had flushed, and his heavy eyes were stern. "You may be a military man, Colonel Grayson, but I'm a business man. We have free enterprise in America. I've been reading very nice accounts of 'free enterprise' in England. That's a lie. There never was free enterprise in England, as we know it here in America. And there probably won't ever be. I don't want to help the English, Colonel Grayson."

The colonel nodded. "But that's not the point. The thing in Europe is now just a powder-keg, waiting for a spark. Something is sure to set it off."

"And if it's set off, the Amalgamated will use my patents to help England? No."

"Perhaps by helping England we'll be helping ourselves."

"Europe's always fighting. There's no reason for us to be embroiled." Angry panic rose in Charles' voice.

"Quite true. We may be able to keep out of it—by helping people who are just expedient, and not insane. You may think them the same thing, but they aren't."

"I don't care what happens to Europe," said Charles, stubbornly. "I care only for America."

Again, the colonel considered what Charles had said. "Let me put it this way: by helping England, if there is a war, we'll also be preparing to defend ourselves."

Charles exclaimed: "It is impossible that you're thinking we'd get into a war!"

"We might. We just possibly might."

Charles said: "It wasn't even a year ago when you asked me not to sell or lease or lend my patents to anyone, under any circumstances."

"Quite true. I'm still asking you that, unless you hear from me to the contrary. But the situation has changed, in Europe. It is changing hour by hour."

"You'll never get the American people to believe that they must embroil themselves in any European struggle for power!"

"The American people will resist war. Let us hope that it will never be necessary for them to change their minds. If there is a war in Europe, we won't be able, I'm afraid, to stay out, passively or actively. Let's hope we'll only need to help arm England, and the other free nations of the world."

"Like England's tacit ally, Russia," Charles sneered.

The colonel sighed. "You don't know what's going on in Europe, Mr. Wittmann." He stood up.

"You're a 'military man,' as you said, Colonel," remarked Charles bitterly. "And military men never have denounced war."

"Mr. Wittmann," said the colonel, "I'm also the father of sons, and the grandfather of my sons' sons." He looked at Charles gravely. "I don't want my sons and their sons to die. I want to protect them, in any way possible. That's why I'm here now."

Charles felt ill. He was feeling ill very often these days. He leaned his forehead on the back of his hand. "I can't think clearly," he muttered. "My brother—" He then thought of Friederich. "I have another brother, here, who wouldn't consent—"

"But you're the president of this company. Mr. Wittmann, try to believe that there might not be any war. I'm just asking you to give your own consent when the Amalgamated Steel Company asks you about the patents. When they do, you'll know it's urgent."

"I can manufacture anything necessary," said Charles.

"I'm sorry, but you aren't a big enough company. The Amalgamated could produce twenty times as much as you could, and more rapidly."

Charles looked up, exhausted. "I'll wait. I'll see," he said.

"There's just one other thing, Mr. Wittmann: Don't let the Bouchards or the Connington have anything. If there is a war, they'll be manu-facturing for Germany, directly, and they'll be sending patents to Ger-many, for manufacture. I happen to know that. They're already doing it, in fact, through their European subsidiaries."

The colonel was a man of sympathy. He studied Charles' shrunken face. He said: "I've got to go at once. And, Mr. Wittmann, I want you to know how terribly sorry I am about your brother."

CHAPTER XXXVII

JIMMY had been accepted at Harvard. There was just the small matter of somewhat low marks in Latin, so again the weary tutor was called in to assist. Jimmy was saying nothing, these days, about seeing Ger-aldine, but Charles knew that the boy often saw the girl. He appreciated Jimmy's thoughtfulness in not telling him of this, or rather, he appre-ciated what Jimmy was trying to do for him. He trod delicately around Jimmy's high opinion of him, and Jimmy's conviction, since the quarrel between his father and uncle, that Charles would prefer him not to see his cousin.

When Jimmy had announced the last day of school Charles had nodded abstractedly. Time passed, now, without visible trace for him. There was too much grief and fear in him, too much apprehension and sense of helplessness. He worked harder than ever. He had not slept well since Wilhelm's death, and when he did sleep he dreamt of his brother. Once he dreamt that he was talking to Wilhelm, and he heard himself saying: "Only when death comes do we realize how much in common we had with the dead. Willie, why didn't we talk about so many things, together?"

There was, of course, Jochen. There was Jochen's plot with Brink-well, which Wilhelm had so easily explained, to Charles' mortification. The estrangement between the two brothers was complete. Charles often said to himself: There is no turning back.

He often heard Jochen's quick but heavy step, lumbering past his office door. There was no hesitation in that step. Plot, Charles would say to himself, savagely. I know, and I'm prepared, and there's nothing you can do about it.

He told himself that he no longer felt regret, and he knew that this was not true. He knew it was not true when he found himself hating Roger Brinkwell more than he hated Jochen. Then one night Charles thought: Why go on deceiving myself? There was bound to be a Brinkwell, eventually, in Jochen's life.

Friends were beginning to invite Charles to "quiet little dinners." But Charles invariably refused. The friends understood; it was very hard on Charles, who had been so fond of Wilhelm. Charles used the long evenings for reading. He read everything he could, long past his bed-time. It's useless, he would think. But he continued to read. Once he thought: I'm helpless, alone, but what if ten million men like myself, all over the world, had applied themselves as I've been doing these last months, and what if we'd all come upon some of the truths simultaneously? Couldn't we have accomplished something, against the murderers?

But America wasn't of age, Charles would think. No one questioned why great mills were suddenly teeming. It was just the depression passing. No newspaper man reported the enormous cargo ships in the Atlantic harbors, being loaded with so many sinister things. No one observed or commented upon the new tone in the newspapers about England. There were "hands across the sea" now, even in those papers which invariably had written fiery editorials against England on the Fourth of July. Charles began to hate the newspapers, which filled five pages with enthusiastic news about sports, three of local "society" news, ten of national news, and only a column or two, occasionally, about foreign news.

But a year ago I didn't read, either, thought Charles. All this was going on a year ago, and I knew nothing. It was to be seen, and I sat here every day at my desk and planned how to outwit my brothers and went home to read the sports news, yawn, and go to bed. Everything has changed for me, since the day the colonel came to my office.

Sometimes he found it hard to work, in his despair. Mr. Parker had to remind him of appointments he had written down, himself, on the big calendar on his desk. He was never conscious of the passing of time. He had not noticed the change in the seasons. Spring had gone; Summer had come. He only knew that Jimmy was at home and that he, himself, did not wear an overcoat any longer. The sun had gone off somewhere, for him, and he never saw it.

He often went to see Phyllis, who was inconsolable until he came. He would just sit and let her cry, and after a while he would talk of Wilhelm and they would, quite often, recall some humorous occasion, and they would laugh together and talk as if Wilhelm were there and listening, and laughing with them. Charles sometimes had the oddest impression that he was, and he knew that Phyllis felt this, too. On other occasions, however, he found friends with Phyllis, and he was annoyed. No one could comfort Phyllis but himself. I must show my annoyance to them, he would think when he was at home, and that's too bad. Only this could explain why some of the friends were pointedly cool or mysterious with him, or overly friendly as if to hide uneasiness, or why they would often leave quite soon after his arrival.

He was not resentful of Mrs. Holt, but she had a way of being quiet with him, when he allowed himself to be driven home in her car on the occasions when he had walked up to Wilhelm's house. He had the impression that she wanted to speak to him, and then when he'd turn to her expectantly she would suddenly become quite red and begin to talk rapidly of some inconsequential thing. Once or twice, in his presence, she had argued heatedly with Phyllis that Phyllis ought to go away for a nice long rest. It was obvious that Phyllis needed "a rest," but Charles could not understand Mrs. Holt's insistence. Charles had not known how much Mrs. Holt had liked Phyllis, and he was grateful. He had also pleaded with Phyllis to go away for a while. But Phyllis would not go. She said that when she was at home she felt that Wilhelm was with her. Mrs. Holt called this morbid. "I'll even go with you, Phyllis," she said, once. But Phyllis would not go.

Mr. Parker came into the office and looked reproachfully at Charles. Charles was now used to that look. "What've I forgot this time, Parker?" he asked resignedly. Mr. Parker pointed to the calendar. June 27th. Under the large letters was a scribble in Charles' own handwriting. "Prepare few words opening Park tomorrow."

"How do you know I haven't already prepared them?" demanded Charles.

"Because, whenever you say a few words, or prepare to say them, you show them to me days beforehand, sometimes, Mr. Wittmann, for any suggestions."

Charles sighed. "Write out something for me, Parker. Something very short. And appropriate. After all, under the circumstances, no one will expect me to give a long speech."

"The Mayor and other city officials, and a number of clergymen, are to be present, sir, and they'll expect more than a word or two. It's a big occasion; there'll be the firemen's band, too."

"It'll be at seven o'clock in the evening, and everyone will be tired. Just a few words, Parker. Not more than two hundred, at the most. And I'll read them."

Mr. Parker was disapproving, if sympathetic. Thousands of people were to be at the opening of the Wittmann Civic Park, and there Mr. Wittmann sat, pale and strained, and with no particular display of interest. Of course, Mr. Wittmann was thinking of his dead brother, Mr. Wilhelm, who would not be present. However, one had certain duties to perform. Mr. Parker nodded, and walked out with quiet stateliness.

There were rapid footsteps outside Charles' door. He winced. Friederich came in, with his look of concentrated excitement. He had been wearing this look for a considerable time, and though Charles found it far more preferable than the old expression of fanaticism and sullenness and suspicion, it was somewhat wearing to him. He loved his shops, and had been giving all his life to them for many years, but sometimes he found it hard to be tolerant and understanding when Friederich acted, as he always did, as if the shops were something new, exhilarating, just revealed, and altogether fascinating. And Friederich's own, personal discovery.

Friederich flung himself into a chair and began to talk. Charles was very tired. It was a hot day. Those sleeping powders old Metzger had given him gave him hardly more than four hours' sleep a night. His eyes, fixed politely on Friederich, began to glaze with weariness. He watched Friederich's mouth move, but it was like being deaf.

"You are not listening, Karl!" exclaimed Friederich.

"I was. I am," said Charles. "But it's hot. It's June 27th," he added, with heavy wonder.

"Yes! You were listening, then. What are you going to say, Karl?"

Charles, after a moment's bafflement, understood. "Frankly, I haven't decided. What do you think?"

Friederich was immediately gratified, and Charles was touched. Friederich leaned back in his chair, though he eyed Charles reproachfully. "Karl! Such an important occasion. Thousands—"

"Yes, yes, I know," said Charles, irritably. "Firemen's band, Mayor, city officials, Et cetera. But—"

Friederich stared at him. "I know. You still think of Wilhelm, all the time." His small brown eyes glinted with jealousy. He had been deeply, and astonishingly, affected by Wilhelm's death, and shocked. It was only later that Charles understood that Friederich had resented his affection for Wilhelm, and had resented it all his life. When Charles understood this he had been moved and he could still be moved. He said: "I always think of Wilhelm, Fred. And you think of him, too. How could we help it?"

Friederich was mollified. "True, true," he muttered. He paused, and brooded for a few moments. "I never understood Wilhelm, Karl. I confess I was perhaps unjust to him at times, and thought him precious."

"He was," said Charles, smiling. "I even think he thought that of himself, too, occasionally. I don't think he considered himself very important."

"He never did anything important," said Friederich, nodding. Charles was about to say, with some irascibility, that that wasn't what he meant at all, but decided that it was too hot for subtleties. "The shops," Friederich went on. "Wilhelm was never interested in the shops, as we always were."

Charles' eyebrows began to rise, but he stopped them. Friederich was deadly serious.

Charles had not told Friederich of that last talk with Wilhelm, nor of Jochen's plot against the shops and his brothers. He did not trust Friederich's instability. Friederich rarely spoke to Jochen, and then only with a patronage which Charles contentedly knew infuriated the other man. If Friederich knew of the plot he would lash out at Jochen, and there would be an upheaval too strenuous to be borne as yet.

"But surely you have in mind something to say, Karl," Friederich said.

"Not much." Charles considered his brother. "Well, have you any suggestions? For instance, what would you say?"

Friederich sat upright, all excitement. "I would be dignified. After all, it is an occasion." He spoke, as usual, in German, with rounded periods. "It is a magnificent occasion. The Wittmann Civic Park. The city is honored, the family is honored. This is a park for the refreshment and the comfort of the people. It is given from the heart of the Wittmanns. It is open to the children, the work-stained, the weary, the mothers of families, the humble man who can bask in the shade of the trees, and walk along the cool paths—"

"You say it," interrupted Charles, suddenly.

Friederich gaped.

"Wonderful!" said Charles. "You say it, Fred. But not in German, of course."

Friederich colored brightly. "Impossible!" he cried. However, he was already glowing.

"Come, now. I've heard you're a magnificent speaker, Fred. Move mountains. That's what George Hadden told me."

Friederich colored even more brightly.

"And Miss Helen is going to be there. You know how she admires you."

Friederich coughed a little. "But you are the president of the company," he murmured.

"But I'm not a speaker. Never was. I'd bungle it. As you said, it's an important occasion. It should be dignified, and in keeping. It's yours, Fred."

Friederich now trusted Charles so completely that he at once believed that it was he, himself, who was responsible for the Park. Charles had said it; it must be so. He cried: "If you insist, then I must not refuse!"

Charles said, cautiously, as Friederich jumped to his feet: "Suppose, then, that you make a few notes, and show them to me, after lunch, and if I have any suggestions I'll be glad to help you."

"I'll write them out at once. It will take me but an hour," said Friederich, and ran out of the office.

Charles lifted his telephone towards him and called George Hadden. George said: "Now, that's strange. I was just going to call you, Charlie, and ask you to have lunch with Oliver Prescott and me. Will you?"

Charles was about to refuse; it was very hard for him to talk to anyone these days. But George Hadden continued: "Charlie, it's important. Oliver and I have decided to talk to you."

"What?"

"Don't sound so alarmed." George laughed, but Charles detected a worried intonation in his laughter. "I don't suppose it's too important. I think, though, that it's time you heard something. Will you come?"

"Yes." Charles paused. Then he said: "George, how are things between Fred and your sister? Of course, he may not occupy—any place —in her mind."

"Oh, he does," said George, cheerfully. "Of course, Helen's a very strait-laced young lady. But I think if he 'spoke' to her in about a couple of months he might be very happy at her answer. And our parents admire him as much as Helen does. They think he has a splendid mind, and is completely without guile, and very plain."

"I'm beginning to think that of him, too," said Charles, with a smile.

"Helen will make a good Quaker out of him, one of these days, Charlie."

"That," said Charles, "would be worth waiting to see."

"Perhaps you won't have too long to wait. He's gone to the Meeting House with Helen half a dozen times, lately."

Charles shook his head incredulously; Friederich among the Quakers! Charles found himself smiling again. A pretty, nice and sedate young woman, with big blue eyes and a calm smile, had been able to accomplish for Friederich what no combination of brothers had been able to do, no reason, no appeals to logic, no argument.

Mr. Parker came in, still stately, and announced that Tom Murphy was waiting to speak to Mr. Wittmann. Tom entered, pulling off his cap, and Charles motioned him to a seat.

"Well, Tom?" Charles asked.

"You don't have to worry about the older fellows, Mr. Wittmann," replied Tom. "It's the young ones, just out of apprenticeship, or the ones on the way. They make me sick, but the Connington is offering them bigger wages, a third more than—we—can afford to pay. Expert tool-makers are hard to come by in this country, sir, as you know."

"And?" prodded Charles.

Tom's face hardened. "I guess we'll just have to make up our minds to losing some of 'em, sir. And after all you've done for 'em, too! The young fellows, as well as the older ones, with sick pay, and insurance, and better wages than anyone else. You'd think the bastards would be grateful!"

"I never heard that gratitude was a common human virtue," Charles said. "And I don't expect it, just for doing what I could do. So, we'll lose some of the men we've trained. Well."

"We'll just have to train new men as fast as we can, and that ain't fast, sir. It's a long, hard training, and a man's got to be bright first of all. That's even harder. And then we'll go on losing them to that damned Connington. You know what they're doing now? The Connington is encouraging their machine-tool makers to form a union! Not a company union. That's funny, coming from the Connington."

Charles tapped a pencil against his teeth. "Then our men will just have to join that union. No more company union."

"But we wouldn't be able to pay what the union would ask."

Charles leaned back in his chair. "Not for too long. No. But the Connington won't pay sick benefits, or insurance, either. If they did, all the hundreds of other workers in their mill would demand it, too. They couldn't just extend those benefits to the machine-tool makers. Discriminatory. There'd be strikes, and the Connington can't afford strikes, just now. A waiting game, Tom."

Tom nodded, but dubiously. Then he stared directly at Charles. "You know something, Mr. Wittmann? I think the Connington's out to smash you."

He expected Charles to express disbelief, but Charles only said: "Of course. I've known that for a long time."

Tom stood up. "I've been working, Mr. Wittmann. I've been talking to the men. I'm doing what I can."

When Tom had gone, Charles glanced at his watch. He had an hour before going to the old Imperial Hotel for lunch with George Hadden and Oliver Prescott. There were some papers he had to sign for Phyllis. Wilhelm had made him his executor. Beyond even his gratitude that Wilhelm had trusted him so, was Charles' enormous relief. He now had sufficient power, given to him in Wilhelm's will, and with Friederich, to do what he must eventually do to Jochen. He hoped that the occasion would never come, but something warned him that it would.

CHAPTER XXXVIII

THE OLD Imperial Hotel had once been the meeting place of politicians, Senators, bankers, doctors, business men, and others of importance in Andersburg. For decades, they had met here for luncheon and for dinner, to discuss business, plot strategy, and to eat heavily and leisurely. But now their sons preferred the "new" Penn-Andersburg Hotel, which had been built in 1908, and which was completely electrified. However, Charles liked the old Imperial, with its incandescent gas-chandeliers, its crimson carpeting, its red velvet draperies over thick, mended lace, and its ponderous air. He liked the dining-room, the mahogany walls, great arched windows, and faint smell of dust and rich German cooking.

The hotel dining-room was very hot, with the yellow June sunlight beating through the curtains which shrouded the windows. He saw that the long wide room was only partially filled, and then he saw Oliver and George rising in a distant corner and waving to him. He went to them, and on the way he looked around him to see if there was anyone here whom he knew. Then he saw old Mr. Heinz, president of the Andersburg City Bank, eating quietly, and alone. Mr. Heinz had known Emil Wittmann well, and had been superintendent of the Sunday school which the Wittmann boys had attended. Charles had not seen him for many weeks; he suddenly remembered that when he had last seen the old gentleman it had been at Wilhelm's funeral.

Charles hesitated. Mr. Heinz was a prosy and precise old bore, even if he was a very shrewd banker. Charles did not bank with him, but they had always been friends. He stopped, and said, "Good afternoon, Mr. Heinz."

The old man turned his big bald head on his short thick neck and looked at Charles. He had the face of a sea lion, with an enormous and drooping gray mustache. The light was none too brilliant in the room, for all the sun at the windows, but Mr. Heinz was noted for his sharp eyesight, even without the rimless spectacles perched on his nose. It was very strange, then, that he did not appear to recognize Charles, that nothing at all moved on his face. He just sat there and looked at Charles impassively, as at a vague and irrelevant intruder, a passing waiter, perhaps. Then he returned to his food and went on eating.

Charles was taken aback. He had halted about six feet from Mr. Heinz; it was impossible that the old gentleman had not recognized him. Then he shrugged and went on. Oliver and George were still standing, and waiting for him. He shook hands with them. Then, as they sat down, he said: "I'm glad I don't bank with old Heinz. It's time they retired him. I've known him all my life, and he used to visit my parents very often. Yet, I spoke to him just now and he didn't know me from a waiter."

He expected the two young men to laugh. They did, but not before Charles saw them exchange a serious glance. Then, while he watched them, slightly frowning, they began to talk rapidly, or, at least, Oliver did.

"I've just been showing George a pamphlet I received in the mail this morning," he said. "Have you gotten one, too? George says he did."

It was a finely bound pamphlet; in fact, it was almost a book. Its cover was of crinkled parchment, stamped with gold letters. The paper was thick and shining, the printing excellent. It was entitled: "The Modern Defender of the Faith." Above this golden title was a group of three flags flowing together, the American Stars and Stripes in the center, to the right of it the German emblem, and to the left, the British Union Jack. The flags were embossed, and so beautifully colored that they appeared painted in enamel.

Charles opened the pamphlet, and he saw a portrait of the Kaiser in full and resplendent uniform, with a lofty and Wagnerian expression on his face.

"Well, well," said Charles, puzzled. "Is our old friend 'The Modern

Defender of the Faith'? Yes, I see he is. One of his lesser roles?" He saw that the pamphlet had been printed in New York. He also saw that the publishing company had an office in London and another in Berlin and still another in Stockholm. He held the pamphlet at a little distance and ran his eye rapidly over a few sentences here and there.

The pamphlet had been written by one Professor Adolph Wittinger, and the professor was evidently a scholar, and one given to stern hero-worship and meticulous research. He outlined the life of the Kaiser since that royal personage had been a very young man. "From the very first His Majesty revealed those noble traits of character necessary for one destined to be a leader of men and to carry out those grave responsibilities which fate, the time and the hour, have laid upon him."

Charles read a little more, and was about to lose interest when a sentence caught his eye: "The manifest destiny of the new world lies with those nations cognate with the Reformation of heroic and death-less memory: Germany, the British Empire, and the United States of America. These nations are the heirs of the mighty traditions of Martin Luther; they have inherited his mantle. For, without him, they would never have been born, or would never have reached their majestic stature. The three sisters stand as one—"

"For God's sake," said Charles.

Another sentence caught his eye: ". . . the depraved inheritors of the Latin medieval tradition, the ecclesiastical and feudalistic decadence of Rome . . ."

Charles read more closely, now. This was no crude and inflammatory denunciation, no barbaric call to riot and to hatred. The periods might be resonant, but they had flow and a dignified tone of reason. It appeared that "the three sisters" who "stand as one" had been called upon by the Most High to follow the Kaiser in a crusade of liberation, "bound as they are by a single tradition, and sharing among them the holiest of all sacraments, the sacrament of an identical blood, the sacra-ment of one splendid race."

That blood, and that race, it developed, was the Teutonic. All other races, implied the professor, had been marked for extinction, not only because they were inferior and effete, but because the scientific and evolutionary process had ceased to operate in them.

"Well," said Charles, "this is an entirely different song from the others I have been hearing. It's original, anyway.

"It's part of the pattern. It fits in, somewhere. It has a purpose." It all returned to the huge and sinister stirring in the dark, to the terrible disease silently attacking the minds of men. Charles came out of his thoughts in time to hear George say to Oliver: "It's just as we've always believed and taught; the scientific materialism that began to rise in the nineteenth century has caught up with us. Herbert Spencer was one of its high priests, with his dogma of 'scientific' laws and inexorable 'evolution.' "

"There is but one God, and His Name is Science, and the Twentieth Century is His prophet," said Oliver.

"Yes," said Charles. "It's all part of the pattern." He looked at the pamphlet. "They called the nineteenth century 'the age of enlightenment.' I think we're now entering on 'the age of enslavement.' There're so many in it. We might not survive what they're planning for us."

The waiter came to take their orders, an ancient waiter who believed that food should not be eaten hastily, but in dignity and in decorum. Charles knew that it would be at least ten minutes before he returned with the first course.

George Hadden lifted his morning paper and unfolded it to a photograph. "Here is one of the boys," he said. Charles took the paper and he saw the face of a very undistinguished man wearing an expression of complete and detached neutrality. "Herbert Belz," said George Hadden. "The face that's everywhere and nowhere. The face that could belong to anybody. The face of dialectic materialism. I've heard him, and I've read his books, too."

The face that could belong to anybody. Charles put on his glasses. "I've seen him, somewhere," he said. He looked closer. Then he remembered. This man had been in "old" Harry Hoffman's Ford that dreadful April day on which Wilhelm had died. He had been going to Roger Brinkwell's house.

Charles looked at Oliver and George, and he told them. Oliver said: "Yes. It's part of the pattern, as you'd say, Charlie."

Charles read aloud a quotation from one of Herbert Belz' books, which appeared under the photograph: " 'It is only just, and it is inevitable, that eventually the people will demand absolute security from the State.' "

"And absolute security is absolute slavery," Charles said. "The pattern grows clear and clearer. It doesn't surprise me now, as it would have a year ago, to know that Belz, the disciple of Marx, Spencer, and Hegel, is a friend, or at least an acquaintance, of Brinkwell's. Great power and wealth have a common denominator with Socialism. They both detest freedom, and believe in the absolute control of the individual."

"We must just remember one thing," said Oliver. "And that is that the safety of America lies in us, our tens of thousands of independent business men, and professional men. Maybe," he added, with a dry smile, "there'll be no literal barricades in the streets, but there'll be ideological ones. I'm ready to man one, myself."

George ran his hand worriedly over his fine light hair. "There's already a tendency, in America, towards centralization in Government, and in industry. You can see that in your business, Charlie. The Connington is determined to put you out of the market."

"They're trying," Charles admitted. "But they won't succeed. Anyway, that's what I'm hoping. I'm counting a great deal on the skilled men they're trying to take away from me, with their wages which I couldn't afford. These men were trained in my shops, and they're intelligent, and they have pride in their craftsmanship."

Oliver's dark face was seriously skeptical. "And you think that they'll finally decide that it is better to be a man, for less money, than a mere tool, for more? Honestly, Charlie, do you believe that?"

"I'm hoping," Charles repeated. He glanced around the room; the tables near them were empty. He looked at Mr. Heinz' table, but the old gentleman had gone. "Heinz told me that when Mr. Wilson was elected in '12 America had come to the end of an era, the era of personal responsibility, adventurousness, and self-respect. I considered him a gloomy old codger, then. Now I'm not so sure but what he was right. Mr. Wilson talks constantly about 'social justice.' He doesn't seem to understand that social justice exists only when government keeps out of the affairs of the people. He'd like to centralize governmental powers in Washington. But he won't succeed, or even begin to succeed, unless—"

"Unless there's a war," said George.

"That'll give the men behind him their chance," added Oliver.

The soup had been eaten, and the braised spareribs and kraut had been brought and partially consumed. Charles noticed that in his absorption he had forgotten that his favorite dish no longer agreed with him. He put down his fork. He furtively felt in his pocket to see if he had his soda-mint tablets with him.

"Old Heinz is a pretty shrewd fellow," said Charles. "But he's failing."

Oliver glanced at George, then said: "No, Charlie, he isn't failing He recognized you, all right."

"What do you mean?"

Oliver leaned towards Charles. "Charlie, I know you've had so many things on your mind, but try to think if you've noticed that other people besides Mr. Heinz have been avoiding or snubbing you for the past couple of months or so. Or even before that."

Charles stared at him blankly. "I don't know what you're talking about." Then he was alarmed. He continued to stare at Oliver. Those times at Wilhelm's house, recently, when he had encountered Phyllis' friends. Those times when he had thought Mrs. Holt had been bursting to say something to him, and then had turned away in red distress. Come to think of it, two of the members of the Church Board had been coolly nodding to him lately, men whom he had known from childhood. Then he remembered more and more cold faces.

Oliver and George watched him gravely. He frowned; his alarm grew. He took out his bottle of soda-mints and swallowed two tablets, drinking water slowly after them.

"Of course," he said, "it's just my imagination, or something. What do you mean?" he demanded.

The two young men were embarrassed. George spoke: "Charlie, you know we are your friends, don't you?"

"Oh, I see," said Charles. "That's always a prelude to some nasty news, or gossip. So, there's been some talk about me in Andersburg, has there? What about?"

The young Quaker said in real distress: "Charlie, we wouldn't be saying this to you now but the thing has gotten out of hand. We've been hearing these—these things—for months, and ignored them. But now we think it's reached a point where it's going to injure you. You, and someone else. This is a small city, Charlie. Scandal can do a lot of harm."

"Scandal?" Charles was amazed. Then he laughed uncomfortably. "I've never done anything scandalous in my life, except on very few occasions, and then it wasn't in this town. Scandal," he repeated. "That always implies sexual adventure, to a small city mind. Who am I suspected of seducing, eh?" Now he was less alarmed. He laughed again, more easily.

"Go on, tell me," he said, with good nature.

"Charlie," said Oliver, "suppose we drop all this now, and suppose George and I do what Mr. Haas has suggested, trace back to the source. Then we'll come to you and tell you. But we didn't want to interfere, without your full knowledge of what we were doing. So you could help us, if necessary."

Charles studied him. Oliver Prescott was a very level-headed young feller. He was the best lawyer in Andersburg. He knew how to weigh anything in the balance and discover if it had value. He would never speak of something unless he had good and sufficient reason to speak.

"You'll have to tell me what the 'scandal' is before I can say whether it is worth hunting down," he said. "After all, gossip is the great human pastime, and no one takes it very seriously. I have friends here, and to my knowledge, I've only two enemies."

"You're right, to a certain extent, Charlie," said George, with discomfort. "And you have a lot of friends here, who are all busy defending you."

"My God, is it as bad as that?" Charles exclaimed in dismay.

"Yes," said Oliver. "It is. Charlie, I'm a lawyer, and I've learned to discount nine-tenths of what I hear. But this thing is getting dangerous. It's true that you have friends in Andersburg, but even friends are very apt to believe in lies if they're juicy enough. Take old Heinz; you've known him all your life. He hasn't anything personal against you, and he's perfectly sound. Yet, he's believing this thing, as you saw, yourself, today. And without giving you a chance to defend your own good name."

My city, my home, thought Charles. Why, they've known me, most of them, since I was born. They know everything I do, and everything I've done. I don't believe it.

"Tell me," he said. It was Brinkwell, of course. What was he saying? Was he deprecating Charles' importance in Andersburg, sneering at the quality of his machine tools, undermining him with innuendo? Of course, that was it. Charles smiled. "Go on. I can see it's Brinkwell. He's trying to wreck me. My friends will know that, and so I'm not too concerned."

"Perhaps it's Brinkwell, as you say," said Oliver. "We'll find out. I've had my suspicions that he was in it, too, for a long time. But I also have my suspicions that he's only repeating what someone else has told him."

He paused, then said with real misery: "Charlie, can't you persuade your sister-in-law to go away for a few months?"

Again, Charles was blank. "My sister-in-law? I have two. Isabel? Phyllis?" Then he remembered that Mrs. Holt had been pleading with Phyllis to go away, for "a nice long rest." He remembered the urgent note in Mrs. Holt's voice. His face, always so pale and drained lately, flushed deeply. "Phyllis?" he repeated.

"Yes," said Oliver.

There was that damned spasm in his stomach again, and a deep sick burning.

"They're talking about Phyllis—and me?" he said.

Oliver moved uncomfortably. He looked down at his hands, which played with a coffee spoon. "Yes," he said.

Phyllis! It was incredible. It was loathsome. But no one would believe it. Everyone knew Phyllis. Phyllis!

"I don't believe it," said Charles. He shook his head. "I don't believe it." He lifted his glass of water and drank unsteadily. "Our friends wouldn't believe anything that foul of Phyllis—"

"And you," George added, wretchedly.

Charles put down his glass, slowly. "What are they saying?" he asked, and now there was a white line about his mouth.

Oliver hesitated. "That you—that you and Mrs. Wittmann have been having an affair for a long time, for at least a year. I'm sorry, Charlie."

"A year?" cried Charles, aghast. "Even while Willie was alive?" He was horrified. "My God! But Willie never knew about these lies!" Then he stopped abruptly. He was remembering the hour before Wilhelm had fallen on the stairs. Wilhelm had asked him to come into the gallery for a talk. He, Charles, and Phyllis, had been convinced that Jochen had been poisoning Wilhelm's mind and they had spoken to Wilhelm before the latter could speak, himself. They had taken it for granted that Jochen had been alienating Wilhelm from Charles in a purely business way, and for purely financial reasons in connection with Brinkwell. Charles, turning paler and paler, was remembering those long months of estrangement, his brother's bitter aversion for him, his look of grief and despair, his flights with Phyllis from Andersburg.

Willie had heard the lies, and he had believed them. That was unendurable to Charles. Willie had suffered agonies. Charles was remembering how ill Wilhelm had looked, how broken. He was remembering his brother, leaning against the gallery wall, with his head fallen on his chest. All the time when he, Charles, had been believing he had reached his brother with the story of Jochen's plots with Brinkwell, he had only been dispelling Wilhelm's suspicion that he and Phyllis—

Charles stood up. He put his hands on the table, and leaned on them. "Willie knew," he said. "He'd been lied to. He'd been made to suffer."

The two young men stood up also, in consternation. Oliver put his hand on Charles' arm. "Charlie, don't look like that," he said. "Charlie. We'll find out who started all this."

"Charlie," pleaded George, deeply alarmed.

But Charles did not hear them. He stared down at the table. "All those months," he said. "He was suffering like hell. And then, he died."

Only about eight or ten diners remained in the room, and these were at a distance. But they were looking at the three men with curiosity. They could not hear what was being said. They saw Charles standing there, however, half-bent over the table, in an attitude of blunt agony, and they saw the younger men trying to shield him from their eyes.

"Let's get out of here," urged Oliver. "Come to my office, Charlie, and you, too, George. We'll map out our plans, we'll find out—"

Charles heard him. He straightened. "No," he said. "We don't have to 'find out' anything. It was my brother Joe." He looked at them. "I know how to deal with this, myself, believe me."

He turned and walked away, and his legs bent a little, weakly, once or twice.

CHAPTER XXXIX

THE SUN pressed heavily on Charles' head and shoulders as he walked back to his office. It seemed to have an iron heat, so that there was a scorched sensation in his throat, a burning in his chest. Charles stared before him, and there was nothing in him but hatred, and a hunger for vengeance so intense that he knew what it was to feel the overpowering urge to kill.

He has brought me to this—Joe, he thought. He is my brother, and I not only want to kill him but feel that I must. Think what he did to Willie! All those months. Willie, who had never harmed him. Willie, with his pictures and his books and his marble busts, and his sharp, fastidious gestures, and his sudden thin humor—and his innocence! Willie, a young man, murdered as surely by Joe as if Joe had shot or strangled him. There was something floating about, hazily and half-guessed, in Charles' mind. Willie had fallen on the stairs; he had begun to hurry; he had said something. He had slipped. Yet Charles knew, in some way, that Wilhelm had been killed, that if what he had been told by Jochen had never been told Wilhelm would be alive, today.

Charles stepped from the curb, unseeing, and was almost run down by a brewer's wagon. He stepped back, and stood there on the crowded curb, panting. Phyllis. They had done this to Phyllis, also. They were so determined to have their way, to ruin him, Charles, that they had murdered Wilhelm, they had heaped slime on Phyllis. He had been too stunned to feel much when Wilhelm had been buried; he had been shaken by grief later. Nothing, however, could compare with this awful sorrow he felt now, this crushed mourning.

Someone spoke to him; he could not stop. He was walking in a nightmare; he pulled his arm furiously from the hand which had touched it, and went on. Now his hatred was like something mad. His friends! He had lived in this city all his life, fatly, stupidly, complacently, and he had thought he had friends! Yet his friends, without any proof, without any sign from him or from Phyllis, had believed this intolerable thing of him. God damn them, thought Charles, and his mind began to clear. Heinz, Stollmann, Wurlitzer—all of them, dozens of them. He saw their averted faces, their eyes filmed over with hostility. Why, a man had no friends, not ever, in all the world! A man smugly prided himself on his neighbors, on their loyalty, their kindness, their generosity, their belief in him, and all the time they were enemies, waiting to fall on him and tear him apart and strike him down, if they could.

Again, a hand touched his arm, this time more firmly. People were passing; he saw them as blurs. Then he saw the anxious young face of Father Hagerty. "Mr. Wittmann!" said the priest. "What is it? I tried to speak to you before. Is something wrong?"

He looked at Charles, so swollen and red, and with such ferocity in his eyes. He had an impulse to step back, then he tightened his hand on Charles' arm. This was a man in the direst distress and torment; he seemed almost out of his mind.

"Go away," said Charles, roughly, and tried to go on. "No," said the priest. "I'll walk on with you. Did you know people are looking at you, Mr. Wittmann? Let me walk along with you, for a little way. There's someone nodding—"

Charles walked faster. The young priest walked beside him, his lean legs, in their shabby trousers, moving rapidly. People stared at Charles, and at Father Hagerty, and their eyes were pointed with curiosity. What was wrong with old Charlie, running along like that, like a madman, with that priest beside him?

They were coming to quieter streets, now, shaded with trees. They were approaching the area of the Wittmann shops. "Mr. Wittmann," said Father Hagerty, when he could get his breath. "Let me help you. Something's wrong; I know it. You helped me; it's my turn, now."

Charles stopped abruptly. His face was streaming with sweat. "You can't help me," he said. "Nobody can help me. Please go away. I don't want to insult you, Father—"

"This isn't like you, Mr. Wittmann," said the priest, calmly and earnestly.

Charles stood there and looked at him. "No," he said at last. "It isn't like me. But who knows what anyone is 'like' until—something—happens? Please go away." He began to walk again, though slower, for his heart was pounding and he was shaking.

The priest followed, desperately tenacious, and again he caught up with Charles. That violence he had seen, that torture—Mr. Wittmann was on his way, somewhere, to do something, not with that considering mind of his, but with powerful emotions that were dangerous. Charles saw the black shadow beside him, and once more he stopped, with huge exasperation. "Father Hagerty," he began. But the priest said: "Mr. Wittmann, stop just a moment. Let me talk with you. Look," and he pointed to a small house nearby almost shrouded in heavy trees. "I must go in there. I'd like you to come in with me for a moment."

"No," said Charles. "I've asked you—"

"In that house lives an old man," said the priest. "He's dying. He received the Last Sacrament a few days ago. This old man is very poor; his neighbors are supporting him, even though they're poor themselves."

Something changed for only an instant in Charles' eyes, but the priest saw it. "Very poor people; they haven't enough to eat, sometimes. But they give everything they can. They're his friends. They thought he was rich," and the priest smiled sadly. "They thought he was a miser, and that he didn't need anybody, and that he was self-sufficient. And so they envied him, and they gossiped about him." The priest said to himself: I don't know whether it is what I've said, but he's listening as though I've told him something he ought to know. "They never thought he was just a man like themselves, and that he needed their help," the priest continued. "You see, he wasn't young when he married, and neither was his wife. They had a son, when they were middle-aged. All they had: a son. They were proud of him; they bragged to their neighbors about him, and they held their heads high, feeling strong."

Charles looked at the sidewalk.

"The mother died, without ever finding out what her son really was," said Father Hagerty. "That was fortunate. So there the old man was alone, with his son; he'd educated him well. He was going to teach geology—the son. Then he went away, to Titusville. That was ten years ago. Somehow, he got into an outfit that was prospecting for oil. He found it. He became rich, almost overnight. It was then that he stopped writing to his father, after the first letter telling what he had done. The father was nearly seventy, then. He wrote to his son, letter after letter, but never heard from him. But he did hear about him, in the newspapers. How he made so much money, and married a wealthy New York girl, and how he lives so fine in New York. The old man couldn't get over it; it was so wonderful. He was prouder than ever. He carried newspaper clippings with him, to show everybody, and he boasted of how much his son loved him, and all the money he sent him." The priest sighed. "The son never sent a cent; he never wrote a single letter. The old man had a little money saved, and he lived on that, when he couldn't work any longer. The money's gone, now. The neighbors found out; they found out he was practically starving. That's when they went to work, these friends of his."

"Very sad," said Charles, bitterly. He took out his wallet, and withdrew three yellow twenty-dollar bills from it, and gave them to the priest. "Thank you," said Father Hagerty, gently. "The friends found someone in New York who would send the old man letters, in his son's name. He's almost blind; he can't see the letters, and they're read to him, and there's always money in the envelope. It's making him very happy, these last days. He's been told his son's in Europe, and he insists that no one inform his son of this illness of his, because he doesn't want to worry him." The priest looked at the bills. "This will help pay for his funeral," he remarked. "His friends have been worrying."

Now he looked directly at Charles. "A man always finds friends when he needs them, provided they know he needs them," he said. "Mr. Wittmann, I'm your friend. So is your minister. Let us help you. You need help. No one's strong enough to go on alone, all the time."

Charles said: "Thank you. Yes, I believe you'd help me, if you could. In a way, you've helped already. Someday I'll tell you." He paused. "There's something I must do, but now I can do it without —well—without rage. Just quietly, reasonably, as it ought to be done."

He walked away then, the heavy flushed look subsiding from his face. Father Hagerty, still wondering what he had said to Charles which had made him stop and listen, went into the tiny house.

Friends, thought Charles. I'm going to need them. I'd forgotten Oliver and George, and this young feller, the priest, and Mr. Haas. And Mrs. Holt. I've never given them a chance to help me before, because I've let them know, all the time, that I would never need them. I've certainly been a dogged kind of cuss.

His rage and sorrow and violence had hardened into cold common sense again. Joe would have to get out, and as soon as possible. Yes. But it would be done sensibly, and sharply. That was all.

When he had entered his office he called Parker and asked him to ask Mr. Jochen to come in, at once. Mr. Parker then informed him that Mr. Jochen had left for the afternoon "on business," and would not return. Charles leaned back in his chair, and the hard muscles sprang out around his mouth. He pointed to the telephone. "Call the Connington Steel Company, and ask if Mr. Jochen is there. No, I don't want to speak to him. Just find out for me, Parker."

Parker, without a glance of surprise, made the call. Then he put his hand over the mouthpiece. "Mr. Jochen's there," he muttered. "Hang up," said Charles. "And now, send Mr. Friederich in to me."

Friederich came in at once, carrying a sheaf of paper. "The speech, Karl!" he exclaimed, beaming. Charles frowned. "You wanted to hear it, remember," added Friederich. He sat down, carefully, so as not to crush his clothing.

Charles said: "I don't—I mean, Friederich, that it isn't necessary. I want to enjoy it, myself, tomorrow. Just surprise me. I know it's very good," he added.

Friederich took off his glasses. "I think so," he said, simply. "Not too long a speech, Karl. But I put my heart into it, as it deserved. The Wittmann Civic Park. It is wonderful."

"I just had lunch with George Hadden," said Charles.

Friederich became very alert. "A fine young man," he said, coloring as usual when he heard the Hadden name.

Charles moved his inkwell carefully on his desk.

"George told me something today, Friederich. I thought of telling you now. But it can wait." He moved the inkwell back. "But I can tell you this: George gave me his advice. I'm going to follow it."

Friederich nodded, solemnly. "You can be sure it's excellent advice, Karl."

Charles thought of the Wittmann Civic Park, and cursed to himself. He had forgotten the Park. This matter would have to wait until the day after tomorrow, the twenty-ninth. Nothing must happen to ruin the opening of the Park. How was a man to live with this inside him for forty-eight hours?

"You don't think George Hadden would lie to me, do you, Fred?" Charles asked.

"Lie?" Friederich was aghast. "George is a Quaker! And he's my friend."

"You think I can trust him, that what he's told me is the truth?"

"You can believe every word!" cried Friederich.

Charles smiled to himself.

"And you'll believe it when you hear it, right in this office, day after tomorrow?"

"If George said it, then I'll believe it, Karl." Friederich stood up, tremendously alarmed. "Why can you not tell me now?"

"Because," said Charles, "George advised against it. That's why I must ask you to trust me." He made himself smile at Friederich. "Sorry I interrupted you. I just wanted to know that you were with me."

When Friederich had gone, Charles called George Hadden, who heard his voice with relief, remembering how Charles had looked only an hour ago. Charles said: "George, I've made up my mind considering everything, considering Brinkwell and Joe's associations with him. And then what you told me today. I'm throwing Joe out, George."

George Hadden was silent for a few moments. Then he said: "But calmly, Charles. Yes, I see it's necessary, as you say, considering everything. You couldn't do otherwise."

"But not until day after tomorrow. The Park, you know."

He then called Mrs. Holt, who was exuberantly glad to hear from him. "Why, Charlie, how nice!" she said. "I was going to call you, myself, about the Park. That Caesar, you know. Braydon's having it hauled there tomorrow morning. Dreadful old thing, and I think it's only a fraud, but it'll look very imposing, in the shrubbery. It really has a nice face; much nicer than Caesar's was, probably."

"I'm sure it is. And you're going to be there, Minnie, and Braydon, too?"

"We wouldn't miss it, Charlie. It's just wonderful. The Mayor, and all. Of course, the Mayor is an old fool, and he'll probably talk for hours and hours. He's coming up for election this fall, you know. Just hours and hours. Charlie," she said, suddenly, "what's the matter?"

Charles kept his voice light. "How much money can you lend me, Minnie?"

Her own voice was quieter: "Bad, Charlie?"

"Very bad. You see, Minnie, I've just found out today, from Oliver Prescott and George Hadden, about the stories that've been going around about me and—about me. And I know who started them, kept them going, and made them bigger. My brother Joe."

"I see." All the joviality had left her voice.

"You've heard the stories, Minnie. You wanted to tell me."

"Yes. But then I thought they'd blow over. Then they've become worse. That's why I tried to persuade—her—to leave for a while. I knew something would come up; I knew you'd find out."

"I never knew," said Charles. "I never knew." He kept a firm control over himself; his hatred and violence were returning, and he struggled with them.

"I know you didn't, Charlie. It's all over. And it's such a relief to talk to you about them. Can you come up for a while, for tea, and we'll discuss this thoroughly?"

"I can't, Minnie. I don't want to talk about it. I only want to know if you and Braydon will lend me some money. I'm afraid I'm going to need it, and I haven't all I need."

Mrs. Holt sighed. "Charlie, you can have anything you want. Anything."

Charles nodded, as if she could see him. "And Minnie, will you persuade—Phyllis—to go away? I can't see Phyllis just now. Invent something. It's going to be hard to see her at the Park, tomorrow. Perhaps you could persuade her not to come."

"I can't think what I ought to say to her," said Mrs. Holt, distressed. "But I'll manage. Leave it to me, Charlie. Oh, Charlie. I'm so awfully sorry. Braydon and I and so many others have just been seething. And we couldn't say anything, because we didn't want you to know."

So many others, thought Charles, after he had said goodbye to Mrs. Holt. They were my friends, in spite of what my enemies believed. I have friends, he said to himself. I knew it, before. But I didn't know I had enemies, too, imbecile that I was. Good old Charlie Wittmann. Everybody loves him.

If I hadn't met that young feller, that priest, thought Charles, I would have called Joe back here, or I'd have rushed up to the Consolidated, and made a fool of myself. It would have been all over town. Horrible, for Phyllis. I would have acted insanely. My God. The things I would have said, the things I would have done.

He tried to work, but a furious headache had set in, behind his forehead. The heat of the June day was almost insupportable to him. He put down his pen. He could not stand the steady heat of the shops. So long as Joe is part of this place, I won't be able to do anything, thought Charles. I'll go home.

Then he reached for the telephone, and called Father Hagerty's house. "That old man," said Charles, after the young priest's stammered words of surprise. "How is he?"

"He died an hour ago, Mr. Wittmann."

Charles moved the inkwell, round and round, in circles. "Father Hagerty, let him have a wonderful funeral. A fine one. All the flowers. And the services—"

"A solemn requiem Mass," said the priest, his voice trembling. "And all the neighbors there, and a fine coffin. You'll come, Mr. Wittmann?"

"I'll come," said Charles. He hesitated. "Order everything, Father Hagerty. I wasn't myself, when I saw you this afternoon." The inkwell stopped moving. "Send all the bills to me. A fine funeral. The cemetery—"

"The Holy Cross, Mr. Wittmann."

"A good fine plot. And later, a headstone. A big one."

"It'll be wonderful for his friends, Mr. Wittmann. They'll go there often, and be proud. It'll be something in their lives, to think of, and remember, as they sit under the trees and look at the monument. They'll bring flowers from their gardens. God bless you, Mr. Wittmann."

Charles went home. It was almost four o'clock, this twenty-seventh of June, 1914.

CHAPTER XL

JIMMY USUALLY called for Charles in the beloved red Oldsmobile at half past five, but as it was only four Charles ordered a station hack and drove home. The leisurely ambling through the green and sun-shot streets calmed him more and more by the minute, though it did not shake his resolution that Jochen must leave the Wittmann Machine Tool Company. This had to be done. His headache became worse, in spite of the subsiding of his unfamiliar violence and passion. He climbed the steps of his house heavily. He heard the strong and dolorous moaning of some somber music inside. Jimmy, then, was at home, and at his gramophone. Charles entered the parlor and found Jimmy and Walter Haas half-lying on the cool carpet, hypnotized by and engrossed in the majestic clamor. Between them, on a huge tray, lay a very light repast consisting of a large apple cake, four great roast-pork sandwiches, six apples, two bananas, two wedges of lemon pie, and two bottles of "cream soda." They had just begun to demolish all this when Charles walked in. The boys scrambled to their feet, and Jimmy cried over the thunder of the music: "Dad!"

"Now, look here," said Charles, irritably, raising his hand. "I don't have a cerebral hemorrhage, a coronary occlusion, uremia, diabetes—though you'll probably have the last, you two, if you eat all that mess there—nor have I had an attack of gallstones, though you both will have, from the looks of what you intend to eat. Or is this a picnic, and are you waiting for about a dozen other boys?"

But Jimmy stopped the music, and then said: "Dad, what's wrong?" His voice was tense with anxiety, and he walked towards Charles. Charles moved to the door.

"Now, Jimmy, I just have a headache. It's the heat. How are you, Walter?"

The minister's stocky blond son replied gravely: "Very well, Mr. Wittmann."

"Your father's lucky that you don't intend to be a doctor, Walter," said Charles. "Jimmy's practicing on me all the time."

Walter smiled solemnly, but Jimmy was not diverted. He said: "All right, Dad. But will you tell me about it, if there's anything I can do?" He looked so young and troubled that Charles went to him and put his hand on his arm. He said: "Yes, Jimmy. I'll do that, honestly I will. And I'll tell you about it soon, even though there's nothing you can do to help me, except"—and now he spoke more lightly—"keeping from getting acute indigestion over that tray of groceries. My God, how can you two—just you two—eat all that?"

"It's just a snack," said Jimmy. "Walter's staying for dinner. Mrs. Meyers is going out early this evening, so we have to eat before six."

Shaking his head, and with a last look at the tray, Charles went upstairs. But he moved less heavily now, remembering the expression in Jimmy's eyes. It was good to have a child, even one who imagined you had a fatal disease when you were only bilious. But, thought Charles, in a way I have a fatal disease. I've developed an imagination.

Nothing could be done until day after tomorrow, he reminded himself, as he took off his coat and shoes and lay down on the bed. Until then, there was no use in thinking. There was no use in remembering Willie, or in hating Joe. There were times when a man just had to stop his thoughts, until the time came for action. He closed his eyes and tried, by will power alone, to stop the bursting pain in his head. He heard a sound, and there was Jimmy with a glass in his hand. "Bromo-seltzer, Dad," said the boy, hurriedly, as Charles sat up, annoyed. "For your headache. You never take care of yourself."

Charles drank the foaming liquid, while Jimmy pulled down the shades against the sunlight which streamed through the trees outside. Then Charles, having drained the glass, bellowed. Jimmy said, appeasingly: "It was just a double dose, Dad. To stop the headache and make you sleep for a while."

"If I never wake up you'll have yourself to blame," said Charles, wrathfully. "A double dose! Why, I never take more than half a single dose!" He glared at the glass. "What else was in it, too? The taste's familiar."

"One of your sleeping powders," said Jimmy, soothingly. "They don't seem to help you, but I thought the bromo and the powder together might make you take a nap."

Charles could not help but laugh. "I ought to write a suicide note, so they won't arrest you for my murder," he remarked. "Now, will you please go away and let me die in peace?"

Jimmy became master of the situation and was full of authority. "Not until you take off your shirt and your trousers and put on your cotton bathrobe," he said. He brought the bathrobe from the closet. "You've got to be comfortable. Why, you've still got your collar on."

Charles allowed his son to take off his collar and help him remove his shirt and other clothing. He put on the bathrobe. He felt his son's solicitude and love all about him. He lay down and watched Jimmy as the boy hung up his clothing neatly. Jimmy moved quietly and expertly, and all at once he was no longer a boy but a man of understanding. I, thought Charles, am the father of a man. The headache was beginning to subside; Charles' inflamed thoughts were becoming softer and dimmer. He wanted to say something to Jimmy which would reach his son and tell him of his deep tenderness. Jimmy stood by the bed, now, watching him. "If you make a single move to feel my pulse, I'll kick you out of the room," said Charles.

Jimmy said: "Things are awfully bad with you, aren't they, Dad? Try not to think about them just now. Try to sleep. Once you told me that nothing looks so bad after a sleep. Remember?"

"I remember," said Charles. "Jimmy—"

There was a silence between them. Then Jimmy nodded soberly. He hesitated. He put out his hand and felt Charles' forehead, and Charles did not move. Jimmy lifted Charles' head and turned the hot pillow over. What did a father say to his son, who was a man, to tell him of his love?

The headache was gone; drowsiness was creeping over Charles like a deep twilit wave. "Jimmy," he said. "I've had a blow today. But you know that, don't you? It was pretty bad, for a while, and I'm afraid that it's going to be worse before it's better. But just so long as I have you there'll be some comfort—"

He closed his eyes. Jimmy tiptoed from the room, and softly closed the door. He went downstairs, and into the kitchen, where Mrs. Meyers was preparing dinner.

"Dad's sick," said Jimmy. "I've given him something to make him rest. We won't wake him to eat. Just put something aside, Mrs. Meyers, and when Dad wakes up I'll fix it for him."

"What did you give him?" asked Mrs. Meyers, alarmed, shaking her floury hands. "Now, Jimmy, you know you killed my cat with that stuff you mixed up, and Tippy was a very good cat and kept the mice away."

"Tippy was dying, anyway," said Jimmy, with dignity. "She was too old. I didn't kill her. It was just her age."

Charles slept under the dark-blue waves. The sun left the windows, and now the sky reddened and robins began to sing for rain, sweetly and purely. The hot room cooled pleasantly, and a breeze moved the curtains. Twilight filled the bedroom with shadows, and Charles slept. The first stars came out.

Then Charles began to move restlessly. He dreamt that he was in some enormous darkness, and that some horrible pain was in him and all about him. It was everywhere. The darkness shook with it. It was not a complete darkness, for every now and then it was torn apart by an enormous slash of scarlet, like lightning, and terrible thunder followed it. Then the scarlet was gone, and the noise, and there was someone in his arms, crying over and over: "Charles! Charles! I'm here. I love you."

It was Phyllis' voice, and he could feel her in his arms, but his arms were powerless and there was nothing in him but desolation and anguish. She continued to call to him, and he could not feel anything, though he knew that she was kissing his mouth, his hands, and his cheek. Then he heard himself say: "Oh, Phyllis, Phyllis." The desolation was not strangling him so mercilessly, now, though it throbbed somewhere, off in the sightless night, as if it belonged to someone else. His arms tightened about Phyllis. There was the weight of her head on his shoulder.

He awoke with a start, dazed and trembling. For a moment he believed he was still dreaming, because of the desolation and the darkness. Then he saw that it was night, and the house was very quiet. He sat up, weak, almost stunned. A horrible nightmare. He forced himself to get out of bed and light the gaslight over his head. He sat on the edge of the bed, and drew several slow deep breaths. He rose and looked at his watch, and saw that it was nine o'clock. That boy and his infernal mixtures! It's a wonder I'm not dead, thought Charles. Then, Charles was at the door in one wild run, and he was shouting downstairs, clutching the banister: "Jimmy! Jimmy!"

There was a light below, and Jimmy came at once from the parlor, calling in alarm: "Yes, Dad! Dad?"

Charles did not know why the sound of his son's voice should make him so weak and should cause his knees to bend, or why, an instant before Jimmy had answered, he should know such a terror, or why, now, he should feel this shattering sense of deliverance. He could only say to himself: That nightmare. That boy and his mixtures. He called down: "It's a wonder I'm not dead, Jimmy." His throat relaxed; it had been so dry and his voice had ripped through it.

Jimmy was at the foot of the stairs, laughing. "Did you have a good sleep?"

"A very good sleep. I'm hungry."

"Everything's laid in the dining-room. I just have to heat up the coffee. Come on down, Dad."

But it was some moments before Charles' legs could carry him down the stairs. And when he sat at the table he could not eat. He moved the food about on his plate, and Jimmy knew that this was for his benefit, and he made no comment. He only sat there and talked, and Charles watched him, and listened to the sound of his voice.

In some way that dream was connected with Jimmy. Charles knew it. Jimmy talked on and looked at his father and saw the beads of sweat on his forehead. The day's been too much for me, thought Charles.

The telephone rang. Jimmy went to answer it, and returned, looking disappointed. "It's for you, Dad," said Jimmy, and Charles went to the telephone.

"Oh, Charlie," said Mrs. Holt. "Please come up here, to my house. I've already sent my chauffeur for you. He'll be there in fifteen minutes. Charlie, it's very important. I haven't succeeded, and I need your help —and there's someone here."

CHAPTER XLI

The big Holt mansion was very quiet. Charles was led into the first enormous drawing-room by a maid, and there he found Mrs. Holt and Phyllis, and no one else. Mrs. Holt came to him and kissed him affectionately, and tapped his shoulders, and said: "Well, what a pleasant surprise, Charlie! Phyllis and I are having such a dull time together, with Braydon talking over some new sculpture with one of his friends down in the city, and we were just about to have some nice cold lemonade, or something— Wonderful, Charlie! Scotch, Charlie?"

Charles sat down and accepted a glass of whiskey and soda, and Phyllis, so silent and preoccupied these wretched days, smiled at him. Her black dress accentuated her thinness and her white face. Her usually bright and springing hair lay flattened about her head, and her eyes were too large, too brilliant. The shock and grief of her husband's death had given her a look of desperate illness. Yet, she could smile at Charles, and some color came into her pale mouth, and she commented on the weather. Mrs. Holt chattered as she passed about some wafers, and pretended to be utterly unaware of how Phyllis' eyes were fixed on Charles as if she were finding in her brother-in-law some strength and surety. Poor Charlie, thought Mrs. Holt, while she talked of the opening of the Park the next day. Poor Phyllis. But it won't be long, it can't be long, now. It's just that it's too soon. And then, all this business, and the ugly stories, and that abominable Jochen, and that trailing Pauline and that really hateful, active Roger!

Charles told of the headache he had developed that afternoon, and how Jimmy had put him to sleep, and even Phyllis laughed a little, and said, with some warmth in her tired, faint voice, that Jimmy was such a marvelous boy. The talk went on and on, while occasionally Mrs. Holt would glance at Charles' haggard face with concern and distress, and then at Phyllis, who always came to life when she met her dead husband's brother. Charles sat and drank as casually as if he had in fact only dropped in on a friend. For some reason or other he told the two women of the story the priest had told him, and they listened with absorbed interest. Then Mrs. Holt nodded. "I think I know who the son is," she said. "And he really is in Europe, now, on business. He's written to Braydon a few times recently, about the oil." Her red face became glazed and bland. "There seems such a call for oil, lately."

Charles heard the long booming of the monstrously large clock in the hall beyond. Half-past ten. "Such a lot of oil, all the wells working night and day," Mrs. Holt went on. Charles' head began to ache again, with that sullen throbbing, and then he thought of his nightmare, and his terror, and his shouting for his son. It was easy to understand the nightmare, now. He looked at Phyllis, and remembered how she had cried to him in his dream, and how she had kissed him, and how his arms had been about her. He could feel the weight of her head on his shoulder. He was not a superstitious man. There is nothing in precognition, he told himself. There doesn't dare to be anything.

He put down his glass; he was disgusted with himself when he saw that his hand was trembling. He looked at Phyllis again, and the light of the crystal chandelier hanging high above shone in those too-brilliant eyes. She was regarding him almost eagerly, her lips parted, as if she only wanted to hear his voice saying anything, anything at all.

He said: "Let them buy oil, in Europe, if they want to. Even if they want it for a war. We are three thousand miles away, and we've never been embroiled in their damn wars, and never shall be."

"Certainly not," said Mrs. Holt, cheerfully. "By the way, Charlie, I've been trying to persuade Phyllis, again, to go away for a while. I'll go with her; she knows that. But not to Europe." She paused. Charles stared down at his empty glass on the table beside him. A cooling mountain wind came through the tremendous arched windows. The chandelier swayed in it, and a frail glittering light swept over Phyllis' face. Mrs. Holt continued, wondering why her handsome drawing-room should suddenly feel so lonely and abandoned. "We could go to California. All those interesting moving-picture studios. We met Charlie Chaplin once, at a party in New York, and Norma Talmadge. We became great friends. I'm sure they'll remember me. California sounds so fascinating."

"Oh, I couldn't go away," said Phyllis, gently. "I'd be lost, dear Minnie."

"Not with me," said Mrs. Holt, firmly. "We'd see the most incredible things."

Phyllis smiled, and shook her head. She held her glass of lemonade in her thin hands, and did not put it to her lips.

"Charles," she said, "would you come up to see me the day after tomorrow? There's something about—about Wilhelm's affairs—which I think you ought to know. I haven't seen you lately."

Charles glanced at Mrs. Holt, and she jumped up with an exclamation. "I forgot. How very terrible of me! I promised Braydon to call him and tell him when I would send the automobile for him. You see, he gets so bored sometimes, and he's so awfully polite, and he'd never let anyone know how much he wanted to come home and go to bed, and so we have this arrangement, and no one's feelings are hurt."

Charles remained standing even when Mrs. Holt had been gone from the room several moments. Phyllis sat on a faded tapestried settee and looked up at him. She saw how drawn he was, and how there was a red flush on his forehead and about his eyes, like a fever. "Charles, what is wrong?" she asked. He went over to her and sat down beside her. Her hands gripped her glass, and very gently he took the glass away from her and put it on a table. Then he held her hand.

"Phyllis," he said, "there is something you must do for me. I can't tell you the reason, but I want you to do what has to be done. I want you to go away with Mrs. Holt, either tomorrow night, or, at the earliest, the next morning."

The hand stiffened in his, in protest, but he held it tighter. "Why, Charles?" she asked.

"I can't tell you, Phyllis. I can only ask you to go away. When you come back, I can explain." The beating in his head had become intense again. "Believe me, I wouldn't ask this of you if I didn't have a grave and serious reason."

The tears had begun to run down her cheeks, one by one. "Don't, Phyllis," he said. "Don't ever try to understand. Just trust me, as you've always trusted me."

"It's something about Wilhelm's will, then, isn't it?" she whispered.

"His will?" Charles frowned.

"Yes. He really did change it, after all, didn't he? Oh, Charles, you can tell me all about it. That's why I wanted you to come up to see me very soon."

The beating had become a roar, and Charles moved his head from side to side so that he could hear, and so that he could see. "Tell me," he said.

"I was just going through his desk, to see if there were any papers we had forgotten," said Phyllis. "And then I found these papers, in his own handwriting. Charles! I don't understand! Why should he have written those things?"

"Tell me." His arm was about her shoulders, and he was almost shaking her.

"They were drafts, I think, for there was a number of them, and he had crossed out some things, and added others." Her white face became scarlet. "I couldn't believe it. And then there was a note on top, a memorandum, for him to call his lawyer, and the date was—the date was for three days after he—"

"Phyllis," said Charles, "you'll have to tell me, as quickly and clearly as you can."

"Charles, I couldn't believe it. The will sounded as if he hated you, and hated me, in a way, too. His money, and all that he had, was to be placed in a trust fund, and Jochen was to set it up, and be his executor, and I was to receive only the income from the fund. Until I died. And then everything was to be settled on Geraldine, except for one-third, which was to go to Jochen. You, Charles"—and her voice became fainter—"were not mentioned at all, as a beneficiary, and Wilhelm's interest in the company, and in the patents, was to be assigned to Jochen. And there was something else added: 'In order that my brother Jochen Wittmann might have controlling interest in the Wittmann Machine Tool Company.'"

"In other words," said Charles, "he had substituted Joe's name for mine, in the original will which was probated."

He stood up, and began to walk about the room, and all the hatred and violence which he had repressed these last few hours came back to him. Phyllis watched him in fear and she murmured a few times: "Oh, Charles. Oh, Charles."

He stopped before her. "Phyllis, there was no signature? He hadn't signed these drafts, any of them?"

"No. I told you, Charles, he had made an appointment with his lawyer, and I suppose he was going to take the drafts with him."

"You're certain there were no witnesses to this—this draft?"

"No, Charles, there was nothing. Just drafts. But how could Wilhelm even think—"

He sat down beside her and took her two hands in his and held them. "Where are those drafts? Are they locked up, safely?"

She was frightened by his expression. "They are back in his desk, Charles, and I have the key."

He breathed slowly and heavily a few times. "Phyllis, they are only drafts. They aren't legal. Even if anyone presented them, they'd not be considered by any court. But they're a danger. To you. To me. So, when you go home tonight you must destroy them, piece by piece, burn them, do anything with them but see that not a single word remains."

"If you say so, then I will. It was just that I thought that perhaps you might think we ought to honor this draft, because he had wanted it that way. And Charles, I thought perhaps he had seen his lawyer earlier, or a lawyer in Philadelphia, and there was really another will."

Charles sat and thought, and he knew that he must tell Phyllis something. He said: "Think back, and remember, Phyllis, that night— You remember how we told Willie how Joe had been lying to him about me, for his own purposes, and how we convinced him, finally, about what Joe was trying to do to me, and to the company, in league with Brinkwell. But for months before that, he had believed Joe's lies, and the drafts were written because of them. However, we convinced him, together, and he'd have destroyed the drafts the next day, if he had not died that night."

Phyllis was crying again, her head bent over her shoulder, her hands in Charles' hands. "Yes, I see you are right," she said. "And I'll destroy those papers the very moment I get home."

Charles wiped her eyes with his own handkerchief, and she sat beside him like a forlorn but vaguely comforted child. Then Charles said: "My wanting you to go away, Phyllis, had nothing whatever to do with any will. I can only tell you that you must go, either tomorrow night, or the morning after."

She hardly heard him. "But why should Wilhelm's notes sound as if he almost hated me, Charles, and did not trust me?" Charles was silent for so long that she lifted her head questioningly. Then when she saw his face she cried: "Charles! Charles! What is it?"

"Hush." He put his arm about her shoulders. "Phyllis, there's something I've got to do, the day after tomorrow. I might as well tell you. I'm throwing Joe out of the company. I don't want you to be here when it happens. My God, Phyllis!"he exclaimed. "Try to understand that I have my reasons for not wanting you here, then!"

She clasped her hands together and looked at him, appalled. "Jochen? You're 'throwing him out,' Charles? Oh, I know, he's been dreadful and sly and scheming. But, does he deserve this? He's your brother. He's Wilhelm's brother."

"He made Willie suffer for months. In a way, he killed him. Yes, he killed him." Charles stood up again, and the rage he was battling made his face swell.

"What are you saying, Charles?" Phyllis could not speak above a whisper. "No doubt the lies he told Wilhelm were bad enough, but how did he make Wilhelm suffer? And you say 'kill'—" Horror sharpened her whisper to shrillness. "Jochen always told lies, and Wilhelm knew he did, and it wasn't very hard to convince him, that night. But Charles, you said 'kill'— You said 'suffer.' Why?"

He did not answer her, and she got to her feet, quickly. She caught his arms in her hands, and shook him. "Charles, you must answer me. There's something terrible, here. I knew that Wilhelm was upset, all those months before, but I thought it was just about the company, and Jochen's lies. It was something else, wasn't it? It was, wasn't it, Charles? You must answer me."

He looked away from her. But she still clutched him. "And it's because of that 'something else' that you want me to go away, while you force Jochen out? Charles?"

The breeze was blowing out one of the long draperies, and Charles watched it. He felt Phyllis' hands leave his arms. He could not look at her. Then he heard her say, feebly: "Oh, my God! My God! So, that's why poor Wilhelm suffered so, and why Jochen has to go, and why you look so, Charles."

He told himself that he could not turn and face her, but he did. He had thought that if she ever knew she would collapse. But she was standing straight and tall before him, and she was stern.

"Yes," she murmured.

"Joe lied, to Willie," Charles said. "He made something—of nothing. Or he made a lot out of what was very little. Phyllis, I've got this far, you've made me, and I might as well tell you the rest. He not only told Willie those things, but he told other people, and it's been repeated over and over, in Andersburg. Brinkwell and his wife helped. It's everywhere. They've dirtied you, Phyllis. They've tried to ruin me, because they wanted the company. But the worst of all was making Willie believe the lies, and torturing him. I think I could overlook almost anything else but that."

"Yes," she said.

"And so, while I kick him out—and don't think there won't be an uproar—you've got to be out of it, Phyllis. It'll make it easier for me, knowing that you aren't here when it happens. For they'll try to strike at me through you."

"Through me?" she repeated.

She looked at him intently when he did not answer her. "You don't want me to be hurt, do you, Charles?"

"That's right, Phyllis."

She said, quietly: "I think I can see it all, now. I can fill in what you haven't told me. Charles, they can't hurt you?"

"No. Not more than they've already done."

"Charles, I can't let you face everything alone."

"You must," he said. "This is something you've got to do for me."

The many weeks of confusion and grief and shock which had stood between them had been cleared away, fully, and they could see each other without that cloud. Phyllis' eyes widened, became brighter. She held out her hand to Charles, and he took it. Then, very simply, she moved towards him and put her head on his shoulder. His arms lifted, and he held her, and they were very still together. Phyllis did not cry or stir, and it was only after some time that Charles turned his head and kissed her hair. "Dear Phyllis," he said. It was so natural, standing like this, and holding her, and when she lifted her head he could kiss her on the mouth.

They sat down together on the settee, and Phyllis' head was again on Charles' shoulder, and he thought that perhaps there was something in precognition, after all. He had experienced so many emotions today, so many storms and rages, that this moment seemed the calmest and gentlest of resting places, and full of fulfillment. His headache was gone. There was tomorrow, and there was this place, and this comfort, and tomorrow could wait.

Mrs. Holt, who had been unashamedly lurking beyond the arch of the doorway, and who had avidly listened to everything, came in, beaming. She sat down opposite Charles and Phyllis, and said: "No, don't move. Well, Charlie, I'm glad you told her. Yes, I heard it all. Why not? Eavesdropping saves so many explanations, so many mis-understandings." She sighed, gustily, then laughed as she saw Phyllis color. "Don't be an idiot, Phyllis. It's very funny, in a way, Jochen Wittmann telling everyone the truth, with exaggerations, of course, and yet having it proved a lie."

"It was proved a lie, to Willie," said Charles, when he felt Phyllis stiffen. "He didn't believe it, at the last. So long as he lived, and if he had lived forever, it would have been a lie. Neither Phyllis nor I would ever have done anything to hurt him."

"Of course not," said Mrs. Holt, sturdily. "Now, Phyllis, don't let yourself start to agonize, and wonder. Your husband trusted you, and he trusted poor Charlie, here. And now we can settle down and be sensible. While Charlie does what he has to do, you've got to be away. Neither of you can do anything rash; I can't imagine Charlie doing anything rash, no matter how I try, and you aren't children. You'll travel around, Phyllis, and then in about a year or so, we can talk about things."

"You are such a friend, Minnie," said Phyllis, and she smiled and her eyes were wet.

"A friend, indeed," added Charles. Then he said: "But there are others, and when I've taken care of Joe, I'll settle with those who were willing to believe anything of me, without proof."

"Now, Charles," said Mrs. Holt, reprovingly. "That's so silly. Your friends believe in you, because we love you. But there are a lot of people about whom I can hear the most frightful stories and relish them. Yes, I really can. It doesn't necessarily mean I don't like those people, or would like to see any harm come to them because of the stories. But good juicy gossip makes life so interesting."

She laughed at Charles and Phyllis. "Why, how silly you two are! I know dozens of people right here, in this town, who've heard all the nasty stories about you, Charlie, and never believed them for a moment, but had a good time pretending they did. As for the others, you'll just have to ignore them. They were never your friends, even if some belonged to your very own church, and had you to dinner. That's life, Charlie. And now I think the automobile is here, and we'll take Phyllis home, and we'll drive you down to your house, and then I'll bring my poor, yawning Braydon back to his bed."

After they had left Phyllis at her lonely home, where only the hall light shone through the fanlight, Charles drove on with Mrs. Holt. She chattered gayly, while Charles absentmindedly dodged the big hatpins in her bigger hat; she did not expect him to listen, and he did not. Her talk just filled and dissipated a silence. He could only see Phyllis waving to him and Mrs. Holt from the steps of her house, with a vague star-sheen on her face, and the light from the hall gilding her hair.

The street was warm and dark, the trees barely moving, and then only with a drowsy whisper. Charles said goodnight to Mrs. Holt, and shook her hand, and she patted his shoulder. He went up the steps of the verandah, and he heard the creaking of the hammock. "Jimmy," said Charles. "Why aren't you in bed? It's after twelve."

The boy untangled his long legs from the hammock and stood up. "I wasn't sleepy," he answered. "Besides, you looked so terrible when you went away in Mrs. Holt's automobile that I thought I'd wait up and find out if there was anything wrong."

Charles opened the screen door, and Jimmy followed him into the house. The door slapped behind them in the midnight quiet. Jimmy turned up the wall gaslight. "Now, look here," said Charles, "you've got to stop this idiotic pampering of me, Jimmy, and acting as if I were a child and you a grandfather. You've got to remember that I lived a considerable time before you were born, and that someway, somehow, I'll manage to go on living in my own feeble-minded way, long after you're married and have a dozen children of your own."

But Jimmy was thoughtfully scrutinizing him, like a physician coming to his own conclusions and not listening to the babblings of a half-witted patient. Then he grinned. "You look better, Dad," he said, with relief.

"I feel better," replied Charles, impatiently. Then he began to smile. "Now run along, son, and get to bed." He pushed Jimmy roughly and affectionately towards the stairway. But Jimmy resisted. "Some hot milk?" he suggested. "Make you sleep."

"No, no hot milk. No anything. If I want some I'll heat it myself. I wouldn't trust you not to put something in it so that I'd never wake up again."

"Well, anyway, what I gave you did make you sleep for almost five hours."

"And gave me a nightmare, too." What had that nightmare been? Charles could not remember very clearly. No matter. He briskly turned out the gaslight, and the parlor became dark, lit only by the street-lamp outside. It was odd that he wasn't tired any longer, and that his mind was refreshed, as if he had just awakened from a long sleep. He and Jimmy went up the stairs, where another light burned very low near the landing. "And I'm going to read," Charles informed his son. "None of this confounded new habit of yours, shuffling past my door at all hours, and then listening near the key-hole to see if I'm uttering my last death-rattle or something."

Jimmy laughed; the laugh was almost a hysterical giggle. Why, I've been worrying the poor kid to death for months, thought Charles, remorseful. It's bad enough to go through hell yourself without dragging someone else with you, too. "I'm feeling fine," he said. Again, the inability of a man to express his love for his son came to him.

"Good night, Jimmy," he said, firmly. He heard Jimmy whistling as he went into his own room. It had been a long time since he had heard that low and happy sound, Charles thought. I've put him through hell, he said to himself, again.

He undressed, went to bed with a book, lit the gaslight. He rubbed his glasses. Tomorrow. There was always tomorrow, and he had once more returned to his old philosophy that it was bad business to fore-live events, or to relive past wretchedness. All that was coming would come, without his help or his hindrance.

It was perhaps unfortunate that this book was by Flaubert, for whom Charles, in his relentless reading, had developed a profound taste. For the first sentence he read was: "The trouble with men is not that they are scoundrels but that they are fools." He put down the book, and frowned.

He turned out the light, and scowled in the darkness. He would go to sleep. He had had enough for one day.

He drowsed uneasily, for the shocks of the past hours invaded his restless sleep like vague forms of menace. Voices, faces, gestures, dim movements, pushed against his eyelids. He turned from side to side, muttering. The early morning wind rose and the trees answered it. The lamplight outside flickered on the drawn shades.

Charles woke with a start, and as he did so he was completely overwhelmed by a horrible foreboding. It was like being struck by an iron fist in the pit of the stomach. This was even worse than the nightmare he had had after Jimmy had put him to sleep. It was so complete, so inexorable, and he had no fortitude with which to meet it.

He heard the rumbling of the first milk-wagon down the street, though it was still hardly dawn. He heard the clock below strike five. Now a buggy rattled a long way off, and a homeless dog barked hopelessly. The trees spoke louder. A first bird chirped sleepily, and then another called.

Charles lay in his bed, rigid and very still and the foreboding crushed him down.

It was only a coincidence, of course, that at that very moment the Archduke Francis Ferdinand, heir to the throne of Austria-Hungary, and his wife, the Duchess of Hohenberg, were being murdered in Sarajevo. It was high noon, there, and the sun was shining hotly, this very hour in Slavic Bosnia.

CHAPTER XLII

CHARLES STARTED to get up at his usual hour to go to church, this Sunday morning, June 28, 1914, and then he knew that it was impossible. He could not begin to live a normal life, or one approaching this, until things were settled. He could not bear the thought of seeing Jochen in the church today. Lately, they had nodded surlily to each other when there was an encounter in the halls, though they continued to communicate mostly by notes and messages through clerks.

Just my nerves, he told himself, as he shaved. Then, still in his nightshirt, he knocked at Jimmy's door. Jimmy was already dressing.

"Jimmy," said Charles, "I oughtn't to have slept yesterday. I didn't sleep well last night. Besides, there'll be things to do at the Park. So I'm not going to church today. And as your tutor will be here later, even though it's Sunday, you need not go either, if you don't want to."

Jimmy gave him a long sharp look. "Now, Dr. Wittmann," said Charles, gravely, "I assure you that I have no symptoms at all. Breakfast in half an hour, eh? We'll sit and talk over our coffee." He added: "I need the rest. We've been working Saturdays the last few months, as you know, with all the orders and things."

He went back to his room. But he was so tired. He looked at his clothing, then lay down on his rumpled bed. One of the pillows was on the floor. He had no energy with which to retrieve it. He lay on his back, his arms folded under his head. The door opened and Jimmy came in. Charles made an irritable movement, attempted to sit up, then lay down. Jimmy sat near him. "Well, Dad," said the boy. "Suppose you tell me all about it, or as much as you can. I'm not a child, you know."

Charles was silent. He stared at the window, which was an oblong of gold. The trees stood in brilliance, outside. It was a warm and lovely Sabbath day, full of softness and peace. Children were already playing and laughing on the sidewalks, and their mothers were scolding them for breaking the Sabbath quiet. The breeze sang.

Charles did not look at his son. "You're right, Jim," he said. You'll hear tomorrow, anyway. Jim, I'm throwing your Uncle Joe out of the company, tomorrow. He's finished."

Jimmy did not comment. Charles turned his head. "Disturbed, son?"

"No," said Jimmy, thoughtfully. "Except about what all this is doing to you. I know it must've taken a long time for you to make up your mind to do all this. You must have your reasons, and they must be good."

Charles said: "About Gerry, Jim. Will it make any difference?"

Jimmy shook his head, and smiled. "No, Dad. Not a bit of difference. Gerry and I understand more than you think." He hesitated. "For instance, I've known, for a long time, what Uncle Joe's been saying about you all over Andersburg."

"What!" exclaimed Charles. He sat up.

"Gerry loves her parents," said Jim, as if Charles had not spoken. "But she loves me, too, and she loves you a lot, also, Dad. The only thing that was wrong was you, and how you had it all bottled up in yourself, and we were worried about you. We knew Uncle Joe had some reason for all these stories, and we came to a pretty good conclusion. It's the Connington, isn't it?"

Charles was dumbfounded. He thought, confusedly: What idiots parents are. They hide things from their children, under the delusion they are protecting them, or something, and the children know all the time and suffer over it.

"The Connington," Charles muttered, helplessly.

Jimmy nodded. "Yes. And Mr. Brinkwell. He's always either over at Uncle Joe's or Uncle Joe and Aunt Isabel are over at Brinkwell's. And there's that Kenneth. Well, Dad, it's all tied up with the Connington, someway, and the company, though what the details are we've never quite found out."

Charles was full of shame. His son, hearing those foul stories! Anyone else hearing them, and it would not have mattered. But his son!

Jimmy said, casually: "I know what you're thinking, Dad. Remember, though, I'm not a little kid. And when people want something they'll do anything."

He began to laugh, gently. "We're in a new age, Dad. The young people know a lot of things you don't dream we know. At first I was mad about those stories, and then I just began to worry about you hearing them. Gerry said that the people concerned are always the last to know."

Now Charles was intensely humiliated. "You ought to have told me, son."

Jimmy shook his head. "No. You know you wouldn't have wanted me to. I just had to wait until you told me, yourself."

Charles said: "Would you believe it, Jim, if I told you that I first heard about them only yesterday?" He picked up his pillows, punched them behind his head. "Your Uncle Willie knew about the stories; Joe had told him. You'll just have to fill in for yourself. But I never knew anything about the tales until Oliver Prescott and George Hadden told me about them—yesterday."

Jimmy had listened seriously. Then, with abstraction, he pulled out a box of Melachrinos from his back pocket, lit one, and smoked with concentration. Charles wanted to protest, saying: "Smoking? When did this begin?" And then he realized his son was truly not a child any longer, but a man. The smell of the warm Turkish tobacco drifted through the room, undisturbed.

"It is the only thing to do, of course," said Jimmy, soberly. "The only thing to do, and as soon as possible. But it'll take a great deal of money, won't it? You'll have to buy him out."

"I have friends," said Charles.

"So," said Jimmy, with almost his father's own tone and mannerism. "Besides, you've got Uncle Fred, and Uncle Willie's will, and everything, behind you."

I almost didn't have, thought Charles. He said: "You know, Jim, that you're your Uncle Willie's ultimate heir—after your Aunt Phyllis. Everything. And—and—"

"My issue," added Jimmy, unperturbed. "Yes, I know. I suppose that's another reason why Uncle Joe wanted to ruin you, if he could."

"Are they so determined that poor little Gerry must marry that Brinkwell feller?"

"Oh, yes. They want to announce the engagement at Christmas. She's going away in September, you know. But we'll see each other! Week-ends, sometimes."

His father was looking better, much better! Good old Dad. Sometimes adults were very childish. Jimmy stood up. "Well, how about some breakfast? Want a tray up here?"

Charles was so relieved, so unaccountably relieved, that he sat up and said explosively: "No! I wouldn't put it past you to dope the coffee, or something. Go on out, and I'll be right down."

Jimmy went away, whistling loudly. No dolorous music, now. Some "rag," gay, catching, lilting. A man. No longer "Jimmy," but "Jim." Charles heard his son thumping away in his room.

Charles avoided glancing at his son when he called George Hadden. He said to George: "Will you do me an innocent favor? Well, innocent in a way, you Quaker! Please call Fred at his home, on some pretext. Tell him you talked to me yesterday about some matters which I am to discuss with Fred tomorrow. Tell him, as mysteriously as you can, that you gave me your 'advice' and that I promised to act on it."

He turned to Jim, as he completed his call. He said: "George is vaguely alarmed. He's afraid I'm jeopardizing his Quaker conscience. But he'll do what I ask."

"It's fine to have a reputation for integrity," said Jim, with a broad smile.

"It is, indeed," agreed Charles, with the utmost seriousness. "By the way, did you know that within a few months or so you'll have an Aunt Helen?"

It was wonderful to have someone in whom to confide in his own house. Father and son lingered a long time over breakfast, while Charles spoke and Jim listened. "To think," said the boy, "that you've carried all this in you all this time and never talked with anyone. It must have been horrible. But here's the tutor now. In the meantime, try to rest, Dad."

Charles went into the garden, and stretched out in the hammock under the trees. He rocked back and forth gently, his hands clasped on his chest. He mapped out his plans. The leaf-pattern of the trees flowed over his face and his closed eyes. He was the picture of relaxation. But his mind churned. Then it was settled. There was nothing to do but to wait for tomorrow. The hammock swayed, the sweet scent of grass and roses moved in the soft breeze, the leaves fluttered, and the sun rose hotter and hotter. He stared at the shifting bits of sky which showed through the trees. He thought of the confused nightmares of the months past. In many ways I've been exaggerating, he said to himself. I became panic-stricken. It needs only to be thought out, and planned—any problem.

He had lunch alone, for Jim and his tutor went on with their lessons. He could hear their voices upstairs, in Jim's room. The day was becoming very hot, and Charles was folded in a deep languor which continued when he went into the garden again. He slept. Mrs. Meyers awakened him; it was almost five. "Mr. Grimsley, of the paper, called, an hour ago," she informed Charles. "He said it was important, and you must call back."

But this Charles refused to do. It was something about the Park, he thought. He ate his dinner, with Jim.

At half-past six he and Jim, with Jim driving the roaring red automobile, started for the Park. A German band, drawn from some other town, hopefully had come to Andersburg. For some reason Charles had the automobile halted, and he sat and listened to the band, which was strenuously playing some old German tunes. They were the songs which Emil Wittmann had sung, and they had a sad nostalgia, keen and disturbing, to Charles. The musicians, all elderly and discouraged, and very shabby, played with a kind of frenzy directed almost exclusively to the gentlemen in the big red automobile. A small crowd of people, on their way to the Park, stopped to listen. Some of the older people began to sing bashfully, in time with the music, and the softened German gutturals also sounded sad and mournful. The sun was beginning to fall behind the distant blue mountains, and long golden shadows lay on the street under the trees. The passing of an era, thought Charles, utterly without reason, but from some instinct. The horns, big and wide-mouthed, shone in the mellow light. The old musicians' mouths puffed at the horns, their fingers ran up and down the flutes. The drum banged with a lonely sound.

Charles, on an impulse, took out his wallet and removed four five-dollar bills. One of the musicians was now moving about with his hat. When Charles dropped the bills in the hat, the old man stared at them, looked at Charles. "Danke schoen," he murmured, stunned. Charles said in German: "Come to the Park, and play there, too. There is a fireman's band, but there'll be hundreds of people there who will like your music." He looked at the faded blue uniforms of the bandsmen, at their caps brave in tarnished gold. He told Jim to drive on, and he wondered why he should feel so heavy-hearted, so grieved. Nerves, he told himself.

During the last few weeks he had visited the Park regularly, to watch its progress. It was a beautiful park. Wilhelm's plans had been followed explicitly. They had been modelled on some German park, in Munich, and they gave an impression of complete naturalness, which Charles understood to be the height of artistry. Not formal, after all. Winding crushed gravel paths led through groups of old fine trees. A spring had been trained into a fountain of white stone dolphins disporting themselves in a wide round pool. Stone and white-painted benches stood under the trees. Openings, here and there, let the river be seen beyond sloping green lawns. There was a refreshment house, discreetly hidden in a small natural wood, where sandwiches could be bought, and coffee and beer, and a band could play on Sundays and holidays. There were tables outside, on a terrace. There was a separate playground for children, with swings and slides and see-saws. Wilhelm had discarded the idea of rigid flower-beds. Flowers grew along the paths, or suddenly appeared in a blaze of color on a stretch of greensward, kindly, old-fashioned flowers, and rock gardens with mossy green plants. The sounds of the city came here muffled and gentled; high above the Park rose the mountains. It was all "foreign" and lovely and simple.

Because of the Wittmann family's recent bereavement the ceremonies were not scheduled to be extensive. There were plenty of flags, and there was a red ribbon drawn between the two graystone gateposts at the entrance of the Park. Charles found a crowd of several thousand people already waiting for the family, and the firemen's band was playing lustily. The old German band, Charles decided, would be requested to perform at the refreshment house, where, tonight, all the sandwiches and cakes and coffee and beer would be free. Japanese lanterns were strung through the trees, and the Park lights would not go on until tomorrow night.

Charles' red automobile was greeted with cheers. There was a place reserved for the Wittmann family. Friederich was there, important and shining, with the Haddens and Oliver Prescott. He was too excited to sit still, and he ignored Jochen and his family, who, with the Brinkwells and other friends, deliberately ignored Friederich in return, and even Charles' arrival. Charles saw at once that Phyllis had not come, and he was relieved. But Mrs. Holt and Braydon Holt greeted him affectionately. Mrs. Holt made a rather large fuss over him, and this was observed by Jochen and Roger Brinkwell, and their friends. Mrs. Holt sat beside Charles, and made a point of leaning animatedly towards him and talking above the music of the band. The sun, now half-fallen behind the mountains, gilded the tops of the trees.

Then all at once the band struck up "America" and everyone rose. The thickening crowds began to sing. The firemen, in their fine uniforms, were a brave sight, and sweated. Charles thought he had never heard a crowd sing with such fervor:

> "My country, 'tis of thee,
> Sweet land of liberty,
> Of thee I sing!
> Land where my fathers died,
> Land of the Pilgrims' pride,
> From every mountainside
> Let freedom ring!"

My country—let freedom ring! Someone was pushing towards Charles. The crowd, somewhat tentatively, were humming the other verses. Charles saw the gnarled face of Ralph Grimsley, and he motioned to the editor to stand beside him. He, too, sang, but the editor was silent. Then Charles felt him pluck at his sleeve, and he bent his head to listen.

". . . called you," said Mr. Grimsley. Charles nodded. Now the music faded from his consciousness, and all the crowds. "Didn't have time," muttered Charles. The little editor pulled at his lip. "It's started," he said. "The Archduke of Austria and his wife were murdered this morning in Sarajevo. The opening gun. Got the news a couple of hours ago, by wire, from New York. Came over the cable about three o'clock. Thought you might want to know, but keep it quiet. Getting out an extra tonight at eleven o'clock."

The crowds were humming loudly, the band was coming, with a flourish, to its final crashing. Everywhere was a sea of women's gay hats, men's stiff straw hats. Laughter, song, and music. The Mayor was rising, importantly, to speak, and Friederich stood beside him. All at once, everything was artificial to Charles, tinted with nightmare, unreal, terrible, desolate.

"It might not mean anything," he said to the editor.

"It does, it does," said Mr. Grimsley.

"They wouldn't—dare," said Charles. He looked over at Jochen and the Brinkwells. Their faces were blurred for him. He saw only one face, sharply, young Geraldine's clear young features under a flower-burdened hat. She was smiling slightly, and she was looking at Jim.

Oh, yes, "they'd" dare. Charles knew it. It had begun. The end of the world had begun.

CHAPTER XLIII

THE MAYOR, poor fellow, isn't really as boring as all that, thought Mrs. Holt, noticing Charles' set face, clamped mouth, and fixed eyes. Tedious, yes; but he certainly was not expressing any opinions that Charlie might dislike; after all, Charlie helped to elect him, and would probably help to elect him this fall, too. Mrs. Holt nudged Charles' arm, and said: "Bored?"

Charles started. And then she knew that he had heard nothing of the prosy sonorousness of the Mayor's pronouncements, that the majestic tributes being paid by "his honor" to the Wittmann family had literally fallen upon one set of closed ears, at least. Concerned, but inquisitive, Mrs. Holt peered around Charles and saw the little spidery form and face of Ralph Grimsley, who was also staring sightlessly at the crowds. Mrs. Holt's heart jumped. Something had happened, something terrible. Charles turned away from her, unaware that she had even spoken to him.

The Mayor tossed his leonine head. The crowd moved restively, but with good humor. All politicians talked; it was too bad that they never said anything worth listening to. Charles' eyes moved slowly over the thousands of faces which stretched everywhere. He picked out a few, automatically; Mr. Haas was here, not far away, on a special bench with his family: his wife, the sober young Walter, and the three little girls; there were members of the Church Board with them. Then, not on a seat, but in the ranks of the crowd, the eager but serious young priest, Father Hagerty. His eyes met Charles' eyes. It was impossible for the priest to know anything yet, but Charles looked at him and the priest looked back, and Father Hagerty thought, as Mrs. Holt had thought: Something terrible has happened.

The sky became a lake of lemon-yellow over the western mountains, and the tops of the trees turned yellow, also, and the faces of the people. There was a polite clapping of hands, and the Mayor, flushed and triumphant, sat down in stately grandeur. Now Friederich was rising, and this time Jochen and the Brinkwells and their friends looked at him, and their expressions became smilingly contemptuous. It had been a surprise that Charles was not to speak. Jochen whispered to Roger: "Look what he's picked out! Now we'll have a dissertation on social justice, or something!"

Charles began to stare intently at his brother Jochen and Roger Brinkwell, when Friederich started to speak. He was only faintly aware that the crowd was no longer restive, and that his brother's voice had a deep and reaching quality, loud and fervent in the silence. He looked at Roger Brinkwell, and he thought: He knows! He looked at Jochen, and now his bitter eyes became speculative, and then startled. Jochen did not know. Charles saw his brother's fat and ruddy cheeks, his double chin, his massive body leaning indolently back in his seat, his thick arms folded over his big chest, his legs crossed, his hat tilted forward over his brow. Why, thought Charles, the fool, the benighted, cunning, plotting fool! He knows nothing of what is going on, or what has happened. The simpleton has been plotting childishly in the shadow of death and never knew what it was that was looking over his shoulder all the time.

Charles hated Jochen with fresh violence, remembering the scandal his brother had spread about him. But, to his own amazement, and disgust, he also felt a wondering and compassionate contempt. He was not shaken in his purpose; Jochen, in his ignorant stupidity, was as dangerous as if he knew. However, there was this sick pity in Charles, this sensation of helplessness.

There was Isabel, handsomely coquettish under her big straw hat, and in her white linen frock, talking to Pauline Brinkwell, all gray chiffon and elegance. There was young Kenneth Brinkwell, whispering to Geraldine, who nodded and smiled, and looked only at Jimmy. There were Ethel and May, Jochen's younger daughters, blooming and buxom, like their mother. There was Brinkwell, slight, black, and dapper, smoking languidly, yet emanating to Charles, even at this distance of some sixty feet, something alert and vicious.

Then Charles became conscious of the deepening attention of the crowd, and Friederich's intense and soaring voice.

"So," Friederich said, and Charles, who had never heard his brother speak, was amazed at the infinite range and eloquence of his voice: "that while every man, everywhere, dies a little when any other man dies, and every man everywhere is guilty of the crime of every other man, so all of us share, collectively, in the good which any single man does, and we are part of the virtue of every saint who has ever lived or will live. While we must cry 'Mea culpa!' when murder is done anywhere in the world, so we may cry 'Eureka!' when we hear of a noble deed or a kindness, or some compassionate act. Not only are we guilty of everything evil, but we share in every heroism and in every justice."

What had he said, before, which had led up to this? Charles did not know, and he did not care. He only listened, and looked at his brother. The lemon-yellow light lay on Friederich's face, and it was the inspired and kindling face of a prophet, and all his mediocrity was gone.

Now Friederich's voice dropped, became deep and portentous: "When Armageddon comes, and it is almost here, then we must say to ourselves, every man singly: 'I have done this.' And when we fight for honor and peace, we must say to ourselves, and every man singly: 'I have done an evil thing, but I have died for mankind, also.' "

He sat down, and the silence was an almost ringing thing over the heads of the crowd. No one applauded; but everyone looked at Friederich. Even Jochen looked, and there was a puzzled frown on his large, fat face. Only one smiled contemptuously, and that one was Roger Brinkwell. Roger leaned towards Jochen and whispered jocularly: "Now, let us pray!" But Jochen looked at Friederich.

Now the crowd was moving uneasily, like a herd of sheep that had smelled an ominous wind and had heard an ominous sound. The Mayor, always a politician, rose at once and announced that Mr. Charles Wittmann would cut the ribbon and admit the people to "their Park." As if he, himself, and he only, were the beginning and the end of this beneficence, he smiled proudly at the crowds, and waved his large white hand. The crowds began to surge towards the gates, like those delivered from some prophesied horror from which they had just escaped.

Charles left as soon as he could, having seen to it that the timorous German band had been firmly established near the terrace of the refreshment house and had begun their sweet German airs. The lanterns had been lit; the crowds were walking along the softly illuminated gravel paths, laughing and admiring, and eventually finding their way to the sandwiches and beer and coffee and cakes. Charles had insisted that

Jim stay. He, himself, wanted to walk home, quietly. He unobtrusively avoided every familiar face, and walked out of the Park.

The river flowed in dark gold past the city; the mountains stood in dark blue majesty in the distance. Charles left the music and the laughter and the voices, and walked through the quiet streets. The lavender twilight was flooding in, everywhere, under the trees, like velvet water. Charles' footsteps echoed. He was in a deserted town, full of dreaming silence. Church bells began to ring, in a warm entrancement.

So, it had come at last, after all the dreadful fear and the waiting. It had come in confusion, and there would be no sharp drawing of lines, no good, no definite evil. The iniquity of man had created this impending death and ruin; this iniquity would blur every issue, make it impossible to say "this is right" or "this is wrong." The collective iniquity of all men, everywhere, had done this thing to the world. The collective and enormous greed, the stupidity, the monstrous blindness!

Ralph Grimsley had said to Charles when he had seen Charles about to leave: "Perhaps we're wrong. Let's hope so. Perhaps Sarajevo will be forgotten in a few days, or weeks. Perhaps we're just having private nightmares." Charles had said nothing. He had just gone away.

Charles walked on, and now he began to hurry, overwhelmed with catastrophe. His heels were loud and sharp on the pavements. No one was about.

Then at a long distance he heard the faint and mournful music of a street organ. He stopped, involuntarily, and listened. He knew that music; he had heard it from Jimmy's gramophone. It was the Miserere.

He listened. Down the long and purple aisles of the streets the music drifted. The lament for men.

CHAPTER XLIV

CHARLES STOPPED in at the home of his friend Dr. Metzger just as the latter was opening his office. It was only half-past eight. "Gustave," said Charles, "I feel like hell. And today I'm no use at all. I've got to be; I have to do perhaps the most serious thing I've ever done in my life, and I'm shaking like a leaf. Can you give me something to quiet me down for a few hours at least?"

Dr. Metzger regarded him with anxiety. "Sit down, Charlie," he said, trying not to sound too alarmed. "Still not sleeping, eh? Well. Let's see what I can do for you." He went into his laboratory. Charles, exhausted, leaned his elbow on the doctor's desk. Two newspapers were there, one the extra edition gotten out last night by the *Clarion*, and the other by the morning paper. The *Clarion* screamed in huge black headlines: "ARCHDUKE OF AUSTRIA AND WIFE MURDERED TODAY IN SARAJEVO!" But the morning paper had only a single column on the left-hand side of the paper, and the heading read, simply, "Murdered in Sarajevo: Austrian Archduke and wife."

The *Clarion* shouted and ejaculated in three front-page columns. The morning paper referred to the whole story as "another mess in the Balkans."

Later, Charles was to wonder if the *Clarion* had been the only paper in the happy, newly prosperous and baseball-absorbed country which had been endowed with any prophetic vision at all. Certainly, he found out in the following few weeks, no other paper had taken June 28, 1914, too seriously.

Charles had not read the *Clarion's* unprecedented Sunday night extra edition. He opened the paper to see if there was any editorial comment on the murders. There was. Charles' tired eyes swam as he read: "There will be very few people today in America who will realize that this dastardly assassination is the overture to a universal calamity." He put aside the paper. Dr. Metzger was entering the office with a glass of water and two pills in his hand.

Charles obediently swallowed the pills. Then he sat there, gasping a little, while Dr. Metzger took his blood pressure, and pursed his lips at the reading. The doctor sat down, thoughtfully tapped his fingers on his desk. "Better go slow, Charlie. You say you've got to do something today. 'Serious.' Put it off until you calm down. You're not doing so well. Why don't you go home and go to bed for a couple of days?"

"Can't," replied Charles, impatiently. He pointed at the *Clarion's* headline. "What do you think of that?"

The doctor considered the *Clarion*, and then the morning paper. He shook his head. "Maybe Grimsley's too excited. 'Universal calamity.' Has he been reading a crystal ball, or something?" But the doctor's face was worried.

"You know Grimsley's right," said Charles.

"Now, now, Charlie. I knew the *Clarion* before Grimsley became editor, and it had a lot of common sense. Grimsley's got a nose for news. But you know how he plays up the least little thing. Someone gets into a hunting accident, and Grimsley hints, in headlines, that perhaps it was murder. Charlie, you go home and read about the Giants, or something." He pointed his big finger at Charles. "How long do you think your heart and blood vessels are going to stand the strain you're putting on them?

"How's Jimmy?" he continued, smiling affectionately as he always did when Charles' son was mentioned.

Charles buttoned his coat. He tucked a newspaper under his arm. "I've been doing a lot of thinking about Jimmy," he said. He looked down at the *Clarion's* headlines.

"Now, now," said the doctor, again.

It was Charles' intention to send for Jochen the moment he arrived at the office. But Friederich was already waiting for him there, and he was in a frightful condition. His cheek twitched as Charles had not seen it twitch for months. He was ghastly pale, and his lips were purplish, and there were dark marks under his eyes. He had the *Clarion* open on his knees, and when he saw Charles he jumped up and cried: "It's come!"

Charles sat down. The sedative had given him some calm. He said: "Yes."

Friederich began to run up and down the office, distracted. "No one will believe it! I never liked Grimsley, because of his sneers at Socialism, but he's right, this time." All his wild fanaticism had returned, and Charles knew what the romantic description of one's heart "sinking" really meant. Socialism. Friederich had not mentioned the word for months.

"Only a Socialized world could have prevented this!" he exclaimed. "But a greedy Capitalistic world has caused this catastrophe, and all the catastrophes that'll follow it." He stopped beside Charles, and panted. Charles closed his eyes for a moment. He tried to find the right words. Then, his eyes still closed, he said faintly: "It's the world, Fred, just the world of men. It always is."

Friederich flung himself into a chair. "You—" he began. Charles lifted his hand. "I just met George Hadden on the street a few minutes ago," he said. He did not open his eyes, but he felt an uneasy quiet fall on his brother. "He told me he had taken you to the Park, yesterday, with Helen, in his new automobile. Incidentally, that was a wonderful speech you made. Wonderful," he added, and he heard his own voice with sincerity. "Armageddon. Yes. You prophesied it. And you know why, and it hasn't anything to do with Capitalism, or anything. You said so, yourself. It's just men."

Friederich opened his mouth to speak, then he closed it.

"Wonderful speech," repeated Charles. "Hope you have a copy of it. It ought to be printed. Helen Hadden told me afterwards that it was the most moving thing she'd ever heard."

He opened his eyes. Friederich was almost smiling, but his color was still very bad and his misery was still very evident. He said: "Thank you, Karl."

Charles spread the newspaper he had been carrying open to a certain page. He struggled with the lassitude which the pills had given him. The most serious day in his life, perhaps. He could not fail, he dared not fail. Inwardly he prayed: You've got to help me. God Almighty, You've got to help me!

He pointed to a photograph. "See this, Fred? Recognize this man?"

Friederich, who was stiff and rigid with agitation, bent forward and looked at the photograph. "It's Herman Belz," he said. He looked at the date, three days ago. "I read it. One of his best speeches."

Oh, God, thought Charles. "I saw this man, here in Andersburg, the day Willie died," he said.

Friederich was incredulous. "Impossible! Belz has not been in Andersburg since—since a year ago."

Charles said, with quiet savagery: "Yes, he was. I met him. He was going up to Brinkwell's in old Harry Hoffmann's hack, and the Ford was stuck in the mud. I helped get it out."

"Brinkwell?" Friederich was aghast, and disbelieving. "Impossible!"

"Not impossible. Fred, can you think of any reason why he'd be visiting Brinkwell, knowing what Brinkwell is, and what he's doing?"

Friederich jumped up again, in wild excitement. "You are mistaken, Karl! He wrote me, about three days before Wilhelm died. He was in Chicago, and he said he could not come to Andersburg for some time."

"He was here," said Charles. "He tried not to show himself." And then he told Friederich of the incident on the mountain road. He looked into Friederich's flickering eyes as he did so, and held them, and Friederich knew that he spoke the truth. Friederich fell once more into his chair, and if he had been an appalling color before, his color was even more terrifying now. As Charles had done, he closed his eyes. Fine beads of sweat appeared over his lips and on his forehead.

"It's all part of the picture," said Charles, in conclusion. "And that's why I wanted to see you today. Fred, you must listen to me. Today, we must come to a decision."

But Friederich, shaken and distraught, kept his eyes shut. "Belz— and Brinkwell," he murmured.

"The man isn't what you think he is," said Charles. "But I think you knew he wasn't, a long time ago. You were miserable, because you knew instinctively that he's one of the men who are trying to destroy all of us."

Friederich's hands clenched and unclenched. He said, simply: "I think I'm going to be sick." He opened his eyes and looked at Charles with the desperate expression of a mortally stricken child. "I'm going to be sick," he repeated. And then he actually retched.

Innocent, thought Charles, with despairing pity. He reached across his desk and took his brother's arm firmly. "No, you're not," he said. "There's too much to be done, today, and I need your help. Today's the day you've got to trust me. Fred, control yourself, and listen."

"I'm controlling myself. I'm listening." Friederich's voice shook. He put his hands over his face, pressed very hard, dragged his hands down. His fingers left red welts on the yellowish skin. Then he braced his thin shoulders, took out his handkerchief, and wiped his damp forehead. "I've had a blow. But I'm listening, Karl."

"You're due for a worse one, so prepare yourself," said Charles. "Today, unless you help me, we're all done. There'll be nothing left in a few weeks, or months. Nothing for you; nothing for me."

Friederich looked at him, affrighted. "What are you saying, Karl?" he stammered.

Charles was laying a long sheaf of papers on his desk, bound in blue. "I'm not using hysterical words, Fred. I'm stating a very simple fact." He pointed to the papers. "Our father's will. Let me quote you a section." Then he read: " 'In full knowledge of the natures of all my sons, I hereby make this provision: In the event one of my sons takes any action whatsoever which will jeopardize my company, which will militate against the financial welfare of this company, to the financial or other ruin of my sons, then the majority of my sons are hereby commanded to oust the offending member and pay him a reasonable and just sum for his interest in the said company, said sum to be established by the majority of my sons, and at least one appraiser.' "

Friederich listened in dull stupefaction, his handkerchief clenched in one of his hands.

"You knew this provision," said Charles. "You heard it read by the lawyers. Now the time has come. Listen, for God's sake. Listen very carefully."

Friederich nodded, dumbly.

Then Charles began to talk. The warm sunlight lay on the windows of the office. It expanded. Then it spread. It touched Charles' back. It seeped onto the desk. Finally it rose higher and struck on Friederich's ghostly face. Charles talked on, doggedly. He kept his voice quiet. He told everything. He told of what he had learned from Oliver Prescott and George Hadden, and when he mentioned Phyllis' name his voice remained without emotion.

Friederich did not speak at all, not to ask a single question, not to make a single exclamation. He made not the slightest gesture of disbelief, or objection. He just sat there. Even when the sun was full in his staring eyes he did not turn aside. Charles' words beat relentlessly on his ears. He saw Charles' face, ruthless and cold.

The sun was fingering the opposite wall when Charles came to the end. "And there you have it all," he said. "You knew some of it, to some extent. But you didn't know how far the villainy had gone, and how complete it was."

He fumbled for the small bottle Dr. Metzger had given him over two hours ago. He took it out of his pocket and looked at it. He shook two pills out into the palm of his hand. Then he said: "Get me a glass of water, Fred. I don't think I can stand up."

It was this one remark that convinced Friederich more than anything else that Charles had been telling the truth, and only the truth. Then he went to the water-bottle and brought Charles a glass of water. He stood over Charles, still trembling, and watched his brother swallow the pills. Charles' shoulders were sagging, and now, for the first time, Friederich felt pity for Charles, the deep pity for a brother who is suffering, and it gave him strength.

He put his hand on Charles' shoulder, awkwardly. His voice was uncertain with this alien compassion, this sense of being stronger than Charles just now, this conviction that Charles needed him and could do nothing without him: "Karl, try to be calm. You are ill. You ought to have told me before. Did you not know you could trust me?"

Something broke in Charles. He put down the glass. He looked up at Friederich. Then he put his own hand on the hand on his shoulder. "I knew," he said. "I knew I could rely upon you." And it seemed to himself that he spoke sincerely.

Friederich sat down. "All those months," he said. "You had all this in you. But you did not speak. Did you think I was so—so wretched a brother that you couldn't trust me?" He paused. "But I was. I was."

Charles could say nothing. He leaned back in his chair and spread his hands flat on the desk.

Friederich's strength grew, as Charles' declined. "We have no other way," said Friederich. "Jochen must go. He must be told at once. No, you are not well enough. Tomorrow—"

"No," said Charles. "Now." He touched the bell on his desk. "I can't stand another day of this." Parker came in, and Charles, almost weakly, said: "Please ask Mr. Jochen to come in at once, Parker."

The sedative began to work again. Charles' eyes closed heavily. He heard Jochen come in, with his ponderous tread. Then he opened his eyes. The two brothers looked at each other in a long silence across the desk. Jochen ignored Friederich.

"Well," he said.

He must have known, Charles remembered, later. Nothing else could have accounted for his profound and sudden loss of color. Nothing else could have caused that sudden shrinking of facial skin and muscles. Jochen sat down in another chair. But he did not cross his knees easily. He sat straight and massive and stiff, his clenched hands on his knees. "Well?" he said again.

Charles lifted his father's will, pointed to the section he had read to Friederich, and said: "Perhaps you remember this?"

Jochen did not take the paper immediately. He seemed fascinated, paralyzed, by Charles' expression. He gave Friederich a glance. Then he made a very slight movement. This was not the Friederich he knew. Still staring at Friederich, he took the paper, and then he read the section Charles had indicated.

If possible, his color became even paler. He licked his lips. The paper shook in his hands. Then he put it down. "What—what has that to do with me?" he asked.

"Everything," Charles said. "Joe, you're through. You are out, out of the Wittmann Machine Tool Company. You know why. Let's not waste time talking about it."

The papers literally fell on Charles' desk from Jochen's big hands. "Are you insane?" he stuttered.

"No," said Charles. "And you know I'm not. I was, on Saturday, after I learned what you had been saying about me and about—about me, all over town. That, on top of what I already knew about you and Brinkwell. And the Connington. And your plot to destroy our father's company, and make it a subsidiary of the Connington, with yourself, probably, as president. That, on top of knowing how you tried to set Willie against me, to make yourselves a majority to get me out. You discounted Fred, here. You thought, at the last, that he was weak, that he could be pulled in by you, when you were ready to tell all your lies to him. You were just about ready, when Willie died, weren't you?"

He said, when Jochen did not answer him: "Yes, I was insane, on Saturday. I wanted to kill you. I might have, if I'd found you. But you were with Brinkwell, weren't you? I made sure of that."

The ruddy Wittmann color did not return to Jochen's face, but all at once its expression was ferocious with hatred. He seemed to swell. His jaws bulged. He clenched his fist and began to beat it very slowly but meatily on Charles' desk. He looked at Charles, and his eyes were full of malignance.

"All right," he said. "You've told your own lies to this—this imitation of a man, Now, I have something to say, myself, and when I've said it you'll give it a lot of thought. A lot of thought."

"There's nothing to say," said Charles. "I refuse to allow you to say anything. Fred and I are agreed that you're getting out. You can't set aside the provisions of that will. Fred and I are a majority. Aren't we?" He turned to Friederich. Jochen automatically turned, also.

Friederich did not hesitate. "We are," he said. Fascinated again, Jochen stared at him.

"And I am the executor of Willie's will," said Charles. "I have been given authority in that will to do what I wish, in so far as Willie's share is concerned. I have power of attorney. I don't want to protract this, Joe. Just—get out. You'll have your share in cash, in a week or so."

Then he said: "Or do you want to make a public issue of this, in the courts, Joe? Do you want me to drag in Brinkwell's name, too? Do you know what will happen, then? Brinkwell wouldn't give you a look after that. He has his own name to protect, and the name of the Connington. Just go, quietly, and take your money when it's ready. Go quietly, and Brinkwell will give you a job in the Connington. After all, you can be valuable to him; you're an able man. Besides, if you keep your mouth shut, he wouldn't dare not to make it up to you handsomely. But just talk, Joe. Just force me to take this to the courts. And Joe, that'll be the end of you."

He pointed at his brother, with one implacable finger. "Joe, don't tempt me. You are tempting me, now. You are driving me dangerously to the point where I'll forget you're my father's son, too. Don't do it, Joe. I don't want to do this to you."

Charles' voice had been quiet, but Jochen heard its undertones. Now terror returned to him, and rage, and hatred. He stood up.

"Is that so?" he shouted. "You've talked and talked, like the smug rascal you are. But I have something to say! I'll say it, too, and you can't stop me. Or"—and now he leaned towards Charles—"would you like me to have my day in court, too?"

"Go on. You have your day, now," said Charles. "Say it. Fred's here. Let him know, too."

But Jochen laughed a little, in an ugly way. "Oh, no, not with him here. I don't want any witnesses. I just want you to hear it, all by yourself, Charlie." He bent over the desk, and again pounded it slowly and meatily. "Just you, Charlie."

Charles was silent. He sat in his chair, stolid and unmoving.

Then Friederich stood up, with dignity. "I'll go, Karl," he said. "If you wish me to. But under no circumstances must you let—let this man—intimidate you." He added this, pleadingly, and with pity.

Charles turned to him. "It's all right, Fred. He can't intimidate me. And he has a right to say something to me in private, if he wants to, and if you don't mind."

Jochen was chuckling. "No, I won't be able to intimidate you, Charlie," he said, jeeringly. "Not at all."

Friederich did not even glance at him as he walked out of the room and closed the door behind him. The two brothers watched him go. Jochen sat down. He was all sudden elation.

"Well?" said Charles.

Jochen reached in his pocket for his cigar case. He took out a cigar. He lit it, leisurely, puffed at it, regarded the volume of smoke critically. "Very nice of you," he said in a conversational tone, "to mention my being my father's son, too. I'm wondering if it's ever occurred to you that perhaps I've remembered you were, also, and that's what's kept my mouth shut."

"About what?" asked Charles.

Jochen grinned at him. "I've really been very kind to you, Charlie. Have you ever thought of that? But after all, I didn't want the family name smeared. I've got three girls. And I've always had a soft spot for Jimmy, too. I didn't want the kids hurt by my exposing you, and having you hanged. As a murderer."

The sun mounted the opposite wall. It struck on the white face of the big wooden clock. The position of the hands indicated fifteen minutes after eleven. It was all these things that Charles saw, in his mundane office, which vibrated continuously with the rumbling of the shops. Something had been said, something incredible, something not to be believed. Words had been spoken that had no meaning for him, like words in a preposterous language, conveying nothing but bafflement and incomprehension. He regarded Jochen with bewilderment.

"What?" he said, in a stupid tone. He was so dazed, partly from the sedative, partly from his disbelief, that he felt no emotion at all.

"You heard me," answered Jochen, with nonchalance. Now his little brown eyes glinted with cunning amusement. "And you've thought about it a lot, I know. I've seen you getting more and more haggard every day, wondering if I had remembered, wondering if I had attached any importance to what happened the night Willie was —killed. And then, when I didn't say anything, you thought you were safe. Well, Charlie, you weren't. You aren't. That's what I want you to keep in mind. Move against me, and I move against you."

"You're out of your mind," said Charles, wonderingly, and still with no emotion except bewilderment. "Would you mind telling me what you're talking about, for God's sake? Have you gone Socialist, or something, and taken up Fred's old jargon, about 'murderers'?"

"Come, come, Charlie," answered Jochen, in tolerant indulgence. "Don't try your tricks on me. I know them all." He pointed at Charles with his cigar. "Let me refresh your memory, though you know it doesn't need refreshing.

"Let's begin with Willie, and his, shall we say—perturbation—about your little indiscretions with a certain lady—" He stopped, for Charles had half risen from his chair and his whole face had turned a dark crimson.

"So," said Charles. Involuntarily, his hand reached out and lifted his heavy glass paper-weight. He felt it in his fingers; he looked down at it, and when he realized what his impulse had been he was horrified. He put the paper-weight on his papers again, but stood up. "I do not intend to discuss with you any of your lies, which you know are lies, and which had a purpose known to both of us." He stood there, shaken. "None of your lies," he repeated. "None of your filth here. Get out, Joe. Get out, before I start remembering what you made Willie suffer for months. I tell you, Joe, you've made a dangerous man out of me. Get out!"

But Jochen, though his grin had disappeared, and though he was no longer nonchalant, did not move.

"All right," he said, as if conceding the point. "We won't discuss the lady. I have the highest respect for her, myself. Whatever you had in mind about her, I'm sure she didn't agree with you. I told Willie that, so help me God. Isabel's heard me say it to Willie a dozen times. I have other witnesses. It's only you, and what you did to Willie, yourself."

Charles sat down. He held the edge of his desk in his hands, and his knuckles whitened. "Go on," he said. "I'm listening." There was something he should hear, he knew. When he had heard it he would call in two men, half a dozen men, and have Joe thrown bodily out of this building. He had only to wait a few minutes longer, and then he could act. Only a little more self-control, and it would be over.

Jochen was not deceived that he had intimidated Charles. He saw those blank dull eyes, that set and heavy mouth, and the deep flush that did not disappear. Here was a man who could kill. Jochen was a big man, but he pushed back his chair a few inches, and held all his muscles tight. He had seen Charles seize the paper-weight, and knew it had been Charles' first intention to smash it full in his face. Something had restrained Charles. It might not restrain him again. Jochen hesitated. Only the complete knowledge of his own desperate condition, his own conviction that Charles meant to throw him out of this company—his own company!—kept Jochen in his chair.

Jochen spoke rapidly, in the high-pitched voice of fear and rage: "I'll make it brief. That Sunday, when Willie died: he'd been at our house, and we'd had a talk. It was his determination, then, to help me get rid of you. I know it was; it was what you deserved. But I won't go into all that. Willie was convinced of your intentions about his wife." He paused. Charles only said: "Go on. I'm listening. But to save you time, I know all about it."

Jochen made himself raise a quizzical eyebrow. "Is that so? Well, it simplifies things then, but it also makes them more difficult for you. We arrived at Willie's house, and there was your car. How did you know he was home? Simple. Phyllis called you. Am I right?"

"Yes," said Charles.

"When we came into the house, Willie asked me to wait, and Phyllis went upstairs, alone. Then he asked you to go upstairs to the gallery with him. Right?"

"Right," said Charles.

"Now," Jochen went on, "I'm not going to pretend that I know what was said between you and Willie, alone up there in the gallery. But I can imagine what it was. Phyllis suddenly appeared on the stairs, after a long while, ahead of you both. You came down, hurrying. Willie came just behind you, or beside you, hurrying, too. I saw his face. If ever a man was close to murder, it was Willie. And you looked close to it, too. I can just imagine what you two said to each other up there!"

"Can you?" asked Charles. "But, go on."

"I'll do that! Then Willie caught up with you, on the stairs. You saw him. You reached out, when you saw him, and pushed him. He knew

what you were about to do, a split second before you did it. He yelled:
'Don't!' But you did, Charlie, you did. You threw him down the
stairs. And killed him. I saw you do it."

There was a sudden silence in the office. Charles did not break it.
Jochen waited, but Charles did not speak.

"So, you have it," said Jochen, almost desperately. "I saw the whole
thing. I've kept quiet, for the sake of all of us, you, me, our families,
the company. I never intended to mention it to you. Never, so help
me God. I never intend to speak of it to anyone, and again, so help
me God! Unless you go on with what you said you are going to do.
Then, I'll have to speak."

Charles thought: Phyllis! He felt no apprehension for himself. He
knew his law too well. His word against Jochen's. It wouldn't matter,
in the long run, even though nothing would ever come to court. He
would never be indicted; he would never be accused. But there was
Phyllis. Charles did not deceive himself that Jochen would not openly
denounce him. In his desperation, he would do this, even though he
must know that nothing would come of it in the way of harm to him,
Charles. It would be Phyllis who would suffer, always and only
Phyllis.

The lies had reached too deeply into the fabric of Andersburg.
Phyllis' name would be used freely, in the papers, in any preliminary
hearing during which Charles would be exonerated. Jochen would
use it.

They understood each other as they looked at each other. Jochen stood
up. He knew that Charles was paralyzed, that he had grasped everything.

"To use your own expression, Charles: 'So.' And so, Charlie, it'll be
you who'll be getting out of the company, not I. I'm giving you two
months, Charlie. I wouldn't have done this if you hadn't pushed me.
But it's you or me, Charlie; there's no compromise, now. Both of us
can't be in this company, together. I'll buy you out, Charlie."

He waited. Charles sat very still, bunched together in his chair.

"A fair price," said Jochen. "But not too fair." Then he stood up,
looked at Charles again, and walked rapidly out of the room.

Charles sat alone for a long time. The flush remained on his forehead
and about his eyes. He began to tap the edge of his desk. Finally, he
reached for his telephone and called Oliver Prescott.

A few minutes later he took his stiff straw hat and went out of the
office. He found Friederich in his own room. He closed the door and
leaned against it, willing himself to breathe normally.

"Yes?" cried Friederich, eagerly. "You've done it? You've told him to get out?"

"Yes," said Charles. "But there're some preliminaries. Fred, if Joe tries to speak to you, to lie to you, don't listen to him. You see, I have to leave the office for a couple of hours. When I come back, I'll tell you the whole story."

CHAPTER XLV

OLIVER PRESCOTT looked only once at Charles' face, and then said: "Don't say anything, Charlie. Just sit down a minute. I have to see old Scott about something. Oh, and in the meantime, how about some brandy?" He opened his desk drawer and brought out an old bottle and a brandy glass. Charles protested feebly, but Oliver poured the brandy with the air of a pleased connoisseur, held up the liquid to the bright sun, and nodded. "Here you are, Charlie. The best. We keep only the best for our best customers."

Charles took the brandy, and Oliver left the room. He was gone for at least five minutes. Charles sipped the brandy, though he was nauseated. In a moment or two the warmth of the liquor began to melt the stiff ice which seemed to have congealed in his stomach. He glanced absently about the big and impressive old room, which he had always liked. It was one of a series of rooms, old-fashioned, dignified, and breathing the ponderousness of law in the nineteenth century. Panelled wood, fireplace, shrouded windows, gas brackets on the walls now holding electric bulbs. This large suite of legal offices had once been called Scott, Meredith, Owens and Prescott. But only old Scott remained of the first three, with Oliver as his partner, an immensely rich ancient with the noblest reputation for immense integrity and aristocracy. Oliver occupied the office once used by Mr. Meredith. Mr. Scott, now in his eighties, acted as judge and counselor to Oliver in especially difficult cases. But he never appeared in court, leaving that to Oliver, who, armed with the old man's wisdom and advice, rarely lost a case.

Oliver came back, serious but smiling, accompanied by Mr. Scott. Charles stood up, holding his empty brandy glass. "How are you, dear Charles?" asked Mr. Scott, affectionately, holding out his little sinewy hand. He was a very small man, quiet and powerful yet frail, with the face of an old eagle. His wardrobe never changed; he wore a dark gray suit, a black silk tie with a black pearl stick-pin, and brilliantly polished boots with gaiters. His clothing might be anachronistic but his mind was as urbane and wise as it had ever been.

"I thought," said Oliver, "that as the matter you want to talk about, Charlie, sounded very grave, Mr. Scott ought to hear it, too."

"I didn't say," began Charles tactlessly. But Oliver was busily seating his distinguished old partner. Then Oliver refilled Charles' glass, after pouring one for Mr. Scott. He then poured a third glass for himself, and sat down.

"Ah," said Mr. Scott, smiling behind his glasses at Charles. "This is what I like. Gentlemen discussing important things in an atmosphere of ease—like gentlemen. None of this modern, hectic rush, in which significant details are overlooked only to be found again, unexpectedly and embarrassingly, in court. Even law has become superficial and tawdry in this age."

Charles' first annoyance at the presence of the old man immediately vanished. He had the middle-class man's aversion to having more than one witness to a terrible confidence, the middle-class man's caution at extending knowledge to too many. Now he realized how subtle Oliver was, and how valuable Mr. Scott's advice might be in this situation.

He began to talk, slowly and awkwardly at first, then more quickly. Mr. Scott watched him. When Charles showed evidence of excitement, or his voice shook, Mr. Scott would lift a calm hand, and say: "Please repeat that more slowly, Charles. Remember, my hearing isn't what it was. Besides, there was a little something there—" Charles would then repeat, more slowly and concisely, and the excitement that threatened to make him ill would retreat.

Both the young and the old man listened gravely, and without comment to Charles' story. In that unhurried atmosphere, carefully muffled from the noises of the street outside, or any sound of typewriters or opening and closing of doors, Charles began to relax. And as he did so, the sick terror and rage subsided in him. Mr. Scott sat very upright in his chair, his hands on the arms, his glasses twinkling in the subdued sunlight, his head cocked.

Finally, Charles had done. He had seen no expression of indignation or incredulity or doubt or censure on Mr. Scott's face. Nothing could have been calmer or more detached. It might have been a dull and routine story of some legal technicality which Charles had been expounding, for all the impression it had made upon Mr. Scott. He sat in silent thought, and Charles and Oliver waited. The old man tapped the arm of his chair.

"Well," he said, after long reflection. He then took out his watch.

"Dear me, past luncheon time. Charles, will you join Oliver and me in my little dining-room here? Just a very light repast, brought in from the Imperial Hotel."

Charles tried to feel anxiety and fear again, but the act of telling his story had relieved him. Mr. Scott rose, and the two younger men rose with him. I won't be able to eat a thing, thought Charles, until this is settled. But he ate a very good lunch, indeed, while Mr. Scott told some humorous stories of old and famous cases which he had handled in his earlier days. It was not for some time that Charles began to realize that the point of all these sharp and pungent anecdotes was that justice was invariably the victor, in the end.

It was half-past three before they returned to Oliver's office. But another ceremony had to take place. Mr. Scott's cigar had to be lighted, and Charles', while Oliver smoked a cigarette. It was cool here, for all the heat outside.

"Now," said Mr. Scott. "To return to your case, Charles." He coughed delicately. "If I were a modern lawyer, for instance, all brash sensationalism and melodrama, I'd stage a very theatrical trick. Mr. Jochen is very sly. He apparently is not anxious to have any witnesses to his accusations, for fear of prosecution for blackmail. He has been shrewd. Blackmail is a very serious crime in Pennsylvania, Charles. A very serious crime, with severe penalties. So, if I were a young and eager sprout of a modern lawyer, I'd advise you to call Mr. Jochen to another consultation, and have witnesses lurking behind every curtain, and notes taken, and then a grand finale of counter threats. All in the wonderful stage tradition, with a last brazen trumpet of triumph over the enemy." He coughed again, and shook his head. He looked at his cigar. "But, of course, there might be a witness, unknown to you and Mr. Jochen."

"There wasn't," said Charles.

Mr. Scott shook his head.

"One of the very first things a lawyer learns is that witnesses have a strange way of leaping up all over the place, when wanted, or not wanted," said Mr. Scott. "Murder in the dark, after midnight, in a forest. No one about, no footstep—everyone asleep. Then the case comes to court, and lo and behold! there are half a dozen witnesses. Apparently the distant community all had insomnia that particular night, and heard strange sounds, saw a figure flitting under the stars, heard a cry. Et cetera. Very disconcerting—or helpful, depending whether or not you are defending or prosecuting." He looked kindly at Charles. "Your chief clerk, Mr. Parker?"

"No," said Charles. "Parker never eavesdrops. Besides, he was in the shops. None of the other clerks, either. They are far down the hall, and have been trained to go about their business."

Mr. Scott watched the smoke curling up from his cigar, and Oliver was alerted. "I've been hearing a lot about your brother, Mr. Fred, Charles. Great improvement, very. Becoming pillar of the community; associated with Quakers, who all have our deepest respect. Wonderful, dignified people, whose word is never doubted. Rumor that Mr. Fred is to marry Miss Hadden. Have heard many approving comments about him, Charles."

"Fred didn't hear a word," said Charles, flatly. "He is the soul of honor. It would never occur to him to eavesdrop, never. No matter how much it concerned him. And I've also never known him to tell a lie. Not even when a lie would have saved him a thrashing, when he was a kid. He's absolutely incapable of it."

"Of course," said Mr. Scott. "Everyone knows that. That is why he would make a valuable witness, if he had overheard anything. You may not remember, but I imagine neither your brother nor you spoke in very hushed voices. And Mr. Fred's office is not too far away from your own, I gather. It is just possible that he did overhear something which might be of importance."

"I saw him before I left the office," said Charles. "If Fred, during the fight between Joe and me, had heard a single sentence, he would have been so aroused that he would have come charging in on Joe."

It was hopeless. But Mr. Scott was looking at Oliver. "One should never overlook a possibility," he murmured. "Definitely not. A little discussion between you and Mr. Fred, Oliver? Ah, yes. In the meantime, however, suppose Charles' story be typed out so that Mr. Fred could glance over it, in the very probable event he had heard anything, and could throw a little corroboration our way."

"He never heard a thing," Charles repeated. "I know he didn't. Typed out? The whole thing?"

"Don't worry, Charlie," said Oliver, who was smiling slightly. "I'll type it out, myself. No one else will read it except you and Fred—and you'll sign it—"

"Sign it!" exclaimed Charles, with loathing and alarm.

"Don't be so frightened and so middle-class," said Oliver. "It'll be filed away, in my own safe, and after it's served its purpose I'll give it to you and you can destroy it."

"Served its purpose?" Charles repeated, baffled. But Mr. Scott was rising. He put his hand on Charles' shoulder. "It's really very odd how there almost always is a witness about, my boy." He turned to Oliver. "While Charles' statement is being typed by you, Oliver, Mr. Fred could be on his way here, after Charles has called him." He walked out, in his majesty.

Oliver held out the telephone to Charles, but Charles, very red, balked. "I can't stand Fred knowing anything about this, Oliver. It makes me sick. Fred's an innocent—"

But Oliver held out the telephone. "We can't overlook anything. Charlie, we must investigate everything." So Charles called Friederich, who was very excited at hearing his brother's reluctant voice. "Oliver Prescott's?" repeated Friederich. "What is it, Karl? What is it?"

"Just a consultation," said Charles, impatiently. "But a very important one. Just slip out. Don't tell anyone where you're going." He hung up. "I tell you, Oliver, Fred doesn't know anything, never heard a word. It's humiliating—I'd rather he didn't know."

Oliver gave Charles a magazine devoted to hunting and fishing. Then he went out with his few notes. Silence and peace brooded in the large quiet office. Charles was at first in a turmoil, but after a few minutes a fatalistic numbness clouded his thoughts. Half an hour went by. Then Oliver, holding a long sheet of paper, entered with Friederich, who was bristling with agitation and impatience.

"Karl, you're alone," he said, accusingly. He swung to Oliver. "Why did you keep me waiting, when I might have been here talking to my brother, and learning what he has to say? All this mystery!"

"I think Charles was talking with Mr. Scott," said Oliver, smoothly. "Besides, he isn't feeling well, and I thought he ought to be alone to collect his thoughts."

Charles glanced at Oliver sharply, but Oliver was making the twitching Friederich comfortable in the best chair. Then the younger man sat down, smiling easily, as if this were only the most casual meeting of friends. Charles' stomach tightened again; he began to sweat as he looked at the paper on Oliver's desk. He wouldn't sign it; God damn, if he'd sign that degrading story. He said: "Oliver, I don't want Fred to read that. I can't have it—"

This was exactly what Oliver wished him to say. He raised his eyebrows, looked wonderingly at Charles, and then at the tense Friederich. "You don't want your brother, your fellow officer and director and co-owner of the Wittmann Machine Tool Company, to know anything so important to his own interests?"

"What's this? What's this?" cried Friederich, filled with the deepest suspicions. "Karl, are you trying to hide things from me again, after all your promises?"

A trick, thought Charles, fuming. Oliver was smiling. Charles said: "It's a personal matter, Fred."

"I disagree," said Oliver. "And if you are right, Charlie, I'm sure you can trust your brother. Can't you?"

"Of course I can," said Charles, angrily.

"Then let him be the judge. Don't change your mind now, Charlie. You, yourself, called Mr. Fred, you remember."

He turned to Friederich, who was regarding Charles with darkly sparkling eyes of reawakened distrust. Charles wanted to get up and leave the room. But God only knew what Oliver might say. Charles checked his rising movement. Oliver held out the paper to Friederich, who was fumbling with his spectacles. "One thing, Mr. Fred. I must ask you to make no comment whatever until you have finished reading this. My object in showing you Charlie's statement is that I believe you, as an important member of the Wittmann Company, ought to know what threatens your company and you, and another object is to see if you overheard anything of this story—inadvertently, of course."

"Overheard?" said Fred.

"You didn't—" Charles began, but Oliver interrupted deftly. "Sometimes it isn't possible to prevent overhearing, Mr. Fred. Then one forgets, until one hears the story again. And then any information is of the most vital importance. Most vital," he repeated, catching Friederich's eye and holding it. "A witness in this case would be invaluable, and would stop everything in its tracks. Without such a witness, even an eavesdropper—accidentally, of course, I can't tell you to what lengths your brother, Jochen, will go."

Friederich stared at Oliver.

"Jochen could ruin all of you," Oliver continued. "Charlie's told me you know the whole story of his plottings against your company, with Mr. Brinkwell. This, I believe, and know, is the final act of the plot. So, you can see how terribly necessary it is for us to know if you heard a single phrase." And he gave the paper to Friederich.

These lawyers, thought Charles, bitterly. They never overlook anything. He sat back in his chair, heat spreading over his face again as Friederich began to read. He watched his brother. After the first few sentences, Friederich sat up, rigidly. The paper began to shake in his hands. He turned it towards the light, holding it almost up to his nose. His face began to jerk, to color, to pale, to assume expressions of incredulity, disgust, excitement, fury. Charles tried to speak, once or twice, but Oliver, with a stern look, repressed him, and held up his hand. The moments ticked away, and no one said a word. Friederich did not utter a single exclamation, and this seemed very strange to Charles.

Then, still without speaking, Friederich placed the paper on Oliver's desk. But he continued to look at it, hunched up in his chair, his body bent forward. His eyebrows twitched, his forehead wrinkled, his face became darkly red, his mouth moved, he inclined his head, straightened it, bent it again, as if conducting a conversation with someone. He did not glance at Charles, or even at Oliver.

"You see," said Oliver, gently, "how important it is for us to know if you overheard anything."

Charles said again: "You didn't—" Oliver said: "Charlie, I must ask you not to speak, to interfere with a possible witness, who might be able to save you and your company. We only want the truth. If you insist upon interrupting, I must ask you to leave me alone with your brother."

Friederich continued to stare at the paper, and no one spoke. Some enormous struggle was going on in the poor man. Charles felt compassion for him. He had only one thought, now, and that was to try to extricate his brother from this situation.

Friederich began to shiver, as if cold. He opened his mouth. No sound came from it. He tried again, and his voice was hoarse and low. Then he lifted a shaking finger and put it on a paragraph. He said: "I—I didn't hear all of it. I knew Karl was going to tell Jochen to get out. It—it was all arranged, between Karl and me. I heard the first part between Karl and Jochen, because I was there, in the room. Karl knows. And then Jochen asked me to leave, and Karl asked me, too. So, I went out."

He still did not look at either of the men. He was swallowing, painfully. His ears were scarlet. He went on, even more hoarsely: "I— I know all Jochen's tricks. He's a bad man. No one can trust him. But, I went into my office, and closed the door. I knew Karl could take care of everything, without me."

Charles sighed, in relief. Oliver frowned.

"And you heard nothing of this very important attempt at blackmail, Mr. Fred?" And then he was no longer frowning, for Friederich's misery became even more evident. His finger was still on one paragraph. He spoke again: "It was a long time. Then I began to be uneasy. I wondered what—what was happening, and if—if Karl needed me. And I wanted to know what had been happening. So—" and he bent his head even lower, "so I went back to Karl's office. The door was still shut. I wondered if Jochen had gone. So I put my ear—my ear— up against the door. And"—now he looked up desperately at Oliver— "I—I heard that."

Charles sat up. But Friederich refused to look at him. Oliver read the paragraph:

" 'So, though readily admitting that he, himself, Jochen Wittmann, had no real or serious grounds for his false accusation, and that his fabricated story would be used only against me, Charles Wittmann, in the event I did not submit to his blackmail—' "

"But, he never said—" said Charles.

Oliver read louder: " '—he, Jochen Wittmann, then said, quote: It'll be you who'll be getting out of the company, not I. I'm giving you two months, Charlie.' " Oliver looked at Charles: "He said that, didn't he? It's in your statement."

"That part, yes," admitted Charles angrily. "But not—"

Friederich said: "I heard that whole—that whole paragraph. Yes. Jochen admitted it was all lies, but said his word was as good as Karl's, in any court." He paused. "There was something else, which isn't in here. Jochen said, and I overheard him, that he'd get Brinkwell to help him with—with stories about Karl, too, because Brinkwell wanted the Wittmann Machine Tool Company."

Charles was aghast. His mouth fell open. Then he shouted: "Fred! That's not true, and you know it!"

Friederich turned to him, fiercely. "Don't try to protect Jochen, Karl, from any scandal. You always played it safe and cautiously, didn't you? But this time I'll tell the truth, myself."

Charles was dumfounded. Oliver said: "You wish to sign a statement as to what you heard, Mr. Fred?"

"Yes!" cried Friederich, with a zealot's fervor.

Oliver smiled broadly. "With two such statements to show to Jochen, nothing will come of all this. He'll be so afraid of prosecution that he'll never open his mouth again. What's that, Charlie? You don't want the truth to come out about him, even at the risk of the destruction of your company, and your own ruin? You'd defend Jochen even against Mr. Fred?"

Charles shouted again: "I won't have—"

Friederich exclaimed: "And you promised me you'd trust me, and that I could trust you, Karl! Is this your trust? How can I go on trusting you, under these circumstances?"

"You know damn well, Fred—"

"I know what I heard, Karl." The poor man's eyes were shining fanatically. "You've forgotten about me, haven't you? I have a stake in this company. And—and you're my brother. The only one I ever trusted."

"I just don't want you to perjure yourself," said Charles, with a savage glance at Oliver. "You don't know what these lawyers are in court. They'd crucify you, Fred."

"It'll never come to court. No one will need to see these papers, Charlie, but Jochen. Then he'll run like mad. I promise you that. No perjury. Are you accusing Mr. Fred of deliberately intending to perjure himself?"

"I told you the truth, in that statement, Oliver!" said Charles furiously. "And nothing else. Fred didn't overhear anything. Joe didn't say what Fred said."

Oliver lifted the telephone, and asked his secretary to request Mr. Scott to come into the office. In the meantime, while Charles sat impotently glaring at him, Oliver wrote out Friederich's statement by hand, very swiftly. He's afraid to leave me alone with old Fred, thought Charles. He tried to catch Friederich's eye, but his brother had half-turned his back upon him, a stiff back full of resolution and denial. Mr. Scott entered, and greeted Friederich, whom he knew slightly, with calm interest and kindness. Oliver finally finished his writing, held out the sheet to Friederich, and presented him with his pen. Friederich rapidly read what had been written. Then he lifted the pen.

"Wait," said Charles. "Fred, I can fight my own battles. I don't want you to do this to yourself."

Friederich signed the paper with a defiant flourish, pushed it towards Oliver. Oliver, then, with the utmost gravity, presented Mr. Scott with the two papers. It's no use, thought Charles. Then he began to smile, in spite of himself. Fred, who less than a year ago would have believed anything of him, who would not have said or done a single thing to help him!

Mr. Scott read both papers serenely, murmuring once or twice, and nodding his head. Then he carefully folded the papers and held them. "I think it would be in order, Oliver, to request Mr. Jochen Wittmann to see me, personally, and immediately, in my own office. I shall ask my secretary to call him for me at once. In the meantime, may I suggest that Charles and Friederich remain here with you until the conclusion of this unfortunate affair? I expect it won't take very long."

"I don't want to see Jochen," said Friederich, excitedly.

"Certainly not. He is not even to know you are here." Then Mr.

Scott did a rare thing. He went to Friederich, and held out his hand. "Friederich," he said, "it is seldom a lawyer meets a man of integrity, and principle."

Friederich was confused, his ears reddening again. He took Mr. Scott's hand. His eyes wrinkled as he watched the old man leave the room. Charles looked at him, and he was suddenly and intensely moved. He forgot Oliver, and said to his brother: "Fred, Mr. Scott is right. I've been a fool all my life." He looked more closely at Friederich, and said, without thinking: "I've always been told you resemble me. But all at once I see you resemble our father more than anyone else in the family."

Friederich's profile softened, smiled. He turned to Charles, and said, eagerly: "Thank you, Karl, thank you!"

"I'll never forget this, Friederich," said Charles, and he spoke in German. "It was a noble thing to do."

Friederich smiled at him fully. "I always prefer the truth," he said. "But you are so careful, Karl. If the truth will not serve, one must use equivocation."

"This," said Oliver, "definitely calls for a toast." And he took out three glasses. "Fred doesn't drink," said Charles. Friederich hesitated only a moment, then he held his glass to his mouth, and remarked: "Karl knows so many things about me which are not true." And he drank, and to Charles' astonishment did not even cough, though he poured the liquor quickly down his throat and struggled unsuccessfully with a grimace. He put the glass on Oliver's desk with a fine gesture of triumph. No one smiled.

Oliver came around his desk and solemnly shook hands with Friederich. Then Charles shook hands with him. The two men slapped Friederich upon the back with great vigor. Charles felt quite heady, and loved both his brother and his friend. He was almost exhilarated. He decided he loved the whole world, except, of course, for a few people.

Nearly an hour went by, and no one noticed it. It was half-past six when the door opened and Mr. Scott returned. He was smiling quite genially. He glanced at each suddenly sober face, and said at once: "It is perfectly all right, gentlemen. I have talked to Mr. Jochen. He has just left. And he tells me that you will have his resignation tomorrow, Charles."

Charles said: "What did he say?"

With something close to airiness, Mr. Scott replied: "Very little. Quite a reasonable man, after all. I did not expect it of him, to be frank. He merely read the papers, then put them down. I then explained to him the penalties for attempted blackmail. A realist. I believe he said something about a man knowing when he was beaten. And, if he was a little bitter, at moments, that is understandable."

Friederich, in his innocence, accepted this, and nodded seriously. Oliver smiled. But Charles, without knowing the reason, felt a great and heavy sickness.

Oliver took Charles home first in his automobile, and then drove off with Friederich. Charles went into the warm dim house, and as he did so the weight of the hot and uproarious day fell on him, and all his wretchedness and flatness and fear. Jimmy greeted him with reserve, then, seeing his father's face, came close to him. Charles shut his eyes. "It's all over, Jim," he said. "Joe's out. Everything's finished. It turned out well, after all. No need to worry."

He sat down, and Jim took his hat. There was a heavy scent of roses in the room, too pressing. Mrs. Meyers, who was a sentimental woman, had taken to putting a bowl of fresh flowers every day under Wilhelm's Picasso. "I wish she'd stop that," said Charles, glancing at the fiery red blooms. "Willie wouldn't like it."

"Oh, yes," said Jimmy, trying to hide his concern for his father. "It's exactly what he'd like. You didn't know much about Uncle Willie, Dad."

Charles reflected on this. He said, at last: "That's true. I'm afraid I never knew much about anything, and still don't know very much."

Three days later the *Clarion* published a very flattering photograph of Jochen Wittmann on its front page, and announced that Mr. Wittmann had resigned from the Wittmann Machine Tool Company to become assistant superintendent of the Connington Steel Company, under Mr. Roger Brinkwell. "My father's company remains in the able hands of my two brothers, Charles and Friederich," said Mr. Wittmann, when interviewed. Andersburg was extremely excited over this news.

PART FIVE

But 'twas a famous victory.
—THE BATTLE OF BLENHEIM.

CHAPTER XLVI

ON JULY 28th, Austria-Hungary, with a flourish of heroic trumpets, declared war on Serbia. On August 1st, the Kaiser solemnly pronounced that Germany was at war with Russia; on August 3rd France was at war with Germany; Germany with Belgium, Great Britain with Germany, on August 4th; Austria-Hungary with Russia, and Serbia with Germany, on August 6th; France with Austria-Hungary and Great Britain with Austria-Hungary, on August 12th.

Armageddon had begun.

"By the Grace of God—" said Emperor Nicholas of Russia.

"A fateful hour," said Kaiser Wilhelm of Germany. "Remember that the German people are the chosen of God—"

"Great fleets in battle, London hears mine sinks British cruiser, 131 lives lost," reported the New York *World* of August 7th.

Terror, agony, death and hate leapt from a million guns in Europe. Armies marched, invaded, murdered, were murdered. Europe spurted into flame.

New York newspapers roared with headlines. The American people were only mildly interested. Something was always going on in Europe. But there were so many more important things to consider at home. After all, the baseball season was in full glory, Colonel Roosevelt's reported illness was causing much concern, Billy Sunday was raving in his huge wooden tabernacles, the "Perils of Pauline" were being excitedly followed in the moving picture houses every Saturday, and Mrs. Niver, unofficial censor of Hollywood, had sternly pronounced that "one yard of film is enough for a kiss." A debate was raging pro and con the feminine corset, various States were voting for Prohibition, and it was rumored that the new Reo runabout was a serious threat to the Ford. The New York newspapers frenziedly reported the progress of the war, but in the hinterland crops were discussed, there was not enough rain or too much rain, the tariff was being cursed or applauded, and there was much indignation over the slit in the long tight skirts of the women. A particularly horrible murder in Chicago— "a crime of passion"—occupied the thoughts and the secret gloatings of millions of readers. Wheat was seventy-five cents a bushel, and there was a tremendous feeling, all over the country, that a new epoch of prosperity had suddenly manifested itself in America.

On August 19th, the President urged that the American people be "impartial" towards the war. The people looked at each other vaguely. "Impartial" about what? Who cared?

Andersburg was no more interested in the war than the rest of the country. If the war was mentioned, it was only spoken of to fill uncomfortable pauses in conversation when entertaining guests. The citizens of Andersburg were happy in the new prosperity brought to the city by the Connington Steel Company. Their interest and speculations centered on the reasons why Joe Wittmann had left his father's company to be assistant to Mr. Brinkwell. Of course, everyone said, it was obvious and he was doing much better for himself at the Connington. "But money isn't everything," said those who had so much money, themselves, that the lack of money in the pockets of others was a matter of no importance.

No one asked why the Connington Steel Company thundered day and night, or what were the products being produced in the great mills. It was enough that unemployment had disappeared, and that the shops were crowded with new faces, and that a building "boom" was on, and that, suddenly, everyone's pockets were jingling. There was a very titillating rumor, too, that Joe Wittmann was now attending the very fashionable Episcopalian church patronized by the Brinkwells.

No, no one thought or cared about the war very much, except Charles and Friederich Wittmann, the Reverend Mr. Haas of the First Lutheran Church, Oliver Prescott and the Haddens, Father Hagerty, and Ralph Grimsley, of the *Clarion*. They thought of little else, and with fear and despair.

In middle August Charles went with Jim to a mountain "lodge" and fished and boated with his son, held long conversations with him about unimportant things, and grew paler and thinner. They did not speak of the war. Jim knew that he must not allow his father to speak of it. He quarrelled with Charles about his loss of appetite, or exulted over the fish they caught. He shared a room with his father, and heard him sighing and turning in the night. The boy pretended to sleep. He told himself the war had nothing to do with them. And he listened in the night to Charles' sighing, or woke Charles when the latter groaned aloud in nightmare. Nothing to do with us, Jim thought over and over, and looked at his father's dinner plate, and talked about baseball and his cousin Geraldine.

When, during the night, Charles got up and stood beside his son's bed, like a terrified ghost, Jimmy feigned sleep, and breathed long and regular breaths. But they never spoke of the war.

They returned to the city, Jim brown and full of vitality and spirits. There were several letters from Phyllis, from San Francisco, Los Angeles, Phoenix, Chicago. Affectionate letters. Mrs. Holt and she were returning home on September 1st. Phyllis did not mention the war, either. She was homesick for Andersburg. Such careful letters, sprightly and casual. Charles read them, and knew what Phyllis was thinking. He put them aside, wearily. He could not think of Phyllis now.

Where was the Germany of Goethe and Schiller and Lessing, of Beethoven and Brahms and Bach, of slumbrous old German cities, of the Grimm Brothers, of poetry and song and philosophy and romantic legend? Had Kant ever lived there? What was this Germany of the "mailed fist," and "the chosen people," and "the Lord's Anointed," and the rape of Belgium? What was this Germany of the mad voice, of the goose-step, of the Uhlans, of the murderers, of the assassins of Liege?

But the madness was not Germany's alone, nor the guilt. Did the men of Europe, in the red nights, ever cry out to their God: "Mea culpa"? Charles was sure they did not.

On August 29th, as he sat in his hot office, he had a visitor.

Mr. Henry J. Dayton. And in small type at the left: The Amalgamated Steel Company, Pittsburgh, Pa. Charles sat and looked at the smooth white card. Then he rang his bell for Mr. Parker. "Send Mr. Friederich in," he said. "Then, in five minutes I'll see Mr. Dayton."

He had told Friederich about Colonel Grayson alias Mr. Lord. He had told him of the colonel's last visit. Friederich had listened, with that new and silent intensity of his, which was now without excitement or hysteria. Friederich had said: "We'll wait. We can do nothing but wait. And then we'll see, Karl."

Friederich entered the office and Charles gave him Mr. Dayton's card. "It's come, Fred. We've got to decide."

He half expected, in spite of everything, that Friederich would become vehement. But Friederich sat down, staring at the card in his hand, and only the muscles along his lean jaw tightened. He said, as he had said weeks ago: "We'll see, Karl. Let him talk."

Mr. Parker ushered Mr. Dayton into the office, and the two brothers did not get up. They only looked at the quiet slender man with the white mustache and the bright quick eyes. If Charles and Friederich disconcerted him with their silent hostilitiy he did not show it. He looked from one to the other and said: "Mr. Charles Wittmann?"

"I'm Charles Wittmann," said Charles. "And this is my brother Friederich."

Mr. Dayton hesitated. He sat down, uninvited. There was a certain repelling stolidity about Charles Wittmann, he saw, and even about the thinner brother. But his business was grave and very important. He said: "Mr. Lord has suggested I see you, Mr. Wittmann."

Charles Wittmann, he saw, was afraid, and the colonel had told him why. A stubborn hard-headed man: but he was afraid. Mr. Dayton glanced quickly at Friederich. An excitable man, he decided, for all his silence. Excitable men were less stubborn than frightened men, but, also, they were harder to convince. Mr. Dayton knew all about the Wittmanns.

He said: "I'll come to the point, Mr. Wittmann. I think you know why I'm here. A mutual friend has already told you." He looked at Charles, because he knew Charles was frightened. "We'd like to have you lease us some of your patents. Especially your aeroplane steering control assembly. And as soon as possible."

It was Friederich who said: "For whom?"

Mr. Dayton opened his brief case and took out a paper. He named some of the Wittmann patents, as well as the aeroplane steering control assembly.

"For whom?" repeated Friederich.

"Not for Germany," said Mr. Dayton.

"For England, or France, or Russia," said Friederich.

"I'm not at liberty to say," Mr. Dayton protested. He tried to smile. The brothers regarded him doggedly.

"Germany," said Friederich, "has ships. This is a neutral country. Why not for Germany, then?"

Mr. Dayton stroked his mustache.

"If we refuse arms for Germany, then we are no longer neutral," Friederich said. "We have become active participants in a war which does not concern us."

"It does concern us, Mr. Wittmann," said Mr. Dayton. "Or it will, eventually."

"Mr. Wilson," said Charles, "has urged the American people to be strictly neutral. I consider," said Charles, "that any company, such as yours, which manufactures war material is violating Mr. Wilson's express wishes. I prefer to follow Mr. Wilson's command. Therefore—"

Mr. Dayton interrupted. He knew that when men like Charles Wittmann were allowed to refuse anything they would stick obstinately by
that refusal. So he said: "The President's wishes will be respected. We
have no intention of violating them. In fact, I can say that they will
be obeyed." Again, he looked from one brother to the other. "By helping—say, one certain country—we can protect our neutrality absolutely.
We can protect ourselves."

Friederich snorted. Now his eyes were afire. "We can put ourselves
in the position of cowards who arm one man against another, then
protest that the quarrel does not concern us. That is hypocrisy, sir.
Shall we just be frank and say that America simply wants to sell arms
to one nation for profits—to the highest bidder?"

Mr. Dayton reflected. How much should these obstinate men know?
He said: "There is really no morality in war, Mr. Wittmann. War
and morality are a contradiction in terms. But let me put it this way:
there are companies in America which are selling war material to
Germany, either directly, or through subsidiaries in every country in
Europe. Yes, even the French steel companies are arming Germany,
right at this minute; coal is being shipped from French mines to Germany, direct through the ranks of the armies. British patents are being
freely used in Germany, and German patents in England. Between
munitions makers there is no quarrel. There never was. I have just recently heard that Russia has received some very excellent patents from
Germany, and within a week after war was declared between the two
countries. French bankers and Austrian bankers are giving credits to
each other, and Swedish ships, carrying excellent Swedish ore, are
passing without hindrance into German ports, while British men-of-
war stand at a discreet distance. Yes. I repeat: war knows no morality."

"And you ask us to enter into a similar infamous agreement?" cried
Friederich.

Mr. Dayton sighed. He took a pipe from his pocket and slowly filled
it. Trouble darkened his face.

"Infamous," he repeated, as if to himself. "Yes."

Charles said only one word: "No."

He had been permitted to say the word. Mr. Dayton put the pipe in
his mouth and carefully lit it. He said, after a few puffs: "I think the
Amalgamated Steel Company was the only large concern in America
which did not help arm any faction in Mexico. I think that answers
your question, Mr. Wittmann." He looked at Friederich.

"So?" said Charles.

Mr. Dayton glanced at the door. There was no help for it. He said:

"The Amalgamated Steel Company will not help any combatant in Europe. We've been told we are quixotic, quite unlike, for instance, the Connington Steel Company, which is sending material to Germany."

Charles turned in his chair, and his eyes met Friederich's. Friederich's sallow face became a darker hue. He wilted.

"We believe in preparedness, Mr. Wittmann," said Mr. Dayton, looking at Charles.

"For what?" exclaimed Friederich. But Charles got up, slowly and heavily, and walked to the window. He stood there, his hands in his pockets, and stared out.

"Preparedness," Charles heard Mr. Dayton say, "is quite often the surest guarantee against attack. We're down to raw fundamentals, now. We must be prepared." He hesitated. "There's madness loose in the world."

Charles said, still looking sightlessly through the window: "Mr. Wilson hasn't said that."

Mr. Dayton dropped his voice: "Mr. Wilson is very frightened. What he says in public is not what he says in private."

Charles turned from the window. "You are trying to tell us that these patents of ours will not be used to help any combatant, but will be held in reserve for America." There were deep furrows in his face.

Mr. Dayton looked at him. Then, very slightly, he nodded.

Charles sat down. He looked at Mr. Dayton directly. "You believe we'll need these patents. You believe we'll get into this hellish thing."

"I didn't say so, Mr. Wittmann. But I do say: I hope not."

"And I say," continued Charles, "that we must have a solemn guarantee that none of our patents will be used to arm any combatant."

Mr. Dayton's lower teeth nibbled at his mustache. "Even if events force Mr. Wilson to agree to the arming of any—combatant?"

"Yes!" cried Friederich.

But Charles said: "It isn't possible that Mr. Wilson will be forced into anything but absolute neutrality."

"If we ever are betrayed into arming England and her allies, then we'll be in the war," said Friederich. "The Kaiser will be forced to regard us as an enemy in fact."

"If events become so dangerous that our own safety is threatened— yes," replied Mr. Dayton. "But by that time the Kaiser will have committed an overt act against us."

"He can be provoked into that 'overt act,'" said Friederich, bitterly. "England can provoke him against America. She's done such things before. Do you trust England, Mr. Dayton?"

"No," said Mr. Dayton, quietly. "I don't. But we are now faced with the frightful facts of reality. We must be prepared. That is our only safety."

Friederich had become wildly excited. "Look at what England is doing now! She is permitting Americans to use her passenger liners to England! And she is carrying war materials in their holds. Americans are being utilized by her as hostages. She believes that the Kaiser will never dare to order those liners torpedoed, because that might provoke American intervention." He shook a finger in Mr. Dayton's face. "And I say that if Germany becomes desperate enough, and if Americans, in their stupidity, still embark on British passenger liners, those liners will be torpedoed!"

"There is that danger, yes," admitted Mr. Dayton. "The President has warned American tourists. But we must remember that the Hague Convention has upheld the freedom of the seas."

"Why doesn't our Government refuse to permit Americans to embark on British liners?" asked Charles.

Friederich turned to him furiously. "Because we have rascals here who wish us to be embroiled in this war—for their own profit!"

Mr. Dayton shook his head. "No. We must uphold the freedom of the seas. It is a point of honor."

"More men have died for 'honor' than have been saved by it," said Charles.

Then no one spoke. Friederich's face was crimson. His fingers beat rapidly on Charles' desk. Charles sagged in his chair. Mr. Dayton looked at the pipe he held in his hand.

Then Charles said: "Speaking of 'honor'— We have your word of honor, your guarantee, that no patent of ours would ever be used either for England or for Germany?"

Friederich exclaimed: "Karl! You are not actually considering—"

Charles said to him: "Fred, if we are prepared, if we have time to be prepared, then no one will attack us."

Mr. Dayton said to Charles: "You have our word of honor, our guarantee."

Friederich jumped to his feet. "There is no honor among thieves! Karl, I will not permit this!"

"We've no other choice," said Charles, sternly. "I don't know what's going to happen. But we can't remain defenseless." He said to Mr. Dayton: "I have another condition: those patents are not to be used until the President himself admits we are in danger, or if we are about to break off diplomatic relations with Germany."

Mr. Dayton stood up. Friederich retreated from him, in impotent rage and detestation. "You shall have that guarantee in writing, Mr. Wittmann."

He held out his hand. Friederich made a gesture of refusal. But Charles shook Mr. Dayton's hand briefly.

"Karl!" cried Friederich. "You've betrayed us!"

"No," said Charles, shaking his head over and over. "We were all betrayed, long ago."

CHAPTER XLVII

The thunder and lightning and storm which tore at the heart of Europe echoed about the White House. Mr. Wilson petulantly, and with secret terror, ignored it. He became more and more absorbed in his program which he had called the "New Freedom." He sponsored a bill reorganizing the banking structure of the country into the Federal Reserve system; he castigated the "Money Trust" in the rounded and eloquent periods of a naïve pedant. In well-bred accents, he denounced "unfair" methods of competition in business and industry. He was preoccupied with the Sherman Anti-Trust law of 1890. He concentrated on lower tariffs, in a world no longer passionately interested in tariffs. He had begun all these things before the war; now, almost hysterical, he pressed Congress to enact all the new and radical panaceas for society of which he had dreamed.

In the meantime, the civilization of Europe dropped, stone by stone, wall by wall, into the fiery seas of hell.

It was not until the last of August, 1914, that the American people, concentrating on all the things which had the desperate attention of their President, became uneasy. Even the most insular began to feel the reverberations of the earthquakes which were rocking the world. Half of the newspapers screamed that it was none of the affair of America; the other half screamed that it was most certainly the affair of America. It was impossible, any longer, to ignore the fact that something had changed in the world, had shifted, that America, whether she wished it or not, was being tilted towards the abyss. The cities began to stir; the countryside murmured. No one knew what this unease was, this quickened movement, this sound of a million voices in the night. The people looked at the photographs of the devastations of Belgium and Alsace, the aeroplanes, the men-of-war, the marching troops of Germany and England and France and Austria-Hungary and Russia and Serbia. One by one, they read of new declarations of war daily.

This happened in Andersburg, also, and Charles was one of the first to see it.

Charles was a man slow to anger and to resentment, but once having become angry and resentful he was unable to free himself easily. He kept to his resolution not to borrow money from the banks, remembering old Mr. Heinz. So, he approached Mr. Holt, who at once, and with pleasure, offered to lend him the money with which to buy out Jochen. Without interest. But Charles never accepted favors. He put up his own stock in the Wittmann Machine Tool Company as collateral. He insisted on full interest. He valued the friendship of the Holts, and would not jeopardize that friendship by accepting a favor which would put him in an inferior position.

Charles had always been very popular in Andersburg, not only with men in his own class, but with all workers and the very wealthy. He was "sound." He was just. He was logical and honorable and trustworthy. He had, personally, preferred his own middle class above any other. But, through Wilhelm, and then through the Holts, he had become greatly admired by the "well-bred" and financially opulent of the city.

Though not conscious of "race," and openly ridiculing it, he had felt more at ease with those of German stock, like himself. He liked German cooking, German uprightness, German solidity. All these things had always been part of his life, and he had never been self-conscious about them, or given them much thought. The newer friends on the mountains had English and Celtic names; they had had different backgrounds. They were Americans, but their traditions were British.

All through August he had been preoccupied with his personal problems, his fears, his dreads, his alarms, and his business. It was not until the end of August that he became aware of the change about him.

It was very subtle, and at first he thought it was his imagination, or because he was abstracted and concerned only with his own affairs. He met his newer friends on the streets, friends with the English and the Celtic names, and they were polite, but cool, to him. He began to wonder if he had offended them in some way, and remembered that he had refused some invitations.

One-third of the congregation of the First Lutheran Church was of English stock. These people had drifted into the church years ago, be-

cause it was a fine church and the Reverend Mr. Haas was an eloquent pastor, and there was a certain éclat in belonging to the congregation, which was composed mainly of the middle-class element. Mr.
Haas believed more in the spirit of the Law than the letter, and his
sermons had never been dogmatic. There was no obvious reason, then,
that by the end of August, 1914, that segment of the congregation
composed of non-German stock should have begun to melt away perceptibly. There was no reason why Mr. Bartlett, one of the members
of the Church Board, should have resigned with the vague excuse that
his health was none too excellent.

Had the congregation which melted away not immediately joined
the Episcopalian, the Presbyterian, the Baptist, and Methodist churches
in the vicinity, no one would have remarked upon this phenomenon.
But they did. Mr. Bartlett became Secretary of the First Presbyterian
Church of Andersburg. Mr. Bartlett, meeting Charles once at the
Imperial Hotel during luncheon, nodded to him coldly, then turned
his back upon him. Charles was disturbed.

Charles, as President of the Board, noticed that the roster of new
names was growing in his church. They were all German names. It
was nothing, of course. But one Sunday he went to the rectory and
talked about the matter with Mr. Haas.

"Are our old people moving out of the neighborhood, or something?" he asked.

Mr. Haas looked at him sadly. "No, Charles," he answered. "Something is happening. The war. German-Americans, in spite of all that
Mr. Wilson has been saying, are becoming unpopular."

Charles was shocked and incredulous. "People can't be such fools!"
he exclaimed.

Mr. Haas smiled sadly. "Folly has never been a minor vice of humanity's," he said.

"I haven't heard anyone speaking highly of England or France,"
protested Charles, unwilling to believe.

"Neither have I, Charles. But something ugly is stirring. Look at
this." And he gave Charles a cheap sheet of paper, a letter which had
been addressed to him anonymously: "Dirty German! We don't want
you in America. Go back to your Kaiser and your Vaterland!"

"It wouldn't matter so much, but our old people, of German stock,
are becoming defensive and truculent," said Mr. Haas. "That's natural,
when you're attacked. They've never thought of themselves as being
Germans. They were Americans, part of everything which was American. Now they are insisting that the schools teach German again.

They are singing hymns in German, a rusty German, and uncertain. Some of them have asked me to revive old German Christmas customs. Some of them have bought pictures of the Kaiser and hung them prominently in their houses, though they've always hated and ridiculed everything that was European-German. They're afraid. Poor people. They are not to blame. The guilt lies with their enemies."

"But they've been Americans, and Americans only, for three, four, and even five generations!" said Charles. "They know nothing of Germany. Many of their ancestors fought in the Civil War; some of them, themselves, fought in the Spanish-American War."

Mr. Haas smiled wearily. "Yes. We know that. But there's something else we must remember. I'm a minister, but I've never believed in the sweetness and light of the human animal. Men wish to hate; it's part of their nature. They wish to oppress, to be cruel, to be savage, to attack. That urge is an instinctual element in all men. It lies in wait, eternally. That is the reason for periodic wars, for pogroms, for individual homicide, for hatred. It is beyond logic, for long before logic was evolved murder had rooted itself in the instincts of man."

He waited for Charles to speak, but Charles only stared at him grimly. Mr. Haas sighed. "Always, at the propitious moment, the animal asserts itself in a flare of surging madness. Later, the man-mind is aghast, remorseful, ashamed. But the damage has been done. We call that damage 'history.' "

Charles suddenly remembered how he had once wanted to kill his brother Jochen. He had had provocation—yes. . . .

"The Animal against God. Yes. It has always been so," added Mr. Haas. "One has only to look at recent history. It is all part of the story of the Animal against God. And now, this war."

Still, Charles could not believe it. He knew it was true, but he did not want to believe it.

Mr. Haas smiled at Charles drearily. "Do you remember that poem by Robert Southey, called 'The Battle of Blenheim'? I don't remember all of it, but I'll quote what I do:

> 'Now tell us what 'twas all about,'
> Young Peterkin he cries;
> And little Wilhelmine looks up
> With wonder-waiting eyes.
> 'Now tell us all about the war,
> And what they fought each other for.'

*　　*　　*　　*　　*　　*　　*

'But what good came of it at last?'
Quoth little Peterkin.
'Why, that I cannot tell,' said he;
'But 'twas a famous victory.'

Charles listened, and his face grew even more grim. Mr. Haas said: "The Animal against God has had so many 'famous victories.' We can only hope that the last victory is with God."

Mr. Haas' sermon, the next Sunday, was announced as "The Battle of Blenheim." The congregation went away, soberly discussing it, shaking their heads. Some of them, at home, stared at the new portraits of the Kaiser on the parlor walls. Some removed the portraits. Some retained them. They were afraid.

America was neutral, and was determined to remain neutral. But the foul wind blew over all the cities and the people murmured restlessly.

On September 1st, Mr. and Mrs. Herbert Hadden announced the engagement of their daughter, Helen, to Mr. Friederich Wittmann, the marriage to take place on January 15th, 1915.

On the same day the engagement was announced, Phyllis and Mrs. Holt came home to Andersburg.

CHAPTER XLVIII

On the morning of September 2nd, Charles called Phyllis. All at once, he wanted to see her. She would speak of nothing he wished to avoid speaking of, he knew. She would understand everything without a single word. She would be the very essence of comfort and serenity and consolation. He had anticipated hearing her voice with pleasure. When he actually did hear it, over the telephone, he was filled with wonder and a quick, releasing delight. He had not know how much he had missed her, and how much he loved her, until he heard her say: "Charles! Oh, Charles."

"Phyllis, I'm coming up to have dinner with you tonight. Alone. I want to talk—talk—"

"Yes," she said. "Of course. Oh, Charles." Had her voice always been so sweet, so alive, and had it always struck at his heart like this, with such tenderness? He was sure it had not. He called his son and told him where he was going. Jim was enthusiastic. "Give Aunt Phyllis a kiss for me, Dad," said the boy. "And tell her to hurry up and marry you." He hung up, chuckling.

Phyllis was waiting for him at the gate where he had once left her. He saw her long before he reached her, a slender figure in mauve voile, waving to him. The early September evening flooded the mountains with warm blue light, and it seemed to Charles that the last sun was all concentrated on Phyllis' hair. He had walked, for in walking he had found some escape from his awful and harassing thoughts, and now he walked faster, waving his straw hat at her, and she waved again and took a few steps into the road. Behind her, the white house stood bright against the green slope, silent but no longer mysterious and retreating.

Charles looked for some change in Phyllis, and found it. Her face was not so tense, now, and not so thin, and there was a vividness in her eyes and in her smile which he had not seen since she had been very young. She appeared very beautiful to him, and all that he had ever wanted; her blue eyes shone at him with unspeakable love. She gave him her hand, and, as she had done the last time he had seen her, she put her head on his shoulder, simply and naturally. There was just one moment when he glanced discreetly at the house, then he recklessly put his arms around her and held her to him. They said nothing. They stood like that for a long time, and Charles knew the first peace he had known for more than a year. She was living and slender in his arms; he kissed her hair, and touched it with his hand. The memory of Wilhelm and Mary was the memory of friends, affectionate and devoted, mourned and loved. But only friends.

They went up the private road to the house, hand in hand, as they had often walked when they had been engaged, swinging their locked hands a little, and smiling at each other. They did not look at the staircase where Wilhelm had fallen to his death. There were no ghosts here, watchful and unfriendly. Just friends. Charles did not glance around instinctively for his brother, as he had done before. Still, Charles was sad, and for an instant or two he could feel a sudden hatred for Jochen, who had caused Wilhelm such suffering.

They went into the music room, and Charles remembered: Etude. Yes: finished, fulfilled, complete in itself. The flower-beds outside glimmered with color in the first twilight; the trees stood still in silence. A few birds were drinking from the white baths on the heavy green grass. The doors were open to the freshness of the evening, and the faint sound of the mountain breeze. Charles and Phyllis lingered on the threshold and looked at the garden. He had his arm about her, holding her close to him, and his tension went from him completely.

Phyllis brought his favorite whiskey and soda, and a glass of wine for herself. They sat near the doors and studied each other, smiling. Charles thought: It's a lovely place, up here, but I don't think she'd mind leaving it. We'll build somewhere. We'll start out fresh, new. He said: "When are you going to marry me, Phyllis?"

She laughed gently. "Next summer. Jimmy will be home then, from Harvard."

Of course. A year must go by. Willie had been dead hardly four months. Charles looked at his glass. He wanted to say: "Not next summer. Now. My son's going away. How can I be alone—with everything?" Then some of his pain came back.

"Yes. Jimmy's going away. I know it's just to school. But it'll be the first time he's left me. Yes, he'll be back for vacations, and in the summers. But it's a going away, after all. It's a change, and even though he'll come back, he's really on his way out of my life. It's nothing to him; it's a beginning. For me, it's an end." He added: "All summer, we've been making plans, and being glad that he's been accepted, and we thought it'd be all right. Perhaps it is, for Jimmy. I wish I'd had more children."

Phyllis regarded him with compassion. "Yes, I know," she said. Then she colored brightly. He wondered at this. Then he thought: I've forgotten. Phyllis is still a young woman. There could be children. She's always wanted them, I know. We can have them. I'm not so old, after all. I'm only forty-one. Lots of men have children in their forties. I could have another son, and perhaps a daughter. He looked at Phyllis shyly. She put out her hand and he took it. The pain retreated.

"This seems—just right. You and me, here," said Charles hopefully.

"Of course, Charles." Her fingers were warm and firm in his. She smiled.

Two years from now, I could have another son, Charles thought again. He drank his whiskey, to hide his elation. He was conscious of an unfamiliar recklessness. He wanted to say, again: Not next summer. Now. Afraid that she would know what he was thinking, he asked her about California, and all the other places where she had been, and she told him some amusing stories about Mrs. Holt in Hollywood, and how Mrs. Holt was so gratified that her friend, Cecil deMille, had allowed her to be part of a mob scene. They said nothing about the war; they did not speak of Jochen, and what had happened during those terrible months Phyllis had been away.

Charles found that Phyllis expected him to sit in Wilhelm's place. He hesitated only briefly, then felt once more that this is what his brother would have wished. The dinner was good and simple, with no wine sauces, no lobster, no consommé. Charles said, as he carved the roast beef: "Willie never liked what he called 'raw blood.'" They laughed. Charles thought: We'll call the boy Wilhelm. Willie'd like that.

Later, Charles asked: "We'll find a place to build, Phyllis? A nice house. Solid. Substantial. We'll look around, very soon, so the house will be ready for us."

Had he said something wrong? For Phyllis was looking troubled and uncertain. She lifted her eyes, and they were blue light in the glow of the candles. "Charles, I've thought I'd like to live in your house. I like it. I couldn't imagine you—us—anywhere else."

"That house?" said Charles, amazed. He glanced about the beautiful dining room. "You can't really mean that, Phyllis." He hardly believed it, and he wondered why he should feel so relieved, so delighted.

"I do mean it. Honestly, my dear. You are part of the house; you were born there. Jimmy was born there. I've always loved it. No, it isn't 'ugly.' It's kind and old. It's a home. Oh, I'll do all sorts of frightful things to it, of course! Fresh bright paper, and new rugs and quite a lot of my furniture and pictures, and things. You'll be horrified." She laughed at him, gayly. "But we'll keep the house, and all those old apple and peach trees, and the garden. I'm homesick for it."

He knew now that it would have been unbearably painful for him to leave his home. He wanted to stay there, to wait for Jim to come back from school. He wanted to sit on the wide verandah, with Phyllis, and hear the summer voices passing in the street. There was so much in that house, so much of his life. He knew, all at once, that Phyllis had never really lived in this lovely house which his brother had built. She had never been happy here. He said: "Has there ever been any time when we haven't loved each other, Phyllis?"

Yes, she thought. There were years when you hardly thought of me. You had Mary, and Jimmy, and you were contented. But I always loved you. She said: "I can't think of a time when we didn't love each other." And she smiled, sadly.

They went to sit on the terrace in the still darkness. A moon stood over the great trees. Charles was drinking another whiskey and soda. He had not wanted to talk of what had happened in the last months. But she was sitting close to him, and their hands were together, and he began to talk. The moonlight lay on her quiet and listening face.

Charles talked on and on, as he had never talked to anyone before. He could not help himself. Sometimes he clutched Phyllis' hand so that her fingers were bruised. But she said nothing, and only listened.

"I wouldn't be able to stand it, if we got into this war—Jimmy'd be just old enough—they'd take him—I don't understand, Phyllis—I've seen the photographs of the English and French and Russian and German troops—boys—laughing, singing, shouting—I don't understand —I suppose I never understood anything—the boys don't know either—"

He went on and on, at times incoherent, passionate, and desperate. He could hide nothing from her now. He could not control himself. He found words, stumbled over some, shook his head numbly. The moon rode higher over the trees, brilliant, swimming in its own light. Crickets were shrilling in the grass. Phyllis listened, aching, but still silent, sometimes putting her head on his shoulder, sometimes watching his face in the white radiance, sometimes sighing. Was this frantic man, speaking so loudly, so bitterly, so despairingly, the old stolid Charles, the "sensible" Charles of the Wittmann Machine Tool Company, the "reliable" and moderating Charles everyone knew? No, this was the real Charles, the Charles kept hidden for over forty years. She lifted his hand to her lips, to comfort him, but he only looked at her for a moment, dazed, then went on talking.

Then he was talking about Jochen, and she shrank a little. "I've been hearing reports," he said, and there was nothing in his voice but misery and gloom. "He's wretched. In our company, he was a big man, a man of consequence, a man who knew his business. What is he now? Assistant to that little black rat Brinkwell! Someone who could be re- placed. What does it matter that he gets a large salary, and is Brink- well's friend, and visits Brinkwell's country house near Philadelphia, and knows so many 'important' people? What does it matter if Isabel is mentioned daily in the newspapers, and goes to New York with Brinkwell's wife, and is reported 'dining' with famous people, and is accepted socially everywhere? I saw Joe, once or twice, at a distance, and he's a broken man—"

You're sorry for him, even if you hate him, even if you wanted to kill him, as he really killed Wilhelm, thought Phyllis. Something ended for you when you forced him out, my poor dear. You are so afraid of things ending. You like the world to stay unchanged.

She said, very gently: "Jochen did these things to himself, dear Charles. You can't control peoples' lives."

"Yes, yes. I suppose you're right, Phyllis," he said. He put his glass to his mouth. It was empty, now, and he stared at it, helplessly. Then he added: "It's this feeling I have, that I can't control anything, no matter how I try—I always thought one could— Things get away from you— Things happen— You try to think what you should have done, and then you know that nobody can do anything. Phyllis, I can't stand this war."

She felt his huge dread, his active terror. She knew the war had just one face, and that was the face of his son. He talked of the Connington Steel Company; he talked of everything. But always, everything was Jimmy. The moon was overhead, and the leaves of the trees were blazing silver, and the mountains were black against a dark blue sky. It is so peaceful here, thought Phyllis, but it is an illusion. I don't suppose there was ever really any peace any time in the world, or in men.

She looked at the moon, and said in herself: Our Father, Who art in Heaven—Man passed in a bloody dream, but God remained. She wanted to tell this to Charles. It might help him. But she could say nothing, and could only think: Deliver us from this evil.

It was almost midnight before they went back into the house. Charles was quieter now. He held Phyllis to him, and his arms were tired. He said, trying to smile: "I had to talk to you, Phyllis. It hasn't solved anything. But it was a relief."

She put her hand to his haggard face, and kissed him. "My poor darling," she said. That was all any woman could ever say to any man. He turned his head and kissed the palm of her hand. "It was a relief," he repeated.

He found Jimmy waiting for him, and he was glad, though it was very late. He said: "It'll be next summer, son." They shook hands solemnly. They went upstairs together, and for the first time in many months Charles fell asleep instantly. Something had happened to him, was his last thought. Something had comforted him. Perhaps things might not be so bad as he had thought.

CHAPTER XLIX

CHARLES AND JIM called for young Walter Haas, and the Reverend Mr. Haas, so that they could all go together to the station in Charles' big red automobile. Both fathers were very jovial with their sons, and warned them of all sorts of interesting temptations to which they were likely to be exposed at Harvard. Jim drove the car, with Walter beside him, and Charles and the minister rode in the rear, amid a vast tangle of baggage and tennis rackets.

The boys were excited; their fathers laughed and exchanged winks with each other. Charles and the minister did not look directly at each other, however. It was unsafe. Jim was slightly worried under his excitement. He was not completely convinced that Charles could drive the automobile safely home, and he wished that he had insisted that Charles' handyman do the driving. Charles thought this very funny; he and the minister laughed loudly. The boys were less exuberant. Young Walter hoped that his father would be a comfort to his mother and would give her a little more time now that her son would be away. He resolved that when he was a minister, himself, he would give his first thoughts to his family; the parishioners would come next. Then he reminded himself that this would be wrong, and he became very sober.

They all got out at the station, and the baggage was untangled and heaped on the hot wooden platform. In five minutes the train would be here. The four stood together, and then no one could speak. Charles thought of his empty house. He looked at the minister enviously. Three little girls at home, and a wife. When a man was young, Charles thought, he congratulated himself if his family was very small, and he had no impediments dragging on his shirt-tails as he struggled towards a hoped-for success. But when he was middle-aged, and had no children at all, or only one or two, and he had a big house and money and security, then he wished that he had at least five children to fill those rooms. Yes, five children around a Christmas tree, five children in the garden, five children and their friends thundering up and down the stairs, five children about the table—and five strong and loving children about one's death-bed—that was the only real fulfillment, the only real reason for living.

Charles looked up and found his son watching him anxiously. Jim said impulsively: "I'll be back at Thanksgiving, Dad." He smiled, and pushed his father's shoulder. "And one of these days I'll get married and I'll give you half a dozen grandchildren, three boys and three girls!" He added, generously: "And you can name them all yourself, too."

The minister smiled at his own son. He took off his pince-nez and rubbed them vigorously, his broad plump face tired but resolutely happy in the hot September sunlight. A minister—my boy, thought Mr. Haas. A very hard life, but a rewarding one. At least, it would be rewarding if people just thought of their pastor as a man like themselves, and had a little patience with him, and a little consideration, and did not expect him to be the social arbiter of the parish, and a grinning politician, and a schemer, and each family's personal property alone. Sheep could play hob with the shepherd, and ruin his disposition, and make him a cynic. Young Walter, so sedate, so earnest, so circumspect, so single-hearted, would find it a hard life. But it has its rewards, thought Mr. Haas, determinedly. Yes, indeed. If the boy just had a little more sense of humor—yes, indeed, said Mr. Haas, firmly, to himself.

They all heard someone coming towards them, and they saw it was young Father Hagerty, smiling eagerly. He was carrying two parcels, and he was shabby in the blazing sunlight. Charles and Mr. Haas shook hands with him, with deep affection, and the boys shook hands with him shyly. "I knew Jimmy was going away, Mr. Wittmann," said the priest. "You told me in the summer. So I thought I'd come down here to give him my best wishes."

He glanced at Jimmy. Charles saw there was considerable resemblance between them. They were both tall and dark and a little too thin, and both were uncertain, and they both had a youthful passion in their eyes. Mr. Haas smiled benignly, and sadly. Such a young feller, this priest. He still believed that sheep could be led, that they could be taught not to butt each other and scramble over each other.

Father Hagerty gave the parcels to Jimmy. He looked at them thoughtfully, as the boy held them. He cleared his throat, and laughed. "When I went away to my seminary some of my parents' friends brought me all sorts of sacred literature," he said. "But the thing I really liked was a box of my mother's penuche, with walnuts. I remembered that. So, one of those parcels contains a book about St. Francis of Assisi, and the other one contains some of my mother's candy."

"Food for the body, and food for the soul," said Mr. Haas, heartily.

Charles thought this very trite, and he wished Mr. Haas had not said something so banal. He was embarrassed for his minister, before these three young men. Then he saw that Mr. Haas was embarrassed, too. Charles felt very compassionate, and nodded solemnly. It must be hell being a minister, thought Charles. He regarded both clergymen with affectionate pity. His son was going to be a doctor.

The five stood together, and tried to talk. It was a miserable effort. I hope the damn train's an hour late, Charles thought. It's always late. But, of course, it would be on time today, he added to himself, as he heard the humming of the rails. In a minute or two the infernal thing would be roaring in upon them, ringing and steaming and roaring, in a cursed hurry to be off again. Passengers were straggling out of the station. Charles moved closer to his son. The train now could be seen, clamoring from around the bend. Jim whispered to his father hurriedly: "I'm glad you're going to have dinner tonight with the Holts and Aunt Phyllis, Dad. But will you go right home from here, before you go to the Holts'? I've left something there for you."

"Eh?" said Charles. "Something for me? Of course I'll go home first." The train was shrieking past them now, and the Pullman cars were slowing down. Other passengers were running for the coaches. The five men moved towards the Pullmans. The time had come. These two young men were loading themselves with baggage, and a porter was coming helpfully towards them. They were already going; they were going out of their fathers' lives. They were rushing into manhood. Charles held himself back from clutching his son's arm. Mr. Haas was all paternal smiles. There was sweat on his wide forehead. Then he was unashamedly hugging Walter, and Charles found himself helplessly pumping Jim's hand and trying to see his face through a mist. The young priest watched sympathetically.

The boys' faces appeared at a Pullman window. The train hesitated. Go on, go on! thought Charles, desperately. I can't stand this. The train was moving, the wheels churning. The boys waved; their fathers waved. Then the train was rushing away. Charles and Mr. Haas watched it until it was out of sight. Then Charles said, and could not help himself: "This is bad. But think how bad it would be if they were going off to fight, to kill, to be killed. Thank God, we've no war here, and pray God we'll never have one."

Mr. Haas bent his head and moved slowly away. Charles said to the priest: "We'll take you home, Father Hagerty. It was very kind of you to—to—"

They went home in silence. Or, at least, it was Charles' impression that no one spoke. Fear rode in the red and brazen splendor of the automobile with them. It was a relief when he found himself alone, and drawing up slowly before his house. Communicated fear was worse than solitary fear, because all knew what was in your mind, and they suffered with you and for themselves.

Before Charles went up the stairs, he looked at his big, old, solid house. It had already taken on an abandoned air. There was nothing inside, nothing, only empty rooms. For days and weeks on end, he, Charles, would sit alone at his table. Jim would be back for the holidays, but he would be a visitor. This house would never be a home again until Phyllis was there. The thick warm green of the great trees fell across the windows. The screen door opened on a cool, shuttered interior. Sighing, Charles went up the stairs and into the house.

Someone stirred in the parlor, and stood up. Charles blinked, the blaze of outdoor sunlight still half blinding him in this dimness. Then he exclaimed: "Gerry! Gerry, my dear!" So, this is what Jim had meant when he had asked his father to go home first.

The tall young girl came towards him timidly. "Uncle Charlie," she said, and her voice shook as if she were about to cry. He took her in his arms and kissed her with deep love. It had been a long time since he had last seen her. Why, he had not seen her since last winter! And how the child had grown. She was as tall as Charles, or even a little taller. Her white blouse and white skirt glimmered in the dusk of the parlor. He saw the shining of her large dark eyes, and he saw the tears on her lashes.

"Jimmy asked me to be here when you came back," she said, as they sat down. "He didn't want you to come in here alone." Her hair was up, in a gleaming mass of black braids around her head, and it gave her slender throat, her young straight shoulders, her gentle young breast, a regal look. Charles thought that nothing could be more gently distinguished than that quiet young face. Why, it was beautiful! A lovely face; a lovely girl. He got up, bent over her, and kissed her again. "Gerry, this is wonderful," he said.

"Has Jimmy told you we've been seeing each other all the time?" she asked, as Charles sat down again. "You see, we have, Uncle Charlie."

"He never told me," answered Charles, laughing. "But I knew. And I was glad."

But the girl was miserable. "There'll never be anyone for me but Jimmy," she said. "Never, never. No matter what happens. I'm going away to school, myself, on Monday. Jimmy and I'll be writing, all the time. And we'll see each other on vacations, and Jimmy says that somehow we'll manage to see each other even during school periods. Jimmy can do almost anything," she added, proudly.

"I wouldn't worry too much about—things," said Charles, comfortingly. "Jimmy's got six years, at least, at school, and then he'll be an interne, and you'll be at school, too. You'll both be growing up. Don't be so sad, Gerry. There'll always be a way, when Jim is a man and you are a woman." He thought of Phyllis, and his voice became stronger. "Yes, there'll always be a way."

I probably sound as foolish as poor Haas sounded at the station, to this child, thought Charles. She thinks I'm an ancient, and how can ancients know anything about anything?

"Papa and Mama want to announce my engagement to Kenneth Brinkwell after Christmas," said Geraldine in so low a voice that Charles had to lean forward to hear her.

"But you're only a child," said Charles, largely, thinking only of comforting her. "It's all nonsense. You've only to tell them you're too young. Why, you're only seventeen, sweetheart."

Geraldine did not lift her head. "I'll be eighteen, next year. They want me to be married to Kenneth, then. Lots of girls I know are already engaged, and they're only my age." Then she was crying, her handkerchief over her face, her shoulders heaving in dreadful sobs.

Charles, appalled, clutching the arms of his chair, stared at her helplessly, unable to move. He listened to her muffled cries; he watched the bent convulsions of her body. And then the slow but huge fire of his rage began to burn in him, and he clenched his hands. He forced himself to his feet; he put his arm about the girl's shoulders; he smoothed her hair.

"Listen to me, Gerry," he said, with sternness. "You don't have to marry anyone you don't want to marry. Your—your father and mother can't force you. This isn't the Middle Ages." He lifted the girl's head and held it against his chest, tightly. "If you and Jim love each other —though you're both too young to be thinking of that yet—then you'll wait for each other. Why, you won't have to wait! We'll settle it—all of us together. When Jim's twenty-one, you can be married, and you can have a little flat near Harvard, and then when he goes to a hospital, you can move again with him. I've got money, sweetheart. You two can have everything you want."

But did this child have the strength and the fortitude to resist Jochen and Isabel—damn them! If she only hated her parents, it would be easy. But she loved them. She was her father's favorite. He would work on her; he would appeal to her. He would use her love for him. Charles thought he had hated his brother with all the force he had had in him; now he knew that that hatred was nothing to what he felt now.

"You're not engaged to young Brinkwell," said Charles. "You don't have to be, Gerry. Try to stop crying, darling. Try to listen. You don't have to be engaged to anyone."

She was still sobbing, but more quietly. Her face was hidden against his vest. She lifted her left hand, such a childish, white hand, and showed him what was on it. It was a gold ring, with the tiniest possible diamond, hardly a twinkle, and it was on her third finger.

Geraldine drew her face away from him; it was blotched and swollen.

"Jimmy gave me that ring last week," she said, and she smiled through her tears.

Why, it was a beautiful ring; it was innocent and touching. It was like these children, themselves. Charles held Geraldine's hand and looked at the ring, and it seemed to him to be the noblest and loveliest of all engagement rings.

"He saved for over a year for it, Uncle Charlie," said Geraldine. "Isn't it lovely? But I have to wear it on a chain, at home, and I hide it under my pillow at night. So, we're really engaged now. Jimmy put it on my finger, so I'd always remember that."

Charles said: "It's the most magnificent ring I've ever seen." And it was. It meant a whole year of careful saving, of self-denial, of love. "This makes me very happy, my dear. I can't tell you how happy."

She stood up, wiping her eyes. She held her hand stiffly in front of her, and smiled with delight on the ring. Then she covered it with her other hand.

"It's going to be awfully hard, Uncle Charlie, opposing Mama and Papa. And perhaps you'll hear I'm engaged to Kenneth Brinkwell. But I won't be, really. Nothing will ever make me be."

She had to leave at once, she told Charles. She was supposed to be shopping for school. She stood near the door and threw her arms about his neck and gave him a child's kiss, fervent and confiding, on his mouth.

Before she ran down the steps, she said breathlessly, not looking at him: "Don't be too angry with Papa, Uncle Charlie. Please! He's so miserable. I can't tell you—"

And then she was running down the street, a flutter of white skirt, a flutter of a white glove. Charles watched her go. He stood on the verandah for a long time.

CHAPTER L

Mrs. Holt assured Charles that she was delighted to be home. Mr. Holt was also delighted that his wife had returned, though the poor man's eyes already showed signs of fond strain. Charles sympathized with him, as he watched Mr. Holt's apprehension whenever his wife spoke. Mr. Holt had spent the summer, while Mrs. Holt had been travelling with Phyllis, visiting friends in Philadelphia and Atlantic City and an area which he vaguely described as "The Mountains."

They had had a very pleasant dinner in the monster dining-room, the three of them, and now they sat in the vast, tapestried living-room, talking. It had begun to rain at sunset, and through the open French doors they could hear the soft whispering of water on the trees, and could feel the mountain wind which filled the house with gusts of pine and grass and verbena.

"So cozy, this," said Mrs. Holt, fanning herself with a handkerchief heavily laden with a perfume she had confided was called "Ashes of Love," and which could not be bought anywhere but in California. "Just the three of us, together. A night at home, with the rain outside."

Charles thought that "cozy" hardly described the great hall. It was like sitting in a museum. But he understood what Mrs. Holt meant, and so he smiled. He was relieved that Phyllis, according to Mrs. Holt, had "told her and Braydon everything." He did not like thrashing and rethrashing old straw. What had been done had been done; there was mold on it, thought Charles—an acrid mold, which stung the nostrils with remembrance.

"But, of course, one expects such wonderful things of you, Charlie," said Mrs. Holt with enthusiasm. "How you managed it all, that horrid Jochen, and everything! How very Machiavellian of you, Charlie!"

Charles was mortified. Mrs. Holt glowed at him admiringly.

"Now, Minnie," said Mr. Holt. " 'Machiavellian' has unpleasant connotations. I don't think Charles relished what he had to do. He did a disagreeable job of work—"

Mrs. Holt slapped her husband's hand affectionately. "Did you hear that, Charlie? 'Job of work.' He must have met some Englishmen, someplace. Braydon keeps forgetting that he was once a fine, brawny, American oil-weller, or whatever you call it, with just one pair of overalls, and a dinner-pail. And did you hear him tell you when you came that he was feeling 'very fit'? Such silly expressions—the English think up. So precious. Did you meet Englishmen in New York, Braydon, my pet?"

"A lot of them," replied Mr. Holt, and now for some unaccountable reason he was uneasy. Charles glanced up, alert.

"That accounts for it," laughed Mrs. Holt. "And those idiot New Yorkers: they're beginning to parrot the English a lot now. Aren't they, Braydon?"

Mr. Holt cleared his throat. He crossed his legs, uncrossed them, crossed them again. "A certain class of New Yorkers—yes, my dear, the 'precious' ones—always did parrot the English, and imitate their mannerisms. They've even begun to speak of 'quiet holidays,' and 'quiet week-ends,' and such."

Charles waited. There was something he was intended to hear. Mrs. Holt's blue eyes had that certain glazed, blank expression. She said, with hearty ridicule: "The Englishmen of 'Merrie England' weren't the 'quiet week-enders,' and the 'quiet hearts' and the 'quiet family men' who are so fashionable in England now. What do you suppose happened to 'Merrie England,' Charlie?"

She was staring at Charles. But Charles looked at Mr. Holt. Mr. Holt's distinguished face had become brooding and harassed. He held his big brandy glass cupped in his hands, and he regarded it as if it were a crystal ball.

Charles replied to Mrs. Holt, very slowly, but he still looked at his host: "Maybe the gaiety and the 'spirit' have gone out of the English, Minnie. But something's still there: the worst of what they are."

Mrs. Holt said: "Well, we all know that the English are hypocrites. They even know it themselves, now, and they've made it a virtue, as they always do with their vices."

"I suppose the Englishmen you met were negotiating for war materials for England, Braydon?" asked Charles.

"Oh, dear, not entirely," Mrs. Holt interrupted, smiling broadly at her husband. "Braydon told me. They were so impartial, the broad-minded dears. There was war material for England, of course, but there was other war material, too. Being loaded on Swedish vessels. The Swedes are so neutral, you know. So intelligent and civilized of them, isn't it? Flag high in all waters: the good, sound Swedish flag. And no one, of course, would be so impolite as to ask where the war material was going, or by whom it had been bought, or with whose money."

Mr. Holt still gazed at his glass. "Yes," he said. Now he looked at Charles, with distress. "Have you been watching the Stock Market, Charles? We shouldn't just blame the English; that isn't entirely fair. We're selling to—to everybody, and taking everybody's money, and making a good thing of it."

Mrs. Holt laughed as if it were the gayest subject in the world. "Germans buying the things which England needs, and the English buying what the Germans need. And the sturdy Swedish vessels plowing the seas diligently, and taking money from everybody, and delivering the goods to exactly the ports which need the war material. Well," added Mrs. Holt, with gusto, "I'm just a woman, and all this agreeable high finance and courtliness between enemies is beyond me." She looked slowly from one face to another. "And the English boys laughing and waving their caps as they rush up gangplanks on the way to the Front, and the French boys singing, and the German boys playing their brassy music and sticking out their legs—the poor children. And Belgium in ruins, and Alsace burning. Well, I'm just a woman, and I don't know."

"I do," said Charles. "This all isn't just 'happening.' It's the strongest blow ever yet struck against man, and against liberty. They're all in it, together. The reported casualty lists tonight—just figures. So many thousands of boys dead, here, there, everywhere. But who cares? Who's yet written what their parents are thinking tonight, or praying, or sobbing out? Who ever wrote a story, even Richard Harding Davis who's having such a fine time writing about the murder of Belgium for us, about what a single mother or father is feeling? Who ever cared, in the history of the world, for a dead son?"

No one answered him.

"If the history of wars was written by parents, if the truth of wars was ever written, a politician who waved a flag, an army officer who mustered his men, a ruler who ever shrieked of the 'destiny' of his country, would be hunted down like the mad dogs they are!" Charles' face swelled and reddened.

Mr. Holt spoke now, faintly. "It gets all muddled. Finally, none of them know what they're fighting for. Except, of course, a few men on top, and they'll never tell the real reason."

" 'But 'twas a famous victory,' " said Charles.

"Well," said Mr. Holt, "we've sometimes got to choose the lesser of evils. A trite aphorism, of course. But it's true."

"I don't like the English; never did," said Mrs. Holt. "But anyway, they aren't as awful as that Kaiser. And just think of the Americans who are helping him! I wonder what would happen if, for instance, there were strikes in some of our big mills and factories, which are selling war materials to Germany?"

"Yes," said Mr. Holt. He and his wife fixed their eyes on Charles. Charles said nothing. The face of his brother Friederich swam before him.

"I'm really in favor of unions," Mrs. Holt prattled. "And the workers are really horribly low-paid. Except for a few craftsmen, the Connington pays the most miserable wages. The company's so strong, too, and so busy. A strike would cripple the whole thing, for days, weeks, months, maybe. The Connington hates unions."

"Yes," said Mr. Holt again, uncomfortably.

Mrs. Holt smiled. "Well, it would be very exciting. Ralph Grimsley knows a lot, too. He's such a friend of yours, Charlie."

"There're dozens of other factories, however," said Charles. "The Connington might be important, but the others would go on manufacturing."

"Strikes," said Mr. Holt, thoughtfully, "have a way of spreading." He stood up, now, and all his hesitation was gone, and a new hard bitterness came into his face. "Charles, you buy your steel from the Sessions Steel Company, don't you? The best high-speed tool steel?"

"Yes. It's a specialized steel, the very best. That's why our tools are so much in demand." Charles stood up, abruptly, and faced his host. "Well?"

"The Connington doesn't have the patent for that steel, Charles." The two men faced each other. "I hate to speak so directly, my boy, but I feel I must. You use Sessions steel. Two weeks ago, I heard, in New York, that Brinkwell and the Sessions people have become very friendly, and Brinkwell's manufacturing machine tools, now."

Charles' mouth went dry. "I wired them, yesterday, for double the amount of tool steel which I ordered at this same time last year. I haven't received a confirmation of the order yet, but I've no doubt I'll be supplied."

Mr. Holt gazed at him in silence.

"So," said Charles. "It's Brinkwell." He looked around, with furious helplessness. "I'll get the steel; I can't run the shops without it. I'll get it!"

He sat down. He was sick with his hate and fear. Tomorrow! He couldn't wait for tomorrow. But he had to wait. He had to wait, and think all night, and plot and plan. He sat in his black silence, and his fingers were numb and cold as they held his coffee cup. His head pounded with his thoughts. I'll stop at nothing, he said to himself.

Then he heard Mrs. Holt say, placidly: "Oh, no, Braydon, I'm sure we won't get into the war. Don't worry."

"So, there it is," said Charles, to Friederich. His right hand rested on the telephone on his desk. His other hand held a telegram. He looked at the telegram again, which had come from the Sessions Steel Company in Windsor: "Regret that previous large orders from other concerns, now straining our capacity to manufacture high speed tool steel, force us to decline your own order for an indefinite period of time."

Charles said: "We have enough steel for five months. That's all."

Friederich said: "Calling them will do no good, Karl." He had listened to Charles for nearly an hour, and so profound was the change in him that only once or twice had he uttered an exclamation, or made a vehement gesture.

"I'm afraid you're right," said Charles. "It won't do any good. They probably won't talk to me, anyway. So. We'll have to bring up our own ammunition. I've talked to Grimsley; he's ready for action at any time, when I give the word. We'll have to use dirty tactics, Fred, and you're not a man who ever liked dirty tactics. And now, as for you: you understand, of course, that no one must know that you are behind the labor organizers who'll come to Andersburg. It's all to be spontaneous."

"I understand," said Friederich. He gnawed briefly at his thumb-nail, and frowned in concentration. "Dirty tactics. But for a good end. We must try to remember that." He paused. "I know just the men we'll need. Honest men. Karl, we could use the same tactics against all the mills and factories which are supplying war materials to Europe."

Charles laughed weakly. "It would take too long. Besides, you and I alone can't fight this monster organization; you know that. We can't even persuade our neutral Government to take a hand in it, though that would promptly stop all wars, of course. But we'd be 'interfering' in business, and nothing must ever interfere in 'free business.' Besides, Mr. Wilson stubbornly persists in ignoring the war; it's so damned ungenteel and distasteful."

"But the newspapers could tell the people."

"They could. But they won't. After all, newspapers don't exist apart from society, and they get their orders. 'Free press.' A high-sounding phrase, but a contradiction in terms. The *Clarion*, here in Andersburg, comes as close to being a free paper as it can be, and that's because Ralph owns it, and nobody else. But even he has to temper his news with a nice appreciation of what he owes to advertisers."

The Sessions Steel Company in Windsor did not call Charles. Instead, the superintendent called Roger Brinkwell. The conversation between the two friends gave much pleasure to Mr. Brinkwell, who went, thereafter, into the fine suite of offices which his assistant, Jochen Wittmann, now occupied.

"Well, Joe, we've got old Charlie on the run," he said, slapping Jochen on his massive shoulder. "Sessions have an idea he has only about two months' supply of steel. At the proper time, we'll close in on him. We'll have him working for us and eating out of our hands and begging us to use his damn patents."

Jochen grunted mirthfully. But his little brown eyes shifted away from Mr. Brinkwell. His big blunt fingers began to beat on his desk. "Serves him right," said Jochen. He looked about his sumptuous private office, with the panelled walls and the draperies at the big windows. He looked at the heavy carpet on the floor, at his large mahogany desk, at the door behind which his secretaries tapped, at the distant view of immense smoking chimneys. He thought of his extraordinary salary, and of the string of oriental pearls he had bought for Isabel, of his new Pierce-Arrow automobile with the silver appointments, of the coming engagement between his daughter Geraldine and Roger Brinkwell's son. He looked, and he thought, and he said to himself: I'm a lackey.

Mr. Brinkwell was in high good humor. He regarded Jochen with affection. An able man, an excellent choice, old Joe. No one could be better.

"Just be patient, Joe," said Mr. Brinkwell, walking towards the door. "Just two months. Charlie won't buy inferior steel; he's too damned proud and stiff-necked about his tools." He stopped as he began to open the door, and grinned back at Jochen. "When you come to dinner tonight Kenneth will show you the ring he's bought for Gerry."

Jochen raised his eyes. The small muddy pupils lifted and showed a large portion of white cornea under them. Mr. Brinkwell could not read their expression. "Good," said Jochen. "Good," he repeated.

"You gave up too easily, when Charlie showed his teeth," said Roger, with indulgence. Then with a wave of his hand he went out.

Damn you, thought Jochen. I didn't give up. I just didn't want to go on with it.

CHAPTER LI

THOUGH President Wilson continued to ostracize the war, as one would ostracize an ill-bred person, the American people uneasily became more and more conscious of it, by October. They could not ignore it. The great guns of European propaganda swung on their pivots and belched their poison gas across the Atlantic. The President could murmur "neutrality," but the people could not pretend that there was not a stench in their nostrils.

The Germans and the French were vociferously, and simultaneously, accusing each other of the foulest atrocities. No sooner did the French produce photographs of murdered civilians and priests, than the Germans produced other photographs (much better) of wounded German soldiers being murdered by the French, and civilians and clergymen also being slaughtered. They had one thing in common: a complete lack of originality.

The Kaiser and France were now too busy to plead the "righteousness" of their cause before America. The British heroically undertook that task. They pitted the wits of their artists, teachers, and scholars against the wits of German artists, teachers, and scholars. "We protest the lies and calumnies (of the Allies) (of the German Government) against us!" they cried. "It is NOT TRUE!" they screamed in chorus. Britain had one advantage: she controlled the news that came by cable across the ocean. She had, in fact, cut the single German cable between Germany and America almost at the moment war was declared. This put her in a very advantageous position, for now Germany had to rely solely on the uncertain wireless and the more uncertain mails. British propaganda, ringing, solemn, and skillful, poured unrestricted into America, from London and from Paris.

The war, a dim nightmare far off in space to America, now brightened daily in scarlet and purple on the horizon of American consciousness. The editors of newspapers now tentatively but still uncertainly began to express cautious indignation against German "Kultur" and German "Junkers" and German "Schrecklichkeit."

Charles Wittmann waited. There was nothing that he could do but wait. Long patience was one of his strongest characteristics, and though he knew the deathly danger all about him, and the imminent menace, he knew that he would have to be patient. He read the New York newspapers and the Philadelphia newspapers minutely, and nothing else. He walked the streets of Andersburg, and he listened. Nothing I can do, yet, he would say to himself. I can only wait. Friederich was working in silence. He never told Charles what he was doing, and Charles never asked him. The supply of high speed tool steel he had on hand was dwindling.

There were letters from Jim, three or four a week, sometimes very short, sometimes very long. These, and visits to Phyllis, were his only pleasure these days. It was not until the end of October that Charles became aware that Jim was not mentioning the war any more, though in the beginning he had casually written of it in his letters. He knows what I'm feeling, and thinking, Charles thought, and he's trying to get my mind off it. He wrote to his son: "You must be hearing a lot about the war at Harvard. What do all the boys up there think of it?" Jim answered the letter, or rather, he answered everything else his father had asked, but he did not write of the war. "It is of no interest to him, thank God," he told Phyllis. "He even forgot I'd asked him the question."

Charles went to see his minister. "What has Walter to say about the war?" asked Charles. Mr. Haas obligingly opened a drawer in his desk and brought out Walter's last letter. "Walter takes everything seriously," said Mr. Haas. "He says he wishes 'there was something a person could do.' "

Charles, transfixed, looked at Mr. Haas. "Now what in the hell does he mean by that?" he demanded. "Excuse me. But what does the kid mean?"

Mr. Haas was perturbed. He looked sharply at the letter to see if there was something in it which he had overlooked. "I can't imagine, Charles," he murmured. "But everyone's talking about peace missions, and things like that, and Walter always did think the clergy could do something about wars, and ought to do it."

"Well, they could, and ought to," said Charles, immensely relieved.

He was very sorry for Mr. Haas, whose son was going to be a minister, also. What clergymen must suffer! he thought, sympathetically amused. Ten days to Thanksgiving. Friederich, when encountering Charles, looked at him in a bemused way, as if wondering who he was. He was to be married in two months, but he did not speak of it during these weeks.

Charles' troubles kept him from noticing, too acutely, that now all his friends were only those of German ancestry, except for Father Hagerty and the Haddens and the Holts. He knew the secret animosity was growing against him and the other "Dutchmen" in the community, but he still believed that Americans had a lot of "common sense" and that when "this thing" was over everyone would forget it.

Then one day old Mr. Leo Schiffhauer, Secretary of the Board of the Church, and owner of the small brewery on the outskirts of Andersburg, came to see him at his home.

Mr. Schiffhauer was seventy-four, small, round as one of his own kegs, with fierce little blue eyes and a gentle mouth under a white mustache. He was a good business man, and his beer was excellent, and he had six married daughters and fourteen grandchildren of whom he was very proud. He was an active politician, a fighter, a man of justice, of stern Lutheranism, and of humor. One of his sons-in-law had died in the Spanish-American War; his young grandsons all belonged to the Boy Scouts, and Mr. Schiffhauer, who still spoke with a slight German accent, was regularly called upon to deliver patriotic speeches on the Fourth of July.

Charles was glad to see this old friend of his father's, for whom he had considerable affection in spite of Mr. Schiffhauer's propensity for obstinate argument, especially concerning matters that related to the Board and the church. He had been somewhat haughty towards Charles for the last few months, because of Charles' disagreement with him over some Board policy. It was Charles' belief that the old man had come to him in private to see if some compromise could be reached, though this was hardly in character.

When Mr. Schiffhauer walked, he put each foot down with determined belligerency, no matter what the occasion. It was his "game-cock" way, in spite of his age. But tonight he almost crept into Charles' house, his head bowed, his manner broken and abstracted. He spoke to Charles in German, to Charles' surprise: "Good evening, Karl. It is bad, this weather, is it not?"

Charles had never heard Mr. Schiffhauer speak German, and this surprised him again, and made him uneasy. However, he replied in the same language: "It is very bad. But November is a disagreeable month." The old man sat down, planted his hands on his knees; his great belly bulged. He sighed; he looked at the fire. He seemed to have aged.

"It is a serious concern which has brought me to you tonight, Karl," he said.

Charles was prepared to be the younger man, and the more indulgent. "Yes, I know. But considering the new high cost of living, I cannot but believe that our minister deserves to receive five hundred dollars more a year."

Mr. Schiffhauer waved a little fat hand, on which a diamond twinkled. "It does not matter. You are right, Karl. A thousand dollars a year would not be too much—extra. It is as you say. The prices! A good man, our reverend minister, but a stubborn one."

Charles smiled. Mr. Schiffhauer, sighing even more deeply, took out his old German pipe, filled it, lit it. "Beer?" suggested Charles. "Your own, and very excellent, Herr Schiffhauer."

"Cold," said Mr. Schiffhauer, nodding.

Charles produced the beer. Mr. Schiffhauer drank long, as if very thirsty. Then he put down his stein, wiped his mustache with a white silk handkerchief. He picked up the stein, and studied it. "It is from Bavaria," he said. "I recognize the fine glaze. Ach, ja, my beer is the best," he added, absently. "It is not good for a man to praise what is his own, but in this case it is justified. One must not let modesty carry him too far."

"Modesty, according to Goethe, is false pride," said Charles.

"Ach, Goethe," said Mr. Schiffhauer, with much mournfulness. "One can read Goethe, forever," continued the old man, "and each time it is new. There is so much meaning. Do you remember, Karl, that he once said that it is impossible to know anything? I am finding things impossible to understand these days."

Charles waited, frowning. Mr. Schiffhauer looked at him with his fiery blue eyes, now so sad but still so indomitable.

"Karl, you are an important man in this city. A revered man—though, of course, you are still young. A man of power. Your word is taken. That is why I have come to you. What you say will inspire thought, consideration. Your father chose well when he made you president of those fine shops."

"Thank you," said Charles.

"So," said Mr. Schiffhauer, drawing a heavy breath, "I could think of no one else who is important enough to form a new society for us. I have given it much thought. We must have our new society, and it must be strong, in this city."

"The town," said Charles, speaking now in English, "crawls with societies. We've got luncheons every day. Masons, Rotarians, God knows what else. Why should we have another society?"

But Mr. Schiffhauer spoke on in German as if Charles had made no comment: "I have discussed this with many friends. We have decided to form a society called 'The American Friends of Germany.' All Americans in the city of German ancestry will be asked to join. We wish to make you head of this society."

Charles stood up, moving rapidly. "What!" he exclaimed.

Mr. Schiffhauer raised his hand. His eyes had become filmed, an old man's tired eyes. "Surely it has not escaped your notice, Karl, that there is now a great prejudice against us of German ancestry, in this city? And my friends in other cities tell me this prejudice is growing there, also. We must defend ourselves. We are being attacked, insulted, ignored, belittled. It is not good. We must defend ourselves."

"You're right," said Charles, "it is not good. I know. I understand. I feel it in the air around me. It is a bad thing, and stupid. But one must remember that madness passes, and common sense eventually always prevails. One must be patient."

Mr. Schiffhauer laughed hoarsely and bitterly. He nodded again. "That is true. But sometimes it is too late for the victim."

Charles walked up and down the room, his hands in his pockets, frowning. Then he stopped before the old man. "Mr. Schiffhauer, you are an American, in spite of idiots who are now taking sides in a neutral country. Your heart is American; your children and your grandchildren are Americans. You are so truly American, for you love America, and America is part of you and you are part of this country."

Mr. Schiffhauer looked at him in silence. Then Charles sat down, leaned towards Mr. Schiffhauer and spoke earnestly.

"Prejudice is a vile thing. But please listen to me. The worst thing that prejudice can do is to the soul of a man. It is worse than what it can do to his body, and his mind. It serves, if allowed, to split off a man from his own community, from his own country. It sets him apart. He has permitted his enemies to make him a 'stranger.' That, he must not allow. That, he must fight, in his own heart. He must refuse to consider himself an alien. In that way he defeats his enemies in the only real victory they can attain against him. Never, for one moment, must he let his enemies make him think: 'I am not really of this country. I am not of this city. I am not of my neighbors. I am a creature foreign to them.'

"You, Herr Schiffhauer, are an American. You are more American than your enemies. For, if they were Americans, they would never say of a neighbor: 'He is a German. He is an Irishman. He is a Jew. He is a Catholic. He is a Pole, a Hungarian, or whatever.' Americans are of many races; they are one people. He who forgets this is not an American."

Mr. Schiffhauer looked at the fire.

"The men who insult you are not Americans," said Charles. "They will never be Americans. They can boast that their ancestors have lived here three hundred years, and they'll still not be Americans. We can say to them, as they say to many others: 'Go back to the place from which you came!' But these bastards have no place to go! They never came from anywhere, except, perhaps, from hell."

Mr. Schiffhauer turned his square white head towards Charles, and blinked.

"No, Mr. Schiffhauer, you mustn't let these people, or anybody, let you suspect for an instant you aren't an American. They want you to think you aren't. They want to put you outside the pale. You mustn't let them. Therefore, you mustn't consider, even for a moment, organizing the kind of society you suggest. Don't you think I know it's hard? I know. But I remember that I'm an American, and they're not."

" 'I am an American, and they are not,' " repeated Mr. Schiffhauer. But he spoke doubtfully. Then he looked at Charles with pleading in his eyes, silent and pathetic.

Charles said: "You don't like the Kaiser, do you? You hated Bismarck, and everything he was. You came to America to be an American. This is your country, Mr. Schiffhauer. Don't let anyone take her away from you, or separate you from her."

Mr. Schiffhauer lifted his head proudly. "I'm an American," he said, in English. "What America is, I am. I chose America. I am better, in a way, than those who were only born here, for I know what America is, and how wonderful. I did not need school-books to tell me this."

He stood up and gave his hand to Charles. "You are a fine boy, Charles. You made me happy when you made me realize that I'm an American." Then he added cautiously: "But I was too hasty when I said we should increase our minister's salary one thousand dollars. Five hundred is enough."

CHAPTER LII

By the fifteenth of November, the madness in Europe had become one enormous confusion. Russia was at war with Turkey, Great Britain was at war with Turkey, and Turkey had declared herself engaged in a "holy, religious war" against Serbia, France, Britain, and Russia. The mighty munitions plants in France and Germany, however, operated peacefully, and were not bombed. The trains ran serenely, loaded with materials of war, from France through Switzerland to Germany, and from Germany through Switzerland to France. There, in Switzerland, in rich secrecy, met the sly, sleek men of England and France and Germany, to dine well, to drink excellently, and to negotiate, not peace, but war, and the profits of war. Later, they discussed available women.

The young men of England, France, and Germany did not go laughing and singing to The Front any longer. The early winter rains washed through their trenches in a gray and stinking river. The rats ate of the bleeding corpses, and the young men watched them, in bewilderment, horror, and despair, and thought of their homes, and why they were here. The air exploded above and about them; the night was red with fire and death. The sleek men laughed in Switzerland, but the boys in their trenches did not laugh. Some of them cried, for they were so young.

As early as September, the Kaiser had written to President Wilson: "The old town of Louvain had to be destroyed for the protection of my troops.—The cruelties practiced in this cruel warfare even by the Belgian women and priests towards my wounded soldiers, doctors, and nurses, were such that eventually my generals were compelled to adopt the strongest measures to punish the guilty and frighten the blood-thirsty population—"

Charles had thought, when reading this letter in the papers: But what were your Junkers, your embroidered generals, your stiff-legged colonels, your arrogant captains and your soldiers, doing there in Belgium in the first place, you madman? Those poor, valiant priests, those poor, beleaguered women—they were only protecting their homes, their churches, and their country. Charles discounted the atrocity stories, but the photographs of ruined Belgian cities were enough to make a decent man hate the sight of a soldier forever, and hate any people who outfited, armed, and glorified him. But he remembered what Colonel Grayson had said, that the guilty were always the nations who tolerated armies.

Charles Wittmann knew that America was not neutral any longer. Americans were beginning to sing British war songs, such as "Tipperary." Except for the great Western plains, where farmers thought more of crops and seasons and wheat than war, Americans became conscious of an uneasy hatred for all that was German. It was very easy to understand, when a man once knew, as Charles did. British propaganda, superbly managed, superbly executed and delivered, filtered into the minds of Americans.

Charles, like millions of other enlightened Americans, understood, and had but one thought: to keep America out of the war. Neutrality was an illusion. Charles surrendered that hope. America could not be neutral. But she might—she must!—be kept out of the war. He, and his fellow Americans, fought a stubborn battle of retreat. The war might end soon. It could not go on much longer. Charles reckoned without the men in Switzerland, who smiled over their wine and laughed through their clouds of cigar smoke, and who figured endlessly, and bartered away the lives and the liberties and the hopes and the dreams of millions of other men. They bartered away the destiny of generations still unborn.

Three days before Thanksgiving, the three thousand men who worked in the shops and the mills of the Connington Steel Company went out on strike. It happened very suddenly. They wanted more wages. They wanted a union. They went to their homes, and sat there, sullenly but determinedly.

On the same day Charles received a letter from Mr. Dayton of the Amalgamated Steel Company. Mr. Dayton ordered a tremendous amount of tools. Charles called him, and said: "It's impossible. I don't have the steel. The Connington has a contract with Sessions, and they've pushed me out. You know why." He listened for a few moments to what Mr. Dayton said, and he smiled grimly. He waited for two hours, while Mr. Dayton discreetly called Washington. Then Charles called Colonel Grayson, himself.

"A little matter of restraint of trade, of monopoly, Colonel," he said.

"I see," said the colonel. "The President won't like that."

On the day before Thanksgiving Charles received a telegram from the Sessions Steel Company, in Windsor: "We find that our output of high speed tool steel exceeds the amount of our contract with certain other companies. We are glad to tell you that your recent orders will be filled at once."

Charles took the telegram to his brother Friederich, who read it and exclaimed bitterly over it. "There isn't even honor among thieves," said Friederich.

"I wouldn't say that," answered Charles. "A profit is always a profit." He did not tell Friederich of his conversations with Mr. Dayton and with the colonel. There were still some things he did not tell his brother. It would have been too confusing. He only said: "I wonder how long the strike will last at the Connington." And he smiled and went away, somewhat cheered.

He tried to forget that Americans were accepting British propaganda with enthusiasm and abject belief, and were rejecting German propaganda, sometimes amazingly the same, with disgust and incredulity.

But still, whatever their sympathies, the American people did not want to be thrust into the pit of war. In fact, many of them were becoming angered at the arrogance of Britain, who was openly violating the "freedom of the seas" long enough to board American and other neutral vessels in order to examine the mails. Charles thought: Idiots and rascals—all of them. Let them die, if they wish. It is none of our affair.

On the night before Thanksgiving he and the Reverend Mr. Haas went to the station to meet their sons. Jim and Walter had been gone only two months, but when their fathers saw them they said to themselves: They're no longer boys. They're men. They shook hands with their sons, and they were shy, and delighted, and did not know what to say. On the way home both Jim and Walter had their own private jokes, their own fraternal laughter. They would patiently explain all this to their fathers. They were on the way to lives of their own, and these lives did not include the minister and Charles.

Jim looked about the house with happy criticism, after he had gone into the kitchen to give Mrs. Meyers a hug. "Never knew the old place was so small," he said.

"Small? Twelve rooms aren't small," replied Charles. He sat down before the fire, and drank his beer. Then he glanced at his son. "Beer?" he suggested, somewhat reluctantly. Jim nodded, went to the kitchen, and came back with a bottle and a glass. He's been gone only two months, Charles thought again, yet he seems twice the size. "Good beer," said Jim. "Old Schiffhauer knows how to make it."

Charles then told him of Mr. Schiffhauer's visit. Jim listened, all seriousness. He sat there, big, black-haired, broad-shouldered—a man. Jim said, looking at his glass: "You gave him good advice, Dad. There's no place in America, now, where Germans are popular, and forming a belligerent German society, in the face of public opinion, would have been a dangerous thing."

Charles was alarmed. But he said as quietly as possible, though with irritation: "You've missed the point entirely. What do you mean by 'public opinion,' Jim? We're a neutral country. At the present time, we're nearer to war with England than with Germany, because of her violation of the freedom of the seas, her censoring of our mail, and her illegal boarding of our ships. Only the fact that we've a pro-Ally Ambassador, Page, keeps the American people from exploding and knocking hell out of England, right now! We went to war with her in 1812 because she did something similar to this—boarding our vessels, and such." Only two months, and his son was a stranger, with strange, unknown friends, a strange life, and strange new ideas! Charles said: "Jim! What's the matter with you?"

Jim looked up, surprised. "There's nothing the matter with me, Dad." He was thoughtful, then. His father, he said to himself, was looking haggard and old and strained. Things were getting too much for the old boy. He supposed that he ought to ask his father all about the shops, as he formerly did, but somehow they were not of much interest to him now. There were other matters more important. The young man said: "It's just that I'm studying very hard. I want to be the best damn doctor in the whole country." And he grinned at Charles affectionately.

"Good," said Charles. "Of course, you'll be that." He drank his beer, with worry. "You still haven't told me what you mean by 'public opinion.' I know the British are doing a good job on us with their propaganda. But we're determined to be neutral. What do the boys at your school think of the war, eh?"

"The men at the college," said Jim, with dignity, "are divided. Some of them are all for going into it, and ending it. On the side of the Allies, of course. Some of them are just as much against it—against all war. They're the bookish fellows. Hate everything but the old ivy and the libraries and the laboratories. And some of them want to fight England. But most of them, I'd say, are all for keeping out of it."

"Sensible," commented Charles. "I remember what Burke said: 'War never leaves, where it found a nation.' The best America can do for the world is to stay at peace, and keep her reason. Jim, I've come to what you might think is a foolish conclusion of my own: This war isn't being fought for what is being given as the ostensible reason. It's being fought, by everybody, to destroy the new ideal of the freedom of man. You'll see, after this war, that this ideal will be scrapped, and old absolutisms will come up like—well, like poisonous mushrooms. America will be able to hold the balance, afterwards; she'll be able to stop all attempts to enslave men again."

Jim looked at his father with deep and shadowy uneasiness, and Charles, with greater alarm, saw it. "In the meantime," said Jim, "men are dying. I wish to God," continued the young man desperately, "that I was a full-fledged doctor. I'd go over there and help take care of the wounded, at least. Any wounded."

Relief came immensely to Charles. "That's fine," he said. "Fine." He reflected, comfortably, that Jim was not a "full-fledged doctor." "I'm thinking of the wounded and dying, too," said Charles, pouring more beer, and this time out of Jim's bottle. "But what can we do? Nothing. Except keep our heads and remain sensible and at peace. Later, we can do something."

He waited for Jim to ask him about the shops, and all that had happened. But Jim stared at the fire, brooding, and he had thoughts his father could not know. Then Jim said suddenly, still staring at the fire: "When are you and Aunt Phyllis going to get married?"

"Next August."

"Not until then?" Jim was annoyed. "Almost a year."

"Well, we have to wait a year from the time your uncle died, to announce the engagement," said Charles, lamely. "And then we have to wait a few months after the announcement."

"It's all nonsense," said Jim, impatiently.

He thinks I'm an old fogey, thought Charles. I know I never thought that about my own father. Or, did I? He could not remember.

"There're some things you can do and some things you can't," said Charles. Yes, he was talking like an "old fogey," and Jim was smiling at him.

"Good old Dad. Always conventional," said Jim. "Nothing new must ever intrude." His black eyes studied Charles indulgently.

"All this talk about the 'new'!" exclaimed Charles, with acerbity. "As if anything new was better than something old, just because it *was* new! Look at ragtime, for instance. That's new. Is it better than Beethoven, or Bach, or Brahms, or Wagner, or Verdi?"

Something was running under the surface of their conversation which Charles could not grasp; something had shifted between him and his son these last eight or ten weeks. We're talking to cover something up, thought Charles. What is it? What has happened to my boy? He's changed.

Dad's changed, thought Jim. He's all nerves. I don't understand him. He's never shouted at me like this before. What's wrong with him?

"The world changes," said Jim, somewhat irrelevantly. He was really anxious about his father, now. He never used to flush up so easily, thought the young man. He never used to be so on edge. He looks sick.

"We must all sing and whistle and scream the same silly imbecilities, because they're new," said Charles. "We must all ride in automobiles— because they're new. We must all think the same thoughts—because they're new. We mustn't have any distinctiveness, any difference, because something 'new' has become the pattern of our existence. We're getting to be faceless. The 'new' collectivism! By God, that's something I'd fight with my last breath!" And Charles stood up, his face a heavy crimson.

"Dad," began Jim, standing up also. He looked down at his father. He did not know why Charles turned away from him, after one glance upwards.

"The Renaissance was 'new,' in its time," said Charles. "But it was a healthy and vigorous newness, and not the newness of inferior and mean-spirited and trivial men. It emphasized an old concept: the importance of the individual over the unimportance of the mass. The Church had always declared that man, himself, was everything, and that anything that debased that individuality was dangerous. Now we have this modern newness, which wants to destroy the individual and make him just part of the mass, a herd-man, a slave. And I think this war is the culmination, or the beginning, of the idea that man, as a thinking individual, ought to be destroyed."

He added bitterly: "You've just got to listen to Wilson! His 'New Freedom,' by God! Freedom was given to humanity by God. But governments, if they can help it, never give freedom. They just hand out slavery with slogans."

"Dad," said Jim, urgently, "you're right. I agree with you. But you don't have to get all worked up like this—" His only thought was to calm his father. "You won't be able to digest your dinner," said the boy. "You'll have indigestion again, as you always do when you get mad. And then out will come that box of bicarbonate of soda, and you'll have gas."

"Much you care," said Charles, and he sat down heavily. Then he said to himself with consternation: I'm quarreling with my son! He's just come home, and I'm quarreling with him, as if he were a stranger! What's wrong with us? There's something under the surface—

"I do care," said Jim, earnestly. "Please, Dad. I know how you've worked; I know how you've worried. You've written me all about it. I ought to be ashamed," he added, with self-disgust. "I oughtn't to have let you get mad like this. It's all my fault."

Charles looked up at him for a long time. His dark flush retreated, and all at once he was pale and very tired, but smiling. "No," he said. "I know what it is. I just resent it that you're growing up. I've just begun to realize you're a man. I don't like it, much. I'm a fool."

The harsh November wind poured down the chimney, and the fire crackled and blew. The November wind battered at the windows; the November rain ran mournfully in the eaves. I've never been so lonely, thought Charles. Not even when I was alone.

"I can't help growing up," said Jim. "But you've got your own life, Dad. You're not so old." He spoke with sympathy, and without conviction, and Charles suddenly laughed.

Mrs. Meyers had prepared a very good dinner, and father and son sat down to it with anticipation. They talked of Jim's studies. They talked of many things. They did not speak of the war. Jim's still too young to understand what's really happening, thought Charles. Besides, it doesn't matter. The war'll never touch him, thank God.

Charles said, later: "The Connington's on strike. Brinkwell's going out of his mind." They did not mention Jochen.

CHAPTER LIII

In December, 1914, the United States was so perilously close to war with Britain that only the strenuous exertions of Ambassador Page prevented it. Britain controlled the seas, and Germany was helpless. Britain had declared that American vessels carrying contraband either openly to

Germany, or to neutral countries, could be, and were, rightfully seized by her. Food, gasoline, copper, rubber, and many other articles were labelled "contraband" by Britain, and British warships halted American vessels, without apology, for search, or took them to British ports for further search.

The American people, aroused, read with incredulity and anger of British ships actually hoisting the American flag on the high seas, in order to protect themselves from German torpedoes, and then proceeding serenely, under the aegis of that flag, with the seized "contraband" or goods bought from America by the British Government. American companies impartially willing to sell to either Britain or Germany were blacklisted by Britain to such effect that American trade with other neutral countries almost ceased. Secretary of State Lansing indignantly exclaimed that Britain's acts were illegal and indefensible, and President Wilson helplessly mourned: "We can do two things: protest or declare war." Notes passed constantly from Washington, notes distinguished for their pleading overtones. But Ambassador Page stood "valiantly" for the "righteousness" of England's "cause." Without subterfuge, without hypocrisy, without valid excuse, he openly announced his hopes for England's victory over Germany. Troubled and aghast, both at this violation of the principles of neutrality and the urbane candor of the diplomat, the American people, through the press, began to demand his recall. But he was not recalled.

To most Americans, all the issues were now so confused, so entangled, so incapable of being understood, that they gave up in despair. They jeered at the futility of the notes sent to both Britain and Germany by President Wilson; they denounced Ambassador Page and ridiculed the Kaiser. But they were firm in their resolution to remain out of the war.

It was odd that the Connington Steel Company, and similar companies, were not blacklisted by Britain. This was possible because these companies, having discovered that they could no longer ship war materials to Germany, now, with fine impartiality, were quite willing to ship them to Britain, using British ships or British lines carrying American citizens, who were eagerly curious to be near the center of the universal storm. Beneath the happy, romping feet of naïve Americans on British passenger vessels lay tons of war material. The Americans were very excited when the liners were externally darkened at night, and they shuddered deliciously in saloons and in their staterooms at the thought of the danger to which they were so childishly exposing themselves. It was exceedingly thrilling. Why, they might be torpedoed! The British captains listened to this infantile prattle, and smiled contemptuously to themselves. They carried hostages for the safe delivery of the steel, guns, ammunition, and explosives in their holds.

Business was very good for the Connington Steel Company's mills, or, rather, it would have been good except for the strike.

The Connington Steel Company's policy had always been determinedly against unions of any kind. They refused to change their policy. "Labor" was becoming "dangerous." It was a "menace" to enterprise. Its leaders were enemies of American freedom.

"They'll come back, crawling, when they see they'll get nothing out of this but starvation," said Roger Brinkwell to Jochen Wittmann.

He and Jochen and their office staff came through the ranks of the pickets, disdainfully, ignoring the ominous shouts and jeers of the hungry men. But Mr. Brinkwell was annoyed at the *Clarion*, which defended the strikers and called the Connington Steel Company "anachronistic." Mr. Grimsley vitriolically attacked Mr. Brinkwell by name, and attacked his superiors in Pittsburgh. Mr. Grimsley was delighted when the parent mills in Pittsburgh shut down as their own workers went out on a sympathy strike. Had the Connington Steel Company in Andersburg been a small concern, the sentiment of the Andersburg citizens might not have been so aroused. But thousands of men, both natives of Andersburg and natives of nearby towns and villages, were suffering. This had a bad effect on the shopkeepers of the city, and an equally bad effect on related business. The Quakers had set up soup kitchens for the destitute workers and their families, and offered their services in mediation. The Connington Steel Company, through Mr. Brinkwell, rejected this offer with derision. "We'll never negotiate with this disorderly rabble," he was reported to have said.

The *Clarion* published the opinions of clergymen and other influential people in Andersburg. The Reverend Mr. Haas was quoted as saying that the Connington had brought misery to the people of Andersburg, that it harbored "medieval" ideas, that its tactics were inhuman and cruel, that it was "high-handed" and brutal in its refusal to negotiate with the leaders of the workers. Mr. Haas prayed for moderation, for understanding, for decency.

Father Hagerty was quoted: "The Popes have always pleaded the cause of labor, of social justice and consideration on the part of the powerful, and of the rights of the working man. One will notice the word 'rights.' Justice is not a concession, to be dispensed grandly by employers, and in their own way, and at their own time. Pope Pius, in

1891, said: 'With criminal injustice they (employers) denied the innate right of forming associations to those who needed them most for self-protection against oppression by the more powerful.' The Connington Steel Company would do well to read the papal document of His Holiness, Leo XIII: 'The Condition of Labor.'—It is un-Christian to deny the right of labor to organize into unions, and to refuse to negotiate with those who desire to form a union."

Prodded by Charles Wittmann, the Mayor, in misery, also urged the Connington Steel Company to "negotiate in a fair spirit of brotherhood and reason." The Mayor remembered that he owed his office to Charles, but he was very unhappy because his wife sedulously courted Pauline Brinkwell, and the latter's friends.

"Sanctimonious rats," said Mr. Brinkwell, to Jochen. "That former minister of yours: He knows we're now sending war material to England, and being a porky Dutchman he's enraged, of course."

Jochen, still fat these days, but flabby and pale, looked at his friend quickly, and with secret hatred. Porky Dutchman! Jochen lit a cigar with big and clumsy fingers, and let the smoke hide his face. Mr. Brinkwell was sitting on the edge of Jochen's desk, and he was reading the various quotations aloud, and laughing contemptuously. Jochen asked: "How would Mr. Haas know we're sending steel, and things, to England?"

Roger Brinkwell laughed again. "Old Charlie must have told him. Old Charlie knows a lot of things, Joe." He added: "Old Charlie always thought of himself as a Dutchman, didn't he? He was never really American, was he?"

Jochen had extended his manner of living from the mildly luxurious to the very luxurious. He had recently bought some land in a very exclusive suburb, and was about to build a very sumptuous house—at Isabel's insistence. His daughters were accepted "everywhere." Geraldine was to marry Kenneth Brinkwell next summer. Jochen did not save any money these days. It went for enormous expenses, commensurate with his new mode of living. He belonged to very expensive clubs, sponsored by Roger Brinkwell. Isabel had her own automobile and her own private chauffeur, and there were seven servants now instead of the former three. For Isabel must have her personal maid, and there was a maid for the girls. Jochen smoked savagely. He said: "I don't remember that Charlie ever particularly cared about Germany, or even spoke of it." Roger's mouth still smiled. Jochen added: "But Charlie never let anyone know what he really thought."

Roger nodded, appeased. "Cunning devil." He opened his gold cigarette case and thoughtfully withdrew a gold-tipped cigarette. "Yes, cunning. One of these days we'll settle with him, when we've knocked hell out of our strikers. And I'll have a word or two to say to the Bouchards, about their subsidiary, Sessions, shipping steel again to your brother. In fact, I've already written to the Bouchards. It's unethical, to say the least."

Jochen was not a man to appreciate irony, or to recognize it. But now he said to himself: Unethical, eh? He blew another cloud of smoke, and there was a feeling of tension in his temples. He had come to hate his employer. He did not remember when this hatred began, or what caused it. He, being a simple man, merely accepted the hatred and the resentment, without seeking for reasons. There was a festering in him, and a dull, constant ache, and a discontent. His salary was almost three times what it had been as vice-president of the Wittmann Machine Tool Company. But he could not save a penny. Isabel! May and Ethel, those silly girls! And Geraldine— Jochen thought of Geraldine's last visit home, at Thanksgiving. He thought of her thin young face, of her listlessness.

Jochen remarked dully: "I never heard that the Bouchards didn't like a profit. I always was under the impression that they'd sell to anybody. They're in a nasty position, themselves, with the Government, with that suit brought against them, accusing them of being a monopoly and acting in restraint of trade."

Roger laughed. "The suit'll come to nothing. The Bouchards have too many Senators in the palms of their hands. And they own two Supreme Court judges." He studied Jochen. "What's the matter, Joe? You look pretty wretched, these days."

"The strike," muttered Jochen.

Roger smoked thoughtfully, nodding. "Well, don't worry. It'll be settled any day now. They're getting pretty hungry, in spite of the Quakers, and the public subscriptions. They'll come back soon, and they'll take what we choose to give them."

Jochen's big Pierce-Arrow automobile called for him, with its uniformed chauffeur. It plunged implacably towards the picketing men, who jumped out of the way. A rock smashed against the rear window, was followed by other rocks, and shouts and curses. Jochen stolidly looked through the window at his right and he saw the faces of the strikers. He saw the pale and sunken cheeks, the starved eyes, the bitter anger, the despair that twisted the mouths of the men. He had never felt any friendliness towards the men who had worked under him at his brother's shops, or at these mills. He had felt only contempt and aloofness, such as one feels for animals. But now he had a sudden, and inexplicable, desire to have the car halted, and to empty his pockets for these poor wretches, to hold out the yellow and the green bills, and the silver, and to say— Say what? My God, thought Jochen, I must be losing my mind! "Drive faster!" he cried to the chauffeur.

The sky was gray and somber, and snow was falling thickly. The house would be warm. Geraldine was home for Christmas; Isabel had met her train that afternoon. Gerry, thought Jochen. He'd take her to their doctor if she still looked ill and thin and tired. She was his darling, his pet. My sweet thing, thought Jochen. She never asks for anything, and I'd give her the world, if I could. But she never tells me anything any more.

He decided that his vague distress was due to his worry about his oldest daughter. He said to the chauffeur: "Can't you go faster?" He sat on the edge of the velvet seat, and then without warning he heard again: "Porky Dutchman!" That was Charlie. It had nothing to do with him, Jochen. His misery became so acute that it was a physical pain. He put his hand on his chest. In spite of what that damned doctor said there must be something wrong with his heart! He knew it.

Charles had his steel, now, thought Jochen. For a time, at least, the Connington Steel Company would not get those patents it wanted so urgently. It would get nothing. The Wittmann Machine Tool Company was safe. Charlie, the dirty dog, was safe. The company would go on, as it had always gone on. My father's company, thought Jochen. He sat back in his seat, drew a deep breath. The pain had vanished, and the tightness.

The house, now so despised by Isabel, was as warm as Jochen had anticipated. It was also silent. The lamps had been lighted, and the curtains drawn against the wind and the snow. A maid told Jochen that Mrs. Wittmann had had to attend a club meeting, and that she would not be home for another hour. Miss May and Miss Ethel were at a pre-Christmas party. Yes, Miss Geraldine had arrived. She was upstairs in her room.

Jochen threw his coat and hat into the hands of the maid, and forgetting his "heart," ran very fast up the wide and carpeted stairs. He called: "Gerry! Gerry!" He forgot that this was a detested nickname, and that Isabel resented it. He called again: "Gerry!" And he burst into his daughter's room, with a delighted smile, and his arms out.

Geraldine had been lying on her bed in her pretty ruffled room, and one wall light was dimly lit. She pushed herself up on one elbow as her father entered, and pressed her hand against her cheek. All her movements were sluggish and full of fatigue. Her black hair had loosened, and rolled on her thin shoulders. Her eyes were very big and heavy and dull, and her face was white and almost gaunt.

"Papa," she said. Then slowly, weakly, she stood up. Jochen stood there and watched her, and the shock of his pain and fear kept him standing mutely, his arms extended. Then she was leaning against his bulky chest, and her head was dropping against his shoulder. He put his arms about her; his heart began to thump loudly in his ears and temples and throat. "Why, Gerry," he said, and held her closer. "Why, Gerry."

He lifted his hands and thrust them almost fiercely through her hair, pulling her head against his shoulder as if to hide her, as if she were a stricken or threatened child. He took up strands of her hair and kissed them; he pushed her hair from her forehead, and kissed it. "Why, Gerry, my sweet," he said, in dismay. He was very frightened. "What's wrong with my girl, home for Christmas? Is my girl sick? What've they been doing to my girl? I knew I shouldn't have let you go away!"

"Nothing's wrong, Papa," she said, feebly. "I'm just tired, I guess. The courses are hard." She began to cry, suddenly, despairingly, and clung to him. "I did miss you so, Papa! I wanted you so, Papa!"

"Why, Gerry," he said again. It hurt him to breathe. "Why—why I'll kill anybody who ever hurts you! You mustn't cry like that, Gerry. Hush, hush, Gerry. See, it's Papa. There's no one here but us, my darling. Let's sit down together and talk, eh? Whatever my girl wants she can have." But Geraldine, he remembered, never asked for any-thing, never had temper tantrums, never demanded. He sat her down on the edge of her bed, and he sat with her, holding her in his arms, wiping her eyes. "You never tell me," he said.

He took her face in his hands; it was blotched, and between the blotches the flesh was a sickly white, and her lips were bluish. "You're sick!" he cried. "You never told me! You'll never go away from me again."

But Geraldine remembered that her school was not far from Har-vard, and that she would not see Jim for months if she remained at home. She stammered: "I—I like the school, Papa. It isn't that."

She fixed her large eyes on her father, and she, too, was frightened. His color was very bad; he had become fatter, yet he was so flabby and worn. He looked as if he had gained years, even since Thanksgiving, and his shoulders, always so broad and thick, sagged. She knew so much about her father. She cried wretchedly, the tears running down her cheeks. "It isn't that," she repeated.

Her father was at Mr. Brinkwell's mercy. She thought of the new home which was to be built in the summer; she thought of her father's huge expenses. She knew he was afraid. She could not tell him that she didn't want to become engaged to Kenneth Brinkwell. Kenneth's father could be so revengeful. She thought of Roger Brinkwell again, and shrank.

"You always told me everything," Jochen was pleading. "Tell me, Gerry, tell me, now."

She could never tell him. Then she heard herself saying, with sick horror: "Papa, I don't want to be engaged to Kenneth. I just can't, Papa."

His hands dropped onto his knees. His jowly face twitched.

"Oh, Papa," said the girl. "I didn't mean that! I didn't mean to say that!" She put her hands on his shoulders, vehemently. "Please forget I said that. I didn't know what I was saying."

He took one of her hands and held it tightly. He stared before him, with bleakness. He said: "I thought you liked Kenneth, Gerry."

"I do like him, Papa. Or, at least, I don't dislike him. He's awfully nice to me. He writes me almost every day. He isn't like his father—" And she stopped, horrified again.

"No," said Jochen. "He isn't like his father. He isn't even very much like his mother. Lucky for him. I always thought he was kind of a nice young fellow, in a way."

The engagement was supposed to be announced on New Year's Eve. The Brinkwells were giving a dance for the young couple. It was to be the "affair of the season." The marriage was to take place next June. Jochen said, apathetically: "You never told me, Gerry. There's the ring, and everything. You ought to have told me before."

"I was going to, Papa," said the young girl, with fresh tears. "And then—"

He turned to his daughter, and his eyes were miserable. All at once, they sharpened, and his whole moonlike face flushed heavily. "And then, I went to the Connington," he said.

It was his heart; he knew it now, more than ever. Only a diseased heart could cause a man such pain. He tried to keep his breathing shallow. He sat, bent and sagging, on the bed, and he said to himself: I'm the cause of this. I'm killing my little girl. She's never said anything, just because of me. She's doing all this, for me. So I could have what I wanted.

"I wouldn't have gone," he said, with a hatred for everything and everyone but his daughter. "But your uncle made me get out. He stole my share of my father's company from me. He robbed me. I had to get out—out of my father's company, where I was somebody, where I was vice-president in charge of production, where I wasn't a hired man. That's what he did to me—your uncle."

"Oh, Papa," said Geraldine, mournfully. "You know Uncle Charlie didn't 'steal' anything from you. He always liked you; he always came here, even when he didn't see Uncle Willie very often, and never saw Uncle Fred. Uncle Charlie wouldn't do any harm to anybody."

He moved away from her. "He robbed me, Gerry. He ruined me. He drove me out." But he did not look at her. He rubbed the back of his hand against his eyes. "No, it wasn't just like that, Gerry." He could not stop himself. "It was Brinkwell, all the time. I must have been out of my mind! Brinkwell wanted our patents; he wanted me to push Charlie. Charlie's an obstinate—" He stopped. ("Porky Dutchman!") Jochen stood up, and then began to pace the room with a ponderous, old man's tread. "He said we'd all make money if Charlie leased the patents— We would have, too. But Charlie wouldn't lease him the patents. I know why, now, and Charlie was right. I've just found out, these last few months. But how could Charlie have known? He never told anybody anything. He just sat there in his office, and I thought he was looking sick and tired because of his liver, and all the time it was—"

"Was what, Papa?" Geraldine asked, eagerly. She got up.

"It was something else," said Jochen. He put his arm about his daughter, and they walked up and down together. "I know now. Brinkwell used me. But he couldn't use Charlie. He tried to stop Charlie from getting steel, but he didn't know Charlie! Charlie got the steel. It was all something too big for me; Brinkwell played me for a fool. But he couldn't play with Charlie!"

"Nobody can play with Uncle Charlie," said Geraldine. Some color had come into her face. "Why don't you go and tell Uncle Charlie all this, Papa?"

"Why, Gerry, I'd die first," said Jochen, simply. "Besides, I hate him. He was my father's favorite. It was always Charlie, Charlie, Charlie. But I suppose my father was right, in a way, but Charlie didn't have to be so bustling and busy and cocksure, in the early days, and being so damned right and smug about everything all the time. It made Willie sick, and that idiot, Fred, too." His resentment made his voice rise.

How much money had he, now? This house—it was mortgage-free. He didn't have to build that damned house for Isabel, which was to cost sixty thousand dollars! There were his stocks and bonds, seventy-five thousand dollars' worth, and the market rising. There were thirty thousand dollars in the bank. No mortgage on the house, and all his insurance paid up. But there was, of course, Isabel, and the other two girls. His money wasn't a fortune. It would be enough for a while. He'd go to Pittsburgh, or Cleveland. He knew the machine tool business better than anybody, even old Charlie. He hated the Connington; he hated Brinkwell, and this stinking town. He was still a young man, and a valuable one. The other steel companies would jump at him. He put his arms about his daughter and hugged her tightly.

"You don't have to marry young Kenneth, my sweetheart," he said, and there was a new strength in his voice. "You don't have to do anything you don't want to do. We'll get out of here; there're better places in this country." He rubbed her under her chin, and he chuckled. "But don't tell anybody anything. It's just between the two of us, eh?"

She burrowed her head in his chest, and her thin young arms clung to him. She had been such a fool. She ought to have told her father before. Then she looked up, and said fearfully: "But the dance, Papa. And the announcement. On New Year's Eve, too."

He had forgotten this. He hesitated. He might use guile and chicanery, himself, but he had never wanted his daughters to be hard or expedient or cunning. Especially not Geraldine. He frowned.

"I know, Papa," said Geraldine, understanding. "We'll go through the engagement party. That'll help. That'll give you time. Six months. And it won't really be hurting Kenneth. He wouldn't want someone to marry him who didn't want to. Why, there're hundreds of girls who'd marry him in a minute. He was almost engaged to a girl in Philadelphia, before he came here, and his mother was angry with him when he began to like me. Mrs. Brinkwell would be only too glad not to have Kenneth marry me."

For no reason at all they began to laugh. Jochen forgot all about his "heart." He felt free, exultant, and young. He tickled Geraldine, as he chased her, and then they went downstairs together, hand in hand, to meet Isabel who was just coming in.

"Well," said Isabel, as the maid helped her remove her rich fur coat. "You two look very happy, I must say. What've you been up to? Jochen, I've just bought the most beautiful Chippendale mirror for our new entrance hall; in really wonderful condition. You must see it. It's at Blake's. And Geraldine, there's a dress you must see, for New Year's Eve. I don't like these ready-made clothes, so cheap, really. But this is from Paris. We'll look at it tomorrow."

CHAPTER LIV

ABRUPTLY, ONLY two days before Christmas, the Connington Steel Company, seriously alarmed at the stubbornness of their workers both in Andersburg and Pittsburgh, and stunned by a large public resentment against it, agreed to negotiate with the leaders of the strike. "There's something going on in this damned country that I can't understand," said Roger Brinkwell to Jochen Wittmann. "This is something unique. But if there wasn't a war going on in Europe we'd sit here, snug, and let them starve themselves to death. We haven't time, just now."

"Rotten business," agreed Jochen.

Charles, when he heard of the end of the strike, called in his brother Friederich and Tom Murphy. He said: "Now, our own men mustn't have a company union any longer. They've got to join the tool-makers at Connington, in one union. That strengthens everybody. And Tom —we're raising our own tool-makers, and everybody else, ten cents on the dollar. We've got the big orders from the Amalgamated Steel Company, now, and more coming in." He told no one that he had already assigned his own personal patents, such as the aeroplane steering control assembly, to the Amalgamated Steel Company, who were re-releasing it to aeroplane companies.

He tried not to think too much. Tomorrow, Jim would be home. There was Friederich's wedding on January fifteenth to plan for, and his hopes for his life with Phyllis. There were times when a man dared not think too much, for there was nothing he could do. He could only temporize. Charles remembered what his father had always quoted to him so admiringly, a saying of Lincoln's: "All government—indeed every human benefit and enjoyment, every virtue and every prudent act—is founded on compromise." But I've always thought that, reflected Charles, with some bitterness.

Jim seemed even bigger when he came home, and when his father mentioned that he was still only eighteen, Jim was prompt in reminding him that within a few weeks he would be nineteen. He appeared wary, at first, but Charles, following his minister's advice, talked only of his son. He could not help but be hurt, however, when Jim asked about the shops only once or twice, and was more interested in the result of the strike.

He said, idly, the day after Christmas: "I understand they're going to announce Gerry's engagement to Kenneth Brinkwell on New Year's." He began to laugh, then stopped, soberly.

"Don't be such an imbecile," said Charles. "Gerry showed me the ring you gave her, before you went away. She's a girl of sense. I suppose she has to go through this thing, but, of course, she'll never marry young Brinkwell."

"You've known about Gerry and me all along," Jim accused his father.

Charles thought that it was hard to be a father. Jim was looking at him reproachfully. So he said: "Gerry made me see it was all right."

They had had Christmas dinner alone, but Phyllis was having dinner with them tonight. For some reason, Jim was not too enthusiastic. Apparently the appalling idea that his father might be capable of be-getting other children had been too much for him. When Phyllis came, he was less affectionate with her than he had ever been before. Phyllis was amused, though Charles was annoyed. "I understand all about it, dear," Phyllis said to Charles, as he drove her home. She patted his hand maternally. He did not care particularly about that, either.

However, by exercising tremendous self-control, Charles found it not too hard to keep from being irritable with his son. He was jealous of Jim's school-life, away from his own, but Jim's deep and passionate devotion to his studies was something so unique that Charles could not help but be proud, though he sometimes smiled when Jim, in this, his freshman year, and still far from beginning his real medical studies, spoke with dignity of his "profession."

"Are you supposed to be studying these books?" Charles asked once, noticing certain books which looked somewhat advanced to him, deal-ing, as they did, with pathology. Jim admitted that these were not the books he was actually studying at the moment; they were simply books he had bought, far in anticipation, because they fascinated him. When Charles, a day or two before Jim left for school, confessed to "another" headache, Jim wanted to know what Dr. Metzger had told him of his blood pressure, and if there were symptoms of hypertension. This seemed so like the old days that Charles was much cheered, especially when he overheard Jim talking learnedly to Dr. Metzger on the tele-phone and discussing systolic and diastolic, with regard to Charles. When Jim lectured him anxiously on "emotional states" Charles knew for certain that his son had not actually left him.

"But he never will," Phyllis said, when Charles told her of these incidents.

Jim returned to attend Friederich's wedding, and had grown at least another five inches, in Charles' estimation. Jim said: "What you've done with old Uncle Fred, Dad! It's amazing."

"I haven't 'done' anything with him," said Charles, annoyed. "No one can do anything for anybody. A man can only do things with or for himself. You make me sound like a schemer."

"Well, you are, in a nice way," said Jim, with elderly and affectionate patronage. "Uncle Fred's a human being, for the first time in his life. And look how clean he is, and how he talks so moderately, and marrying that nice Helen, too. He hardly ever gets excited, except for his eyes. I heard him and George Hadden talking about the war, and Uncle Fred didn't once scream, or talk about Socialism, and 'capitalistic evils.' He didn't once yell about 'Germany's wrongs,' as he did a couple of years ago. Now he just says—and I heard him saying it to George— that everybody's guilty of this war, and that the Kaiser ought to be in an insane asylum."

Charles said: "Sometimes a man understands in his youth, sometimes he understands in his manhood, and sometimes he never understands. Your uncle came to understanding pretty late, but he came."

"Yes," said Jim. He did not speak of the war again, but looked at his father anxiously. "I try not to think of the damned war," said Charles. "At the present time the American people haven't decided whether they ought to be fighting England or Germany, and that's a good thing."

Charles, at least temporarily, was able to sleep without nightmares. The American people were angered against all the combatants, though they were moved at the plight of Belgium. All the churches held special peace services regularly, and prayed for the end of the war. Besides, everybody was now prophesying the end of the war by the spring. "It couldn't go on."

Very few people, and very few newspapers, talked of Russia's part in this war. The prophets had declared that if the Russian people once "got their hands on guns" the rule of the Czars would be over, and a modern and civilized government would be established. The prophets, up to date, had been wrong. If the Russians were doing very much it was not recorded prominently. No one knew very much about Russia. Just as Charles was falling asleep one night he remembered what his father had said to him, nearly two decades ago: "One of these days the Russian bear will walk, then God help the rest of the world!" His father, thought Charles, just falling into unconsciousness, was as bad a prophet as the rest of them.

Charles slept. The April trees, newly leafed, moved their gentle shadows on the window shades. The April moon poured down a cataract of silver on the cities of America, on new wheatfields, on quiet roads, on farm-houses and villages, on mountains and prairies. There was no sound of marching armies here, no alarms, no red skies, no flight of refugees, no weeping over the murdered dead, no drums, no trumpets. If there was an evil stirring in the night, few Americans knew it.

CHAPTER LV

FRIEDERICH'S MARRIAGE to Helen Hadden had aroused considerable derision in Andersburg, among Charles' enemies. "Well, he tamed *that* fanatic," they said. "He's lucky. One brother is killed, he robs and drives out another brother, and he gets the last brother to eating out of his hand. Now he's all there is of the Wittmann Machine Tool Company."

Charles had learned, after Wilhelm's death, that a man's integrity, his decency, his tolerance towards his fellowmen, his friendship for his neighbors, a more or less exemplary life, his earnest affection for his city, his refraining from engaging in any sort of nasty chicanery, his devotion to his family and to his church—in short, his exercising of his duties as a good citizen and a good man—did not necessarily exempt him from hatred, envy, and enmity. Rather, he had discovered to his dismay, that sometimes these virtues were the very things that aroused animosity, not only among rascals but in "good" men, themselves. Some of them were members of his own church, and he had talked with Mr. Haas about this.

"Well," said the Reverend Mr. Haas, ruefully, "I've been sermonizing about this off and on for at least twenty-five years, now, Charlie, but it seems that you've never heard a single word I've said. That looks bad for all my other sermons, too. Sometimes," said the minister, "I wonder if anyone ever listens to anything his pastor says, at any time. You come to church on Sundays, all of you, and you sing the hymns, and you give your responses, and you pray—or do you?—and you all sit there like bags of meal while I deliver the sermon I've sweated over for days. And what happens, then? You, and others, too, come to me later all amazed, and ask me questions I've answered a dozen times." He shook his head. "Sometimes—" he repeated, and he was not in the least amused.

"Charles," he went on, when Charles looked properly embarrassed, "I often think that people just don't deserve to have churches at all. They don't deserve to have priests and ministers. We give up our lives to you, and the best we can hope is that you won't beat your wives or murder your neighbors. Perhaps that's an advance, for which we can be thankful. Very few of you do beat your wives, and only occasionally do you murder a neighbor. But nothing we can be too proud of, after two thousand years.

"You see, Charles, men don't like their neighbors to succeed, brothers don't rejoice too much when their brothers rise a little higher, sisters resent another sister who is prettier than themselves or who has made a more profitable marriage, and even fathers have been embittered when sons did better with their businesses than they did, themselves. If I were a homespun philosopher I'd say: 'That's the way people are,' and I'd let it go, thinking I'd said a wise thing. And maybe the homespun philosopher is right. That's the way people are, and that's why ministers and priests pray and hope their parishioners will learn a little charity one of these days, by the grace of God. And not 'be the way they are.' "

He took off his glasses, polished them, sighed. "We've learned to fly, in the air, but how many of us fly with the spirit? Modern man has advanced in science; in so far as his soul is concerned it is still grappling with the saber-toothed tiger."

Charles tried to be a Christian when he felt the sneers and suspected innuendoes and jibes following the announcement, by Mr. and Mrs. Braydon Holt, of his engagement to Phyllis, on April 30, 1915. It was hard to meet congratulatory smiles blandly, and know them not to be congratulatory at all; it was hard to pretend not to see a quirked eyebrow or a tilted mouth-corner. He knew that many of the alleged wishers for his happiness also wished that his business would fail, or were remembering the cruel scandals they had broadcast about Phyllis, and hoping they were true. Sometimes Charles wanted to say to them, bitterly: "Why do you resent a man being happy? You are happy, aren't you?" After he had thought this a number of times, he, one day, felt a sudden surge of compassion, and said to the hand-shakers, silently: "If you aren't happy, I damn well wish you were!" He meant it, much to his surprise, and thereafter he was no longer disgusted. At least, not too often.

When the announcement appeared in the *Clarion*, Isabel called her husband and said with a light scream of malicious delight: "What do you think, Jochen! Those Holts, who've been snubbing us so constantly, have just announced that your brother Charles and Phyllis are going to be married on August tenth! Isn't that delicious? What a scandal! Everybody will be remembering the stories about them."

Jochen said: "I didn't quite hear you, Isabel." But he had heard. He only wanted time to think. "The stories about them." But he, Jochen, had invented the stories, had disseminated them. They were lies.

"——And I really do hope they'll come to realize how much people will despise them now," Isabel was saying. "Absolutely disgraceful. No shame. But then, what would you expect of Charles and Phyllis, anyway?"

Jochen looked about his office. It was the thirtieth of April, and he had done nothing, yet. He had been afraid. Afraid of his wife, afraid of "talk," afraid of Brinkwell. Afraid of everything, when there was no reason for fear except in himself. He said: "Isabel, don't say that. You know what my personal feelings are about Charlie, but all the rest— the stories and such—were lies."

"What!" cried Isabel, incredulously. "You told them to me, yourself, Jochen!"

Again, Jochen looked about his office, and hated it. "I told you lies," said Jochen. "I wanted what Charlie had, that's all. It's about time you knew it, Isabel. It's about time you knew a lot of things. I'll tell you about it. Tonight."

All the way home, this lilac-colored April evening, he thought of Isabel and himself. He thought of their youth together, and the affection they had had for each other, and the trust. The youth was gone. He was no longer sure even of the affection and trust. He rarely saw Isabel these days. She was always so tired and hurried and irritable, so worn out and harassed. She had been spending weeks on the preparations for the marriage of her daughter and Kenneth Brinkwell. May and Ethel, always close to her, were now so exigent, so indifferent and selfish and greedy, that Jochen often caught a confused expression of bewilderment and hurt on his wife's strained face. I've let it go on too long, thought Jochen. It's all my fault. If Isabel hates me, after I tell her everything, she'll have a right to. I've done something to my wife and my family; I've done something to myself. Maybe it's too late for anything now. But I've got to risk it.

Isabel would be waiting for him in tearfulness when he came home. She would demand to know, instantly, what he had meant by his curious words over the telephone. Later, she would look at him with aversion and shock and rage. She would become hysterical. It is something I'll have to endure, Jochen thought. I've brought it on myself, he added. I've got to fight it out, no matter what happens.

He was told that Isabel was up in her room, when he entered the house. Very quietly, and with a very pale face, he went upstairs, and knocked at her door. (I never used to have to knock, he thought.) She said: "Come in, Jochen." She would be on her bed, crying. But Isabel was sitting by a window, and she was white, and she said: "Jochen, come sit near me. You look so tired. I'll have the tea sent up, and then we can talk."

He stood and looked at her and he could not speak. She smiled at him, sadly, after a long moment, and said: "Poor Jochen. My poor dear. See, I have a chair right beside me. And now I'll ring for the tea, and they'll bring up your favorite little cakes, too." She gestured for him to sit down.

He sat down beside her. He put his hands on his knees, and looked at her again. Then he said, like a child: "You still love me, don't you, Isabel?"

She bent sideways and kissed his cheek. "I never stopped, darling. But I thought you had."

She was so handsome, so composed, sitting there, and for the first time in many months he saw a shining in her pretty hazel eyes. She gave him her hand and he held it tightly. "I knew, when you said that to me this morning, that something awful had been happening to you, Jochen. You see, I've seen it, for a long time, and I wondered what it was. But here's the tea, and you must have it, first."

They drank their tea, and Jochen ate his "favorite little cakes," though they stuck in his throat. Isabel spoke of everything that was unimportant, in a very soft voice, and she never once uttered a belittling remark or a word of gossip about anyone. This, in itself, would have made Jochen wonder, for, at one time, he had overheard some woman say a little scornfully: "Isabel's the town-cryer, isn't she?"

From time to time, as they sat in the long spring twilight together, Isabel would lovingly and sympathetically touch Jochen's hand; it was a light touch, but very comforting.

She's trying to tell me ahead of time that nothing matters but us, he thought. How much does she know? Isabel turned on a lamp near her, and the golden light shone on the ripples of her rich hair. When she looked at her husband her eyes became large and intent, and full of pitying knowledge.

The maid took away the tea-tray, and Isabel held Jochen's hand firmly in both of hers and said: "Now, tell me. Tell me everything, and I won't even ask a question."

Jochen was afraid again. How would it be possible for Isabel to re-arrange her carefully arranged life? She lived for social triumphs. What her neighbors and friends thought of her house, and especially her clothes, was a matter of the gravest import to her.

"Please," said Isabel, in a pleading voice. Jochen looked at her search-ingly. He had never seen this expression on Isabel's face before, so tender, so tired, so understanding.

"You'll hate me, and I won't blame you," he said. "It'll be terribly hard on you," he added. She smiled. "Not so hard on me as watching you becoming more and more wretched every day," she said. "Nothing means as much to me as you, Jochen. Men are so silly; they always think their wives want more than they really do. But they always give their wives what they don't actually want."

So Jochen, still hardly believing, began to talk. It took a long time. It was harder than he expected. Isabel still held his hand warmly. Her smile did not change, or the sadness in her eyes. Once or twice he wanted to hold back something, then Isabel would press his hand, and he would blurt it out. The twilight became night; they heard the voices of May and Ethel in the hall outside. There was a sound of quickening dinner preparations below.

Then Jochen said, exhausted: "Well, there it is, all of it, Bella. Noth-ing left out. You see where we are, now. I've brought it all down on us. Hate me, if you want to. It's what I deserve, for failing you and the girls."

Isabel pulled the bell-rope, and when the maid came in, she said: "Mr. Wittmann and I won't be down to dinner tonight, Mabel. We'll have two trays up here, please." She said to Jochen: "Don't say anything for a few minutes, darling. I just want to think. I suspected a lot of this, but there are a few other things I hadn't known. I've got to con-sider them; after all, they affect other people besides ourselves."

She bent her head, and her face became stern and reflective with her thoughts. Jochen waited. There was a quick tap on the door, and May looked in at them petulantly, all auburn hair, rosy cheeks, and predatory hazel eyes. "What do you mean, saying you aren't coming down to din-ner, Mama?" she demanded, without a glance at her father.

Isabel lifted her head. "I meant it, May. Your father and I have things to discuss, very important things. By the way, I see you haven't noticed he's here."

She had never spoken so sharply and harshly to her daughter before, and Jochen felt such relief that he lay back in his chair. May was startled. "Oh, hello, Papa," she muttered. "Run along, dear," said Isabel. "And don't disturb us, either you or Ethel. Children are important, but not when their parents have something *more* important on their minds. Run along; close the door after you."

Again, she began to think. Then she turned to Jochen, and smiled. "So, it comes down to this, very simply: We have enough money to give us a permanent income of at least six thousand dollars a year, even if you do nothing at all, Sweet. We have this house all paid for. When we married, Jochen, we had only eighteen hundred dollars a year. That's almost twenty years ago, and times have changed. However, six thousand dollars, at least, is quite a lot of money. Not to live as we live now, or expected to live, but still quite a lot."

She sounded brisk and practical, but then, Jochen thought with gratitude, she belongs to a very practical sex. Isabel continued to take stock: "As you say, you can't stand being a hired man to a super hired man. I've known that a long time. You'll never be able to be a hireling again, my pet. So, what is the best thing to do? Why, go to some other city and invest in a machine tool business, and be a partner, or something! Very simple.

"You've admitted that Charles did not actually 'throw you out.' I had a feeling all along he didn't. After all, we both wanted you to be president of the company, and we both had a share in trying to undermine Charles. I still think you ought to have been president. I've never liked him or Phyllis; we tried to injure them. I'm sorry about that. However, that's modern competition, and people do that to each other every day, and I imagine that's bad, if natural. But that's something we can't help. We're made that way. Charles had to make you leave the company—after everything. You'd do that yourself. He won, instead of you. So, we won't be silly enough to be maudlin about the whole thing. We can be a little sorry, but not enough to cripple us."

Jochen had a moment's wish that women weren't so "damned sensible." He was in a mood for sackcloth and ashes. Women, he suspected, did not regard sackcloth and ashes as fashionable, or even intelligent. Isabel was going on: "I never told you I was worried about Geraldine. How little sense the child has! She let this business of the wedding go on, and drooped all over the place instead of just telling me. I can't help but be hurt that she went to you instead of to me. Oh, yes, I know!

She was 'doing it for us'! As if real parents would ever want their children hurt. Such a sentimental little fool! Well," said Isabel, with a sigh. "Not too much harm's been done. We'll simply talk it over with the Brinkwells and then issue an announcement in the papers that the wedding is indefinitely postponed. It might be a relief to Pauline," and Isabel laughed, drily.

She looked affectionately at Jochen, and laughed again. "All right, I'll tell Pauline. You won't have to discuss it with Roger!"

Jochen said: "You don't care at all, do you, Isabel?" He spoke marvelingly.

"Of course, I care! Don't be ridiculous, Jochen. But we have just one important problem. Your happiness, your success, what you want."

She stood up, and Jochen got to his feet. He always rose so weightily and slowly, these days. He could not understand how it was that he could get up so easily now, with a sense of lightness and buoyancy. He put his arms about his wife. "I've been such a fool," he said.

"Of course you have. That's what comes of a man not knowing a single thing about women." But she smiled, and her eyes were full of tears. She kissed him. "Well, it's all over. And I hear our trays coming, and tonight, for once, you're going to eat a decent meal and not look as if every forkful was poison."

CHAPTER LVI

ROGER BRINKWELL let Jochen talk without making any comment of any kind. They sat in Mr. Brinkwell's elaborate office, and the clerks had been told not to interrupt. The early May sunshine ran in waves of light over the polished windows, and the long deep roaring of the mills could hardly be heard here. Jochen had found it easier to talk to his superior than he had thought; in fact, as he continued, he lost all his first nervousness and embarrassment, and gained confidence. He had long ago learned that it was impossible to guess what Brinkwell was thinking, for he was almost always smiling.

The sunlight lay on Brinkwell's big head with its crisp black hair, and there was a certain boyishness about him, which was due to his small and active body, his quick and energetic ways, his manner of speaking which was like the brisk snapping of fingers. Only the eyes that watched Jochen thoughtfully had no youth in them. They were shrewd and considering, and, to Jochen's surprise, they were not in the least unfriendly.

"Well," said Jochen, "I think that's all, Roger. And, as I said, it hasn't anything to do with that announcement of my daughter's marriage to your son being 'indefinitely postponed.' I want you to believe that."

"Of course, I do believe it," said Brinkwell. He lit another monogrammed cigarette from the burning stub in his small fingers. He put down the stub and crushed it in a silver ash tray. All his movements were swift and decisive.

"But, you're more important just now, Joe, than those kids. I don't want you to leave me. Oh, yes, I've listened when you said you just couldn't work for anyone at all, and that you want to get into something of your own. That's natural. I understand. You're an independent devil," and Brinkwell smiled, with real friendliness. "Like all Germans," he added.

Now, why the hell did old Joe look so sullen all at once, thought Brinkwell, genuinely puzzled. Then, being an intuitive man, he said: "That is, the best kind of German."

"I'm an American," said Jochen, flatly. His sullenness gave his massive face a heavy obstinacy. His little brown eyes looked at Brinkwell with something hostile in them.

"There's no reason to be ashamed of one's racial heritage," said Brinkwell.

"I don't give a damn about anybody's racial heritage," said Jochen, and believed he meant it. "All I care about is whether or not he's an American."

Brinkwell was silent. The wrinkles about his eyes deepened, giving them a sardonic expression. Jochen saw this, and his flabby cheeks colored unhealthily. He took out a cigar, in order not to have to look at Brinkwell, and lit it.

Then Brinkwell spoke lightly: "I'm all for being an American, too, unless it interferes with profits." He laughed, as if at some mutual joke. Jochen did not laugh. He seemed to be having some trouble making his cigar draw.

"All right, all right," said Brinkwell, in a lively voice. "But we're wandering away from the subject. Joe, let's be sensible. I know you're not a poor man; you could go to Cincinnati or some other place, and invest in one of those machine tool shops. They'd be glad to have you; I know that. But this is your town; you've got a home here, even though you've told me you're going to sell the land you bought and aren't going to build that new house. You've got an investment in this town, Joe, a real one. Your friends, Isabel's friends, your daughters' friends. You think you won't miss your town and your home and your friends, but you will. After thirty, it's hard for a man to pull up roots and move somewhere else, into unknown territory. I know. I still think of myself as living in Pittsburgh, that's why I go back there as often as I can.

"But, that's the emotional side. There's a more practical one. The machine tool shops in Ohio, though excellent, are still small concerns. Even if you invest in one of them, and are a partner, or an officer, it'll be years before you'll be making any real money. You've said you don't care, and that Isabel doesn't care, either. You think that now. Later, you'll care like hell. You're under forty, still, but you're not what is meant by a really young man. It needs enthusiasm to begin all over again in a new place, among strangers.

"Now, I'm not going to pretend to think that you'll fail. You won't. You'll just begin to remember the money you'll have lost by leaving us. Joe, you haven't begun to make money, yet! Believe me, I know it." For some reason he glanced at the framed calendar on the wall: May 5, 1915. "I can almost guarantee that your salary would be double in less than two years—double what it is now. Do you have the right to throw up such a future for independence, when you know what that independence will eventually cost you, and what it'll cost your family?"

Jochen did not answer him; he was staring at his cigar. Brinkwell shrugged, good-humoredly. "I haven't mentioned the fact that I need you, Joe, need you like hell. You know what the men in Pittsburgh think about you. Why, sometimes I've been afraid they'd give you my job, if I didn't watch out!" He laughed. "We need you here. You're worth anything to us."

"Even without the Wittmann Machine Tool Company," said Jochen.

"Even without the Wittmann Machine Tool Company," repeated Brinkwell. "Our machine tools are every bit as good as your brother's, or, at least, they serve their purpose, which is all that has mattered, and is going to matter. I'm not asking you to stay because of anything I might think you can do for us, with your brother's company. But you know that."

"Yes," said Jochen, somberly. "I know it." He moved uneasily in his chair. "I can't stay, Roger. I can't. I've got to be in something for myself. That's all there is to it. I'm glad that you want me to stay. It—it's given me even more confidence in myself."

Brinkwell said, softly: "You don't think that if you went into one of those concerns in Ohio, they wouldn't be making tools for—shall we say—friends?" He began to laugh. "We're neutral, Joe. We sell to anybody who has the money to pay, and who can cart off our goods. The machine tool companies will be just as neutral. Or did you think they wouldn't be?"

Jochen said simply: "I don't know. It's just that I think we shouldn't be supplying anybody with anything. The Amalgamated, for instance, isn't selling to either England or Germany, but only to neutral countries." Now he flushed again, and said violently: "And if England keeps on boarding our vessels, and confiscating our goods, and hoisting our flag over her damned ships—well, I think we should knock hell out of her! If Germany did that to us only once, we'd be right in, shooting! Sure, some of our seamen have been killed, when they've been working on British ships, but that was their own fault; they oughtn't to have been on those ships in the first place. Oh, I know!" he cried. "It's all figured out. And that's another reason I'm leaving." His eyes, inflamed now, could not conceal his hatred.

So, thought Brinkwell, you're a Dutchman, after all. Scratch a German's hide and you'll find the pork underneath. But he smiled soothingly.

"Joe, you're a sensible man, aren't you? And you've said you were an American, and had no concern with anything that was German. All you have to do is to remember that."

Jochen stood up. He pointed to a paper on Brinkwell's desk. "There's my resignation, Roger. I'm sorry, but I've got to do it." He paused. "And Roger—I don't want you to think, even for a minute, that anything I've found out here will ever be told by me, to anybody."

Roger shrugged again. "Oh, that wouldn't matter, Joe. Not in the least. You see, there're so many in Washington who do know. They just haven't let Mr. Wilson in on the secret." He stood up, and moved actively to the calendar. He lifted the pages, scrutinized them, nodded as if satisfied. He came back to his desk, and looked up at Jochen.

"Joe, if you go now, everyone will think it has something to do with the delaying of the marriage of our children. You don't want people to laugh at you. You want to leave on June first. That isn't fair to me. Why don't you stay until September first? In the meantime, if you want to, you can be getting in touch with those Ohio concerns, while drawing your salary. It might be months before you find out just where you want to go. Months without any income. That isn't intelligent, and you know it. And, if you remain here until September you'll have had time to think it all over, and to have come to some considered, instead of impulsive, decision."

"It isn't impulsive," said Jochen, stubbornly. But he was thinking. "All right," he said at last. "I'll stay till September, if you really want me. I suppose it isn't the right thing to leave as abruptly as I intended. Just consider that my resignation takes place on the first of September."

"Good!" exclaimed Brinkwell. He stood up, smiling delightedly, and held out his hand.

Jochen looked at that small, neat hand. He looked at Brinkwell's face, affable, friendly. He took the extended hand and shook it briefly.

All German ships of all German lines in New York had been empty of prospective passengers for many, many months. All German ships were either in the shelter of their home ports, in Germany, or idle in neutral ports. But British lines calmly rode the seas, majestic and placid.

The Cunard Line advertised sailings of its proudest liner, the *Lusitania*, on various dates in May, 1915. Directly under this advertisement in the New York newspapers appeared a warning from the Imperial German Embassy in Washington: "Travellers intending to embark on the Atlantic voyage are reminded that a state of war exists between Germany and her allies and Great Britain and her allies; that the zone of war includes the waters adjacent to the British Isles; that, in accordance with formal notice given by the Imperial German Government, vessels flying the flag of Great Britain, or of any of her allies, are liable to destruction in those waters and that travellers sailing do so at their own risk."

On May 7, 1915, the *Lusitania*, unprotected by any British convoy, was sunk off the coast of Ireland by a submarine, and 1198 men, women, and children lost their lives. There was also lost a considerable amount of "contraband," which lay in the vast hold of the ship.

CHAPTER LVII

"NOTHING," SAID Ralph Grimsley to Charles Wittmann, "but God's intervention can keep us out of the war now, Charlie."

They sat in Mr. Grimsley's gritty office; there were piles of news telegrams all over the big roll-top desk. Charles held some of them in his hands, and read them doggedly. Some of them were excerpts from editorials in many influential American newspapers: "The sinking of the *Lusitania* was murder!"

Charles threw down these telegrams. He picked up another. Theodore Roosevelt was quoted: "It is inconceivable that we should refrain from action. We owe it not only to humanity but to our own national self-respect."

Other telegrams told of accounts of naturalized, and unnaturalized people, of German stock being attacked by "unknown gangs of youths and men" in many American cities. Mobs shouted for war against Germany in other towns, and in a number of villages. Hatred, rage, and fury against all that was German were reported in still other telegrams, from all points in the nation. Washington, it was said, was full of dazed men.

Mr. Grimsley shook his head drearily. He watched Charles as he read. How was it possible for a man to become so wizened, so gray of face, so sunken of eye, in only a few days? Especially a man like old Charlie? Well, now, if old Charlie didn't know so much, and hadn't understood so much, these past two years, he, too, might be shouting for war. He was horrified, it was true, as all decent Americans were, since the sinking of the *Lusitania*, and he was also bitterly angry. But still—he knew too much.

Charles threw down the telegrams. He looked at his friend in a long and brooding silence. Mr. Grimsley waited. Then Charles made an effort to speak, coughed weakly, and finally said in a stifled voice: "I haven't read anything yet which explains why the *Lusitania* wasn't convoyed by British destroyers, as the other liners have been convoyed right along. Where were the destroyers?"

Mr. Grimsley said, quietly: "Yes, where were they?"

They stared at each other with grim, sick eyes.

Charles said: "All the other liners—they were convoyed. But this one, carrying so many hundreds of Americans—the biggest lot of them all—wasn't convoyed." He coughed again. "Yes. Murder. Deliberate. And all the murderers aren't being named."

"No," Mr. Grimsley admitted, "they aren't."

"The bastards, the bastards!" said Charles. The words sounded even more violent because his voice was so low, almost indistinct.

"All of them," agreed the editor. "And too many of us, too, in Washington—everywhere. The torpedo that sank the *Lusitania* had many stamps of approval on it, and not only the one stamped in Germany."

Charles sat, appalled, and looked at the floor, blinking his sleepless eyes. Jim—nineteen, now. Jim—in a war not of his making. Jim—

dying—for what, whom? The torpedo that had struck down that giant ship had been directed against thousands of American lives in every city, every town, every village, every home. Thousands of young men in their schools, their fathers' homes, their factories and their mills, had been marked to die—for what, for whom?

Nothing worth living for, nothing worth fighting for, nothing worth dying for, in all the world. Nowhere, in the world, a fixed point for a man's faith. Nowhere, honor or justice or mercy. What could a man do, how could he go on living, knowing this, understanding, even if only a little, of what real motivations lay behind this war, what real shadows fell on a million walls, what real ghosts marched throughout the earth?

"It would be easier, not knowing," said Charles. "It would be much better to be fooled. Then you could listen to the murderers and wave your flag, and feel noble and exalted, and go out to kill, thinking you were doing a good and holy thing. You could even give up your—your —son, 'for his country.' I wish to God," he said, "that I had never found out!"

He rubbed his eyes with the blunt tips of his fingers. "There is one thing no government will let its people know—the truth. No, there's nothing a man can hold to, or believe in."

The editor said, looking at Charles with alarmed sympathy: "Yes. Yes. But your own minister said, on Sunday, that a man can't ever put his trust in anything, in anyone, but God. Look, Charlie, I'm not a religious man," he added, with embarrassment. "But you might think of what Mr. Haas said."

Charles got up so abruptly that the pile of telegrams near his elbow were jolted, and slithered down to the floor. Then Charles walked out of the office without another word, out into the warm May sunshine he never saw or felt, out past faces he could not see. It was a work day, but he went home, and he went upstairs to his room and lay on the bed. Mrs. Meyers, hearing him, crept up to the door; it was slightly ajar. She saw Charles staring blindly at the ceiling, and she crept away again, crying.

She heard the telephone ringing, and hurried downstairs to answer it. It was Friederich, who asked for his brother in a worried voice. "Yes, Mr. Wittmann, he's here. But you know he won't talk to anyone. Mrs. Wittmann has called every day, but he won't answer her. Yes, he's lying down. I think he just wants to rest. I'll tell him you called."

The poor woman sat on the telephone chair, and bowed her head and shook it with grief for Charles. He was thinking of his boy. How many fathers were thinking of their sons just now?

The postman knocked at the screen door, and Mrs. Meyers went for the mail. There was only one letter of importance, and that was from Jim. Mrs. Meyers ran with it, upstairs again, to Charles' room, tapped at the door, and called eagerly: "A letter for you, from Jim, Mr. Wittmann!"

Charles was up at once, holding out his hand, without a word. Mrs. Meyers gave him the letter, and asked anxiously: "You haven't had any lunch, Mr. Wittmann. Let me bring you some coffee and a sandwich, or something."

"No," said Charles. He was already opening the letter. He shut the door in Mrs. Meyers' face.

He had written a long letter to Jim five days ago, a letter incoherent here and there, and imploring and vehement. He had said: "I know all you young fellows will be shouting for war, or talking about it, and reading the papers, and studying the cartoons, and quoting Roosevelt, and the editorials, and everybody. But Jim, I want you to remember the things I've told you for the past two years. I want you to re-member—"

The envelope fluttered to the floor. Charles carried Jim's letter to the window. The shadow of moving green leaves fell upon it. Charles could hardly read that clear, small writing, for his eyes kept blurring, and there was a savage ache behind them. He bent his head over the single page.

"Dear Dad—I didn't have to wait for a letter from you to know what you've been thinking and feeling, all these days. But I'd hoped that you wouldn't feel so awful—you've so many things worrying you—I've understood, right along, and I've known what was in your mind when I was home, and so I didn't want to talk to you about the war—I see I was wrong. I should have talked it out, and then you wouldn't have had me to sweat and stew about—you would have known what I've been thinking, too. We shouldn't hide anything that bothers us from each other; we aren't doing each other a favor at all. I'm especially doing you a wrong, and I ought to have remembered your blood pressure and what old Doc Metzger has told me about you. But I thought if I didn't talk about the war you'd believe it doesn't matter to me.—Dad, I can promise you this, and I mean it sincerely: I'll never go to war. I remember what you've told me. I promise you, so help me God, that no one is ever going to put a rifle in my hand and make me kill another man—"

Mrs. Meyers was sitting dolefully in her kitchen when she heard Charles enter the dining-room. She hurried into the room, also, full of fear. But Charles, though still terribly haggard and pale, was smiling. "I think," he said, "that I'll have that coffee and that sandwich, after all, Mrs. Meyers. Will you hurry with it? I have to go back to the office."

Charles went to the telephone and called Phyllis. When she heard his voice, her own caught in her throat, and she could only murmur: "Oh, Charles!"

"I'm all right, Phyllis. I'm sorry I didn't answer your calls. But, there was Jim; I was afraid. You know, all this war hysteria. I haven't worked, or done anything. But I had a letter from Jim, just now. And he tells me I mustn't worry, that they'll never send him out to kill. Yes, my darling, I'll come for dinner, tonight. I'm a wreck, but when I see you I'll forget all about it."

He carried his unread New York and Philadelphia newspapers to the table. They had quieted down considerably. They quoted a speech of the President's:

"The example of America must be a special example—the example not merely of peace because it will not fight, but of peace because peace is the healing and elevating influence of the world and strife is not.— There is such a thing as a man being too proud to fight."

"Trust the President," was the editorial comment of all the newspapers. Yesterday, they had screamed for war. Today, they pleaded: "Trust the President."

Charles ate his lunch, and for the first time in days there was no clenching terror in him, no fear or despair. Perhaps, in his thoughts, and in the things he had said to others, he had done the American people a great injustice. Was it possible, as his father had often said, that a people was often far more intelligent than its Government?

Now, thought Charles, if the damned Germans will only stop openly and defiantly being "glad" that the *Lusitania* was sunk! If that damned Embassy in Washington will only shut its mouth! If that idiot of a Kaiser will stop striking his chest and shouting: "Deutschland über Alles!" And if Americans will just stop sailing on British vessels! Just a few things to do, and the plotters would be impotent, and the plan against the freedom of man, all over the world, would lie and mold away in secret drawers.

Jochen, in his office, sometimes would not lift a pen or a finger for as long as half an hour at a time. He would just look vacantly before him, running his tongue over his dry lips, lighting a cigar only to let it die out, unsmoked, in its tray, wiping his forehead, and thinking, thinking.

CHAPTER LVIII

BEFORE THE date of his return from Harvard, Jim had asked his father if he would "mind" if he, Jim, paid a visit of a few days to the home of fellow freshmen in upper New York State. Walter Haas, Jim wrote, was also going to visit these friends. "Of course," Jim ended the letter, "if you'd rather I didn't, Dad, I'll come home immediately." There was a long-suffering and patient note to the letter which irked Charles.

But, I suppose, thought Charles, this is part of the separation which began last September, part of the separation that will continue as long as I live. So Charles, irked again at the tone of the letter, wrote back: "Enjoy yourself, son. But be back in time for my wedding, on August tenth. If you feel that is too early, I'll understand."

"It's only five or six days, after all, Charles," said Phyllis, soothingly, when Charles complained to her, out of his disappointment.

The extra few days passed, and on the night before the day Jim was to arrive home Charles gave a dinner for Mr. and Mrs. George Hadden, Friederich and his wife, Helen, and Phyllis. It was a hot June evening, and there were long and soundless flashes of heat lightning in the summer sky which outlined the distant mountains and blazed for an instant or two on the tops of the thick trees of the streets. After dinner, they sat in the parlor, and Charles was amused at the furtive and considering glances Phyllis kept giving the room. He knew that she was already deciding what pieces of furniture might be retained and what discarded. The next week she was going to Philadelphia and New York with Mrs. Holt for her trousseau, and what she vaguely called "other affairs." The house which Wilhelm had built had already been sold, and the furniture, except for the best paintings, and a few cherished chairs and tables and mirrors and carpets, also was to be sold.

Mrs. Meyers had cooked a very good dinner; Phyllis had arrived at Charles' house earlier in the afternoon, and had supervised both dinner and table. Charles was very happy with his guests, and he looked at little Edith Hadden and his new sister-in-law, Helen, and at Phyllis, with affection. But inevitably, George Hadden and he and Friederich unobtrusively moved to one end of the room, leaving the women together. Helen gave them a smiling but irritated glance, and was grateful that, if she were being deserted, she at least had two women to talk to who were not "comfy" fools who could chatter about nothing but clothes and children and servants. She, herself, was three months pregnant; however, she did not discuss this with her brother's wife, or Phyllis.

"Well," said Charles, "it seems the war scare is passing. Everybody's settling down, reasonably, following the President's lead. I hope though"—and Charles laughed—"that he won't run out of paper for his notes."

He was very much at ease, now. The country, in general, was showing great restraint and caution and common sense. Many newspapers, in their cartoons and editorials, published inflammatory jibes, sneers, and insults against the Kaiser and Germany and "Kultur." The anti-British attacks had become much milder, however, even in the few papers openly defending Germany. The "neutral" press had almost entirely ceased to mention anything derogatory about Great Britain. Mr. Grimsley knew this, if Charles did not, but Mr. Grimsley did not tell his friend. Old Charlie had enough to worry him as it was. And too, if the press in general was very overheated, the people displayed admirable calm. There might be "Aid for Britain" bazaars and "benefits" and such, but this was only a sign of the immense good nature of Americans. Besides, next year there was to be another Presidential election, and the people turned from the news of the European war to news about prospective candidates. It was firmly believed, in some quarters, that Mr. Wilson's "New Freedom" program was the opening of an enlightened age, and it was just as firmly believed, in other quarters, that it was the beginning of "anarchy." Besides, there was the baseball season to consider.

George and Friederich made no comment after Charles' remark. They only gave each other a sober glance, which Charles did not see.

"This thing can't go on," Charles continued. "There're rumors every day of the end of the war. No one's winning."

Friederich frowned. "The Russians were, Karl, until just recently. Have you forgotten the fall of Przemysl, in March, after a four months' siege? The Russians captured nearly 100,000 men, and it was thought, at that time, that this would put Austria out of the war. It did not. Then Russia took 50,000 more Austrian prisoners, the latter part of the same month, in the Carpathian passes, and Germany had to go to Austria's aid, with two million men."

"Well, you see, it's just as I said: nobody's winning. They just shuffle the armies about," said Charles. "Of course, the German offensive against Russia started a couple of months ago, but—"

Friederich looked at George challengingly. Charles, lately, had been in a very optimistic mood. It did not do, Friederich thought, to let anyone be optimistic these days. It was too dangerous. So Friederich said: "Yes. And the Germans won every battle against the Russians, thereafter, and by May 11th their lines were at Przemysl, again. And the Russians have been retreating ever since."

Charles moved uncomfortably in his chair. "Oh, the Russians will rally again. When Russia gets Mackensen in her mouth she'll close her jaws on him. As she closed her jaws on Napoleon."

George Hadden saw that Friederich was not going to permit his brother to be complacent. Perhaps Friederich was right. George looked at Charles and said, gently: "I wonder if you've given any thought as to why Russia, who was carrying everything before her only a few months ago, should be now retreating, Charlie? Retreating, as if at a signal, with victory before her?"

"Mackensen," said Charles, "and his two million men—"

"But the Russians were advancing steadily. It isn't easy to stop a huge army in its tracks, suddenly. And not as easily as this. Why, Charlie?"

All Charles' pleasure in the evening was gone. Something ominous had moved close to him, in this warm bright room. He could hear the women "gossiping," and the sound of the night wind in the trees, and the flutter of the curtains, and the distant note of a gramophone, and the softened slaps of screen doors as people came in and out of their houses. He could hear the friendly voices of his neighbors, the creak of hammocks and rockers on the porches. It was comfortable, and it was home, and here were his friends and relatives. Yet, something was standing over him again, faceless and evil.

"What do you mean by 'why,' George?" he demanded.

George answered seriously: "There are ways to get reports, Charlie. We know, now, that something is happening in Russia. What it is we don't know as yet. But a signal was given for the Russian armies to retreat. And we do know that the Russian regiments are miserably armed, those which have been moved up. We know that ammunition in Russia is being sent off to sidings in Russian towns, and left standing there. No effort is being made to supply the men. Mackensen is approaching Lemberg, and Russia has half a million dead. Why was this permitted?"

Charles decided he did not like George tonight. His nerves had quieted down lately; he was sleeping better. Now here was the sinister thing again, the universal and almost soundless booming of secret drums under the shrill trumpets of war.

"There might be some," said George, when Charles did not speak but only eyed him bitterly, "who don't want Russia to overcome Germany, or even Germany to overcome Russia." He turned to Friederich, and said: "Friederich, I think you can tell us a little."

Friederich flushed miserably. Charles looked at him: "Well?" he demanded.

"Karl," said the other man. "You've forgotten. We talked about this, all during the past year or so. When I was a—I mean, when I had slightly different ideas, I heard a great deal. All Europe was to be socialized. That was the plan. Then America, and then the rest of the world. 'The death of freedom for all men, everywhere.' You said it yourself, Karl. Those were your words."

"I know," said Charles. He put down his cigar. "But I'd hoped the plotters were done with, now. I'd hoped—"

George leaned towards him, earnestly. "Charlie, let's look at pre-war Europe. England, France and Germany, and Scandinavia: what has distinguished them from most of the other countries during the past one hundred years or so? The rise of a strong and vigorous middle class. What, in the main, does the middle class, anywhere, stand for? Moderation, progress, peace, and freedom. This religion of the middle class has become very strong in the major nations of Europe, even in Germany. Now, it has been decided that in one way or another the middle class must be destroyed. After it is destroyed, there'll be no freedom, anywhere. Call it Socialism or Marxism, or whatever—it'll still be slavery." The young Quaker sighed.

Phyllis, smiling at some remark little Mrs. Hadden had made, glanced at Charles. Where was the "good color" which he had had all evening? Phyllis heard him say: "We won't get in! If we do, it's the end of us." She stood up, alarmed, and went to him and put her hand on his shoulder. He did not look at her. "I insist that you men have stayed away from us too long," she said. "Now, we're coming up here with you, or you're coming back with us." She made her voice light and gay.

They heard the screen door open, then slap shut. Charles did not move. Then he heard Phyllis exclaim, joyfully: "Jim!"

At the sound of that name, Charles was electrified. He jumped to his feet. Jim was actually there, without warning, with his bags in his hands. Charles almost ran to him. "Son! I didn't expect you until

tomorrow! Why, you rascal, you're home at last! Wanted to give me
a surprise, I suppose!" He caught his son's hand and shook it vigorously, and looked about for the others to share his delight.

They crowded about Jim, shaking his hand. Phyllis and Helen
kissed him. It was only the women who saw that the boy was pale
and strained, and seemed very tired. All the time that his hand was
being shaken, and Phyllis and Helen were kissing him, he looked at
nobody but his father, and his young eyes were grave and afraid.

"Leave the bags right there!" Charles said. "Sit, sit down. Have you
had any dinner? There's some cold lemonade in the ice-box, or some
beer, perhaps. Sit down, son. Why do you stand there like that?"

Jim glanced at the faces around him. "I'm glad you're all here. It
makes it easier," he said. "Easier for me, and perhaps for Dad." Again
he fixed his eyes on Charles. "Dad, I've got to tell you. Now. When
I was upstate in New York, visiting some friends—with Walter—we
met a brother of one of the fellows. He's with an ambulance unit, for
the Canadian Red Cross. Dad, Walter and I are going. In a few days.
Dad? You see, we had to do it. All those people being killed. The Red
Cross needs drivers, for its ambulances. We've got to help. I don't care
about England or Germany, or anybody. Just the men who've got to
get to hospitals. Dad? Why don't you say something?"

But nobody said anything. No one looked at Charles. Jim took a
step towards his father, and held out his hand pleadingly. "Dad, it
won't be long. Three or four months, or so. Or even six months. I
won't be missing much, at school. Why, I'll probably be back in September, in time! Everybody says the war's nearly over, now. Dad, why
do you look at me like that?"

It was long after midnight, and the heat lightning had given way
to real lightning, and there was a dull muttering in the hot air. Charles
had said very little. He had said nothing much at all, except: "No."
His friends and relatives sat around him and Jim, and Charles stared
at them all, slowly, terribly, doggedly. He stared at his son. And each
time he said: "No."

He could not say anything else. He looked to George Hadden and
Friederich for help. He was like a dying man. At last, after all these
hours, George said: "What's done can't be undone, Charlie. After
all, the boy won't be in much danger, if any. No one fires on the Red
Cross. It's against international law. And there's the matter of Jim's
conscience to consider. He is a human being, and he has his rights
as such, and it's an errand of mercy."

Charles regarded him with hatred. He said: "Go away, Hadden. I don't want to talk to you any longer. I've asked your help, and you've turned against me."

George sighed. "I know how you feel, Charlie. We'll go home." He stood up, and his little wife, who had been crying, as Phyllis and Helen had been crying, too, came up to him. The two Haddens left the house, silently.

Charles turned to Friederich, with fierceness. "I've told him. He knows! Tell him yourself, Fred."

Friederich was utterly wretched. "If you have told him, Karl, I can tell him no more. Let us think of this for a moment. George is correct in saying one cannot interfere with a man's conscience. And help is needed. But I do think"—and Friederich tried to frown with ferocity at his nephew—"that the father should have been consulted, first, before the decision was made, and the journey taken to Canada, and all commitments agreed to—that the father should have known, it should have been discussed. It is the American way, now, to disregard the father, though it is not so in Europe. The father is nothing, in America."

"Uncle Fred, I didn't disregard Dad," said poor Jim, almost weeping. "When we talked to this friend's brother, Walter and I saw what we had to do. There was no time to talk to anyone. So, we went to Toronto."

Friederich shook his head sorrowfully. "The father only gives life. He is not to be respected."

Helen said softly: "I don't think Jim felt like that. He acted very hastily, and though I understand, I think he ought to have talked it over with his father."

"Dad," said Jim, with simplicity, "would have talked me out of it. And all the time, back at school, I'd have been thinking of how much I was needed, and I'd have hated myself. The Red Cross isn't an army. It's a mercy organization. I'll be saving lives, not taking them."

"No," said Charles, and he beat his knee with his fist.

"Jim," murmured Phyllis, helplessly. All her pain was for Charles. She did not touch him; she only sat as close to him as possible.

"Aunt Phyllis, you've got to help me and Dad," said Jim, desperately. "He has a life of his own, too. I've just begun to realize. You'll be getting married to each other; you can do such a lot for Dad."

"No," said Phyllis, shaking her head with sadness. "That's the worst of it. You can't do anything for anybody you love."

Jim stood up. He looked down at his father. "I've only got a few days home, Dad. Don't make it too hard on me. I've got to go; everything's arranged. Let's have these few days together. Look, Dad, we'll go fishing; we'll go everywhere together—"

"No!" cried Charles, and now his shock and dread made his face swell and grow darkly congested. "No, no, in the name of God!"

CHAPTER LIX

JIM TOLD himself that he was a coward, but he was afraid to be alone with his father. He went upstairs while Phyllis, Helen, and Friederich were still with Charles, and he undressed hurriedly, turned off the light, and went to bed. A long time later, Jim heard his relatives leaving. He pulled the sheet over his head, childishly. But his father did not come into the room. Jim turned over and listened; he heard Charles moving about in his own room. Finally there was a monotonous beat through the walls; Charles was walking up and down, back and forth. To the young man, it was the most mournful sound he could hear: the exhausted pacing of his father, growing slower and heavier, but never stopping. Once Jim, worn out, fell into a doze, woke with a start to see the gray line of the morning under his shade. Charles was still walking, feebly. Jim sat up. He said to himself that he couldn't stand it any longer. His father would die of this. He began to get out of bed, then he heard the creak of the springs in Charles' room, the sudden weighty drop of Charles' body on the mattress. Jim did not doze again, this Sunday morning.

He got up, finally, red-eyed and aching, dressed and crept downstairs. He could smell the coffee and the bacon, the toast and the pancakes. He went into the kitchen and Mrs. Meyers was there, crying. She looked at the young man reproachfully. "Now, don't start on me," said Jim, with haste. "I see you know all about it. Dad's sleeping—I guess. I'm going to church, so I'll just eat here in the kitchen."

"I should think you would go to church," said Mrs. Meyers. "You'll be the death of your poor father. But that's the way with children, break your heart after they take all you've got." Nevertheless, when she saw how little Jim could eat, and how heart-broken he was, she was remorseful.

Jim went to church, and looked about for the Haas family. Mrs. Haas, a little plump woman, sat with her daughters and her son, and her face was puffy and red with past crying. She held Walter's hand tightly, and from time to time she would try to smile at him. A moment later she would put up her handkerchief to her lips. After the services, which Jim did not hear at all, he went to the minister in the latter's study, and a few minutes later they left together.

They found Charles in his bathrobe, in the parlor, with the morning paper, unread, on his knees. All the life and strength has gone out of him, thought Mr. Haas, as Charles looked at them silently and did not move. Jim exchanged a glance with the minister, then went to his room, and Mr. Haas sat down near Charles.

He polished his glasses, studied Charles gravely. "I see I'm not the only father who didn't sleep all night, Charles," he said. "I thought I'd never get through the services this morning. Luckily, I had written out the complete sermon, and read it verbatim."

Charles said, incredulously: "You conducted the services—today?"

"Well, who else?" asked Mr. Haas. "My assistant is taking his vacation this week, and next. Who was to take my place? All those people depended on me. They have their own troubles. I can't put mine on their shoulders, too."

Charles looked away from him.

"My wife was there, also," went on the minister, gently. "She and I and Walter sat together all night, and I think we all cried."

Charles turned to him. The minister said: "I'm glad my boy can feel so deeply for those who are suffering, all the other boys who are in a war not of their own making. I'm glad he wants to help them. He has the true spirit of a minister, just as Jim has the true spirit of a doctor. It is terrible for us, but we can be proud of them."

All Charles' features seemed to squeeze together with agony. The minister went on: "It's not like an army—the Red Cross. I have a feeling the boys will be home by Christmas. In fact, I think that is the general arrangement, unless, of course, the war ends sooner. At the very worst, they'll only be missing a year of college. What is that, compared with what they intend to do? Besides, they'll be men when they return; they'll have seen so much that they'll be a better minister and a better doctor for it."

Charles rested his elbows suddenly on his knees and dropped his face into his hands.

Mr. Haas looked at him with compassion. "What does it matter, when young men are wounded and need help, that this war's an evil thing and ought not to have happened? Walter has no romantic notions about the 'rightness' of this war; he knows all the background of it, for I've told him, as you'd told Jim, Charles. The boys think it piteous that boys like themselves must be torn and killed for—what? So, they want to do what they can for the young men of their own generation, to give them a chance for life again."

"They'll be killed," said Charles, from behind his hands.

"No," said the minister, and his voice broke. "No. We mustn't think that, Charles. We mustn't let the boys see that we could ever think it. I suppose it would break their hearts, knowing we were suffering, too. In the meantime, Charles, let us make their few days with us very happy ones. We must keep telling them how proud we are."

Charles dropped his hands. He said: "I'm not proud. I'm scared to death. I'll read the papers, and then—how can I pretend to be proud, when I know what this war's about? When the very worst thing I've feared has happened to me? I should have known. It came out of nowhere—but Phyllis told me she believes that they've had it in mind, or something like this for a long time—I think they have—the deceit, the hiding, the not telling me—I—"

"Charles," said the minister, "do you realize that you've said, all the time: 'I,' 'me'? You've not been thinking of Jim very much, except in relation to yourself. That's wrong. It's even cruel." He waited for Charles to speak, and then when Charles remained silent, the minister said, with simplicity: "I'm scared to death, too, Charles. But I'm thinking of Walter, also."

Confused thoughts ran through Charles' mind: The minister had only one son. The minister loved his son. The minister was a brave man, and a good one. He wasn't burdening his son with his grief and fear. His very love would be used to make Walter stronger. The boy would do his duty in the knowledge that his father had pride in him.

Mr. Haas said: "And time passes so fast, Charles, as you know. In six weeks you and Phyllis will be married in my church. You'll have a wife again. Before you know it, before you've both settled down, Jim will be back. In the meantime, help him. God give you the strength to help him."

Jim, standing despondently at his window, saw the minister go. He did not hear Charles climbing wearily up the stairs. His door opened, and Charles said: "Son." Jim whirled about. Charles tried to smile, he tried to speak. He held out one of his hands. Then in a moment father and son were in each other's arms, and Jim was saying: "Dad. Dad." And he was crying as he had cried, sometimes, when he was nine, and not nineteen, and then Charles was saying: "Here, stop that. If that's the way you're going to act, then I'll write the Red Cross today and tell them that you haven't grown up yet, and they can't have you!"

Charles took the next few days off, and he and Jim went fishing and boating, and he had a dinner for his son, and he smiled and smiled and smiled. He did not walk at night, for Jim must not hear him; he kept his terror to himself, and when Jim's anxious eyes met his, he would grimace paternally. They never spoke of the war, even when they were alone. They talked of Geraldine, and Harvard, and how Jim, next summer, would have a tutor at home, or perhaps remain for the summer session, to catch up, and how much money he would need while away. They parted at night, sunburned and smiling, and with loud words of raillery. And Charles would swallow two, and sometimes three, of the tablets Dr. Metzger had given him, and then he would doze and have nightmares and wake up in a cold sweat. The nights were the worst; but they were just the beginning of the nights of anguish. Charles knew this. Jim must not suspect that his father had this knowledge. They talked only of the coming wedding, and Jim bought a gift for Phyllis and his father, to be opened only on the wedding day.

The days went fast. It was impossible for any days to go so fast. Jim seemed to be uneasy, and Charles guessed the reason. The day before the last, he said: "Jim, why don't you take the automobile and get Gerry out of her house in some way, and go for a ride? Take the whole day off. Go out into the country, somewhere, and be alone for a while."

"You're sure you don't mind?" asked Jim with joy, but looking at his father searchingly.

"I wouldn't have suggested it if I did," said Charles. "The poor girl's probably eaten up with anxiety now, especially since Grimsley published that fine article about you and Walter. Now, get in touch with her, in whatever code you two use."

So Jim took the automobile, and Charles went to the office. Friederich was so relieved to see him that tears came into his eyes behind his glasses. Charles said: "It's all right, Fred." He put his hand on his brother's shoulder, and added: "Fred, I'm glad we're together, for a dozen very important reasons, but I think this is the most important. I'm going to need you."

"A nice boy, a good boy, that one of yours, Karl," said Friederich, much moved. "A boy to be proud of—yes. I hope I shall have such a boy. And in the meantime, Karl, we must work and do all we can so that there shall never be another war. And so my boy won't be taken. I'm not so strong as you, Karl. I could not say to my boy, as you have said to yours: 'I am proud of you. Go in peace, and forget me.' "

"I've said it, yes," answered Charles, wryly. "But, so help me God, I haven't meant it!"

The worst day of all was the day of departure, when the minister and Charles and the two young men went to the station together. Father Hagerty was there, again, and he gave a medal to each of the boys, and told them that he was praying for their quick return. The train was a little late, and this was the hardest thing to bear for the fathers, for this last hour with their sons had been almost unendurable.

Then the train came, and the boys went into their coach. The window was open, and they stood there, smiling down at their fathers, smiling at the priest, and pushing each other like children. The wide sedate face of young Walter was pale, and Jim kept coughing, and Charles and the minister laughed at them. The train began to move. Charles and the minister walked beside it, waving. Then Jim, very white, put his face out through the window again, and called: "Dad! Dad! I'll be home soon! And Dad, take care of Gerry for me—she'll tell you—" The train roared, went faster and faster, and then it was gone. The two fathers looked after it for a long time, then turned away and could not look at each other.

They took Father Hagerty home in the big red automobile, in silence. When they had reached the priest's house, Father Hagerty said: "I'll remember the boys in my prayers, Mr. Haas."

"Do, please," said the minister, humbly. "I've tried to pray, but somehow, it's impossible. A terrible thing, but I couldn't really pray, these last days."

Charles thought: A million, a hundred million, prayers, haven't stopped this war. There is nothing prayer can do, nothing. I don't suppose even God could do anything, either. He said: "Thank you, Father Hagerty. And don't forget the minister and me, too."

Charles went back to his office, as usual, the next day. Then began for him that agonized waiting so familiar to so many fathers now, in Europe, in Canada, in dozens of raging countries, all over the world. Charles wondered if that agony of parents could not be diverted in some way to blast apart the bodies and the souls, if any, of the war-makers, the statesmen, the brass-plated generals and officers, the men in Switzerland who laughed.

He told himself, during the weeks that followed, that all would be well with Jim. He dared not think of any other possibility. No one fired on the Red Cross! But that was not true, now. He knew it, in spite of the fact that he read that the hospital ships sailed fully lighted and unharmed on the oceans, and were respected. But what of the battlefields, the shells, the guns, the fire, the flame? Charles forced himself to work, to go about his business. He tried to pray. He attended parties given for him and Phyllis, and daily he grew gaunter, and his eyes became more sunken. He sat with Phyllis in her house, and she and Mrs. Holt visited him together, this first week in August before the wedding, and the two women often were unreal to Charles, like painted figures, flat and voiceless, and there was such a numbness in him that he sometimes wondered if he were paralyzed, and would cautiously lift his arm or open and shut his hands, to test them.

The nights were not so terrible, in spite of what he had feared. Perhaps the sedatives, stronger now, which the doctor had given him, were blurring the outlines of his thoughts and his dreams, or perhaps he had reached the state where his exhausted mind could not feel too acutely.

He had one letter from Jim, in Canada, and one only. It was a cheerful letter. Cautiously, it implied that Jim would soon be on his way. There was a postscript: "And when you see Gerry, she'll tell you all about it. I wanted to tell you before, as a surprise, but she wanted to do it, herself. Take care of yourself, Dad. You know what I think of you. The best Dad in the world." Charles, eagerly reading the letter, trying to discover something which would tell him when Jim would be leaving, hoping to find in it the full strength of his son's love for him, did not suspect for a moment that the letter was a little cryptic.

Phyllis saw him almost every day, and called him at least twice. Slowly, he began to find his deepest comfort in her. He began to talk again, more easily. They walked at night over the mountain paths. Her presence was healing to him. He sometimes said: "It won't be so bad when you're with me, Phyllis. It won't be so hard, waiting, and watching for letters. Another five days! I'm glad we've put off the honeymoon until Jim comes home. I couldn't go away, wondering if a letter had arrived for me. It was thoughtful of you, to suggest waiting for the honeymoon."

Another five days, thought Phyllis. Her house no longer belonged to her; soon, the furniture would be gone, also, except what she had saved. She walked through the beautiful rooms, and saw her reflection in the long mirrors, and she knew it was the reflection of a stranger who had no right in this house any longer. The stranger lived in that other house with Charles, slept in that old-fashioned bed, ate her breakfasts and her dinners with Charles.

She would think this, and wish the five days were over, and she were Charles' wife. Phyllis' impatience grew. Now the house which had been hers and Wilhelm's took on a waiting quality, not happy and tranquil, but uneasy and ominous.

CHAPTER LX

THE WEDDING was to be a very quiet one, and only a few invitations had been issued for the reception in the Holts' mansion. But many presents had been sent, even from those who had been invited only to the church ceremony. Charles was touched by this, for some of the best gifts were from those who had stared at him coldly during the past year, or had avoided him. Phyllis had laid out all the presents in the Holts' second "drawing-room," and Charles would examine them, marvelling. "I can't get over old Heinz sending us a dozen hand-chased silver demi-tasse cups!" he would say. "Must have cost the old miser a fortune."

It was hard to leave Phyllis at night, and go home to that empty house. He often stayed very late with her, and no one gossiped. The people in Andersburg talked of him with sympathy, and they sincerely wished him happiness. Most of them could imagine, with dread, what it must mean to this father not to know where his son was, or what his son was doing. They would look at their own sons, and say passionately to each other: "No war for us! They'll never get us into their damned war!"

Jochen and Isabel talked of Charles often and soberly. Once Isabel said: "That boy! To do this to his father! I can't like Charles, ever, Jochen, but I pray for him. I really do. That awful boy!"

To which Jochen replied: "Isabel, he isn't 'awful.' He's a nice kid. Glad, though, we haven't boys of our own." He often thought regretfully of Jim. Once he had wanted him for a son-in-law. If only the Brinkwells had never appeared in Andersburg! Everything had gone wrong, with their coming. Geraldine and Jimmy might be engaged now, and planning on an early marriage. If that had happened, the boy would not now be somewhere in that accursed Europe; he would never have left Geraldine. And he, Jochen, would still be vice-president of the Wittmann Machine Tool Company, complaining, not content, but at least safe and important.

It was very strange that Geraldine, though relieved as she was of any plans for a marriage to Kenneth Brinkwell, should seem to grow whiter daily, and more silent. Jochen told himself that it was all his imagination. He hoped it was, for he had little time to think of anything these days except the fact that he had not found anything, anywhere, which attracted him. Once he was sure that his search was over, in Cincinnati. Once he even came to the point of discussing financial matters and even arrangements with the owners of a good small machine tool company. Then mysteriously, a few days later, he received an apologetic telegram announcing that the owners had, for some inexplicable reason or other, changed their minds. Jochen was extremely disappointed. But he went on searching. After one or more such odd last-minute rejections of his terms and his suggestions, he became panic-stricken. He never once suspected that Roger Brinkwell had something to do with this, so he continued to confide in his friend and employer, who listened sympathetically and suggested another concern, or concerns, and expressed himself as annoyed or baffled when the inevitable refusal arrived.

"They don't know a good man and a sound offer when they see them," Mr. Brinkwell would say, frowning. "But, let's consider the Goodwin Company, Joe. I'll write them myself for you, if you want me to. Why don't you go about it this way—?"

August eighth, and still no connection. Jochen's panic grew. When Mr. Brinkwell offered to extend the date of Jochen's resignation Jochen did not refuse. Isabel, however, and much to Jochen's surprise, opposed this.

"No," she said, "it must definitely be September first. You can give all your time to it then, Jochen. You can push it through, personally, waiting in those cities until they make up their minds, or forcing them to make up their minds at once."

No, it was no time to think much of one's daughter's imagined pallor and listlessness, especially when one was trying to find some secure future for that daughter. Besides, Jochen would think gratefully, a man's first duty was towards his wife, especially a wife who knew the worst about a man and who still loved and admired him, and was ready to accept anything for his sake.

Two days before the wedding, Charles received a letter on the Canadian Red Cross stationery from Jim. It was from London, and it was dated the early part of July. It was the most satisfactory present Charles could have received, and he read it eagerly. All was well with Jim and Walter. They did not know when they would be sent to "Somewhere in France." They only hoped it would be soon.

"Dad," Jim wrote, "if you could see the poor fellows here in the hospitals! It would almost kill you. I only know it's convinced Walter and me more than ever that we were right to come. Lots of these kids wouldn't be dying now, in the hospitals, if they had been picked up earlier. They wouldn't have developed gangrene and septicemia. Everyone's talking of the end of the war, confidently, and it can't end too quickly for me."

London, in wartime, was more than a little exciting. He had seen the Zeppelins a few times, "big, bloated balloons, like silver sausages," floating in the twilight skies over the city, and dropping down their cargo of fire and death. The Germans called it "strafing" London; the bombs did not cause too much damage, according to Jim. He liked London. "But it's worse than home, on Sundays. Everyone dies. You hardly see anyone on the streets. There's a joke here, about where the people go on Sundays, but I wouldn't soil the eyes of the censor by telling you the joke in a letter."

Jim had also gone to Westminster Abbey, which he had not apparently liked. The day, though in July, was gloomy, bitterly cold, and rainy. "They can keep their Abbey," Jim wrote. "Tombs back to Edward, King of the East Saxons. Cloisters, disintegrating, sifting into dust. The Abbey's shaped like a cross, with here and there a dim lantern on dank decay. Smell of death. Some of the fellows here get sentimental about the place, and say 'home of my ancestors.' Well, the endless Edwards and Henrys and the others meant nothing to me, with the tattered standards drooping over the tombs. Not the home of my ancestors!" He had also toured the Tower of London, which found even less favor with him than the Abbey. The torture chambers, the beheading blocks, the armor perched on wooden horses—all the debris of dead kings who had gained honored fame by the red ax of murder.

"I'll write you when I can, Dad, but letters will be even slower than this, in the future. Don't worry. I'll be very careful. Be happy, Dad. You'll probably get this letter about the time you'll be marrying Aunt Phyllis, and you'll know how much I'm wishing I could be there, too. But, anyway, as the old song says, I'll be there in spirit. Be happy, Dad—"

He ended, then, with this message: "Please take care of Gerry for me, Dad. I get letters from her, and she's very anxious. Tell her to take care of you, for me, too."

Charles called up his minister, who joyously reported that he, too, had just received a letter from Walter. Mr. Haas read the letter to Charles, who thought it was much less colorful than Jim's, much more flat and monotonous. Charles read Jim's letter to Mr. Haas, who said, flatteringly: "Why, the boy's quite a poet! But poor Walter never had much imagination. Perhaps that will help him when he becomes a minister. I don't know. But it might save him a lot of trouble."

Charles called up Phyllis, to read the letter to her, and she, too, flattered him with her admiration. She was very relieved that Charles had heard from his son. It was a very happy circumstance that the letter had arrived just before the wedding.

Yet, when Phyllis was alone, she remembered only one phrase in that letter: "Be happy, Dad." She sat alone in the early evening, in her silent living-room, and listened to the sound of the soft rain, and she felt melancholy and sadness move over her like water. "Be happy—" It had a mournful sound, not gay or boyish or loving. It was like an admonition, an urging— Phyllis got to her feet, and went to the French windows. The wet gardens were a green and shadowy blur in the rain. She told herself that the day after tomorrow she would be Charles' wife, and she would be with him. No matter what happened.

Charles, however, was not in the least sorrowful. He was more at peace than he had been for almost two months. He read and reread Jim's letter. Then he went upstairs to his room, to look about him with satisfaction. The day after tomorrow he would be married to Phyllis, and then no more empty bed, no empty house, no unshared fear, no unshared waiting. The warm summer rain outside, and the long green and lilac shadows, did not bring any premonition to him as they had brought to Phyllis. He enjoyed the sound of the rain rustling through the trees. The fresh scent of the earth came to him, as he opened the windows a little wider. He saw a figure running up the steps of his verandah, and wondered who was calling. He heard the bell ring below, then Mrs. Meyers hurrying from the kitchen, and muttering, as she always did when the door needed answering.

Charles, still looking at the rain and the trees, heard Mrs. Meyers cry out. It was only a single cry, but it was sharp and loud. He ran from the room, and down the stairs. He knew instantly, knew it all even before he saw Mrs. Meyers below, looking up the stairway at him, her mouth stark and open, her eyes stark and open, too. There was a messenger boy on the threshold of the hall. But Charles did not see him, for a moment.

Yes, he had known it all, at the instant of the cry, before seeing Mrs. Meyers or the messenger or the yellow envelope in Mrs. Meyers' hand, which she was holding up to him. He was running down the stairs, an endless well of dark stairs, and he knew he had always known it, from the very beginning, two years ago. He had lived a long death. This was only the culmination, this cablegram which came no nearer to him no matter how fast he ran, this oblong of yellow nightmare glimmering under the hall light.

He had always known it. He could take the envelope quite calmly. He could even scan the words "—regrets—killed while on ambulance duty—somewhere in France—" He could even turn away, still holding the cablegram, and go upstairs again, steadily. At the door of his room he stopped. No, not in there.

He went into Jim's room, and he sat down in Jim's chair, and he looked out at the rain, the cablegram in his hand.

CHAPTER LXI

To ALL the distorted faces, to all the retreating and approaching and disappearing and recurring figures, to every light and to every vague, distant voice, Charles said only: "Go away."

Nightmares of sound, of motion, of glasses being put into his hand, of hands on his arms, his shoulders. Nightmares of weeping, of urges, of attempts to move him from Jim's room. He said to everything: "Go away." Then there would be darkness, as he lay on Jim's bed, and he would feel that he was undressed, that someone had spoken to him. He was never alone. That was the most terrible part of it. Someone was always with him, just out of sight, in a chair, and that someone would not leave him. He only wanted to be alone, in the night. There would be an acrid taste in his mouth, as of sleeping powders or other sedatives, and he would close his eyes and drift out for a while on the darkness. But always, there was someone with him, someone who came creeping to the bed when he moved. Sometimes there was a cold wetness on his face, from which he turned, or a hand on his forehead, which he pushed aside. He heard his name being called many times, but not the name he wanted to hear. There was always someone he wanted, but he never came.

Were the faces he saw dreams? The faces of Friederich, the minister, the priest, Phyllis, all his friends? He never knew. Why did they not pull down the shade to keep out the sun? But it was not the sun, it was the moon. Why was he undressed one minute, and completely dressed the next? Who was laying a tray on his knees, a tray with food at which he stared blankly? Food must have gone into his mouth, but he could never remember. Day and night, footsteps came and went up the stairs, but not the ones he knew. Then there would be more faces, more figures, more lights, more hands on him, more voices asking him to go into his own room, more sounds of crying. "Charles!" "Charlie!" "Karl!" He kept shaking his head, for that was not the name he wanted to hear himself called. He could not quite remember what the name was, but he understood if he once heard it all this vague and numbing death would leave him immediately, and he could rest.

He had dreams of great hollow voices, like voices calling over mountains: "But 'twas a famous victory!" A victory. But when he asked what victory, the phrase was only repeated like a long boom in his ears.

And then there was a morning when the sun was brilliant in his eyes and he could see more clearly. Phyllis was with him, too vivid, and his brother Friederich and the minister. He looked at them wonderingly, and Phyllis got up and stood beside his chair—Jim's chair— and her arms were about his neck and her head was on his shoulder. She said: "Oh, Charles, Charles." But that had been another dream, a long time ago. He patted her back, feebly, and said: "Don't cry, Phyllis. It was only a dream."

She straightened up, and she was not Phyllis at all, but Dr. Metzger, and the minister and Friederich and Phyllis were gone, and there was another glass in his hand. And there was someone else coming into the room. His brother Jochen. That was absurd. Jochen would not come here, so it was a dream, after all. It was all a dream. He said to his brother: "Joe." The sickly powder was dry and choking in his throat. It was Jochen who was putting the glass of water to his lips, and he drank, and then he said: "Thanks, Joe. How is Gerry?" There was some message for Gerry. He frowned intently, and tried to remember. "Still blacked out, thank God," Dr. Metzger was saying. Charles looked up at him and asked: "Who?" But it was not Dr. Metzger, and Jochen was not there. It was Phyllis again. Charles repeated: "Who?" But everyone was gone, and he was in darkness again, with a little pale light in the distance, and an unseen watcher was with him. Someone who cried.

There was finally a morning when he came out of a stupor, but did not open his eyes. He felt the sun on them, warm and searching. Then all at once he was floating on a sea of black smoke or mist, and it boiled up all about him. He saw the puffs of it, the waves and streamers of it. He said to himself: "I hate. I hate." He was rolled in this black smoke, and he knew it was hatred of an immeasurable intensity. Now he had the name he was always remembering and forgetting: Jim. Jim had been murdered.

He opened his eyes. Phyllis and Friederich were beside Jim's bed, on which he lay. He saw them clearly, without that too sharp brilliance. He saw every object in the room. He sat up, and Friederich tried to help him. He pushed his brother away. "I'm all right," he said. He sat on the edge of the bed, bent over so that his shoulders almost touched his knees. He asked: "How long—?"

Phyllis knelt beside him, in silence, but did not reach out to him. He saw her face, blanched and shrivelled. He saw Friederich's face, blotched, the eyes swollen. Friederich said: "Karl. Five days, Karl."

"Five days," Charles repeated. He said: "I remember, now."

There must have been times when he had left Jim's room, but all memory of that was gone. There was not even a memory of pain, but he felt pain waiting for him, a huge monster like something hiding just beyond vision. He would have to look for it, and take it, though it wasn't time as yet. And when he took it, it would be with hatred.

"I'm all right," he said. His arms were sore and stiff. They had given him injections, then, besides the other sedatives, to send him out in the darkness. He moved his arms languidly. He said: "I'll get up, and shave and dress. I'm all right."

It was a hot August morning. His wedding day had come and gone, and he had been here all the time. But nothing mattered, nothing at all but this hatred.

Father Hagerty hung up the telephone, after having called Phyllis, and he was deeply relieved. Charles had awakened from his stuporous state, was quite calm, had even dressed by himself, and though weak, was now downstairs in his parlor. His brother Friederich had stayed with him for a while, then had gone to his offices. She, Phyllis, was with Charles. She thought that Charles was now in a condition to see some of his friends, and that it would be a good thing for him. No, he did not talk about his son. Father Hagerty, remembering that, was less relieved. He decided to call Mr. Haas. He lifted the telephone receiver again.

Phyllis sat with Charles in the shaded parlor. He had eaten some breakfast. He had even talked to her intermittently. Then he had read a little of the morning newspaper. He sat so still, so listless, and now for nearly an hour he had not spoken. He had just sat, looking before him, his pale mouth a line in his face, his cheeks and jaws lined and furrowed. He was an old man; he had become old in these terrible five days. If only he would talk about it, thought Phyllis desperately. If only he could cry, or rage. But Charles sat as if asleep, except that his eyes were open, and they moved very slightly once in a while. Dr. Metzger had come in after breakfast, and he had told Phyllis that Charles was still in a state of shock, though perfectly conscious. Phyllis did not believe that he was in shock. There was something in the movement of his eyes. He was holding himself against pain, bending rigidly against it. He needed the pain, if he was to get well again.

So Phyllis sat with him, patiently, praying silently, hoping that he would look at her and tell her about Jim. She was numb with fatigue. It was an effort to breathe, to hold up her head. She wore a thin black dress, but the day was already so warm that the light fabric clung to her thin shoulders and breasts. There were no more tears left in her. Her hands lay in her lap, the palms upturned. She saw the strong patches of sunlight outside, between the jagged shadows of the trees; she heard mourning doves near the house. The curtains fluttered slightly, and there was a smell of roses in the room. Phyllis looked up at the Picasso which Wilhelm had given Charles. Its stark colors shone dazzlingly even in the shade. Below the picture stood a bowl of red roses, burningly alive, and hurting to the eyes.

Then she heard a carriage drawing up before the house. Two men were getting out, in clerical garb, one the Reverend Mr. Haas and the other the young priest who had been here so often. Father Hagerty jumped out of the carriage, and then helped Mr. Haas. Why did Mr. Haas, who was hardly much older than Charles, need helping? He stepped down from the carriage like a blind man, fumbling on the step. His hand was on the priest's shoulder, and he leaned heavily on it. Then Phyllis saw the minister's face, waxen, collapsed. Phyllis got up and went swiftly from the room, out into the hall, and then out into the heat that enveloped the verandah. The two men came slowly up the stairs, the priest supporting the older man.

Charles had seen and heard nothing. It seemed to him, however, that he had been alone for a long time. He heard the silken flow of leaves in the hot wind, the doves, the faint sound of voices. None of this concerned him. None of it would ever concern him again, not living, not being, not caring. That was the sun, out there, but there would never be any sun for him, no moon, no day, no night, no peace. He would go away, and be alone. He would then have time to think, and after that—what? Nothing, world without end.

People were coming into the parlor, and he frowned at them, and looked away from them. Mr. Haas, and that young priest who was too young to know anything, and who resembled Jim so closely. Charles did not want to see them. Keeping his head averted, he said: "I'm sorry. But I can't talk to anyone. Please let me alone."

The priest, however, helped Mr. Haas into a chair, and then he stood beside the older clergyman, not speaking. Mr. Haas sat in his chair, his chin on his chest, as lifeless as Charles. It was a long time before he spoke:

"Charles, I had to come to you today. I had to talk to you. When a man loses his child, when a man loses his only child, when a man loses his only son, then his grief is worse than any other grief. Because the death seems so senseless and so futile. The world is full of old people, and useless and wicked ones, and people who want to be dead. But they live, and the child dies, and what is there for a man then? His whole life was in that son, all his hopes for the future, all his worldly immortality, all his pride and his love. Then, all at once the child is gone, and where there was meaning there's only emptiness. Unless a man has his God and his faith."

Charles listened. He said to himself: The clergy talk their platitudes but they don't know anything about anything. They are anesthetized with their own words, which don't have any meaning. They even think by rote. Why does this fool waste his time with me? He has his son. Nothing has happened to his son. His son will be back one of these days, perhaps very soon, alive and well. But my son was murdered. He'll never come back. There's his room upstairs, and all his clothes, his chairs, his bed, his books, his school papers. And his dreams. I'll never hear Jim's voice again. I'll never hear him running up the stairs, and calling me. Dr. Wittmann. But now there'll never be a Dr. Wittmann. There'll never be anything.

He said, in a dull voice: "Thank you for coming, Mr. Haas. But I'm very tired."

Mr. Haas said, as if Charles had not spoken: "A man has his God. He must remember that. Everything comes and goes, but God remains. One should never forget that. Never. Never!" And now the minister's voice broke.

He stood up, and staggered a little. The priest caught his arm strongly, and held it. Mr. Haas looked at Charles, and there was something in his eyes so compelling that Charles had to turn to him. He saw the minister, then, with the tears on his cheeks, the mouth falling and quivering. The minister raised his hand:

"The Lord giveth, and the Lord taketh away—"

His head fell. The priest put his arm about him, supporting him. The minister was weeping. Slowly, Charles rose from his seat, his eyes fixed on the minister. Something was stirring in him, something rising with an awful pain. He held the back of his chair.

Very slowly, the minister raised his head. He did not look at Charles now. His lips were moving. The priest nodded, mournfully, and smiled with infinite compassion.

Mr. Haas spoke, and he faltered: "—Blessed be the Name of the Lord!"

Then the priest was supporting him entirely, his head fallen on the younger man's shoulder.

"No!" said Charles. He took his hand from his chair, and began to walk unsteadily towards the minister. Then he stopped, turned with dread and grief to Father Hagerty.

"He heard, only an hour or so ago. About Walter," said the priest. "I called him, to ask him to come here to see you, Mr. Wittman. Then when the maid at his house told me, I wanted to hang up. But Mr. Haas came to the telephone, and said that he would come to see you immediately." The priest paused. "Jim—went instantly, it seems. The boys were in the same ambulance together. It was a shell, or something, on the battlefield. Walter was wounded. He must have lived a few days after—Jim."

"No," said Charles. The pain was something alive in him, twisting. "No," he repeated. And then he was silent, looking at the minister.

This man, newly bereaved, newly broken, had come to him, his friend, his parishioner. He had come to comfort Charles, he who needed comfort himself. He had come to say the only thing that could be said.

"He left his wife—for me," Charles said. "He left his home, after hearing about Walter—for me. He could come—for me."

He could reach the minister now. Mr. Haas raised his head. The two fathers regarded each other. Then they were holding to each other and weeping, and they were trying to comfort each other incoherently, patting each other's shoulder, giving way to their mutual pain and sorrow.

They sat down, close together, and the priest sat at a distance, praying for them, praying for the souls of the young men who had died while trying to help their brothers.

No one saw Phyllis, who watched from the hall, crying when she had thought she could never cry again. She saw the priest's bowed head, as he prayed. She put her hands over her face, and her body bent in grief.

Someone was touching her arm. It was the minister, and he was trying to smile at her. "I think Charles is all right, now," he was saying.

"But, Mrs. Haas," whispered Phyllis. "Oh, my God, my God."

"Yes," said the minister. "Yes, my God, my God."

Then she was alone with Charles, and she saw his shattered face. She went to him and knelt down beside him, and he put his hand on her head. "Poor Phyllis," he muttered. "You've been here with me all the time, haven't you?"

She pressed her cheek against his arm. "Yes, of course, my darling. Besides, I had no home." She laughed faintly, and forlornly. "I had to leave on August tenth. So I came here. To my home. I've been sleeping in your room, Charles, when I could. Our room, dear."

She put her arms about him. "I won't ever go away again. Never. And Charles, you must do what I want you to do. I want you to marry me the day after tomorrow."

He held her to him. He rubbed his cheek against her hair. "Why, yes, of course, my dearest. Of course."

The pain was coming to him, huge and monstrous, and he let it come. He held Phyllis tightly, and he kept repeating: "Of course, of course."

CHAPTER LXII

It was Phyllis who arranged the details of her marriage to Charles in Mr. Haas' study. Only the Holts, the Haddens, Friederich, and Helen were there. Later, they had a quiet dinner at the Holts' mansion, and then Phyllis and Charles went home. It was understood that Charles, because of his enfeebled condition, must rest for a few days, then the honeymoon, which no longer needed to be postponed, would follow. Phyllis was determined that this honeymoon would not be in the form of a "rest" for Charles. He dare not be idle just now. She arranged that they would travel rapidly from city to city, from resort to resort.

When Charles and Phyllis returned from the Holt's dinner, they found that Mrs. Meyers had lit up the lights in all the rooms, and there was coffee waiting for them, and dump cake. Mrs. Meyers cried a little when Phyllis kissed her, and cried even more when Charles shook her hands.

Then, Phyllis and Charles, arm in arm, went upstairs together. They passed Jim's room. The lights were all brilliantly burning in there, and the door was open. Charles stopped on the threshold, and Phyllis stood beside him in silence. Charles looked at everything in the room, and it seemed to him that the room was not empty at all. Jim had left it only a few minutes ago, for a forage in the kitchen. He would return in a moment or two.

"Let's leave the lights on," said Phyllis.

Charles turned to her. He said: "You always understand, don't you, Phyllis?"

They left the brightly lit room, and they left the door ajar, and went into their own room. Charles took Phyllis' hand and led her in. Here only a light or two had been lit. Charles and Phyllis stood in the center of the room, their hands together, and the light blue of Phyllis' silk dress was the color of her smiling eyes. Her lips smiled, also, and she did not seem to be watching Charles with passionate anxiety. Even he did not know it. He drew her to him and held her to him tightly, and she could hear his breath in her hair.

She thought that he had brought a wife to his room and to this bed, before, the bed in which he had been born. His wife, Mary, had given him a son from this bed, and a daughter, who had died, in this bed, also, and she, Mary, had died in it. The house was full of ghosts. This door was shut, but beyond it a room was lighted for a boy who would never enter it again. Phyllis was afraid.

She waited for Charles to speak, or not to speak at all. She did not know which she preferred, just at this moment. Was he, too, remembering the ghosts of those he had loved? Was he listening for them? Charles took Phyllis' face in his hands, and he kissed her gently on the mouth.

"I've been waiting all my life for this," he said. "Now, I won't be alone any more."

He had said the one thing she had wanted him to say. Then he added: "I'll turn off the lights in Jim's room."

She let him go. She saw the hall go dark. Then she heard Charles shut the door of Jim's room, very softly and slowly, as someone might close the room where another slept. Then he came back to her, and she was waiting for him and holding out her arms to him.

Charles protested after the first two weeks of the four-week honeymoon. It was "silly" to go "tearing around after only one or two days in one place." But Phyllis kept him moving. She no sooner saw the gray bitterness returning to his face, or the sodden grief, than she began to repack her suitcases furiously, and Charles was whirled off. In the confusion, strangeness, and change of renewed travel, he had little time to think. And when the nights came he was so exhausted that he almost immediately fell asleep beside her.

Phyllis had hoped that Charles would talk a great deal about his dead son. But he did not. She became afraid again. He was taking up his life once more, but he would not talk, even to her, about Jim. Sometimes in the night, as he slept, he would cry out, and once or twice he called wildly for his son, and on another occasion or two he had sobbed drily. In the morning, however, he smiled at his wife, and discussed where they should go that day. They had already visited Atlantic City, Philadelphia, and New York. Now, they would go to Washington. "And then anywhere else we can think of," Phyllis would laugh.

She was giving him comfort, and all her tenderness and devotion. Over and over, he would say: "Without you, Phyllis, there'd have been no use in going on. And when I look back, I can see that there never was any going on, without you, all those years." She knew he meant this. But he would not let her talk to him about his son. Sometimes she was close to it, and he knew, and he would get up abruptly and suggest a walk or a late supper.

"You are taking a hard road, Phyllis," Mr. Haas had told her before her marriage. "You must remember that. It might be months before Charles can talk to you; it might even be a year or two. You must be patient, and you must just keep praying, that's all."

Charles no longer bought or read newspapers, not even to look at the Stock Market. The newsboys shrilled "extras" on the streets of New York, Philadelphia, Atlantic City, Washington, Baltimore, and all the other cities they visited. But Charles passed the boys as if they did not exist, without a glance at the papers they offered. This, to Phyllis, was very disquieting. She said nothing, and, as the minister had suggested, she prayed.

Then, the four weeks were over, and they were returning home.

They stopped in Philadelphia for a night, and the next morning they took a cab to the station. They passed a high school, and the cab had to stop to let the streams of young boys and girls cross the street. Charles looked through the windows, idly, then held himself stiffly as he heard the shouts of the youths and saw their rush. The cab still stood, but Charles let himself fall back against the seat. He had forgotten Phyllis. He stared emptily before him and his face was again a ruin of agony. Phyllis put her hand over his, and her eyes blurred with tears.

Charles said: "I hope that Fred's been able to manage all right without me."

The cab moved slowly on, the school doors were open, and the boisterous children fell behind. Their shouts became fainter and fainter. The cab turned a corner and the station was just ahead.

It will be this way for a long time, thought Phyllis. Every time he hears a boy's voice, or sees a boy Jim's age, or someone who resembles him, it will be frightful for him. He will remember when Jim was graduated from high school; he will remember him shouting and laughing and running. He will look at these other boys and wonder why his boy, of them all, had to die. Phyllis thought of all the hundreds of thousands, even millions, perhaps, of boys who would die in this war. But she thought more of their fathers and their mothers, and asked silently, with her own bitterness, why no one ever wrote of the anguish of these parents who could see no "glory" in the death of their lives and their hopes, their pride and all their work. She thought of the countless thousands of painful births which had taken place hardly two decades ago—to end in a bloody and fiery death—for nothing. She thought of the planning of parents, the sacrifices, the tears and prayers—for nothing. The drums and the banners, the reports of victories, the end of the war, itself, would mean nothing at all to men and women who stared hopelessly at empty chairs, who put away books which would never be used again, and closed doors— thousands of doors—as Charles had closed the door of Jim's room. It was horrible that millions of young eyes would never see the sun again. It was more horrible that millions of older eyes could see the sun, but would refuse to see it. Who had said: "The tragedy of war is not in the death of the young men alone; it is in the lives of their fathers"?

Such a rage and hatred came to Phyllis then, such an overpowering sorrow, that her gloved hands clenched and tears ran down her face. She forgot Charles, for he had become only one of those fathers whose sons were being murdered daily in Europe. His tragedy was the tragedy of the whole world, a monstrous and futile tragedy. Even worse, it was a planned tragedy.

She became aware that Charles was unclenching her hands, very gently. He said: "Don't, Phyllis. It can't be helped, now. I suppose I'll just have to force myself to look at other boys, and not feel too much about Jim. Besides, I have you. I must remember that."

He had spoken of Jim, voluntarily, to her. It was the first turning away from the darkness. No one could help him much; he would have to help himself. But when he would turn again and again from his suffering, she, Phyllis, would be waiting for him.

When they reached home, and were going up the stairs of the house, Charles said: "You can't know, Phyllis, how often I've hated to come back here. But when I leave the office, every night, you'll be here, waiting for me. How did I get along without you before?"

But a few days later, he said to her: "Once, a long time ago, I hoped that when we were married we might have a child or two, Phyllis. I don't want that, now. Let's get what comfort and contentment we can out of existence, and let it end there. Once I read that having children is an affirmation of life. I don't want to affirm anything again. It's no use."

CHAPTER LXIII

FRIEDERICH COULD only shake hands with Charles when the latter returned to the offices. Like all deeply emotional people, Friederich was intuitive. He saw that Charles looked much better than when he had left for his honeymoon, that his old balance was returning, and that he had regained quite a good deal of his old solid poise. However, a certain sturdy vigor he had had, a certain vital energy, had gone from him.

Charles was honestly interested in the affairs of his company, and became involved in them immediately. That was his nature. He complimented Friederich on the really extraordinary efficiency the latter had displayed. He said, smiling at his brother: "I'd never have thought it, candidly, Fred! But scratch a Wittmann and you'll find a business man, every time. You're a real burgher, Fred, a real sound bourgeois."

Two years ago Friederich would have become inflamed with rage and affront at this. Now, he blushed like a young girl, with pleasure.

The two men were sitting in Charles' office. Friederich, haltingly, told Charles that he was glad he was pleased. He had done his best. Of course, there were a few little things— "Nothing," said Charles, "compared with the big things you've done. The sound judgment." He added, and his voice was smooth and without emotion: "I hope your boy, when he is born, will have your qualities. We've got to keep this business in the family, you know."

He wondered why Friederich, all at once, looked distressed, and why he began to bite his lips. Now what? thought Charles. He waited. Friederich began to twiddle his fingers. "Something happened while you were away, Karl. The whole city is buzzing with it." He paused. "Jochen left the Connington Steel Company. On September first. He resigned."

"What!"

"Yes. And there was a newspaper interview. Jochen said that as he had always been a partner in business, an officer, he had made up his mind to look for an investment of his time and money in another machine tool company. He hinted that there were some good prospects in Cincinnati, for him."

Charles was astounded. He could only stare at his brother. Friederich went on: "You know I neither hear nor spread rumors unless they are substantiated. However, there has been gossip that Jochen wanted to resign months ago, but that Brinkwell persuaded him to remain until he had found some suitable company in which he could invest, and become a partner. And the gossip continues that he has not found such a company, though Brinkwell has been trying to help him."

Charles leaned back in his chair, and thought. His hand began to tap slowly on his desk. His little brown eyes quickened. He said at last: "So. Brinkwell's been trying to 'help' Joe, has he? I doubt it. If anything, he's been trying to keep him from leaving. I know Brinkwell. Anything else, Fred, from your bag of gossip?"

"It isn't gossip, Karl," replied Friederich, indignantly. "I've gotten much of this from George Hadden, who got it from his wife, who got it from a friend of Isabel's. Now, it is very superior of you to smile like that! But women," Friederich continued with the wise and serious air of a married man, "often hear authentic things long before they penetrate to the duller ears of men. An obscure German poet once said: 'Women's rumors run like the fire in grass before the major catastrophes, and they are the tolling of the church bells before the first sound of battle is heard.'" He regarded Charles severely. "I am almost of a mind not to tell you anything more."

Charles was properly penitent. "Oh, go on, Fred. What else?"

"Isabel, I've heard, has been insisting that Jochen leave on September first, and go in things for himself. In spite of Jochen's large salary. Don't look so incredulous. And it was, indeed, Isabel's and Jochen's doing that broke off the engagement between their daughter and Brinkwell's son. It is said that Jochen, at Isabel's demand, gave his resignation to Brinkwell."

"Well," said Charles, "if that is so, Isabel's been 'converted,' to use the whacking Fundamentalist term. What caused that, I wonder? She was getting along famously with Pauline Brinkwell. What turned Isabel from a society leader and a grande dame into a woman concerned with her husband's welfare? And what made Jochen want to resign, anyway?"

Friederich, however, had no opinion to offer. But Charles knew that Friederich had his own secret convictions, even if he did not want to express them. This is what made him look so troubled and uncertain, and obstinate. Friederich, having emptied his "bag of gossip" got up, very dignified, and left Charles' office.

Charles gave a lot of thought to Jochen's affairs, and to the unbelievable story Friederich had told him. He was still somewhat incredulous. After some time he called the Willoughby and Jameson Machine Tool Company in Cincinnati. He was an old friend of Willoughby's, and he knew he would get the truth. In an hour or so, he was connected with his friend.

"Jack," he said, "I wonder if you can give me some confidential information. I've just heard, and it's probably not true, that my brother Joe is trying to connect with a concern or two in your city."

Even over the telephone Charles could detect the other man's discomfort, for he was silent for some moments. Then he coughed, as if embarrassed, and said: "Well, yes, Charlie, it's so. He wanted to come in here. We gave some thought to his proposition. We know he is a very valuable man. He approached us last June."

"Well?" demanded Charles. "Why didn't you take him?"

"I can't go into details, Charlie," said the other man, lamely. "It—it just wasn't expedient, at the time."

"Could you mean that Brinkwell, of the Connington, persuaded you it wasn't?"

"Now, Charlie," said Mr. Willoughby.

"That's all I wanted to know," said Charles, and hung up abruptly.

Something had happened to Joe, he thought. He hadn't been thrown out of the Connington. In the first place, Brinkwell needed such a man as Jochen Wittmann. In the second place, Jochen knew too much about the Connington's affairs. Charles rubbed his forehead until it was red. There was something back in his mind— He could not remember. Something insistent. It hung there, wanting conscious thought. It was irritating that it would not express itself, and it left a gnawing uneasiness in Charles.

The first day went well enough. One could do almost anything if one did not think. The horror and the grief were like clouds in the back of his mind. It was no use, however. If a man wanted to live— and Charles wanted to live now—he could not let himself think. One had to lift himself from the place he had fallen and go on, shattered, it is true, but still breathing and existing. One had to spin a web, like a cocoon, around a terrible event, and immobilize it, so that it wasn't always fluttering around to make a man sick of living and wanting only to die.

At five o'clock, Charles' big red automobile, which had been the delight of Jim's life, called for him, and he was driven home. Charles had the automobile stopped for a moment to buy the first newspaper he had bought since he had reecived the news of Jim's death. He scanned the headlines remotely. It had nothing to do with him now. He threw the paper away. He began to think of Phyllis, waiting for him. There was a sudden stir in him, as if something frozen was moving and awakening.

He pictured Phyllis on the verendah, in this bright and golden September evening, smiling at him as he got out of the automobile. But the verandah, the door, were empty as they had been for so long. There was no sign of Phyllis. Charles ran up the steps of the verandah, and, in the manner of men who had been before visited by calamity, he felt a premonition of disaster. He threw open the door, and did not know how loud his voice was when he cried: "Phyllis! Phyllis! Where are you?"

Then he heard her voice from upstairs: "Charles! I'll be down at once."

He went into the parlor and sat down, breathing unevenly. Disaster had passed him by this time. Was he always to feel like this, when something did not happen as he had expected? How could a man go on living, under the shadow of such fear?

Phyllis came running down the stairway, and he heard the starched rustling of her gray cotton dress. She came into the parlor, and saw him sitting there, spent and drained. The first day at the office had been too much for him, she thought. She saw that he had to make a powerful effort to get up. She kissed him and said: "I didn't notice the time." There was something in her voice, troubled and constrained, which made him loosen her arms and put her away from him. Disaster, then, had not gone by. What form would it take this time?

She was, indeed, very pale and tense. "What's the matter, Phyllis?" he demanded. "Something's wrong with you."

"Not with me, dear," she said at once, understanding, and full of pity. "I'm splendid. And nothing wrong with you, I hope. Darling?"

"I'm all right," he answered, impatiently. "But there's something you want to tell me, isn't there?"

She hesitated. Then she tried to smile, and took his hand. "Let's go upstairs, Charles. There's someone here who has been waiting an hour for you." He let her lead him upstairs, flaccidly. He had no curiosity, only renewed dread. Jim's door was open. A girl, Geraldine, was sitting in Jim's chair, and she was crying silently.

"Gerry!" exclaimed Charles. He had forgotten Geraldine, who loved Jimmy, who was engaged to Jimmy. He had never once thought of this child, who must have had her own suffering. Full of remorse, he went to her, saying over and over: "My poor dear, my poor dear, my poor little girl."

She did not stand up, even when he was close to her. She could only look at him with swollen eyes and terror and grief. She let him kiss her. She was so thin, so distraught, that Charles was deeply moved. He pulled up a chair to sit near her, while Phyllis stood beside them. "Oh, Gerry," he said. He took her hand; it was trembling, and it was very cold. She regarded him with the wide pupils of distraction, and her lips shook.

"Uncle Charlie," she murmured, then burst into wild tears, bowing her head, her whole body shaking. Charles looked helplessly at Phyllis, who began to stroke the girl's dark hair.

"She told me she had to see you. She wouldn't tell me why, poor little thing," said Phyllis. "But, of course, I understand."

"You mustn't cry like that, Gerry. You'll make yourself ill," said Charles, putting his arm about Geraldine. "It won't bring Jim back." And then he thought of an old story he had heard one time. A man was weeping inconsolably for his dead son. He had wept for days. And then his friends, kindly but impatiently, said to him: "Why do you weep? Nothing will bring your son back to you." The man replied: "That is why I weep."

He forgot Geraldine again, and thought of Jim. Why had he ever thought that he might be able to isolate his despair and his sorrow, and go on living naturally? It was impossible. There were Jim's best pair of military brushes on the dresser; there was Jim's Harvard banner on the wall. There was Jim's bookcase, with a pair of shoes still standing under it. There was Jim's old globe of the world in the corner, and Jim's desk, with the useless school papers piled neatly upon it. The door of the clothes closet was slightly open: Charles could see the rack of Jim's ties, and the row of Jim's suits, and the silly walking-stick he had bought, with the silver knob, and the bat and tennis-racket which he had cherished. He had once belonged to the "Andersburg Devils," a youthful baseball club; his red-and-yellow cap hung on a hook within plain sight.

He heard Geraldine cry: "What shall I do, Uncle Charlie! What shall I do?"

Charles stared at the baseball cap. "There's nothing else to do, Gerry, except bear it. You're young. You'll forget. In a year, two years, you'll have forgotten." He did not know how bitterly he was speaking.

"But how can I forget?" Geraldine was sobbing. "I can't, ever. And I'm so afraid."

Charles shook his head, and repeated: "You'll forget. You're young."

She grasped his arm. "Uncle Charlie! I'll never forget Jimmy, never. I know that. But now I've got to think of me, and the baby."

Charles did not understand what she was saying for a moment, and then he was stunned.

"The baby!"

Geraldine was crying again. "Jim's baby, and mine. I'm so afraid. Mama and Papa— And Papa is so worried, now. This will just kill them. Oh, Uncle Charlie, I wish I were dead!"

Charles could only look at her, shocked and desperate. He turned to Phyllis, dumbly, and she put her hand on his shoulder. Charles tried to speak, but his throat was too dry. He shook his head, again and again, and his body dropped once more into the lines of sorrow and agony.

"How could—I didn't know—why should Jimmy do this to you, Gerry?" he stammered at last. "I didn't think Jimmy would do a thing like that—it isn't like Jimmy—"

Geraldine's eyes opened wide; her mouth fell open, also. She regarded Charles, stunned also.

"Why—why, Uncle Charlie! What are you saying about Jimmy? He told me he told you— he wrote me a letter from England—he said he'd told you just before his train pulled out of the station—he said he'd asked you to take care of me, and then he wrote I should go to you immediately. But I didn't. I was afraid of hurting poor Mama and Papa. I didn't know, then, that I was going to have a baby—"

"What are you trying to tell me, Gerry?" asked Charles. He took the girl's shoulders in his hands and shook her. "Tell me!"

"Charles," said Phyllis, urgently. "You're hurting her."

But Charles, as if he could not help it, continued to shake the girl. In the meantime, she was fumbling in her purse, and her face was blank. She found a slip of paper, wrenched herself from Charles' grasp, and pushed the paper in his hand. "Uncle Charlie, how could you think anything wrong of Jimmy? How terrible of you! We were married in Weston, the next to the last day he was here." Her voice rose clear and loud, with horrified indignation. Her eyes fixed themselves with brilliant repulsion on him. "Jimmy wrote he'd told you. On the train. And he wrote me that he'd written you from England, and said that he'd asked you to take care of me, and that I was to take care of you, too— for him."

Charles looked at the narrow piece of paper, stupefied.

"And then we drove back home," said Geraldine, simply. "But before we got into Andersburg, we stopped in a woods. It was so beautiful. Jimmy and I had no time. No time at all." She did not color or look ashamed or embarrassed. She lifted her young head with pride. "And I'm glad I'm going to have something of Jimmy's forever. It's just that I feel so sorry for Mama and Papa."

Charles was now remembering Jim's letters. Jim had thought his father had understood. He thought that Geraldine had told him, also. He had left this girl to his father. He must have known, somehow, that he was not coming home. He had begged his father to take care of this young girl, and protect her. It was all so plain, now. And Charles thought of this terrified child, alone with her grief, and then alone with her knowledge that she was to have a baby. There had been no one to comfort her, or to know. He, Charles, had Phyllis, and his friends. This girl had had nothing but her fear and her sorrow, in silence, and there had been no consolation for her.

"Oh, my God," said Charles, with compassion. "Oh, my poor little girl."

He smoothed the slip of paper in his hands. It was dated in June. He had told Jim to take the automobile and spend a day with Gerry. A day of a secret and impulsive marriage, and an innocent mating in a wood. "No time at all." No time for youth and joy. There never was. There was only time for age and regret and death.

Charles lifted the crying girl from her chair, and sat her down on his knee. He held her to him almost fiercely. He pressed her head against his own. He rocked with her in his arms. He wiped her eyes, and kissed her. It was frightful. It was not to be stood. And then Charles stopped rocking. His hand stroked Geraldine's head slower and slower.

Jim's child. Jim's son! In a few months—Jim's son! Jim had not died completely, after all. Jim was not dead. Something of Jim's would live, was living now. A Wittmann would be born. It would be part of him, Charles. His life had not stopped with Jim's death. It would go on, full and strong again, after this brief pause. Jim would go on. Jim was alive, in this new child.

Something was beginning to pound in Charles' body, triumphant and vital. His pale face flushed. He began to smile. "Well, now, Gerry," he said. "It's not so awful. Try to stop crying. You'll have Jim, again. A baby, yours and Jim's. It—why, it's wonderful! If only you'd told me before. I didn't understand Jim's letters. And the train drowned out what he was trying to tell me at the last minute. I wasn't thinking of anybody but Jim. And now I can't tell you how happy I am, and how glad I am."

Phyllis sighed, and smiled. "Affirm nothing," Charles had told her. And here he was, affirming life once more, with vigor and strength. She smiled even more. Dear Charles!

Charles was looking at Phyllis with life in his eyes, and joy. "Isn't it wonderful, Phyllis? Just when I was beginning to think I couldn't go on, after all."

Phyllis hid her own sudden hurt, and said: "Yes, darling, it's wonderful."

Then Charles was no longer smiling. His eyes took on a remote expression. "Phyllis," he said. "There was something I was trying to remember. I thought it was a dream. Tell me, did Joe come to see me? When I was ill?"

"Yes," she said. "He did. Not once, but several times. And he stayed with you for two whole nights, taking care of you. And Isabel was here, too. She relieved me one afternoon. They wouldn't listen to Dr. Metzger's suggestion of getting a nurse."

"So," said Charles. He got up, vigorous and decisive. He put Geraldine into Phyllis' arms. He went out of the room, not slowly, but with firmness and determination. He went downstairs, and called Jochen's number.

"Joe," he said, and he had a hard time keeping his voice down to a normal level. "Charlie. Can you and Isabel come home, at once?"

EPILOGUE

"You're an obstinate devil," said Jochen, to Charles, angrily. "Everyone says this is the time to expand, to prepare for a boom."

"No," said Charles. "This is the time to retrench. We're in for a depression, short or long, I don't know. This is the time to mend our fences, economize. I don't care what the rest of the country is doing. I'm not that optimistic, and won't be until the inflation is deflated, and things settle down. The world's out of equilibrium, lop-sided. As after an earthquake. I prefer to be cautious, and watch how the wind is going to blow."

"I agree with Karl," said Friederich. "Things have changed. It's wiser to see what permanent pattern will emerge—"

"There'll never be any permanent pattern," insisted Jochen. "Never again. It'll be a constant process of improvising, adjusting. If we just sit, we'll find ourselves sitting alone—flat broke."

"Now," said Charles, patiently. "I don't expect the world'll be the same as it was. I expect we'll see constant changes. But I don't expect chaos. There'll be some sort of a pattern underneath all the superficial runnings back and forth—"

It was like old times—almost. Charles and Phyllis, Isabel and Jochen, Friederich and Helen, and Geraldine Wittmann, were sitting in the old garden of Charles' house, under the apple trees. They sat on wooden chairs and iron settees, heaped with pillows. The hot July sunshine was blurred, greened, and softened here. The haphazard rose-bed and other flower-beds brightened the shadowed grass. Nearby played Geraldine and Jim's son, Jochen Charles, and Charles and Phyllis' son, Jimmy, and Friederich and Helen's son, Emil. The children were busily inspecting everything in the garden, running about, screaming, chasing each other, crying momentarily, laughing, shouting.

Now everyone stopped talking to watch the children contentedly. Helen rocked her little daughter, one year old, Greta Louise, in her arms, and she smiled at her son, Emil, who was some months past his third birthday. The boy had her light hair, big square frame, and blue eyes. "Emil!" she called to him, affectionately, when he fell on his knees and howled.

The two other little boys stopped to look scornfully at Emil. "Cry-baby," said little Jimmy, Charles' son. "Cry-baby," repeated Jochen

Charles (little Joe). Emil looked at them savagely, jumped up and pursued the others with a cry of vengeance. The adults under the trees laughed.

It was the occasion of little Jimmy's third birthday. He might be Jim, at three, thought Charles. His boy was dark and tall and slender, with a thick mop of curls. But he had Phyllis' blue eyes and Phyllis' smile. However, he had Jim's ways, eager yet thoughtful. It was kind of Joe and Isabel, who had understood, and had not insisted that their grandson be christened until Charles' son had been born. It had been agreed that if Charles' child were a girl, Geraldine and Jim's son would be christened James. When Phyllis had given birth to a boy, Charles was quite willing that his grandson be named after the two grandfathers. And so his second son had been named after the child's dead brother.

Little Joe was not like his young parents at all. He "favored" Isabel remarkably, which did not reduce Isabel's affection for him. In fact, she and Jochen regarded their grandson as their own direct son, they who had had only girls. They were in the process, at this time, of being rather stately and cool to Geraldine, who was insisting that when she married young Albert Hadden (Helen's cousin) in September, she and her new husband would move to a new little fieldstone house on Elm Tree Road, thus taking her son with her. Jochen and Isabel, who had argued incessantly that their own home was more than large enough to house the young married couple and Geraldine's son, especially as May and Ethel were preparing for their own coming weddings, had finally begged Geraldine to allow little Joe to remain with his grandparents. A compromise had been reached: Geraldine and Albert would permit little Joe to stay with Jochen and Isabel for at least six months, until the honeymoon was over and routine established in the new house.

However, Jochen and Isabel were quite convinced that they would have little trouble in keeping their grandson. Doubtless, there would be a new child on the way in six months. Geraldine would be grateful to her parents for their care of Jim's son. At the very worst, he would be with his grandparents very often. Elm Tree Road was only five streets away. Besides, little Joe called his mother by her nickname, and he called his grandparents "Mama and Papa." Geraldine had been annoyed at first. Now she thought it very touching.

Wounds don't heal as fast as superficial people think, Charles reflected, as he watched little Jim stop to inspect, very gravely, a brilliant red rose. In fact, they never really heal at all. Scar tissue forms, but it keeps on breaking. To the end of your life. Look at the little feller, now: he was bending his head for a closer inspection of the rose, and he had a way of tilting his head which was exactly like Jim's, at his age. The scar tissue throbbed, and broke. Charles called out: "Jim!" The little boy looked at him alertly and smiled. "Jim," repeated Charles, more gently. The throbbing stopped.

He looked at his grandson, little Joe—Jim's son. He was deeply devoted to the child, whom he visited very often. Geraldine also brought the boy to Charles on every possible occasion, when she could remove him from the jealous possessiveness of her own parents. Then there were two boys in the house, quarreling, playing together, racing up and down the stairs, clamoring, demanding, rushing to Charles to settle disputes. He would take them both on his knees, with contentment. He called them indiscriminately "My boys." In four months, Phyllis would have another child. Charles hoped for a girl this time. He rocked slowly in the grass, watched the children, and smiled.

The war was over. The "plotters" hadn't succeeded after all. The Kaiser had run away to exile, in Holland. Germany was apparently settling down in the slow process of accepting a truly democratic government. She would never tolerate tyranny again. Russia—well, the Bolsheviks were trying to destroy what small middle class they had, and were apparently succeeding, too, according to the fitful reports which came intermittently from that mysterious country. But the Russians had had their little taste of freedom, and the Bolsheviks would pass as the Czar had passed. Once give a nation a sharp vision of liberty, and she would never be content with anything else again. Bolshevism was a temporary nightmare in medieval Russia.

The war had shattered the old systems of Europe, had destroyed the ancient concept of "the divine right of kings." It had cost Europe and America billions of dollars, millions of lives. A frightful thing. But perhaps not too high a cost for the new enfranchisement and liberation of mankind. No, there'd never be tyranny in Germany again, no more despots, no more deified autocrats. The people who had given Kant, Goethe, Beethoven, and Brahms to the world were on their way, at last, into the free family of nations. In two years, three years, Russia, too, would eliminate her new, raving enslavers. And America—it would take only a little time until America realized that she should belong to the League of Nations.

The mighty blow struck at the universal freedom of man had failed. Now, the process of deliverance would go on, surely and steadily. There would be no more wars, no more agony, no more despair, no more fathers and mothers crying in the nights. The long terrors which had gripped the centuries had passed in a bloody cloud. No more war. No more enslavement. Perhaps it had been a "famous victory" after all.

Charles dreamed and smiled, and watched the three little boys. Time moved fast. Let me see, he thought. In twenty years—1939—little Emil will be twenty-four. He'll have been out of college for two years. He'll be with Fred, his father, in the Wittmann Machine Tool Company. Little Joe, and my boy, Jim, will be twenty-three. Finished with school. Unless Jim has decided to be a doctor. Dr. James Wittmann! Charles was certain this would be so. He felt quite clairvoyant. Little Joe will be big Joe by then, and also with his grandfather in the company. Continuity. That gave a man a sense of permanence. There could be no break in that continuity. By 1939 the world would have established the gigantic pattern of eternal peace and freedom. Prosperity. Progress. Scientific advancement. The conquest of disease. The "federation of man, the parliament of the world." Perhaps, after all, the grief and death had not been too high a cost. The murderers and the plotters had failed. Mankind had refused to accept the prison-house again, and imperialism, and all the other madnesses. Man had come of age. The world was "safe for democracy."

Charles glanced at his brother Jochen, who was once again vice-president of the Wittmann Machine Tool Company. It was an old platitude, but blood was indeed thicker than water. He might still hate Jochen, and Jochen might still hate him, but under the hatred and the disagreements and the quarrels was the deep tide of blood-affection and understanding. We won't be so old, in 1939, thought Charles. I'll only be sixty-six, and my brothers are both younger than I. We'll have joy and pleasure in our children, in the new world.

Jochen said, with irritation: "I still think you're an obstinate devil, Charlie—" Everybody still called Charles the balance wheel. It was infuriating.

But Charles did not hear his brother. He was again watching the children. There would be no terror by night for them, no death by day. They had been ransomed. Life and liberty and peace—these were theirs. For there would be no more war.

AD INFINITUM